# Wereworld

# Wereworld

## SHADOW OF THE HAWK

BOOK 3

# CURTIS JOBLING

VIKING

An Imprint of Penguin Group (USA) Inc.

VIKING

Published by Penguin Group

Penguin Young Readers Group, 345 Hudson Street, New York, New York 10014, U.S.A.

Penguin Group (Canada), 90 Eglinton Avenue East, Suite 700, Toronto, Ontario, Canada M4P 2Y3

(a division of Pearson Penguin Canada Inc.)

Penguin Books Ltd, 80 Strand, London WC2R 0RL, England

Penguin Ireland, 25 St Stephen's Green, Dublin 2, Ireland (a division of Penguin Books Ltd)

Penguin Group (Australia), 250 Camberwell Road, Camberwell, Victoria 3124, Australia

(a division of Pearson Australia Group Pty Ltd)

Penguin Books India Pvt Ltd, 11 Community Center, Panchsheel Park, New Delhi – 110 017, India

Penguin Group (NZ), 67 Apollo Drive, Rosedale, Auckland 0632, New Zealand

(a division of Pearson New Zealand Ltd.)

Penguin Books (South Africa) (Pty) Ltd, 24 Sturdee Avenue, Rosebank,

Johannesburg 2196, South Africa

Penguin Books Ltd, Registered Offices: 80 Strand, London WC2R 0RL, England

First published in 2011 by Puffin UK, a division of Penguin Books Ltd.

This edition published in 2012 by Viking, a division of Penguin Young Readers Group

1   3   5   7   9   10   8   6   4   2

Text and map copyright © Curtis Jobling, 2012

Excerpt from *Wereworld: Nest of Serpents* copyright © Curtis Jobling, 2012

All rights reserved

LIBRARY OF CONGRESS CATALOGING-IN-PUBLICATION DATA

Jobling, Curtis.

Shadow of the Hawk / by Curtis Jobling.

p. cm. — (Wereworld ; bk. 3)

Summary: Enslaved by the Goatlord Kesslar, young werewolf Drew finds himself on the volcanic
isle of Scoria, forced to fight in the arena for the Lizardlords.

ISBN 978-0-670-78455-4 (hardcover)

[1. Werewolves—Fiction. 2. Adventure and adventurers—Fiction. 3. Fantasy.]  I. Title.

PZ7.J5785Sh 2012

[Fic]—dc23

2011046347

Printed in the USA    Set in Elysium Book    Book design by Jim Hoover

ALWAYS LEARNING                                              PEARSON

*For Mum and Dad*

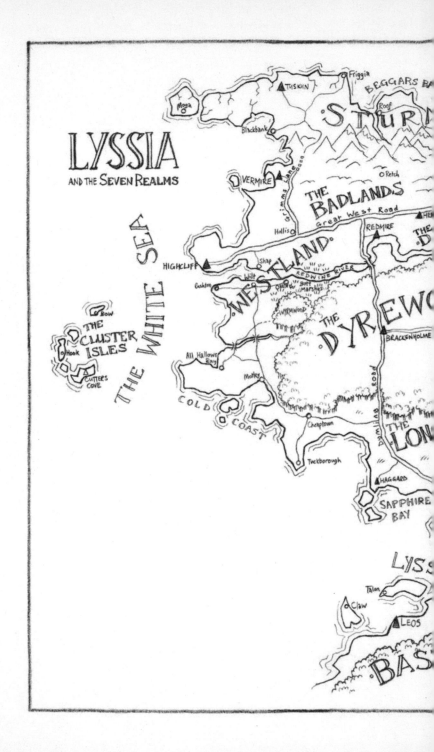

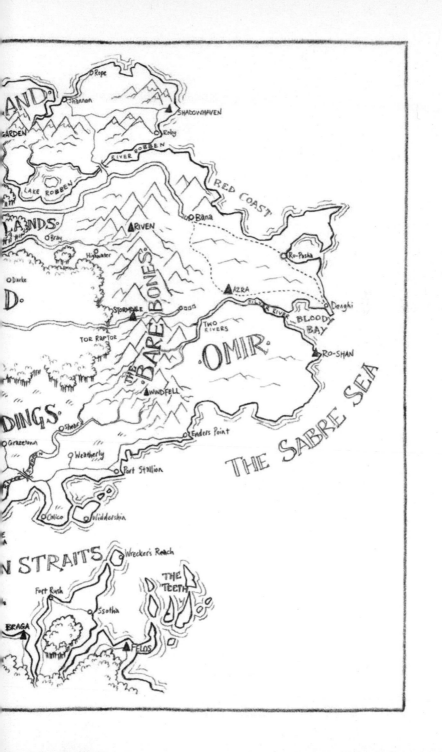

# CONTENTS

# PART I

## SURVIVORS

# I

# SAVAGE SHORES

**THE SHRIEKS OF** strange beasts heralded his approach: a chorus of barks, booms, and bellows that echoed through the jungle. Creatures dotting the riverbanks ran for cover in the dense forest, dashing out of sight at the figure's frantic approach. His legs powered through the brackish water, feet struggling for purchase on the sandy riverbed as he put distance between himself and the beach behind him at the mouth of the shallow river. Spots of sunlight broke through the emerald canopy overhead, illuminating him briefly as he passed, leaving frothing waves in his wake.

Drew Ferran looked back all the while, eyes searching the landscape for those who followed. He had to keep moving, couldn't stop for one moment. If they found him it would be back into the belly of the slave ship. The harsh cry of a nearby animal surprised him, causing him to stumble with a splash. Indistinct shapes darted from tree to tree on either side of him, leaping through branches, shadowing his every step. Not so far away he could hear the shouts of Count Kesslar's men tracking him. Drew pushed on; he much preferred taking his chances in the wild.

He'd left chaos behind on the beach. The *Banshee* had dropped anchor only to allow the quartermaster to take men ashore to gather provisions. Those crew members remaining had made the most of the break, swimming in the bay or relaxing on deck. When the ship's cook had brought Drew his meal—foul-smelling strips of rancid meat on a heavy steel dish—the guard had casually unlocked his cell door. Drew had acted fast. Within moments both cook and guard lay unconscious, the dish having proved a surprisingly adequate improvised weapon.

Emerging on a deck loaded with slavers, Drew hadn't stopped for good-byes. He'd instantly spied the nearby jungle-covered shore and had leaped overboard. The chill ocean had been a shock to his system, but Drew was made of hardy stuff; growing up, he and his brother, Trent, had frequently swum in the White Sea. These clear waters had nothing on the Cold Coast. When he'd surfaced he'd kept his head down, swimming hard, not looking back as he headed for the beach. His newly missing hand caused him grief and made it difficult to swim, but the promise of freedom more than made up for this hindrance, granting him unexpected energy.

Manacled by the Ratlord Vanmorten in the palace of High Stable and surrounded by a horde of approaching undead, Drew had been left with little choice. By biting his own hand from his wrist, he'd lived to fight another day, but the phantom pains in the stump were a constant reminder of his loss.

Scrambling up the golden sand he'd glanced back to see rowing boats making for the shore, men-at-arms shouting to one another as they made to recapture him. Farther along the beach he'd seen the quartermaster's team emerge from the trees, dropping their baskets of fruit and giving chase when they spotted Drew dashing toward the jungle's edge.

The river he was following had emerged into the sea from deep within the jungle. As the tropical forest on each bank looked impenetrable, Drew had opted to follow the river itself away from the beach. He scratched at his throat, cursing the collar Kesslar's slavers had secured around it. With the metal ring removed he would have been free to change, to embrace the Werewolf. He was amazed how quickly he'd come to rely upon his lycanthropic ability. A relatively short time ago he'd been a simple farm boy, content with his lot in life. With the discovery of his powers and the events that had followed, he'd initially resented his true identity—the last of the shape-shifting Wolflords. In time he'd learned to control the beast, call upon it in times of need, to save his friends and defeat his enemies.

5

Drew's feet caught against something hard on the river-bed, sending him tumbling forward, face disappearing beneath the turbulent water. Frantically, he spluttered back to the sur-face, struggling for air in a panic. Something large brushed against his side before hitting his legs hard. Drew was pro-pelled through the air and then back beneath the water, unable to tell up from down. He opened his eyes, squinting against the storm of churning water and sand. A dark shape emerged, huge mouth opening wide to reveal rows of jagged teeth. Drew found his bearings at the last moment, kicking clear and dodg-ing the jaws as they snapped shut.

Rising from the water, Drew gasped for breath, realizing with horror that he had been propelled into a lake. He caught a full view of the circling monster. Perhaps fifteen feet long, it bore no resemblance to anything he'd ever seen. Its skin was dark green with tough, gnarled ridges rising along the length of its body down to its great, swishing tail. Its head briefly surfaced and the beast's yellow eyes regarded him. Dozens of filthy teeth interlocked the length of its immense three-foot-long jaws, clasped together like miserly fingers. It seemed rep-tilian, like the rock lizards that inhabited the cliffs back home, but owed more in its terrifying appearance to the dragons from Drew's childhood storybooks.

The water erupted as the monster propelled itself at Drew, causing him to scramble backward. Teeth took hold of his leg, threatening to pull him under as the creature began to roll.

Drew disappeared beneath the foaming surface, his body spinning as the beast turned ferociously, trying to drown him. Drew felt his trousers tear, realizing with relief that the monster had only taken hold of the tattered material. With a kick he was free, propelling himself away from the chaos.

He hit the bank, scrambling against the muddy incline, struggling to find a purchase. The fingers on his remaining hand tore into the wet clay, the bank falling away around him. Exposed roots hung overhead, agonizingly out of reach. He leaped up, snatching at them before splashing pathetically back into the water. Drew staggered to his feet, working his way along the muddy slope, slipping and sliding as he searched vainly for an escape route. He caught a branch that was floating by and used it to try and hook the roots, pull them down within reach. Then the sound of surging water caused him to turn.

The monster's jaws had emerged from the water; the beast was launching itself at Drew. He turned the branch quickly, shoving it into the creature's open maw as it came in for the kill. The branch disappeared into its red fleshy gullet like a sword into its sheath. Instantly the monster broke away, thrashing and snapping its teeth, trying to dislodge the maddening branch. Drew didn't wait around. He kicked on, swimming once more as he headed for the lake mouth. Behind, he could hear crunching and splintering as the creature turned the branch into kindling. *Move, Drew, it'll be your bones next!*

Drew had no strength left, exhausted from fleeing his captors and then fighting the ferocious animal. He collapsed against a fallen tree that ran down from the jungle into the water, the monster racing up behind him. Drew tried to climb the trunk, crying out loud when a strip of bark came away in his hand.

But the killing blow never arrived. A rope net sailed through the air, weighted down along its edges by lead balls. The net descended over the creature, swiftly entangling the beast as it rolled. The more it struggled, the tighter the net bound. More ropes flew into the lagoon, lassoing the monster and holding it fast as the crew of the *Banshee* appeared along the banks of the lake.

The fallen tree trunk shuddered as something landed overhead. Drew turned, backing away while looking up its length and squinting. The unmistakable figure of the slaver Djogo stood silhouetted in a shaft of sunlight. The leather patch over his left eye covered the empty socket Drew had left him with back in Haggard. For the first time, Drew saw an unusual scar on Djogo's bare shoulder, a triangle within a circle. *Like a brand we'd give the animals back home on the farm.*

"Nearly got yourself killed, Wolf."

Drew looked back at the beast as the sailors subdued it, securing its limbs together, binding its jaws shut. "What kind of monster is it?"

"A crocodile. If you think that's monstrous you'll love the Furnace!"

The crack of Djogo's whip made everyone in the water jump, as the long lash of leather snared Drew around the throat. His hand went to the noose as he struggled to breathe. Djogo tugged at the whip, the cord tightening its hold around the captive therian's throat, causing his eyes to bulge from their sockets.

"Struggle all you like, boy," said the slaver, grinning as he yanked the lash tight, winding the whip in and hauling the choking Wolflord ever closer to him. "It's back to the *Banshee* for you!"

# 2

# PRISONERS OF WAR

**THE TWO CAPTAINS** knelt on the *Maelstrom*'s deck, each showing very different spirit. The older man kept his head bowed, although his eyes scanned the surrounding audience, weighing up the futile situation. In his twilight years, he should have been in some distant port, warming himself by a roaring fire instead of cowering on the pitching deck of a pirate ship. The fellow at his side kept his back straight, chest out, staring his enemies down, shouting and swearing all the while. Younger, cockier, and with far too much to say, it looked increasingly likely he'd get them both killed.

Count Vega paced back and forth in front of them, letting the younger captain exhaust himself with his torrent of abuse. Behind Vega stood Duke Manfred, the Werestag of Stormdale, watching impassively. Queen Amelie stood beside the duke, leaning on his arm for support as the ship lurched against the waves. Bethwyn, her lady-in-waiting and constant shadow, stood at her shoulder. The Werelords were ringed by a crowd of pirates who kept a respectful distance.

Baron Hector, the young Boarlord of Redmire, stood behind the two kneeling men, watching the pacing Sharklord. Hector and his fellow therianthropes had fled Highcliff in the wake of the attack by the Doglords of Omir and the Catlords of Bast. As founding members of the Wolf's Council, he, Vega, and Manfred had been instrumental in supporting Drew Ferran, the young Werewolf and rightful heir to the throne of Westland, as they defeated King Leopold, the Werelion. With the Lion trapped within Highcliff Keep, the Wolf's Council had held control of the city, laying siege to the overthrown king and waiting for his surrender. After the unexpected arrival of Leopold's allies, the group had narrowly escaped Highcliff with their lives. Their enemy had given chase, the remaining allies of the Wolf jumping on board the pirate ship, the *Maelstrom*, as the Wereshark captain tried to spirit them away from their foes.

The prisoners knew him. Vega's reputation as Pirate Prince of the Cluster Isles ensured he was known across the White Sea. When the small, ragtag fleet that had escaped Highcliff had been spotted off Vermire, three ships had come after them. Knowing that their companion vessels weren't built for battle,

Vega had sent them on ahead, with the plan to regroup at the Sturmish port of Roof. The *Maelstrom* had then turned about and engaged the enemy. She'd charged into their midst, breaking their formation, leading them back toward the coast, away from the fleeing civilian ships.

"When the Kraken gets a hold of you he'll drag you down to Sosha's bed, leave you there for the crabs. You'd save Ghul a lot of time by dropping on your sword," spat the younger captain, while his companion remained silent.

Vega sighed. "I would, dear boy, but I fear it wouldn't kill me."

*He's not wrong,* mused Hector. As a therianthrope the Sharklord was immune to most injuries, his accelerated healing repairing wounds that would be fatal for a mortal. There were exceptions to the rule, of course; silver and the physical attack of another werecreature could each lead directly to death, as could any very grave injury.

*There's always magick, too, brother,* hissed the Vincent-vile in Hector's ear. *Can't forget the magick now, can we?*

Hector shivered, shrugging the dark spirit away. It was unnerving to have the disembodied voice of one's dead brother following him around, especially as only Hector could hear him. The Boarlord had played his part in the death of his twin, and he paid the price each and every day. Hector rubbed the gloved palm of his left hand with the thumb of his right nervously, the leather squeaking as he circled the dark mark that stained the flesh beneath. The black spot had appeared the first time he had communed with the dead Wylderman shaman, back in the Wyrmwood. Talking with the dead was forbidden to all magisters, but desperate measures had been called for in order that he and Drew could save their friend Lady Gretchen from the wild men and their mistress, the Wereserpent. Each following occasion when he'd dabbled in communing, the dark spot had grown, the flesh corrupting with every dark act. Shivering, he clenched his gloved hands into fists and returned his gaze to the captured pirates.

"You think you're smart, Vega, but you're just lucky! It was rocks what ripped the belly out of the *Ace o' Clubs*, not any fancy move on the *Maelstrom*'s part!"

The captain was bitter that his ship had struck the submerged rocks, and understandably so. The following vessel had plowed into the back of it, the two keeling over as men dived away from the wreckage of twisted timber and lashing ropes. That had left one ship for the *Maelstrom* to engage: the bigger, slower *Leviathan*. Pitched against the deadliest crew and craftiest captain of all the Cluster Isles, the big boat hadn't stood a chance. Vega's ship had outmaneuvered it, dodging its catapults and sending flaming arrows, cannon fire, and heavy bolts into masts and deck. The battle was over and the white flag now fluttered from the mainmast—the *Leviathan*'s captain having had no choice but to surrender to the count.

"Luck didn't enter into it, Fisk," said the elderly Ransome, captain of the *Leviathan*. "It wasn't chance that you were led into those rocks. Your enemy knew the battlefield. If you'd held back as I commanded, the *Ace* might not have been reduced to driftwood. Stop whining; you were well beaten."

Vega smiled. "What can I say? I know these waters. Now if you're quite done, I'd like to hear about your masters."

Captain Fisk laughed haughtily, spitting at the Sharklord. "We won't tell you nothin', fish! The Kraken'll fillet you when he finds you!"

Hector shivered to think about what fate the Wolf's Council might face should they fall into the hands of the Squidlord Ghul, known throughout Lyssia by his nickname "the Kraken." Ghul's reputation was fearsome, built upon a lifetime of tyranny across the White Sea, showing little mercy to those poor souls he plundered. The Squidlord had been the eyes and ears of King Leopold, the Werelion, for many years, taking all that had once belonged to Count Vega in the process.

Vega nodded. "Yes, yes, so you keep saying. The Kraken this, Ghul that, blah blah, cut me up—all very tiresome! You forget that forty-faced fool used to work for me; I know the squid *all* too well."

"Then you know he don't take kindly to disappointment."

"Well he should prepare himself for a world of disappointment if he thinks his army of sprats will ever catch the *Maelstrom*. Last chance, Fisk: what are Ghul's plans? What does his fleet consist of? Tell me and I'll spare your life."

"I'd sooner embrace Sosha," snarled Fisk defiantly, throwing the sea goddess's name in the Sharklord's face once more.

Vega's cutlass flew from its scabbard, sliding gracefully into the man's heart and out again in a fluid motion. The assembled crowd gasped, none louder than Queen Amelie. The captain of the *Ace o' Clubs* collapsed to the deck, dying eyes wide with disbelief.

*He's a cold-hearted monster*, whispered Vincent to Hector. The young Boarlord nodded slowly as the Sharklord flicked the blood from his blade. His chief mate, Figgis, stepped over Fisk's body, giving it a couple of kicks as he rolled it along the deck and hauled it over the side. Vega turned to Captain Ransome, who stared back calmly.

"Been a while, Eric," said Vega.

"Indeed, lad. You're still painting the sea red, then?"

"Only when I have to, old friend."

"Spare the talk of friendship, Vega, if you're going to do me in like that idiot Fisk."

"He had it coming. Parlay will only protect a pirate for so long, Captain. This is war, after all."

"You're on the wrong side, Vega." Ransome sighed. "You saw what sailed north from Bast. I heard what the Catlords did to your sorry fleet. There's good money to be made working for the Cats. Perhaps it's not too late. Maybe Lord Onyx can find a place for you in his navy."

"I've burned my bridges there, Ransome. I've sided with the Wolf, if you couldn't already tell. I'm not sure the Catlords are as forgiving as you believe. A man is judged by the company he keeps, and I fear my choice of friends tells a terribly sorry tale." He waved a hand in the direction of Hector, Manfred, and Amelie.

Ransome nodded. "Shame. You're a good captain. It would have been nice to sail alongside you once again."

Vega crouched in front of the old pirate. His skin had taken on a gray hue, eyes darkening. Sharp white teeth glinted within the shadows of his face. "Ghul's plans, Ransome?"

The captain of the *Leviathan* shivered, a lifetime serving the Werelords of the Sea still no preparation for the sight of one on the change. "Half of Onyx's fleet has returned to Bast, the remainder is mooring up in Highcliff. It's unlikely they'll leave port until their cargo returns."

"Their cargo?" asked Hector.

"Bastian warriors—thousands of 'em. Seems the Cats are making Westland their own."

"So who patrols the White Sea?" said Vega.

"A handful of Bastian dreadnoughts are out there, but for the most part it's the pirates of the Cluster Isles. Ghul's sat on his backside for too long, growing fat on taxes he claimed in Leopold's name. Onyx has set him to work, now."

"Doing what?" asked Manfred.

"Hunting you."

Amelie gripped the Staglord's arm, face blanching.

"There were only three of you," said the Sharklord. "Where's the rest of your fleet, Ransome?"

16

"There's maybe twenty ships between Vermire and Blackbank, putting the word out that the *Maelstrom*'s a wanted vessel. There's a bounty, too; you'll have every privateer in Lyssia hunting you before long."

"He sees the *Maelstrom* as that much of a threat?" marveled Vega.

"He sees the Wolf's Council as the threat. As long as the councilors live he fears Lucas's kingship is in peril."

Hector's ears pricked up at mention of Werelion Prince Lucas. Having served his magister's apprenticeship under the Ratlord Vankaskan, the young Boarlord had spent a great deal of time in the prince's company. He had endured the young Werelion's violent temper throughout his teenage years and had finally been saved from the Catlord's cruelty when Drew had crashed headlong into their lives. A bully and a brat, Lucas had been spoiled by his father, and his planned marriage to the Werefox Lady Gretchen had been scuppered by the uprising of the Wolf's Council.

*But what has happened to Leopold if his son now stands to inherit the throne?* Hector thought, glancing at Queen Amelie, the Lion Prince's mother.

"Lucas?" said Amelie. "What of Leopold?"

"Dead, Your Majesty," said Ransome respectfully. He might have been a pirate, but he recognized royalty when he saw it. Manfred embraced her as she buckled at the news.

*It sounds like the Werepanther has taken the Lion cub under his* wing, hissed the vile. *See how the old woman sobs! Her record for keeping husbands alive is decidedly poor!*

"How did he die?" whispered the queen.

"Duke Bergan killed him, they say, although the king slayed the Bearlord in the process."

Hector felt dizzy suddenly, the news of Bergan's demise hitting him like a hammer blow. He glanced at Manfred, who looked back pale faced. The Stag and the Bear had been like brothers. Such news so soon after the death of his younger brother, Earl Mikkel, would wound Manfred deeply.

"What was Ghul's last command?" asked Vega, pushing past the dreadful news.

"Follow the coast. Get word to the Isle of Moga, bring the Sturmish pirates on board. If the price is right Baron Bosa might aid us."

"He'll never join the fray," said Vega confidently. "He's a die-hard neutral; that'll never change."

Vega had told Hector about the Whalelord Bosa on the journey. Another old friend of his father's—the Sharklords were well known across the White Sea, it appeared—Bosa would deal with any party when there was money to be made. He'd retired from piracy long ago, although there were many villains who took their booty to the old Whale. Vega had intended to visit Bosa, but Hector now wondered whether avoiding Moga altogether might not be a better idea.

Ransome shook his head, smiling grimly. "Your old man

might have been friendly with Bosa once upon a time, Vega, but that's history. Onyx is confident Bosa will sign up: it's join him or sleep with Sosha. There are only friends and enemies in the Catlords' world."

Vega flexed his cutlass blade in his hands, sharing a look with Hector and Manfred. Ransome looked up, eyeing the sword worriedly.

"If you're going to run me through, get it done would you!"

Vega sheathed the blade, smiling at the *Leviathan*'s captain. "Fisk was an arrogant thug. He had it coming. You, on the other hand, Ransome, have my respect. I doubt you take a great deal of pleasure in hunting the *Maelstrom* and a few boatloads of townsfolk. I give you the *Leviathan* back, your crew, and the survivors of the *Ace o' Clubs* and the *Wild Fiddler*. Your lives are your own. I don't expect you to follow us; not only are you overladen with bodies, you have to replace those burned sails before you can go anywhere."

Ransome looked astonished. "Thought you were going to do me in . . ."

"You thought wrong," said Vega. "I *do* suggest you reconsider your decision, however, and certainly think twice about rejoining the hunt. If we should encounter one another again under these circumstances, I'll take great pleasure in tearing your throat from your body and feeding your guts to the gulls."

Ransome nodded, struggling to his feet as Figgis cut his bonds. "You won't see me again," said the captain, but Vega was no longer listening, leading the Werelords away toward the rear of the ship.

Hector fell in behind, passing his own men, Ringlin and Ibal, once henchmen of his brother, as he followed. The two men of the Boarguard looked up, acknowledging him briefly with nods.

*You seem to have straightened those two out*, the Vincent-vile chimed in. *Do you trust them?*

"More than some," murmured Hector, his eyes on Vega ahead. Hector had once admired the count, the only fellow beside Drew who had ever stood up to Duke Bergan and the Wolf's Council. He'd looked out for Hector when all others had deserted him. Drew was gone and the Bearlord had turned his back on him. Vega had been there for him when Vincent had been slain, disposing of the body, tidying up loose ends, and remaining silent throughout.

But as time went on, the debt he owed the count became oppressive, weighing heavy on the young magister's shoulders. Vega had betrayed his "friends" before: the Sharklord had been the one to leave Highcliff undefended when King Leopold took the throne from the old king, Wergar the Wolf. Could Hector truly trust him? What was to stop Vega from selling Hector out and revealing his dirty secret, if the price was right? The idea of owing anyone anything, especially the Wereshark, was unbearable. He needed to pay the debt. He needed to be free of Vega.

The nobles gathered on the quarterdeck, away from the activity below. Ransome and his men were already being transferred back to the *Leviathan*, which remained lashed to the *Maelstrom* by boarding ropes. None of the ship's sails remained, the smoldering remnants hanging limply from the masts.

"It'll be days before they get her moving again," said Vega, looking down at the sea chart that was laid out over a raised hatch.

"You realize he'll send word straight to his masters?" said Manfred.

"By the time that old girl limps back into harbor, we'll be long gone."

"Is Bergan really dead?" whispered Hector suddenly. Manfred and Vega looked at him, their faces grim as they nodded.

"So it sounds, Brenn bless his soul," said Manfred.

Vega placed a hand on Hector's shoulder and gave him a squeeze. "Bergan would have wanted us to continue, Hector. We need to go on to Icegarden."

"Is that still the plan, then?" asked the Staglord.

"It has to be," said Hector. "We need to seek audience with Duke Henrik and find where his allegiance lies."

"Let's hope he's feeling hospitable," said Manfred. "There'll be plenty of folk looking for refuge in the Whitepeaks once the Catlords march through Westland. I'd imagine half of the

Dalelands are already on their way after the Omiri Dogs tore a path across Lyssia."

"Death everywhere," murmured Amelie, staring at the map, her eyes moist. "It's hopeless."

*What think you, brother? Does she weep for Lyssia or her dead Lion?*

Hector ignored the vile, reaching a black-gloved hand across to take hold of the queen's. She looked up at the young Boarlord.

"Your Majesty, we must stay together, stay strong. We need to show the people that they don't have to serve the Catlords—they have a choice. And Drew is out there, somewhere—he lives, I'm sure of it."

Amelie looked warily at Vega, who kept his eyes fixed on the chart. "Do you feel no remorse, Count?" she asked. "Captain Fisk was unarmed; you could have thrown him in irons. You didn't have to kill him."

"Please don't shed tears for Fisk, Your Majesty. He was a killer."

"As are you, Vega."

He looked up from the map, nodding. "As am I, Your Majesty. Only I'm a killer who is on *your* side. We are at war. Fisk's fate helped loosen Ransome's tongue, I'm sure you'll agree. Please don't lecture me on board my ship. The kings you married were hardly shy of bloodshed."

Amelie shuddered, releasing her hand from Hector's and turned to her lady-in-waiting. "Come, Bethwyn," she said. "Let us return to our cabin. We might be stuck on board this cursed ship, but we can still choose the company we keep."

Lady Bethwyn curtsied to the men and followed the angry Amelie as she departed. She flashed her big brown eyes at Hector as she passed, causing his heart to flutter.

*That cow-eyed girl, Hector? And I thought you were toughening up. It seems you're still soft inside.* Vincent chuckled.

"This 'cursed ship' is the reason we still live," muttered Vega. He looked across to Manfred, who was watching the queen depart.

"Do you want to go with her, Manfred? Make sure she gets to her quarters all right?"

The Staglord glowered back at Vega. Hector watched the two Werelords, the air crackling with tension. Manfred's brow darkened, bumps beginning to appear beneath the skin.

*The antlers,* gasped the vile. *Here they come!*

"Watch your tongue, Vega," said the duke slowly, trying to keep the beast in check. "I don't appreciate what you're insinuating."

"I insinuate nothing, Manfred. It's clear to me you care for her, that's all. As a friend, of course, nothing more," said the Sharklord.

*Your ridiculous little council is tearing itself apart,* said the vile.

*Look at them, bickering over that old widow like schoolchildren. You're doomed, Hector. All of you: doomed.*

"Shut up!" he shouted, his black-gloved fist striking the map. Manfred and Vega both looked at him in surprise. Vega smiled before returning his attention to the sea chart.

"Moga," he said at last, poking at the island on the map. Hector avoided Manfred's gaze. His cheeks were flushed with embarrassment, but also something else. He might have spoken out of turn, but they'd listened to him; he'd silenced them. *Am I indeed their equal?*

"Moga? Really?" asked the Lord of Stormdale gruffly.

"Onyx has yet to make the Whale his offer. If we get in early, who knows? Perhaps he'll be struck by a rare moment of conscience. Maybe he'll do the right thing."

"I would suggest we avoid Moga altogether," said Manfred. "Continue straight on to Sturmland. You're inviting danger by going ashore in such a dangerous port. The forces of the Werewalrus, Lady Slotha, are harbored there, are they not?"

Hector had heard all about Slotha, the Walrus of Tuskun. The tribal people of her remote region were known as the Ugri, fiercely loyal, owing more to the Wyldermen of the Dyrewood than the more civilized people of Sturmland. When Leopold had overthrown the old king, Wergar the Wolf, she had sided with the Lion, gaining governance over the northwestern tip of Lyssia in return for the muscle she added to the fight. In the following years she'd fortified her position in the frozen wastes, waging war on her neighbors in the Whitepeaks and striking fear into the hearts of sea traders. There was no love lost between the Walrus and the Wolf's Council.

"She has forces there, certainly, but Moga itself is still considered a free port. If anyone rules there, it's Bosa. Let me speak with him, see if I can win his aid before Onyx comes knocking."

"We should sail on," said Manfred. "Hector, your thoughts?"

"We're low on supplies, Your Grace. We should stock up on fresh water and food. The few provisions we had on board when we left Highcliff are virtually gone."

"Besides which," said Vega, "our five fellow ships that fled Highcliff are ahead of us, somewhere. Chances are good that someone in Moga will have sighted them. Bosa has answers. Trust me, Manfred; we need to pay him a visit."

The Staglord massaged his brow between thumb and forefinger, the argument lost. "I think we're making a mistake."

"We'll take a couple of boats ashore. Hector—can you oversee the securing of provisions? Manfred—you and I shall speak with Bosa. We keep our heads down, keep a low profile."

*Look at him*, hissed Vincent. *He's enjoying this. Skulking about, piracy—he's in his element. He's pulling the strings, Hector. He's in control now.*

Vega grinned at the Boarlord and winked slyly. "In and out. The Werewalrus Slotha won't even know we're there."

# 3

# THE BLACK STAIRCASE

**THE DRIVERS CRACKED** their whips, urging the procession of wagons and horses onward and away from the curving cliff edge. The wagon wheels found their way into the ancient ruts worn into the dark rock road by centuries of traffic. To the people of the island the circling road was known as the Black Staircase, running all the way from the harbor below, through the city, around the mountainous island.

Drew pushed his face against the bamboo bars, looking down the cliff as the wagon he traveled in drove ever higher. There were six of them in the jail wagon, each equally miserable. No doubt Drew's fellow slaves had been picked up by Kesslar on his travels, and each bore the scars of the journey. Battered and beaten, the men were weary from the long time spent in the hold of the slave ship. The Goatlord Kesslar traveled at the front of the procession in a sumptuous caravan, his ill-gotten gains of blood, flesh, and bone following miserably behind.

The Black Staircase rose from the docks through the strange city, past bazaars and merchants' stalls, before winding through the town houses higher up. Far below in the harbor Drew spied the *Banshee*, bobbing lazily in the crystal-clear water, her cargo delivered.

At the highest point of the Black Staircase there was no sign of vegetation; the slopes of the mountain were covered with rocks and boulders as dark as jet. The road leveled out briefly as they reached the summit, turning in toward the mountain's center. Here the wagons passed through a tall, white gatehouse. Lightly armored guards stood to either side, inspecting the carts and their slaves as they trundled past. The people of the island reminded Drew of Djogo, Kesslar's captain, tall and rangy with dark, leathery skin. *Perhaps this is where the brute hails from?*

The wagons were moving downhill now into a bowl-shaped valley that marked the mountain's summit, a palace sitting at its center. An outer wall curved around the grand palace structure, echoing the concentric circles of the Black Staircase. Terra-cotta rooftops dipped in toward its center, the courtyard beyond not yet visible on the approach. Towers thrust up from the outer wall toward the clouds, their brickwork an ornate

tapestry of black and white banded marble. The heat was oppressive; Drew felt it roll over him in waves. Occasional jets of steam
broke through fissures in the ground on either side of the road,
and hot gases belched violently from the earth. He held his hand
to his mouth, gagging at a familiar scent in the air.

Drew's mind flew back to Hector's communing. He blanched
as he remembered his dear friend's necromancy, speaking with
the souls of the departed. The Boarlord had used a foul-smelling
yellow powder, tracing out warding symbols and binding circles
as part of the ritual. Despite the heat, Drew shivered. He remembered the undead playthings of Vankaskan in Cape Gala, and
how they had cost him his hand. With a manacle fastened tight
around his hand and a crowd of monsters hungry for his flesh,
the choice between life and death had been a torturous one to
make. When he closed his eyes, he could imagine the hand was
still connected, could feel the flexing of ghostly fingertips. It was
going to take some getting used to. Drew stared at his wrist,
fully healed now, a scarred stump of flesh and bone. He sniffed
at the air once again.

"Brimstone," he said, as much to himself as to anyone who
might listen.

"That's right," said another slave, leaning against the bars
on the opposite side of the wagon. "Sulfur. What else would
you expect from a volcano?"

"Welcome to Scoria!"

If the heat outdoors was stifling, inside the palace it was unbearable. Guards had led the shackled slaves into the colossal building, past crowds of onlookers into a huge, circular hall. Stone tables ringed the room, littered with food from the previous night's feasting. Flies buzzed over discarded pieces of meat, adding to the grim atmosphere. Torches burned along the wall, while a large metal grille covered the center of the chamber, riveted to the polished basalt floor. A steady flow of steam emerged through the grating, turning the chamber into a sauna. A metal brazier, stacked with red-hot coals, stood beside the grille, long-handled brands buried deep within the glowing embers. Drew winced as he spied them, imagining what they might be used for.

The man who addressed the slaves rose from a tall, marble chair. He was wearing no more than a loincloth, gold jewelry, and a wide, slick smile. Three similarly garbed figures stood behind his throne, cloaked in shadow and steam. There wasn't a trace of hair on the speaker's body—the man didn't even have eyebrows, giving his face a permanently surprised look. His oiled skin glistened in the torchlight, reflecting different colors in the glow of the flames. Drew squinted, convinced his eyes were playing tricks on him. The man's flesh seemed to shimmer, first gray and then green, with a brief flash of blue before darkening once more.

Count Kesslar finally appeared from the rear of the group of slaves, accompanied by the Werehawk Shah, and made his way directly to the almost naked man. Djogo stood beside Drew, his one good eye fixed upon the young Wolflord. Kesslar and the bald, barely dressed man embraced, shaking hands heartily and laughing all the while.

"My dear Kesslar," said the man in the loincloth. "By the Wyrms, you've brought the enchanting Lady Shah with you, too! How is the Goat treating you, my lady?" He licked his lips, reaching a hand toward her. She backed away a step.

"Well enough," she said pointedly. "I trust you have kept *your* end of our bargain, Ignus?"

The bald man nodded, stroking his fingers over his smooth, oily chest. "Like family, Shah. Like family."

Drew didn't follow what they were discussing, but he paid attention nonetheless. He needed to return to Lyssia, to his friends and his people, so any information he could glean might hasten his escape. Shah was a strange one, staying close to Kesslar at all times. *Odd*, thought Drew, *considering the dark looks she always throws him.* He had his suspicions about her. The Werehawk had rescued him from certain death at the hands of the Catlords and carried him through the air, out of Cape Gala, bloodied and broken, only for him to wake up as Kesslar's prisoner. The notion made his head spin.

Ignus turned to Kesslar, pulling his eyes away from Shah. "I feared you weren't returning. I was ready to send your remaining stock into the arena to celebrate your demise!"

"I wouldn't make it that easy for you, Ignus," said the Goatlord. "I need every one of those souls in the Furnace, especially our brother therians. I've brought them a *true* champion to fight!"

"Really?" said Ignus, walking toward the crowd of slaves. "Bring them forward so I may better see."

The guards lowered their spears, jabbing at the slaves, forcing them to walk across the metal grille. Drew grimaced at the feel of hot iron against his feet, but he pushed the pain to the back of his mind. All those hours training to be a warrior under the watchful eye of Manfred back in Buck House were standing the young Wolflord in good stead.

He walked forward and stood before the man in the loincloth.

"So you're Kesslar's prize specimen, then?" said Ignus. Drew turned, looking back to the others who all struggled, stumbling, none daring to cross the hot metal floor. He stared back at Ignus, getting a good look at their oily host.

Ignus was maybe in his eighth decade. His neck looked deformed, strangely long, and he had a wide mouth with reed-thin lips that seemed to stretch almost back to his ears. His eyes were bulbous, pale, and honey colored with misshapen pupils.

Ignus peered down at Drew's arm. Djogo had clapped his stump in a smaller, tighter iron, just to ensure he couldn't slip his handless arm from the manacle.

"He has only one hand, Kesslar," Ignus said dismissively. "Damaged goods. You really expect me to buy this one from you? This boy probably can't even wipe his own rear; he's not fit for slavery, let alone my ludus. I take only the *best* in my gladiatorial school."

Drew's ears pricked up at mention of Ignus's ludus: *A gladiatorial school?* he wondered. *Is this connected to the Furnace that Kesslar and his cronies keep mentioning?*

"I'd be careful what you say, Ignus," said the Goatlord, stroking his short, forked beard. "There's more than one weapon a therian can use in battle, as well you know. This one bites!"

Ignus chortled. "Go on then, Kesslar. Tell me what beast you've brought to Scoria, and I'll tell you what he's worth."

"No, Ignus," said Kesslar, wandering over to one of the tables and picking up a rotten piece of meat. He batted the flies away and collapsed into a marble chair, tearing into the rancid hunk with splintered yellow teeth. "You guess what he is and I'll tell you what you're going to pay me."

Ignus glanced at his companions who hovered behind his throne. The three other men were also bald, bug-eyed, and smooth-skinned; no doubt, Drew thought, relatives of the ugly fellow. Ignus returned his gaze to Drew, looking him up and down, standing back to better judge him.

"From Lyssia?"

Kesslar nodded, devouring the meat.

"The north, I'd say. A Ramlord?"

Kesslar spat on the ground. The spittle hit the metal grille, sizzling where it landed.

"The next Ram I see I'll fleece and gut. I've had all I can stomach from my pathetic cousins."

"A Wereboar then?"

"Too lean," said Kesslar. "Look at his physique. He's built for the kill."

"Some kind of Doglord?"

"Bigger."

"A Bearlord!" exclaimed Ignus, clapping his hands together triumphantly. "Have you brought me a Bearlord?"

"You were closer with dog . . ."

Ignus turned slowly, looking at Drew with a fresh, inquisitive gaze. He stepped closer, their faces inches apart. Ignus's bulbous eyes narrowed and his thin lips peeled back, his foul breath washing over Drew.

"Wolf?"

Kesslar began a slow handclap from the marble chair.

Ignus spun around. "I don't believe you! The Wolves are dead. Wergar was the last, the Lion made sure of that!"

"He missed one of them in his eagerness to put them to the sword!"

"You're lying!"

"He's telling the truth," snapped Shah. "You could take the

silver collar off and see for yourself, if you're so confident."

Djogo reached into a pouch at his hip, withdrawing a short hammer and flat-headed chisel, used by the captain to remove his slaves' collars. He held them out to Ignus. The Lord of Scoria shook his head, sneering at the tall slaver.

"I see you're still making use of this beast," he said to Kesslar.

"Djogo? Of course. One of the finest deals we ever made."

"He's not bitten your hand yet as he did mine?"

"No, he's been dutiful to the last."

Ignus puffed his chest out, oiled skin rippling as he suddenly grew in size. Djogo, for all his height, took a faltering step back as Ignus towered over him. He was threatening to change, intimidating Djogo, keeping the beast in check. *Interesting*, thought Drew. *Another therianthrope—but what kind?*

"I should have fed you to the volcano when I had the chance," said Ignus. He dismissed the slaver with a shove, sending Djogo stumbling backward.

"If you break him, you pay for him," joked Kesslar. Shah kept her attention fixed on Drew, as Ignus rounded on him once more.

"Your master says you're a Werewolf?"

"He's not my master," said Drew, after a long pause.

Ignus laughed. "Very confident for one who is destined for the Furnace, aren't you?"

"If I knew what the Furnace was, I might tremble for you."

"You'll tremble soon enough," said Ignus. He looked Drew over again like a piece of meat, licking his lips. The swollen eyes blinked quickly. He called back to Kesslar.

"How much then?"

"Remember what you paid for Stamm? Double it!"

Ignus spluttered. "You're not serious?"

"Oh I am, Ignus. You wouldn't *believe* the lengths I've gone to, bringing this Werelord to Scoria. He's the most wanted therian in Lyssia, Bast, too, no doubt, now that the Catlords are after him. He's the last of the Gray Wolves—disputed heir to the throne of Westland!"

Kesslar rose and joined Ignus. He offered an open palm to the Lord of Scoria. Ignus moved to take it, snatching at thin air as Kesslar withdrew it for a moment. He stroked his short beard, nodding to himself and giving Drew a sly look.

"Twice Stamm's fee? No, I'm cheating myself." He held out his hand once more. "Make it *three* times, and we have a deal!"

Ignus took the Goatlord's palm and shook it firmly. "You'll cheat me out of house and home, Kesslar, if I'm not careful."

The slave trader grinned as one of Ignus's guards walked to the brazier of coals. Two more took hold of Drew by his shoulders, holding him in a tight grip as the guard stoked the embers.

"You'll need the silver one for the Wolf," said Ignus, as the man withdrew a metal poker from the coals. Drew recognized the glowing silver symbol on the end of the device, a triangle within a circle; the same as the one Djogo bore on his shoulder. His rage rose, the thought of these villains scarring his flesh— the last of the Gray Wolves and rightful king of Westland— almost bringing on the change. To shapeshift now, with a collar about his throat, would prove fatal. He struggled as the guard advanced. A punch to his stomach from one of the soldiers sent him wheezing to the metal-grilled floor as the men held him still and the brand seared his flesh.

Drew's scream could be heard far below in the harbor.

# 4

# HOUSE OF THE WHITE WHALE

**A BITTER WIND** blew through Moga's cobbled streets, sending shutters rattling and townsfolk scurrying for shelter. The autumnal weather was shifting across Lyssia, winter drawing ever nearer, and the north was always the first to feel the change. Inns and taverns crowded the seafront, jostling for the affections of passing sailors and fishermen, offering food, drink, and company on this grim evening. The Torch of Moga, an ancient watchtower, stood proud on the town's natural stone jetty. Forty feet tall, the monolith rose from the promontory, centuries old steps carved around its perimeter leading to a timber platform. A solitary lookout stood atop, watching over the town and harbor.

The grandest tavern of all was the House of the White

Whale, its style owing more to a castle than a drinking establishment. Three stories high and taking up the space of four regular inns, the roof was bordered with granite battlements, complete with turrets on each of the four corners. While providing fine food and ale to the wealthy of Moga, the White Whale was also famed for its gambling hall, where a man could bet on and with anything his heart desired, from the toss of a coin to the blood in his veins.

At the rear of the hall, beyond the gamblers and gluttons for punishment, a flight of steps rose to a mezzanine that overlooked the tables and bars, protected by a gaggle of roughnecks who looked more like pirates than guards. Here, on two huge satin cushions, sat Count Vega and Duke Manfred before the imposing figure of Baron Bosa. The Whale of Moga was busy decanting wine into three golden goblets. Manfred struggled to keep his balance—and dignity—on the cushion, while Vega sat cross-legged, looking annoyingly at ease. Bosa took a drink in each hand, rings and jewels jangling, and passed them across. Taking up the third, he raised it into the air.

"A toast," he said, in a deep, fruity voice that belonged on a stage. "To my dear old boating chum, Vega, and his delightful friend, Manfred!"

Manfred looked surprised by the baron's flowery language, but Vega didn't hold back.

"To the glorious health and long life of our most gracious host, the divine Bosa!"

This made the baron squeal with delight. He was the most unlikely looking pirate Lord Manfred had ever seen. Bosa was a giant, a whale in every aspect. His vast mass filled a chaise longue, his enormous belly resting on his thighs. His arms were lost within a black silk blouse that wouldn't have looked out of place on a dancing girl. Wobbling jowls linked up with a roll of double chins, his face a picture of jollity.

"It's been too long since we last shared a drink, dear Vega," said Bosa, sinking his goblet of claret. His men stood nearby, keeping a respectful distance, but watching the two guests' every move.

"Indeed it has. I've been busy, in case you hadn't noticed. There was the small matter of Leopold stealing my islands from me."

"Heard all about that, dear chap. Terrible business. Sounds like the Kraken's been riding roughshod over your archipelago with impunity!"

"He's a mollusc on the rear end of the Cluster Isles."

"Is that any way to speak of a fellow Werelord?"

"Fifteen years, Bosa," said Vega, sucking his teeth as he swilled the wine in his goblet. "That's an awful long time for bad blood to fester."

The Whalelord looked to Manfred and smiled. "I must

say it is a *tremendous* honor to have the Lord of Stormdale visit my little establishment. You're a long way from home, Duke Manfred. I can't imagine what drama has brought you all the way to Moga."

Manfred could feel the color rise in his cheeks and cleared his throat with a gruff cough. "I'm sure you know full well what's brought us here, Baron Bosa."

Vega raised a hand, making to apologize for his friend's straight talking, but the baron waved him away.

"They don't mince their words, these mountain men, do they, Vega?"

"I don't play these games very well either," added Manfred. "I'm not one for dancing around the issues."

"You don't love dance?" gasped Bosa dramatically, before leaning over toward them, his face suddenly more serious, the fat cheeks hardening and his jaw now set. The smell of roses washed over the Werelords like a wave.

Bosa's voice was quiet when he spoke again, the playfulness gone. "No more games, then. Tell me why you're here."

Vega shuffled forward, trying to diffuse the tension between the Whale and the Stag. "You'll be aware of the events in Highcliff. I'm sure word has reached every rock in the White Sea by now. The Catlords of Bast have marched to the Lion's aid; though Leopold is now dead, they're putting Lucas on the throne."

"But *why* did they come to Lyssia?" The Whalelord jabbed

his fat forefinger at the two Werelords. "Did you not turn on the king and take the throne as yours? Is this not lawful retaliation by the Cats?"

"Not so," said Manfred. "Leopold had imprisoned the last surviving son of Wergar, a boy named Drew Ferran. He was rescued from the Lion's murderous rampage when he was a babe-in-arms, and had grown up as a farmer's boy on the Cold Coast. The king was about to execute the lad on the eve of his son's marriage to Lady Gretchen. We ensured that didn't happen."

"Wergar really has an heir? So, the rumors are true?"

"Indeed," said Vega. "The rightful king of Westland. That's why Onyx came to Lyssia, to ensure a felinthrope of his choosing remains on the throne and controls the Seven Realms."

"Where is this son of Wergar now?"

Manfred and Vega looked at one another awkwardly.

"We don't know," said the Sharklord. "It's complicated."

"You've *misplaced* your king?" said Bosa, hiding a smirk.

"The boy is strong-willed," said Manfred. "He's his father's son, but with something else. He headed south recklessly, no army at his back, to save the life of a friend. He knows right from wrong, but has an empathy with others that's rare among the Werelords: he has the common touch."

The three therians were quiet for a moment, each staring out over the gambling hall as the music played.

"My dear, sweet Vega," said Bosa eventually. "If you and your allies came here seeking sanctuary, I'm afraid you came to the wrong place. I won't stand in the way of these Bastians, and I'm certainly not looking to pick a fight with Ghul. It's been many a year since my rear sat in a ship; I'm not sure it would fit anymore!"

"We're not seeking your swords or support, old friend," said Vega. "I know what kind of hoard you sit on here, Bosa. You've the wealth of ten Werelords on this island, hidden Sosha knows where, the spoils of half a century's piracy in the Sturmish seas. You're sitting on a war chest."

"I make no apologies for my good fortune. It's been hard earned, Vega. I'm a trader, a gambler, an opportunist; make your point."

"The Beast of Bast will come knocking, Bosa. I merely ask you *not* to be drawn into this coming war on the side of the Catlords. I respect your decision not to fight alongside us, but please, don't assist those who'd see us dead."

Bosa rubbed his jowls, tweaking the flesh between thumb and finger.

"Agreed, my dear Vega; I give you my word. If Ghul and the Catlords *do* come ashore, they can expect a dazzling smile, sparkling wit, and a glass of the Redwine's finest, nothing more."

Vega and Manfred rose from their cushions, each offering hands to shake on the deal. Bosa staggered to his feet, batting the hands away and embracing the Werelords, one in each arm. Manfred could just about see the count's smiling face over the

Whalelord's shoulder; it appeared the Wereshark found great amusement in the Stag's embarrassment.

Below the mezzanine, toward the front of the gambling hall, Vega noticed a crowd was gathering, looking out of the huge bay windows that faced out on to the harbor street. He recognized a mob when he saw one, men and women jeering excitedly at a commotion outdoors. He pulled away from Bosa as all three Werelords turned to look.

"Moga might be my home, and a freeport aligned to no Realm, but there are other dangerous individuals on my isle. Did you bring anyone else ashore from the *Maelstrom*?" asked Bosa.

Manfred looked at Vega, answering for both of them.

"Hector."

"Back to the *Maelstrom*!"

A dozen of Vega's men ran along the harbor front, struggling to carry barrels and sacks between them, the wind in their faces and the battle at their backs. Hector remained in the middle of them, urging them back to the landing boats. Half the goods they'd picked up lay abandoned in the marketplace, dropped in their hasty flight. Behind the fleeing sailors the fight continued, swords clashing as the rear guard covered their retreat. Hector cursed his ill luck.

His mission should have been straightforward. While

Vega talked with Bosa, Hector was to requisition provisions for the *Maelstrom*. Vega's mate, Figgis, had accompanied him, guiding Hector to his regular supplier and leaving the Boarlord to strike the deal. It should have been uneventful; pay the man and take the goods back to the ship. Hector hadn't accounted for the distractions the port had on offer.

While he, Figgis, and the more reputable crew members had got on with their job, a few of the men had slipped into a tavern for a stolen drink. One drink had led to five, and by the time they were ready to return to the *Maelstrom* an altercation had taken place. Unfortunately for Hector, his men, Ringlin and Ibal, were at the heart of the disagreement. The argument had become a fist fight, and the fists had led to knives. Two men lay dead on the stoop of the Lucky Nine tavern, cut open by the Boarguard. Chaos had erupted.

Passing beneath the Torch of Moga, the sailors ignored the shouts of the guard in the watchtower, instead concentrating on getting what goods they'd saved onto their craft. The fight drew ever closer, Hector making his way toward the battle to hasten the men along.

*What fools they were to trust the Baron of Redmire with such a daring mission*, rasped the Vincent-vile. *Who'd have thought a shopping errand could result in such bloodshed?*

Ringlin and Ibal were in the thick of it, three of Vega's men shoulder to shoulder with them engaged with ten Moga men, two-deep along the stone jetty, jabbing and hacking with knives and cutlasses. More appeared, rushing toward the melee, reinforcing the enemy.

"Disengage!" shouted Hector, his voice lost in the commotion. The goods were on the boats now; they had to beat a retreat and fast. There was no sign of Manfred and Vega, but they had to move—if they stayed they'd be cut down. He yelled again, but his orders fell on deaf ears. Ringlin and Ibal seemed to be enjoying the fight a little too much.

*They're not listening, brother! Can you not command your own men?*

Hector glanced down the jetty to where Figgis waited, beckoning him to get on the boat. The Boarlord turned back to the fight, slipping on the wet stone floor just as a cutlass ripped down across his torso. An opponent had broken the line, having felled one of Vega's pirates. The man had intended to slash the magister's belly open. Hector's hapless balance might just have saved his life, his jerkin torn open as he landed on his rear.

The attacker was instantly on top of him, striking Hector's forehead with the basket handle of his cutlass. The Boarlord saw stars, throwing his arms up and clawing at the man's eyes in desperation. The man screamed as Hector's fingers found their targets, raking his face. The sound of battle was all around him, the air thick with screams and curses. A stray boot connected with Hector's temple, sending fresh shockwaves racing through his skull. He brought a knee up, connecting with the enemy's nether regions, making him release his grip with a cry.

*Run, brother! Run!*

Hector rolled over, crawling on all fours through puddles, vision yet to return. He could just make out Figgis ahead, calling him frantically. Then an impact in the small of his back flattened him, the knees of his foe crushing his kidneys. The man grabbed a handful of his hair, yanking Hector's head back, throat taut, exposed. He'd have unleashed the vile on the man, but all control was lost. Since the death of Vincent by his hand, Hector had been haunted by his brother's tormented spirit. However, with Hector's knowledge of dark magistry growing, he'd learned to control the vile, acquiring an ability to project the shadowy specter forward like an attack dog. In the heat of battle, though, he now found his composure lost. Hector felt the touch of cold steel at his neck.

No sooner had the blade touched his throat than it was gone, along with the man from his back. He heard a shrill wail and a *snap*, very possibly from his attacker. Hector rolled over. Both Vega and Manfred were in the middle of the mob, transformed into beasts. While many of the enemy leaped clear of the changed therians, some of the braver, more foolish souls stayed for the fight.

The Werestag threw his fists into the men, dropping his antlers to catch and launch them aside. Bodies flew as he made short work of those who stood in his way. The Wereshark was more reckless, not caring how gravely he harmed his enemy. Limbs were torn free, fountains of blood erupting as Vega went into a frenzy. Within moments the pier was clear, the men from the *Maelstrom* regaining their composure, their foes defeated.

"Thanks for coming when you did, Captain—"

Vega, still transformed, backhanded the speaker across the face, sending him sliding along the wet stone pier.

"Shut your rattle, Carney," roared Vega. "If I didn't need you on the *Maelstrom*, I'd have left you here to be skinned alive! They'll be back shortly, and there'll be more of them. Get to the ship, we sail immediately!"

The men didn't move, staring at the transformed Sharklord fearfully.

"Are you deaf?" he screamed furiously, death-black eyes bulging, rows of razor-sharp teeth bared. "Move it!"

The men moved quickly, all but Ringlin and Ibal who had a self-satisfied swagger about them as they passed a prostrate Hector by. The short, fat one patted the other on the back as they returned their weapons to their belts. Vega lunged, catching each by the throat and lifting them high. The men kicked at thin air, hands raking at the Sharklord's muscular gray forearms. Manfred stepped forward to stop him, but the Pirate Prince wouldn't be halted.

"Back off, Manfred," said Vega, focusing on the two rogues. "This is your doing, isn't it? Pick a fight in Moga? They were Slotha's men. *Slotha's!* My boys are many things, but they're not suicidal!"

"They . . . dishonored us . . ." gasped Ringlin.

"You have no honor!" yelled Vega. "Why shouldn't I kill you both here and now?" He tightened his dark claws in their throats, a squeeze away from ending their lives.

"Because they're the Boarguard," said Hector, over the mournful wail of the wind. He was back on his feet again, and Vega looked at him with disbelief. "An attack on my men is an attack on Redmire. And on me."

Vega let go of them, the two men crumpling to the ground in a heap. Both scrambled over one another to get away, scurrying to the end of the long pier and joining the other men on the rowboats. Only the three Werelords remained on the stone promontory, in an uneasy standoff. They could hear Slotha's men calling for assistance, the beaten mob quickly growing into a fighting force.

"We need to return to the *Maelstrom*," said Manfred, taking Vega by the upper arm. The Sharklord shrugged him loose, looking overhead at the Torch of Moga. The lookout had already set light to the pyre on top, the fire burning hungrily and devouring the stacked timber. Bright flames and dark smoke belched into the stormy night sky.

"Your idiot Boarguard might just have drawn Lady Slotha on to our wake. If you ever reprimand me again . . ." Vega choked on his words, furious with the young Baron of Redmire. He pointed at Hector. "Control your dogs, magister. Or I'll control them for you."

# 5

# THE EIGHTH WONDER

**THE SPEAR STRUCK** Drew's temple. The skin split as his head recoiled and he crashed into the dust, ears ringing and head spinning. The weapon may have been blunt and fashioned from wood, but it was deadly enough. Drew scrambled clear as the spear stabbed into the ground where his head had been a second earlier. His attacker let the weapon glance off the floor and pirouetted, bringing it back down to Drew's new position on the baked earth of the ludus. Another roll from the young Wolf enabled him to evade the next lunge, this one destined for his bare belly. His enemy anticipated Drew's next tumble, jumping swiftly ahead of him to place a well-aimed kick at his jaw.

Just as Drew had hoped.

His hand was already coming up, snatching the foot from the air as it swung down. At the same moment he scissor-kicked his combatant's standing ankle, sweeping her legs from beneath her. She landed beside him, the wind knocked from her lungs. He reached for her, momentarily forgetting that he no longer had both hands, his left arm flailing at thin air. Cursing to himself, Drew rolled across, pinning her body while throwing his handless forearm over her throat. One of her arms was trapped beneath her, while the other was held in Drew's grasp. He needed to strike her one more time to the head. Currently, their contest stood at two strikes apiece, the next hit being the winner.

She struggled, writhing to break free, but he held her fast. She gnashed her teeth, trying to bite at his forearm, but he kept his flesh clear of her teeth. They were bright white, and sharp. Her eyes were amber, the black pupils narrowing into slits. He looked at the collar around her throat, silver like his own. *If she changes, she'll die.*

"Finish it!" shouted their gladiator master, a wiry, old fellow named Griffyn. He cracked his whip at the earth a foot from them. A cloud of dust exploded into their faces, and Drew chose the moment to release his opponent and roll away.

She was on her feet quickly, hissing at Drew while reaching for her wooden spear. Drew remained on his knees, panting heavily, looking up at the cruel sky. His skin was slick with sweat, the flesh sore from hours under the sun's burning glare.

"I won't fight her!" shouted Drew, glaring at Griffyn. The old man shook his head and readied another whiplash. The girl moved fast, leaping and landing behind Drew. He made no effort to evade her. They were both prisoners, both victims, being made to perform this foul game for the amusement of Kesslar and Ignus. He hoped his mercy might strike a chord with the girl.

He was mistaken.

"Then you'll die," she said, striking the wooden spear shaft hard across his head.

The clattering of plates and pots stirred Drew from his slumber, stabbing his skull like hot knives. He had the mother of all headaches, every noise hitting home as a hammer strikes an anvil. He'd been deposited on a trestle table in the mess, a corner of the ludus that doubled as both dining area and surgery. His presence hadn't prevented his fellow slaves and gladiators from taking their seats. They surrounded him, glowering as he tried to shuffle clear. A canopy of palm fronds overhead protected them from the worst of the midday heat, the training having halted while the gladiators ate and drank.

Drew swung his feet around from the end of the table and stood up gingerly, scanning the ludus. The other therians stood out against the rest of the slaves, together at a table of their own. While the humans wore their dull pig-iron collars, the therians wore silver chokers. Drew noticed that all gladiators and slaves bore the same mark upon their arms—the triangle within the circle—just as he'd seen upon Djogo. He looked at the scar upon his own left shoulder. His anger at Ignus and Kesslar for further disfiguring him remained undiminished. When he closed his eyes he could still feel the touch of the hot metal against his skin. The flesh was raised, the silver brand having done its damage well. *Djogo was a slave also, then? Or a gladiator?*

Shah stood nearby, in conversation with Griffyn. Both looked across when they saw him rise. Shah came over immediately, but the old man remained a distance away, watching keenly.

"Well, if it isn't the Eighth Wonder of the Furnace, a new Werelord the crowds can cheer for. You nearly got yourself killed out there this morning," she said.

"They were wooden weapons," said Drew, rubbing the back of his head. "What harm could they really do?"

"Don't be arrogant, Wolf. Taboo has other weapons, remember—her claws could have removed your throat if she'd so desired."

"Whatever therianthrope she is, she'd have risked death if she'd changed, and she didn't strike me as suicidal." He looked across the ludus to where the woman sat dining with the other therians. "Ungrateful. But not suicidal."

"You underestimate your opponent. Had you not considered she has more control of her therianthropy than you?"

Drew glowered at Shah. "I didn't expect my kindness to be thrown back in my face."

"Kindness will get you killed."

"Excuse me," said Drew stiffly. He didn't much like Shah and was in no mood to be patronized by one of Kesslar's cronies. He passed by a serving table where a couple of the slaves were dishing out the gruel. Drew snatched up a pot of the anemic-looking slop and made his way to the therian table. There were seven seated in all.

"Mind if I join you?" he asked, his voice unsteady.

Each figure was fearsome looking, and none seemed especially pleased to see him. A look passed between two on the end who appeared to be brothers, heavy-set men with broad shoulders and massive hairy arms. One of them opened the palm of his hand and gestured toward a seat opposite. Drew smiled and sat down beside another large man who left him little room on the end of the bench. He glowered briefly at Drew, his broad nose and lips curling with contempt before turning away.

"Don't mind Krieg," said one of the hairy brothers. "The Rhino can be a bad-tempered beast at the best of times."

"What's a Rhino?"

The brothers looked at each other in disbelief. Even the brute named Krieg allowed Drew a glance before shaking his head. Drew slunk low in his seat, embarrassed by his ignorance, scooping up the gruel with his fingers and shoveling it into his mouth hungrily.

"You're a Lyssian, then?" asked the other brother.

"They say he's a Wolf," said the first. "Is that right?"

Drew nodded, wondering where the conversation was headed.

"You're a long way from home," said number two. "Got a lot to learn, too."

"What do you mean?"

"Well, firstly, showing Taboo down there kindness is a surefire way of getting yourself killed."

The young woman with the amber eyes at the opposite end of the table shot them a glare. The two brothers laughed.

"She doesn't play nice with others, poor little princess!" said the second brother.

"Shut your mouth, Balk, or I'll shut it for you!" she shouted. Balk waved her away dismissively.

"Save your boasts for the Furnace, little girl," said Balk's brother. "My brother and I will teach you some manners in the dust."

Drew noticed that none of the others joined the conversation, each concentrating on their eating and ignoring the bickering.

54

"You're brave when you're with your brother, Arik," the girl said. "I'd watch your back; you can't always hide in his shadow."

Arik grinned aggressively at the girl, baring all his teeth.

"Secondly, sleep with one eye open, Wolf," continued Balk. "I haven't seen you in the Furnace yet, but I suspect you can fight. Makes sense that your rivals will try to dispose of you in the night rather than risk death by tooth and claw beneath the sun."

Drew looked at the others at the table, shivering to think that any one of them might happily murder him.

"And lastly," said Balk, whispering the final piece of advice. Drew leaned closer to hear the words. The big man's breath was rancid. "You'll find no friends here."

Without warning Balk smashed Drew's face down into the bowl of gruel. His head bounced up back into the waiting fist of Arik. This time he flew back, the brother's knuckles catching him across the jaw. Drew toppled off the bench, his body slumping into the baked earth as the brothers tossed their bowls onto him, laughing and clapping as they departed. Drew lay in a heap, shaken and angry.

"Here."

He looked up and saw the open hand of Krieg. Drew eyed it warily.

"Or stay down there like a dog. The choice is yours."

Drew snatched at the hand, the big fingers closing around

his palm. Krieg lifted him as if he were a child, plonking him back on to the bench.

"Thanks," said Drew sheepishly.

"Don't get used to helping hands, boy," grumbled the broad-nosed man. The Werelord opposite him chuckled. If Krieg was large, the other man was a giant—over seven feet tall, Drew guessed. He'd seen these two massive therians sparring in the ludus, hammering at one another with all their might.

"You should give the Apes a wide berth," said the giant. "They single out the weak. They're relentless once they get their teeth into you."

"You sound like you speak from experience."

"They've baited everyone here. They move on if you ignore them." He looked down the table to the girl at the end. "Taboo has yet to learn this lesson."

The young woman snarled. "They bite me, I bite back. They'll learn soon enough."

The giant shook his head sadly. "Seems felinthropes are incapable of turning the other cheek."

"Felinthrope?" said Drew, shuddering. "You're a Catlord?"

"What of it?" she asked sharply. "You've met my kind before?"

"I've had my run-ins."

A shaggy-haired fellow the other side of Krieg leaned around the Rhino.

"You might want to put your differences aside. Once you get into the Furnace, you may depend on one another."

Drew kept hearing mention of the Furnace. This was the arena where combat would take place, so named because of the battleground's location, Scoria's volcanic plateau.

"Depend on each other?" asked Drew. "I thought he wanted us to fight each other?"

"That happens occasionally, if Ignus and his guests are in a sadistic mood, but for the most part we therians are the main attraction," said the shaggy man. Even in human form, the fellow's shoulders were oversized and stacked with muscles, his mass of dark-brown hair framing his head like a matted thatch. His eyes were dark and heavy-lidded, his lips wide and downturned, giving his face a somber, thoughtful appearance. "The Lord of Scoria owns you, as he owns all of us. Our lives are over beyond the walls of the Furnace. We fight whatever they send out, be it human, beast, or monster."

"Monster?"

"You heard Stamm right," said Krieg.

Drew had heard the roars of whatever animals Ignus kept for the arena. They were housed within the circular walls of the Furnace, out of sight of Drew and the other gladiators.

"So we look out for one another?" said Drew, struggling to make sense of the situation. The Apes, as the giant had described them, were clearly a wicked pair, and he doubted they'd spare a moment's thought for Drew if he got into trouble in the Furnace. The girl, Taboo, seemed likewise unhinged, waiting to explode.

The giant sighed, long and hard. He was around Bergan's age, but time and the arena hadn't been kind to him. He was heavily scarred, his leathery skin dusty and gray. His dark eyes seemed sad, their lids downturned.

"You do what you must to survive. If you're looking for wise words, you've come to the wrong table. If you survive your first fight, take it from there. Live for each day, that's the only advice I have for you. Don't make plans for the future."

The giant rose, nodding to Krieg and Stamm before lumbering slowly away.

"The Behemoth speaks the truth," came a voice from the far end of the table. The last of the seven Werelord gladiators was a lean, languid youth around Drew's age, lying on his back on the bench. He drummed his fingers against his stomach, the sound like the rapping of a woodpecker's beak, the flesh hard as teak.

"The Behemoth? Is that his name?"

"It's the name we know him by. I'm Drake, by the way. Just so you know . . . when I have to kill you."

Drew chuckled, causing the others to look up. Even Drake leaned up from where he lay, twisting to stare as Drew's laughter grew in volume. The young Wolflord slapped his hand on to the table top.

"I get it," he said, wiping a tear from his eye and rising to his feet.

"You get what?" asked Stamm, confused.

"All of this. I'm the new arrival. Some of you, like the Ape brothers, will be the cruel ones who'll taunt me. Then there'll be the one who I can't get close to for fear of losing my throat—that'd be you, Taboo."

The woman remained seated, her face twisting angrily.

"Which brings us to the old timers: you, the Behemoth, and Stamm, right, Krieg? I guess you've been here the longest? That just leaves the sarcastic, smart-mouthed loose blade at the end there . . ."

Drake was already up off the bench and leaping across the table at Drew. Stamm and Krieg wrestled him back, while Taboo squealed excitedly at the conflict. Drew stood still, defiantly. He could feel the bile in his throat, thought he might vomit at any moment. His heart pounded, willing him to change, to embrace the Wolf. He couldn't show them how scared he was, couldn't let them see that they'd got to him.

"I see only one *smart mouth* here, Wolf!" spat Drake. "Who do you think you are? Where's your respect for your betters?"

"I was prepared to give my fellow Werelords all the respect they deserved. You each threw that back at me. It's good to know that therians are the same the world over; arrogance isn't unique to Lyssia!"

"You jumped up little turd!" grunted Stamm, letting go of Drake to reach over the table himself now. Stamm's huge mane of matted hair shook as the therian snatched at Drew, the young Wolf just dodging clear of a great, dirty hand. Taboo punched the table with delight. Krieg found himself holding back both of his fellow gladiators now.

"Don't you see?" said Drew, his confidence now shifting to a heartfelt plea. "You're *letting* Ignus treat you like animals. It doesn't have to be this way!"

"Spare your breath, child," said Krieg wearily. "Many have uttered similar words and all are now turned to dust."

"Just so *you* know," said Drew, staring at the therianthropes, "I don't intend to remain here, let alone die in this sun-baked pit in the middle of the ocean. I'll be leaving Scoria as soon as I find a way. It's up to you whether you'll join me or not. I lost a hand in Lyssia, was beaten, tortured, and terrorized by my enemies. I need to return there, to help my people and settle some scores. You may be broken at the moment, but if you remember what it was that once made you great Werelords, come find me. I could do with some tooth and claw at my side."

With that, Drew turned and walked away, leaving the therians staring at one another, lost for words.

On the outside Drew might have been the rightful king of Westland and the best hope for a free Lyssia, but on the inside he was still a farmer's son from the Cold Coast. *I just faced down a gang of Werelord warriors*, he thought. *They could kill me as quick as blinking.* It took every piece of will and nerve on the shepherd boy's part not to stumble as he went.

# 6

# BLAZETOWN

**HIS MOUTH WAS** thick with the taste of smoke. Hacking up a glob of dark spittle, he smeared it on the dirty material of his red cloak. He shuddered, thinking about the homes they had burned, the villages they had sacked, all in the name of the cause; all in the hope of finding the Wolf.

Trent Ferran looked at the burning farms around him. The sound of families sobbing mixed with the crackling of their blazing homesteads. He recognized the people, not so dissimilar from those he'd grown up around back on the Cold Coast; simple folk, for the most part, who busied themselves with tending their flocks and fields. But these people of the Longridings had aligned themselves with the enemy, siding with the Wolf and his allies. He would shed no tears for those who stood against the Lion.

Nearby, a large group of townsfolk gathered in a huddle, a dozen Bastian warriors surrounding them. They looked pitiful, faces smeared with soot and tears, holding one another fearfully. Grazetown was one of the Longridings' largest settlements, a glorified village compared to other towns in Lyssia. They had no defensive walls, and the small militia had resisted as best they could, but they were vastly inexperienced compared to the Bastians and Redcloaks, and the fight had been brief and bloody. The surviving militia had been shackled. Trent didn't know what the plans were for them, but he hoped their families would be spared. He'd spilled enough blood for one night.

Trent looked at the Wolfshead blade in his hands, the sword stained dark from battle; his father's sword, found in the bloody ruins of Cape Gala, left behind by his traitorous brother, Drew. He wondered how many men Mack Ferran had killed with it in battle, fighting for the old Wolf Wergar many years ago. He thought back to the night he and his father had found his mother, freshly murdered by Drew after he'd transformed into the beast. Trent and Mack had had no other choice than to join the Lionguard to seek revenge. The old man had spent his life trying to dissuade Trent from a military life. But with his wife so brutally taken from him, he'd had no qualms in letting Trent sign up alongside him. While Mack was fast-tracked into the Royal Guard of Highcliff, Trent found himself a new recruit for the Lionguard, his skill at horsemanship ensuring a position as an outrider for the army.

When Highcliff was taken by Drew and his allies, Mack had been killed in the initial skirmishes, apparently at the hands of the young Wolf's friends. Trent shivered to think about Drew. They'd been as close as any brothers could be. He hadn't known what kind of monster Drew really was. When the change came and the beast took over, Trent had been help-less to stop him, as Drew betrayed his family and destroyed his world. Drew had taken both his mother and father from him. How many others would the Wolf murder? Trent had to stop him. He was no longer afraid of death. The cause was just, the Wolf his mortal enemy.

Sliding the Wolfshead blade into its sheath, he strode past the soldiers and their prisoners. Some nodded respectfully. He'd proven himself to his brother warriors now; there was no doubting his allegiance, his loyalty. Some had questioned whether he'd be able to stand up and be counted when the fight was on them; after all, he *was* the Wolf's brother. Those con-cerns had been quashed since their forces had left Cape Gala and begun their search of the Longridings; he was every bit the equal of his comrades.

An elderly woman broke from the huddle and rushed to-ward him, cradling a crying baby. She snatched at his cloak, bony knuckles clinging to the deep red material.

"Please," she implored. "Winter approaches and you leave us with nothing!"

The child wailed in her embrace. The mop of curly blond

hair was filthy, the face a mask of misery. The baby's cries cut Trent to the bone. Here was one of the few innocents of Grazetown. Trent tore the woman's hand loose.

"I'm sorry," he said regretfully, pushing the woman away. "I can't help you."

With that Trent strode away, the child's screams haunting him as he departed. He walked between the torched homes toward the tall wooden building at the town's heart. This was the seat of power for Grazetown. The doors were wide open, soldiers carrying provisions and whatever else they could find from within—crates of food, barrels of wine, golden candlesticks, precious tapestries. He entered the building.

The Lord's hall had been stripped of all valuables. Bodies of slain militiamen lay about, including a few soldiers wearing the garb of the Horseguard of the Longridings. Trent stepped over the bodies as he made his way toward the soldiers gathered in front of the Lord's Table. Two figures knelt before them.

Lord Gallen and Lady Jenna, the masters of Grazetown, were broken figures. Gallen's long gray hair had been shorn off, a sign of disrespect to the Horselords. His wife sobbed quietly at his side. To the rear of the table the remaining family members stood, helpless at the hands of the Lionguard. Sorin stood directly behind the Lord and Lady, a grin as wide as the Lyssian Straits filling his broken-nosed face. The Redcloak captain remained at loggerheads with Trent, having still not forgiven the young outrider for snatching Mack Ferran's Wolfshead blade from him back in Cape Gala. Sorin made no attempt to disguise his contempt for Trent, taunting him for being the Wolf's brother whenever the opportunity arose. He nodded at Trent, throwing him a filthy wink. Trent disliked the man, but he was an accomplished soldier.

"I ask you again: where's the Wolf?" said Frost.

The albino Catlord paced in front of the kneeling Horselords, every movement smooth, almost lazy. He carried his staff in his hands. Gallen lifted his gaze to Frost.

"I've told you already, we don't know his whereabouts. Since your people sacked Cape Gala, my wife and I have been on the road, heading home. We were not party to the violence that took place there."

"Come now, my lord," said Frost. "This isn't a difficult question, yet you insist on telling mistruths. You were seen fleeing the city with your fellow Horselords, those who had revolted against Lord Vankaskan."

"He was no lord to us!" spat Jenna tearfully, instantly catching a look of warning from her husband.

"Now we're getting somewhere. I know he was an unpopular choice as Protector of the city in my family's absence, but he was your lord nonetheless. I do not seek a confession here; we know all we need to know from the noble Viscount Colt. He has very honorably told us *exactly* who participated in the revolt."

Jenna sneered. "That old nag is a traitor to the Longridings!"

"Yet he sits on the throne in Cape Gala now—imagine that!" The albino stopped pacing, swinging his staff behind his back and hooking it between his crooked elbows.

"Where—is—the—Wolf?" he said slowly.

Gallen sighed. "We don't know. Brenn be my witness, we don't know."

"You must know! You and your cohorts freed him!"

"Drew was gone when we arrived in the courtroom. All that remained were the dead and unliving, thanks to your friend the Ratlord!"

Trent trembled at the memory of the risen dead they'd encountered in Cape Gala, the handiwork of the Ratlord Vankaskan. The dark magister hadn't been content with killing his enemies in High Stable, instead raising them from death to torment them anew. Sorin withdrew his sword, the sound of the metal against scabbard causing the husband and wife to look warily over their shoulders. The sword shone, silver runes catching the light of the fires that burned beyond the hall's windows. Trent watched Sorin. He'd seen him question people every day since they'd left Cape Gala. It always ended the same way.

Gallen's eyes widened.

"I swear to you, we don't know where he went!"

"Wait," said Trent, interrupting the interrogation. "Perhaps he doesn't know the whereabouts of the Wolf. But there were others present who might."

"Go on," said Frost, gesturing to Trent to continue. Trent stepped forward.

"The Wolf had friends in Cape Gala, did he not? Lady Gretchen of Hedgemoor—the Werefox was close to him, wasn't she? She was with you when you left your city. Where did she head to?"

Jenna nodded at Trent, tears flowing as she looked at him imploringly.

"Wife, please—" began Gallen, but she spoke over him.

"If I tell you, how do I know you won't kill me? You have slaughtered so many of our people!"

"You have my word we shan't harm you, my lady," promised Trent, his face grim. "Please, answer the question and this torment shall be finished."

"Calico," she stammered. "She heads to the coast."

Trent straightened, turning to Frost. "If she heads to Calico, then the Wolf will follow."

"You're sure of this, Ferran?"

"He chased her all the way to Cape Gala. If he lives, he'll find her, I guarantee it."

"Good," said Frost, spinning his staff. "Find the Fox, find the Wolf."

He banged the base of his staff on the floor, the metal-shod end striking the stone flags. An eight-inch spike projected from the top, the silver blade appearing in a flash. Frost turned the staff and lunged, the blade sinking deep into Gallen's heart.

Frost held it there as the Horselord spluttered, his wife and family screaming in horror. The Lord of Grazetown slid from the end of the silver spear, collapsing on to the cold floor. Frost flicked off the blood before striking the base once more and the blade disappeared from whence it came. He turned, putting an arm around Trent and walked away, as Lady Jenna wailed mournfully over the body of her dead husband.

"You promised you'd spare us!" she screamed as they left.

"He said we'd spare *you*, my lady," called Frost as he stalked out of the room, the young outrider at his side. "Be grateful we're men of our word!"

Trent looked back at the Horselord's family grieving around their slain father.

"Well played, Ferran." The albino chuckled. "You're a shrewd young man. Come with me; that sword of yours is missing something."

# PART II

## RED SAND, DEAD SEA

# I

# A BEAST AT ONE'S BACK

**FOR A MOMENT** he didn't recognize his own reflection. His face was tanned, beaten by the elements, while his black hair hung over his eyes, cloaking them in shadow. The water rippled as he ran his fingertips across the surface, the image fracturing with their passing, soon gone from sight.

Clasping the barrel's edge with his one hand, Drew dipped his face forward, submerging his whole head beneath the water. Although it was dusk, the water was warm after standing all day beneath the hot Scorian sun. He shook his head from side to side, the water cleansing the blood, dust, and filth from his face.

When his head came up he was momentarily blinded, dragging his mutilated left arm across his eyes, blinking the water away. Slowly, he was adjusting to life without the hand,

relying on his right for every little task. The phantom sensa-
tions would probably never leave him, but he could learn to
tolerate them in time. As his vision returned he realized he
was no longer alone. The roofless bathhouse was deserted; the
human and therian gladiators had disappeared to the ludus to
eat. Having spent the day surrounded by others, fighting and
sparring, Drew had taken a moment for himself, disappearing
into the baths of the gladiator school to reflect in solitude on
his predicament. He should have known better. Privacy was a
luxury he no longer enjoyed, and a lone soul separated from the
pack would always be a target for predators.

Arik and Balk had appeared at the far end of the open
chamber, casting long shadows in Drew's direction as they
watched him, waiting for him to move. Drew could feel the
adrenaline coursing through his exhausted body, preparing
him for the coming fight. He wasn't ready for this. His body
was battered and bruised from hours of punishing drills and
contests. He eyeballed each of the brothers, baring his teeth,
putting on a show of strength. But it was bravado.

The Apes had both sparred with him over the course of
the day, and he'd bested each of them under the watchful eye
of Griffyn, the old gladiator master. Drew had put his victories
down to good luck and survival instinct. He was approaching
each fight as if it were his last, each opponent in the ludus an
obstacle to overcome if he was ever to see Lyssia again. Beating
the Wereapes in single combat was one thing; defeating them

both at once, however, was a feat that no gladiator had ever accomplished. The two brutes grinned, their huge white teeth shining within their ugly faces as they stepped forward.

Then they halted.

Their smiles transformed into sneers. Arik spat on the floor and Balk stalked away. The remaining Wereape growled, the sound deep and bassy, bouncing off the bathhouse walls and making Drew's guts quake. Then the warrior turned and lumbered after his brother. Drew remained motionless, suddenly realizing that he'd been holding his breath. Slowly he exhaled, his lips trembling as the air escaped in a steady, relieved stream. His extremities shook, his body still prepared for a fight that wasn't going to happen. *What had made them stop?*

"I can't always have your back, Wolf."

Drew turned at the voice, surprised to see Drake standing a few feet behind him.

"I didn't see you there."

Drake pointed after the departed Wereapes. "They did."

He walked past Drew toward the water barrel, grasping the wooden frame before plunging his head beneath the water's surface. For the first time, Drew got a good look at him. Drake was perhaps a year older than he, and by the look of his body he'd spent a great deal of time in the Furnace. As toned and muscular as he was, his torso was hatchmarked with old injuries, a grisly map of scars. Drew thought about his own awful injuries—the severed hand, the whipmarks on his back from

Highcliff, his brand from the Furnace—and felt an empathy for another person that until that moment had been missing since he left Lyssia.

With alarm, he realized that Drake's head had been submerged for a dreadfully long time. Was Drake trying to take his own life? Drew lurched forward, grabbing the other therian by the shoulder and yanking him back out of the barrel. The two tumbled into the dirt, Drake beating Drew away with an expression of deep irritation on his face.

"What are you doing?"

"You'd been under for ages," said Drew. "I thought . . ."

"You thought what? I'd drowned?"

Drake got to his feet, shaking himself off, his torso and head soaking. He ran his hands through his hair, slicking it away from his face.

"You've got a lot to learn about the therians of Bast, Wolf." Drake chuckled. "I'm a Werecrocodile. Water is the least of my worries."

Drew gasped. "I fought one of those croc-creatures. They're like *dragons*!"

Drake laughed. "I suppose so. My father always told me we were descended from the dragons. Perhaps he was on to something."

Drake held his hand out to Drew, snatching his arm and helping him to his feet.

"I'm not the only Reptilelord—there are a few of us," he

said wearily, glancing toward the open archway that led from the baths back into the ludus.

"You're different when you're away from the others," said Drew, warming to the other therian.

"I have a reputation to keep up, Wolf. I'm a killer. It'd do me no good if they all thought I was stepping into everyone else's fight. They'd think I was going soft."

"So what was this? A rare moment of compassion?"

Drake looked hard at Drew. "You and I aren't so different."

"You feel that, too?" said Drew. "It's been so long since I've had a proper conversation with someone, I'd almost forgotten what it felt like. This was the last place I expected to find friendship."

Drake arched a thin eyebrow at Drew's words. "Friendship? You're getting ahead of yourself, Wolf. I see myself in you, back when I first arrived on Scoria."

"When was that?"

"Nine years ago."

"Nine years?" exclaimed Drew, unable to hide his astonishment. He tried to imagine what he was doing nine years ago. He was probably playing with the lambs on the farm, or hanging off his mother's apron strings. Drake had been in the ludus all that time, a child, just like Drew?

"I know," replied Drake, thinking for a moment. "I've spent half my life in this hellhole. I can hardly remember my life before the Furnace."

Drew expected to see a change in Drake's mood, but it didn't happen. The Crocodile simply leaned back against the stone wall of the baths and stared up into the darkening sky.

"What was your story, before all this?" Drake asked.

Now it was Drew's turn to smile. "How long do you have?"

He gave Drake a brief summary of his life, from growing up on the farm to the discovery of his lycanthropy and all that had followed.

"The last of the Gray Wolves of Lyssia, eh?" said Drake, sucking his teeth. "You know, your old man was like a bogeyman to the people of Bast. He was 'the enemy across the water,' the monster who was going to sail south and attack our lands. Little did we know the real foe was closer to home."

"Closer to home?"

"The Catlords," muttered Drake. "They're the reason I'm here. They conquered my people, took our land for their own, and stole hundreds of children, like me. I often wonder what became of my family, whether the Cats spared my mother's life or killed her as they did my father."

"Have you been fighting since then?"

"By the Wyrm's teeth, no! After I was brought to Scoria, I was put to work as a slave in Ignus's palace. When I began to change from child into youth they tired of me quickly—I was a liability. The last thing they needed was a Werecrocodile on the cusp of the change wandering around the palace. They sent me down here, under Griffyn's tutelage. I started in the ludus the same time as Taboo."

"He seems strict."

"Griffyn? I suppose he is. The old man's doing you a favor. If he cracks his whip or shoves you back into the sand to spar one more time, just remember: he's helping you stay alive. If he shows you no mercy, that's because you can expect none in the Furnace. Believe me, if anyone knows how to survive the arena, it's him."

"Griffyn? Why?"

"He was a gladiator once himself, possibly the greatest to ever fight in the Furnace. Five years or so he fought for Ignus and his brothers. He was the crowd's favorite, a true champion. If ever a gladiator earned his freedom, it was him."

"He doesn't look free to me."

Drake shrugged. "He's as free as you can ever expect to be when you're owned by Ignus. He no longer wakes each morning wondering whether the day will be his last. You and I don't have that luxury."

Drew thought about the old man, finding it hard to imagine how he had ever been a gladiator, let alone a champion.

"How is it that Taboo is here—a prisoner, a gladiator—if she's a Felinthrope?"

"That's a question you need to ask Taboo. She'll tear my throat out if I go blabbing about her past."

"You know her well, then?"

"Well enough, Wolf. She's the closest thing to a friend I'll ever have."

"That's sweet."

Drake cackled. "Don't talk soft, Wolf. I'll still have to kill her if we come face to face in the Furnace."

Drew shivered at the Crocodile's cold words. "How can you say that so matter-of-factly?"

Drake turned to Drew and prodded a finger in the young Wolflord's chest. "You need to wake up, and fast," he said. "This—you and me shooting our mouths off—this is fun. This feels almost normal, like how folk talk to one another beyond the walls of the Furnace. Only we'll never get to experience that, will we? We're stuck here, and thinking about any other life is sheer folly. You're a gladiator, Drew, and gladiators fight and die. Don't ever forget that."

He was about to jab Drew in the chest again with his final comment when Drew caught his finger.

"There's something you've forgotten, Drake. We may be prisoners for now, at the mercy of Ignus and Kesslar, but we're Werelords. Think of the power each of us possesses, and what we could do if we worked together. There *is* a life for us beyond these walls. And I intend to return to it."

Drew turned toward the ludus. "Thanks for stepping in with the Ape brothers," he added over his shoulder as he made for the archway from the bathhouse. "But if you're worried about losing face in front of the other gladiators, next time feel free to leave me to fight my own battles."

The Werecrocodile watched the Wolf go. "You're on your own, Wolf!" he shouted after him, chuckling hollowly as Drew disappeared.

## 2
# DEADLY WATERS

**THE *MAELSTROM* REMAINED** tantalizingly out of reach of the two chasing ships' cannons, her eight white sails faintly visible in the dim light of dusk. The pursuers had been dogging the pirate ship for days now, hot on her heels since she'd fled Moga in a mist of blood. The ships represented the twin enemies of the *Maelstrom* on the high seas: the *Rainbow Serpent* of Lady Slotha and the *Quiet Death* from the Cluster Isles. Slotha had not sat idle since hearing of the bloodshed in Moga, sending the *Rainbow Serpent* out immediately. The *Quiet Death* had joined the chase not long afterward, the lead ship in the Weresquid Ghul's fearsome fleet.

While the captain of the *Rainbow Serpent* wasn't known to the crew of the *Maelstrom*, they knew the *Quiet Death*'s commander all too well. Captain Klay was another of the Sealords, a therian of the ocean like Vega and Ghul. A pirate first and a Werelord second, the Barracuda was a butcher of men and a maker of widows. Sticking close to the *Rainbow Serpent*, Lord Klay was determined to be the Werelord to capture the elusive Count Vega and, better still, put the Shark to the sword.

Klay stood at the prow of the *Quiet Death*, as she sailed slightly ahead and to starboard of the *Rainbow Serpent*, willing his vessel to greater speeds, but his ship remained at a distance from the *Maelstrom*. Vega's ship was the fastest for sure, but the *Quiet Death* was a close second. If Klay could capture the count's ship, he might even end up with the two fastest pirate ships in the known seas. Imagine that! And here was the *Quiet Death*, keeping apace with the Shark. He grinned to himself. Klay had been waiting for his chance to come up against Vega. The man was a braggart and a showman, grown soft over the years on a fading reputation. His time was over. Vega didn't have the nerve to cut it as a pirate anymore, better suited to flouncing around in the courts of Lyssia. *Leave the piracy to the true Sealords, Vega.*

An explosion of fire along the port side of the *Rainbow Serpent* caused Klay's head to whip around. The Sealord ran to the *Quiet Death*'s starboard to better see the destruction, the other ship only forty feet from his own. Two more eruptions along the *Rainbow Serpent*'s flank sent fire racing across her frame, snaking through the cannon hatches below deck. The screams from the men within mixed with the roar of the hungry flames. In moments the ship was careering wildly out of control as the deckhands rushed to put out fires, abandoning their posts—the Tuskun ship was lurching toward the *Quiet Death*.

"Hard to port!" screamed Klay as his own crew rushed to their posts, their pursuit of the *Maelstrom* halted by the devastation that had struck their companion vessel. Fire now covered the decks of the *Rainbow Serpent*, her crew desperately trying to tame the inferno. The *Quiet Death* was able to turn aside just in time as the other lunged across her bow, wails and flames trailing in her wake. A loud *boom* within the middle of the ship sent timbers splintering into the night sky as something exploded in the *Rainbow Serpent*'s belly. Klay's crew watched in horror as burning men leaped from the other warship into the sea.

Fire and yelling on board the *Quiet Death* now caused fresh chaos as Klay's men rushed about in a panic. The Sealord saw his mizzenmast aflame, the orange fire licking up the sails and devouring them hungrily. How could this be happening? He snatched hold of his first mate by the throat, shaking him like a doll.

"What's going on?"

"The fire, Captain!" cried the man. "The fire and the monster!"

*Monster?* Klay tossed him aside into the path of more fleeing men. They looked over their shoulders, clearly fearful of whatever awaited them there.

"Get back, you dogs!" Klay yelled, his face morphing as he began to channel the Barracuda. He whipped out his saber as his eyes grew luminescent, teeth sharpening into long white needles. His skin took on a pale silver pallor, his mouth splitting the flesh as the jaw receded toward his ears.

"Screaming like women—I'm the only monster here! I see you running to the foredecks and I'll cut you in two myself! Get that mast down, and quench those fires!"

To emphasize the point he took a swipe at the air in front of them, the saber scything inches from the men's throats. They fell back as one, terrified into returning to the flames, the first mate leading the way. Buckets were hurried along lines as the crew of the *Quiet Death* was forced to clamber up the burning rigging. Flaming sails fell to the deck as the men struggled to kill the fire. Captain Klay nodded contentedly, pleased that his men were now shaping up.

He was about to return to the rest of his crew when the wet *thunk* of something hitting the deck made him halt. Klay glanced down, thinking a bucket had fallen from a sailor's grasp. The sight of a decapitated head staring back at him did not instantly register.

He looked up as a severed arm spun through the air, narrowly missing his face. Through the smoke and shadows he could see shapes moving frantically, men running, swords slashing, as a melee broke out beneath the flaming mast. He shifted his saber in his grip before stalking through the choking gray clouds. An arc of blood sprayed him as he emerged into the fight. His first mate's carotid artery had been opened up like a bottle of the Redwine's finest. As the body tumbled onto a pile of equally lifeless corpses, Klay squinted through the smoke, trying to spot the killer. He opened his mouth wide, teeth glistening, an armory of shining daggers. He tried to call his men to him, rally them to his aid, but no sound came forth. With surprise and horror he felt a wet sensation washing down his chest and soaking his shirt. He reached a faltering hand up to his throat, finding a gaping hole where it used to be.

The Werefish Klay, commander of the Kraken Ghul's fleet, tumbled onto the corpses of his shipmates. As his life slipped away he stared up at the monstrous silhouette that towered over him; broad gray head, dead black eyes, and razor-sharp teeth that went on forever. *So fast: never saw him coming.* The Wereshark, Count Vega, tossed the lump of torn throat and severed vocal cords on to the Barracuda's body. The last thing Klay heard was the captain of the *Maelstrom*'s voice, dark as the night.

"How's that for your *Quiet Death*, Klay?"


Hector watched the burning ships from the rear deck, the crew of the *Maelstrom* cheering all around him. The ship's rocking left him feeling constantly ill; a life at sea didn't suit the young magister's weak constitution. Hector had found it impossible to keep a meal down since boarding the *Maelstrom* and couldn't

85

wait until they hit land once more. Lady Bethwyn stood at his side, shivering despite her thick cloak. He wanted to put a comforting arm around her but found his limbs unwilling.

*What are you afraid of? She won't bite!*

Hector snarled at the taunts of the Vincent-vile, and Bethwyn heard the noise that escaped his lips. He smiled awkwardly, embarrassment never far away. A commotion on the main deck caused a crowd to gather. Bethwyn turned and followed the men as they rushed to their returning captain. Vega was soaking, his white shirt clinging to his torso as he shook the excess water from his body. Duke Manfred passed the Sharklord his cloak.

"That was some piece of work, Vega," said the Staglord, impressed.

"I did what had to be done. That's put their lead ships off our tail for the time being. We might be able to put some distance between ourselves and the remaining pack."

"Klay's dead, then?" asked Hector as he approached.

Vega looked up, tousling his long, dark locks dry with the cloak.

"Very much so," said the Shark, his characteristic smile not present. "Klay's reputation was built upon hitting hard and showing no mercy. He got what he deserved."

Vega's plan had been as cunning as one might have expected from the Pirate Prince of the Cluster Isles. As twilight fell they'd lowered a small boat overboard, loaded up with flasks of Spyr Oil and a hooded lantern. The Shark had then clambered in and rowed silently back toward the pursuing ships, ensuring he ended up between the two.

Once in position he'd lit the flasks and launched them at the *Rainbow Serpent*, saving the last to throw at the *Quiet Death*. Diving from the boats he'd clambered onto the pirate ship while the crew were distracted by the fires. Transformed into his therian form, he'd added to the madness, slaughtering the enemy and dispatching their captain, the terrible Lord Klay.

Vega clapped his hands, attracting the crew's attention. "Enough lollygagging, lads! We need to make the most of Sosha's blessings. Ghul and Slotha aren't far behind. These are uncharted waters and we mean to reach Roof—let's not get complacent!"

The crew immediately dispersed back to their posts, leaving the Werelords to return to the aft deck. Queen Amelie stared at the burning ships in the west.

"Will there be survivors?"

"I should think so," said Vega. "I'm not a *monster*, Your Majesty. But their fate isn't our concern."

"That's cold," said the queen.

"That's war." Vega sighed. "With respect, Your Majesty, it's the business we're in."

"Don't patronize me, Vega. You forget my people are from this part of the world. The White Wolves of Sturmland are a tough breed."

"So tough they were chased out of Shadowhaven when the Lionguard arrived."

Amelie slapped the Sharklord hard across the face.

"Do not mock me! The White Wolves were lucky to escape Shadowhaven with their lives. If I hadn't agreed to wed Leopold, he'd have slaughtered all my people. Who knows where my brethren are now? My people are *lost*, Vega!"

*See how poisonous the Sharklord is to your precious Council? I can't imagine the Wolf would be pleased to hear how the Shark speaks to his mother!*

"Show some respect to the queen, Vega," said Hector, the words out before he'd even considered them. He wished he could take them back, but it was too late.

*Very good, brother!*

Vega looked up, his left eyebrow threatening to lift off his head. Even Manfred was surprised to hear Hector speak to the Sharklord in such a manner. Vega bowed to Hector, smiling through a split lip he'd sustained in the melee.

"My apologies," said the sea marshal. "I meant no offense."

"This quarreling does us no good," said Manfred. "We need to remain unified. If we're at one another's throats, then we're doomed. With my brother and Bergan gone and Drew still lost, we only have each other."

"I'm sorry, Count Vega. I spoke out of turn," said the queen. "I worry about all lives in these terrible times, even those of our enemy."

"That's understandable, Your Majesty," said Vega, his voice now respectful. "The beast sometimes gets the better of me."

"The hour's late, gentlemen. We shall retire for the evening and see you at first light."

The three male Werelords all bowed as the queen and Bethwyn departed. Hector watched Bethwyn go, the girl glancing back just once before disappearing belowdecks. His heart briefly skipped a beat.

"Speaking to her wouldn't hurt," said Vega, causing Hector to start. The sea marshal didn't look up, unfurling his sketchy maps and inspecting them hopefully by lantern light. Hector's anger flared at Vega's remark, but he remained tight-lipped.

"I'd have thought we'd have encountered one of our own ships by now," said Manfred, casting his thumb across the waters ahead of them on the parchment. "They're out here somewhere, Brenn help them."

"If they're lost then they're at Sosha's mercy," said Vega. "Hopefully they'll all make it to Roof and we can regroup there."

Hector looked away, back toward the door that led to the cabins.

*Yes, go and speak with her, Hector. She won't be able to resist you: you're the Baron of Redmire now, remember?*

Hector shivered, stepping away from the two therians as they looked back to the faded sea charts. He made his way down the staircase back to the main deck, stepping aside as sailors rushed about. The sails clapped as the wind caught them, speeding them away from the burning ships.

He spied Ringlin and Ibal, skulking in the shadows before the poop deck. Since the fight in Moga, Hector had been forced to show control over the duo, ordering them to work alongside Vega's men.

They nodded briefly as he passed them by, but didn't speak.

*They don't trust you anymore, brother, and who can blame them? Letting Vega take a whip to them? Flogging them in front of his crew? You're lucky they haven't slit your throat in your sleep!*

"They had to be punished," said Hector under his breath. He strode to the side of the ship, gloved hands clutching the rail. He could feel his evening meal rising in his throat, the sickness returning.

*Yes, but by you, surely? Not by the Shark!*

"Don't worry about me, Vincent. I know what I'm doing."

The vile's gurgling laughter made Hector's skin crawl. He felt its cold breath rasp against his ear, while bile raced toward his mouth.

"I'll be fine," he whispered to himself, but his words felt hollow.

# 3
# Blood in the Dust

**"YOU'RE UP, WOLF!"**

Drew remained seated, ignoring Griffyn's words. The din was deafening, dust falling from the ceiling into his holding pen. A grilled door barred his entrance into the Furnace, beyond which he could hear the bloodthirsty crowd's cheers. Drew had just witnessed the Wereapes, Balk and Arik, tear through ten gladiators. The brothers now stood in the center of the arena, caked in blood and gore, roaring triumphantly at the ghoulish spectators.

"I shall not fight innocent men."

"Then you'll die."

Drew looked around. The old gladiator master stood behind bars at his back, there to ensure the Wolf entered the arena. He held Drew's collar in his hand, having removed the silver choker once he'd been locked into the cell. Two of Ignus's warriors stood either side of Griffyn, each carrying polearms. The foot-long blades on their ends shone brilliantly, the silver reflecting flashes of sunlight into Drew's face. He winced, raising his wrist stump to his eyes.

"Pick up your weapons, boy," said Griffyn, insistent now. The guards began to lower their weapons toward the grilled door. "Kesslar didn't bring you all this way to be run through in this stinking pen."

"Then he's in for a disappointment."

"Banish all thought of these men being innocent," said Griffyn. "They're killers, Wolf. Gladiators. They live to fight and die."

The Apes had now departed and the bodies of their opponents had been removed. Drew heard the grating of metal cogs as the door mechanism ground into action. The metal bars rose, hard clay falling from the spiked ends that had been buried in the baked earth. Drew choked as the hot dust blew into the cell, catching in his throat.

Griffyn reached through the bars for one of the weapons lying on the floor that had been given to the Werewolf. Drew snatched the old man's forearm, holding him fast. The two glared at one another.

"If you want to live, Wolf, pick up the weapons," he said quietly.

"Why do you care if I live or die?"

Griffyn smiled. "You remind me of someone I used to know."

A guard grabbed hold of Griffyn's shoulder, trying to pull the gladiator master back.

"Pick them up and *fight!*" said Griffyn.

With that, the warriors pulled Griffyn clear and readied their polearms to strike. Drew could hear the crowd chanting and booing now, growing restless with the delay. He examined his weapons.

The two blades were old and pitted, each caked with dried blood and rust. The first was a trident dagger with a basket handle, no doubt formerly the property of some other single-armed gladiator. Drew pulled it over his stump, using the pommel of the other weapon, a shortsword, to bang it home. The fit was tight.

Rising, Drew took a couple of deep breaths before looking back at Griffyn. The old gladiator nodded to Drew, pointing toward the exit. Saying a silent prayer to Brenn, he turned and stepped out into the Furnace.

The first thing that hit Drew was the unbearable heat. The sun glared down, while the ground felt like a bed of hot coals. The sulfurous smell was overwhelming, pockets of the noxious gas leaking from the cracked arena floor. The sand was stained crimson and brown from the day's earlier battles, the blood drying swiftly in the soaring temperature. He was walking into the heart of hell, with no turning back.

The mob filled the seating all around, a mixture of the wealthy and poor of Scoria, all united in their bloodlust. They bayed at Drew as he walked into the center of the Furnace, screaming obscenities and howling wildly. One side of the terrace was taken up by guests from the palace of Lord Ignus, the viewing deck jutting out from the black and white marble walls. Great sails of colorful cloth kept the heat from Ignus's guests while they lounged and feasted, enjoying their sport.

On the opposite side of the arena, Drew saw a trio of figures entering the Furnace. The heat haze caused them to shimmer into focus as they approached. One carried a net and trident, a broad helmet covering his face. Another carried a spear and shield, a pot helm hiding his head from view. The last carried a pair of shortswords, spinning them in his hands as he advanced.

"Behold!" cried Ignus from his viewing deck. He wore a long white robe, open to his midriff, baring his smooth, oiled chest. His three brothers stood leaning on the balcony, similarly undressed, ugly and misshapen. Beside Ignus, Drew spied Kesslar, Shah, and Djogo.

"I give you Drew of the Dyrewood, the last Gray Wolf of Lyssia!"

The mob found new volumes, roaring their approval and chanting for blood.

"He faces Haxur of the Teeth; Obliss of Ro-Shann; and our very own Galtus, the Swords of Scoria!"

The crowd chanted the gladiators' names, each having their favorites. The one named Galtus—whom Drew had to assume carried the two swords—seemed to be popular, clearly one of Scoria's champions. They each raised their weapons to the crowd, soaking up their adulation. *They're* enjoying *this madness!*

The gladiators split formation, fanning out as they circled Drew. Each was clearly a seasoned slayer of men—better armed and armored than the ten the Apes had slaughtered—and they moved with deadly grace. Nevertheless, Drew had no intention of killing anyone. His fight was with Ignus and Kesslar.

"I don't want to fight you . . ." began Drew, but the one with the trident moved quickly. The net flew through the air landing over Drew, the lead balls clattering about his waist as he became entangled.

"Too bad!" yelled Obliss, leaping forward to drive his pronged spear home. Drew twisted clear as the weapon ripped through the air where his stomach had been a second previously. He dived into a roll, arms pinned by the netting as he powered himself toward the spot Obliss had vacated, just as Haxur's spear struck the earth where he'd stood.

"See how he runs with his tail between his legs!" Haxur laughed.

Drew scrambled to his knees, sawing at the net with sword

and parrying dagger, desperate to free himself. The crowd laughed and jeered, disappointed to see how quickly this great Wolf from the Northern continent had fallen. The gladiators laughed, clapping Galtus on the back as he stepped forward.

"You're a long way from home, Lyssian cur," said the Scorian champion. Drew scrambled back, toppling and kicking into the dirt as he retreated. Galtus relentlessly closed in.

"Change for me, dog, and I'll have your pelt as a cloak!"

Galtus kicked Drew, sending him rolling across the hot clay. The last thing he wanted was to let the Wolf loose, but it looked increasingly like he was going to have to. Drew's shortsword arm suddenly came free from the netting, allowing him to bring it up as Galtus bore down. He parried the first sword away, but the second scored a wound across his bicep, causing the shortsword to fly from his grasp. The crowd booed, throwing stones and bits of rubbish into the Furnace.

Galtus held his swords out to either side, turning on the spot as he looked around the arena.

"This is the best Lyssia has to offer?" he bellowed. "Let me kill him, Lord Ignus! Let me end this embarrassment before he ridicules the Furnace any further!"

Ignus stood on the platform, the subject of much of the crowd's booing. They had come to see battle, see blood. He glared across the terrace at Kesslar, then marched over to him, his face red with fury. His brothers joined him, circling the Goatlord.

"You make a mockery of my arena!" spat the outraged Lord of Scoria. "You sell me this worthless hound for a king's ransom and have the gall to watch as I'm humiliated!"

The Scorians continued to curse and bay. Fights broke out as the mob turned on one another in anger. From where Drew lay, surrounded by killers, he could see the confrontation on the balcony, Kesslar shifting back as Ignus and his brothers began to transform. Shah and Djogo took a step away from the enraged Werelords.

Ignus's neck elongated, his jaws widening and cracking. His thin lips ripped even farther back, the flesh tearing as he opened his mouth wide. His gray oily skin rippled, shifting quickly to a sickly green, while his bulbous eyes almost popped from their sockets. He brought his hands up, now transformed into scaly claws, readying a fist to strike the Goatlord. Kesslar stood his ground, horns breaking free as the therians put on a show of their own. Even the gladiators looked up, their attention pulled away from Drew.

"You steal from me, Kesslar, and I would seek recompense!" yelled the Lizardlord of Scoria, his black tongue flicking over serrated teeth.

"You bought the Wolf fair and square," brayed Kesslar, stamping a hoof angrily. "It's not my fault if he won't fight for you!"

"I'll take what you owe me, Kesslar!" roared Ignus. "In blood if I have to!"

With that, the Scorian swung around with lightning speed and grabbed Djogo by his throat. In one savage motion he hurled him off the viewing deck.

"No!" shouted Shah as Kesslar's captain landed twenty feet below on the red clay floor of the Furnace. Before she could move, the three other Werelizards took hold of her, wrestling her into submission.

"Now we'll see a show!" Ignus laughed as his warriors joined his brothers, forming a ring around Kesslar and Shah.

"He can't *do* this!" cried Shah. The Goatlord made no effort to intervene.

Djogo struggled to rise as the Lizard bellowed: "Scoria shall have blood!"

From where he lay on the floor of the Furnace, entangled in the net, Drew watched the desperate Djogo struggling to rise. *How quickly loyalty can shift,* he thought. The slaver hobbled gingerly to his feet, scrabbling for a weapon as Obliss and Haxur advanced. *They'll kill him,* Drew mused, for a moment seized by inaction. Here was the man who had tormented him in Haggard and aboard the *Banshee*. Djogo was a monster—why should Drew care if the trio of gladiators ran the killer through? Finding only his whip, Djogo looked up to the balcony.

"Throw me a blade, I beg you!"

Ignus picked up a blunt knife from his banquet table and tossed it below, the tiny sliver of metal plinking on the hard clay. The crowd roared with laughter as Djogo ignored the insult and cracked his whip overhead, trying to ward off the gladiators.

"Been a while since you fought in the Furnace, Djogo," sneered Obliss, avoiding the lash.

"I bet you thought you were done with the arena once the old Goat bought you!" Haxur laughed as he moved to flank the slaver. Djogo got one more whiplash away before they lunged in and brought him down, spear and trident slashing and stabbings sending him to the dirt.

The lanky ex-gladiator was brought to his knees to a chorus of roars from the crowd. Galtus raised his swords in the air as his companions held Djogo down. The spectators suddenly went wild. Too late, Galtus realized the mob was agitated not by the imminent slaughter of the slaver, but by what was happening directly behind him. He turned quickly, but not quick enough. A powerful lupine leg kicked out, connecting with Galtus's knee and breaking it at the joint. The leg buckled back at an impossible angle, sending the gladiator tumbling in a fit of wailing agony.

The transformation had taken place swiftly, Drew's body now more than accustomed to the change. He rose with the net still wrapped about his dark torso, snarling at the man and roaring in his face. Spittle hit Galtus as he slashed out with his blades, the swords tearing through net and fur as they cut into the Werewolf's flesh. The net fell away like a tattered cloak as Drew shook it loose, ignoring the fresh wounds. A mighty fist caught the man in the jaw, sending him skidding along the dirt, a cloud of dust erupting in his wake.

The two other gladiators stared at the scene, shocked at the sudden and violent metamorphosis and the dramatic reversal of fortune for their fellow gladiator. Djogo winced, his body checkered with cuts as the gladiators disengaged from their fight with him to face the Wolf. They moved to flank Drew, Haxur banging his spear against his shield, calling for the Wolf to attack while Obliss readied to lunge. Drew feinted to attack Haxur, stepping forward on his left before leaping back toward Obliss. The man was already committed, throwing his weight behind his trident. Knowing what the gladiator's move would be allowed Drew to leap above the blow, high into the air as his opponent passed beneath.

Obliss looked up as the shadow descended, the Werewolf landing on him from on high. His companion having taken Drew's attack, Haxur tried to skewer the beast on his spear, a blow that would surely find its home in the therian. Instead he halted mid-thrust, the crack of Djogo's whip signaling the attack. The whip coiled around Haxur's throat, catching fast. Djogo rose in the dust, pulling hard, the throttled man spinning toward him, spear flying from his grasp. Pirouetting across the Furnace floor, Haxur whirled inexorably toward Djogo to be caught in the slaver's arms.

Haxur's eyes widened as he looked down at his chest, the blunt banquet knife piercing deep through his breastplate and

into his heart. Djogo let the body fall to the floor as Drew rose
from the unconscious form of Obliss.

The crowd were silent for a brief, dreadful moment, before
bursting into rapturous applause. Drew stood opposite Djogo,
still changed, chest heaving, as he weighed the slaver up. Djogo
teetered, torso bloody, ready to collapse at any moment. He fell
forward as Drew lunged, changing as he moved. Back in human
form, Drew caught the slaver as they landed, the beast receding as the guards of Ignus emerged from the pens, advancing
toward the combatants.

"Thank you," panted the one-eyed warrior through bloodied teeth.

"Don't thank me yet, Djogo," said the young therian as the
guards surrounded them. "The enemy of my enemy is still my
enemy."

# 4
# THE BOLD THUNDER

**THE CREW OF** the *Maelstrom* had never seen anything like it. The fog that surrounded the ship was the thickest they'd ever encountered, a great bank of sea mist that swallowed everything in its path. The crew stood around every rail, squinting into the gloom. Men muttered prayers, some chanting, others whispering, the atmosphere sinister. A dread sense of foreboding filled the soul of everyone. Nobody, human or therian, was immune.

It had come on fast. The ship's lookout boy, Casper, spied it easily enough, pointing it out to Count Vega and allowing the *Maelstrom* to change course and avoid it. But somehow the fog had still intercepted them. Few ships sailed through the Sturmish Sea, its grim reputation making it a body of water to avoid whenever possible. The sails were lowered as they cut their speed, at the mercy of the mysterious fog. With Figgis holding the wheel, Vega, Duke Manfred, and Baron Hector all stood on the foredeck, looking out into the mist.

"Ship ahead!" cried out a crewman as a black shape appeared out of nowhere. Figgis turned the wheel hard, bringing the *Maelstrom* about to avoid a collision. Manfred and Hector backed away as Vega stood firm on the prow, feet apart and legs locked as the other vessel drew ever closer. The *Maelstrom* ran beside it, the distance between the ships a matter of mere feet. To their relief, the other ship wasn't in flight, simply drifting on the currents.

The ship's name painted down the side proclaimed her to be *Bold Thunder*. She was one of theirs, another escapee from Highcliff that had carried civilians when they'd fled. This was the first ship from their tiny fleet the *Maelstrom* had encountered.

"Grapples and ropes!" cried out Vega as he paced along the deck, Manfred and Hector close at his heel. Lines were hastily thrown, securing the *Bold Thunder* to the *Maelstrom* and bringing her alongside.

"Captain Crowley!" called out Vega, hailing the other ship's skipper. He waited for an answer, but none came—the ship appeared deserted. The sea marshal turned to look at his puzzled companions.

"Perhaps they're all sleeping in their cabins," said Vega

with a grim smile, unsheathing his cutlass. "After me, lads—and stay on your toes!"

With that, Vega placed his blade between his teeth before taking hold of a mooring rope and beginning to drag himself across. Hector looked at Manfred worriedly.

"I think he means us to follow, Hector," said the Staglord, taking hold of the rope and clambering after the count.

Hector watched him go, his insides knotting, hands sweating inside the leather gloves.

*Well? Aren't you going to follow, brother? Afraid of what you'll find?*

The young magister ignored the vile's taunts, stepping up onto the rails and taking a grip on the rope. It bounced in his grasp as Manfred disappeared into the fog ahead. Hector threw his legs around it, letting his body swing until he was suspended beneath it, gripping with his arms and legs. The waves lapped ten feet below him between the two ships, clapping against the hulls in anticipation of his falling.

Hector glanced back before setting off, spying Queen Amelie and Bethwyn at the edge of the rail. He'd summoned enough courage to speak to Bethwyn in the last few days—only small talk, light banter that didn't lead anywhere—but it was a start. His life felt empty without his friends: Drew, Gretchen, and Whitley were lost to him, possibly forever. A blossoming friendship with Bethwyn might fill that void.

"Be careful," whispered Bethwyn, her eyes never leaving him.

His heart beat faster now, the weight of expectation having doubled suddenly with this unexpected audience. He just needed to get across without making a fool of himself. He began to move.

At the middle point between the ships, the rope sagged, swinging wildly. Hector closed his eyes, inching his hands forward one over the other, dragging his knees onward while gripping on for dear life. He could swear he felt the waves slapping his back, could imagine the horrors lurking in the depths waiting to take a bite. Nearing the *Bold Thunder* he found his grip slipping. Panic rising, he feared he might fall at any moment.

A firm hand took hold of his jerkin, hefting him up through the air, away from the rope, and down on to the deck of the *Bold Thunder* in one motion. His legs wobbled as he steadied himself. Vega patted him down.

"Are you all right, Hector?" asked the count.

"I'm fine, thank you, Vega," he replied, trying to sound confident while his trembling voice betrayed him. He looked around as more men from the *Maelstrom* joined them.

The *Bold Thunder* was a ghost ship.

There was no sign of anyone on deck, the wheel unmanned and the sails flapping idly in the faint breeze. The men fanned out, calling to one another, remaining in earshot when the fog threatened to hide them from their shipmates. Hector unsheathed his dagger, holding it warily before him. The Lord of

Stormdale pulled a lantern from its housing on the main mast, and taking out his flint and steel he set about lighting it.

"Have you seen anything like this before, Vega?" asked the Staglord as he worked on his tinderbox.

"Very rarely; sometimes piracy can be the cause of an abandoned ship, but more often than not the pirates take the ship." He smiled at his fellow therians. "I've done it myself!"

Hector walked toward the cabin hatch that led belowdecks. He flexed his left hand, the black skin of his palm rippling beneath the glove as he held it toward the handle. A hand on his shoulder caused him to jump.

"You want me to go first?"

It was Vega again; ever present, shadowing his every move. *And you thought I was bad?* said the vile in his ear.

Hector turned to the captain as assuredly as he could. "You're welcome to accompany me, Vega."

The sea marshal looked impressed, gesturing to the door. "After you, dear baron."

Hector grasped the handle and opened the door. The dark below was impenetrable. Hector shivered, his courage deserting him. He was about to turn and suggest Vega lead when the lighted lantern was offered by Manfred.

"Here, Hector. Looks like you'll need light down there."

Hector smiled, gratefully taking the lantern before proceeding down into the belly of the *Bold Thunder*. He heard the footsteps of the following Werelords, relieved he had them at his back. The stairs led down into a cramped corridor that ran to the officers' cabins at the rear, and forward to a cargo hold.

"The *Bold Thunder*'s a merchant ship," said Vega, ducking as he entered the corridor behind Hector. "Crowley's been a regular trader along the Cold Coast since I was a boy. He'd never leave his ship, not under any circumstances. This is his home, his life."

He slapped the wall as if to emphasize the point, as Hector entered the cargo hold. Crates and barrels were lashed down against the walls, provisions that had been stowed in the hold before the violence had broken out in Highcliff. Crowley had taken as many civilians onto the *Bold Thunder* as possible, crowding them belowdecks as the ship had set sail. Empty bedrolls littered the floor, with not a single body occupying them.

"Where *is* everybody?" gasped Hector.

"It's like a tomb down here," said Manfred.

"A tomb without any bodies," added Vega quietly.

Manfred pulled his cloak tight around his chin. "I don't like this one bit."

Hector inspected the lashed-down goods, checking what Crowley had been shipping. Manfred followed, reading the words aloud that marked each crate and barrel.

"Grain, vegetables, wine; there's enough here to feed the *Maelstrom* for a couple of weeks. Why would they leave it behind?"

"Crowley wouldn't," said Vega, rubbing his jaw thoughtfully. He headed toward the cabins. Manfred and Hector hurried along behind him.

The captain's quarters were well furnished. A leather-backed chair swiveled lazily behind his huge desk; ledgers, sea charts, and maps remained unfurled on the table, open ink-pots holding them in place. Vega skirted the desk and went over to the bunk. Rummaging beneath it he found a chest. He pulled out a knife and jammed it into the lock. With a crack the box opened, revealing gold, silver, and personal artifacts; all of Crowley's worldly possessions. Vega stared up at his companions.

The three men returned above deck, where the *Maelstrom*'s away party had gathered. Vega addressed the group.

"There are goods below that we need aboard the *Maelstrom*. Whatever happened to the crew and civilians of the *Bold Thunder*, we can't neglect the fact that we left Moga in a hurry, without anywhere near the provisions we required."

Vega couldn't help but glance Hector's way at the mention of the disastrous encounter in Moga. Hector simmered silently.

*Any opportunity to stick the knife in . . . and twist . . .*

Hector looked at the gaudy dagger he always carried with him—the dagger that had ended Vincent's life. Thin wisps of black smoke materialized before his eyes as the vile's thin hand appeared to claw at its hilt.

Vega continued, aware that his men were uneasy aboard the abandoned vessel. "I know none of you wants to be on this ship any longer than need be, so be quick about it. Peavney, you're in charge."

One of the *Maelstrom*'s mates stepped forward as the three Werelords paced back toward the mooring ropes that held the two vessels together. Hector spied Ringlin and Ibal among them, lurking at the rear of the bunch. Both men nodded to their lord.

*Seems they've found their respect again*, whispered the vile. *But for how long, brother?*

Hector skidded on the deck, his legs threatening to fly from beneath him, his dagger flashing wildly as he steadied himself.

The duke and the count caught him, "Careful, Hector." Vega grinned. "You could have someone's eye out."

The vile hissed in Hector's ear. *Every barbed word the Shark says hides a meaning just for you, brother!*

"I know what I'm doing, thank you, Vega."

Vega didn't respond to the riposte, instead crouching and inspecting the deck. He traced his hand across the timber planks where Hector had slid, his fingers slick with brackish slime. He flicked it, the gelatinous liquid spattering on to the deck a few feet away.

"What is it?" asked Manfred, frowning.

"I have no idea," said Vega, the mischief in his voice replaced by concern. "I have absolutely no idea."

# 5

# RECRIMINATION
# AND RECUPERATION

**THE LIZARD LOUNGED** in his stone chair, alone, staring at the open balcony that overlooked the Furnace. The last of his guests from yesterday were finally gone, having remained during the night to share in the debauched entertainment. His brothers had retired to their own quarters in the palace, nursing their heads and stomachs after their excesses.

The rap of a spear on the door, followed by it swinging open, brought the Lizardlord's attention back to the rear of the hall.

"Count Kesslar and Lady Shah, my lord," the guard announced.

"Send them in."

The guard stepped into the chamber, followed by the Goatlord and the raven-haired lady, and three more warriors fell in behind them. They came to a halt before the metal grate. The guards stood to the side of the pair, not retreating from the chamber. Kesslar eyed them, stroking his gray beard between bony knuckles.

"You took your time," snapped Ignus, reaching down beside his throne to pick up a terra-cotta bowl. He scooped up a handful of yellow oil out of it, slapped it onto his chest, and began to massage it into his skin. Shah wrinkled her nose at the sight.

"I didn't realize we were to come rushing like your lackeys, Ignus. We are still guests, are we not?"

"For the time being," said the Lizardlord, the threat evident in his voice. "I plan another contest in two days' time and don't want the same debacle we witnessed yesterday. What guarantees do you give that this Wolf will cause no further chaos?"

"None, Ignus. He's troublesome, but it's not my place to break him to your will. That's *your* job. I simply supply the raw meat."

Ignus threw the bowl at Kesslar, the pot shattering against his shoulder and sending the hot oil over his face. The Goatlord cried out, wiping the amber liquid from his eyes.

"Do not dare to enter *my* home and tell me how *I* should

run my affairs, Goatlord! You made a mockery of my arena with your incompetence! I'll make a gladiator out of the Wolf, mark my words, but our business isn't finished. You still owe me for the shame you brought to the Furnace."

"I owe you nothing," said Kesslar.

The guards shifted at his words, spears twitching menacingly. A jet of sulfurous steam erupted from the grate, as if the volcano was adding its voice to the proceedings. Ignus pointed a clawed finger at the slave trader, his face contorting as his rage rose.

"Say that one more time, Kesslar, and you'll pay with more than blood, flesh, and bone!"

The Goatlord sulked, smearing the last of the oil's residue from his face on to his sleeve. Shah remained silent, watching the guards warily.

"Good," said the Lizard, reclining on his throne once more. "I think you know what I ask of you."

"Consider it done," muttered Kesslar.

"Speak up!"

"He's yours once more!" shouted the Goat. "Do with him as you please!"

Shah suddenly understood and became animated. "You can't do this, he's a free man!"

"Be quiet, Shah," snapped Kesslar. "Have you not yet learned? None who are in my service are truly free. What part of being a slaver do you not yet grasp?"

"But he's your friend! This is unfair!"

"This is business," said the Goat, glaring at Ignus.

"That's the spirit, Kesslar," said the Lizardlord. "And I'd mind your tongue if I were you, Shah. You forget that I hold your father still. His wings may be clipped but I can do an awful lot more if I so please!"

Shah looked between them, unable to decide which she despised more.

"If you're done with me, I would like to retire to my room," she said, her voice raw with anger.

Ignus nodded and waved a hand dismissively. Kesslar snatched at Shah's arm as she turned to depart.

"Do not do anything foolish, woman. I'd hate to lose you, too."

Shah tugged herself free, tearing her sleeve. She took a staggering step away from Kesslar before storming from the foul hall.

Drew stared into his bowl, his stomach knotting as the grains shifted. He deftly picked out the tiny grubs from the two-day-old rice, flicking them away before proceeding to eat. His insides rumbled, hunger ensuring his search for unwanted visitors in the meal was short-lived. If there were any more of the creatures in the gloopy mush, they'd be dead soon enough once they hit his belly.

He kept his head down, not wanting to attract further attention. It had been a chaotic time since his appearance in the Furnace. Many of the human gladiators had given him a wide berth, wary of what he was capable of after defeating three of their best. Galtus and Obliss glowered at him from across the ludus, still mourning the death of Haxur and blaming the young Werewolf for his part in the gladiator's demise. Galtus's right leg was strapped in a splint, and the man never took his eyes off Drew.

The therians had been less evasive, Arik and Balk wasting no time in continuing their taunts. Drew gave them nothing, taking their insults. The remaining Werelords had kept a respectful distance, although he'd sparred in the ludus with Krieg the Rhino and Stamm the Buffalo. He'd trained alongside them for hours that afternoon, trading blows, parrying, and wrestling, but not a word had passed between them. Presently the pair sat down at Drew's table.

"You fought well in the Furnace the other day," said Stamm from beneath his shaggy mane. For once, the Buffalo's somber face seemed a touch less miserable. His sad eyes twinkled as he looked at Drew with newfound respect from beneath his thick fringe.

"When you finally fought, that is." Krieg laughed. "I thought they were going to finish you in the pen before you got out of the gate!"

Drew wondered whether this was the precursor to more insults like the cruel games of the Ape brothers. Neither therian showed signs of aggression. Indeed, Stamm was now smiling, his thick, matted hair shaking as he rocked in his seat, his laughter low and rumbling.

"I didn't know how that would play out," Drew muttered. "I won't take a life without just reason."

"I could have told you the crimes those three committed in the outside world before you were led into your pen, Wolf," said Krieg. "That may have made your decision to fight that bit easier."

"What do you mean?"

"All three were murderers. They were bought by Ignus to perform. None will leave alive."

"Seems Ignus might have done something right there," said Drew.

"Ignus serves himself when buying the lives of these killers," said Stamm. "His reasons are entirely selfish. He wants the very *best* killers to walk on to the red clay and do battle."

Drew looked over his shoulder, spying the human gladiators still watching him.

"They knew Djogo. Did the slaver fight here in the past?"

"He used to be one of them, a gladiator, and a fine one for a human," said the Wererhino, snorting as he threw his rice down his throat. "Kesslar struck a deal with Ignus, buying the man and making him his own. Djogo's worked his way into a position of power for the Goat by all accounts. He's the exception to the rule."

"He's a ruthless killer," said Drew. He hadn't seen the slaver since the fight in the Furnace. He wondered what had become of him.

"The young Wolf catches on fast." Stamm chuckled, scooping the remainder of the rice out of his own bowl. The Buffalo shoved it into his wide mouth, slurping the last grains from his thick, dirty fingertips.

Drew shook his head. "Why did Ignus throw him into the arena?"

Krieg leaned across the table, keeping his voice low. "Ignus and his brothers own *everything* on Scoria. Anyone who comes here is a guest of the Lizards so long as they remain in favor. It appears Kesslar displeased Ignus when his star gladiator failed to live up to expectations. That would be you, of course."

Stamm added his voice. "In Ignus's eyes, the Goatlord deceived him. He took Djogo as payment for Kesslar's bad business. You cost the Lizard a great deal of gold, Wolf."

Just then the Behemoth came over, sitting down at the opposite end of the table from them. Drew felt the bench bow as he took his seat.

"Won't you join us?" asked Drew, making the most of the thaw in relations between the therians.

The Behemoth turned slowly as he was about to take his first mouthful of food. The man's eyes were spaced farther apart than one might expect on a human, and his skin had a hard, hide-like quality, as if whatever beast he was remained hidden just below the surface. Without speaking, the Behemoth rose. Any fears Drew had that he'd offended the giant disappeared, as he paced farther down the long table to join them, the ground trembling beneath his footsteps.

"Thank you," said the Behemoth as he sat. "Am I joining you to dine, or for something else?"

Stamm and Krieg looked at one another, unsure what to make of the Behemoth's question. Drew wasted no time.

"What else could you be joining us for?"

"The grand speech you made the other day—I dismissed it as sunstroke initially. But now I see you're a man of conviction. You really intend to escape the Furnace, don't you?"

"I do."

Stamm waved his hand dismissively. "You waste your words; talk of escape is futile."

"How is it futile?" said Drew urgently. "I was told the Werelords were noble; look what you've been reduced to!"

"Be quiet, boy," said Krieg, big lips curling back to reveal teeth like blocks of granite. The therians may all have been wearing silver collars, but each was more than capable of killing Drew in human form if they put their mind to it. Nevertheless, Drew would not back down.

"You've become used to fighting alone, looking after your own skin in the Furnace. But imagine what we could do if we were to *combine* our strength and make a stand! Do you not want to see your homelands again?"

"Our homelands are enslaved, just as we are, Wolf," said Stamm. The laughter that had earlier been evident had disappeared, the Werebuffalo's thick mane casting shadows over his face once again, sad eyes drooping as he stared at the floor. "Do you think Lyssia is the first of the Catlords' conquests?"

"The boy does not speak for me," said Krieg, shaking his head.

"If we escape the arena, we can work together, Krieg. We can unite against our common enemy. You risk your life every time you enter the Furnace. Why not risk it for something noble for once?"

Krieg snatched angrily at Drew, but the young Werewolf was too quick for the Rhino, dodging out of reach. The debate was descending into a fight.

"Leave the Wolf alone, Krieg," said the Behemoth. Krieg growled and snorted, bringing his fist back but keeping his glare on the young man.

"He's right," the giant continued quietly. "Each of us has been dragged to this purgatory. We all have scores to settle with Ignus and his friends, like Kesslar and the Catlords."

"And where would your grand plan start?" asked Stamm, his voice a whisper.

The Behemoth sighed. "Thinking was never my strength. My strength . . . would be my strength."

Drew looked around the ludus at the other gladiators. Galtus and Obliss couldn't be trusted, but there had to be other

118

humans present who wanted to escape. He saw Taboo eating at another table with Drake. His eyes suddenly recognized a familiar face being led out of the small surgery tent at the rear of the ludus by master Griffyn.

"Excuse me," said Drew, rising immediately and making his way between the tables, ignoring the jeers of Galtus and Obliss on one side and the Apes on the other.

Griffyn was in deep conversation with his man, heads close together as they spoke quietly. Drew slowed his pace. The two appeared to know each other very well. The aged gladiator had his arm around the other's shoulder in a fashion more familiar than Drew might have expected. *Almost paternal*, thought Drew. He thought back to the rare occasions as a boy when Mack Ferran would put a consoling arm around him when he was hurt. He stepped before the two men, who looked up with a mixture of surprise and shock. Griffyn seemed flustered.

"Can I help you, boy?" asked the wiry old man, his hands scratching at the silver collar that encircled his ragged throat. *So Griffyn's a therian*, thought Drew. *Yet Ignus ensures the collar remains around his neck. It seems freedom in Scoria still comes with conditions attached.* The man beside him wore a newly forged collar of iron.

"You might be able to," said Drew, before turning to the Furnace's latest recruit. The man stared back at Drew with one good eye, the other missing from a recent fight. "But it's Djogo I really wanted to talk to."

# 6

# SONG OF THE SIRENS

**SHE SWAM IN** a lake, crystal-clear waters breaking with each stroke of her arms. The shore was comfortingly close by; the silence deafening yet beautiful. She was alone, the only soul in the world, content with her solitude. Rolling over, she made a series of backstrokes, her hands cutting through the heavenly water and propelling her gently backward. She looked up at the sun, its warm rays invigorating and caressing her from above. She let her arms trail as she kicked her feet, turning once more on to her chest, allowing a giggle to escape her lips. She dipped her head beneath the water and opened her eyes.

The darkness consumed her. If the surface world was the beautiful day, the terrible night lurked in the depths. Black shapes moved in the deep, snaking their way up, up through the black water, up toward her. Slits of light broke the shadows, opening into round globes of light.

*Eyes: terrible pale eyes with pinprick pupils. She struggled to return to the surface, hitting a sheet of glassy ice above. Beyond, she could see the sunlight, tantalizingly out of reach. She hammered the ice with the balls of her fists, her lungs bursting, trying to find an escape route. She looked down once more into the darkness, as the first of the phantoms took a grip on her legs, its claws cutting deep into her flesh, and a scream burst from her mouth in a cloud of bubbles.*

Bethwyn's eyes flicked open, the nightmare replaced by the cabin's darkness. She looked to the bunk opposite, the sleeping form of Queen Amelie faintly visible in the gloom. She reached a hand beneath the covers to feel her legs, the sensation of the monster's claws still evident on her skin. Finding no wounds, she relaxed once more, her head collapsing onto her pillow.

Sleeping on board the *Maelstrom* was proving difficult for the young Wildcat. She had grown up on an island in the middle of a lake, and her father, Baron Mervin, the Lord of Robben, had regularly taken her boating. They were good times, happy times. But life on board the pirate ship was quite different from a lazy day on the lake.

She'd felt no split loyalties when Leopold had been overthrown. Although she shared the felinthrope heritage of the Catlords, their similarities ended there. The Wildcats were creatures of the north, native to Lyssia; they had as little in common with the Cats of Bast as with the Dogs of Omir.

Mervin had wasted no time in swearing allegiance to Lord Drew, returning home to Lake Robben after the uprising, leaving his daughter behind to care for his queen.

With only Amelie and the staff of Buck House for company, Bethwyn had found herself looking forward to the visits of Baron Hector. He'd been a frequent visitor to the Staglord mansion in Highcliff, often on official business with Drew. She sensed he'd wanted to make a formal introduction to her, but the shy Boarlord had never seized the moment back in the city. Even now, on board Count Vega's ship, he struggled to find something to talk about with her.

She made a silent promise to make more effort with the magister, starting in the morning. There was something there—it just needed coaxing out. Bethwyn's heartbeat began to slow again, as sleep promised to return.

Then she heard it.

Initially she dismissed it as the sound of the waves lapping against the *Maelstrom*, sloshing against the thick timber hull. Yet the noise was constant, a gurgling sound shifting from high to low, as water might disappear down a drain. There was something musical about the sound, an undulating rhythm that built gradually, as if in a chorus. Soon the noise was all around her, crawling through the cabin and creeping through the shadows.

Bethwyn swung her legs out of the bunk and dropped to the floor. She reached for the lamp that swung from the ceiling, unhooking it and turning up the burner. The light chased the darkness away as the queen stirred in her cot.

"What is it?" she whispered. "What's the matter, Bethwyn?"

"Don't you hear it, Your Majesty?"

Amelie lay still, a hand shielding the light from her face, listening intently. Her eyes widened as the gurgling sound registered. The queen pushed the covers away and climbed out of her bed, joining Bethwyn barefoot on the floorboards. She took her robe, wrapping it about herself, while her lady-in-waiting picked up her own cloak.

"That song," said the queen. "Where's it coming from?"

The girl opened the cabin door a crack, expecting to see crew members rushing by to investigate the strange sounds. The corridor was empty.

Bethwyn turned to the queen. "Please, Your Majesty, remain here while I investigate."

Amelie shook her head. "If you think I'm going to allow you to go up there alone, you're sorely mistaken, my girl. I'm coming with you."

The women walked along the corridor, the ship's constant creaking adding to the sinister chorus that filled the air. Bethwyn leaned against the wall as she advanced, one hand trailing along the varnished wood as she drew closer to the steps that led to the main deck. Taking hold of the rail in her free hand she rose up the staircase toward the open air. The hatch door was swinging on its hinges, left open to the night.

The men of the *Maelstrom* were gathered on the deck, standing like statues in the fog. They swayed with the motion of the ship, shifting like a field of barley. The sound was louder now, clearly coming from the sea, surrounding the ship.

"What's the matter with them?" asked the queen.

Each man stood as if under a spell, mesmerized by the gurgling drone as it came high and low through the cold night air. Bethwyn spied Hector and Manfred among them, the Boarlord and old Stag still wearing their nightshirts. She moved through the crew toward the magister, maneuvering in front of him.

Hector's face was slack, his mouth parted slightly, eyes staring through her like she wasn't there. She waved her hand across his field of vision, but he didn't even blink, as if hypnotized. Bethwyn took his hand in hers, giving it a squeeze— nothing. She raised his wrist up and gripped harder, digging her nails in—no reaction. She glanced down at the palm, usually hidden by a glove, and was shocked to see a dark mark that filled it like an ink stain.

"Bethwyn!" called Amelie fearfully.

Bethwyn looked for the queen, unable to see her through the bewitched crew and the unnatural fog. She kept hold of Hector's hand and began to lead him, his steps clumsy and staggering, as if sleepwalking.

"Your Majesty?"

"Bethwyn!" A scream now.

She moved fast, dragging Hector behind her like a stumbling corpse, bumping into the crew, none showing any reaction. Bethwyn burst from their midst, the magister coming to an immediate halt beside her. Queen Amelie was retreating from the railing on the port side of the *Maelstrom*. The gurgling chorus had grown louder still, rising from the depths and rolling over the decks. Bethwyn moved in front of her queen, raising the lantern to provide illumination.

A scaly green hand clung to the rails, webbing spanning the gaps between each clawed finger. Another hand lurched up beside it, this time the forearm reaching over to grasp an upright post. A dark shape followed, its head looming from the mist as its torso came over the side. Scales covered the creature's entire body, its squat skull sunk low between the shoulder blades, merging with its chest. Two enormous eyes the size of saucers blinked at the lantern light, as the beast's mouth hung open, the terrible song guttering from its throat through a maw of needle-sharp teeth. Seaweed hung from the creature like an emerald shawl, clinging to its skin as it landed with a wet *thump* on the deck.

Bethwyn and Amelie screamed and clung to each other as the monster crawled toward them. Below its waist they could see the beast had a fish's body that snaked along the deck, flapping movements propelling it forward as its clawed hands dug into the decking. A long spiked dorsal fin ran along its spine to an enormous tail, the fin rattling as it advanced. Bethwyn spied pendulous breasts hanging from its chest.

"Get back!" she screamed, swinging the lantern, causing the beast to back up, its song lifting into a gurgling screech. The chorus grew from every side of the ship as Bethwyn and Amelie looked about. With rising dread the women saw more of the shapes emerging over the side. Still the crew remained motionless, oblivious to the nightmare that unfolded around them.

"What are they?" came a shout above. Bethwyn glanced up, spying the shape of the lookout boy, Casper, straddling the spar overhead. Like the women, he seemed immune to the ghastly song of the creatures.

"Stay where you are, child!" warned Amelie.

The women moved closer to the sailors, bumping into them as the creature nearest closed in. Another joined it, this one slightly different in shape and color, its skin a mottled red. She could hear them crawling over the decks, surrounding the crew.

"There must be nearly twenty of them, my lady!" gasped Casper, his voice tearful. "They're going for the lads!"

One of the sailors suddenly went down, caught in the grip of one of the sea creatures. He was quickly followed by another and in seconds, six of the men had been thinned from the crowd. None cried out. All the while the creatures sang as they tossed the sailors over the side.

The swinging hatch door slammed open suddenly as Count Vega emerged on deck. He wore his leather breeches and nothing else, having been rudely woken by the commotion and not a moment too soon. Cutlass in hand he leaped forward toward the nearest creature, which reared up on its tail. He lunged in, catching the creature across the belly, the cutlass splitting the flesh. The monster's arms shot out, grabbing the sea captain by his shoulders and pulling him toward its jaws. Vega began to transform instantly, chest and shoulders rippling and causing the beast to lose its grasp. He brought his head down, mid-change, butting it in the face, its teeth scraping furrows across his brow as its mouth crumpled. The two tumbled to the deck, Vega having badly underestimated the strength of the beast.

"Captain!" Bethwyn cried, moving to help the Wereshark, whose changed head now emerged from the violent struggle.

"Get back!" he yelled, his monstrous mouth flying down to bite at the creature's throat. Black blood fountained, spraying the count and the deck around him as the beast clawed wildly at the Shark's face.

More creatures appeared, avoiding the two women, skirting around them as they went for the men instead. Bethwyn stepped forward as the one they'd first encountered hissed, clawing at the motionless Hector beside her.

"No you don't!" she shouted, smashing the lantern over the creature's head. The Spyr Oil within erupted, sending flames over the beast and back across Hector. Monster and magister shrieked at the fire, Hector waking instantly. He swiftly patted down the flames, trying to comprehend what was happening.

"What in Brenn's name is that?" he gasped as the burning sea creature thrashed about, its face aflame.

Bethwyn noticed that the guttural singing had ceased, the creatures now distracted by their fight with the Wereshark and her fire.

"The lantern!" called Amelie. "They're afraid of the flames!"

Bethwyn snatched up the broken lantern from the floor, sloshing the remaining oil at another beast. It roared and recoiled as the oil burst into flame, scuttling away in terror. Still it was not enough. The men continued to fall and the creatures departed with their prizes. But now the crew were being woken up by the noise and heat of the battle. They were confused and terrified but instead of being dragged over the side, limp and lifeless, they screamed, kicking and clawing at the creatures as they tried to wrestle them overboard.

Bethwyn and Amelie moved swiftly through the men now, waking them up, the song's spell broken. The creatures were among them, bringing the men down quickly. They screeched as they attacked, huge eyes closing each time they clamped their jaws around the pirates.

"Into them, lads!" bellowed Vega as the crew of the *Maelstrom* rallied, aiding him in the fight. They picked up cudgels, knives, axes—whatever was to hand—weighing in to battle against the monstrous creatures. Duke Manfred charged into the fray, his head lowered, transformed, antlers tossing the beasts from the decks, tearing them in two in the process.

Feet thundered across the deck around Bethwyn as the crew of the *Maelstrom* fought back. A clawed hand grabbed hold of her leg, in exactly the same place where she was seized in her nightmare. She shrieked as she fell, the creature crawling up her legs and hips, over her stomach toward her face. Bethwyn raised a hand, claws springing from her fingertips as she slashed down at the monster, tearing strips from its wide face. The huge milky eyes didn't even blink, its cavernous mouth yawning open as it came to bite her. Putrid, salty breath rolled over her in a tide. She tried to scream but nothing came out, gripped as she was by fear and the beast from the deep.

Suddenly the creature halted as if on a choke chain, huge eyes bulging. Bethwyn held it away from her, still gnashing its teeth, but instead of her it bit at the air, snatching and clawing at an invisible foe. Its hands went to its throat, Bethwyn watched as it struggled for breath. Then, with a harsh *crack* its head spun around, slime and seaweed spraying the young Wildcat as its corpse collapsed on top of her.

All around her limbs were snapped and severed as gradually Vega's men pushed the foul creatures back, forcing them off the gore-slicked deck. Through the crowd of fighting men and monsters, Bethwyn saw Hector. *Had he saved her?* The magister's left arm was raised, the black-stained palm open toward her, fingers splayed, a look of deadly concentration on his face. He was ten yards away from her. *How in the world could he have stopped the beast?*

129

# 7

# Hunter's Moon

**THE LUDUS WAS** quiet, the hour late, and the palace of Ignus asleep. Inside the labyrinth of chambers that riddled the volcano's cone, the Lizardlord's gladiators slumbered in bunks and bedrolls within the hot, carved rock. Locked away from the outside world, they were alone with one another, brother warriors who might die at each other's hand in the morning, for tomorrow Lord Ignus would bless Scoria with the blood of his finest gladiators.

One solitary figure stood in the paddock, clad in only a loincloth, his skin scarred from battle, staring at the full moon overhead. Drew took in the heavens, the moon huge and bloody in a dark sky. It reminded him of his childhood on the Cold Coast. Mack Ferran would take his boys hunting on nights like this during the autumn equinox; the "Hunter's Moon" it was known as in Lyssia. He couldn't think of his father without thinking of the others he'd lost. He said a silent prayer to the old man, willing him to look after his mother in the afterlife. Mack Ferran had saved his life, just when it had appeared that Leopold might execute him, losing his own in the process. The little solace he took from his father's passing was that the man had absolved him of any guilt he might have felt over his mother's death. He thought of his brother, Trent, hoping he was far away from whatever war and misery the Catlords had brought upon his homeland. Most of all, he wished he could see him again.

He grimaced as he eyeballed the moon. There'd been a time when the moon had been something for Drew to fear, the beginning stages of a sickness that had transformed him into the Werewolf, setting him upon his epic path. He'd resented his destiny once, but that seemed long ago. He was the last of the Wolves of Westland, and a survivor. Now the full moon wasn't to be feared; it was his friend.

But the Hunter's Moon had its own meaning for the Scorians. When the moon was full and blood red, their volcano demanded a sacrifice. Tomorrow the fire mountain would be served a feast.

Standing with a silver collar around his throat, standing before a full moon and resisting the change, was the ultimate test of will for Drew. The Werewolf was dying to rip free. Drew was pushing his body to its limits, toughening it up for what lay ahead. His muscles flexed as he curled his hand into a fist, the stump on his other arm trembling. He could feel the moon's rays across his flesh, their touch electric. A bank of clouds passed, casting shadows over the paddock and releasing the moon's grip on Drew momentarily.

"A dangerous game you play, Wolf."

Drew hadn't heard Djogo approach, turning suddenly to find the slaver a few yards away. Drew panted, the strain proving great, his skin slick with sweat on the humid red night.

"Do you always creep around?" he rasped to the slaver.

Djogo didn't answer, walking closer to stand beside Drew and look up at the sky.

"Have you considered my offer?" asked Drew, dragging his forearm across his wet brow.

"I have indeed, and I still say you're a lunatic, Wolf."

"That's not an answer. Yes or no, Djogo; I'm not looking for your opinion of my sanity."

"Your plan is madness."

"To a broken man, perhaps, but not to a man who has hope in his heart. Which are you, Djogo?"

The slaver sneered at Drew. "Watch what you say. We're equals now, and wearing that silver collar means you've no beast to call upon."

"You're right. We *are* equals. How does it feel to be an owned man?"

"It's nothing new. I was a slave and gladiator before, until Kesslar freed me from the Furnace. The Goatlord let me rise."

"And now he's let you fall. He's discarded you. If he'd respected you he wouldn't have handed you over to Ignus!"

"He'll barter with Ignus to have me released."

"You believe that? How long have you worked for the Goat? You know what Kesslar's capable of. Can you really afford to wait?"

"There's too much to lose . . ."

"You've nothing to lose!" cried Drew, reaching out to grab the man's arm.

"I've everything to lose," spat Djogo, shoving Drew away angrily. "There are more ways to wound a man than with a sword."

Drew shook his head. "I don't understand."

Djogo turned his back on Drew. "He can hurt those I care about."

Drew considered the man's words. "You fought here for many years, Djogo. You know the Furnace and the palace better than anybody. The old master—Griffyn—I've seen you with him. You care about him, don't you?"

Djogo said nothing.

"I don't know what your relationship is. I don't *care*, truth be told. You and I have been enemies since we first met. I don't see how the pair of us being gladiators now makes us brothers. Tomorrow I fight back, and I hope those who share my desire to be free of Scoria will stand up and be counted."

Djogo paced back to the sleeping chambers silently. Drew watched him go, wondering if he'd angered the man further. He looked up. The sky was clear again, the moon casting her spell over the young Werewolf once more. He snarled through clenched teeth as he basked in her cold white light.

# 8

# A WORLD AWAY

**THE GROUND WAS** hard and uneven beneath his bedroll, promising an uncomfortable night's sleep, but Trent Ferran didn't care. He stared at the Hunter's Moon overhead. Not so long ago they'd run through fields and meadows, stalking deer under the bright night sky: Trent, his father, and his brother, Drew. He sucked his teeth, thinking of the young man who had ruined his life. He sighed, closing his eyes and willing the memories from his mind.

This had been the first day for weeks that he and his men had seen no combat. While his companions seemed indifferent, it was a relief for Trent. He'd joined the Lionguard for one reason: revenge. He hadn't signed up to burn people out of their farms and turn wives into widows. Of the hundred or so fighters he traveled with, the majority were Bastians. They were emotionless, carrying out their officer's instructions to the letter and never breaking rank. The Lionguard were sadly less disciplined than their southern counterparts, recklessly meting out their own justice in Prince Lucas's name.

It was only a matter of time before Lucas was made king: the Pantherlords from Bast, Onyx, and Opal would ensure that. While Onyx marched across Lyssia, Opal was in Highcliff watching over the prince's education while he awaited confirmation of his ascension. Trent had met Onyx briefly in the Horselords' plundered court of High Stable. The Beast of Bast cut a monstrous figure, a giant among men. It chilled Trent's heart to imagine how fearsome the transformed Werepanther might look in battle. King Leopold had been slain in the fight for Highcliff, and Queen Amelie had been kidnapped by Duke Manfred and Count Vega, two Werelords whose names now topped the kingdom's most-wanted list alongside Drew's. Lucas was now without a father or a mother. With Lyssia in such a state of flux, the vacuum was waiting to be filled. As Trent's fellow Redcloaks often said, the sooner Lucas was crowned the better.

"Asleep so soon?"

Trent opened his eyes. The Catlord Frost was standing over him. He sat up, instantly alert.

"Resting my eyes is all, sire."

"Did your blade get blessed as I said?"

"With silver, sire." Trent made to stand up.

Frost waved his hand, dropping on to his haunches beside the youth.

"Drop the titles, Trent. Frost will suffice. I like you, and see no need for you to jump to attention whenever I'm close by. You're not like the other Lyssians. You're honest and true, like the best Bast has to offer."

Trent felt his heart swell at Frost's words, recognition for his efforts warming his spirit. He felt honored that the Catlord could be so informal in his company. He began to relax a little.

"Any word from Westland?" asked Trent.

"Onyx makes huge strides. The Great West Road is ours already, and whatever resistance the Wolf's army had provided is all but broken. Our main force marches east, through the Dalelands. I don't expect them to find much of a fight there. The real battle lies ahead with the Barebones and the Dyrewood. This war will be over once we crush the Stags and the Bears."

Frost smiled as he stared at the moon, pink eyes glowing with an unearthly light.

"Does it have an effect on you, as it does the Wolf?" Trent asked.

"The moon? It affects all therians in different ways. The more passive Werelords find calm and clarity under her light. For the more aggressive, it stirs the blood, fires passion and power." He clapped his hands. "I could fight an army of Lyssian turncoats presently without breaking sweat." He laughed. "As for the Wolves? Different beasts altogether. They're more connected to the lunar cycles than any of us. I'm too young to have ever faced Wergar, but those who fought him said he was at his most ferocious while the moon was full."

"Is Drew really the last one left?"

"The last of the Gray Wolves, most certainly. But your queen, Amelie, she's a White Wolf of the north. They were always fewer in number, so I'm told, but fled their home of Shadowhaven when Leopold came to power. There may be some left, vagabonds. But I'd be surprised if any other White Wolves still survive, to be honest. The queen and Drew may be the last of the true Werewolves."

"We'll find him, Frost. I promise."

The albino put an arm around the youth. "I'm sure we will. If anyone can sniff the beast out it's you. It sickens me to think of what he did to those who raised him as their own. The Wolves of Westland are a vile breed—a blight on your land. They need to be extinguished. Utterly."

Trent nodded. "He won't stray far from Lady Gretchen," he promised Frost. "He stole her from Prince Lucas once, and no doubt he'll try it again. We just need to find her, quickly."

"That's the spirit, Trent," said Frost, clapping his back. "And when we do, hiding in Calico no doubt, I want you by my side. Then your blade can truly be blessed, with the Wolf's blood."

Trent's smile was bittersweet. "That's the greatest gift I could receive."

Frost held his open palm out, head bowed and voice low. "You have my word, Trent. Lead us to him and the Wolf is yours."

Trent took Frost's hand and shook it heartily.

"Now rest, my friend. We've another march tomorrow. The Longridings are riddled with the Wolf's allies. The Werefox may be heading to Calico, but who knows where she might be hiding along the road as she makes her way there. We can leave no stone unturned."

Trent nodded as the Catlord rose gracefully before stalking away through the tall grass toward his tent.

"So you think you're his favorite now?"

The voice was Sorin's, from his bedroll nearby.

"I wouldn't say that," muttered Trent, relaxing onto his mat. He pulled his blanket back up, staring up at the moon once again.

"Don't get me wrong, Ferran, you're a good soldier. But a Werelord calling you his friend? That's laughable, you have to admit!"

Trent tried to block Sorin's words from his head, but he went on.

"He's plumping you up, making you feel more than you are. You're a grunt, Ferran, like the rest of us. Don't think just because his lordship says you can call him 'Frost' he means anything he says."

Sorin rustled through the grass toward him, his voice low.

"He doesn't trust you," he said jealously. "At the end of the day you're the Wolf's brother. When push comes to shove, Frost worries you'll betray him, betray all of us."

Trent closed his eyes, but Sorin's words were poisonous. He heard Sorin crawl closer, his voice inches away when he next spoke.

"I think he's right."

Trent was out of his bedroll and on top of Sorin in an instant, hunting knife at the other's throat. Sorin chuckled, his eyes wide as he looked down. Trent followed his gaze to where Sorin held his own knife to Trent's belly, ready to be driven home.

"You've got me wrong," spat Trent angrily. "I want the Wolf dead."

"So you say," snarled the broken-nosed captain of the Lionguard.

"Nobody has more reason to see Drew Ferran dead than I!"

Sorin pushed him off, the knife fight over before it had begun.

"It might be argued . . . *Ferran*," said Sorin, slinking back toward his bedroll, "that nobody would have more reason than you to see him live."

Trent collapsed back on to his mat, shaking his head. *Sorin knows nothing. Drew's a monster. Monsters need to be killed.* What did Sorin know about him? Trent tried to push his captain's malignant words away, but they just kept coming back at him.

# 9
# BITTER BLOWS

**"SIRENS⸮"**

Duke Manfred was incredulous. He stood beside the two Wereladies in the captain's quarters.

"Some call them that," said Vega from behind his desk. "Others call them the Fishwives. Either way I thought they were creatures of myth before last night."

"They were vile." Queen Amelie shuddered, her arm around Lady Bethwyn. It was dawn, but the previous night's encounter was still all too fresh in their minds.

Hector winced at Amelie's mention of the word "vile."

*If she only knew the true meaning of the word now, eh, brother?*

Hector spoke over Vincent's whispered words. "They were like no therians I've seen before."

"Some therians turn their back on their human form, fully embracing the beast," said Vega. "Legend has it the Sirens did that very thing; the once noble wives of the Fishlords swam to the seabed, accepting their bestial nature totally. Is it really so unlikely, Hector? Didn't you face and defeat the Wereserpent, Vala, in the Wyrmwood not so long ago?"

Hector nodded, his thoughts returning to the encounter with the giant Snake. He'd had Drew at his side then, his tower of strength. It seemed a distant memory.

"How was it that some were affected by their song while others weren't?" asked the magister.

"I can't explain it," said Vega, "although I have a theory. The Sirens of nautical mythology can enchant only males, not females. Alluring beauties, so tales tell. If these beasts are in any way connected to those of legend, that would explain why Queen Amelie and Lady Bethwyn were unaffected by their dreadful chorus."

"But their song had no effect on you, Count," said Amelie.

"Hazarding a guess, perhaps it's because I, like them, am a beast of the sea. Maybe the Sealords are immune to their enchantments?"

"And the boy, Casper?" added Manfred, pointing out the only other member of the crew who had not been captivated by the Siren song.

Vega shrugged. "He's still a child, not yet grown. Maybe that's why he was spared their spell."

"The Sturmish Sea is a dreadful place," muttered Manfred. "The sooner we reach land the better. Where are we, Vega?"

The count looked at the map on his desk, shaking his head.

"Hard to say. These are waters I've never ventured through. My charts are old and that cursed fog has thrown out our navigation. I reckon we're somewhere north of Tuskun, but I'd wager nothing!"

"Manfred's right," said Amelie. "We need to find the mainland soon. Who knows what else lurks in this awful sea?"

"Your guess is as good as mine." Vega sighed, scratching his head and running his hand through his long dark locks. He stretched in his chair, exhausted from the night's activities, as was everyone.

"The *Maelstrom* is eighteen souls light after last night. I can't decide what's best for her when we reach Roof. Do I crew up and head back out to sea? Or disembark and continue on with you, to Icegarden?"

"That's for you to decide," said Manfred, not about to be drawn on Vega's tormented morals.

"Thank you, Your Grace. Ever helpful with your counsel," said the Sealord sarcastically.

"Your Majesty," said Bethwyn, turning to the queen, a tired smile across her face, "if you could excuse me, may I head above decks?"

"You look exhausted, my dear," said Amelie.

"Here," said Hector, seizing the moment to step forward and offer his arm. "Let me escort you."

Amelie smiled at the Boarlord approvingly, while Bethwyn blushed at the show of courtesy.

"Really, Baron Hector, I'm quite all right," replied the girl. "Please don't mistake me for a damsel in distress. I merely need to take some air."

"Sounds like a fine idea," said Hector. "If you'd allow me to join you?"

"Persistent fellow, isn't he?" said Vega with a grin.

*See how he can't resist making a joke at your expense, brother?* hissed the Vincent-vile.

Hector ignored his brother's voice and held a gloved hand out to Bethwyn. The young woman looked at it tentatively before taking it.

"Your Majesty," she said to Amelie, managing a clumsy curtsy before allowing herself to be led away by Hector.

The two made their way to the main deck.

*She's putty in your hands*, the vile persisted.

Hector shivered, trying to shake the spirit loose.

"Are you cold?" Bethwyn asked.

"A little, my lady," he said awkwardly, hating his tormenting brother with every step.

They emerged on deck into bright daylight, the cold morning air bracing. The remaining crew were busy, rushing about their business with even greater industry than before. Figgis stood steady at the wheel, keeping the *Maelstrom's* course steady. Casper stood beside him, watching Hector with suspicious eyes.

*Even that wretched urchin distrusts you, brother.*

Hector walked Bethwyn over to the rail and out of the way of the busy crew, many of whom were still scrubbing the gore and slime from the decks. The corpses of the Sirens had been tossed overboard once the battle was over, Vega waiting until they'd put some distance between themselves and the scene before burying his slain crew at sea.

"Your hand," said Bethwyn, holding the railing. "Is it wounded?"

"Pardon?" asked Hector, alarmed by the question.

"Your left hand: I saw it last night. You've a burn in your palm, a big one. What happened?"

"Oh, that," said Hector, flustered. "I burned it on a lamp. I know; I'm a fool."

"It should be looked at."

"Don't worry, really," said Hector. "I'm a magister after all. It's nothing I can't take care of."

She nodded, seeming to accept his answer. She looked pale, exhaustion and terror having chased the warmth from her face. The crew had begun to sing a shanty, sailors chiming in as they worked to the tune's rhythm. Hector spied Ringlin and Ibal near the ship's aft, apart from their fellows, shying away from work again.

"I'd have thought we'd heard enough singing after last night," said Bethwyn.

"They're a tough breed, aren't they? They buried their brothers only hours ago and they're finding their voices again."

Hector rapped his gloved fingers along the rail's edge to the beat of the shanty, trying to look relaxed while his insides were in turmoil.

"You were very brave," he finally said. "If you and the queen hadn't acted so swiftly, who knows what might have become of us. Thank you, Bethwyn."

"It's I who should thank you, Hector. You stopped the Siren that would have killed me, didn't you? How did you *do* that?"

Hector smiled nervously.

"I don't follow."

"I saw you: you strangled it! You broke its neck, yet you were a great distance away. How could that be?"

*She's on to us, Hector. She saw your little parlor trick, sending me out to do your dirty work. Tell her about me, brother. Tell her about your shadow hand . . .*

"I wasn't so far away, my lady. Perhaps it seemed farther from where you lay?"

"I could've sworn you were many yards from my struggle," she said, raising a hand to rub her brow.

"I can't remember the night's events clearly myself. In the chaos of battle it's hard to see straight, let alone recall what happened."

He plucked up the courage to place his hand over hers on the rail. He gave it a reassuring squeeze.

"You're safe now, my lady. That's all that matters."

Vega, Manfred, and Amelie emerged from the cabins nearby, the captain heading to the wheel while the duke and queen promenaded along the deck.

*If this is courtship, brother, I was getting it* wrong *all these years.* The vile laughed.

"You've been the queen's lady-in-waiting for some years now," said Hector, his hand still on top of Bethwyn's. "Do you not long for your own life, away from service?"

"I'm the queen's confidante," replied the young Wildcat. "I was appointed her companion, and that's more important than ever now."

"How long must you remain with her?"

She turned, puzzled, her big brown eyes narrowing. He kept his hand over hers, Bethwyn having not yet pulled away.

"For as long as she needs me. In Highcliff my responsibilities were manifold: music, languages, writing letters for the queen. Out here, however, I do whatever she asks."

Hector nodded.

"You're most noble, Bethwyn. You do your father and Robben proud."

"I do my duty, Hector."

*Don't make a fool out of yourself, piggy. What could she ever see in you? A sickly bookworm with a penchant for dark magistry . . .*

Hector cleared his throat, taking a big lungful of sea air. His heart felt like it might leap from his chest as he squeezed her hand once more.

"I would speak with Baron Mervin once this war is over, my lady."

"Regarding what?"

"Regarding your hand, Lady Bethwyn."

She didn't react immediately, but when his words registered, a shocked look flew across her face as she whipped her hand away. Hector raised his black-gloved palms by way of apology.

"My lady, I'm sorry if my words cause offense!"

*You clumsy oaf! Do you really think this is how one asks a Werelady for her hand in marriage? Stick to your books and scrolls, fool!*

"You caught me unawares, my lord," she gasped, bringing her hands to her bosom and clenching them together. She backed away, the color having returned to her cheeks in a crimson blush. Her big brown eyes looked anywhere but at Hector. He took a step forward as she retreated.

"My lady—" he began, but he was interrupted by her flustered response.

"I must return to the queen. Thank you, again, for your kindness last night, and just now. Walking up. Thank you. The fresh air . . ."

With that she was hurrying after the queen, leaving

Hector alone by the rail. He turned, grinding his fists into the timber banister, shaking his head.

*That went well, I thought!*

"Curse you, Vincent! Cease your incessant chatter!"

*Too late, brother: I'm already cursed!*

Hector opened his left hand, the black leather creaking as he splayed his fingers. His head was splitting, an ache cutting into his temple. He could feel anger rising, threatening to erupt in glorious fury: anger at their predicament, at Vega, at Bethwyn, and at his own hapless attempts to charm her.

Hector clenched his hand tight, his eyes alone seeing the black smoke curling around it, the vile in his grasp, choked in his fist.

"Hold your tongue, vile. You forget the control I have over you. The Siren last night was a reminder. You're mine, Vincent, to do my bidding, as and when I please!"

Hector waited for a smart-mouthed response from the vile, but nothing came. He kept his fist closed, thumping it on to the rail as he closed his eyes, letting his head slump miserably into his chest.

Count Vega looked down from the poop deck, watching the Boarlord of Redmire rage. He winced as Hector snarled and spat, holding a heated discussion with himself. Vega worried about the magister, after all he'd been through—continued to go through. He knew Hector had a good heart, and prayed the young man stayed out of the shadows.

The cabin boy, Casper, handed the sea marshal his goblet. Vega smiled as he took it, washing the day's first brandy down his throat. He'd purloined a bottle from the *Bold Thunder* for himself, while handing the rest over to Cook. He'd make sure the lads had a drink this day. They'd earned it after last night's horrors.

"Captain," said the boy, still at the count's side.

"What is it, lad?" asked Vega, giving the cabin boy his full attention.

"Last night, those Mermaids—I saw what happened."

Vega put a hand on the boy's head, ruffling his hair.

"Saw what, lad?"

Casper looked across the deck. Vega followed his gaze as it settled upon the irate Boarlord.

"I saw what he did to that monster."

Vega's cheery mood vanished in an instant. He crouched down beside the boy, turning him to face him. Casper looked shocked, and more than a little frightened. When Vega spoke again, his voice was a whisper.

"What did you see, Casper?"

"Wasn't natural, the way he killed it. His hand, Captain: that black hand. It was dark magick, I swear to Sosha. The magister scares me."

"Then stay close to me, my boy," said the Wereshark. The boy smiled nervously at Vega, the captain, his hero, his every-thing. The count brushed Casper's mop of dark hair out of his eyes.

"Stay close to me."

# PART III

## THE FIRES OF THE FURNACE

# I

# BATTLE OF THE BEASTS

**THE CROWD HAD** enjoyed their fill of blood. Fifty gladiators had entered the Furnace and only twenty-five had walked away. Every appetite had been catered to. Horseback warriors had jousted, boxers had dueled with bare fists, bowmen had peppered opponents with arrows, while spearmen had launched their javelins. Swords, scimitars, axes, and tridents had clashed across the volcanic earth, limbs and heads severed and hoisted as trophies. The Bestiari, specialists in fighting animals, had come up against lions, bears, jackals, and wolves. The cruelest contests involved two recently condemned criminals pitted against each other: one armed but blindfolded, the other unarmed but clear-sighted. The blindfold ultimately proved too great a handicap. Now the Scorians quieted as Lord Ignus appeared upon his balcony.

"People of Scoria, I give you the rarest gift. I show the fire mountain the greatest generosity—my therian warriors from across the known world. You all saw the Blood Moon last night, signaling the need for sacrifice. Those gladiators who have fallen thus far today have gone some way to quench the mountain's thirst, but she hungers for yet more. We must honor Scoria with the mightiest offerings in order to appease her fire. My Eight Wonders enter the Furnace. The contest is over when only five remain standing."

He cast his hands over the arena below, oily skin glistening in the midday sun.

"Behold: the Battle of the Beasts!"

Eight iron gates were cranked open around the Furnace, each one sending clouds of dust billowing into the arena. From out of the pens the therian gladiators strode forward. Ignus clapped his hands, turning to his fellow nobles and Lizardlords who had gathered as honored guests. He'd just witnessed his most recent acquisition from Kesslar provide the fight of his life. Djogo had triumphed against the trident-wielding Obliss of Ro-Shann. Of the Goatlord there had been no sign. Ignus suspected Kesslar was still smarting from the humiliation he'd dealt him.

Drew squinted through the dust clouds as he looked

around the Furnace. He'd seen Djogo moments earlier when the gladiator had returned to the gates, the two sharing a look as they'd passed. Drew walked forward as the sand settled, taking in the combatants. The Behemoth had entered from a gate directly opposite. To his side the Wereapes, Arik and Balk, had appeared, immediately moving together into a pair. Between Drew and the brothers stood Taboo, limbering up as she prepared for the fight. To the other side of Drew stood the Rhino, Krieg, flanked by the lean figure of Drake. The Werecrocodile looked the most relaxed of all, turning to look toward the chanting crowd. Last of all, between Drake and the Behemoth, Stamm could be seen, the Buffalo shaking the dust from his shaggy mane. Drew wondered who—if any—would follow his lead.

None of the other Werelords carried weapons. In a cruel twist devised by Ignus, they were to use tooth, claw, and their therian strength alone to best their opponents. Only Drew's trident dagger remained on his stumped wrist. Drew hoped to avoid the Behemoth in the coming fight. The giant had been responsive to the idea of breaking out, but that was yesterday. Here, in the heat of the arena, it might count for naught. There had to be a fight, and that fight would separate those who were with Drew and those who were against him. Arik and Balk were certain enemies, while questions remained over Drake and Taboo.

Then the battle began.

It happened so fast, triggered by the two brothers. As if reacting to Drew's thoughts, the Apelords wasted no time, rushing Taboo as their opening gambit. As they charged they changed, forearms exploding with muscles while their backs expanded, silver bristles bursting from their skin. Within seconds the brothers flanked the young woman, their mouths open to reveal huge, deadly canines.

Taboo was ready. She kicked up the dust, sending a cloud into the air to provide cover. By the time Arik brought his huge hand down at her, the girl had gone. She shot a lithe leg through the dusty air, her clawed foot striking and piercing the Ape's shoulder, sending him tumbling away. When Balk's fist flew through the air where he'd imagined she stood, Taboo rolled out of the dust, transformed, her body shimmering with dark black stripes across orange skin. The Weretiger snarled, unfazed by the brutes.

Drew turned just in time to see the bowed head of Krieg charging him. The Rhino was transformed, head down and shoulders thick with hide armor. Dodging the great horn, Drew caught the brunt of the attack from the Rhino's shoulder. The collision was colossal, the pain immense. Drew was catapulted into the air and back toward his gate and landed in the dirt. As he flew he tried to breathe, the air having been crushed from his lungs.

Drew rolled, choking and gasping as he saw Krieg skid, changing his angle of attack. The head was his primary weapon and the ground thundered as he sped back toward Drew.

"Krieg!" he yelled, his breath returned. "What are you doing? We can fight *together*!"

"It can't work, boy!" Krieg snorted as he charged. "Better let me finish you, end this quickly. Three of us have to die, and I won't be one of them!"

Drew hadn't wanted to fight Krieg. He had believed he'd be an ally, but he'd got it wrong. Drew let the Wolf in, and the transformation was rapid. He leaped up from the floor on powerful, lupine legs, his clawed feet digging into the dirt for extra purchase. The specially built trident dagger sat snugly on his left arm, while his clawed right hand was open. His yellow eyes blazed with purpose as he peeled back his lips to reveal deadly teeth. He let out a deafening roar to alert Krieg.

The crowd screamed deliriously as Drew changed, but he ignored their cheers, his attention focused on the Rhino. The armor plating over Krieg's head, shoulders, and back afforded him a confidence in battle that few therians would know.

Drew's trident dagger bounced off the main horn, sending his arm ringing with shock. He dropped to one side as the brute raced to the center of the Furnace, allowing his clawed hand to rake the Rhino's flank. Drew felt the claws struggle for any purchase, scraping harmlessly over Krieg's armored skin.

The Rhino was far bigger than the Wolf, but what Drew lacked in size he made up for in agility. He readied himself for Krieg's next attack using the same defense as before, raising the dagger again. At the last moment, with Krieg almost on top of him, Drew leaped in the air, spinning and coming down to land on the Rhino's shoulders. Krieg snorted, swinging his head, legs still pumping, momentum carrying him forward. Drew held on tight, his arms around the Rhino's throat as Krieg charged on.

Krieg looked up suddenly as the arena wall appeared before him. He felt Drew's feet dig into the armor of his back as he sprang away to safety, the Rhino struggling vainly to slow down. He crashed into the wall with a sickening crunch, rocks and rubble coming loose and showering him as he collapsed to the Furnace floor in a heap.

Drew landed gracefully, looking around the arena at the other battles that raged. Taboo had been joined by Stamm, evening up the fight against the Apes. The Crocodile, Drake, was darting around the Behemoth, who now stood transformed. Drew was amazed by the sight.

He'd heard about mammoths as a child, giant beasts from Bast, dismissing them as being as mythical as dragons. The animals the other therians were brethren to—crocodile, rhino, ape, and buffalo—he could comprehend. But the Weremammoth was beyond all his experience. He was monstrously impressive—twice Drew's height, with legs like battering rams, the Behemoth dominated everything around him. Enormous fists smashed down, narrowly missing his opponent. Huge ears flapped from the side of his boulder-sized head, while curling ivory tusks jutted from his mouth. A snaking trunk swung through the air, smacking Drake across his long, toothy snout and sending the Werecrocodile flying.

The Apes were brutal. Their silver backs rippled with muscles as their powerful arms lashed out at their enemies. While Stamm was holding his own with Arik, Taboo was faring less well with Balk, tiring under the relentless blows of the Wereape, as his fists connected with alarming frequency.

Having assessed the field, Drew chose his opponent.

With a couple of bounds he bowled into Balk, hitting him square in the back and the two of them went down.

"Dog!" snarled the Ape. "The Cat can wait! Let's see the color of your blood!"

Drew didn't answer, squirming out of reach of the Ape's mighty arms. He'd made a mistake, choosing to wrestle the monster. Balk bit into his shoulder. Drew roared, snapping his own jaws down the side of the Ape's face. A black ear came away with a wet rip. Wailing, Balk disengaged, lifting a hand to the wound.

"I see yours is red," spat the Werewolf, poised for the next attack. Then suddenly an arm slid over his throat from behind, muscles flexing as Arik snatched hold. *I thought he was fighting Stamm!* Drew's head thundered as the blood struggled to find a way through his restricted arteries.

Balk was about to join the attack when his jaw cracked, a flying kick from Taboo sending his head recoiling. Teeth flew as the Tiger landed, panting hard. The Ape went for her, drawn away from his brother's fight with the Wolf.

Drew was seeing lights—fading fast. With a desperate burst he yanked his left arm free of Arik's other fist, burying the trident dagger in the Ape's forearm. The beast roared, releasing its grip, the dagger tearing a lump of flesh with it. The enraged Ape smashed his other arm down on to Drew's back, flattening him. He rolled over in time to see both Arik's arms raised, fists curled and about to strike.

Then without warning, the horns of the Buffalo, Stamm, crashed into Arik's back, the two Werelords going down beside the stunned Drew. He saw the damage the Apes had done to Stamm, one of his arms broken and limp at his side, his torso ripped and torn. Balk now returned to the fracas, while some distance away, Drew saw Taboo lying wounded and still.

Seizing Stamm's curling horns, Balk hauled the Buffalo's head up, holding the neck exposed. From beneath, Arik opened his jaws wide as his teeth connected with Stamm's throat. Drew caught a despairing look in Stamm's eyes as his neck was torn open.

Drew pounced, his heart full of rage. He had known Stamm from only their few exchanges in the ludus, but the Buffalo's valiant assistance had struck deep. Balk tried to bat Drew away, but the Wolf wouldn't be halted. He took three, four more punches as he dragged the Ape off Stamm, the butchered

Buffalo landing on Arik beneath him. The fifth punch came and Drew opened his mouth, closing his jaws around Balk's fist. Bones, knuckles, and tendons crunched as he ground his muzzle closed.

Balk screamed, trying to prize the Wolf's jaws apart with his other hand, but Drew's teeth snapped together, taking four fat fingers off with two quick bites. The bloodied Ape fell, kicking at the Wolf, but Drew was too swift, his clawed hand snatching hold of Balk's jaw. The monster grasped at him with broken, bloody hands, but Drew's grip was solid. He raised his powerful leg and brought his foot down hard on Balk's chest. A sickening crunch sounded above the noise of combat in the Furnace, and the Wereape lay dead in the dust.

Drew turned to see Arik struggle from beneath the slain Buffalo, letting loose a despairing wail at the sight of his brother's demise. The Ape bounded high, blotting out the sun as he came down toward Drew.

The Werewolf readied himself for the impact, but the expected blow didn't come from above, but from the side—Drew was thrown clear of Arik's attack. Krieg had replaced him, taking the Ape's barrage. The two went down, Arik landing directly on top of Krieg with a wet *crack*, throwing a cloud of red dust into the air. The combat between the Ape and Rhino was over instantly. As the cloud settled, Drew could see Krieg's huge horn, standing proud from the silverback of the Wereape.

Krieg pushed him back, the dead Arik sliding off his horn into the bloody dust.

"Thank you," Drew whispered, embracing Krieg. Taboo stood nearby, battered but not beaten. The bloodthirsty crowd were wild with excitement. Ignoring the mob of onlookers, the three therians walked across the Furnace toward the two who still fought.

The Behemoth and Drake still battled, trading blows, but not dealing any true damage to each other. This combat took place beneath the viewing balcony of the palace, but all eyes had been fixed upon Drew's battle.

"Enough!" yelled Ignus. "We have our victors!"

Drake and the Behemoth parted as Drew joined them, Krieg and Taboo following.

"The fire mountain has been appeased!" cried Ignus as the audience cheered. "We are blessed for another year. The glorious death of these noble Werelords has sated Scoria's hunger!"

The Lizardlord was so busy performing to the crowd that he paid little attention to the five therians who stood below. Drew stepped in front of the Behemoth and nodded to him.

"You're sure?" asked the Weremammoth.

Drew smiled, grimly. The Behemoth bent his head, allowing Drew to clamber on to his tusks, crouching low.

"Today the Furnace has witnessed the greatest contest Scoria has ever seen!" continued Ignus, arms open and enjoy-

163

ing his oratory. "The fire mountain has had her fill of blood, both human *and* therian!"

The Weremammoth swung his head, tossing Drew skyward. The lycanthrope, springing from his haunches to gain extra speed, flew through the air toward the balcony.

"Not quite!" he shouted, landing on the balcony with deadly grace to a chorus of frantic screams. "Your fire mountain is still thirsty!"

# 2

# THE UPPER CLAW

**THE GUESTS ON** the balcony fled as the Werewolf of Westland rose to his full height. Instantly the palace guards rushed him, sending him leaping clear onto the stone banquet table. Plates and goblets scattered beneath his clawed feet, clattering across the floor as the rich and powerful of Scoria screamed. The guards fanned out, trying to anticipate the Wolf's next move, but Drew was on the prowl, making his way closer to Lord Ignus, who was already changing.

The Lizardlord shook off his robe, his long neck ballooning as it stretched and twisted, mouth gaping open. His skin turned a mottled green, and hooked, black claws burst from his fingers as a reptilian tail snaked out behind him. Panic increased as Drake landed on the balcony to join the fray, and then Taboo followed her brother therians into the palace.

Below, the Furnace gates broke open. Scoria's human glad-iators surged through, carrying poles, ladders, anything that might help them clamber out of the arena. Deep within the walls of the coliseum, fighting had broken out as others chose different escape routes. The cage doors that had kept them im-prisoned had been mysteriously unlocked, allowing them to surge over any astonished soldiers who dared stand in their way. The wild beasts were freed from their pens, running riot through the corridors that encircled the arena. Soldiers, civil-ians—all fell beneath their teeth and claws. The breakout had caught the Scorians by surprise.

Drake and Taboo darted between the guards' spears, strik-ing home with ease, filling the air with a fine red spray. The guards, so used to bullying manacled slaves around, struggled to hold the therian warriors back. With the guards preoccu-pied, that left Drew facing just the Lizardlord.

"Where's Kesslar?" snarled Drew as Ignus stood trans-formed, bathed in the sulfurous steam that billowed through the floor grate. His eyes bulged, thin rubbery lips peeling back to reveal jagged teeth.

"Kesslar isn't your concern, Wolf! You'll put your collar back on if you know what's good for you!"

Ignus's three siblings emerged through the yellow mist behind him, Lizards like their brother. None looked lean or fit like Drew and his companions. The Lizards of Scoria had grown used to a life of gluttonous luxury, feeding their addictions with whatever took their fancy. One was a tall, skinny wretch, while his fat brother loped beside him. The third one was top heavy with stunted legs, and then there was Ignus, their glorious leader, too used to letting others fight his battles.

The Lizardmen rushed Drew, all four attacking in clumsy unison. *These weren't the odds I'd hoped for*, thought Drew, bounding over their heads as they dived across the stone table. He landed with a *clang* on the grille, just behind the slowest of them. He lashed out his leg, clawed feet tearing the top-heavy one's hamstring in two and putting him out of action.

*Down to three.*

The fattest Lizard leaped back over the table, directly on top of Drew, but the Werewolf was ready for him, catching him on his clawed feet. His knees compressed up to his chin as the monstrous mouth snapped inches from his face and scaly hands clawed at Drew's throat. The grille vent groaned and buckled beneath the impact of their combined weight. Drew snarled and kicked back. The fat Lizardlord's eyes widened as he was propelled through the air, disappearing over the balcony's edge.

*Two down. Two to go.*

Drew jumped away from the grille, landing before the stone throne. Ignus and his last sibling separated, the lanky one snatching a silver spear from a fallen guard.

"It's been a while since I slew another therian," the Lizard rasped, Ignus grinning at his side.

"I'd like to say the same," said Drew.

The Lizard lunged, but Drew parried the spear away with the trident dagger. The reptile came a second time, and Drew knocked him the other way. Snarling, the Lizard put his weight behind the spear, stabbing high at Drew's chest. The Wolf caught hold of the spear in the crux of the trident dagger, its progress halting. His foe looked shocked as Drew bit down on the wooden pole, snapping the gleaming blade off. Before he could react, Drew buried the spearhead in the Lizard's chest, the hapless therian still clutching the broken spear shaft as black blood gushed from his bosom.

*And then there was one.*

Ignus screamed to his men for assistance, but they were occupied by the therian gladiators. Silver weapons or not, none was a seasoned warrior like Taboo and Drake. The pile of Scorian corpses grew.

Drew was about to offer Ignus a chance to surrender, to end the bloodshed, but he was spared the speech. Ignus ducked low, flicking his tail out and around, whipping Drew's legs from beneath him. The Wolf toppled backward, crashing on to the throne. Before he could rise, Ignus had leaped, straddling him, pinning Drew to the chair.

The Wolf struggled to escape the Lizard's hold, but the hooked claws were buried in his arms, fixing him in place. He snapped his jaws at Ignus's reptilian face, the Lizard's eyes blinking as a wicked grin spread across his reed-thin lips. The

Lord of Scoria's bony forehead came down like a hammer blow, cracking Drew's muzzle and leaving the Werewolf stunned. He was aware of the Lizard's mouth gaping open, its jaws separating, but he was helpless to stop it.

Darkness enveloped him, the world hot, wet, and terrible. With sick dread he realized his head was in the Lizardlord's gullet. He tried to shake it loose, open his jaws to bite the monster from the inside, but the Lizard's constrictive mouth was too powerful, too tight. He could smell Ignus's stomach acids, noxious and overwhelming, heavy with the stench of bacteria and infection. The monster meant to suffocate him, and was close to succeeding.

Drew's feet scrabbled at the base of the chair, struggling for purchase on the polished stone floor. His clawed toes found a crack in the flags. Digging in with all his might, he pushed back, straightening his legs. Slowly, the stone throne rocked. With each push the chair shifted looser off its back legs. He felt the Lizard's tongue flickering over his closed jaws inside its throat. A final shove sent the throne back hard, crashing into the wall behind before lurching forward, sending Wolf and Lizard flying from the seat.

They landed on the grilled floor, the iron grate buckling again. Drew's arms were now free and he jabbed with the trident dagger and clawed with his hand as he pounded Ignus's leathery torso. The Lizard choked and gagged, coughing the strangulated Werewolf's head from its ballooned throat. Drew shook the reptilian Werelord's saliva from his eyes, glancing up in time to see the stone throne rocking back toward them, sheering from its plinth.

The Wolf rolled clear on to the polished stone floor as the throne crashed down on to Ignus. It landed with a bone-crunching *clang*, metal screeching as the grate tore free from its housing. Lizard, throne, and twisted grille all disappeared into the sulfurous hole, the screaming of iron against rock mixing with the wails of Ignus as the Lord of Scoria plummeted to his doom.

Black smoke rolled through the palace of the Lizardlords and fires raged deep within the ludus, the house of the gladiators burning out of control. The corridors that encircled the Furnace were a scene of carnage and the sounds of combat still rang from the vaulted walls. An enormous lion lay on a pile of bodies, chewing on a corpse as if relaxing with its kill in the wild. Screams echoed through the thoroughfare as the coliseum burned.

Drew and his companions emerged into the sunlight. The air was parched and dry, unlike the humid, chemical atmosphere in the throne room, and Drew could feel his sweat already drying. He looked at Taboo and Drake at his side, his fellow therians shifting back to their human forms. All three bore many wounds, but most were superficial.

They headed away from the smoking palace, the curved black and white walls cracking as the fires raged at their backs. Huge portions of the terra-cotta roof broke away, crumbling into the arena, as Ignus's coliseum threatened to collapse in on itself. The survivors of the battle, a crowd of gladiators and slaves, had gathered by the gatehouse at the top of the Black Staircase.

"Friends, we feared the Furnace had taken you!"

Krieg smiled as he greeted them. Beside him stood the Behemoth and a hundred or so fighters.

"That's the first time I've seen you smile," said Drew, shaking the Rhinolord's hand. The greeting was warm and earnest. Drew looked up at the Behemoth, nodding respectfully.

"Thank you. We couldn't have done that without you."

"We couldn't have done that without many people," said the Behemoth, standing to one side as three other figures emerged from the crowd.

Shah walked with her arm around Griffyn, the wizened trainer weary as he leaned on her. Drew could see the family resemblance now, the same shaped nose and sharp cheekbones.

"Your grandfather?"

"Father," corrected Shah.

Drew was shocked. He'd have put sixty years between the old man and his daughter. He could only imagine how hard the trainer's life must have been beneath the boot of Ignus.

"You risked a great deal unlocking the gates in the house

of gladiators, Shah. If Ignus or Kesslar had discovered your complicity, you'd have been killed."

"Strange how the actions of one can inspire others, Drew of the Dyrewood," she said, smiling as she glanced up at the other man beside her. The one-eyed warrior looked down at Drew.

"Come, Wolf," said Djogo. "We need to get you back to Lyssia."

# 3
# THE WHITE ISLE

**IT MIGHT HAVE** been missed had it not been for the keen eyesight of the cabin boy, Casper, perched atop the *Maelstrom's* crow's nest. Count Vega extended his spyglass to better see the island—a barren stack of chalk-white rocks that erupted from the gray waters. It looked unremarkable, a pile of bleached bones floating on the Sturmish Sea, the flesh picked bare from a long-dead leviathan.

"It's land all right," said Vega, "but I've seen more life hanging from a gallows."

"Can we not alight there, even if only briefly?" asked Baron Hector.

Vega stared at the Boarlord as if he'd grown another head. "For what possible reason?"

"This life at sea is all too familiar to you and your crew, Vega. You forget that myself, Manfred, and the ladies are *land-lubbers*, as your crew so eloquently put it." Hector smiled. "Solid ground beneath our feet would make a welcome interruption to our journey."

Vega rubbed his chin and looked at Manfred. "You feel this way, too?"

The Duke tipped his head to one side. "To be honest I'd rather we kept going until we hit the mainland. The longer we're in these foul waters, the less safe I feel. Hanging around out here, we're giving Ghul and Slotha every opportunity to capture us."

Hector turned to the Staglord, opening his gloved hands in a show of reasoning.

"Vega *did* say we needed to plot a new route, calculate where we are. Where better than a spot of dry land? Don't worry about our enemies. Anyone who follows us through that green fog will struggle to emerge on this side anywhere near us. Besides, think of Queen Amelie and Lady Bethwyn. Wouldn't this provide a pleasant, albeit brief, distraction from their journey?"

The Duke looked over his shoulder as if the queen might suddenly appear. He rubbed a hand over his stubbled jaw.

"Hector may have a point there."

"Exactly," said Hector, smiling as he clapped his hands

together. "Then it's agreed. We stop to take some air. Really, what harm can it do?"

There was a knock at Hector's cabin door. He hurriedly threw the blanket over the satchel on his bunk.

"Enter."

The door swung open and the tall figure of Ringlin stepped in, ducking beneath the low door frame.

"Close it behind you," said Hector, waiting for his man to shut the door before pulling his blanket back once again. The Boarguard rogue looked over the magister's shoulder, watching Hector as he packed his bag. Hector's ungloved hands rolled bottles and jars over the rough mattress, glass containers clinking as they collided, his fingers hurriedly sorting what was needed. There was also the narrow mahogany box containing the silver arrow that Bergan had entrusted to him in Highcliff. Hector's hands hovered over the black candlestick, fingers brushing the dark wax before stowing it in the satchel.

"You're packing a lot of gear there if you're only going to stretch your legs, my lord," observed Ringlin slyly.

"If I were visiting the island for a constitutional, I'd hardly need you accompanying me, Ringlin."

The tall man smiled.

"Is Ibal also ready?"

"He is, my lord. He's on deck now, making sure he gets us a spot together on the same landing boat."

"Good," said Hector, fastening the clasps on his bag and throwing it over his shoulder. He was about to pass Ringlin when the tall man placed a hand on his chest, stopping him. Hector's face instantly darkened.

"Your hands, my lord," reminded the Boarguard. Hector glanced back to the bunk, spying the black leather gloves by the pillow.

Hector smiled nervously, snatching them up and pulling them on. Ringlin watched as his master tugged the glove over the left hand, the black scar now almost filling the palm.

"On the island," said Hector, taking hold of the door handle, "you and Ibal are to stay close to me. You'll be my eyes and ears if need be."

"I don't follow."

"You will," said the magister, opening the door.

Two longboats rowed away from the *Maelstrom* in the twilight, the ship anchored a safe distance from the White Isle. Vega was on the first, accompanying Manfred, Amelie, and Bethwyn, as six of his men rowed them ever nearer the rocky outcrop. Behind came Hector's boat, Ringlin and Ibal helping with the rowing.

*Very clever, brother,* whispered Vincent's vile. *You've got them all dancing to your tune. You're getting good at this.*

Hector sat at the rear, his knees drawn up, satchel on his lap, arms crossed over it. The men were too busy rowing to hear or notice him muttering to himself.

"Hardly. There was some truth to my suggestion. Stretching one's legs on solid ground is a good idea."

*But stretching one's legs on* this *solid ground, brother? Why did you not tell them of the voice? Do you fear they'll think you mad?*

Hector had heard the voice for the last two nights, calling him across the water, teasing him as to the White Isle's whereabouts. Hector winced, thinking about the sensation. Voice wasn't the correct word, as no true words were recognizable within the call. More it was a series of images lancing through his mind, feelings and flashes of knowledge tantalizingly out of reach. The strange language was archaic, but somehow Hector recognized it. In his heart he knew the call held the answers to a world of questions, answers that he'd find in no ancient tomes or scrolls. It was connected to the communing, he was sure, the telepathy similar to his bond with Vincent's vile. But there was a great power behind this; the call promised something. Hector needed to discover what.

"Is it mad to search for the answers to one's questions?"

*Perhaps if it means putting those you care for in peril, brother. But what do I know? I'm just a wicked spirit sent here to torment you. It's not my place to suffer from a guilty conscience. I'll leave that to you. . . .*

The launches drew closer. The rocks thrust skyward at jagged angles, reaching up like bony fingers. The island was perhaps half a mile long and maybe a hundred feet tall at its highest point, a pyramid of splintered stone, bereft of plant life. As the boats searched for a mooring point, the sailors took special care to avoid the rocks beneath the surface, faintly visible through the waves. If the *Maelstrom* had drawn nearer, such hidden dangers could have ripped a hole in her hull.

As if to prove this point, the call came up from the lead boat as the shell of a wrecked ship was spied. The vessel was on her side, broken masts clinging onto the rocks, a jagged wound in her belly suffering the constant pounding of the waves. Beyond the wreck, the crew could see a rocky stretch of beach, perhaps a few hundred feet long and the perfect place to get ashore.

Hector felt the call again, an alien tongue rich in old magick, luring him closer. He looked at the crewmen, checking their reactions, convinced they too heard the summons. But the sailors rowed on, oblivious, the message inaudible to all but the magister. As the lead boat hit the shore, Vega leaped off the prow, his booted feet landing on the shingle beach. At this precise moment Hector felt a stabbing pain behind his eyes, as if a blade had been slipped into his skull. He wavered at the rear of the boat, one hand grasping the seat while the other snatched at his temple.

Images flashed: *skin against rock; blood on stone; a black eye opening suddenly. A recognizable word:* welcome.

Hector opened his eyes, snorting for breath. His throat burned as if scorched by acid. Ringlin glanced up, catching sight of his master's shocked expression.

"You all right, my lord?"

*You're not all right, are you, brother? I heard it, too. It's expecting you.*

The second boat hit the beach, the sailors jumping out and dragging it onto the pebbles alongside the first. Amelie and Bethwyn were already ashore, their winter cloaks wrapped tightly around them. Vega stood beside Manfred, looking up and down the length of beach.

"Everybody stay close," said the captain. "No wandering off. Keep a shipmate at your side at all times. Last thing we need is to lose anyone on this white rock."

Casper appeared between the count and the duke, a wooden case on his back. The captain removed it and laid it flat on the beach, opening it up.

"What's this then, Vega?" asked Manfred, watching the sea marshal at work.

"Our best bet at working out where in Sosha's big blue we are," said Vega, removing a sextant from the box and placing it gently to one side. The navigational artifacts were all utterly fascinating to Manfred, who reached a tentative hand toward one. Vega smacked at the hand, shooing the duke away.

"An astrolabe, Your Grace," said Vega. "You know how to use one?"

"Um . . ." muttered Manfred sheepishly as Amelie watched, smiling.

"Might be best if you leave it to someone who does, eh, Manfred?" The Sharklord grinned.

Manfred managed a chuckle despite the admonishment.

"This is actually the best time of day for me to take a sighting," said Vega. "It may be only twilight, but the sun's still up and the first stars are in the sky. I should be able to pinpoint our whereabouts. Seems Hector was paying attention after all when he recommended we stop here."

"Talking of our Boarlord," said Manfred, looking about. "Where's he got to?"

Hector paced along the shore, Ringlin and Ibal at his side, the landing party left behind around the bluff. The pebbles disappeared now, replaced by sheets of seaweed-slicked rock that sloped off beneath the surface of the waves. Hector slipped occasionally but wouldn't be slowed.

"Take care, my lord," said Ringlin as he caught a stumbling Ibal. "It's treacherous here; you need to watch your footing."

*Oh, bless him*, hissed Vincent. *See how he cares? He doesn't want you breaking your neck. Not while they still need paying, anyway!*

Hector didn't answer either soul, instead keeping up his pace. He could feel the pull, close now, promising answers.

Images flashed again: *the dark, a black curtain, a mouth, a kiss.*

Hector could feel his heart quicken as he slipped over the rocky ledge, dropping into a rock pool up to his knees. He clambered up again, and his gloved hands scrabbled over the white stone as he rounded the next outcrop, revealing another smaller cove beyond. The beach was empty and gloomy, broken in its center by a tall, thin crevice in the rock. The black crack snaked twenty feet up the stunted chalk cliff, the high-tide water washing in through its entrance and rushing out once again. Hector dropped from the ledge into the water and waded the remaining distance, the Boarguard joining him.

Hector stood ankle deep in the water as the sea surged into the cave. Perhaps a foot across, the gap was just wide enough to allow single file entrance. As the tide sluiced back between his feet, he could have sworn he heard the word again: *welcome.*

He turned to his henchmen. Ibal held his sickle in his hand, turning the blade nervously in his grasp while glancing at Ringlin. The tall man simply stared at the thin cave entrance, his serrated long knife still sheathed.

"You're going in there, aren't you?"

Hector nodded.

"And you won't follow, unless you hear me scream. Understand?"

Ringlin and Ibal nodded, the short man letting loose a nervous giggle before throwing a fat hand over his mouth.

"Brenn be with you," muttered the tall man.

*Don't count on it, brother,* whispered Vincent as Hector squeezed through the gap. *Brenn deserted you long, long ago.*

# 4

# NEW OATHS

**SCORIA WAS A** changed island. It had once known law and order, albeit the bloodthirsty variety of the Lizardlords. But now chaos reigned. The mansions of the Black Staircase had been sacked, stripped of all their worth, the merchants and nobles who lived there long gone. When the Werewolf and his allies had leaped on to Lord Ignus's balcony, the island's wealthiest had fled the coliseum with their guards and entourages in tow, grabbed what they could carry, and raced to the harbor, sailing on the first ships they found. All else was left to those who remained: the slaves, prisoners, and gladiators.

With the Lizardlords gone, it had been left to Drew and the surviving therians to assume control; there were few on Scoria who would argue with their word.

Those freed slaves who could work as sailors were guaranteed passage, crewing up on the remaining ships as, one by one, they set sail from Scoria. Those with trades or families also secured transport, with the remainder forced to stay on the island.

By now, only one ship remained in the harbor, anchored beyond the cove. She was all too familiar to Drew: the *Banshee*, the commandeered slave vessel that had belonged to Count Kesslar and would now take the young Wolflord home to Lyssia. Drew stood on the harbor walls, staring at the black ship, her decks alive with activity. The boat had been his prison as the Goatlord transported him to Scoria. Now she was going to return him to his homeland.

"She's ugly," came a voice from behind. Drew turned and found Djogo stood there, smiling grimly. "Though I'm one to talk."

Drew might have laughed if Djogo's words weren't so barbed. He looked at the eye patch.

"The eye, Djogo . . ." said Drew, trying to find the words to apologize for the wound he'd inflicted back in Haggard.

Djogo snorted, ignoring the young therian as he stared at the *Banshee*.

"Still no sign of Kesslar," he said. "His face is known throughout Scoria—if he remained he'd have been spotted by now. I think we can assume he was behind the theft."

While Drew and his companions had led their revolt

against the Lizardlords, Ignus's private chambers had been burgled, the true wealth of Scoria stolen from his personal vault. The rarest jewels and gems that the Lizard had stashed away down the years, ill-gotten gains from a lifetime trading in the misfortune of others, had been kept secure in a long-box under constant watch. The four warriors who guarded the hoard were found slain, gored from throat to navel or run clean through. Drew had no doubt whatsoever that the horns of the Goat were responsible. The treasure of Scoria was gone, and so was the count.

"Why didn't he take the *Banshee*?" asked Drew.

"Dragging that loot down the Black Staircase would have slowed his escape. By the time he hit the harbor he'd have been with the other rich pigs, struggling to get away. With the *Banshee* anchored so far from the shore, he must have jumped on to another ship."

Drew shook his head. "The Goat has so much to answer for. How many innocent souls fought and died in the Furnace so he could make a coin?"

Djogo nodded slowly. "He'd have happily harmed those closest to me. There can be no forgiveness."

"Who would he have harmed?" said Drew, although he already knew the answer: the Hawklady.

"Kesslar has never tolerated any divided loyalties within his ranks. My—friendship—with Lady Shah would have enraged him if he'd ever known how deep my feelings ran for her. Once he allowed Ignus to throw me into the Furnace, she was on her own, her safety hanging in the balance. Even her own father couldn't protect her from Kesslar because he was left languishing in the ludus. I would have my revenge on the Goatlord."

"With respect, Djogo—finding Kesslar's like searching for a needle in a haystack. Don't devote your life to hunting Kesslar down. Find a new future, with Shah."

Djogo grimaced. "She's a Werelady. What future would she want with a human?"

"It's clear she cares for you. You've a chance at a new beginning now."

"She needs to choose a therian as her mate. It is her duty as a Werehawk, is it not?"

"I'm not the best person to speak to about duty—I've run away from it at every opportunity. Only now do I see what I must do. I need to return to Lyssia."

"And I'll be at your side," said Djogo, staring at the black ship. Drew glanced sharply at the tall warrior. *Did I hear him correctly?*

"You'd accompany me?"

Djogo turned, his face deadly serious, one good eye trained on the Wolf.

"I worked for Kesslar for many years, first as his slave, then as his soldier. I've done many things in the Goat's name that I'm not proud of, terrible things that should've seen me put to the sword. The balance needs redressing. By serving you, Drew of the Dyrewood, I can set that in motion."

Drew was speechless. Here stood Djogo, Kesslar's own killing machine, offering his services. Did Drew *want* to have such a man associated with him—*serving* him? Could he stand shoulder to shoulder with the murderer who'd been his mortal enemy? Could Drew *trust* Djogo?

"I absolve you of any debt you feel you owe me, Djogo. You should go where you wish."

Djogo smiled, the expression hitting Drew like a slap to the face. He'd grown too used to seeing the tall warrior sneering.

"I'm not alone in wanting to aid you, Wolflord; there are others who'd benefit from hearing your words."

The Werelords had gathered aboard the *Banshee*, Djogo the only human present. The former slaver stood beside Drew, trying not to look across at where Shah stood with her father, Baron Griffyn. Taboo and Drake stood on either side of a large porthole that looked out toward Scoria, while the Behemoth towered behind Krieg.

Drew faced the assembly. "Are you certain this is what you want to do with your freedom?"

Krieg spoke up. "We have our freedom thanks to you. If it weren't for your courage, we'd still be in the coliseum fighting for our miserable lives, or worse, dead. We'll stand by you, Drew.

We're all therian brothers—and sisters—of the Furnace."

"You didn't treat me like a brother when I arrived," said Drew.

"Do you think we were met with open arms when we first came to Scoria, Wolf?" Drake laughed. "You got the measure of the Ape brothers pretty quickly—they'd have killed you in your sleep if you'd trusted them."

"If you'd looked for friendship," said Krieg, "you'd be dead now. You're tough, Drew, as tough as any of us."

"This is my fight, though," said Drew. "Lyssia isn't your homeland."

A huge hand landed gently on Drew's shoulder and the Behemoth's deep voice made Drew's bones rattle. "Our home-lands are enslaved. Do you not think our people would have sailed to Scoria to free us if they could? We share the same foe. The Catlords must be stopped."

"I don't understand," said Drew to Taboo. "Why would Onyx and the Catlords allow one of their own to fight in the Furnace? They're your family, aren't they?"

The Tiger looked up, baring her teeth. They all looked away, except Drew, who held her gaze.

"I have no family."

Drew hastily moved the subject away from Taboo's story.

"If you join me, you join my mission," Drew told the group. "Rescue Lyssia from these vicious Cats and restore power to the Lyssians—therians and humans alike. You've all tasted the bitterness of slavery; you know how it feels to live in servitude to another. We must unite with the people, start treating them as our equals. It's time for us, the Werelords, to serve the people." He held out his hand.

The therians looked at one another, Krieg nodding to each in turn as they bowed their heads in agreement.

Each of the therians stepped forward, placing their hands on the Wolf's single hand.

"What happens now?" said Drew, unsure of what they'd agreed to.

"You sail to Lyssia, and we go with you," said Krieg. "We fight at your side, Drew. Fight or die. The Furnace is behind us, but the battle goes on."

Drew smiled and nodded, looking at each of them in turn.

"You have my word, brothers and sisters. When Lyssia is won, we shall return to Bast and your homelands. We'll free your people from the reign of the Catlords."

# 5
# THE HOST

**WITH DAYLIGHT FADING** behind him, Hector felt he'd stepped into the dead of night. A little illumination was provided by phosphorescent lichen that pockmarked the cave walls, covering the pale rock beyond the tide mark's reach. He'd expected to find sea creatures scuttling away in the shallow rock pools, but like the rest of the island the cave was devoid of life, barring the strange lichen. At its widest the cave was ten feet across, the fissure broadening like an opening eye, before closing once more at its rearmost point.

*Where's your host?* teased Vincent. *All alone again . . .*

Hector shook his head, dismissing the vile's words as his hands played over the chamber's walls. He leaned close, squinting, tracing the white stone with his gloved fingertips. The pale light revealed strange markings, symbols scrawled into the chalk that resonated with Hector.

"Language," muttered Hector to himself. He tilted his head, trying to translate the archaic shapes. To the magister, the markings read vertically, from floor to ceiling—or the other way around—and the more he stared, the more they struck a chord with the images that had flashed through his mind's eye.

He sensed Vincent's vile was still listening, and half expected it to chime in, but the phantom remained unusually silent, as if it knew Hector was approaching the truth. The higher Hector looked up the cavern walls, the more markings he discovered.

"A scripture, perhaps. Or a diary. But who wrote it?"

Still no responses were forthcoming from the vile. With the greatest mass of symbols being higher up, Hector tottered on tiptoe in the shallow pools, craning his neck to better examine the ceiling. The hanging stalactites were jagged and broken, severed in places where whoever marked the walls had smashed them from the roof in order to reach bare wall. Hector marveled at the many markings, the symbols crossing over one another, runes illegible, as if the author had gone mad over a tremendous period of time.

One long black stalactite hung in the ceiling's center, directly above Hector's head, the rock black and gnarly as opposed to smooth and white.

"Different from the others . . ." When Hector whispered to himself again, Vincent finally responded.

*You don't know the half of it, brother.*

Two long, skeletal arms separated from the dark mass like a threadbare fan, foot-long fingers splaying out as a pair of hands yawned open. Hector gasped, quickly realizing the figure was suspended upside down, the arms connecting with the shoulders at the base of the body mass. A bulbous head slowly swung down from where it had been tucked away close to the chest. Hector looked straight into the creature's face, nose to nose, trembling chin to pale white forehead.

The face was smooth and hairless, the skin almost translucent. Blue veins were faintly visible, like wisps of pale smoke frozen within marble flesh. It had no nose to speak of, just two angry-looking red holes puncturing the middle of its face. A pair of dark slits widened, revealing cloudy black eyes that stared soullessly at the magister. Then its mouth creaked slowly open. Long teeth, splintered like a graveyard fence, emerged from behind blood-red lips, the creature's fetid breath catching Hector fully in the face. The stench of death was unmistakable, causing the Boarlord to gag, but he couldn't pull his eyes away from those of the creature.

*"Welcome."*

Casper sat on the shingle beach, skimming pebbles into the water. He looked up the shore toward his captain and the Staglord, the two therians having finished consulting the captain's navigation equipment. The duke held a sea chart over the wooden case, the Sharklord scribbling on the map feverishly with an inked quill. Casper looked the other way down the beach, spying the queen and her lady.

Casper had taken quite a shine to Bethwyn. The noblewoman had been happy to talk with the cabin boy, answering his many questions about the fascinating continent of Lyssia. Casper was used to the sea—the mainland was a world he couldn't wait to explore once the *Maelstrom* reached Roof.

The sun had dropped below the horizon, the sky turning a deep indigo as night came on fast. Casper was ready to return to the ship now, regretting not bringing his cloak. Winter seemed especially bitter on the Sturmish Sea. He'd hoped to catch sight of an iceberg so far north, but when Figgis had mentioned how an ice floe could tear open the greatest warship, that had killed his interest swiftly. He reached down and grabbed at a thin white pebble, but it was rooted in the beach, resisting his attempts to pull it free. Another identical stone popped up beside it, and then another. They looked like razor shells at first glance, four of them side by side. It was only when a fifth emerged and closed tight around his hand that he realized they weren't pebbles at all.

They were fingers.

Casper's scream was heard on the *Maelstrom*.


The creature's mouth hung open, its voice as clear in Hector's head as that of his dead brother, although the vile was silent. The pale white head was connected to ragged shoulder blades by the scrawniest length of neck, giving the impression that the skull might tear loose with the slightest provocation. The black eyes remained fixed on Hector as a dark tongue emerged from between the teeth, flickering over the Boarlord's face like a serpent's kiss. Hector swayed, staring at his suspended host, moving left to right, wanting to pull away but locked into its gaze.

*"Why have you sought me out?"*

"I . . . I . . ." stammered Hector nervously, fear snatching the words from his throat. "I heard your call."

Again the tongue flickered, but still Hector couldn't step away. He had no trouble understanding the words now, in such close proximity. The telepathy that had drawn him to the island was now abandoned. The language was new and unnatural to Hector, yet somehow he was able to follow and respond.

*"But you are not one of my kin. What are you?"*

"I'm a Boarlord."

*"Boarlord."*

There was silence as the creature considered this. Hector

glanced at the rest of the body. The beast's head seemed to glow compared to the rest of its form, skeletal with black skin drawn tight across the bones. The torso was an emaciated bag of bones, while the creature's feet remained clamped to the ceiling.

*"How is it you know the tongue of my kin? I have called them for many moons and they fail to come. Now you hear my call?"*

"I can't explain," said Hector, his eyes on the creature's black pupils once more. They held him like a rabbit in a snare. Hector waved his hands toward the walls.

"This language—I recognize it, though I've never studied it. And I *know* languages. Where are you from?"

*"My home is the isle."*

"This island?"

*"I dwell here, but this is not my home. Our isle is bigger. Much bigger. Another white isle."*

"How did you come here? You mention others, but you seem alone. Are you lost? Separated from your people?"

*"People."*

His host made a sound, somewhere between a growl and a laugh. Hector shivered as if someone had walked over his tomb. He sensed that, fragile though the creature seemed, it was more powerful than anything he'd ever encountered, and that included the Wereserpent, Vala. This beast was born from old magicks, while somehow still being connected to theriankind like the Boarlord.

"Perhaps I can help you get home?"

*"In return for what?"*

"I don't know. What do you offer?"

*"You have an understanding, Boarlord, that is rare beyond my kin. A magister, are you not? You are not the first of your order who has visited me seeking answers. You know some dark magick, Boarlord, but you only scratch the surface. Tell me: what do you know of the Children of the Blue Flame?"*

Hector had to think for a moment. He was about to shrug and shake his head, about to say that he knew nothing, when his left hand spasmed involuntarily. He raised it before his face, black leather creaking as the palm and fingers clenched.

Images flashed: *the shaman of the Wyrmwood; the risen corpse of Captain Brutus in the Pits; pale blue eyes that flashed in the night.*

"The undead," whispered Hector.

The creature made the noise again.

*"You are no stranger to the Children of the Blue Flame. You do not fear them?"*

Hector puffed his chest out, confident he had the answers to the creature's riddles. He pulled the glove off his hand, showing the beast the black mark.

"Fear them? I command them!"

The creature's tongue snaked out, perhaps a foot in length, stroking the palm of Hector's hand. He shuddered at the touch but kept his arm up, elbow locked. He couldn't let the host see his fear.

*"You do not understand them, Blackhand. You do not see how they can help you."*

"What is there to understand? How can they help me?"

Again, the growling laughter from the creature.

*"For one who hungers for knowledge, your appetite is easily sated."*

"Tell me what I'm missing, then. Show me what you know!"

*"Good,"* said the host. *"We have our bargain."*

"We do?" asked Hector. He was unsure where this was heading. Beyond the cave, Hector could hear screaming.

*"We have a bargain, Blackhand. I show you what may come to pass, what can be yours."*

"In return for what?"

*"An embrace, magister."*

The creature's mouth opened wider now, the splintered teeth trembling with anticipation. Again, a scream outside. Shouting from the beach. Hector had no time to waste.

"We have a deal," he said. The host's long, skeletal arms swept down toward him, enormous fingers reaching about Hector's skull. Its touch was as cold as death itself.

"Get back on the boats!"

Vega dashed along the shore, grabbing his men and tossing them toward the sea and away from the beach. He was partly transformed, his skin darkening as his hands and teeth sharp-ened with every step. In the eerie twilight moans rose from the beach as the bleached and buried dead hauled themselves from the shingle. Rocks and pebbles tumbled away from hands and heads emerging from the ground, grasping hungrily at the living.

Casper held tight onto Vega's torso like a limpet. He'd been the first to encounter the corpses, but not the last. Amelie and Bethwyn had been dragged to the ground, decayed hands tugging at them. Manfred had dashed to their aid as Vega hauled the boy out of danger, but more of the *Maelstrom*'s men were falling foul of the creatures.

One of the cursed souls had risen fully, taking hold of one of Vega's less agile crewmen. Its skin was parchment thin and clung to every bone on the dead man's body, drained of all fluid. Tattered breeches hinted at the dead man's life; perhaps it had once been a sailor from the wrecked ship. Twin blue fires danced in its eyes as it brought its mouth to the screaming sailor's throat, burying its teeth in warm flesh.

"Move!" screamed Vega as more of the dead emerged from their pebbly graves. Those who got too close took a blow from his clawed fingers, but Vega had no intention of tarrying. They had to get off this devil's rock, and quick.

He waded through the water toward the boats, where the last of his men struggled to clamber aboard.

"Did anyone see Hector?"

"Went around the shore with his men, captain," replied a sailor, pointing. "Beyond that outcrop."

Vega was waist high in the water now and passed Casper to Manfred.

He looked at the beach, counting around twenty of the shambling dead sailors, a clutch of them gathering around the body of his fallen shipmate and tearing hungrily into him. Their moans echoed across the island.

"Keep away from the shore, but try and get around that outcrop. I'll go ahead, see if I can find them."

Vega dived below the surface and swam, skirting the jagged rocks around the White Isle's coastline before heading back toward the beach. As he emerged from the waves he could see Hector's henchmen standing on guard before a tall, thin cave entrance. Both looked startled to see the transformed Sharklord, each of them glancing warily around their small stretch of beach.

"Why all the screaming?" asked Ringlin nervously. "It's enough to wake the dead!"

Ibal's giggles were cut short when Vega threw him a dark and serious look.

"Where's Hector?"

"The master said he wasn't to be interrupted," said Ringlin cockily, sneering at Vega defiantly. "Them's our orders."

"Out of my way," said Vega, making to push past them.

Both men raised their hands to bar his progress, but neither was a match for an angry Sharklord. He punched each in the stomach, grabbed them by their necks, and hurled them back into the water just as the first rowboat emerged into the cove.

"I don't have time for your idiotic loyalty!" he snarled. "Get on the boats. *Now!*"

As if on cue, the first of the risen dead crawled around the outcrop, blue eyes glowing in the dark. Ringlin and Ibal needed no further prompting, running to the boat as Vega disappeared into the cave.

Beyond, in the dark, Vega could hear movements. It was the sound of glass clinking against glass. Gradually the fissure opened into a tall, bell-shaped chamber. The seawater sloshed around his ankles. Vega shook his head, trying to comprehend what he witnessed.

Hector hung in the air, held tight in the long black arms of some creature that was suspended from the cavern's ceiling. The beast was upside down. Its thin fingers with bony knuckles reminded Vega of the spindly legs of a spider crab. He could see the bald white dome of its skull against Hector's neck, its face buried in his throat, the Boarlord's head lolling to one side. The glassy clinking sound came from the magister's satchel, which still hung around his shoulder, banging against his hip as his legs and feet trembled in the air above the rushing tide.

Vega raised up his hands to grab at Hector's shoulder.

Instantly the beast raised its head, still upside-down, revealing its hideous visage with a hiss. Its waxy skin was stretched over its smooth skull, enlarged black eyes narrowing at the Sharklord's interruption. The lower portion of its head was dedicated to a maw of sharp, splintered teeth that ran red with the Boarlord's blood. Vega recoiled, the wound bubbling at Hector's neck.

"Hector!" cried the Sharklord, as the creature screeched something unintelligible.

"No, Vega," said Hector, his voice weak, body trembling spasmodically in the monster's embrace.

*What? He* wants *this?* Vega shook his head, his mind collapsing at the notion that the young magister might have *willingly* let the creature attack him. The captain of the *Maelstrom* had seen men take leave of their minds enough times to know when they needed saving from themselves. He whipped out his cutlass, plunging it swiftly into the monster's chest.

The beast thrashed, screeching as it dropped the Boarlord. Hector landed in the swirling water below with a splash. Vega snatched at him with his free hand as he lunged in once more with his cutlass.

"No!" shouted the Boarlord, but the Wereshark took no notice, standing over the stricken magister as the creature lashed out with its long arms. A thin sheet of black flesh began to appear beneath the beast's arms and between its fingers, a dark elastic membrane that connected joint to joint. Its head snapped toward Vega, blood pooling in the two sword wounds in its torso. Its movements were frantic as its body continued its change. Vega wasn't about to wait and see any further transformation—if it was anything like a therian, then his cutlass would have caused it no harm at all. He brought his open hand back and swung.

The white, skeletal head ripped free from the creature's shoulders with the impact of the Wereshark's blow. The skull went flying across the cave and shattered against the scarred chalk wall. The decapitated body shook uncontrollably as Vega picked up Hector, the young man's eyes wild with madness as he stared over the Pirate Prince's shoulder.

"No," the magister whispered as Vega carried him from the host's cave, out into the cold night.

# PART IV

## THE KISS OF SILVER

# I

# THE HAWKLORD'S TALE

**IF THE SURVIVORS** of Scoria had hoped for a peaceful crossing to Lyssia, they were sorely disappointed. The farther the *Banshee* sailed north, the more restless the Saber Sea became. It was a credit to the crew that they handled the conditions without complaint, content to be out from under the cruel hoof of Count Kesslar. Djogo had assumed captaincy of the vessel, a position he'd held under the Goatlord, and this time the sailors were cooperative and his whip remained in his belt.

Slaves were no longer the cargo of the *Banshee*. Instead, her hold and decks were packed with warriors—former gladiators who had sworn allegiance to the Wolflord. They came from all across the world, each with his own story of enslavement and sorrow to tell. But now their spirits were high, and their loyalty to Drew seemed absolute. His small army numbered over a hundred, each man promising his blade to the cause. Not a moment of the journey was spent idle, with the soldiers training throughout, ensuring that they remained combat ready and fighting fit. Drills and exercises were overseen by the Werelords, with Baron Griffyn pulling the strings. When he wasn't training the Wolf's army, the Hawklord was deep in conversation with Drew.

"Was my father a good man?"

Griffyn sat on one side of the enormous window that spanned the rear of the *Banshee*, with Drew at the opposite end of the sill. The spacious quarters had once been home to Kesslar, but the Goat's belongings had been stripped from the cabin and now lay on the seabed in Scoria's harbor. Practical furniture, such as the captain's desk, chairs, table, and bunks had remained in place, now providing a home to Drew's Werelord companions, the seven therians sharing the cabin and making it their own. It was crowded, but still infinitely better than the labyrinth of the Furnace. While the others slept, the old Hawk and the young Wolf sat quietly, talking in whispered tones.

"I'd love to tell you a string of beautiful lies, Drew, truly I would. Wergar was a hard man. He'd never back out of a fight or argument; he was stubborn, hotheaded, and as tough as Sturmish steel. There was never a more fearsome sight than the Werewolf charging into battle, howling and roaring, scything Moonbrand through the bloody air. You couldn't imagine a more beautiful sword than your father's white blade. Wergar had friends and enemies and nothing in between."

Griffyn took a sip from the tankard he held in his gnarled hand. "I was honored to be considered his friend."

"The more I hear, the more he sounds like a brute."

"He was a man of conviction, Drew, and he was the king."

"King of Westland though, not the Barebones."

"It mattered little back then, just as now; whosoever ruled in Highcliff ruled over all the Seven Realms. Consider Westland as the head of a great beast, and the remaining realms the body. It's long been acknowledged that there's only one king in Lyssia, and that's the one who sits on the throne in Highcliff. The Wolves ruled for two hundred years, Drew; nobody ever contested their place until the Lion arrived."

Drew chewed his thumb as he stared out of the window, watching the churning waves as they flashed moonlight in the *Banshee*'s wake.

"So you knew Bergan, Manfred, and Mikkel then? Were they your friends, too?"

Griffyn smiled. "They were once."

"What changed?"

"Allegiances." The old Hawk sighed. "I'm sure you know all about Bergan's quandary when Leopold took power. He and the Staglords all played their parts in persuading Wergar to surrender his crown. They didn't know the Lion would go back on his word, but each of them deserted Wergar, and I hope each feels the pain of that betrayal to this day."

"You've got them wrong, Griffyn. They're good men; they were my Wolf's Council, my advisers after we took Highcliff. It's cruel to hope they still suffer for something that happened so long ago."

Griffyn looked surprised. "I apologize, Lord Drew. I didn't mean to offend, but my opinion stands. I've earned it."

"How?"

Griffyn rose stiffly, unfastening his jerkin. "I was a loyal Kingsman, right until the last, to the moment Leopold chopped off your father's head. And I continued to remain loyal afterward."

Drew flinched at mention of Wergar's execution. He'd never known the man, but they were still joined by the bond of blood. The old Hawklord shook off his jerkin, popping the buttons of his shirt. Drew shifted uncomfortably.

"The Hawklords would —and did—die for your father, Drew. We were his staunchest allies and one of the fiercest weapons Wergar had in his arsenal. '*Death from above*' our enemies would scream when we soared into battle."

Griffyn's face was wistful as he shrugged off the shirt. "The other Werelords bowed and swore fealty to whoever sat on the throne. Not so the Hawklords, even after the Wolf and his pack were slain. We remained loyal to the dead king. This enraged the Lion, so much so that he made an example of me."

Griffyn turned, the moonlight that streamed through the window illuminating his back. Two enormous scars ran from his shoulders down to the base of his spine, great discolored swathes of pale, colorless skin. There was nothing neat or orderly about the old wounds, the torn flesh undulating in and out, jagged and angry, where his skin had been hacked away many years ago.

"Leopold took my wings. They held me down in the Court of Highcliff, the stench of your murdered and burned family still thick in the air, while the Bear and Stags watched. All the Werelords were there: Horses, Rams, Boars, the lot of them. The Lion took a silver blade to my beautiful wings. He carved them off."

Drew was nauseated. He turned away, unable to look at the Hawklord's awful scars. The image was there in his mind: Leopold holding Griffyn down while he sawed the Werehawk's wings from his back. When he looked back, Griffyn was already rebuttoning his shirt.

"So, as you can imagine, I find it difficult to forgive after all these years."

"I'm sorry, my Lord, I didn't . . ."

"You weren't to know," said Griffyn, dismissing Drew. "Bergan and Manfred are good men who were put in an awful situation. They escaped the Lion's wrath with their bodies intact but their pride battered. I might not have suffered this fate if I hadn't been so stubborn."

Griffyn grimaced as he continued. "Leopold's Lionguard dragged me back to Windfell, accompanied by the lickspittle Skeer—one of my Hawklord brothers—parading me before my people as a warning to all; if any Hawk should show their wings again, they were signing their own death warrant. Skeer was the only Hawk who sided with the Lion, happily swearing allegiance long before Wergar's murder. I was forced to deliver the message on behalf of Leopold. While the Lionguard displayed my severed wings to the Hawklords I recounted Leopold's decree, outlawing my people's falconthropy."

"Falconthropy?"

"The therianthropy of the Hawklords, Drew. You have your lycanthropes, felinthropes, caninthropes, and the like. The Hawks are the falconthropes."

"Leopold outlawed your transformation?"

"That's right," said Griffyn, sitting down again on the windowsill. "In addition, for their treasonous behavior, the Hawklords were forbidden to return to the Barebones. We were banished, chased from our homeland, to be executed should we return. Leopold's army put Windfell under Skeer's command, and I was kept in court as a plaything for the new baron, a reminder to our people of what insubordination led to."

"Where are the Hawklords now?"

"Dead. Gone. Forgotten. I honestly don't know. Leopold and Skeer destroyed my people. Windfell was emptied of Hawklords overnight, never to return. We were powerful and great in number, manning towers and keeps along the spine of the Barebones, acting as commanders and scouts in every army of the Seven Realms. But Leopold put us to the sword."

"But Scoria? How did you get from Windfell to the Furnace?"

"That's where our mutual acquaintance Kesslar comes in," said the Hawk, smacking his bony hand against the window frame.

"Kesslar and Skeer were friends from long, long ago. Opportunists, liars, thieves—they had so much in common. Kesslar was a frequent visitor to Windfell, the only place he was welcome, having taken advantage of his brother therians' kindness in the other courts of the Seven Realms. The Goat took a shine not just to me, but my daughter."

Griffyn paused, glancing toward where Shah slept in her bunk.

"How old was she?"

"Twelve, just a child. Kesslar made Skeer an offer and the old Falcon couldn't say no. Deal done, the Goat had me shipped over to Scoria to fight in the Furnace, while he kept Shah as his own."

Drew tried to imagine what kind of life that must have been for the young Shah. She'd been in a dark mood since he'd met her, and even with their freedom secured, a shadow still hung over Shah's head.

"She must have been terrified."

"I don't doubt it for a moment, but we Hawklords are made of strong stuff. After four years in the Furnace, I'd earned the respect of my masters and freedom from the arena. I'd earned gold for my achievements, as well as lodging of my own away from the slaves and gladiators. While I moved into the ludus to train the Lizards' gladiators, my daughter was by then working for Kesslar, the eyes and wings that got him into places nobody else could reach."

"How did she and Djogo come to know each other?"

"She saw him fight in the Furnace," said the Hawklord. "He was the greatest human gladiator I ever trained. When Kesslar bought him from Ignus, he and Shah began to spend time together, aboard this ship while Kesslar traveled, picking up slaves. A fondness grew, surrounded by the misery the Goatlord thrived upon."

"She seems troubled," whispered Drew, staring at her dark form in the recesses of the cabin.

"If she could get her talons into Kesslar, she'd tear his throat out."

"Because of what he did to you?"

"No." The Hawk sighed. "Because of what happened to her child."

"Child?" gasped Drew.

"Hush, lad," said Griffyn, his voice low. He edged closer along the window seat toward Drew.

"She and Djogo have a child?"

"No, Drew, this was long before Djogo. My daughter met a fellow while she traveled with Kesslar, a charming, dangerous man who thought a little too much of himself—certainly not a marriageable prospect. She was a teenage girl and thought she was in love. Perhaps they were; we'll never know. Anyway, a child came from this union, unbeknown to Kesslar. The father was gone before my daughter even knew she was expecting. We hid the pregnancy from the Goat, Shah remaining in Scoria for the final months while Kesslar was away.

"The baby was born days before the Goat returned with the *Banshee* full of fresh slaves. Shah had no time at all with the child. I had it—him—taken away, using what coin I'd saved to have the baby taken to his father. If Kesslar had found my daughter with a child, Brenn knows what he'd have done with them. Punish her? Sell the child? I only hope the baby was delivered to the father. To this day I worry about what became of him. That child is my only regret."

Drew put a hand on the old Hawk's crooked shoulder. "You did what you had to, protecting your daughter and grandchild."

"If I had that time again, I'd have killed Kesslar before surrendering one of my own. My only regret," he repeated.

Drew wanted to comfort the old Hawklord but was unable to find the words.

"We all have regrets," he said eventually, thinking back to Whitley and Gretchen, how he'd never had the chance to say good-bye to them. He wondered where Hector was, what had become of his dear friend, whether he'd ever see him again.

Griffyn smiled, the grin creasing his weather-beaten face.

"You're too young for regrets, Drew. You've got time on your side. You can make changes and right your wrongs. Better still, right *others'* wrongs. And as long as I live and breathe I shall be by your side to help you do just that."

# 2

# THE GAME

**DIGGING HIS FEET** into the loose earth, Trent scrambled the remaining distance up the hillside. He'd left the campsite behind him, his comrades' calls still echoing at his back as they searched for the escaped prisoners. They'd had forty captured men of the Longridings and Romari, all manacled and chained, and three of them had escaped. They had originally been caught in the grasslands, drawing ever nearer to Calico where Lady Gretchen no doubt hid.

For one prisoner to go missing was extraordinary; for three to have escaped sounded like there might have been a traitor in the camp. Not one to let the tracks go cold, Trent was immediately up and away once the shout went out.

The footprints disappeared up the bluff to the east of the

camp. Looking up, Trent could see a swaying rank of grass silhouetted against the moonlight, marking the highest point of
the snaking ridge. He hauled himself to the summit, snatching
at tufts of grass to stop himself from tumbling back. Breathing
hard, he staggered to his feet and looked down. A huge
meadow of unspoiled long grass disappeared into the darkness.
The bluff was rocky on this side, a steep, treacherous bank of
rough stones and loose earth filling the slope to the north and
south. Trent watched his step as the rocks skittered underfoot,
the scree plummeting sixty feet to the grasslands below.

He glanced along the ridge to see two figures to the north,
a hundred feet or so feet away. By the clear night sky he recognized Sorin as one of them. The other was having his manacles
removed, before being handed a shortsword by Sorin. With a
hearty shove the prisoner was then sent tumbling down the
embankment, a cloud of earth and stones erupting in his wake
as he rolled and spun down into the grass.

"Wait!" called Trent, scrambling along the ridge, but by the
time he'd caught up with Sorin the prisoner had disappeared
from view below.

"What in Brenn's name are you doing? Are you behind
this, Sorin? There's *three* of them that have escaped!"

"That's right, farmboy," said Sorin, winking at Trent. Three
pairs of unlocked manacles lay at his feet. "Was me what freed
them, wasn't it."

Trent struck the broken-nosed captain in the face, his

217

knuckles cracking as the two of them went down.

"Get off me, you fool!" shouted Sorin, hammering the side of Trent's head with his fists as the younger man tried to pin him down.

"Traitor!" yelled Trent, finding fresh strength as he grappled with his senior officer. He couldn't hear the captain's voice; his mind and struggle was focused on Sorin the traitor. Traitor, just like Drew.

Sorin's fist caught Trent across the jaw, sending the young outrider over the ridge and down the rocky embankment. He bounced and twirled, losing all sense of up and down, his body a whirling mass of limbs. His head struck hard rock—once, twice—his temple splitting before he shuddered to a halt in the grass at the base of the scree.

Trent tried to focus his eyes, stars spinning overhead. He lifted a hand, feeling the torn flesh over his eye, his fingertips coming away crimson.

"You'd call *me* a traitor, Ferran?" Sorin laughed from above, staggering back to his feet. "I was obeying orders. Lord Pinkeye told me to have three picked out and sent down here. For the game."

"The game?" called up Trent, dabbing at his streaming brow.

"Our lordship needs to hunt, Ferran. That's why I brought them away from the camp. He can lose control when his blood's up."

Trent rolled on to his belly and began to crawl up the

embankment, the loose earth falling down on top of him. He struggled frantically, trying to find purchase in the scree, but it was impossible. A scream from the long grass behind made him stop and turn, his eyes wide and fearful.

"You gave them swords?" he shouted to Sorin.

"Pinkeye likes his prey to have a little fight in 'em, doesn't he?" called down the captain, crouching over the incline. "I hope you brought your pa's Wolfshead blade with you, Ferran. Best of luck, eh?"

With that, Sorin turned and disappeared from view.

"Sorin!" Trent cried in vain. "Sorin!"

Trent looked up and down the ridge base, desperate to find a way of climbing out. He was blind to a means of escape; the tall grass to his right was as high as his head and constantly swaying. Reluctantly, he unsheathed the Wolfshead blade and started to follow the stony bank northward. He glanced up as he went, constantly searching for a route out.

Sorin had played the situation perfectly. He'd let Trent leap to his own conclusions, and before he knew it, he was lying at the bottom of an impossible slope waiting for the Catlord to tear him to pieces. The captain was a sly fellow.

"Brenn, help me . . ."

A gurgling cry came from the long grass nearby. Trent recognized the wet sound in the voice; blood, pooling at the back of the man's throat. He shook his head and moved onward. *Not your concern, Trent.*

"The beast," a voice sobbed. "Dear Brenn, the beast . . ."

Trent ground his teeth, ignoring the man's pleas. He had to look after his own skin, thanks to Sorin. The sobbing man's cries tugged at him as he walked past, like hooks beneath his skin. *Keep going, Trent. Don't stop now. You can't stop. The man's a traitor. His death rattle's on its way. He got what was coming.*

But with each step, the begging cries of the man snagged hold of Trent's conscience. He couldn't leave *anything* to die— that much Mack Ferran had taught him on the Cold Coast.

He cursed angrily, wiping the blood from his temple along his sleeve as he turned and set off into the long grass. Away from the ridge he strode, cutting the grass back with his long- sword, staggering hesitantly toward the cries of a scared and dying man.

Thirty or so paces from the slope, Trent found him, lying on a flattened bed of grass. The tall, feathery fronds lay bent and broken about him, his limbs spread-eagled as if he'd pre- pared a nest for the night. The man still held the shortsword that Sorin had given him, his right hand feebly raising it as Trent appeared. The man's head remained still against the floor, although his eyes stayed fixed on the Ferran boy as his lips trembled.

The man's mouth was awash with blood, pink spittle foam- ing between his teeth, his belly torn wide open. Trent gagged, the food from his evening meal racing up his throat. He turned away, trying to hold it down but only partly succeeding.

"Please . . ." begged the man, finding his words again. "Kill . . . me . . ."

Trent turned back, his face a mask of pity and horror. He raised the Wolfshead blade and faltered, unable to put the poor man out of his misery. Before he could act decisively, the grasses split to his right as a white shape sprang from the darkness, the moonlight catching the beast's shining fur as it flew. Trent just had time to parry the monster away, before the sword flew from his grasp and the two tumbled into the bloody grass.

The Catlord's white head was huge, the width of Trent's torso. The jaws snapped at his face, teeth the size of daggers. Claws held Trent's shoulders, pinning him to the ground and preventing his escape. He raised his left forearm toward the monster, catching the Cat's bite with it before it tore at his skull. The teeth clamped down hard, cutting into the steel-armored bracer and threatening to snap his arm in two. Trent screamed as the Cat's pink eyes shone, demonic in the moonlight; Frost was possessed by the change, by the hunt, by the kill. The bracer bowed, the metal sleeve groaning, about to break. Trent jabbed at the Catlord's eyes with his free hand, hooking his thumb in and striking home.

With a roar, Frost released his grip on the Redcloak, leaping off the boy and bounding back into the grasses. The shouting of soldiers echoed down from the ridge, as Bastians and Lionguard investigated the commotion. Trent rolled over on to the body of the dying man, but the beast was gone. The light had gone from the prisoner's eyes, life's last breath steaming from his still lips.

Trent scrambled about on the bloody ground, fingers searching for his dropped blade. A low growl emanated from the shadows; the beast was still close by. Did Frost know that it was Trent he was facing? *Surely he recognizes me?* Trent's hand brushed cold steel, fingers racing along its length until they found the handle. Snatching it up he tracked back through the grass, toward the voices on the ridge.

He stumbled from the tall grass, collapsing against the pebbled hillside. Above he heard Bastians and Lyssians alike, shouting for him to climb up, to keep moving. He resheathed the Wolfshead blade and began his ascent again, hands and feet clawing at the bank, every handful of loose earth sending him sliding back again. The growling sound drew closer as his comrades shouted their support, looking on with morbid fascination as the beast closed in.

"Keep moving, Ferran!"

"It's coming, man!"

"Climb for your life!"

Trent wanted to scream, but that was wasted energy. He was fighting for survival now—the changed Catlord behind him was out of his mind with bloodlust. Trent was just one more human delivered by Sorin, a mouse for the cat to play with until it stopped twitching.

Trent's hand caught a flat rock overhead, a few feet below a larger boulder that protruded from the scree bank. He didn't have time to check its suitability. His muscles strained and burned as he trusted his body weight to the flat ledge. It remained in place, deeply embedded, allowing him to finally make progress.

"It's on you, Ferran!"

"I can see it in the grass!"

Trent threw his right hand forward toward the larger boulder, his fingers scrabbling for purchase as he launched himself toward the higher point. The men cheered overhead, willing him on. This would put him clear of the grasses, give him the chance to find a route out while Frost regained his senses.

The boulder ripped free as it took Trent's weight, the bank collapsing as he fell in a shower of dirt, rock, and pebbles back to the base of the ridge. Trent spluttered, the dust cloud blinding and choking him as he struggled to rise from the debris. The grasses parted in front of him as a figure emerged.

Trent had expected a clawed paw to strike out, tear his throat, his stomach, put an end to his fight. Instead, a smooth, human hand was extended before him, as the lithe outline of Frost stood over him, naked in the moonlight. The albino Catlord flexed his fingers, beckoning Trent to take his offered palm. He rubbed his other hand against his injured eye, squinting and blinking as he focused on the terrified outrider.

"Got me good there, Trent," said the felinthrope, smiling through bloodied teeth. He nodded at his hand. The Redcloak hesitantly took it as Frost hauled him to his feet.

"A word of warning: never get in the way of a Catlord when he's hunting game. Come, let's return to camp. I owe you a hundred apologies."

# 3

# THE BLOODY BAY

**AT A GLANCE** he looked like any other sailor on ship's watch in Denghi. A fringe of black hair poked out from the rim of his kash, the headdress popular with the men of the desert. A white scarf was wrapped around his face in the Omiri style, gray eyes peering out from the narrow slit, watching all who passed along the wharf. His bare torso was weather-beaten and tanned; three-quarter length white leggings covered his legs, leaving his bare feet exposed to the elements. His right hand rested on his hip, a shortsword lodged within the sash, while his left was missing, a basket-handled trident dagger sitting on the stump in its place. He stood between the rails at the head of the *Banshee*'s gangway, apparently relaxed. There were few captains in Denghi who could boast the rightful king of Westland as their watchman.

The port was crowded with a variety of ships, greater in number than any Drew had seen before. All Hallows Bay, Highcliff, and Cape Gala had been busy, bustling harbors, but there was a manic energy to Denghi. Griffyn had explained to Drew that this port on the Bloody Bay was the only truly neutral city in Omir. Ro-Pasha to the north was under the control of Lord Canan's Doglords, while Ro-Shann to the south was home to Lady Hayfa, the Hyena. Both Canan and Hayfa were enemies of the true ruler of Omir, King Faisal of Azra, but each respected the neutrality of Denghi. It was the only place in Omir where one could find agents of all three factions rubbing shoulders with one another.

The choice of where they should land had been limited. As predicted, they'd passed patrolling Bastian warships while they slunk across the Saber Sea. As the *Banshee* was known to the Bastians as a slaver, she was allowed on her way with little interference. Djogo and Shah had welcomed the captain of one such vessel aboard while the Werelords and small army of gladiators hid in the hold. They'd made their excuses for Kesslar's absence, telling the Bastians that the Goat was sleeping off a barrel of wine belowdecks. The captain had warned Djogo to steer clear of the southern waters, due to the military activity in the Lyssian Straits. The *Banshee* had no other option than to head for Denghi.

The former slave vessel was moored at the end of the port's longest pier, a five-hundred-foot-stretch of wharf that reached out into the Bloody Bay. Every inch of the pier was crowded with merchants, fishermen, sailors, and ne'er-do-wells, haggling with one another over goods. The air was alive with sounds and smells: music from cantinas clashing with shouting traders, monkeys chattering, dogs barking, spices burning, meats cooking. Apart from one Bastian warship, anchored a little farther around the bay, there was no sign of the military within the harbor. Lyssia may have been at war, but there seemed to be little conflict in Denghi.

Three figures approached the gangplank from the pier. Djogo came first, his face open, identity unhidden. He was known in Omir, with a fearsome reputation hard-earned. Denghi had been a regular stop-off for Kesslar down the years for buying and selling slaves. Behind came Griffyn and Krieg, their faces obscured by kashes. The trio traversed the gangway, Drew nodding as they passed. He followed them as they disappeared below, another sailor replacing him at the top of the planked walkway.

The Werelords gathered around the desk in the captain's cabin, Djogo standing by the door. A crude map of Lyssia was carved into the tabletop, which the Goat had used to plot his raids around the continent. The allies of the Wolf now used it to plan their next move.

Griffyn cast his hand across the map wearily.

"Lyssia is turbulent, more so than ever before," said the Hawklord, pinching his sharp nose between thumb and fore-finger.

"Turbulent?" asked Drew. "Beyond that Bastian frigate, there's no sign of war in Denghi."

"The battle rages beneath calm waters," said Krieg. "It would appear the seaport has dodged much of Omir's fighting, but that could change at any moment."

"You said Denghi was neutral."

"So it is. But news is that Lord Canan is allied with the Catlords," said the Rhino.

"Cats and Dogs, unified?" The Behemoth chuckled, the noise like a grinding millstone.

"I know," agreed Griffyn. "Unlikely unions have sprung up across Lyssia. There is talk that Lady Hayfa has also agreed terms with Canan. Her forces are already mobilizing, ensuring that Faisal is surrounded to the north and south by powerful enemies allied against him. They mean to attack Azra."

"Are they powerful enough to succeed?" asked Drake.

"If the Catlords lend their claws, this Desert King will die," said Taboo, sneering out of the porthole toward the Bastian warship.

"Grim days indeed for the Jackal," said Drake.

"And the rest of Lyssia?" said Drew, keen to hear news of the west.

"Broken," said Djogo. "Highcliff has fallen to the Catlords, your Wolf's Council chased from Westland. Lucas sits on the throne in place of his dead father."

"Leopold, dead?" said Drew, clearly shocked.

"It's said that Duke Bergan killed him," said the old Hawklord.

*Good old Bergan. I knew he wouldn't let us down if he got the chance.*

Drew noticed Griffyn was avoiding eye contact. "What is it?"

"The duke is dead, too, Drew; killed in his battle with Leopold."

Drew stared at Griffyn's bowed head, the old man's words not sinking in straight away.

"The whereabouts of your mother and others—Duke Manfred and Baron Hector—aren't known, though Earl Mikkel was slain by the Doglords. The remains of your Wolf's Council are being bruited about as Lyssia's 'most wanted'; there's a price on their heads—and your own."

Drew hardly heard Griffyn. Mikkel and his dear friend and mentor, Bergan, dead. He'd always felt certain he would see the Bearlord again, didn't imagine that he would never get to make amends to the giant, bearded duke for fleeing Highcliff in secret.

Krieg tugged at the kash around Drew's face.

"It's more important than ever we keep your identity secret, my friend," said the Rhino, before placing a consoling hand on the Wolf's shoulder. "If Onyx offers riches in return for your head, you'll have fewer friends than ever."

"Hector and Whitley," said Drew, his attention still on the Hawklord. "And Gretchen. Any news?"

"As I said, Hector fled Highcliff when Onyx took the city. I couldn't tell you if he's alive. Lady Gretchen and Lady Whitley disappeared from Cape Gala after you were taken by Kesslar. Their whereabouts are unknown, but many of the Horselords fled Cape Gala to Calico on the coast, so your friends may have joined them. Duke Brand, the Bull, reigns there, his fortress city one of the few that makes a stand against the Bastians. A fleet of the Catlord's warships gathers off the coast, blockading the Lyssian Straits."

"Have the other realms not come to Westland's aid? What of Sturmland? The Barebones?"

Krieg raised his voice now as Griffyn shook his head. "The Lords of Sturmland have taken no side, while the Barebones are split—the Stags of Stormdale and Highwater stand in favor of the Wolf, while the Crows of Riven supposedly remain neutral."

"Supposedly?"

"Their contempt for the other Werelords of the Barebones is famous—they want the realm for themselves. I find it hard to believe they aren't involved in some way with the attacks on Highwater."

"Highwater's been attacked?" asked Drew.

"The Staglord cities are without their lords, one brother dead, the other missing," replied Griffyn, pointing a bony finger at the mountain range on the map. "Even now Onyx moves his pieces into play, his army having taken the Dalelands and now laying siege to Highwater."

"But surely Highwater is full of civilians?"

"Not so. Word reached the remaining Stags that a combined army of Bastians and Omiri approached. The innocents have evacuated south to the safety of Stormdale. Brenn willing, the civilians will be spared this conflict and the battle will play out in Highwater. The men of the Barebones are a tough bunch, and Highwater is well protected: they'll be prepared for a long siege."

"Is there *nobody* who can aid them?"

"The Stags have no allies. The Bear is gone from Brackenholme, and Windfell to the south remains deserted." Griffyn sighed. "My homeland is no more than a ghost town, while the Lion's lackey, Skeer, rules the roost."

Shah, at her father's side, now spoke up. "Not for long. Skeer's time is running out. When we return to Windfell, we'll turn the traitorous old bird out of the nest and make it our own again."

"Brave words, Hawk," said Krieg. "But what hope do you and your father have of defeating whatever force awaits you in Windfell? Where are your fellow Hawklords in your time of need?"

Griffyn looked up from the table, his eyes settling upon Drew again, who stared straight back, shocked at the old warrior's tide of bad news.

"Where are the Hawklords, Baron?" asked Drew, his voice quiet as he struggled with his grief.

"Scattered," replied Griffyn. "Many took on lives as normal, mortal men—like you, Drew, before you discovered your lycanthropy. Can you imagine? Forbidden to embrace the beast? Having your gift denied you? My people were broken just as Windfell was. They're lost."

"Is there no way of reaching them?"

Griffyn wavered, his eyes narrowing. The Hawklord sat down, looking back to the map. His finger traced a line up the Silver River from Denghi, past Azra, to the Barebones, coming to a halt. The Werelords were silent as they watched him, waiting for Griffyn to speak. He closed his eyes and spoke.

"There is a place most sacred to my people, the great mountain of Tor Raptor, ancient tomb of the Hawklords of Windfell. Only the just and rightful lord may safely enter the Screaming Peak."

"Screaming Peak?" Drew asked.

"It's a cavern within Tor Raptor's summit. When the stones are lifted, Tor Raptor screams to her children."

"Screams?" Krieg was fascinated, as were the others.

"It's the one way in which the true Lord of Windfell may call the Hawklords home. The only way."

232

"Sounds like a legend to me, old timer." Drake sighed. "We need more than wailing mountains to best our foes."

The Hawklord opened his eyes, settling them upon Drew. The young Wolf nodded.

"We need an army."

# 4

# BACK FROM THE DEAD

**"COME IN," CALLED** Count Vega, as a series of knocks on the door took his attention away from his desk. A heavily cloaked Duke Manfred entered the cabin, stamping his feet and clapping his hands, tiny snowflakes shaking loose from his shoulders.

"Is it chilly outside, Your Grace?"

"It's as cold as Ragnor's chin!" grunted the duke miserably.

"Interesting you mention old Henrik's father. We're close to the coast of Sturmland again by my reckoning, maybe a day or two out of Friggia. That business with the Sirens and then the White Isle almost did for us—thank Sosha that I was able to get my bearings."

The two Werelords were silent for a moment, memories of their brief visit to the lonely island all too vivid. Vega reached into a cabinet and pulled out a bottle and glass, pushing them across the table toward Manfred.

"There really was no need for you to take a watch, you know. The last thing I need is a frozen Stag tumbling on to the deck, shattering into a thousand pieces. Would scare the lives out of my men."

"It's the least I can do, mucking in with your crew," said the old Duke, unstoppering the bottle and pouring himself a glass with shivering hands. He threw it down his throat swiftly, barking a spluttering cough at the drink.

"Friggia, you say?" muttered the duke. "Do you plan to stop there?"

"I'd hoped we could make it straight to Roof. Perhaps we still can. Stopping in Friggia would be dangerous. It's one of Slotha's ports; we want to bypass it if possible. There's no way Onyx's forces could have reached this far north yet. We should get to Icegarden through the back door, so to speak."

"How's Amelie?"

Vega smiled, a rakish grin breaking his handsome features. The captain of the *Maelstrom* had watched the tender friendship between Manfred and the queen blossom into something else. Neither of the therians would admit to such feelings—they'd deny it instantly—but there was no fooling the Sharklord.

"I invited her into my company, but she still needs rest. It appears the encounters on the White Isle have left their scars upon her."

Manfred nodded, staring back into the open stove, the flames warming his hands and soul.

"And Hector?" said the Staglord. "Any news?"

Vega ran a hand through his long black hair, wincing at the thought of the young magister. "He still sleeps."

"Sleep is a good thing. I thought he was dead."

"He might have killed us all."

"How can you say that, Vega? The poor lad was attacked by that creature, wasn't he?"

The count scratched at his scalp. "He was and he wasn't."

"Don't start with the cryptic talk, Vega!"

"Yes, the creature attacked him, could easily have killed him. But I think he deliberately allowed the beast to assault him."

"How so?" The duke sounded shocked.

"We landed on the White Isle on Hector's insistence. I suspect he wanted us to go there, knew what awaited us, and put all our lives in danger."

"How could he have possibly known what was on the island? That's preposterous, Vega!"

"I don't know. This communing he's confessed to carrying out, this necromancy—who knows what he's tapped into? You can't tell me Hector isn't a changed man. He *knew* there was something on that island. His actions led to one of my men getting killed. It has something to do with dark magistry, I'm sure of it. I don't have the answers, Manfred, but I believe Hector does."

The duke scratched at the gray stubble on his jaw, saddened to hear Vega's accusations, but he didn't defend the Boarlord. It was plain for all to see that the sickly Hector bore little resemblance to the happy young boy he'd first met ten years ago in the court of Redmire.

"Does Lady Bethwyn still attend him?"

"She has a soft spot for our magister," said Vega, staring at the cabin door, his thoughts distant. "She is another therian of the Dalelands after all. She seems a lovely girl, very trusting. I hope Hector doesn't betray that trust."

"What on earth do you mean?"

The count shook his head wearily and then smiled at the duke. "I'm thinking aloud, that's all. He's a complex character, our Baron of Redmire, Manfred."

"You worry too much," said Manfred, unfastening his cloak at last as his body warmed up. "He's not as misguided as you suggest, my friend. Just a little misunderstood."

Vega nodded but said nothing, his mind lingering on the memory of two bickering brothers on the staircase of Bevan's tower, arguing over their father's throne for a final, fatal time.

Bethwyn clenched the cloth in her fist, her knuckles turning white as she squeezed the excess water from it. Beyond the porthole, sleet raced past, blurring streaks of white against the pitch-black night. Bethwyn moved her hand over Hector's head, gently mopping his brow with the damp cloth, the warm scented water settling across his clammy skin. For seven days and nights she'd kept vigil over the Boarlord, Queen Amelie relieving her of her other responsibilities in order to care for the magister. She wondered if his terrible fever would ever break.

By the time the rowboats had returned to the *Maelstrom* from the White Isle, many had assumed the baron was bound for a watery grave, few giving him any chance of survival. His throat was torn and his blood loss great, the wound refusing to heal as a normal injury would for a therian. Using what medicinal knowledge she and others had, Bethwyn had patched Hector up, cleaning, staunching, and dressing the bite as best she could. She'd changed the bandage frequently over the following days, but the festering smell never went away. The Boarguard, Ringlin and Ibal, always lurked nearby, making Bethwyn uncomfortable. The tall one didn't have a nice word to say about anyone, and the looks the fat giggling one gave her made her skin crawl. All the while the Boarlord had clung to the sliver of life, refusing to give up his fight.

Bethwyn brushed the matted hair from Hector's brow. He'd lost a lot of weight since she'd first met him in Highcliff, his puppy fat all gone as his skin clung tightly to his cheekbones. His skin had a deathly pallor to it, almost yellow beneath the lantern light. She shivered, throwing another piece of wood on to the stove. She closed the grille door with the poker before facing the sickly Boarlord once more.

Hector's left arm had found its way out of the covers. She picked it up at the wrist and elbow and was about to tuck it back below the blanket when she paused. She turned it over in her hands, revealing the palm. The black mark she'd seen when they'd encountered the Sirens had grown, the entire palm now blackened and the skin darkening between each finger. This wasn't the first time she'd examined the hand while Hector slept. While the rest of his body burned with a fever, the corrupted palm remained cold to the touch. *As cold as death itself,* thought Bethwyn.

Suddenly the hand snatched at her wrist, causing her to cry out in shock. It clasped hard, the chill flesh tight on her skin, fingers holding her in their grasp. Hector's eyes were open, watching her, his head motionless on the pillow.

"Gretchen."

His voice was a whisper, cracked lips trembling as he tried to smile. Bethwyn should have been happy to see his eyes and hear his voice, but she couldn't get over the shock of his grip. *He's mistaken me for another.* She tugged back, trying to free her wrist.

239

"I dreamed it was you. So caring and kind," he said slowly and quietly.

"Please, Hector; it's me, Bethwyn," she said, but he wouldn't relinquish his hold.

"I was in such a dark place, Gretchen, so cold and alone. And you were the warmth I could cling to. It was your light that brought me back from the darkness. It was your love."

"Hector, you're hurting me," she cried, as the magister's hand tightened its grip. *Can he not hear me?* It was as if he were unaware of his hand's action while her words simply didn't register.

"I knew you wouldn't abandon me to the dark," he said, eyes closing as tears rolled down his face. "I knew you'd save me from the nightmare, Gretchen . . ."

Bethwyn was crying out now, trying to prize his fingers away, but the more she struggled the tighter he held on. His words were rambling, making no sense, as if he were sleep talking. *Is he even conscious? Does he* know *he's hurting me?*

"I would speak with your father when the time comes, Gretchen. I would seek your hand my love, for we should be together. We *belong* together."

Bethwyn shrieked, frantically trying to shake him loose, as the door burst open. Vega was between the two of them immediately, trying to bat Hector's hand away. When he realized the Boar wouldn't relinquish his grip, he took his own fingers to Hector's, pulling them back hard. The Sharklord was surprised by the magister's strength, the hold like a trap. Finally the fingers opened enough to allow the girl to pull her arm free, the flesh of her wrist livid with red welts.

"What are you *thinking*?" shouted Vega, shaking Hector by the shoulders in his cot.

"What?" muttered Hector, his eyes blinking as if waking from a dream. "I didn't . . ."

"You were *hurting* her!" said the count as Manfred and Amelie appeared in the doorway. Bethwyn rushed into the queen's arms.

"Bethwyn?" gasped Hector, deeply confused.

Manfred stood to one side, escorting Amelie and Bethwyn from the room. He passed Ringlin and Ibal entering as he left, the Staglord unable to resist glowering at the Boarguard. The men watched the three leave before joining Vega in their sickly master's cabin.

"I didn't know," whispered Hector. "I was dreaming . . ."

"Dreaming or not, Hector, that girl has tended to you for the last seven days."

Vega leaned over the bed and brought his face close to Hector's. "Tell me, Hector: did you *know* what was waiting for us on that island? What kind of monster was that in the cavern? One of my men died on that beach, devoured by the dead, while you explored that cave."

"I don't know . . . what you're talking . . ." stammered Hector, but the captain of the *Maelstrom* continued.

"I thought you and I had an understanding, Hector. I was there in Bevan's Tower, remember? I helped you with that mess. I thought it was an accident . . ."

"It *was* an accident, Vega!" cried Hector, fully awake now, his face contorting with resentment.

"That may be," said the Sharklord. "But our visit to the White Isle was no accident. Your encounter with that monster didn't look like a struggle to me, Hector. It looked like . . . like an *embrace* . . ."

Vega stood up, straightening his collar.

"I'm disappointed, Hector. I've looked out for you, shown you nothing but compassion and friendship, and this is how you repay me. Well, I'm watching you. You know more than you're telling us, only I'm not as foolish as the others. I know your secrets, just remember that."

Count Vega turned, barging between the Boarguard and slamming the cabin door shut as he left. Ringlin and Ibal watched him leave, then looked back to the Lord of Redmire as he lay in his sickbed. Hector's face darkened as he lifted his blackened hand to his throat. He took hold of the bandages, yanking them loose, the stained dressing crunching as he pulled it from his wound. The scar was scabbed over, slowly on the mend. He rubbed his black hand across his neck and heaved himself upright, swaying woozily on the bed. He looked at the two men, his face full of thunder, eyes bright with fury and revenge. The stare spoke volumes to the Boarguard. Ibal giggled and Ringlin nodded.

Hector's whisper hissed from his broken lips. "Vega must die."

# 5

# OVERWHELMING ODDS

**OPENING INTO THE** ocean at Bloody Bay, the Silver River had earned its name on two counts. Firstly, as the main tributary from the Barebones to the Saber Sea, it was the swiftest and most profitable trade route for moving precious metals out of the mountains. It was said that whoever controlled the Silver River controlled Omir, the stewardship of the waterway being a constant bone of contention between the Werelords of the Desert Realm.

As Drew stood on the poop deck of the *Banshee* and looked east toward the sunrise, he marveled at the other cause for the river's name. With the sun's first rays breaking over the horizon, the mighty river threw its light back to the heavens. Drew squinted, raising his hand to shield his eyes from the metallic glare of the water.

"It's something else, isn't it?"

He blinked as his eyes slowly refocused on Lady Shah at his side.

"A jewel in the desert's crown," agreed Drew, turning from the blinding vision.

The crew made the most of the fair weather and unfurled the sails, grateful for the wind that spirited them westward up the river. Djogo stood at the wheel on the deck below, the former slaver enjoying his newfound freedom, even managing to share a rare joke with Drake, who lounged nearby. The sun's rays were warm on Drew's back, a welcome change from the freezing night. They might have been in the land of sand, but the night reminded him of the Cold Coast. Winter had arrived across Lyssia, even flirting with Omir. The snow-capped mountains of the Barebones straddled the horizon, their ultimate destination.

"When did you last visit the mountains?"

"Fifteen years ago," replied Shah, pausing to think about the long absence. "I was but a girl, handed over to Kesslar by Skeer, along with my father."

"And you've encountered no other Hawklords in your travels since then?"

"None. I hear mention of them occasionally, reported

sightings, but their spirits were broken when my father's wings were taken. We were a shamed species to King Leopold, lower than humans in his eyes."

"Do you really think your father can call them home? This Screaming Peak—it sounds like something from a storybook."

"He was taken there as a child by his father, its secrets passed on to him. I just hope we can find it."

The *Banshee* wasn't a huge ship, but she looked out of place on the Silver River. Her big black prow cut a great wake through the water, sending the smaller fishing vessels, barges, and skiffs toward the shores. The waterway was wide and deep, navigable to big ships such as the *Banshee* to where the river split at Two Rivers. This wild port town at the foot of the Barebones, where mountain met desert, was where the Werelords now headed. From Two Rivers they would disembark and hike on toward Tor Raptor. Drew's eyes settled on the former slaver who commanded the ship's wheel on the deck below, his thoughts returning to the private talks the two had shared.

"Djogo seems to be very fond of you," said Drew.

"What's he told you?"

"He says you're friends—that's all you can ever be, he a human, you a therian."

Shah shivered and smiled. "I've loved before, Drew, and it didn't end well . . ." Her voice trailed off as she stared upriver to where a number of craft jostled against one another.

"What is it?" said Drake as he walked up to the poop deck to join them.

"A massacre," said Shah, still looking ahead, her face impassive. "An ambush."

"You can see *that*?" asked Drew, suddenly anxious. They had to retain their anonymity and stay out of the fray—the last thing the group needed was a fight, especially someone else's. He strained his eyes, seeing only blurs aboard the boats ahead, plus the occasional glint of steel.

"You have your nose, Wolf. I have my sight."

"Who's fighting?" asked Drake.

"Hard to tell, but the skiff in the middle is under attack from two others. They're badly outnumbered."

She arched an eyebrow. "A Doglord of some kind leads the assault."

"Really?" said Drew, mention of a therian so similar to his own kind piquing his interest. His instinct told him they should step in. The men of the *Banshee* had noticed the commotion as well, stopping their work to watch.

Shah saw that Drew was agitated. She placed a hand on his shoulder. "You cannot join every fight."

"It feels wrong," he growled as they watched the skirmish. He was about to say more when her fingers dug into his skin. He winced, noticing her nails had transformed into talons.

"What's the matter?" Drew gasped.

"A child's in danger!"

Before Drew could respond, Drake had taken a running jump, launching himself from the deck of the *Banshee*.

"Drake!" cried Shah, but the Crocodile was already gone, swimming speedily toward the fracas. The pair could see his long dark shape powering through the water in the direction of the three boats, transforming as he swam.

"He'll get himself killed!" fretted Shah.

"How many are there?" asked Drew.

"Too many."

Shah arched her back, gray wings emerging with a flourish. Her head was changing, features growing sharper, her nose and mouth blending together into an amber beak as a frill of charcoal feathers emerged through her black hair. A large avian eye stared down at Drew as he stood in the Hawklady's shadow.

She prepared to take flight, taking to the air from the *Banshee*'s wooden deck. Drew needed no invitation, catching hold of her legs as she took off. The Werehawk looked down, surprised at the presence of a passenger.

"You've carried me once before!" he shouted, as if to persuade her not to drop him. Shah shook him loose, his one hand not strong enough to keep hold, only to snatch him up again in her powerful talons. They quickly put the *Banshee* behind them as they closed in on the battle. Drake was there already, wading into the midst of the combatants, turning the air red around him. As they neared, Drew felt the change coming, the

Wolf's aspects gradually shifting through his body. By the time Shah was flying over the ambushed skiff, she was launching a changed Werewolf into a gang of shocked swordsmen.

Drew's claws flew, the lycanthrope spinning as he scattered the mob of attacking warriors along the deck. His foot crunched into a torso, ribs crumpling as the man was catapulted overboard. Drew's hand battered another, sending him colliding into his companion's blade, the two toppling in a bloody mess. A scimitar sailed down, one fighter finding a way past the claws toward the Werewolf's throat. Drew's trident dagger flashed, deflecting the blade off the basket hilt.

Drew took in the scene. The skiff's oarsmen lay dead, some floating facedown in the river, butchered in the attack. Two sleeker boats were moored alongside the skiff, grapples having hauled it in so the warriors could board. The dozen or so invaders wore crimson kashes, the splash of red reminding Drew of the Lionguard. He looked to the prow. A girl no more than ten years old cowered there, two warriors in white valiantly standing between her and the enemy, their dead comrades littering the deck.

Drake tried to cut his way through the red-kashed warriors toward the girl, but the attackers were ready for him, throwing their blades up as he tore into them. Drew was drawn to the towering dog-headed warrior in the middle of the skiff. He held an enormous spear in one hand, barking orders as he faced the therians.

"You've nothing to fear!" cried the Doglord to his soldiers. "Silver or not, they'll still bleed from your blades!"

The warriors attacked, spurred on by their master. Scimitars rained down on Drew and Shah. The Hawklady leaped off the boat to hover over the water, lashing out with her talons. Drew ducked and weaved, returning his own volley of claw, tooth, and dagger at the warriors. He glanced up to see the two brave defenders at the front of the skiff tumble lifelessly to their knees, the attackers' numerous scimitars too much for them. With mighty wing beats Shah rushed to the prow, landing over the girl and snatching up a pair of swords.

"Leave the girl alone!"

The red-kashed warriors hesitated for a moment, facing the transformed Werehawk armed with twin blades. The Doglord urged them forward, Shah's swords finding the first few who got too close, before the caninthrope turned to face the Werecrocodile. Bodies, oars, scimitars, and benches made the battleground uneven for all the combatants. The *Banshee* remained too far away, leaving the three therians alone in their fight against the men in red kashes. The Doglord's giant spear lanced through the air toward Drake, but the Crocodile stumbled clear and into the enemy mob. He went down beneath them as the Doglord turned his attention on Drew.

The spear splintered the deck where the Wolf had stood a moment earlier. Drew hurdled the weapon and leaped, kicking the Dog's jaw. The beast's head snapped back, the blow sending him crashing into his men. They pushed him forward once more, allowing him to take another stab at Drew. The Werehound was fast, and deadly with his spear, the blade finding Drew as he tried to dodge clear. The foot-long silver dagger tore deep into Drew's shoulder, tearing the flesh and glancing off bone. The Wolf howled in agony, dizzy with nausea from the deadly blade.

"You must be the Werewolf everyone's so keen to meet. Let's see what they make of you when I'm wearing your skin as a cloak!" the Doglord taunted.

The spear jabbed forward again, but Drew threw his head out of the way just in time, the blade missing his face by a hair's breadth. He took hold of the spear shaft as it passed, hooking it under his arm and throwing his weight behind it as he swung it hard to one side. The Doglord kept hold of the other end, unable to stop himself from being propelled into his own men. Three of them tumbled overboard and the Hound narrowly avoided joining them. But before Drew could press home his advantage the remaining red-kashed warriors leaped on him.

Drew lashed out blindly, but scimitar cuts crisscrossed his back as his attackers slashed at him, and blood pumped relentlessly from his shoulder wound. He was overwhelmed, knocking one red-kashed fighter off only to see two more take his place. The longer he remained on the deck, the more chance the fight would end badly. More sword blows were finding their mark now, the Doglord's warriors proving fearless and blindly obedient under his command.

But just as it began to look hopeless, the men in red started to fall away, their blows becoming less frequent as their numbers were thinned. Drew looked up to see hands, limbs, fingers, and flesh flying as Drake tore a path through the warriors toward him. The Doglord brought his spear around, striking out at the Werecrocodile, but Drake was too fast, his reptilian tail whipped out from behind. Two men went overboard, legs broken, before the tail struck the Doglord, sending him bouncing on to the deck, spear clattering down on top of him.

Two more soldiers stood over Drew, one aiming an executioner's blow to his neck. Drew knew all too well that no therian healing could replace a missing head. Drake was on them instantly, his reptilian body blocking the blows as he put himself in harm's way. The red warriors were strong but no match for a transformed therian gladiator. The executioner suddenly found he was missing a hand, Drake spitting it back at him as he toppled. The last man let loose a wail as the Crocodile's jaws closed around his neck and snapped closed. He let the body collapse to the deck before turning to his friend.

"Quick, Drew," gasped Drake, extending his clawed hand. "On your feet!"

One moment the Werecrocodile stood over Drew, the epitome of the heroic warrior, lit by the rising sun. The next,

a foot-long silver spearhead burst from Drake's puffing chest.
The Crocodile's face froze in agony. Drake's eyes rolled down to
look at the bloody blade that protruded from his sternum. As
Drew watched in horror the spearhead was savagely twisted
before the Doglord whipped it free from behind with a roar of
triumph.

Drew didn't wait for Drake's body to land.

The Wolf dived across the skiff to where the Doglord lay
against the gunwales in a pile of broken oars, past the spear,
hitting the monster with a ferocious impact. The hull splintered open, sending the wrestling therians into the Silver River,
struggling for dominance as they sank. Drew's teeth found the
Dog's muzzle and nose, biting down hard.

The Dog reached up, trying desperately to prize the jaws
open, but it was hopeless. The struggling slowed, Drew's own
head and chest thundering as he felt his last breaths escape
his body. He released his hold and kicked back toward the surface, but not before he caught sight of the Doglord, choked and
drowned on blood and water, sinking toward the bottom of the
cold river.

Drew resurfaced as the *Banshee* neared, the two enemy
boats having disengaged from the skiff now, beating a hasty
retreat to the southern bank. Drew threw his arm over the
skiff's broken side, taking a great lungful of air, his body already returning to human form. He clambered aboard, spying
Shah with the girl in her arms, struggling to stand upright on

the gore-slicked deck. Her face was ashen as she stared aft.

Drake lay on a bed of dead warriors, clawed hands over the hole in his chest. He, too, was returning to his human form while he clung to life, his lips smacking clumsily as he tried to smile at Drew. The young Wolflord crawled to him, placing his hand over the fatal wound.

"Never doubt it, Wolf . . ." whispered the dying therian as his eyes began to close. "I had your back . . ."

A tear rolled down Drew's cheek as he held Drake in his arms, the young Werecrocodile drifting off to sleep for the final time.

# 6

# STRAIGHT AND TRUE

**THE CANDLELIGHT CAST** long shadows over the captain's desk as Count Vega dipped his quill pen into the ink-pot. The nib swept across the open page, the Sharklord's handwriting as flamboyant as one would expect from the Pirate Prince. He'd kept a journal since his first commission as a captain, thirty of the leather-bound volumes filling the bookcase in his cabin. He was aware that the crew, many of whom were illiterate, considered the habit eccentric, but it was one of the few things that kept Vega feeling civilized during his travels.

The hour was late and the night quiet. With most aboard the *Maelstrom* asleep bar the skeleton crew, it was the perfect time to write uninterrupted. The ship, of course, was more crowded than usual; Vega had to wonder if he'd ever truly have it back for himself. Although it was pleasant to spend time in the company of other Werelords, especially Manfred, his guests were beginning to overstay their welcomes. *Typical dirtwalkers*, his mother would have said. He'd get them to Roof all right, but he wasn't sure where his own path led. Perhaps he'd leave the *Maelstrom* with Figgis as he went inland with the queen and the duke—he couldn't abandon the Wolf's Council now.

Vega wondered if anyone truly considered him a changed character. He'd been described as "the count without a court," shamed for betraying Wergar to help Leopold rise to power. There was more to the story than that, of course. Bergan and Manfred had recovered well enough after bowing before Leopold, although Vega suspected the parts they'd played in the Wolf's downfall had kept them awake at night. He hoped so, anyway—he'd be cursed if he was the only Werelord who carried a guilty conscience wherever he went.

Vega's respect for Drew was a new feeling for the Sharklord. He'd sworn an oath of loyalty to the boy's father years ago, and Leopold since, but he'd taken those vows lightly. Young and impetuous, he'd been more concerned with gold, swashbuckling his way across the White Sea. Now, older and wiser, the count took his promise to the young Wolf seriously—to aid Wergar's son as they set about righting past wrongs and making Lyssia a safe place for all. With Bergan and Mikkel gone and Drew's whereabouts unknown, he held on to the hope that the Wolf's

Council still stood for something. He prayed to Sosha that the boy lived.

The ink burst from the nib suddenly, sending a small black puddle over his script. He cursed, blotting at it with a piece of paper. The stain slowly drying, Vega stared at the inkblot, and his thoughts drifted toward the last member of the Wolf's Council, the Baron of Redmire. Vega had seen Hector's palm while poor Bethwyn had nursed him. The girl had tried to keep the scarred hand hidden, possibly due to some misguided sense of loyalty, but the sea marshal had spied it all the same: a black mark. Hector's flesh was corrupted by something—but what?

Vega wasn't sure when it had happened, but things had gone very wrong for the Boarlord. The young man had been losing control long before the dreadful encounter on the White Isle. Had he started to unravel after the death of his brother? It had been an accident, of course. At least, Vega had *assumed* that was the case. He shook his head. No, Vincent was wicked; he'd have killed Hector that night if fate hadn't intervened. Perhaps Hector's ill luck had begun when he'd first communed with the dead Wylderman shaman in the Wyrmwood.

Hector's decline had really spiraled after Drew's departure. When they were all living in Highcliff, Vega had enjoyed the company of both young men, as had the entire Wolf's Council. It had been good to watch the boys' friendship blossom, each benefiting from the other's best traits. Drew had become more worldly wise with the Boarlord's help, whereas time with the Wolf had allowed Hector to become more confident, more vocal. Hector had changed further without Drew, but it was all for the worse.

The rapping of a loose rope against his cabin window pulled Vega away from his dark thoughts. He swiveled in his seat, staring back at the small panels of glass that filled the rear wall of the captain's quarters. The rope flashed faintly into view as it whipped down and struck the window. Vega grimaced: some fool hadn't tied the thing off. He hated seeing such lazy attention to detail on the *Maelstrom*, and if he did nothing about it now, it'd be sure to keep him awake all night. Replacing the quill in the inkpot, Vega rose from his desk, taking his black cape and fastening it around his throat. He checked the carriage clock that was fixed to his desk, which told him it was the second hour after midnight. Leaving the cabin he made his way above deck, heading aft.

Arriving aloft, Vega caught sight of a couple of crew members working on the foredeck. Only one sailor paid attention to the captain's arrival, the chief mate Figgis, who acknowledged him with a brief nod. The count glanced up the main mast, spying Casper on his way down from the midnight watch. Vega was proud of how seriously the lad took his duties as a cabin boy and lookout. He'd been up there for three hours, earning himself a warm bunk on his return. Marching up the steps to the poop deck, Vega passed the wheel, lashed down for the night, stepping through the darkness toward the stern.

Vega stopped at the railing. He'd expected the offending rope to be attached to a working part of the ship. Instead it was a relatively short length tied to the rail, serving no purpose. He looked over the side, spying the tattered end banging against his cabin windows as the water churned white below. *Who'd fasten a length of rope to the aft of the ship?* What good did it do other than annoy the count and bring him aloft? Vega looked at how the rope was tied; it wasn't a nautical knot, which meant it wasn't one of his crew. The Sharklord suddenly felt a sick, cold feeling in his stomach. He turned.

Hector stood behind him, flanked by two other figures in the shadows. His men kept an eye toward the prow of the *Maelstrom*, on the lookout for passersby, while the Boarlord's eyes were fixed on the count.

"What is this, Hector?" asked Vega, trying to keep his voice calm while his guts were in knots. *Why did he feel so anxious? How could Hector put him so on edge?*

"I needed to see you, Vega."

"Why the rope trick? You could have come and knocked for me. Don't you know, by now? My door's always open to friends, Hector."

Vega glanced past the trio, trying to spy anyone beyond them, but could see no one. They were alone.

"I needed you up here. On deck."

Hector's voice was rough from disuse. He'd not ventured

on to the deck since he'd awoken from his weeklong coma. Clearly, the Boarlord had chosen the time of this meeting carefully.

"Well," said Vega, opening his arms. "You have my attention. What do you want?"

Vega smiled, but it was a mask. The poop deck seemed charged with energy, the Sharklord's ears threatening to pop as if a great pressure was in the air.

"You kept pushing, Vega."

"What?"

"You kept poking, belittling me."

"What are you talking about, Hector?"

"You treat me like a child, a foolish boy who can't do anything right. Is that how you see me?"

Hector took a couple of steps forward. If he'd been in awe of Vega previously, he wasn't showing it. Hector didn't seem the least bit nervous about challenging the Wereshark.

"Hold on," said Vega, wanting to raise his voice but sensing that, if he did, something very bad might happen. The Sharklord's hunches rarely steered him wrong. "I don't know what you're talking about, but you're mistaken. I've stood by your side, my young friend, through every cursed thing that's happened."

"Don't patronize me, *friend*," spat Hector. "As for being at my side, perhaps *you're* the cursed one. Perhaps it's *you* who brings misery and death to all you touch."

Vega saw the young Boarlord's hands curled into fists at his side. His men were no calmer, each of them agitated as they shadowed him. Vega could see where this was heading.

"Hector," he said calmly. "Before you do anything stupid, just think—"

"*Silence!*" hissed Hector, throwing his ungloved hand up, palm open toward the captain of the *Maelstrom*.

Vega couldn't get another word out. His throat felt restricted, closed tight as if held by some invisible force. He clawed at his neck, fingers scratching the skin, trying to sever whatever constricted him but finding nothing. The sensation was sickening, an invisible noose around his throat, tightening as he struggled. He wanted to shout, to scream, but Hector had silenced him utterly. He took a step forward, grabbing Hector by the shoulders. He tried to mouth the word *please*, but all that came forth was spittle.

Vega's eyes widened as he felt something cold and sharp in his gut. He felt it cut through his flesh, burying itself among his internal organs as the blood flowed out around it. Hector's face contorted with both horror and sadness, eyes red with tears.

"Getting rid of Vincent," whispered Hector. "Did you think you could keep me in your debt forever? You're just like the others, Vega. Worse: you're a two-faced serpent. You belong on the seabed with the other bottom-dwellers."

Hector stepped back, as Vega, still spluttering, looked

down. In his hands the Boarlord held an arrow, its beautifully crafted silver head slick with blood. Where had Hector got it from? *It doesn't matter now*, thought Vega, his fingers fumbling over his stomach as his white shirt turned crimson.

Ringlin and Ibal stepped forward, the fat one giggling quietly as he handed a burlap sack with an attached rope to the tall one. Ringlin lifted the rope over Vega's head, a noose that fitted snugly around the count's neck. He pulled it tight before releasing it. Vega instantly staggered at the weight of the sack, recognizing the unmistakable clang of the heavy balls of shot from the *Maelstrom*'s cannons.

Hector snapped his left hand shut, black hand vanishing out of sight, as Vega struggled to breathe with the sack around his throat. He wanted to beg Hector, ask him to stop the madness, apologize for whatever wrongs the lad imagined the count had done him. But he didn't get the chance.

Hector nodded to his henchmen, who stepped forward and grabbed Count Vega, fearsome captain of the *Maelstrom*, Pirate Prince of the Cluster Isles and terror of the White Sea. They gave him a hearty shove, sending him flying back over the aft rail of the ship.

Hector turned away before Vega had even gone over the side. To his shock and horror he saw the cabin boy, Casper, barge past him out of nowhere and sprint between Ringlin and Ibal as they deposited the Sharklord into the cold Sturmish Sea.

Ibal was quick with his sickle, grabbing the boy by his mop of hair and whipping the curved blade to his throat.

"No!" gasped Hector, his old self returning briefly.

*Kill the boy!* snarled the Vincent-vile gleefully, fresh from throttling the Sharklord. *He's seen too much!*

Before Hector could issue any command, the lad bit down hard on the fat man's hand and stamped on his foot, Ibal relinquished his grip instantly and Casper didn't hesitate, leaping overboard after his captain.

Hector rushed to the rail and looked over, astonished by the boy's suicidal act of blind loyalty. All he saw was the white water disappearing behind the *Maelstrom*, the great ship leaving her dying captain to the ocean as a lonely length of rope whipped behind her in the black night.

# 7

# THE JEWEL OF OMIR

**IF HIGHCLIFF'S DEFENSES** had once impressed Drew, the walls of Azra put them firmly in the shade. The shining city walls rose fifty feet high, encircling Omir's capital like a steel crown. Sandblasted by fierce winds, the mighty walls were polished like glass, breathtaking to the eye and intimidating to the enemy. The battlements were manned by gold-helmeted warriors, looking down at the people who crowded around the River Gate. Drew couldn't help but stare as he and his companions approached, jaw slack with awe behind his kash.

The *Banshee* remained moored in Kaza, a small port a mile south of Azra and used by the great city for access to the river. The Silver Road that ran between the two was marked by many small shops, inns, and trade posts, effectively forming a ramshackle town of its own. Those who couldn't gain access to Azra had settled on the Silver Road, waiting for their chance to enter, and many had put down roots, now calling the road their home.

Merchants from the river traveled up the road to queue and seek entrance into King Faisal's city. But there were others present: families with children, fearful-looking people who sought refuge in Azra. Drew was shocked by the number of slaves they also encountered, shackled to one another by chain and collar. Some ferried goods up and down the Silver Road, while others carried their masters and mistresses in silk-covered chairs over the heads of the crowd. It was in the middle of this throng where Drew found himself, jostled by slave and trader as he and his companions pushed toward the gate.

"Bringing the girl to the Jackal's door was a mistake. We should have handed her over to the port authorities," growled Djogo.

"I'd sooner leave her with Kesslar," said Drew, thinking back to the unruly dockers they'd encountered in Kaza. The girl was in a state of shock after the fight on the river that morning, too traumatized to speak. The Werelords had taken the slain body of Drake to the shore, breaking the journey to bury the brave Werecrocodile. They had worked alongside one another, digging deep into the hot sand as they prepared the grave. Krieg had said a few words for their fallen brother while the rest watched in silent respect. None would forget the sacrifice Drake had made in saving the lives of both Drew and the child. The young Wolflord and his companions had decided to take the girl to the city, delivering her safely to the gate guards. They would know what to do with her.

Walking beside Drew, Lady Shah carried the girl in her arms. The girl had warmed to Shah, and the Hawklady had taken her under her wing. In addition to the slain soldiers who'd accompanied the girl, Djogo had found the body of an older, noble-looking gentleman, a silver javelin piercing his chest. Judging by the choice of weapon, Drew assumed he'd been a known Werelord, the girl perhaps a relative. Either way, Azra was the safest place for her.

"Are random attacks common on the Silver River?" Drew asked Djogo as Shah pushed on ahead through the crowd, the exhausted girl sleeping in her arms.

"Yes, but they're usually river pirates, not Doglords and Omiri warriors. That was a coordinated attack; seems the dead Werelord back there had enemies."

Four warriors from the *Banshee* followed them, pulling a covered cart along behind. The body of the slain nobleman lay beneath the tarpaulin.

"Are there not safer ways to travel than the river?"

The tall warrior shrugged.

"In the Desert Realm? It's a balancing act. The smaller your group, the more chance you have of traveling unnoticed, but if you're attacked, you're in trouble. The larger your number, the more noticeable you are to your enemies, but the likelier you are to get there in one piece. The Omiri are a secretive people—they've turned subterfuge into a fine art. Misdirection and smokescreens have won numerous wars in the desert."

Djogo clapped the boards of the wagon behind them. "If war is on Omir's doorstep, then the realm's therians will be returning to their respective homes, quickly and quietly. Our friend here wasn't as well versed in subterfuge as his brethren."

"Perhaps he was betrayed?"

"Not our problem now. Let's drop the child and corpse off and be on our way."

"I can't believe how many slaves I'm seeing. I hadn't expected to see this outside of Scoria."

"I'll say one thing for the Jackals," whispered Djogo. "They treat their slaves better than the Lizards do. But that wouldn't take much, would it?"

"Sounds like you don't want to be here."

"You don't know the half of it, Wolf," said the warrior as they neared the gate, pulling his kash across his face.

A dozen soldiers stood at the gate, checking the papers of anyone who sought admittance into Azra. Wearing golden helmets that rose to sharp points, some carried scimitars at their hips. Others carried the long spears that the Omiri favored. At nine feet long they were somewhere between a pike and javelin. The guards wore yolk-yellow capes around their shoulders. All in all, they looked both regal and lethal.

Suddenly, the crowd shuffling up toward the gate seemed to get thicker, and Drew found himself separated by the pushing throng, which drove a wedge between him and his companions.

"Djogo," called Drew, trying to catch the tall warrior's attention, but he and the other crew members pulling the cart had fallen behind. Looking forward, Drew saw Shah had reached the guards and was trying to reason with a man who appeared to be an officer. The girl shifted in the Hawklady's grasp, beginning to wake with the din of the crowd.

Drew found himself shoved to the front of the shouting and bickering traders, face-to-face with some more of the guards. One of them said something unintelligible to Drew.

"I'm sorry," he said. "I don't understand."

The guard's officer overheard Drew's remark, and left Shah momentarily, stepping closer to speak with the young Westlander.

"You're not Omiri?" he asked, his voice thickly accented but understandable.

"No." Drew smiled awkwardly.

"I tried to explain . . ." called Shah, but the man ignored her.

"Only Omiri enter Azra!" said the man harshly.

"I don't seek entrance!" said Drew, aware that he was shouting and struggling to be heard. Both the officer and Drew caught sight of a scuffle taking place, beyond where Djogo and the men from the *Banshee* stood with the handcart. An alter-cation between merchants had descended into a fistfight. The officer looked back at Drew.

"Then what do you seek?"

"If you'd let me finish . . ." yelled Shah, but the officer's attention returned to the brawl. Many in the crowd were jeering as the merchants fought, the guards standing back while the men exhausted themselves. A fat slaver watched from his silk-covered sedan chair, clapping with glee. The fight was spreading as one of the merchants knocked into a woman carrying a tall basket of fruit. The basket tumbled, clattering into Djogo and the *Banshee*'s men, sending an avalanche of lemons over them. More fists flew as the woman's companions joined the melee.

"Who is this man?" said the captain to Shah as he poked Drew's chest.

At that moment, the crowd barged into the fat slaver's lit-ter and sent it over, crashing into the handcart. A wheel sheared off, clattering over onto the wailing slaver's body, while the Werelord's corpse toppled from the broken cart on to the road. Several women in the crowd screamed, spurring the guards to push forward through the panicking mob. Soldiers and civil-ians instantly recognized the slain therian. Acting quickly, half the guards tried to hold the crowd back while others moved toward the men from the *Banshee*.

At that moment, Djogo's kash fell loose as he was jostled by the crowd.

*"Djogo!"*

The guards' cries of recognition were not happy ones. *They know him,* realized Drew. *Curse the man and his business with Kesslar!*

The soldiers immediately lowered their long spears and unsheathed their scimitars. In response, the tall, one-eyed warrior whipped out his own weapons. The crowd parted as the fistfight suddenly escalated into sword fight. Not prepared to leave their man outnumbered, the warriors from the *Banshee* withdrew their daggers and shortswords.

"Wait!" cried Shah, making a grab at the officer. With the fight spiraling out of control, the captain mistook Shah's hand as an assault. He swung his arm back, scimitar pommel crashing into Shah's forehead, sending woman and girl to the ground, instantly lost in the crowd.

"Don't harm them!" shouted Drew, pushing past the guards to get to them.

To his horror Drew found the commander now turning on him, taking hold and twisting Drew's forearm in his grasp. He stumbled onto one knee, surprised at the other's strength. The officer forced Drew's hand up his back, the young man bellowing as he threatened to collapse. He couldn't get into a fight, yet he couldn't allow his companions to be harmed.

"You don't understand! We just want to leave the girl with you!"

He tried to plead, but the soldier wouldn't listen. Feet stamped around him as another turbaned warrior came forward, striking Drew over his head with the flat of his blade. Drew's head rang as he collapsed on to the sand-covered flags and the officer jumped on him. Through the legs of the crowd, he could see Shah, trampled by the wild mob.

Drew had no choice.

The first notion the captain had that he was no longer wrestling with a human was when the arm he held twisted violently, throwing him one hundred and eighty degrees through the air. He landed with a crunch, his view of the world on its head as the beast rose to its full height, towering over him. The crowd screamed as the Werewolf roared.

Drew's eyes scanned the crowd around the overturned cart as they backed away. Djogo and the gladiators were being overpowered by superior numbers, and the guards had already removed Shah from the chaos. Of the child, there was no sign. Drew felt sick, having brought the girl to the gates of Azra only for her to be lost.

Reinforcements flooded out of the gate as the Omiri circled him, scimitars and spears raised. They'd clearly fought Werelords before, and were treating Drew with a healthy dose of respect. He snapped his jaws, lashing out with the trident dagger while he frantically tried to decide what to do. Overhead, bowmen lined the walls, taking aim at the Wolf.

*Fools*, he thought. *Can't they see we were bringing an innocent to them?* But all the guards saw was a target to take down. He needed to get back to the *Banshee*, regroup with the others, and find a way of rescuing their companions. He couldn't be drawn into a fight here. These men were innocent—foolish, but innocent. He couldn't take their lives.

Dropping into a crouch he sprang backward, high, narrowly avoiding the guards' long spears before landing behind them. A dozen arrows rained down from the walls, half of them finding their target. The Werewolf crashed to the floor, the wind taken from his sails. The arrows weren't silver, but they hurt. Drew cried with agony as he scrambled to his feet, body still aching from the river battle wounds.

Drew stumbled down the Silver Road toward the port of Kaza, onlookers screaming and moving clear as he lurched along. The long spears flew, most hitting the paved road or bouncing off Drew's thick, furred skin, but a couple punched their way home, breaking flesh and jarring bone. He howled, going down again.

Booted Omiri feet surrounded him now as, dizzied, he tried to keep moving, willing his body on.

"Wolf!"

The shout came from the captain of the guard behind. The Werewolf looked back, guards parting to reveal the captured men of the *Banshee*. The captain forced Djogo to his knees, the prisoner's hands tied behind his back. Raising his scimitar high, the blade hovered in the air above the ex-slaver's neck, ready to fly.

# PART V

## DANGEROUS GAMES

# I
## WITNESS

**LOOKING BACK NERVOUSLY**, the young woman checked she wasn't being followed as she hurried along the lurching corridor. Clutching the bottle of water, Bethwyn walked past the queen's cabin and continued on, deeper into the belly of the *Maelstrom*. With a final glance to ensure she was alone, the girl from Robben opened the door to the dark cargo hold and slipped inside.

Closing the door firmly, Bethwyn weaved between the lashed-down crates and barrels, gingerly making her way toward the prow. The hold's contents were severely depleted, many weeks at sea having exhausted the *Maelstrom*'s provisions, leaving the pirates surviving on short rations and in desperate need of making land. Upon hearing the queen was thirsty, the ship's cook, a gaunt fellow named Holman, had handed over the bottle to the lady-in-waiting, telling her to make it last; fresh water was a luxury, more precious than food.

As Bethwyn neared the prow, she felt guilty for taking the bottle from Holman. He was a kind man who had always ensured she got a little extra when serving up the crew's meager portions of food. But she'd needed the bottle, an excuse to go belowdecks and disappear for a while, attending her mistress. There were prying eyes aloft that might question her absence without any plausible reason. She finally arrived at the thick curved wall that marked the head of the hold and the prow of the *Maelstrom*. The others waited, gathered around a hooded lantern that gave out a tiny amount of light.

"Nobody followed you?" asked Amelie, moving up along the crate where she sat to make room. Bethwyn collapsed beside her, shaking her head.

"He doesn't suspect you?" asked Duke Manfred.

"He asked where I was going. If he follows that up, Master Holman will tell him the same thing—I'm with the queen, not to be disturbed." Bethwyn raised the bottle as if to emphasize the ruse.

"Good," said Manfred, rubbing his knuckles against his temple. "What we discuss must never reach Hector's ears."

"Murderous traitor," said Figgis, eyes narrowing in his leathery old face.

"Steady on," said Manfred. "We don't know for sure he's a killer."

"You call me a liar? I saw it with my own eyes!"

"What on earth would young Hector gain from killing Vega? The count was his friend. I question what you saw. I have to. I owe that to Hector."

The first mate spat at mention of the magister's name.

"Gentlemen," said Amelie, raising her hand gently.

Figgis bowed to his queen before nodding to Manfred. The duke returned the gesture, to Bethwyn's relief. She'd watched the old pirate trying to hold his nerve over the course of the day. He'd reported what he'd seen directly to Amelie late last night, hot on the heels of the captain disappearing. A search of the boat had followed, whereupon the crew discovered that Casper was gone, too. Everyone aboard the *Maelstrom* was suspicious, none more so than Figgis, who'd stared daggers at Hector and his men all day long. It was only now, the following night, that the four had the opportunity to discuss the events in detail.

"It's as I said last night," said Figgis, his wiry arms sagging as he recounted what he'd seen. "I was doing my rounds when the captain come aloft, disappeared up to the poop deck, and never came back. The boy followed him up there, too. Then the three of them—Hector and his men—came down. Asked them where the captain was, I did. They said they'd never seen him.

When I got up there they was nowhere to be seen, neither the captain nor the boy."

Bethwyn was surprised to see tears rolling down Figgis's cheeks. The old man was as hard as they came, a long life of piracy behind him and many years by Vega's side. As first mate he'd taken command of the *Maelstrom*, but the responsibility didn't sit easy on his gnarled shoulders.

"Why didn't you challenge Hector at the time?" said Amelie.

"Question the Boarlord, Your Majesty?" Figgis shook his head. "I didn't know right away what had gone on. I went up there to find the captain gone, a bloodstain on the deck. By the time I returned your Lord of Redmire had scarpered to his cabin, along with his men."

Manfred shook his head wearily.

"It makes no sense. *Why* would Hector harm one of us, especially one who's looked out for him these recent months?"

"May well be that the captain looked out for him," said Figgis. "But look at what happened in Moga. Then we had the White Isle—that was his doing, too, so the captain said. That traitor let us land there when he knew it was cursed. He's a bad one, that boy."

"How can you say that? Hector's given everything in the service of the Wolf's Council, Figgis."

*Manfred can't help himself*, thought Bethwyn. *He has to defend*

*Hector. He knows there's good in him, and can't believe there's any bad.*

The Staglord continued. "Couldn't it be that Vega slipped? Struck his head? Fell overboard?"

Figgis laughed. "This is a Wereshark you're talking about, my lord. The captain knew every inch of the *Maelstrom* blindfolded. I never saw him slip on this deck in all the years I've been with him. And even if he fell overboard, he's a shark. He'd have swum back to the ship, wouldn't he?"

"Unless he was injured," said Amelie.

"Exactly, Your Majesty," said the first mate. "And regardless of whether the captain fell overboard or not, there's Casper going missing, too. Two going overboard and not a trace of either?"

"I have to agree with Duke Manfred here," Amelie put in. "Captain Figgis, I believe you saw what you say, I truly do. But the notion that this dear young man could have done something so out of character? It's simply too much."

Figgis looked like he might scream, his face shifting from bloodless white through angry red and then furious purple.

"I believe Figgis."

Manfred and Amelie turned to look at Bethwyn, the girl's big brown eyes wide with fright, but chin set with determination.

"You believe him?" asked Manfred incredulously. "But Hector's your friend!"

"I cannot let friendship stand in the way of the truth, Your Grace."

"What makes you think this is true, my dear?" said Amelie, placing her palms over the trembling lady-in-waiting's hands. "Is this on account of what happened when he woke from his long slumber? Surely you realized that was his fever talking?"

"That was upsetting, Your Majesty, but there were other things. His hand . . ."

"What about it?" said Manfred.

"Something . . . something *bad* has got into it. His hand is blackened, Your Grace. It's so cold to the touch, too. It reminds me of dead skin, all the life leached from it. I saw it well enough when I tended him."

"A diseased hand doesn't make for a diseased mind," said Amelie, but the girl from Robben continued.

"When the Sirens attacked the ship, Hector killed one that would have slain me, only from a great distance away. His left hand, the black palm—he had it open, as if controlling something. I know Hector's a magister, and I know he uses magicks and cantrips to heal, but this was something else."

Manfred sighed. "The communing."

Amelie looked at the Staglord with horror. "Hector has *communed*? When?"

"The first occasion was in the Wyrmwood, when he, Drew, and Gretchen encountered Vala."

"The *first* occasion?" gasped the queen. "This has happened more than once?"

"Yes, regrettably. We thought we'd steered him off that course, but perhaps he has continued to commune in secret."

The four were silent. Bethwyn tried to stifle her tears, holding them back with all her will. She felt as though she'd betrayed Hector, but he was a changed boy from the bumbling Boarlord who'd made his bashful appearances at Buck House. She feared for him.

"So," said Amelie quietly. "What do we do with him?"

"I've been on ships where the likes of him would've been thrown overboard like bait," spat Figgis. "So long as he's aboard the *Maelstrom* he's cursing us all. Who knows what he might do next?"

Amelie and Bethwyn shivered at the thought of the pirate's justice, but neither spoke up.

"No, we won't execute him," said the Staglord. "He'd need a trial before his peers and besides, we still have no evidence. If he *did* send Vega and the boy overboard, how did he do it? And how did he make sure the count never came back?"

"He can't stay on board," said Figgis, his voice calm. "The men already whisper. They won't hold back forever."

Manfred rose, stretching. "We need to return to our quarters, show our faces aloft before our absence alerts Hector."

The others stood, Manfred helping Amelie to her feet.

Figgis picked the lantern up, peering through the dark hold and checking the path ahead.

"Lead the way, Captain Figgis," said Manfred, placing a hand on the old man's shoulder.

"I wish you wouldn't call me that," muttered the old pirate. "There's only one captain of the *Maelstrom*, the best man I ever sailed with, and he's in Sosha's arms now."

The old pirate stopped, his free hand scratching at the thin white hair at the back of his head. He turned back to the therians, his eyes catching the lantern light and glowing like embers.

"There's one more thing I'd wanted to tell you, my lord and lady, but feared not on account of an oath."

"An oath?"

"Aye, my lord. To Captain Vega. Only thing is, he's dead now, ain't he? So, where does that leave my oath?"

Manfred glanced to Amelie and Bethwyn, but the women had no answer.

"If there's something you need to tell us, Figgis, go ahead man."

"The captain . . . he *did* something for your baron. He got rid of something for him."

"What's that supposed to mean?" said Manfred.

"We thought it was an accident, y'see? Captain didn't think it was done on purpose, but the more I think about it, the more I think Hector *meant* to kill him."

"Kill who?" said Amelie.

"Lord Vincent," said Figgis. "Hector killed his brother."

Amelie gasped.

"Why would Vega help Hector cover this up?" asked Manfred, shaking with shock.

"Like I say, the captain believed it was an accident, but he could see others thinking otherwise. If word got out, Hector's life would be as good as over. I got rid of the Boarlord's body myself, Sosha forgive me. What a fool I was."

Manfred patted Figgis on the shoulder. "Your loyalty to Vega, even in death, is commendable, but you've done the right thing by telling us."

The Staglord fixed each of them with a steady gaze. "It's more important than ever before that we remain tight-lipped over what we've discussed here tonight. This is a dangerous game we play with the Boarlord. Hector appears deadlier than I could've ever imagined. He can never know our plans."

"But what *are* our plans?" said Amelie.

"I need to inspect the count's sea charts," said Manfred. "Vega may yet be able to help us, from beyond the grave."

# 2

# IN THE JAWS OF THE JACKAL

**"YOU'RE A LONG** way from home, Wolf."

The two captives stood alongside one another, surrounded by the royal court and twenty of Azra's finest warriors. While Djogo's gaze was fixed on his feet, Drew's eyes lingered on the frescoed domed ceiling above, the centuries-old art predating anything he'd seen in the galleries of Highcliff. He looked around. Majestic marble pillars and busts of ancient kings, fluttering curtains laced with gold and priceless artifacts from Lyssia and beyond—the show of opulence wasn't missed by Drew. He'd grown up under the mistaken belief that the Omiri were savages. A quick glance around the palace revealed that nothing could have been further from the truth. Here was an ancient, rich culture to rival anything in the Seven Realms.

Drew let his gaze return to the figure on the throne who had spoken: King Faisal, the Jackal of Omir.

"Not by choice. I'm sorry if my arrival has caused you any concern," Drew said, raising his bound arms toward the seated figure. His forearms had been lashed together, knotted behind his elbows. "If you could remove these ropes, I'll be on my way."

The crowd laughed, all except the king, who rose from his throne. The audience quieted instantly as he strode gracefully down the dais steps toward Drew and his companion. By Drew's reckoning, Faisal had to be as old as Bergan if he'd fought Wergar during the Werewar. If so, he wore his years well, the Werejackal's tanned skin smooth without scars and wrinkles, his features fine and unspoiled. He wore a simple white toga and a crown of twined golden rope. His feet were bare and paced silently across the polished marble floor. Beautiful wasn't a word Drew would ordinarily use to describe a man, but in Faisal's case no other would fit. The king came to a halt before Drew, his almond eyes inspecting the Wolf intently.

"You have your father's arrogance." His voice was rich and honey-toned, matching his appearance. Although Western wasn't his first language, he was as fluent as any lord of Lyssia in the tongue.

"If I do, it's dumb luck," said Drew. "I never met Wergar."

"Then your arrogance is your own, Wolf. Your dead, arrogant father would be proud."

Drew prickled. He'd never known Wergar and stories of his exploits were mixed, his role ranging from hero to barbarian. Regardless, Faisal's words cut deep.

"I understand Wergar waged war with Omir, Your Majesty," said Drew. "But that was his war. Not mine."

"Your father was the only Werelord ever to break the defenses of Azra, and without the forces of Brackenholme and Stormdale to assist him. It cost him the lives of many. For months he campaigned in my burning deserts, his men dying of thirst and starvation. If he hadn't had the help of the Hawklords, his bones would have joined those of his Wolfguard in the sand."

There was mention of the Hawks of the Barebones again, loyal to Wergar.

"The Hawklords helped him win that war?"

"The Hawklords would side with anyone who might help feather their nest!" shouted a pale-skinned, stocky man in a long black cloak. He looked out of place in the Omiri palace.

"I don't believe that," said Drew. "Griffyn's a good man, a noble therian, one of the last of his kind."

"You claim to know the old Hawk?" scoffed the man in black. "He's probably dead now, a relic of the past. There are few of them left, and the only good one sits in Windfell: Baron Skeer!"

Faisal smiled. "You'll have to forgive my guest, Lord Rook. The Crowlords have never seen eye to eye with the Hawklords. I'd have to say I agree with him. Then again, the Crows never attacked my city, did they?

"I swore fealty to the Wolf to end the siege of Azra, but that agreement didn't last long. By the time he limped home to Westland, bloodied and battered from the fight in Omir, his therian brothers had turned on him, handing his head to the Lion on a platter. They tell me you consider those who betrayed your father your friends and allies: the Bearlord and Staglords?"

"Bergan explained what happened long ago. He kept no secrets from me. If you're hoping to make me doubt my friends, you're barking up the wrong tree, King Faisal."

The king sneered, disappointed. "No doubt you now know that your precious Wolf's Council is broken? The Bearlord's dead, I hear, and the surviving Staglord lost. You'd be the last flame the Catlords need to snuff out, and then Lyssia will finally be rid of the Wolf."

Drew hung his head, the blow hitting home. Faisal nodded, content to see the youth's heartache.

"How have I wronged you, Your Majesty?"

Faisal's laughter was musical, joined by the guffaws of his courtiers. The king shook his head and sighed.

"It's bad enough you come to my city, the son of the only therian ever to defeat me in battle. Yet look who *accompanies* you."

The king turned to face Djogo, his hand reaching out and gently taking the tall warrior's jaw in his slender fingers. He lifted the brute's head, almond eyes widening as he stared into Djogo's one good eye.

"Djogo," he whispered. "Kesslar's hound, returning to the scene of the crime."

"What crime?" asked Drew.

"Your companions didn't explain what business they'd had in Azra previously, then? Splendid. Let me elaborate."

Djogo glanced at Drew briefly, the look apologetic. *What in Brenn's name did you do, Djogo?*

"The Goatlord, Kesslar, lodged here for a time," continued the king, pacing around the bound men. "Initially, he was a generous, thoughtful guest, and we were most gracious hosts."

"He was a slaver!" interrupted Drew.

"Look around you, Wolf. Azra is built on slaves. They're a currency like any other in Omir.

"It didn't take him long to betray our trust. He invited three of my cousins aboard his ship to dine. They took gifts, as is our tradition: gold, jewels, and spices. My cousins and their entourages stayed with him aboard his vessel as guests that night.

"When the morning came, they were gone. The bodies of several guards were found in the Silver River, throats slit. Your work, Djogo?"

The ex-slaver said nothing, his eyes returning to the floor.

"Where are they now, fiend? My people, my cousins? Do they live, or did they die in some distant arena, for the amusement of Kesslar and his friends?"

Djogo spoke at last. "All were sold into slavery, but only the strongest went to the arena. Two Jackals died in the Furnace in Scoria. The third, the youngest, was sold to a Bastian Catlord."

"Brenn, no," muttered Drew miserably. "Why, Djogo?"

The tall warrior looked at Drew, his face emotionless. "I worked for Kesslar. I was a slaver. It was the only world I knew. There was no right or wrong; it was my job."

Drew thought Faisal might strike Djogo at any moment, the king's face shimmering with fury. He bared his teeth as he looked at each of them, speaking clearly and with deadly purpose.

"I see you each bear the mark of gladiator upon your shoulders. That pleases me greatly."

As he spoke, the crowd backed away, while the golden-helmed palace guard stepped forward, long spears and scimitars raised.

"You've got us wrong, Faisal," said Drew. "We're not friends of Kesslar's—we're his enemies, as are you!"

"Finding your voice now, Wolf? Do you plead for forgiveness?"

Drew growled as he answered. "I've done you no wrong. We brought a child to your gate, a girl who'd been attacked upon the river."

"You brought the body of Prince Fier to our gates, Wolf!" shouted the king. "The child who accompanied him was nowhere to be seen!"

"That's not true! We had no idea who that corpse was,

only that he was heading to Azra when he was attacked! Why *else* would we bring his body to you? The girl was the only survivor—"

"They killed Prince Fier," interrupted Rook. "You can't trust the Wolf—no wonder half of Lyssia hunts him. No doubt he and Kesslar's people are agents of the Doglords, sent here to cause your family further harm. Kill him now, Your Majesty. Do every realm a favor."

"The child!" cried Drew. "Someone must have *seen* her! We brought her here along with your slain lord!"

"There was no child," said Faisal. "What? You thought you could show us the body of my uncle and demand a ransom for my daughter?"

"Your daughter? We brought her back to you! Search for her; you'll find her!"

"Just words!" cried Faisal as he paced back up the marble steps to his throne. "Even now my warriors make their way to Kaza to seize your ship. I'll find my daughter, wherever you've hidden her, so beg away, Wolf. You'll say anything now to spare your life!" He turned to his guards adding, "And throw the cyclops a weapon; he'll need it."

Two guards hastily untied the captives. As they stepped back, one threw a scimitar on to the floor, the blade ringing as it struck the marble. Djogo glanced at it and then back to Drew.

"We won't fight," said the ex-slaver, standing shoulder to shoulder with the man he'd sworn his allegiance to.

Drew spoke. "The Djogo you knew may have been a killer, Faisal, but he's a changed man now."

"Nobody ever truly changes. Bring the woman."

Drew and Djogo watched in alarm as the struggling figure of Lady Shah was dragged into the throne room. She kicked and fought as she was hauled before the king, her hands bound and her face bearing bruises. A white gag was looped around her face, muffling her screams.

"I never forget a face. Lady Shah, isn't it? A friend of yours and Kesslar's?" said Faisal. He aimed the question at Djogo.

Lord Rook walked over to Shah and gripped her tightly by the arms. The Crow held his cheek close to hers, as a lover might in an embrace.

"Lady Shah," he whispered. "Daughter of Baron Griffyn. How the Hawks fall . . ."

Rook raised a stubby silver dagger to Shah's throat, placing the point into the hollow beneath her chin. Her eyes widened, pleading for him to stop.

"You *will* fight," said Faisal. "Or the woman dies."

"Don't do this, Faisal!" yelled Drew.

His words were wasted though and should have been directed at Djogo. The tall warrior bent down to the ground, snatching up the scimitar. His good eye blinked, as he shook his head.

"I'm so sorry, Drew," said the ex-slaver.

The scimitar scythed through the air.

# 3
# DUEL

DREW AND DJOGO paced around one another across the patterned throne room floor, a black marble mosaic flecked with the bright white stars of the heavens.

"We don't have to do this," said Drew, his feet moving, keeping the distance between them constant. The guards formed a circular wall of spears and swords around them, weapons lashing out when the combatants got too close. A transformed Drew might have bounded over them, but he didn't fancy his odds of clearing the long spears from a standing jump.

"We do," said Djogo, shifting the scimitar in his grip.

"If either of us dies, it's for what?"

"If you die, it's so that Shah lives," said the warrior. "If I die, it's Brenn's wish that you go on from here."

"And if neither of us dies?"

"If neither of us dies . . . they kill Shah." Djogo glanced to where Rook held the Hawklady, the knife jutting into her neck. "You heard what he said."

Faisal watched from his throne as the other nobles gathered around him, fellow Jackals who shared his hatred for the Wolf and the Goat.

Rook suddenly shouted, jabbing Shah in the jaw, the blade breaking the surface of her flesh.

"Fight!"

Shah kicked her heels, boots squeaking as they scraped the marble, unable to writhe away from the Crow's grip.

That was enough for Djogo.

The warrior lunged at Drew, the scimitar cutting an X through the air. Though still weary from their encounter at the River Gate, both men were recovered enough to fight for their lives.

Drew rolled clear as a sword blow hit the marble floor, sending sparks flying. A chunk of the ancient mosaic broke away, skittering across the court. Drew had to keep moving, evading, while he thought of a plan. *I can't kill Djogo. He's shown faith in me. What kind of man would I be if I betrayed that trust now? He might be blinded by his love for Shah, but there has to be another way!*

Of all the human foes Drew had faced in battle, Djogo was the one he feared the most. He'd been relieved when the tall warrior pledged his allegiance on Scoria, removing the threat that he'd ever fight him again. Drew had given his all, but this was different; he didn't want to see the man dead. He wanted him to live. He wanted the *three* of them to live.

Djogo brought the scimitar down lightning fast toward Drew's chest. The young Wolflord leaped back, narrowly missing having his stomach opened, only to feel the cold bite of a spearhead in his back. The guard propelled him forward toward Djogo's return swing, leaving Drew with no option but to dive at him, tackling him around the chest and wrestling him to the floor.

The two rolled, Drew's one hand his only means of holding the scimitar back.

"Please, Djogo!"

"There's no other way!" grunted the ex-slaver.

Djogo butted Drew in the face, sending him reeling away, blinded. Instincts kicked in as the Wolflord scrambled, eyes streaming as blood poured from his nose. The scimitar clanged against the floor inches from where he'd landed. The therian shook his head and prayed his vision would return. He heard the scrape of the scimitar as Djogo got to his feet, the blade dragging along the floor. Drew scrambled away from the telltale noise, foolishly forgetting the other perils that faced him in the arena. A guard's scimitar ripped across his back, felling him with a scream of pain just as his vision cleared.

Surrounded by a wall of armed warriors, he faced an

opponent focused on slaying him. That's all the Omiri nobles wanted—two hated enemies fighting to the death, slaver versus Werewolf. Drew spat blood on to the marble floor, letting loose a monstrous growl that caused the guards to shift warily.

*Time to give the people what they want.*

The guard with the scimitar took another potshot at Drew, but his timing couldn't have been worse. Drew had embraced the change, and all he now saw was a room full of enemies. His clawed foot shot up from the floor, kicking the warrior hard in his chest, sending him flying back through the air. He hit a marble pillar, landing in a crumpled heap, his polished breastplate battered out of shape. By the time his scimitar fell from his unconscious grasp, Drew had fully transformed, the Werewolf crouching on the floor, ready for battle.

Djogo swung at a surprised guard, disarming him with a deft flick of his scimitar. The guard's weapon flipped through the air and into Djogo's other hand, the Werewolf now facing an even deadlier foe. The ex-slaver spun the scimitars at his sides as he closed on the therian.

Drew watched Djogo's swirling blades, searching for a way past them. They weren't silver, but Djogo was adept enough with any weapon to open him up in moments. No therian healing would help him against such serious wounds. The warriors who ringed them were ready now, should either combatant turn on them again. Spears and scimitars hovered, ready to strike out at therian or human should they stagger too close.

"You can't win this fight!" growled Drew, moving quickly around the arena.

"One of us has to," said Djogo, his voice laden with anger and regret.

Djogo ran at Drew, preparing to leap into the air to cut down at the Wolf. At the last moment, Drew realized it was a bluff, the warrior hitting the marble floor in a diving slide aimed at taking out the Werewolf's legs. Drew hurdled the swordsman, narrowly missing his booted feet, but the scimitars left a trail of red mist in their wake as they scored the Wolf and he hit the floor with a snarl.

The Jackals cheered at the sight of the Wolf's blood. Drew looked down at his torso, his dark, clawed hand dabbing at the wounds the scimitars had left behind. *They won't be content until either Djogo or I lies dead.*

Djogo leaped back again, blades cutting downward in deadly swipes. When Drew ducked one way the warrior followed, closing off his escape route. He'd switch to the other, only to find him waiting. Years of fighting in the Furnace and across Lyssia had honed Djogo into a formidable fighter, predicting Drew's every move.

With an imperceptible glance, Drew marked two spearmen next to one another in the wall, their long weapons poised. Quickly he maneuvered toward them, avoiding Djogo's blows while ensuring the two were eventually at his back.

The Werewolf allowed his huge, clawed feet to strike the ground loudly, black claws scraping the marble and drawing attention. He retreated, one step after another, his head dipped at such an angle that he could still see the guards behind through the corner of his eye. One was unable to resist any longer, bringing his long spear back and stabbing at the Wolf.

The lycanthrope twisted, turning on his haunches and snatching hold of the spear. With a hard tug on the shaft Drew brought the man flying forward, the guard releasing his grip on the spear and flailing toward Djogo. The one-eyed warrior deflected the hapless spearman with his forearms as the guard struck him, the two hitting the marble together.

Drew was moving before they'd landed, whipping the long spear around and sprinting. He lowered the spear haft, praying it would find purchase. The hard, wooden end of the weapon clunked into a hole in the broken mosaic, halting his run instantly and sending the Werewolf into the air. To his relief, the spear buckled but didn't break, launching Drew skyward, vaulting him high over the guards. Their long spears jabbed up but in vain; the monstrous, gray Wolflord sailed above and beyond them.

And landed on the throne.

The nobles roared at the sight of the Wolf straddling King Faisal, pinning him to his seat. Canine features appeared in a wave, the Jackal-lords changing and howling for the Wolf's blood. Faisal bellowed with shock as Drew snatched him around the throat, his clawed feet digging into the king's thighs, drawing blood through the once-pristine white robes. Though the king's head expanded, transforming into the Jackal as his features distorted, his throat remained the size of a mortal man's in Drew's lupine grip. Faisal choked, his airway cut off. The Jackal's eyes bulged as Drew bared his teeth, holding his grip as the king floundered in a blind panic.

While many warriors rushed to their king's aid, others overpowered Djogo, tearing the scimitars from his grip before he was inspired to do anything foolish. He looked on with awe as the Wolf held Omir to ransom.

"Kill the Wolf!" screamed Rook from nearby, baring Shah's throat once more, a jagged red cut now visible where he'd sliced her with the blade.

"Call off your dogs!" said Drew, his lips peeled back as he growled into the Werejackal's ear.

Faisal glanced frantically from side to side, his hands out to his family, warning them to retreat. Drew allowed his grip to relax, enough to allow the Jackal to breathe. He gasped at the air, struggling to get oxygen past the Werewolf's claws.

"Tell the Crow to release Shah," said Drew. "*Now!*"

"Let . . . her . . . go!" whispered the king through his clenched throat.

Rook watched with disbelief, shaking Shah like a rag doll.

"But, Your Majesty . . ."

"Release her!" said Faisal.

Reluctantly the Crowlord let Shah go, the Hawklady stumbling to Djogo, who pulled himself free of the guards and tore her gag away. The two held each other as if their lives depended upon it.

"You won't get out of this palace alive, Wolf!" spat Faisal, strangled in Drew's grip.

The Werewolf tightened his hold again. "I'll get all the way to Westland with my hand around your throat if I have to, Faisal!" snarled Drew. "It didn't have to be like this," he went on, the fury momentarily gone from his voice. "I told you the truth, Faisal, and you chose to ignore me. We came here in peace, but you ensure we leave as enemies. . . ."

"She's returned!"

The woman's cry echoed through the throne room as her footsteps raced through the hall toward the throne. Whoever she was, she was oblivious to the drama that played out in front of her. Her voice was cheery as she approached, more guards accompanying her into the chamber.

"See, my love! She's returned to us!"

The woman looked up at last. Jackals' heads looked down upon her as her shocked eyes landed upon the king, helpless in the Werewolf's grip. She held the girl from the skiff in her arms, the child's big almond eyes wide as she clutched the woman's chest.

"My daughter . . ." Faisal choked out, the fight instantly gone from his body.

Drew looked from the king down to the child, who raised a trembling finger toward the Werewolf.

"It's him, mother," she said, sniffing back the tears. The girl's featured softened suddenly, from fear to admiration.

"He's the one who saved me."

# 4

# THE PORT AT THE END
# OF THE WORLD

**THERE WERE FEW** places in Lyssia as remote and in-hospitable as Friggia. Situated on the northernmost point of Beggars' Bay, it was the one port in Sturmland that the Sturmish people avoided. The Walrus had claimed the town linked by road to the Rat city of Vermire and Lady Slotha's city of Tuskun, for herself. While the majority of the Tuskun fleet was harbored in Blackbank on the southern coast of the Sturm Peninsula, a few of her warships considered Friggia, on the northern coast, their home, launching raids against those brave souls who dared sail the Sturmish Sea. Like their neighbors in Vermire, the Tuskuns were pirates to the core.

With a snowstorm having descended, any other harbor

in Lyssia would have been deserted, but not Friggia. The hour was late and the weather grim, but the Tuskun port was in no mood to sleep, with both streets and ships busy with activity. However, while the largest piers and docks that housed the bigger ships were bustling, the smaller jetties were quieter, all but deserted, with fishing boats moored for the night. Three figures stood on the end of one such jetty, shrouded in swirling snow. Behind them, a rowing boat was being tied up, and a handful of men clambered up from it on to the wooden walkway.

"By Brenn's whiskers," said Manfred. "I thought it was cold in the Barebones but this is something else!"

"You're in the north now, Your Grace," said Hector. "They don't do anything by half measures up here."

The reluctant new captain of the *Maelstrom*, Figgis, had nothing to say, watching the six other men finish securing the rowboat before they came over to join them.

"Are we clear as to our tasks?" asked Manfred, looking to each of them. "Captain Figgis is to remain here with the boat while we split into two groups."

Manfred pointed to the ship's cook, Holman, and the gray-looking fellow nodded back. "Master Holman, I'll accompany you while you see about getting some fresh produce for the stores—meat, vegetables, whatever passes for food up here in the rear end of nowhere. Hector"—Manfred nodded at the young Boarlord—"you'll procure drinking water for the ship, in addition to something a bit stronger as a reward for the boys. Let's keep it quiet, eh? Last thing we want to do is attract unwanted attention to our visit."

Hector's face was stoic and humorless. "You can count on me, Your Grace."

Ringlin and Ibal waited for their master a short distance away along the jetty. Both were well wrapped up against the elements, while Hector wore his cloak hood down, careless of the bitter snowstorm. The magister was about to follow his men when he stopped, turning to Manfred and placing his gloved left hand on the duke's arm.

"Is everything all right, Manfred?" asked Hector quietly and earnestly, dropping the formalities he'd used before the men.

"Whatever do you mean, Hector?" blustered the Staglord, glancing at the magister's hand on his wrist.

"You haven't seemed yourself lately, especially since that awful business with Vega and that poor boy going missing."

Manfred sighed, wearily staring at the young Boarlord from beneath his bushy gray brow.

"Which of us *has* been ourselves since the disappearance of the count, Hector? It's a terrible thing to come to terms with. It's . . . unbelievable . . . that something so tragic could befall our friend on his own ship, no?"

"Unbelievable," said Hector, nodding. "Just so you know,

I'm always here to talk to, should you wish to unburden your-self of anything. We friends must stick together."

"Friends," agreed Manfred, smiling sadly. "Together."

The duke shook the baron's hand before turning back to his complement of men from the *Maelstrom*. With no further word, the group split up, setting off into Friggia with their own very different agendas.

"That wasn't the agreed upon price," said Hector, wagging a finger at the innkeeper.

The two men stood on the frozen cobbles of the alleyway that ran the length of the Black Gate Tavern, cellar doors open at their feet. Lantern light from below was cast skyward, il-luminating the haggling pair, their men working together be-neath the inn.

"That's the price now," said the innkeeper, jutting his jowls out confidently.

"Is that how you do things up here? Renege on business deals at your whim?"

"That's how we're doing things tonight. I don't give a tin-ker's cuss how you do things in . . . Highcliff . . ."

The innkeeper let his sentence trail away, grinning.

*So*, whispered the Vincent-vile. *He knows where we're from, eh? Sounds like a threat, brother. He's a cocky one, isn't he?*

A solitary dray horse stood nearby harnessed to a cart, its head bowed, eyes fixed on the men in dispute. Ringlin and Ibal were working with the innkeeper's hulking barrel boy in the cellar, rolling three large barrels toward the hatch ramp. The barrel boy was a mute giant of a man who said nothing and did all his master commanded; a child trapped in a man's body was the expression that leaped to Hector's mind. The two rogues glanced up as Hector negotiated, paying close attention to where the conversation was heading.

"It sounds like you're getting greedy, sir," said Hector, his gaunt cheekbones lifting slightly as he managed a sickly smile.

"I'm a businessman, that's all. Way I see it you're not just paying me for the barrels of brandy, boy." He lowered his voice. "You're paying for my silence."

Hector shook his head from side to side. "I swear, why does it always have to end this way?" he said in a tired and irritated voice. He lifted his left hand and opened his palm.

Instantly the innkeeper was spluttering as he struggled with the invisible force tangled around his throat. Hector tightened his grip in the air, watching his brother's vile twist around the neck of the innkeeper like a deadly black noose.

"You had every chance of doing a nice bit of business with me tonight and walking away with your life. Three barrels of brandy, that's all I asked for. We had a deal; we shook on it. I distinctly recall shaking on it, don't you?"

The man collapsed to his knees, eyes bulging as his fingernails clawed at his fat throat, tearing the skin away in strips.

"Greed, sir; a terrible, ugly thing, I'm sure you'll agree. I'd love to say it was pleasant doing business with you, but . . ."

Hector clenched his fist tight, mind focused solely on the vile as he saw the phantom's attack through to its grisly end. Whereas previously, back in Highcliff, his control over the vile had been sporadic, inspired by surging emotions, since his encounter with the host on the White Isle he had a deeper understanding of his abilities. He yanked his hand back through the air, as if tugging a rope. The innkeeper's throat made a wet snapping sound before he fell to the floor, neck broken.

Hector looked into the cellar where Ringlin, Ibal, and the barrel boy stared back. The man-child looked worried now, the realization of what had just happened suddenly dawning on him. He stared at the Boarguard, who let the final barrel roll to a halt at the base of the ramp. Ibal pulled his sickle from his belt, while Ringlin gently unsheathed his long knife, twirling the blade as they advanced on the barrel boy. From his vantage point above, Hector lost sight of the trio as the giant mute retreated fearfully into the recesses of the cellar.

*Done, brother.*

Hector was surprised at Vincent. There was a new understanding between magister and vile, as if the spirit realized its master had unlocked a great many secrets. The Vincent-vile was showing a newfound respect for Hector, fear playing a large part in that. The host had hinted many things to Hector as it fed from his throat. It had shown him how to inflict pain, not just on the living, but the dead.

Even with a world of dark magick at his fingertips waiting to be explored, Hector found himself wavering. He'd done what had to be done to get rid of Vega. He knew the Sharklord would have betrayed him in time; he'd already humiliated him in front of Bethwyn at every opportunity. Hector only regretted the fact that he'd allowed the sea marshal to get so close to him. He wouldn't make the same mistake again. For the first time ever, Hector felt in control of his magistry.

The innkeeper had brought it on himself. He'd been an enemy of the Wolf's Council, and Hector had to eliminate him. Who could have imagined that his knowledge of dark magicks could actually be used for *good*? Despite the freezing cold that bit at his face, Hector felt a warmth in his heart that had been missing for too long. He was helping Drew once again, helping what was left of the Wolf's Council, with his Brenn-given gift.

Stepping over the dead body, Hector made his way toward the street, where the singing of folk inside the Black Gate Tavern spilled out of the door. It was only a matter of time before the innkeeper's clientele realized he was missing. Hector looked back over his shoulder as the first barrel emerged from the cellar, the Boarguard working it into the alley. It was time to return to the *Maelstrom*. Hurriedly, the two rogues loaded up the wagon before setting off back to the harbor.

Ibal cracked his whip over the nag's head and the dray

horse picked up its pace along the slippery dock road. With their task completed quicker than expected, Hector was hopeful they'd be back at the rowboat first. It'd be good to show Manfred how capable he was, after everything that had gone on in the recent weeks. The duke's people had looked after Hector in Highcliff when he'd been taken ill, allowing him to convalesce in Buck House. After the chaos in Moga and the White Isle, and with Vega finally out of the way, Hector felt it was time to repay the Staglord for the many kindnesses he'd shown him. Arriving back at the boat, mission accomplished, was the first step toward Hector proving his trustworthiness to Manfred once more.

Three barrels of brandy and four casks of fresh water sat in the back of the cart with Hector, his men riding up front. As they pulled away, the magister couldn't help but stare back in the direction of the Black Gate Tavern. Customers were already exiting the inn as they'd left, in search of the fat oaf who had run the place after he'd failed to return to the bar. Judging by the shouting that had begun to chase them down the lane, they'd found his body, and that of the slain simpleton in the cellar. Hector glanced back nervously at the thick grooves the wagon wheels had cut into the snow-covered floor of the lane. A trail to follow: the sooner they were back aboard the *Maelstrom*, the better. The last thing Hector needed was a hue and cry on his back with the miserable servants of Slotha hunting him.

Pulling up at the jetty where Figgis had moored the boat,

the Boarguard jumped into the back of the dray, clambering past Hector to unload the barrels. The distant cries of angry men told the Boarlord all he needed to know. *Here's hoping old Manfred's right behind us, then*, thought Hector as he jumped down on to the frozen cobbles.

He walked up the jetty, boots slapping the frosty timber planks as he strode through the stiff gale. He slowed as he neared the remaining length of the wooden pier, coming to a staggering halt.

The rowboat was gone.

Initially Hector thought he'd come to the wrong jetty, but that was impossible; there were only a couple at this end of the harbor, and this was certainly the one. He then noticed the other vessels that had been moored along the jetty had been cut free—coracles, fishing boats, and the like. A couple drifted some distance away in the choppy, black water.

Cut free.

He looked across to the next pier; again, the rowboats had been released, their only means of returning to the *Maelstrom* snatched away. He ran back to the dock road, finding his two companions rolling the first barrel along the planking toward him.

"Stop what you're doing," he said. "The boat's gone. We need to find Manfred, let him know Figgis has abandoned us."

But even as he said it, he knew what had happened.

"What's that, my lord?" asked Ringlin, his face white with worry. Ibal gave a sickly, nervous giggle, looking back up the docks toward where torches and lanterns had begun to appear. Ringlin was shocked to see his master smile.

"So that was your game then, Manfred?" Hector said, to himself as much as anyone else.

If his men understood, they didn't respond, instead drawing their weapons.

*The Stag shows his true colors, brother; the last of the Wolf's Council stabs you in the back. You can trust nobody.*

"You're right for once, Vincent," Hector said, walking past Ringlin and Ibal to stand in front of the horse and cart.

"What are you doing, my lord?" said Ringlin, his voice etched with panic as the approaching mob materialized through the swirling snowstorm, following the telltale passage of the dray through the white streets.

Hector stood calmly as the men appeared. Within moments they had surrounded the Boarlord and his henchmen. Ringlin and Ibal held their weapons at the ready; if they were to die, they'd take some of the Walrus's men with them. The locals were already shouting, calling to see the color of the Westlanders' innards.

Hector raised his hands, palms out to the mob. "Silence," he said simply.

A cold unlike anything the men of Friggia had experienced

before suddenly descended over the mob. To each man it felt as if Death's skeletal hand had traced a bony finger across their hearts, silencing them instantly. Hector smiled.

"Take me to Lady Slotha."

"It is done," said Manfred as he clambered back aboard the *Maelstrom*, the crew helping the elderly duke find his footing on the icy deck. Amelie and Bethwyn stood waiting for them, arms around one another as the frosty wind whipped around them.

"He cannot follow?" asked Amelie.

"Not unless he fancies a bracing swim," replied Figgis, the last man to climb up from the rowboat.

"I hope to Brenn we've done the right thing," said the queen, squeezing her lady-in-waiting in a fearful embrace.

"Don't you be worryin' about nothin,'" said Figgis, before turning to the Staglord. "Where to, Your Grace?"

"Onward to Roof, dear Captain," said Manfred. "And from there to Icegarden, and the protection of Duke Henrik. I pray he's in a generous mood."

# 5

# A Captive Audience

**FROM THE LOFTY** balcony, Drew's view of Omir was as great as any in the Desert Realm. To the east the Saber Sea bled across the horizon, separating sand from sky. To the west the Barebone Mountains stood tantalizingly close, their snow-capped peaks glistening like diamonds. Drew glanced down. The city sprawled below the palace, while the gleaming outer wall of Azra kept it safe. A road ran atop the wall's entire circumference, with soldiers, wagons, and teams of horses moving along it, above the city. Only two gatehouses allowed entrance to the city: Copper Gate to the north and Silver Gate to the south. These structures were as big as many castles in the west, housing garrisons of warriors who manned the defenses; so long as the walls stood, Azra remained Faisal's.

The *Banshee* was still in Kaza under armed guard. Regardless of the fact that Drew's company had brought the king's daughter safely home, the Omiri took no chances. Drew wanted to be away as soon as possible but realized that he wouldn't be able to leave now. Not while an army gathered in the north.

Tents of all sizes dotted the desert several miles from Azra, the amassed force as huge as any Drew had seen. Siege engines intermittently towered into the sky, their definition wavering in the intense heat haze. He counted at least thirty of the machines, the sole purpose of each to break down Azra's fabled walls. Drew looked down at the city's defenses once more. Faisal's force was overwhelmingly outnumbered, the wall just about evening up the contest. *One wall to stop this mighty army.*

"Impressive, no?" said King Faisal as he joined Drew at the balcony.

"The walls? Or the army on your doorstep?"

"Both."

"How long have they been there?"

"They began to gather a week ago. More arrive each day, so our scouts report. Who knows how many more shall arrive or when they intend to attack?"

"Who are they?"

"It's Lord Canan and the Doglords. For ten years he's waged war in Omir, each year taking more of the desert from me. While fighting has intensified recently, he's never dared an assault upon Azra before. I wonder what now makes him so brazen. . . ."

Faisal turned and walked back through his throne room. Drew followed, the yellow-cloaked warriors of the palace guard shadowing him all the while. He wore no manacles, but he was their prisoner nonetheless. *Does Faisal know about the Dogs' alliance with the Cats? Has he heard the rumor of Hayfa joining forces with Canan?* Drew had a terrible feeling in the pit of his stomach. *Three armies against Azra? This city will fall. . . .*

After yesterday's drama, the king was a changed man. Drew and his companions might have been captives, but that didn't stop Faisal from extending every courtesy to them. The three had been taken to separate quarters under armed guard, where they could bathe, dine, and sleep. Drew's body cried out for rest and the time to allow his injuries to heal properly, but they needed to be moving again, and swiftly. It was mid-morning when they finally returned to Faisal's throne room. Shah now stood with Djogo, the two talking quietly while courtiers eyed them suspiciously.

"How's your daughter this morning?" asked Drew, as Faisal went to sit on his throne. A slave knelt at his feet with a tray of olives and grapes at the ready, raising them up instinctively whenever the king's hand reached out.

"Kara is better. Thank you again for bringing her safely home. My wife is herself once more."

"I wasn't alone," said Drew, casting his hand toward his companions. "It's Shah you must thank. It was her superior vision that allowed us to stop the Doglord's attack when we did. Without her, the outcome might not have been so joyous."

Faisal nodded to the Werehawk, his smile forced.

"You must understand, Lady Shah, I find it . . . difficult, to express my thanks to a Hawklord, after the part your kind played in breaking Azra's walls so many years ago."

"Understandable," said Shah, stepping beside Drew. "But it's alarming that your enemies might attack your own so close to home. What was your daughter *doing* on that boat in the first place?"

"Being brought home." Faisal's face was serious as he considered how close he'd come to losing his daughter. "The body you returned was that of my uncle, Prince Fier. He'd been schooling Kara in Denghi, where he served as my envoy. Word had reached us that Canan's forces were marching on Azra. We had no choice but to have them return."

"How was it they came under attack?" asked Drew.

Faisal frowned. Before he could answer Lord Rook stepped forward and spoke for him. "The king's enemies have a long and deadly reach, Wolf."

"But it was Doglords who attacked the skiff," said Drew. He watched the black-robed man carefully, the Crow having taken far too much delight in tormenting Shah the previous day.

"We have only *your* word that it was the Dogs who attacked them," said Rook. "It was probably just river pirates. Either way, she's safe now."

"It was a Doglord, all right, your daughter will vouch for that, Your Majesty," said Drew. "I left one at the bottom of the Silver River."

"I would imagine poor Kara can remember little from the traumatic event. The child is still in shock. How very convenient that you left the villain's corpse on the riverbed," said the Crowlord.

"Let's talk about convenient," said Drew, facing Rook. "How did the Dogs know that the king's daughter was traveling to Azra? I know maps and I understand distance: how did word reach the Doglords in the north, alerting them that the child was on her way? To get a message to the Dogs so swiftly? That sounds like something that would require *wings*, don't you agree, Lord Rook?"

"Mind what you insinuate, pup," said Rook. "They were simply pirates; bandits, Your Majesty."

Drew turned to the king, fed up with the Crow's interruptions.

"Armed with silver weapons? They're wealthy bandits Rook speaks of," said Drew. "This sounds like a coordinated attack. Your enemies are mobilizing against you, Your Majesty, and I fear their number is far greater than you imagine, and that some are closer than you know."

Rook took hold of Drew, turning him about so they were face-to-face.

"You think the king isn't *worried* about yesterday's events? You assume an awful lot, son of Wergar. Your greatest concern should be your own immediate future."

"As I understood, this is the court of King Faisal, not the Crows of Riven," Drew snapped. "While your interest in my welfare is appreciated, Rook, it's the king I sought audience with. Not some visiting dignitary from a small town in the Barebones."

"Mind your tongue, Wolf!" said Rook. "You and your *friends* are enemies of Omir. The good people of the Desert Realm have long memories. They remember Wergar's war all too well."

Drew ignored the man, speaking directly to Faisal.

"You have Kara back, Your Majesty, thanks to our actions. One of my companions, Drake, died saving her. A brave man and a Werelord of the first rank, he gave his life for a complete stranger, many miles from his homeland. Surely you can let us go?"

Faisal stroked his jaw as Drew spoke, pondering the young Wolflord's words.

"You're the reason there's a war in the west, boy," said the king finally. "The Seven Realms fight over Highcliff's throne. Some say it should be yours. I've yet to hear your thoughts on the matter."

Drew grimaced. The Jackal understood all too well the young Werewolf's value.

"Up until recently I'd no interest in the throne of Westland. But that was before I saw the cruelty that takes place across Lyssia in the names of monsters like Leopold, Lucas, and Kesslar."

Djogo and Shah looked down, ashamed, when Drew mentioned the Goatlord.

"The people of Lyssia have made a stand; they've rallied behind the Wolf's banner, risen in my name. I'd betray them all if I didn't fight now to free them from tyranny. Brackenholme, Westland, the Longridings, and the Barebones—"

"Don't mention my homeland as your ally, Wolf," said Rook. "The Staglords might have made a stand at your side, but what good did it do their home?"

Drew cocked his head at mention of the Stags. "Why? What's happened?"

The Crowlord jutted out his jaw as he relayed the news from the Barebones. "Highwater is surrounded by Onyx's forces, and sure to fall. As for your Staglords, no doubt you're aware that one brother's dead and the other's disappeared. So please, Wolf, don't tell me you've friends in the Mountain Realm. You'll find none there."

Shah stepped toward the Rook. "Highwater laid siege to? Tell me, Crow, where do the black birds of Riven fit into this picture. Highwater is on your doorstep, is it not?"

Rook prickled at the Hawklady's words.

"We Crowlords remain removed from conflict. We seek nothing but peace and neutrality."

Shah laughed out loud, but when she looked back at Rook her face was stony.

"How can you stand there and say the Crows of Riven want nothing but peace? Your father, Count Croke, has perched on that pile of slate for almost a century. In all those years he's bullied and bickered with his neighbors, trying to wrestle control of the Barebones away from the Stags of Stormdale. You expect me to believe he sits neutral while his lifelong nemeses are beaten black and blue by the Catlords? Tell me: how soon before a Crow resides in Stormdale, Rook?"

Rook lurched toward Shah, lashing out with a fist, only the swift action of the palace guards restraining him in time.

"You witch!" spat the Crowlord. "You dare lecture me on what's best for the Barebones? Your kind don't belong in my mountains any more than a fish belongs in a tree! You're relics, Shah—you and whatever Hawklord scum remain! Skeer's the best of your bad bunch, and he did right striking a deal with Leopold back in the day. He rules Windfell now, the last of the Hawks. Soon enough we'll see how Windfell looks with black feathers on the throne!"

Ignoring the Crow, Drew turned to Faisal. "A Doglord army approaches, Your Majesty, possibly the same one that was allied to the Catlords that attacked Westland. Now they gather north of Azra, the Cats returning the favor to the

Dogs. I wager you'll find Bastians fighting alongside Omiri."

"Let them come!" cried one of Faisal's cousins. "Their bodies will litter the base of Azra's walls!"

"We can defeat this army from the north!" shouted another.

"And the one from the south?" asked Drew, turning to the crowd. "Talk spreads like wildfire in Denghi. Lady Hayfa has struck a bargain with Lord Canan. Her army will come to the aid of the Doglords as well. Send scouts south—I guarantee you'll find her. That's three armies, my lords, surrounding your city. They're going to carve Azra up between them!"

"Preposterous!" scoffed Rook. "Don't listen to him, Your Majesty. He spreads mistrust and fear. You should have killed this monster and his companions when they landed here."

"Let us continue our quest," Drew went on. "We head into the Barebones with Baron Griffyn's blessing. He will lead us to the ancient tomb of his forefathers, the Screaming Peak. From there, the baron shall summon the Hawklords from every corner of Lyssia."

Drew held the king's gaze as he spoke, the room quiet but for the spluttering of Lord Rook.

"Your aid won't be forgotten, King Faisal. We'll return, in number, and help you defeat the army that approaches Azra, be they Dogs, Cats, or any other kind of beast. You shall have the Hawklords as allies this time!"

Rook moved past Drew, bringing his lips closer to Faisal's ear. But Drew still heard his whispers to the king.

"The Wolf will promise you anything to save his hide, Your Majesty. Kill him now and let all Lyssia know—you'll be a hero throughout the Seven Realms! With one thrust of your blade you can end this war!"

Slowly, the king turned to the Crowlord. "My dear Lord Rook," he said, smiling as he spoke. "I think you may have just outstayed your welcome."

"You're not serious," said Rook, his face frozen in a shocked smile.

"I'm very serious. I shall be closing the gates of Azra tonight for the last time to all but my allies. Anyone else should leave. That would include you."

"But I'm here on my father's behalf. We *are* your allies."

"These are turbulent times, Lord Rook. Your father would no doubt appreciate your presence in Riven, with war threatening us all. I want only those loyal to Azra within these walls."

Rook was furious, spittle frothing at his lips as he looked around the room snarling, his eyes settling on Drew and his companions.

"You side with your prisoners, Faisal? Is this how little you think of my kind? You take a Wolf's word over mine?"

Faisal rose and walked toward the enraged Lord of Riven.

"This has nothing to do with the Wolf and everything to do with the Crow. Many questions remain unanswered regarding the enemy at my gates and allegiances in the Barebones. You offer little to put my mind at ease."

"Don't be fooled by the Wolf's gossip," said Rook, but he choked on his words, struggling for conviction.

"I gave you every chance to walk away from Azra with your reputation intact. I tolerated your actions yesterday, taking such delight in holding the Hawklady hostage. I thought the Wolf and Hawk were my enemies—"

"They *are* your enemies!" said Rook. "You should kill them!"

"And now you attack a guest in my palace, a lady no less."

"She's no lady!" squawked Rook. The Crowlord was now surrounded by palace guards, the other nobles having moved clear of the volatile therian.

"What good does your presence here do me and my people, Rook? Why do you wish the Wolf dead so dearly? Whom do you truly serve?"

"If you don't kill them . . ."

"If I don't kill them, what exactly?" exclaimed the king, releasing the Jackal at last.

He arched his back, letting the white robes that draped across his shoulders tumble away as his tanned torso tripled in size. His arms popped with muscles, fingers shifting into claws that pointed menacingly toward Rook. His neck and head broadened, the smooth fur of the Jackal racing through his flesh as sharp ears rose and a long, canine snout worked its way through his face.

"Hold your tongue, Crowlord, before you say something you regret," growled the Werejackal.

Drew heard the snarls of the other therians in the court. A cloud passed in front of the sun, darkening the throne room. His cousins and fellow Jackal-lords growled in unison, the beasts all too visible in their angry faces.

"You have one hour, Crow," said Faisal. "The death of my dear uncle Lord Fier is shrouded by the stench of treachery, and the young Wolflord's words have allowed me to see clearly. Gather your belongings and leave my city. If you're still here after that, I shan't be responsible for my fellow Jackals' actions. A threat against their king is a threat to all."

Rook looked quickly around the room, noticing the assembled Jackal-lords' state of agitation. He backed up warily, eyes flitting between the warriors and therians.

"You've made a grave mistake siding with these beasts, Faisal," warned the Werecrow as he retreated through the throne room, armed guards escorting him closely. Turning on his heel, the Lord of Riven stormed from the chamber, long robe billowing as he left a shower of black feathers in his wake.

Drew kept his distance as the transformed Werejackal watched the Crow disappear. Faisal's broad shoulders heaved up and down. Gradually he returned to human form, the Jackal and his temper subsiding.

Finally the king looked back at Drew. "The black bird says I'm mistaken to trust you," said Faisal, his narrow eyes studying the young therian carefully. The look he gave the Wolf seemed as if he were laying down a challenge as he continued: "Prove him wrong."

# 6

# NOWHERE TO RUN

**THE CALLS OF** the chasing pack seemed distant, their cries carried away on the chill wind that raced across the Longridings. Their torches were visible, flaming brands held aloft by the riders as they scoured the grasslands for fugitives. Trent spurred Storm on through the long grass, keen to put distance between himself and his comrades. With their constant shouting they were making enough noise to wake the dead, and if their enemies were to be caught, stealth had to play a large part.

The tall fronds whipped at horse and youth as they sped along, Trent's eyes picking out the broken grass ahead that marked the route his quarry had taken. Once again, his mind raced back to the Cold Coast where he and his father—and brother—had hunted by night, often on foot, occasionally on

horseback, but always by the light of the moon. The pale light of
the heavenly body illuminated the path ahead—the saw grass
clumsily broken in his foe's desperate desire to escape. The man
was injured, of that much he was sure, judging by the blood he
caught sight of on the pale yellow blades of grass.

The trail came to a halt as the grass fell away suddenly before him. Trent reined Storm in, the horse snorting as she skidded to an abrupt stop, her hooves kicking at the frozen earth
and sending a shower of pebbles skittering off the lip of the ravine. Trent lurched forward in his saddle, patting Storm's neck
as clouds of steam snorted from her nostrils. Directly below
them a small gorge cut through the grasslands, rocky inclines
rising steeply from either side of a rushing, bubbling brook.
Storm stepped nervously as Trent surveyed the terrain, looking north and south up the length of the rocky valley.

"He went down here," he said, as much to the horse as himself. "And so do we."

He gently prodded his heels into Storm's flanks, urging
her over the edge of the ravine. Reluctantly, the horse pro-
ceeded, hooves gingerly picking a path down the steep, rocky
slope. Occasionally they passed a bloodied rock, a red hand-
print smeared against a slab of stone where the fugitive had
scrambled down to the gorge's bottom. Arriving at the base of
the slope, Trent hopped down out of the saddle for a moment,
leading Storm to the stream, his eyes wide and alert, searching
the shadowy valley for a sighting of the enemy. He let Storm

drink from the noisy stream momentarily, jumping across to the other side and searching the other bank. There was no bloody trail, no telltale marks left behind on the rocks. He glanced south down the ravine where the brook disappeared into the distance, back in the direction of the rest of his force.

"He won't have gone back that way, not after he witnessed what was done to his companions."

He jumped back up into his saddle, his horse refreshed by the cold water. "North it is. We follow the stream."

Lord Frost's force had encountered a large band of travelers earlier that day, around dusk, making their way west through the Longridings. The group had numbered nearly two hundred, mainly civilians—farmers, traders, and a smattering of Romari. There were also a number of Horselords within their ranks, the Werelords immediately rushing to the defense of their companions when the Lionguard launched an unprovoked attack against the caravan. The initial offensive had left a sour taste in Trent's mouth. The fact that Romari were present had been enough for the Redcloaks to decide that the group was the enemy, the travelers' loyalty to the Wolf and their antics in Cape Gala still fresh in their minds. As it transpired, their hunch had been correct, but Trent had put that down to blind luck rather than reasoned deduction.

The initial battle had been fierce, the Romari and Horselords engaging Redcloaks and Bastians while the remaining refugees fled across the grasslands. Once the enemy had been defeated, at some cost to Frost's small army, the Catlord had questioned the surviving prisoners. With the aid of Sorin, he had prised a great deal of information from the group, including the knowledge that more Werelords had been traveling with the group, escaping with the other civilians when the battle had commenced. Putting the prisoners to the sword, the Lionguard and Bastians had given chase, gradually picking up those who had fled. The soldiers had cheered as one after another of the refugees had been rounded up and clapped in irons. Only a handful remained at large, and Trent was determined to return to the camp with a trophy of his own.

Trent pushed on along the banks of the brook, Storm picking up pace as the outrider grew in confidence. *This is the only way he could have gone. Nowhere left to run. I have you now.* The foe must have thought the stream would mask his passage, which it would have done ordinarily. However, the noise of the water rushing over the rocks would also conceal Trent's approach, the constant gurgling covering the approach of Storm's hooves. He unsheathed the Wolfshead blade as he rode, controlling his horse by his thighs and heels alone, letting the longsword trail through the air to his right. He sat up in his saddle straight, eyes searching the ravine ahead.

"There you are."

The figure had collapsed ahead, leaning hard against a boulder that sat in the middle of the stream. The fugitive looked up as he caught sight of the approaching rider. The bearded man grunted, clutching his chest as if in pain. Then he was off, running along the shallow streambed. Trent kicked Storm's flanks, forcing the horse into a canter.

The fleeing man tripped and stumbled, feet splashing through the icy water. He glanced over his shoulder as Storm thundered closer, gaining on him swiftly. Trent allowed the horse to charge past, her hooves narrowly missing the man but frightening him enough to send him spread-eagled into the stream. He landed face first in the cold water, momentarily blinded as he surfaced, gasping for air. Trent turned Storm around, squeezing his thighs against her back and urging her to rear up, her hooves threatening to strike the enemy.

The fugitive began to change, heavy horns emerged from the old man's skull, twisting and curling about his head. His short gray beard began to lengthen as his ribcage cracked within his chest, a sound like hammer hitting steel. Trent showed no fear. Here was the trophy he had sought: an enemy therian, a traitorous Werelord. He expertly prompted Storm to lash out, the horse's hooves connecting with the shifting Werelord's horned head with a hollow *crack.*

The man went down on his side, his head bouncing off the rocks on the streambed, his face half submerged in the water. Trent could see the cold liquid rushing through his enemy's slack mouth, racing into his airways and threatening to fill his lungs. He quickly dismounted, landing beside the Werelord in the water, hooking his arms beneath the fellow's partially transformed torso. He heaved the therian on to the bank, throwing him on to his stomach and binding him swiftly with ropes.

More riders arrived, the snorting of horses mingling with the cheers and jeers of the soldiers as they looked down at the hog-tied Werelord. The horns around his head reminded Trent of the old ram they had kept on the farm, the tuft of a gray beard beneath his chin further enhancing the resemblance. A Ramlord? There had been one in Cape Gala, at the court of High Stable. Was this the one of the Werelords they'd been searching for? Trent looked back at his companions, smiling proudly. The old therian snorted, rolling on to his side to view his captors.

"Well done, boys," the aged Ramlord spluttered. "You chased down an old man."

"Chased down a traitor," replied Frost, his voice rich and smooth. The Catlord jumped from his horse and landed in the stream, hardly making a splash. His pink eyes widened as he waded toward the bank where the Ram lay, coming to stand beside Trent. He patted the young outrider's back.

"Good work, Sergeant Ferran."

"Ferran?" said the Ram incredulously, but the only reply he received was the albino's boot to the temple. Trent stared down at the bound captive as two of the Bastian warriors hauled him onto the back of one of their horses, puzzling over the prisoner's reaction to his name.

*He knows my name,* Trent mused as he clambered back on Storm's back. *He knows Drew.*

# 7

# THE STARS OVER AZRA

**ALONE IN THE** heavens, with only the stars for company, the young Wolflord was transported through time and space. He was a child, back at the farmhouse on the Cold Coast, Tilly Ferran rocking him in her chair while the two of them gazed into the night sky. His mother had the gift, so old Mack always told him: she could read the stars, divine a person's fortune on a clear, cloudless night. He tried to recall the things she'd promised him, the events she predicted would come to pass, but all he could remember was the smell of her hair and the feel of her hand over his. For the first time in months, Drew felt a tear roll down his cheek.

"I'm not interrupting you, am I?"

Drew glanced up from the star chart mosaic, wiping the

tear from his face with the flat of his hand, as King Faisal paced through the darkness toward him. The rest of the king's guests were still gathered at the far end of the throne room, feasting one last time on the eve of war. Djogo and Shah were with them, the frosty relations between the two factions thawing, speeded along by fine food and drink. The Hawklady occasionally looked across the room, concerned by the Wolf's dark mood. Drew had no appetite for feasting, and even less for company.

"I'm sorry, Your Majesty. I was a world away."

Faisal walked around the mosaic, circling Drew as he remained rooted in the middle.

"They say Azra is the home of all Lyssia's knowledge. The art of magistry began here. The libraries beneath the palace would rival any in the Seven Realms, Drew. This city was the seat of learning for Brenn's wisest children at one time. Terrifying to think that this could all be lost if the Dogs and the Cats overrun our walls."

"I recognize the stars," said Drew, gesturing to the marble constellations. "There's the Stag, the Serpent. Over there are the Twin Boars."

"And you're standing on the Wolf," said Faisal, smiling.

Drew took a step back.

"So I am."

"Not in the mood for a feast? You surprise me. The morning brings danger to all of us; you, with your journey, and us, with impending war. We Jackals always dine as if it's our last meal on the eve of battle."

"I can't stomach it." Drew sighed. "Have you heard back from your scouts?"

"You were right, Wolf. The Hyena's forces amass to the south of the Silver River. You'll have to leave swiftly at first light if you're to sail out of Kaza before they take the port town."

"Are you prepared for them?"

"Azra is always ready for war. This is the Jewel of Omir. It's been fought over for centuries. This is just one more chapter in this city's rich history."

"You sound as if you're looking forward to war."

"I look forward to action. It's the waiting I can't abide. My warriors are ready. Azra's ready."

"But still . . ." said Drew, scratching the back of his head as he stared out of the archway that led to the balcony. Hundreds of fires dotted the horizon to the north, twinkling like fireflies over a pitch-black meadow.

"Don't hold your tongue now, Drew. If you truly are the king of Westland, then speak freely. It's been long years since another king has been my guest."

Drew looked wearily at the handsome Jackal. "There are so many of them. You're badly outnumbered."

"You underestimate our defenses. Besides, the people will man the walls should the warriors fall."

"I fear for your people."

"This is their home. They take pride in their land."

"Even the slaves?"

Faisal grimaced, shaking his head at the Wolflord. "I wouldn't bring such a matter up if I were you, Drew. We're just getting to know one another. Politics have killed the greatest friendships as sure as swords before now."

Drew bit his lip, shaking his head. His mind went back to the belly of the *Banshee*, to the Furnace and the cruel antics of Kesslar and the Lizardlords. "I can't stand here silent. It goes against all I believe in. I've *been* a slave, Faisal. Walk even one step with a collar around your throat and you may change your tune. No man should be owned by another."

"We shall have to agree to disagree, Wolf Cub."

"Don't mock me, Faisal," said Drew, angry now. "I haven't fought my way back to Lyssia just to sit quietly while a fool spouts barbaric beliefs at me, be he a beggar or a king."

The Jackal snarled. If any of the palace guard had been present, they might have seized Drew for offending the king so. But the two were alone, facing one another across the ancient mosaic.

"This is my land, Wolf—my city. Your place is in the West. Keep your so-called enlightened thinking on the other side of the Barebones."

Drew stepped forward, eyeballing the king. "How many slaves are there in this city?"

"I've no idea, they are too many to count."

"Estimate for me, Your Majesty."

"Tens of thousands, I should imagine."

"Tomorrow, your city will be overrun, even if we can call the Hawklords to our side. You haven't enough warriors to man the walls against three armies."

"And what would you propose?"

"Free them."

Faisal recoiled as if he'd been slapped in the face.

"Release the slaves. Grant them citizenship of Azra as free men. Free the slaves and you'll save your city."

Faisal stared at Drew, weighing the youth up. He clearly hadn't expected Drew to speak so frankly to him. Perhaps Drew might have kept silent if he hadn't been so weary. The thought of journeying to Tor Raptor made his legs feel heavy suddenly. He stifled a yawn.

"It's been a long day, Your Majesty, and I must be away before dawn's first light. I thank you for your hospitality, and your understanding. Until I return, with the Hawklords . . ."

Drew bowed, turning to walk away, as King Faisal called after him.

"I don't understand how turning slaves into free men will save Azra."

The Wolflord continued to walk away, calling back as he went. "Put a roof over a man's head and you give him a home. Put a sword in his hand and pride in his heart—you give him something to fight for. You give him hope."

The fire had burned low by the time Drew returned to his bedchamber, just a handful of coals still kicking out heat as the cold air of the desert spread through the room. The guest quarters could have housed the entire Ferran family and their neighbors, the opulence on a scale Drew had never seen before, not even in Scoria. An enormous round bed dominated the room, circular steps leading up to it like a sacrificial altar. The carvings around the marble fireplace were as intricate as anything he'd seen in the Temple of Brenn in Highcliff. Bejeweled curtains billowed around the door on to the balcony, gems flashing like the stars in the night sky beyond. The Azrans did nothing by half-measures.

Even with the thick doors closed at Drew's back, the noise from the throne room below still echoed through the walls of the palace. Faisal wasn't lying when he said the Jackals liked to feast the night before a battle. He looked around the room, a nagging sensation descending over him. *Something isn't right.* He paused, trying to figure out what irked him, but couldn't put his finger on it.

Drew shivered, striding toward the balcony, the freezing air raising goose bumps on his flesh. The room felt like a mausoleum, the cold marble only enhancing the sensation. He stared at the fires of the enemy encampments beyond the walls, spreading east to west as far as the eye could see. *Does Faisal truly understand the magnitude of what he's facing? Will he take the advice of a boy like me?*

Drew grabbed the handle and pulled the balcony door closed, stopping before he dropped the latch. He suddenly realized what was nagging him: the doors had been closed when he'd left the bedchamber. Drew turned quickly, eyes searching the room. He channeled the Wolf's senses, his vision heightening instantly as he sniffed at the air. Stepping carefully across the chamber, he reached over to the chest at the foot of the bed. A sheathed longsword rested atop it, a gift from the king and a small token of apology for the treatment Drew and his friends had endured. Drew snatched the handle, shaking the scabbard from the blade where it fell quietly on to the rug.

He snorted at the air once more, picking up the scent of the intruder. With his lupine eyes now adjusted to the dim light, he could see through the gloom as if it were day. He pulled at the jewel-encrusted curtains, tearing them clear of the windows to reveal what they hid, but found nothing. He leaped across the room toward the tall closet, flicking the door open only to find it empty. Lastly he dashed back toward the bed, dancing up the steps and pulling back the sheets from where they hung to the marble floor. Ducking down, Drew looked beneath the bed. There was nobody there. The prowler was gone.

He collapsed onto the enormous bed, his heart beating fast, relieved to not be caught in a fight once more but disappointed to have not captured his intruder. He turned his head, the moonlight that streamed through the glass doors illuminating the clean white sheets that spread out before him. Drew's eyes widened. *There you are.*

A single long feather lay on his pillow, black as night itself. Drew shivered as he reached across and picked it up, the waxy texture sliding against his skin. He turned it between his fingertips, considering the gift's meaning. Rook was watching him. There would be no hiding from the Crowlord.

# 8

# A Welcome in Tuskun

**THE DOGS' PAWS** pounded through the deep snow, hauling the sleds through the blizzard, whipcracks urging them on their way. Hector lay on his side, lashed to the sledge as a hunter might bind his kill. Goyt, an old Sturmish pelt trader caught trapping in the queen's woods, lay strapped down before him, head tucked to his chest, the cold and exhaustion having taken their toll on him. Hector felt Ibal's fat belly at his back; the magister was grateful for the warmth of his portly Boarguard. The rogue's giggles had ceased two days ago back in Friggia, the mob having worked some of their anger out on the three southerners before throwing them in the jail for the remainder of the night. They'd departed the Sturmish port at first light, heading inland on a handful of dogsleds, toward the City of the Walrus.

Ringlin was on one of the other sledges, bound to some other criminals who were being transported to Tuskun. The cold was unbearable, the temperature having remained well below freezing during their entire journey. Hector's teeth chattered incessantly, his entire body struggling with the extreme conditions. Who could have imagined the warmth of Ibal's fat belly might keep him alive? His show of strength in Friggia had struck awe into his captors' hearts, the chill touch of his Dark Magistry unnerving the angry mob. But Hector was no fool, and neither were the Tuskuns; they had numbers on their side. Had the Boarlord tried to fight his way out of his predicament, he might have brought two or three of the enemy to their knees before he and his men were overpowered, probably killed. No; surrendering was the only way he could gain audience with Slotha. There were six of them in all being taken to her, each responsible for very different crimes. The queen of Tuskun was a notoriously ill-tempered, violent woman: he hoped the Walrus would allow him the chance to speak in his defense.

The driver let out a cheer, the noise echoing over on the chasing sleds. Hector craned his neck, looking up ahead to where they headed. The blizzard lifted briefly, allowing the magister a clear view of Tuskun's jagged black walls as they loomed into view. To describe the outer defense as a wall was an exaggeration; giant slabs of gray slate had been driven into the ground around the entire city, dozens of tall wooden watchtowers dotted around its circumference. The sharp, splintered defenses reminded Hector of Vega's teeth when the Sharklord was transformed: fearsome and deadly.

*Not so deadly in the end, eh, brother?* whispered the Vincentvile slyly.

Timber gates groaned open, a portcullis grinding clear out of the sleds' path as they raced past beneath it. The city within bore little resemblance to any civilized settlement Hector had ever visited. It was little more than a shantytown, a crowded slum, the locals standing aside as the dogsleds raced up the slippery, stinking streets, a river of feculence steadily streaming beside the road. Hector gagged at the stench as the whip cracked overhead and the driver yelled at his hounds.

The buildings in the city were wooden for the most part, though the Boarlord spotted the occasional stone structure as they raced by. Bones of all shapes and sizes featured everywhere, the skulls of wild beasts adorning doors, giant animal ribs and femurs woven into the rooftops, walls, and windows of the houses. Clearly, this was a city of hunters. These people lived to kill.

The sledge jostled up the rutted avenue, slush and filth splashing off the road surface into the faces of the prisoners. Hector thought he might vomit, smearing the sewage from his face against Goyt's shoulder at his side. The driver pulled hard at the reins, the dogs yelping and barking as they slowed, the sled grinding to a halt in the blackened slush before a great black building. Enormous whale jawbones formed an arch above the open doors of Slotha's Longhouse. Two heavy-set guards stood at either side of the entrance, each carrying a long barbed harpoon. The pair didn't move as the driver jumped off the sled, waiting for the others to join him.

"Goyt. Ibal. We're here," Hector whispered. The fat Boarguard grunted a brief acknowledgment.

Hector gave Goyt a shove with his knee. The impact was enough to jar Goyt's head, which lolled back from his chest with a *crack*. The old trapper's face was blue, his eyes wide and frozen over.

*Welcome to Tuskun, brother.*


The Longhouse resembled the hull of an upturned ship, the interior an arched tunnel that disappeared into darkness. An enormous firepit dominated the hall, belching clouds of black smoke to the ceiling where it struggled to escape through a single round hole. Guards like those at the entrance occupied the chamber, each carrying harpoons and axes, and clad in seal-skins and furs. Their faces were leathery, with long drooping black mustaches and beards obscuring their mouths. Each of them stared intently at the five prisoners as they were marched toward the roaring fire, manacles jangling, and forced to their knees.

Hector looked back over his shoulder. Outside, beyond the open doors, he could hear the snarling of sled dogs as they tore into Goyt's corpse, an unexpected reward for their hard run to Tuskun. Hector shivered, despite the heat, and turned back. Beyond the fire he saw a great mass advancing through the shadows. As she got closer her form was illuminated by the dancing flames. Her flesh was on show to all, between tattered leather strips pulled tight across her broad frame, the skin bulging between the straps. A bearskin robe was draped from her shoulder.

"So," grunted Slotha, the Werewalrus, as she strode around the firepit and made her way behind her captives. "These are the prisoners the good people of Friggia have delivered to me? This is the *fresh meat. . . .*"

*I don't like the sound of this, dear brother. . . .*

The sled drivers standing to one side bowed, their hands clasped together as if in prayer.

"Go get yourselves fed."

The three departed, apparently happy to be away from their queen, while a man who looked like a councilor unrolled a scroll. The vicious-looking Ugri warriors stepped forward, one standing in front of each prisoner as Slotha maneuvered behind them.

"What crimes?" asked the therian lady as she settled behind the first man to Hector's right. The man's eyes were fearful, darting from the guard to the councilor and then back to the magister.

"Defamation of Your Majesty's character in a tavern," said the councilor, sneering as he read the charge.

"What did you say, man?" whispered Slotha, momentarily lowering her head between the terrified man and Hector, her lips wobbling as she muttered into his ear. Hector got a whiff of the woman's breath, as foul as a bucket of rotting fish.

"I . . . I . . . but I . . ." The man couldn't speak, his whole body trembling as he began to shuffle forward away from her. The warrior standing in front of him reached over, clasping the man's hair in his fist and holding him firmly in his place. Hector could hear Slotha grunting behind him now, her bones cracking as her body shifted. He recognized the noise of a therianthrope on the change instantly. The councilor finished the stuttering man's sentence for him.

"He called you a 'fat cow,' Your Majesty."

The man's eyes widened further as the wet sound of blades tearing through flesh cut through the air beside Hector. The Boarlord took a brief glance at the man as he spluttered blood from his trembling lips before the guard released his head, allowing the body to topple forward to the floor. Two great gashes were visible in the man's back, his spine exposed where a pair of blades had sunk through his body, butchering him

345

on the spot. With a grunt, Slotha moved behind Hector.

"Next," she snarled, her voice deep and wet, her teeth grating.

"Murder," said the councilor. "He and his companions killed an innkeeper and his man."

Hector heard the queen shift her bulk behind him, as a warrior reached forward and took hold of his scalp in a dirty hand.

"A moment, I beg of you!" said Hector quickly.

The councilor arched his eyebrows as Hector struggled in the warrior's grasp.

"The charge is quite straightforward; you apparently admitted to your crime in Friggia."

"I believe Her Majesty would benefit from the full story!"

"Spit it out, then!" she said, smacking her lips.

"I'm Baron Hector, the Boarlord of Redmire. I'm one of the Wolf's Council."

The councilor looked astonished as Slotha grabbed Hector by the shoulder and spun him about, his hair tearing from his scalp as he turned to face the queen of Tuskun.

"Oh, but what good fortune!" she roared, clapping her hands together. "Sosha smiles up at me!"

Nothing had prepared Hector for the sight of the monstrous Werewalrus. The scraps of clothing that had clung to her had been ripped away; her pasty, pale skin was now mottled dark brown and covered in calluses, her stocky legs having transformed into huge, flat flippers. Her clawed fingers were long and webbed, her hands wide and wobbling as she clapped them together. Her long, greasy hair hung down her back, neck and lips bristling with oily whiskers. A pair of yard-long tusks protruded down from her top lip, ivory blades that dripped crimson with the dead man's blood.

"You have the look of your father," she grunted, clawing at his face with a flippered hand. "He was an ugly pig, too!"

*You have my permission to roar at the irony,* chuckled the Vincent-vile to Hector.

"Hold him still," she gushed excitedly as her warrior grabbed his head once again. "I want to look into this one's eyes while I run him through. Imagine Prince Lucas's joy when I deliver a spitted Boarlord to him!"

"Wait!" shouted Hector, as Slotha raised her tusks, ready to strike his chest. She paused, waiting for him to speak.

"I know there's a price on my head, but grant my sorry life a few more days, I beg of you, Your Majesty. Killing me would be too easy—the prince would prefer it if you delivered me alive, I can promise you. I know him, I served him for years. Let him do what he will with me. I guarantee he'll be doubly grateful. . . ."

Slotha looked from Hector to her councilor. The man shrugged, leaving the decision entirely to her whim.

"You say I should let you live and go to Highcliff?"

"Hand me over as a gift alive rather than dead. I have information that will aid the Catlords in their war."

"Tell *me* your information then, Piglord."

Hector managed a thin smile.

*Roll the bones, brother!*

"My information is for Prince Lucas and him alone. Deliver me to him and your reward shall be greater than you could possibly imagine, Lady Slotha."

"That's *Queen* Slotha," she snorted.

"I know," said Hector as the warrior's grip on his hair tightened. "The queen of the North and the king of Westland; can you *imagine* what you might discuss together?"

Slotha smacked her lips as if savoring a previously unknown taste. Hector kept his eyes fixed on her.

*She's taken the bait, Hector! Well done!*

"I deliver you alive to Highcliff?"

"Myself and my two men." Hector gestured to Ringlin and Ibal at his side with a quick glance.

"Very well," said the Werewalrus, shuffling past the two rogues who breathed audible sighs of relief at their temporary pardon. She settled behind the last prisoner, who was afforded no such kindness.

"That one's a thief, Your Majesty," said the councilor, answering her unvoiced question.

"But remember, Piglord . . ." she said, rearing up behind the bound man as he knelt before her. The Ugri warrior held the prisoner's head as he kicked out, trying to roll clear. She lunged down fast, the tusks puncturing the man's back and disappearing up to her gums. The blood erupted as she tore them free.

"No tricks."

Hector bowed on his knees, his heart near exploding.

"Ready the *Myrmidon*," said the Walrus of Tuskun. "We sail to Highcliff to meet the prince."

# PART VI

## TALONS AND TURNCOATS

# I

# TWO RIVERS

**ANY OBSERVER WITNESSING** the *Banshee* disembarking into the border town of Two Rivers would have been hard-pressed to imagine a more unusual party of people. Drew led the way, the mountainous figure of the Behemoth, over seven feet of towering muscle, following behind him. The Weremammoth carried an enormous stone mallet across one shoulder, a weapon the strongest man would struggle to lift with both hands. Following him came the crooked figure of Baron Griffyn alongside the Catlady, Taboo.

Krieg awaited them at the head of the docks, his spiked mace swinging from his hip, grimacing as they approached. A chill wind blew through the ramshackle harbor, sending sand through the air like a shower of broken glass.

"Good to be off that wretched boat, isn't it?"

"It's good to be on our way again," said Drew, the passing townsfolk eyeing them suspiciously. "I just hope our friends are safe in Azra. Did you find horses?"

The Rhino nodded and set off up the street, Drew at his shoulder and the others behind.

"How's the old man?" asked Krieg, without looking back.

"He misses her, which is understandable, but she has Djogo. She'll be fine."

Faisal had insisted the Hawklady and Djogo remain behind in Azra as his guests. Effectively, the Jackal was holding her ransom, a guarantee that the Hawklords would return and fight for him, honoring the promise Drew made on their behalf. There had never been any doubt in Drew's mind that the Hawklords, *if* they could summon them, would aid them, but that clearly hadn't been the case for Faisal. Considering the previous visit of Wolf and Hawk to Azra years ago, the king had fair reason to feel that way.

Faisal had passed a decree that very night, granting every single slave in the city of Azra his or her permanent freedom. While the therian lords of the city had accepted this without challenge, the merchant classes had been horrified; it would take all of Faisal's political know-how to put their minds at ease in the following days. Delighted, Drew was in no doubt that the Jackal would bring his people in line; overnight their militia had swelled by tens of thousands as former slaves volunteered to help protect their city. Suddenly, the odds for the people of Azra against the three advancing armies didn't seem so grim.

Furthermore, the hundred gladiators who had journeyed from Scoria had joined Djogo and Shah in the desert city. The men were an elite fighting force who could be put to good use by Faisal, under Djogo's command. There was no need for Drew to drag his small army up into the Barebones. It seemed a far sounder plan to leave them in Azra to aid the Jackal in any way they could. As shows of goodwill went, it was much appreciated by Faisal, who immediately set them to work alongside his own soldiers, training and drilling the civilians and former slaves in preparation for battle. A skeleton crew had remained on the *Banshee*, transporting the remaining therians to Two Rivers.

A prospecting town, Two Rivers was the last place a ship the size of the *Banshee* could navigate up to on the Silver River. Being on the border of the Desert and Mountain Realms, it was a wild old town with little law or order, home to gem diggers, bounty hunters, the crazed, and the criminal. Drew hoped they could pass through the town quickly. A ramshackle avenue ran through its center, low buildings lining the pitted road on either side. Trading posts and taverns made up the majority of businesses, jostling for the attention of passersby. The group kept their heads down as they followed Krieg, aware they were being watched, the townsfolk making no attempt to hide their interest in the travelers. Krieg led them to the end of the street, marching up to a squat stable block with paddocks attached.

The wind stirred up dust devils, sand whipping through the air as they hurried toward the horse trader's establishment.

As they approached, Drew pulled up short, placing his hand on Krieg's shoulder.

"You're sure he can be trusted?"

"As trusted as anyone can be in a fleapit like Two Rivers. Why?"

Drew shivered as he tried to shake off the uneasy feeling. "No matter, Krieg. Lead on," he said as the Rhino entered the building.

The stable was split down the middle by a filthy path, with camels on one side and horses on the other. A bearded man in brown robes emerged down the passage, dragging a sack of grain behind him. He looked up, recognizing Krieg immediately.

"These your friends, then?" he said in a thick Omiri accent.

The man straightened, looking past Krieg toward his companions. His eyes seemed a little too large for his features, as if his face had frozen mid-choke and refused to return to normal.

"The horses," said Krieg, wasting no time on banter. The Rhino unstrung a pouch from his hip, jingling it in his hand. "I have the money, as agreed."

"Is that everything?" said the big-eyed man, watching Krieg weigh the bag of coins. Krieg tossed it, the trader catching it midair.

"Count them, if you distrust me," said the Rhino, his voice serious.

Drew took a moment to look around the interior of the building while the horse trader rooted through the money pouch. It was the largest structure they'd seen in Two Rivers, with a hayloft above that ran around the entire stable. Bright though it was outdoors, it was dark in here, a couple of lanterns keeping the filthy walkway illuminated, but all else shrouded in darkness. Taboo and Griffyn held a quiet conversation at Drew's back while the Behemoth stood to the rear, staring back at the doors.

Drew still felt on edge. Although the atmosphere in the stable was heavy with the smell of captive animals, a gut feeling told him that something wasn't right. Not wanting to alarm the horse trader, Drew let a little of the Wolf in. His heightened sense of smell revealed something else beyond the stench of animal feces. He smelled alcohol, sweat, and steel. His ears pricked as he concentrated, listening beyond the snorting horses and spitting camels. Floorboards creaked in the loft above.

"Do you work here alone?" asked Drew.

The man looked up, lips smacking nervously as Drew's eyes remained fixed upon the shadowy first floor overhead.

"Indeed. Why do you ask?"

"It sounds like you've rats in your hayloft, in that case. Big ones, judging by the noise they're making up there."

Instantly Krieg had his spiked mace out, while Taboo raised her spear. Drew kept his eyes focused upon the hayloft, catching sight of movements now as would-be assassins darted through the darkness.

"What treachery is this?" spat Krieg. "I make a deal with you in good faith."

The trader's eyes widened further as Krieg stepped toward him, twirling the mace in his grasp, the spikes spinning menacingly.

"They . . . they saw you come!" stammered the man, his eyes looking up. "This isn't my . . ."

The trader collapsed to the floor, unable to complete his sentence, the feathered flight of an arrow sticking out of his throat as the coins showered down on top of him. An arrow hit Griffyn's back, while Krieg crashed through the partition fence, an arrow protruding from his chest. Instantly the therians dived into the pens, camels and horses panicking at the intruders in their enclosures. Taboo had found a ladder on the rear wall, and leaped halfway up in one bound. She thrust her spear up through the hatch, a foe screaming as it struck home.

Feet hammered along the walkway above, the ambushers scrambling to find better positions from which to strike. Drew stayed close to Griffyn, supporting the winded Hawklord as they dashed for cover. A horse whinnied beside him as an arrow punched into its flank with a wet snap. It kicked out, striking another animal at its side, the pen transformed into a deadly arena.

"They could have avoided this," said Drew, the Hawklord grimacing as they ducked behind a post.

"It appears they'd rather fight," said Griffyn. "There must be quite a reward on your head!"

Drew pulled the arrow from the Hawklord's back, the tip embedded in the leather strapping of his breastplate. Griffyn grunted as the pair stared in shock at the shining silver arrowhead.

"These are no regular bandits, young Wolf."

"Stay here!"

A mountain of crates lined the rear of the horse enclosure, providing Drew with a means to reach the first floor. He changed as he bounded, feet elongating into gray, clawed paws as he raced up the stacked boxes toward the hayloft. He burst onto the dark landing, and his longsword arced through the air, striking a drawn bow from an assassin's hands. The man in black reached for a scimitar on his hip but was already flying through the air, the Werewolf catching him in the chest with a kick. The attacker disappeared over the hayloft rail, vanishing into the enclosure below.

Another black-kashed warrior lunged at Drew, his silver scimitar tearing a cut down the Werewolf's back. Drew roared, bringing his trident dagger around to disarm the man on his following blow. The scimitar flew from the man's grasp as Drew's longsword struck home.

On the opposite hayloft Drew caught a glimpse of Taboo,

the Weretiger cornered, jabbing with her spear and slashing with her claws. She was outnumbered three to one, and if her enemies had silver weapons, she was in terrible danger.

Glancing below Drew spied the Behemoth, dragging the wounded Krieg to safety through a crowd of alarmed camels. By Brenn's grace the silver arrow embedded in the Rhino's chest hadn't proved fatal. The Weremammoth looked up, noticing Drew as he pointed across to the other hayloft with his sword.

"Take its legs!" shouted Drew, and the giant instantly understood.

Leaning Krieg against the wall, the Weremammoth swung his enormous stone mallet around his head. The therianthrope transformed with each rotation, the weapon's speed increasing with the Mammoth's burgeoning muscles. Finally he brought it around into one of the supporting posts that held the hayloft up. The mallet's stone head shattered the pillar in two, sending the ceiling crashing down around him. Fearless, the Behemoth remained where he was, raising a huge arm over his head as beams and floorboards crashed down on top of him, along with the trio of assassins.

As the dust settled, Drew looked across the stable, searching the debris below for Taboo. There was no sign of her, only the broken-limbed corpses of the black-kashed warriors.

"Up here, Wolf!"

To his relief, Drew saw the Weretiger suspended from a

rafter across the way. She hauled herself over the beam, holding a hand to her bloodied side. Drew leaned on the balcony, chest heaving as he returned to human form. Below, Griffyn staggered over to Krieg, the two Werelords comparing their near-fatal wounds. The Behemoth, cloaked in sawdust and splintered wood, waved a mighty hand up toward Drew, his voice rumbling through the devastation.

"We need to go."

By the time the people of Two Rivers had investigated why camels were roaming their miserable, dust-ridden streets, the five therians had departed. Taking the sturdiest mounts they could find, the riders took a trail through the foothills that followed the southern branch of the river, leaving the barter town behind them.

The terrain was barren and rocky, vegetation sparse, the environment utterly inhospitable. Here and there the odd gnarled tree had managed to survive against the odds, its roots gripping the rocky slopes for dear life as the cold winds battered it.

The Behemoth brought up the rear of the group, riding the stockiest workhorse any of the therians had ever seen. Taller and uglier than the mountain ponies the others were riding, it had a broad back, thick legs, and a desire to carry heavy burdens. None came heavier than the Behemoth, or less experienced at riding for that matter. After suffering the horse's attempts to buck him off, the Weremammoth had struck an uneasy alliance with his mount, riding in stalemated silence. His companions bit their lips, resisting the temptation to tease him over his newfound friend.

Griffyn led the way, with Drew at his back. Taboo followed the Wolf, with Krieg close behind. Taboo had declined her companions' attention, insisting the cut along her side was a mere graze. *I've never encountered a tougher woman*, thought Drew, ever amazed by both her strength and her stubbornness. The Rhino had taken care of his chest wound while the others readied their horses, Griffyn staunching the bleeding with dressings from his pack. In obvious discomfort, Krieg had stifled his complaints on the uncomfortable ride.

"So who were they?" said Drew, his pony shadowing Griffyn's in front.

"I doubt we'll ever know," replied the Hawklord. "They carried no clues as to who was behind the ambush."

"They could have been anyone's agents: Dog, Cat, Hyena . . . Crow!"

"Their choice of weapons is most alarming: silver. The Scorians used it to keep therian gladiators in check, but in Lyssia? It was outlawed across the entire continent, yet these assassins used it by blade and bow. Such a deadly metal doesn't come cheap; our enemies have wealthy benefactors."

Drew thought back to the scars on his back from his time

as a prisoner in Highcliff, whipped by the silver-studded whip of Captain Brutus.

"The Catlords reintroduced silver to Lyssia."

"Another connection then, tying your enemies together, Wolf," said Griffyn, kicking his pony's flanks to encourage her on.

The night was beginning to close in as Drew looked back. The lights of Two Rivers shone below; would anybody follow them, seeking retribution for the death of the men in the stable? Farther back, across the desert, the horizon glowed: Azra. *Are those the fires of the enemy camps? Or does the city burn?* Drew looked ahead once more at the trail disappearing into the distance, following the stream that tumbled down the rocky slope toward them. He stared up at the mountains, their snow-capped summits glowing dully in the twilight.

"I just hope we stay well ahead of our enemies," said Drew, urging his mount after Griffyn's.

"We must remain alert, Drew," said Griffyn, his eyes scanning the mountains in front of them. *His mountains.* "I fear we've been watched since we first set foot on to Omir's sands, young Wolf. The enemy follows our every move."

# 2
# THE WRONG ANSWERS

**THE SOLDIERS OF** the Lionguard were in a relaxed mood, gathered around their fires, playing cards and tossing bones. Sorin led the festivities, winning more than his fair share of coin from his men. The Bastian contingent of Lord Frost's force remained removed from their comrades, polishing armor and sharpening weapons. The albino Catlord had retired to his tent, dining on the best food that his warriors had confiscated from the people of the Longridings. With the camp preoccupied, it was relatively easy for Trent to enter the prisoner's tent unnoticed. Letting the door flap swing shut behind him, he looked down upon the captive Werelord.

"Tell me," Trent said, standing over the bound prisoner. "What was he like?"

Baron Ewan looked up slowly. The Ramlord's face was a rich palette of bruises, a mask of purple, black, and blue. Sorin had used the flat of his silver-blessed longsword on the Lord of Haggard, beating the old man about head and body, dealing him injuries that could only heal over a mortal span of time. Nobody had tended the old man's wounds.

"Who?" asked Ewan, through broken lips. His left eye was closed shut, while his bloodshot right was fixed squarely on Trent.

"The Wolf—Drew," replied Trent, trying to sound cold and impassive.

The old Werelord studied him. "Why so interested?"

"What kind of man is he? We hear so many things. How did you find him?"

Ewan smiled, his swollen lips tearing anew through the bruising. He winced, arching his back, catching his breath.

"What's the matter?" asked Trent, concern creeping into his voice.

"Chest," said the Ram.

Lord Frost had ensured that his interrogators had worked Ewan over thoroughly. The Catlord had even participated himself, the Ram's greatest screams caused by the albino. Trent hadn't the stomach to witness the torturing of prisoners. He could kill a man, at the command of his superior officers, but torture wasn't why he'd signed up to the Lionguard.

Trent could see the rolls of tightly bound ropes that wound

around the beaten old man, securing him to the stake in the ground. Therianthrope or not, the bonds were excessive. Sorin and his cronies had battered the baron to within an inch of his life, his hands broken by the cruel captain's zealous work. Trent crouched and loosened the ropes, letting a clutch of them fall to the ground.

Ewan relaxed a little, leaning back and straightening his bent legs, bringing his bound hands up before him to massage his chest. Trent filled a mug of water for the Werelord, holding it to his lips as Ewan drank thirstily.

"My boy," he whispered. "Thank you."

"Why?"

"That was the greatest drink I've ever savored in my long and glorious life. A barrel of the Redwine's finest couldn't compete with it."

Trent smiled, taking the cup away. "The Wolf," he said again. "What of him?"

"He came to me in Haggard, a prisoner of the Goatlord, Kesslar. He was thrown into the cells beneath my keep alongside my people and me. We got to know one another. He had no reason to lie when he recounted all he'd been through. The death of his parents at the hands of the Lion and the Rats—"

"*He* killed his mother!" interrupted Trent.

Ewan sighed. "Did you want to hear my story?"

Trent grimaced, before nodding.

The Ramlord continued. "Drew was instrumental in freeing my people, helping us rise against our enemies. He then rode south, and I accompanied him as he sought to save Lady Gretchen from the claws of Prince Lucas."

Ewan paused, expecting the young Redcloak to cut in once more. When he didn't, he carried on.

"Lucas and Vanmorten took Cape Gala from the Horselords, stole the sovereign state from the people of the Longridings— *my people*—with the help of the Bastian invaders. While the majority sailed north to attack Highcliff, a small force was left behind in Cape Gala. Once again, Drew came to the aid of his friends, trying to rescue them from Vankaskan."

Ewan hung his head.

"I betrayed him. I handed him over to the monster Vankaskan. I recognize that villain, Sorin, as one of his. My boy, they turned High Stable into a monstrous circus, slaying Werelords and humans alike. Only their torment didn't end there. The Rat did such vile things . . ."

"What more of the Wolf?"

"He was gone," whispered Ewan. "Disappeared. At one moment, he was on the balcony; the next, gone. Vanished on the wind. I don't know what happened to him."

Trent couldn't look at the baron. He didn't want to believe him, but much of what the old therian said made sense. Still, he'd seen what had happened back on the family farm. *Drew had turned on Ma.*

"But Drew," said Trent, "he's a monster! He's a Werewolf, for Brenn's sake!"

"There are monsters across Lyssia—human and therian alike. Your brother's a good man."

"He killed our moth—" Trent stopped, biting his lip. "How did you know he was my brother?"

"You didn't say as much, but I'd heard mention of a Sergeant Ferran." Ewan sighed. "They might have beaten me, but not entirely senseless. My hearing works well enough. You and Drew are brothers?"

"*Were* brothers," corrected Trent. "Until he killed my ma."

Ewan shook his head sadly. "You believe everything you're told, lad?"

"I saw her corpse with my own *eyes*, old man! Don't think to lecture me on the Wolf's true nature. Nobody knows Drew better than I!"

"I fear you believe what you want to, Master Ferran. Could it be you're mistaken?"

"You know nothing. He's pulled the wool over your eyes, Sheeplord, clearly. My brother could charm his way into any fool's heart."

"There you go," said the old man. "*My brother*—the bond is strong between you. Search your heart, boy. You know I'm telling you the truth . . ."

Ewan was cut short as Trent stepped forward, his fist

raised above his head, ready to strike. The Ramlord's bruised eyes went as wide as the swelling would allow, the aged therian shrinking back in anticipation of the blow. Trent wavered, snarling. He stepped behind him swiftly, binding Ewan's ropes once again. Trent knew rope mastery as well as anyone, having learned under his father back on the Ferran farm. He gave them a sharp tug, the Ramlord's battered arms creaking as he was secured once more.

Trent got up. "Keep your poisonous words to yourself in future, you old fool," he said.

"It was you who came to me, seeking answers," said Ewan as Trent strode out of the tent—straight into Lord Frost, chewing on a haunch of bloody meat. Trent jumped with shock.

"It's lamb," said the Catlord, offering it to Trent. The youth looked at the meat: any rarer and it would still be bleating.

"No thank you, my lord," replied Trent, regaining his composure. "My appetite is lacking."

"Speaking with the prisoner, eh? Did he offer us anything new?"

"No, my lord."

"It's Frost, remember. You and I are friends now, Trent, just remember that." The Catlord took another bite of the lamb and looked at the tent door. "You've just reminded me. Our prisoner should never be left unguarded. I'll speak with Sorin; arrange for a guard to be posted on the Ram at all times. Good man, Trent. Go get yourself some rest."

Trent bowed nervously, his cheeks flushed with color at having been discovered speaking with the prisoner. He strode away in the direction of the corral; his horse, Storm, needed bedding down for the night. He glanced back as he walked away. Frost watched him go, tearing another mouthful of meat from the joint of lamb. Trent turned his gaze to the ground, feeling the Catlord's eyes burning holes in his back.

*Fool, Trent,* he berated himself. *Giving Frost cause to distrust me. That's the last time I seek answers.*

# 3

# TOR RAPTOR'S MERCY

**IF THE FOOTHILLS** of Omir appeared treacherous, nothing had prepared the travelers for the perilous trail through the Barebones. Another old mountain road had led to Windfell, but the group had passed it by. The city of the Hawklords wasn't their destination; it was their tomb they sought, high up in the sky. Only Griffyn seemed at ease, the old Hawk returning home for the first time in fifteen years, while his fellow therians gripped the reins of their mounts with white knuckles. At the rear, the Behemoth was slumped in the saddle of his stocky horse. Krieg and Taboo were in front of him, the ravine drop to their right bringing on terrible bouts of vertigo. Farther ahead, Drew followed Griffyn closely, his reins wrapped around his trident dagger.

Occasionally Drew glanced into the chasm, a morbid fascination with the deadly drop luring him like a moth to candlelight. With each of his horse's steps, the hooves dislodged stones that skittered away from the path, bouncing off the sloping rock and disappearing into space. Drew brought his eyes back to Griffyn ahead, smacking his lips as he breathed the cold, thin air. The wind changed direction with alarming frequency, sudden updrafts replaced by blustering downdrafts that threatened to knock the riders from their saddles. As they climbed Tor Raptor the Mighty, giant of the Barebones, wispy clouds drifted all about her and the surrounding peaks.

Griffyn twisted around, smiling at the pale-faced Wolflord. "Breathtaking?"

"Literally," replied Drew as another gust of wind hit him. "I'm struggling to breathe, here. How much farther?"

"Some way yet, cub. See that?"

Griffyn pointed ahead to where the cliffs of Tor Raptor appeared to collide with those of the neighboring mountain, as if the two giant landmasses had collapsed against each other. The path was all but invisible, with a thin sliver of vertical light the only indication that the trail emerged on the other side. The drop between the two vanished into gloomy blackness, swallowed up by the enormous ravine's dark depths.

"I see it," shouted Drew over the wind. "But I don't like it!"

"The Falling Road: it's not to be liked, it's to be endured!

We travel to the tomb of my fathers. Look about you, Wolf—see the burial sites and barrows of my kinsmen."

Drew looked up, scouring the cliffs for sign of human or therian touch. There they were, dotting the mountain hundreds of feet above. At first glance they appeared to be rock formations, but closer inspection revealed them to be cairns, tall spires of rocks that the Hawklords had placed to mark out the chambers of the dead.

"The tombs of the Hawklords, Baron Griffyn? Left unguarded on a mountainside?"

"You think we fear graverobbers in the Barebones? If the mountain doesn't kill you, there are other things on Tor Raptor that protect our tombs. My forefathers do not readily relinquish their worldly goods, even in death . . ."

Griffyn let this last statement hang in the air, the sinister implication not lost on Drew. *Even in death?*

The Hawklord swung in his saddle, leaning precariously out to see around Drew. The Wolflord blanched when he imagined the old man tumbling from his seat.

"Our friends look unwell," chortled Griffyn. "It appears the Barebones aren't for the fainthearted!"

"You might feel like them if you weren't a Hawklord!" said Drew in their defense.

"You forget, young Wolf," said Griffyn, gesturing at his shoulders with a hooked thumb. "My wings were taken from me many years ago. If I fall here, I'd be as dead as anyone else.

Lean forward in your saddle, respect the path, and pray the mountain remains merciful."

The Hawklord cast his hand heavenward, the snowcapped giant of the Barebones towering above them.

"You are in Tor Raptor's talons now!"

As fierce as the winds had been on the cliff path an hour before, nothing had prepared the therians for the gale that greeted them on the Falling Road. Dismounting when they approached the monstrous chasm, Drew had marveled at the sheer cliffs on either side as they reached across to one another. He whispered a brief, heartfelt prayer to Brenn as he followed Griffyn into the darkness, leading his pony along behind.

The Hawklord had warned them to keep their voices low when traversing the Falling Road. Avalanches were commonplace, where massive boulders had caught between the cliffs, weighed down with packed ice, waiting for the chance to break free and plummet toward the road. As if the threat from above and raging winds weren't enough, the path was nothing more than scree. The therians' feet and ponies' hooves scrambled for purchase as they passed over the ice and gravel. Frequently, Drew found himself casting his trident dagger out, grateful for the barbed weapon as he snatched hold of the cliff wall to stop himself from falling.

While Griffyn had little trouble on the path, the same could not be said for Taboo, Krieg, and the Behemoth. The Weremammoth had taken some persuading to traverse the treacherous road, and his companions shared his concerns. These people were from jungles and savannas, not freezing mountains. This world was alien to them. With words of encouragement from Drew and Griffyn they'd continued on, none wishing to break their oath to the young Wolflord. Their loyalty and courage filled Drew's heart with hope.

Ahead, Griffyn waited, cloak wrapped around his body as defense against the freezing wind. His pony hunkered against the cliff face, sheltering as best it could, as Drew slowly and carefully approached. His voice was controlled when he spoke over the howling gale.

"We need to pick up our pace, Drew. The night closes in. If we can get beyond the Falling Road, we may find somewhere to pitch camp before tackling the summit tomorrow."

Drew looked back, spying Taboo appearing around the cliff path a hundred yards or so behind. The others were behind the Weretiger, somewhere—hopefully making steady and safe progress.

He turned back to Griffyn, squinting as sleet peppered his face.

"How far to the end?"

"We're halfway through," replied the Hawklord.

*Only halfway*, thought Drew. *And we've been on this murderous road for over an hour.*

His nerves were shot, his body on the brink of exhaustion, adrenaline the only thing keeping him moving. Drew noticed that Griffyn was looking up. He followed the Hawk's gaze. The black wall of rock rose at a skewed angle overhead, meeting the opposing cliff high above, boulders the size of houses buttressed and braced against one another. It looked like a monstrous cathedral ceiling, hewn crudely from the mountains. With such an awe-inspiring, religious feel to the place, it was no wonder the Hawklords had chosen Tor Raptor as the site of their oldest tombs.

As he watched, a few blocks of ice came away from the natural ceiling, falling from where they'd been packed in place. They were closely followed by a large slab. Drew leaned back against the cliff wall as the frozen debris rushed by. The sound of them crashing on to the ravine bottom bounced back up toward them from hundreds of feet below. Drew held his breath as the reverberations disturbed the ice overhead, cracking noises from the strained ceiling audible over the wind, but was relieved to see nothing else break free.

The Hawklord beckoned him frantically now, urging him to follow swiftly. Drew's booted feet scrambled along the smooth path, the rock pitched at an angle ensuring that one false step would send the Wolflord slipping to his doom.

Then a sudden, terrible shriek echoed overhead, as if the mountain itself cried out in agony. After a couple of awful, ponderous heartbeats, the scream was joined by the sound of the monstrous ceiling cracking. The noise shook Drew's body as he pressed himself once more against the cliff, the rock at his back trembling and shuddering as stone, ice, and snow high above them buckled and began to fall. He looked up in horror as the crashing cascade of black and white death hurtled toward him. Drew glanced back along the ledge as Taboo was suddenly engulfed by the icy downpour, disappearing from view in the blink of an eye. Rocks and snow rained down around him. A fist-sized block of ice hit his shoulder, narrowly missing his skull but still sending him staggering to his knees, while a great lance of granite fell like a guillotine, shearing his pony in two and dragging it over the edge. Boulders hit the path, smashing and tearing the narrow trail away all around him. Drew's scream was cut short as the deafening roar of the avalanche choked the breath from his battered body.

# 4

# THE SCENE OF THE CRIME

AS THE *MYRMIDON* eased into Highcliff, six of Tuskun's finest Ugri warriors stood to attention on the icy foredeck. Before them, Hector took in the city, the night casting a brooding menace over the all-too-quiet port. This city had been his home for a time, a metropolis that brimmed with life from all over Lyssia. Before the curfew of the Wolf's Council, Highcliff had been a city that rarely slept. Now, with the Lord Protector and his friends gone, as well as the majority of the city's inhabitants, Highcliff was a ghost town. Hector placed his black-gloved hands on the frosted rail, manacles jangling between them, as he surveyed the results of the Lion's vengeance.

The pier that the *Myrmidon* pulled alongside had once sported tall lanterns that lit the way for sailors and fishermen alike. Now it was dotted with gibbets that contained the dead and dying. Hector stared at the rusting cages, crows and gulls squawking as they bickered over the morsels within. The unmistakable Graycloaks of the Wolfguard hung around the throats of corpses and captives alike. The moans of the unfortunate souls could be heard by the crew of the warship, but the Tuskuns ignored them. The Ugri were the toughest, most fearsome men the frozen north had spawned, each over six feet tall and seemingly as broad. During the journey, Hector couldn't so much as scratch his nose without one of them glowering or growling. They stood to one side as the heavy barefoot steps of their queen approached.

"Is it as you remember, Piglord?" Slotha, the Walrus of Tuskun, laughed. While many of Lyssia's Werelords chose to keep their human appearance on most occasions, saving their shape-shifting for when the time arose, Slotha held no such discipline. Her hold over the Ugri warriors was to the result of her many victories in battle combined with her intimidating presence. Easily the tallest woman Hector had ever met, and as broad as any barbarian who worked in her service, she revelled in her frightening therian image. While not completely transformed, there were enough elements of the Werewalrus on show to strike fear into the hearts of most men. Her large hands were still webbed, her fingernails sharp claws, and her wide feet slapped the deck with each step. Her muscular arms held the dark, mottled texture of the beast, while her head kept the key features of the walrus, dark whiskers sprouted from around her lips while a suggestion of her tusks remained in evidence, protruding from her upper jaw.

"It's quite . . . changed," managed Hector, trying not to look at the monstrous woman. He'd endured days at sea in her company, and every additional moment in her presence made him fearful she'd back down on their agreement. He'd seen first-hand how vicious she could be with her prisoners. Here was a therian who enjoyed the kill.

"Changed how?"

Hector looked back at the swinging bodies in their cages. "They've done away with the sea lanterns, I notice," he said calmly.

Slotha snorted at Hector's dark humor.

The *Myrmidon* secured, the crew extended their gangway across to the stone pier. Two dozen torch-carrying Lionguard awaited them, alongside half as many Bastian warriors. More cavalry gathered on the docks, along with an empty carriage awaiting the visitors. The Ugri grunted, unimpressed by the southerners' show of strength.

"Take him ashore," grunted Slotha, shifting her great mass to one side. "We've an audience with Prince Lucas."

As the procession climbed through the steep city toward Highcliff Keep, Hector's mind cast back to the frantic escape he'd endured, chased through the streets by Omiri warriors. That seemed like another life now, the youth who'd fled bearing little resemblance to the man who returned.

Looking out of the carriage he noticed the city was far from deserted. Lights were on in many homes and taverns, showing that Highcliff was still inhabited, but the streets were devoid of life, the curfew he'd helped set in place still standing. A veil of fear had settled over the city.

An Ugri warrior sat on either side of him, while opposite the huge frame of Slotha filled the entire padded bench.

"What's the matter, Piglord? Upset with what they've done to your city?" asked the Walrus.

"This isn't my city, Your Majesty. My home is far to the east of here—Redmire, capital of the Dalelands. But I'd be lying if I said Highcliff meant nothing to me. This is the city where I learned who my friends were."

His voice was clipped, the words catching in his throat.

Slotha smiled. "You've got a world full of regrets, boy."

"Only one," answered Hector, looking at his manacled hands. "I never truly said good-bye to him."

Since Friggia, Hector had tried not to think about Drew, but it was impossible. The Stags, Shark, and Bear might have betrayed him, but Drew had been long gone by then. He'd heard the rumors about Drew falling to his death in Cape Gala. The Wolf had been the only true friend he'd ever known. But his hatred for the things done in the Wolf's name, in his absence, remained undiminished. Each of the other Werelords had betrayed him over time and each had paid the price. First the selfish Earl Mikkel had fallen, the Doglords of Omir having slain the Staglord as he'd fled to his home in the Barebones. Then Duke Bergan, the Lord Protector who had humiliated him, stripping him of power within the Wolf's Council, had been slain in Highcliff. Count Vega had held Hector to ransom, dangling the grisly truth of Vincent's death over his head like a guillotine. The Sharklord's reputation had been built upon dishonesty— Hector had done the right thing, getting rid of the count before the Shark could bite.

The last of the quartet had disappointed him most of all, Duke Manfred having left him for dead in Friggia. With dear Drew no doubt dead and those he'd once considered friends having turned on him, what choice did Hector have but to switch his allegiance to the Catlords? They wouldn't punish him for the power he commanded. They would embrace his magistry. And Manfred? He would pay for his betrayal.

*That's it, dear brother,* whispered the Vincent-vile. *A reckoning comes . . .*

"Sounds like the Piglord was in love," teased the Walrus.

Hector directed the conversation back at her. "I know very little about love, Your Majesty," he said. "A lifetime with my head buried in books has allowed me few opportunities to enjoy the company of the fairer sex."

"A bookworm, like your father was, then?"

"You knew him?"

"Lord Huth visited Tuskun when I was in my youth. For a while my father petitioned his to arrange marriage."

Hector coughed suddenly, shocked at the news that his father might have been wed to such a fearsome warrior queen as Slotha. Never could a match be more misplaced. The Werewalrus glowered at her captive Boarlord.

"And what stopped the marriage from taking place?"

"Your father's constitution, apparently," she said, strangely wistful for the briefest moment at what might have been. "The cold northern air played havoc with his breathing."

"That sounds about right," said Hector, slowly regaining his composure.

Slotha sneered at him. "Weakling Boars: it was the best thing that could have happened. Any child of that union would have polluted the bloodlines of the Walruses. My father did right by me. He spared me the embarrassment of a marriage with your kind, and saved me for something greater."

"You mean to impress Prince Lucas?"

"He's a Prince," she said stiffly. "I'm the queen in the North.

Who knows what . . . *alliance* we can agree upon. This is my first visit to Highcliff. I intend to make it memorable."

"I'm sure it will be," said Hector, dabbing at his lips as he reclined in his seat. "The Court of Highcliff won't forget you in a hurry."

# 5

# THE SCREAMING PEAK

**THE TRIDENT DAGGER** remained buried within the ice, the battered old blade the only thing stopping Drew from sliding off the slope into thin air. The muscles in his left arm strained, his elbow locked as he struggled to remain motionless. The toes of his torn boots were braced against the ice as if they might somehow stop his body from falling should the trident dagger snap. The blade was bowing, the metal bending back on itself as it threatened to break. Drew looked up, grimacing, as the old Hawklord skidded down the incline toward him, somehow keeping his balance.

The avalanche on the Falling Road had been no accident. A loud shriek had set the rock- and icefall in motion, timed to perfection. While Drew and Griffyn had avoided the deadly deluge, what fate had befallen their companions wasn't known. The path behind them had been cut off, choked in a cloud of dusty ice and broken stone. Drew's stomach lurched when he thought about Krieg, Taboo, and the Behemoth. The trio had followed him to Lyssia to fight by his side: that the mountain might have killed them broke his heart. The two survivors had continued on alone, minus their ponies and provisions, which had been carried away by the barrage of boulders. Drew and Griffyn were left to pray that their friends had survived and could find their way back to the lower path to Windfell.

"Your hand!" called Griffyn, reaching his out, palm open.

Drew threw his body forward, the hands of the two Werelords clamping over one another's wrists. The baron deftly hauled Drew back up the slope and onto the sliver of a path they'd been following. The young Wolflord collapsed against the cliff, body trembling as he struggled to regain his composure, while the Hawklord seemed perversely relaxed.

"I can't go on!" Drew cried, gasping for breath, the air so thin his lungs ached.

Griffyn looked down, fine hair whipping across his face as he smiled. "It appears youth counts for nothing: experience everything. Remember, these are *my* mountains, Drew. Come, we mustn't delay. We approach the summit, my friend. We must try and reach the Screaming Peak before nightfall and find shelter by the tomb. The last place one wants to be stranded at night is on Tor Raptor's back!"

385

Drew rubbed the strained muscles of his arms. "Any sign of our enemy?"

"None," said Griffyn.

"Perhaps we've lost them. You did say this path's location was guarded by the Hawklords, didn't you?"

"Yes, but that's not to say our enemy hasn't found another route to the summit."

"Are you sure the Hawklords will hear your call?"

Griffyn stroked his grizzled jaw, glancing at the sky around them. Below, the clouds rolled like a smoky sea, the jagged peaks of Tor Raptor's sisters visible like islands through the fading light.

"They'll hear it, Drew, no matter where they are. How many still live, however, is another question entirely."

Griffyn helped Drew to his feet, the young Wolf craning his neck to look toward the summit. Drew shook his head, trying not to linger on the dizzying sight.

"If I don't die of a broken neck, the vertigo might give me a heart attack," he murmured. "How in Brenn's name did you get your dead to the summit?"

"How do you think?" The Hawklord smiled grimly. "We flew them."

The dark settled over the Barebones as the two therians struggled on, their hopes of beating the sunset long gone. Drew caught sight of Griffyn disappearing over a ledge above. There were hand and footholds aplenty here, but they were hidden by the ice and the night. Drew waited a moment for the old man to reappear, to offer a hand to help him climb up, but Griffyn didn't appear.

Cursing, Drew hacked at the ice, forcing the trident dagger in once again, crying in pain as the cold metal rubbed against the stump of his wrist. He thought he'd got used to the feel of the basket handle against the sheared bones, but the freezing weather that crowned Tor Raptor caused a new, unknown discomfort. He reached up with his right hand, black and blue fingertips desperately trying to catch the ledge.

He could feel his will slipping, along with his grip on the mountainside. His eyes drifted down into the empty sky. Death would be swift if he fell. There were worse ways to die.

*I can't stop now, I have to fight on. For my friends and my people! For Taboo and Krieg and the Behemoth!*

Drew brought his head up and stared at the moon.

Her light might have been cold, but the warmth he felt inside was unmistakable, and he let it flood through him. Not for the first time on the mountain, Drew let the Wolf in, just enough to feel his fingers tearing into claws, a lupine hand taking a firm grip on the overhang. With a growl he hauled himself high, ripping the dagger free as he kicked back against the rocks below.

His torso landed on the ledge, the rock digging deep into

the fur that covered his stomach. Drew grunted as he scrambled and snatched at the darkness ahead, legs kicking out into space, threatening to send him toppling back into nothingness. The bent and battered trident dagger bounced off the ledge ahead, causing the sheet ice to shatter in great shards. Gradually, he inched forward, his right leg finally finding its way above the overhang, his knee finding purchase as he rolled his exhausted body on to the ledge.

"You took your time, Wolf."

Drew turned his head, looking toward the voice as the wind tugged at his legs where they dangled across the overhang. The ledge opened onto a rocky platform perhaps twenty feet across, receding toward a sheer wall of rock that rose the remaining fifty feet to Tor Raptor's peak. A jagged, triangular crack was visible at the wall's base, rising ten feet up to a point, a dark doorway that disappeared into the mountain. A figure stepped out of the shadows into the moonlight, Baron Griffyn held before him, with his head pulled back and a familiar short, silver knife pressed to his throat.

"We've been here before, Rook," said Drew to the Crowlord, rolling over on to his stomach, inching away from the overhang. "Only last time it was a woman you threatened as opposed to an old man. Let the Hawk go. Face me like a therian."

"Hawk? This cripple? If he was a Hawk, he'd have wings! Let's see how he flies, eh?" To emphasize the point, Rook skirted Drew and marched toward the edge, instantly causing the young Wolflord to raise his hand.

"No, wait!"

"What do you want?" gasped Griffyn, his feet struggling in vain to halt the Werecrow's progress toward the drop.

Drew looked about frantically, his hand catching hold of a long dagger of broken ice.

"Riven, Stormdale, Windfell: everything! I want the Bare-bones, Griffyn!" shouted Rook, propelling the old man forward.

The dagger of ice hit Rook square in the face; Drew's aim was faultless. The Crow cawed furiously, instantly releasing Griffyn, who hit the ice and slid toward the edge. Rook collapsed, screaming obscenities as his hands went to his shattered face. Drew dived for the Hawklord's arms, catching Griffyn's hand as he disappeared from the ledge. The old man hung there for a moment, the weight of his body drawing the young Wolflord ever closer to the edge. Behind, Drew heard the screams of the Crowlord as Rook began to change.

"Release me, Drew, before we both fall!" shouted Griffyn, eyes wide with fearful sincerity.

"I won't let you go," gasped Drew, tears streaming as he struggled to keep hold of the Hawklord, his body still sliding closer to oblivion.

"Beware the dead, Drew. Open the windows; call my people

to you and take what's yours by rights. I brought it here," whispered Griffyn. "I kept it safe."

Drew growled, calling upon whatever lycanthropic strength remained inside, but it was no use. The Werewolf's clawed hand was gripping at the Hawklord's tearing sleeve. Griffyn glanced past Drew's shoulder, his face a mask of alarm as his eyes settled on the enemy at Drew's back.

"Brenn protect you, Drew!" he cried as he tore his arm loose and fell into the night, swallowed by the darkness below.

Drew rolled quickly, almost following Griffyn over the edge as the ice shattered beside him, a longsword crashing into the ledge. He looked up to see clouds pass over the moon above.

With a blood-curdling screech the Werecrow threw his arms out, wings erupting from his back in an explosion of feathers. The lord of Riven had fully changed—Rook's features had utterly gone, replaced by the monstrous head, sharp black beak open and tongue rattling within. His arm came back down, the sword smashing into the ground where Drew had lain moments earlier. The Wolflord scrambled across the ice, making toward the rock face as the Werecrow followed. Rook was in no danger of slipping, his feet having shifted into long, dark talons that gripped the ice securely.

"Where do you run to?" squawked Rook, his huge chest rippling, muscles and feathers ruffling as he stalked closer. "Wolves don't belong in the sky!"

Drew reached the rock wall. Every muscle burned, every

ounce of energy had been spent climbing Tor Raptor. He tried to call on the Wolf, but there was little left. Tugging his longsword from its battered scabbard, he glanced at the dark doorway. A series of runes were carved around the triangular entrance.

*Beware the dead, Drew . . .*

The Werecrow leaped suddenly, closing on the Wolf with a beat of his enormous wings. Rook's sword came down, Drew raising his own in defense, the metal ringing in his grasp with the full weight of the Crowlord behind it. With the steel shattering, the weapon flew from his grip, the blade broken in two. Drew didn't wait, crawling quickly through the dark arch. As he passed over the threshold, the runes began to glow with a pale silver light, their ghostly illumination bouncing off the rock walls within.

Behind, Drew heard the Werecrow laugh, a wheezing screech of glee, as it followed him into the tomb. He scrambled on, staggering briefly to his feet before tumbling down a flight of stone steps. Drew rolled to a halt in the center of a great round chamber, the walls of which were inscribed with silver sigils like those that glowed outside. A large window was cut through the rock overhead, open to the night sky beyond. The runes seemed to beat with a rising rhythm, the thrum of which reverberated through Drew's ears, causing his teeth to chatter and his bones to ache. It was like a slow, drawn-out heartbeat, as if Tor Raptor's summit were alive, awakening with his arrival. The noise gripped his chest. Drew wearily climbed to his feet, squinting through the otherworldly light.

At first glance it looked as if a series of caves were carved within the domed walls, but then he saw the wrapped bodies set within each of the alcoves: the mummified remains of the Hawklords of old. He counted twelve such catacombs pockmarking the chamber, with chests laid at the feet and head of each mummy. He might have stared at them in wonder longer if it had not been for the dark, feathered monster that descended the steps into the room.

Rook let his wings flap once more, sending clouds of dust swirling through the air. His feet scraped against the cold stone floor, talons grating and sending shivers racing up Drew's spine. The young Wolflord retreated, soon finding the wall at his back.

"Done running, Wolf?" sneered the Werecrow. "Griffyn will have to make do with the mountainside. You can have his bed in this dead birds' nest."

Rook took another step into the chamber just as moonlight began to stream in through the window above. The disturbed dust glittered in the air like tiny silver stars as the light settled on the catacomb behind Drew. The alcove glowed suddenly as the moon's rays landed upon it, and a shaft of pale blue light glowed dimly on the mummy's chest; it held a sword in its grasp.

"What dark magistry is this?" squawked Rook, taking another step closer to Drew, but less steadily now, looking over his mighty winged shoulders around the room.

Drew's instincts told him what to do. He reached behind, his fingers settling around the sword's handle. The mummy instantly released its grip. With his hand closing around the sword, the blade glowed brighter, its pale blue light flashing bright white in Drew's grasp.

"There's nothing dark about it," said Drew breathlessly, his eyes fixed on the shining blade in astonishment. The young Wolflord was so entranced by the weapon that he didn't notice Rook raise his own blade.

Before the Crow could strike, a sudden, violent wind whipped through the tomb, throwing the young Wolf to the ground. He looked up, his left arm sheltering his eyes from the blinding gale. Lord Rook teetered forward and backward as the wind hurtled around him, buffeting him from side to side and lifting him into the air.

Drew could make out a series of dark shadows racing from each of the alcoves and joining the cyclone. The Werecrow let out a scream as the speeding winds smashed into his wings, cartilage snapping and feathers flying in a ghastly black shower. His cry increased in pitch as cuts began to appear across his body, first his arms and legs, flesh tearing and bones breaking. Next the wounds appeared across his chest and back, as shadowy talons slashed into his torso. As the feathers and blood flew, the Crowlord of Riven's screams reached a deafening roar, forcing Drew to look away.

The wind dropped suddenly, as did the body of the Crowlord. Spluttering and coughing, Drew looked back into the center of the tomb, his eyes settling on the corpse of Rook, his head back-to-front and his body sliced to ribbons. Feathers floated through the blood-misted air as the moon continued to shine into the chamber. Drew felt his heart constricting once more as the shadows that had joined the deadly whirlwind began to take a more solid form.

Twelve dark figures appeared, their form shifting all the time as they closed in around him. Drew's mouth was dry, and when he tried to breathe he felt the pressure growing in his chest. Skeletal black hands emerged from the wraiths, reaching out toward him, their taloned fingers grasping. He brought the white sword around, holding it in his trembling grasp, a hopeless attempt at warding the demons away.

As one, the phantoms retreated, and the air returned to Drew's lungs in a surging, life-giving wave. His chest heaved as he watched the dozen shapes suddenly switch from grim black wraiths into ethereal white angels. Dazzled by the stunning light, Drew looked on as the dozen figures seemed to shrink in height. The Wolf righted himself, standing gingerly as he looked over the glowing shapes. *Are they kneeling? Bowing?*

Beyond the sentinels, Drew could see twelve runes carved

into the tomb wall shining as bright as the sword in his hand, forming a perfect circle. He limped over, between the ghosts, taking care to avoid touching them. The runes encircled a round stone set in the rock, similar to a small millstone, with a dimple carved into the middle. Hooking the sword beneath his left arm, he tried to prize the stone's edge, but there was nothing to take hold of. Returning the sword to his hand, he smashed the twisted end off the trident dagger, sending it to the floor with a clatter. He then placed the metal-capped stump into the hollow and pushed. The stone grated, sliding back against the rock around it. With a sudden *clang* the stone fell away, revealing a tunnel that began to rip the air from the room.

Drew dropped to the floor, his tattered cloak flapping and shearing free from his shoulders, sucked away through the hole and out into the dark space beyond the mountain. One after another the white ghosts were drawn through the hole, screeching and screaming as they went, the sound deafening, their light blinding, as Drew gripped the cold stone wall for fear of being torn through the tunnel after them.

# 6

# A Gift from the North

**HECTOR COULDN'T BELIEVE** the change that had taken place in the prince. Having spent a torturous time in Lucas's service under the tutelage of the wicked Vankaskan, he'd seen the young Lionlord change from a boy to a man well before his years. An expert warrior with blade in hand, with total mastery of his felinthropy, he was the image of his dead father, King Leopold, a worthy successor to the Lion King's crown. But the figure that sat on the throne before him was a shadow of that bold, impetuous youth, a ghost of the Werelord he'd once known and feared. Where was the old Lucas?

*He's in there, brother. Just you wait and see. . . .*

Prince Lucas had remained silent when the Tuskun party arrived. He'd stayed silent while Queen Slotha had announced, with much bluster, that she'd brought a gift from the north to the Lion of Westland. The Lord Chancellor, Vanmorten, had gone through the formalities with the Werewalrus, willing her to hurry to the end of her grand speech, his eyes fixed on the young Boarlord who stood manacled between her guards. The Ugri warriors propelled the magister forward, sending Hector to his knees.

"Kill him."

Lucas's voice was clear and calm. This was new to Hector— the prince he'd served had been prone to great emotional rants and tantrums. Vanmorten turned slowly and stared at the throne. His face was hidden within his cowl, the scars from his battles with Drew having left him hideously disfigured twice over.

Lucas was sitting upright in the stone chair, spine stiff against its back. The rear of the hall was shrouded in darkness, the torches unlit in their sconces around the throne. Lucas's hands rested on the carved snakes on the chair's arms as he stared at Hector. Leopold's iron crown sat firmly upon his head, his son's blond hair lank and lifeless beneath it.

"I don't think so," replied a voice from behind the throne. "Let's hear what the Boarlord says before rushing to any judgment, Lucas."

The woman who stepped into the light was the polar opposite to the queen of Tuskun. Whereas Slotha was a towering figure who cast a huge, intimidating shadow, the other was slight and slender. Hector had seen nobody like her in all of Lyssia, her skin so black it seemed to glow with a dull purple light, while her eyes shone yellow like the sun. She came to a halt before him, looking down at the kneeling magister. Her head was shaved smooth, every bump of her skull visible in the torchlight. While others in the chamber avoided eye contact with her, Hector was unable to draw his eyes away. He'd heard the tales about her, and she was even more fascinating in the flesh: Opal, the Catlady of Bast. She arched her eyebrow in surprise as the Boarlord fixed his gaze upon her.

"I would have his head on a spike, to go with those of other traitors," spat the young Lion, his lips peeling back to show a full set of sharp, white teeth. "What can he possibly say that will spare him my wrath?"

"It might be wise to listen to his final words, Your Highness," said Vanmorten, trying to reason with the impatient prince. "Think of it as an amusement!"

"If the prince wants him dead, so be it," declared Slotha, clapping her huge hands. An Ugri stepped forward, unhitching an ax from his belt. The audience gasped as he raised it over Hector's head.

"Put that away!" shouted Vanmorten.

"He's *my* prisoner," growled Slotha, bearing her tusks in a jutting snarl.

"He *was* your prisoner," corrected Vanmorten. "Until you presented him as a gift to Prince Lucas."

The Ugri warrior glanced at his queen who, with a nod of the head, commanded he step down. She glared at the Wererat as the Lord Chancellor turned back to the prince. Opal watched, smiling, enjoying the tension in the great hall.

"Hear what he says, Your Highness, then do what you will," said the Ratlord.

Lucas nodded. He looked tired to Hector, his former vigor and energy having all but disappeared, to be replaced by pale flesh and red-ringed eyes. Something wasn't right.

"Go ahead, Piggy. Speak your mind for the last time."

Hector struggled to his feet, the manacled hands making the task awkward. He pulled his eyes from Opal, focusing on the prince.

"Your Highness," he said, which caused Lucas to chuckle.

"You dare call me that after your betrayal . . ."

Vanmorten and Opal looked at the prince, their glares encouraging him to quieten. Miraculously, this seemed to work.

*The prince pays heed to his advisers' words, brother,* whispered Vincent. *Let's hope his advisers in turn are open to suggestion. . . .*

Hector cleared his throat, the interruption having thrown him. His guts were knotted, twisted around themselves with anxiety. He'd placed his throat in the Lion's jaws on an all-or-nothing roll of the bones.

"As Baron of Redmire and Lord of the Dalelands, I offer the Emerald Realm to you, Prince Lucas, as well as my services as magister and councilor."

The room was quiet as the members of Lucas's court looked at one another in astonishment.

Finally, Vanmorten spoke. "Is this some kind of trick, Boarlord?"

"It's no trick. I'm giving you the Dalelands, Prince Lucas: hilt, blade, and scabbard. You have our allegiance and my support as you secure lordship over Lyssia. What does that give you: Westland, the Cluster Isles, the Longridings, and now the Dalelands? That's four of the Seven Realms: the throne is yours, Your Highness."

"I've already taken the Dalelands, Piggy," said Lucas, glaring at Hector with utter contempt. "It's no longer yours to give."

"But it is, Your Highness," said Hector. "You can attack the Dales, but Brenn's law stands above all others: the Boars of Redmire rule the Dalelands, and as Baron of Redmire I speak on behalf of all my people. The support of the Emerald Realm is mine to give, and mine alone. You have our fealty."

"Do I hear you correctly?" said the Ratlord. "This is the same young Boar who was a founding member of the Wolf's Council, a traitor who turned against the House of Lions and all that was lawful? Why the change of heart, boy? Why the sudden allegiance to your rightful monarch? It doesn't have anything to do with your capture in the north and your friends being defeated, does it?"

The manacles jangled as Hector lifted his arms, right hand raised as he begged permission to speak.

"I wasn't *captured* in the north. Had I chosen to, I could have left Friggia at any point in time. I asked to be escorted to Slotha in . . ."

"That's *Queen* Slotha!" shouted the Walrus, backhanding him.

Hector looked up at the massive Werelady as she hulked over him. He winced, his split lip torn and streaming as he spoke through gritted, bloodied teeth.

"I asked to be escorted to *Queen* Slotha, so I could be brought here to parlay with you. I was never caught by the Tuskuns. I come here willingly. I'm worth more to you alive than dead."

"What possible value do you have?" asked Vanmorten. "I could have you sign a declaration right now, declaring your allegiance, before removing your head from your shoulders. You're a bumpkin, Hector—a child of the country who has wandered into a man's city. You offer nothing. You're out of your depth."

Vanmorten stepped up to the magister, his face inches from Hector's. The young therian could smell the awful cocktail of flowers and rotten flesh, the rose water applied to mask the Ratlord's ghoulish stench. He could see inside the cowl now, one half of the Lord Chancellor's face bare skull, the other blackened flesh. The Rat spoke again through his lipless mouth.

"You're drowning."

*They don't fear you, brother. They don't respect you. They mock you. I fear you may join me, Hector, all too soon. . . .*

401

Hector could sense the mood shifting in the chamber. They'd heard enough. They'd take his signature and then his life. *Last chance to shine.* He raised his voice so all could hear.

"I'm your ally, Prince Lucas, whether you like it or not. My foes are your foes, and I've already slain one of them."

Lucas leaned forward and guffawed, his weariness lifting for a moment before he collapsed into the stone chair once again. Vanmorten and Slotha also laughed, joined by a chorus of jeers from the Lionguard. Only Opal remained straight-faced.

"Who've you killed?" she asked.

"Vega. I killed him aboard the *Maelstrom*. The count is dead."

"Lies!" shouted Vanmorten.

"Kill him!" Slotha laughed. "I'll do it myself," she added, snatching the ax from her Ugri bodyguard.

"Stay your hand, woman," growled the Werepanther.

The Ugri and their queen stared at the woman in shock, but her command was followed. Slotha reluctantly released her hand from the ax haft, glowering at the Catlady.

"How in Brenn's name do you expect us to believe you killed Vega?" asked the prince.

"As much as I hate to admit it, Vega's the most cunning captain on the White Sea," said Slotha. "There's no way this wetling fool could've killed him, my dear prince."

*Oh she is keen, isn't she?* hissed Vincent. *Perhaps there'll be a royal marriage after all, although Slotha's quite a step down from Gretchen.*

"Unlikely," said Hector, accidentally aloud.

"What's unlikely?" said Vanmorten.

"My killing Vega," replied Hector, covering his tracks. "Unlikely, but not impossible: I buried a silver arrow within him, and then I had my men toss him overboard. That arrow is still in my possession, stained dark with the Sharklord's blood. That is, if Slotha hasn't taken it from my belongings. The Wolf's Council is dead to me. My future lies in your service, Your Highness."

"You've worked for the prince before, young magister, and it didn't end . . . well," said the Lord Chancellor. "Even if his Highness were to allow you to live, a notion that I struggle with, what guarantee do we have that you wouldn't bite your master's hand again?"

Lucas nodded. "I've heard enough," he said, turning to the Wererat. "Get him to sign over the Dalelands, and a confession while he's at it. Cut him up into tiny pieces if he resists, Vanmorten."

The Ratlord bowed low as Hector felt the hands of the Ugri warriors on his shoulders.

"You're making a mistake!" cried Hector, struggling against the men as Slotha stepped in front of him.

"You're the same dreadful wretch who sniveled around in my shadow, Piggy!" shouted Lucas, waving his hand dismissively. "You haven't changed one bit!"

"I enjoyed our time together, Boarlord," said Slotha, smiling, unable to resist one last slap. Her clawed fingernails raked across Hector's face, leaving bright red ribbons of torn flesh in their wake. The magister broke free of the Ugri's grasp, raising both his hands, gloved fingers splayed wide, the manacles taut. The prince jumped back in his throne suddenly, the old Lucas coming to the fore as he growled defensively. But if he feared Hector might attack him, he was mistaken. The Boarlord had another target.

The Vincent-vile flew from his grasp, fast as an arrow, whipping around the enormous throat of Lady Slotha. Her huge jaw hung open as the spirit coiled around her thick neck, slipping between the folds of her chin like an invisible garrotte. She stumbled toward the throne, staggering up the dais steps, hands grasping at Lucas. The prince leaped up to stand on the stone chair and lashed out, striking her hands away. He roared to try and warn her off, but she was wild beyond reasoning.

The Ugri warriors realized what was happening, the magister's hands moving as they manipulated the space before him, black leather fingers throttling thin air. They leaped, but not quickly enough; Opal was before them in a flash, her face shifting into that of the Werepanther, clawed hands ready to rip into them if they moved an inch closer. The Ugri stepped back, neutered and helpless as their mistress fell to her knees.

Her tongue lolled from her mouth now, purple and snake-like, as her bulging eyes rolled in her head. The tusks of the Walrus jutted down, ivory sabers that sawed vainly at the air.

Hector yanked his hands back, as if pulling a rug from beneath a giant's feet, hauling the vile back with all his might. The neck of the Werewalrus made an awful, wet cracking sound as her huge head collapsed into her shoulders. With a wheezing death rattle, the queen of Tuskun fell to the flagged floor with a loud thud.

*Brilliant, dear brother,* panted Vincent, fresh from the kill.

Hector's heart shook like a rattle within his chest, his skin covered in sweat as he looked at the Lion, the Rat, and the Panther.

"You're wrong, Lucas," he said, sounding calmer than he felt. "I've changed more than you could ever know."

"Whatever . . . whatever he just did," stammered Lucas. "He could do that again. Kill him. Kill him now, before he uses his dark magick upon me!"

Opal raised her hand to the prince, demanding silence.

*She's the one you need to talk to, brother. She's the one who makes the decisions around here.*

"I've seen dark magistry before," said Opal. "In Cape Gala. Your old mentor, Vankaskan, he knew a thing or two. But that trick you just played. That wasn't one of his, was it?"

"I heard he died," said Hector, avoiding answering the question.

"He was slain by your friend the Wolf," snarled Vanmorten, stepping forward and towering over the Boarlord. If he feared Hector's power, he didn't show it.

"I would pay my respects to him," said Hector. "He set me on my path."

"Then let me escort you up Grimm's Lane to Vermire, Pig. Visit his skull in my father's tomb and see how my brothers greet you!"

"Quiet, Vanmorten," said Opal calmly. She looked at Hector, her big yellow eyes unblinking. And she smiled.

"You risk much allowing yourself to be brought to Highcliff by the Walrus, offering yourself to us. What you bring—this great power of magistry—would make our enemies quake. What do you want in return, Hector?"

All eyes were on the Boarlord.

*Take the leap, brother. Leave the Wolf. Embrace your own destiny.*

"I want a pardon," said Hector, "a guarantee that no harm will befall me at the hands of your forces. I need unhindered access throughout the realms, no restrictions on my movements. There's much I need to research if my magistry is to be a true weapon at your disposal. The Wolf's Council saw it as an aberration. They were feeble-minded fools."

*Good, Hector, keep going.*

"And I'll need a position within the royal court; Lord Magister to the king would be nice."

"Never," spat Lucas, while Opal raised her hand to silence him again.

"Go on," she said.

"Duke Manfred's the only remaining member of the Wolf's

Council, discounting myself. He wronged me, and I'd have his life, too. He's taken your mother to Icegarden, Your Highness. I want to be there when we capture him, to play my part in bringing the Stag down. Then, finally, your enemies will all have been defeated."

"Not all of them," said the prince. "The Wolf. What of him?"

Hector's bloody lips felt suddenly dry as he cleared his throat. "They say he fell to his death. But if he yet lives, I'll help you bring him down."

*You really mean that, brother? If it came to it, you'd kill Drew?*

Opal looked to Vanmorten and the prince. While Lucas sneered, Vanmorten allowed the briefest of nods. Opal turned back to Hector.

"We appear to have an agreement, Boarlord," she said, her yellow eyes finally narrowing as she grinned. The Catlady leaped over the corpse of the Walrus and extended her hand to Hector. He reached a gloved palm out and shook it.

Vanmorten watched, his face hidden within his cowl. Hector couldn't tell whether the look he gave them was one of approval or disgust.

"So, Icegarden," said Lucas. "That's where they've taken my mother. We'll wipe those Sturmish scum off the map for harboring traitors."

Lucas stood, uneasy on his feet as if drunk. Hector watched the young Lion warily; he'd never seen him like this. He could see him by torchlight, unkempt and disheveled. The old Lucas would never have allowed himself to be seen in such a state. The look in his eyes was wild.

"I wouldn't have just four of these realms bowing down before me. We must assemble our armies, Opal: the Lions, the Cats, the Rats, and the Dogs. I'll have all of the Seven Realms kneeling before me, with my foot on their backs and my sword at their throats if that's what it takes!"

"And we'll have the Boars to assist us, too," Vanmorten sneered.

"You shall," said Hector, turning to the Ratlord and smiling. "But first, I'll take you up on your offer, Lord Chancellor. Please, take me to Vermire."

# 7

# RETURN TO THE PACK

**THE BAREBONES LOOMED** large over the eastern horizon, their snow-capped peaks faintly visible by the starlight. Trent Ferran found himself staring at the distant mountain range as the wind raced through the Longridings around him. His red cloak flapped, clapping at the air, as he gripped it tightly about his throat. He shivered as he glanced at the peaks one last time, the hairs prickling on his arms, before turning and pacing through the camp toward the prison tent.

One guard stood to attention in front of the weighted door flaps. Trent quickened his pace into a brisk, officious stride as he approached. He made to walk past the guard.

"Sergeant," said the man, older than the young outrider

and clearly resenting having to call him his superior. He remained barring Trent's path.

"Stand aside, Eaves," said Trent, staring the man down.

"Can't do that, Sergeant," said the man, revealing a hint of a smug smile. Very few of Captain Sorin's friends in the camp respected the young sergeant, Trent having received the promotion at Lord Frost's insistence. The albino Catlord had his favorites, none more blessed than the youth from the Cold Coast.

"Why's that, Eaves?"

"Captain's orders."

"Forget Sorin. I'm here on the command of Lord Frost, to question the prisoner. You want to take that up with his lordship?"

Trent eyeballed the man. He might have been twenty years his junior, but he was the same height, and equally as broad; the apple hadn't fallen far from the tree with Mack Ferran's son. Reluctantly, Eaves stood aside. Trent stepped past, glowering as he went, allowing the tent flap to swing shut behind him. The young soldier paused for a moment to tie the door cords, fastening it tight so it couldn't be opened in a hurry. Satisfied it was secured, he walked quietly into the heart of the dark tent, to the beaten figure kneeling in a slumped heap.

"One more thing," said Trent as he stood over Baron Ewan.

The Ramlord looked up. "You came back?" he whispered through broken lips.

"You don't believe Drew killed my mother. Then who did?"

"The Wererat Vanmorten killed your mother, lad."

Ewan's voice was serious and hard.

"How can you *know* that, though?"

"Drew's word would have been enough for me. I wouldn't doubt anything that lad told me. But you forget: I spent time in Cape Gala, while the Wererat Vankaskan lorded it around High Stable. That one couldn't hold a secret if his life depended upon it; his brother's murder of your mother was something they were proud of. I heard him gloat as much with my own ears."

Trent's skin felt suddenly cold all over, a clamminess that spread from his extremities up toward his chest and throat. He felt a chill seize his heart, fearing the broken Ramlord spoke the truth.

*He* has *to be lying!*

"You'll say anything if it spares you Sorin's beatings," said Trent, struggling to hold back the tears. But his voice was trembling, the young outrider assailed by doubt.

"What more can possibly be done to me?" The Ramlord laughed quietly. "My body and heart are weak after your captain's work. I am already at Death's dark door. The long sleep would be a blessed relief after what your *friends* have done to me."

"This can't be true," sobbed Trent, unable to hold back his emotions any longer.

"Not a day has passed since your mother was murdered when Drew hasn't thought about the horror done to his family.

And that his own father—*and brother*—should think he'd killed her? Can you imagine the torment?"

Tears rolled down Trent's cheeks, a steady stream that couldn't be stopped. He hunched double, retching, a dry heave causing his back to shudder. He dropped to his knees, choking, wanting to shout, but instead silently screaming. *What have I done?*

"I've hunted him," he whispered. "Hunted him for . . . for those who killed my family! What have I done? I'm damned . . ."

"All is not in vain," urged Ewan. "You can still help him. Lady Gretchen and Lady Whitley: your masters believe they've fled to the south, to Calico or Port Stallion."

"They haven't?"

"No! They've gone north, to Brackenholme! Go after them, help them, boy: they're in grave danger!"

A slow handclap caused both of them to look up. The lithe figure of Lord Frost prowled into the room, the severed cords that had bound the door shut fluttering behind him. Trent looked back at Ewan, the look on his face as surprised as the Ramlord's. Ewan smiled sadly at the young man, Trent's eyes wide with horror as the full ramifications of Frost's presence dawned on him. He'd heard *everything*. The Catlord wore a pair of leather breeches and nothing else, his pale feet padding silently across the earth floor. Sorin followed at his shoulder, the broken-nosed captain grinning broadly.

"Excellent work, Trent," said the albino. "Excellent!"

He placed his white hand on Trent's shoulder and gave him a squeeze. Trent felt the Catlord's claws through the material of his cloak, digging into his flesh.

"You've outdone yourself, my friend. I didn't hear it all, but you unearthed the gem at the end: Brackenholme."

Trent wearily rose to his feet, red-ringed eyes still wet with tears. Ewan looked up, his broken face trembling but forgiving. Sorin paced across and launched a vicious kick at the old therian, his booted heel hitting him square in the breast. Ewan collapsed, slumped against his ropes.

"Kill him," said Frost, clapping Trent's back.

The young man's hand hovered over the pommel of the Wolfshead in his scabbard. *All this time, helping my enemy, hunting my brother, betraying my family . . .*

The Wolfshead blade slid out of its sheath, rising up in the air over the Ramlord in a smooth motion. It hovered there, the executioner's steel poised to fall. Every ounce of Trent's rage was unleashed as he let the sword fly in a furious swing, not down toward the Ramlord, but around him in a fluid arc.

Frost stood motionless, his pink eyes widening in wonder as he stared at the young outrider, poised to strike again. The Catlord's eyes settled on the Redcloak's sword, the edge of the blade dark with blood. He glanced down to his stomach, disbelief spreading across his face as a widening red line appeared across the toned flesh. The albino changed quickly, calling upon his felinthrope healing to try and halt the wound's

413

progress, but it was hopeless; the Wolfshead blade was blessed with silver, at the Catlord's own command.

As Frost fell to his knees, mid-change, Sorin leaped past him, his own sword meeting Trent's as the young sergeant defended himself.

"You traitorous scum!" shouted Sorin, raining blows down on Trent as the younger man parried. "You're as bad as the other Ferrans! A Wolf, just like your brother and father!"

Trent had heard enough insults. He could take the barrage of sword blows, but he wouldn't listen to Sorin besmirch the Ferran name. The next time Sorin's sword struck Trent's, the young man dived forward, catching him in the ribs with his shoulder. The air exploded from Sorin's lungs as the two crashed down to earth, both swords flying, Trent on top of the captain.

Sorin threw a wild punch upward, but with little power, and the young man batted it away and landed a flurry of blows on Sorin's face. The captain stopped moving, his features battered, as Trent rolled away, panting and panicked.

The tent flaps swung open as the guard entered, stumbling blindly into the scene. Trent wasted no time on Sorin's man, snatching up the Wolfshead blade and leaping up from the floor in a savage lunge. The sword disappeared through Eaves's stomach, rising up out of his back. The guard fell to the floor, dead in an instant.

Trent scrambled across to Ewan, cutting the Ramlord's bonds as he tumbled into his arms.

"Come, my lord," said Trent. "We need to go."

Before Ewan could answer, another voice cut in.

"They'll find you and your kin. They'll kill you all. My brothers and sisters won't stop."

Trent looked up and saw Lord Frost yet lived, the albino Catlord kneeling, his clawed fingers failing to hold his open stomach in place. He'd partly changed, the White Panther visible throughout, but he looked paler than ever, like a ghost, the enormous puddle of blood that he knelt in steadily growing. His pink eyes fluttered as he stared at Trent, head lolling, a sickly smile across his jagged feline mouth.

Trent rose and walked over to him, dragging the Wolfshead blade behind him.

"You strike a blow against a Catlord, you strike a blow against all my kind."

Trent lifted the sword high before answering. "You strike a blow against a Ferran, you strike a blow against our whole family."

The sword sliced down, the severed head of Lord Frost rolling to a halt beside the body of Eaves. Trent looked back to Ewan in time to see Sorin at his back, risen from the floor, his face a red mask, his sword raised to strike. The captain's face was twisted, bloody skin broken by white snarling teeth and even brighter eyes. Trent began the turn, bringing the Wolfshead blade up to parry the below, but he was too slow, his poise all wrong. Sorin's sword was descending.

The killing blow never struck, the sword clattering from the captain's dying grasp. A horn burst from Sorin's chest, his ribcage splintering, as the changed Ramlord launched himself from the floor into his back. Shock, agony, and horror flashed in Sorin's eyes as he and Baron Ewan collapsed. The Lionguard captain was dead before he hit the dirt. Trent skidded along the ground to catch Ewan as he rolled away from Sorin's corpse, wheezing with the strain of the transformation. The Ramlord was heavy, his head lolling against the youth's chest as his strength faded fast.

"We need to go," cried Trent.

"No, boy," he said. "Go on your own."

"I can take you with me, if we leave now!"

"Slow you down," spluttered the wheezing old Ram.

Trent shook his head, dragging the Werelord toward the wall of the tent, but Ewan was right. Fully transformed, he was a deadweight in Trent's arms, his limbs useless.

"My time's up," said Ewan. "The long sleep awaits me. Go. Help your brother. His friends."

Trent choked back the tears, nodding. Outside he could hear shouting, the commotion in the tent not having been missed by the rest of the camp.

"The girls," whispered Ewan, his voice trailing away.

"What?" asked Trent, bending his ear closer to the Wereram's battered face.

"In danger. Gretchen, Whitley . . . Brackenholme."

A rattling wheeze escaped Ewan's chest as his voice trailed away. His eyes stared at the tent ceiling, the light fading from them.

"They travel . . . with . . . Baba Korga . . ."

Then he was gone, his broken chest no longer moving, the fight over.

Trent didn't wait. More shouting from the camp told him he'd overstayed his welcome. He rushed over to the wall of the tent, slashing through it with a swing of the Wolfshead blade. Trent slipped out of the tent, pacing swiftly through the camp, striding between his fellow soldiers as he headed to where the horses were tethered. Bastian and Lionguard alike hurried past him in the opposite direction as the cry went up from the prison tent. He was sure they were looking at him, could feel their questioning gaze as he strode by, but none stopped him.

When Trent found his horse, Storm, the rest of the camp had descended upon the prison tent. By the time the Bastians and Lionguard began looking for the culprit, the outrider was already on his way, galloping across the Longridings, toward the Dyrewood.

Toward Brackenholme.

# 8

# THE HEIRS AND
# THE HONEST

**TALONED FINGERS SQUEEZED** Drew's windpipe, rousing him from his fevered slumber, threatening to tear his throat out in a flash. His eyes were instantly open, feet scrambling against the freezing stone floor of the Hawklords' tomb as he struggled in vain to slip free of the deadly hold. He brought his hand up to prize his attacker's fingers loose, but the other's free hand shoved him away, the grip tightening suddenly and shutting off Drew's airway. Drew went limp in surrender, eyes fixed firmly on his foe.

The therian was unmistakably a Hawklord, although dramatically different in appearance from Shah. When Griffyn's daughter had transformed she had looked elegant, majestic, a true mistress of the sky. The falconthrope who held Drew's life in his talons was a rougher-looking character. Rusty brown wings folded behind his back. The red feathers were tattered and threadbare in places, old wounds visible beneath missing plumage. A shortbow swung from his hip as he towered over Drew, his head craning in close to better inspect the young Wolflord. One long scar ran down the left side of the Hawklord's face, from the top of his crown, over his eye, disappearing beneath his jaw. His razor-sharp yellow beak snapped at Drew's face, and his big, black killer's eyes blinked suspiciously.

"You're well off the beaten track, boy," croaked the Hawk. "Thought you'd try and take from our kin, did ya?"

Drew's mouth gasped at the air like a fish out of water, no words escaping. Changing into the Wolf wasn't an option—the clawed fingers of the Hawk would puncture his neck like a knife through soft fruit. He could sense unconsciousness—and ultimately death—fast approaching. The Hawk looked across at Rook's corpse where it lay on the floor, illuminated by a shaft of morning sunlight from the window above.

"Thieves!" snapped the Werehawk, shaking Drew like a rag doll. "The Crow promised you a fortune if you helped 'im rob our tomb, did he? Well the Crow's dead, boy, and you're about to join 'im . . ."

"Red Rufus!"

The Hawk bobbed his head, opening his beak to hiss in

419

the direction of the staircase that led into the Screaming Peak. Another figure descended the steps, striding over toward the rust-feathered falconthrope and his prisoner.

"Let him breathe," commanded the newcomer, a blur before Drew's cloudy vision as he was about to pass out.

Reluctantly, Red Rufus released his grip, letting Drew collapse on to the floor, snatching great lungfuls of air.

"Let me kill 'im, Carsten," said Red Rufus, flexing his talons, ready to lash out. "Let's see 'is gizzard, eh?"

The one called Carsten raised his hand, silencing Red Rufus. "Let the lad speak first, Red Rufus, hear what he's got to say. Then you can open him up."

As Drew's vision recovered, Carsten shifted into focus. In his fifth decade, he was stocky and broad-shouldered, with a mop of thick black hair. His eyes were bright blue, trained keenly on Drew, while his hands remained folded over the pommel of an upright broadsword, the blade turned down to the floor. Drew rubbed his throat, massaging life back into his vocal chords.

"Seems like the tombwraiths took care of your master, thief," said Carsten, stepping over Rook's body.

"I'm not . . . a thief!" gasped Drew.

"Lost your way did you, lad?" said Carsten. "Happens all the time up here. A boy's just wandering around through the vales and grasslands, takes a wrong turn, ends up on top of Tor Raptor. Easy mistake to make."

"I came here . . . with Baron Griffyn . . ."

Carsten gave Rook's body a kick, the corpse rolling over, black feathers fluttering around it.

"Rubbish!" sneered Red Rufus, clenching his taloned hands, ready to strike. "Griffyn died years ago. You're one of the Crow's men."

Red Rufus brought his hand back, fingers open, his big black eyes narrowing to slits.

"You're a dead man . . ."

"Wait!" shouted Carsten, causing Red Rufus to turn.

Another figure had descended the staircase. A tall, partly-changed Hawklord staggered down the steps. His wings were already retreating into his back, the beak grinding back into his jaw and skull, feathers disappearing beneath his skin. He was bald with a full black beard, a little taller than Carsten, but they had the look of family. In his arms he carried a body.

"Is that . . . ?" said Carsten, stepping closer.

"It's Griffyn," said the newcomer, his head bowed, beard bristling as he grimaced. "Dead: I found him below the cliffs."

Carsten and Red Rufus looked back to Drew where he lay on the floor, his eyes darting between them all.

"I told you I came with him!"

"And yet you live while my lord lies dead?" said Carsten.

"Let me do 'im, Your Grace," said Red Rufus, hopping from foot to foot now, keen to be on with the business of killing.

"Who is this?" asked the bald, bearded Hawklord.

"My name's Drew. Drew Ferran."

Red Rufus was about to strike when Carsten snatched him by the forearm, causing the red-feathered bird to squawk at his liege. *"You're* Drew Ferran?" he said in disbelief, ignoring Red Rufus. "Half of Lyssia is searching for a boy by that name."

"This is Wergar's son?" asked the bearded falconthrope.

"Just words, Baum," replied Carsten. "I still think he's an agent of this dead Crow, sent here thieving. He'll say anything to live . . ."

"How *does* he live though, brother?" said Baum. "The Screaming Peak and the tombwraiths: *'None but the Heirs and the Honest may enter'*? This Crow lies dead, but the boy survives."

Carsten cocked his head to one side, aspects of the hawk never far away. He crouched on his haunches in front of Drew while Red Rufus paced anxiously behind him.

"Good question, Baum. Boy, how *do* you live while the Crow lies dead?"

Drew reached behind his back, his torn cloak falling to one side to reveal the sword he'd found in the tomb.

Carsten and Baum both gasped, while Red Rufus stuck his avian neck over his lord's shoulder, his eyes running along the length of the blade. Carsten moved from his crouch, dropping onto one knee, while his brother gently placed Griffyn's body onto the floor and did the same.

"What is it?" said Red Rufus, agitated by his falconthrope cousins' show of reverence.

"The sword," whispered Baum, recognizing the blade straightaway.

"He's Wergar's son, all right," said Carsten, taking hold of Red Rufus and drawing the old bird to the ground into a bow. "He's the rightful king of Westland."

Drew staggered to his feet, looking down on the three Hawklords who knelt before him. They reminded him of the tombwraiths he'd encountered that night, striking the same poses that the phantoms had when they'd seen the sword.

"I don't . . . please, I don't understand. And for Brenn's sake, my lords, don't kneel before me!"

The three rose, Red Rufus a little quicker than the other two, stalking to the rear of the tomb.

"The runes beyond this crypt are a warning," Baum said. "None may enter the Screaming Peak but the Heirs and the Honest: this law the tombwraiths honor."

*Only the just and rightful lord may enter*: that's what Baron Griffyn had told Drew about the tomb.

"How did the tombwraiths know I wasn't a thief, come here to steal the sword? They tore Rook to pieces!"

"That sword," Carsten said, pointing to the gray metal blade, "was the weapon of Wergar the Wolf: Moonbrand, forged for his ancestors in Icegarden by Sturmland's greatest smiths centuries ago. The wraiths wouldn't have allowed you to pass if you weren't truly Wergar's heir. Did it glow when you touched it, lad?"

"It was already glowing, but when I picked it up it shone with a white light."

"The Sturmish enchanted the weapons of the Werelords," said Baum. "The steel glows like a torch under moonlight."

"And the rest," muttered Red Rufus cryptically.

"But what's it doing here?" Drew asked, trying to piece together the jigsaw.

"It would appear our dear, departed Griffyn brought it here for safekeeping after Leopold took the throne. Who could have known that one day Wergar's child would climb Tor Raptor and reclaim it as his own?"

Drew thought back to Griffyn's words once more: *I brought it here. I kept it safe.*

Drew had heard the sword's name before. Queen Amelie had mentioned it in Highcliff. *My father's sword.*

"My lords," said Drew, sliding Moonbrand into his battered weapon belt. It was his turn to kneel now, Baum and Carsten looking to one another in surprise while Red Rufus watched distrustfully. "I was here with Baron Griffyn's blessing. We came to the Screaming Peak because we needed to call you back. The war that has taken hold of Lyssia, we, the army that stands before the Catlords of Bast, are in dire need!"

"In need of what, son of Wergar?" asked Carsten, his blue eyes shining like ice.

"We need the Hawklords."

# PART VII

## DEATH FROM ABOVE

# I

# THE GUEST

**THE FIRST RAYS** of sunlight illuminated Windfell Keep as a trio of servants stood in the lord's chamber, watching their master frantically rifle through his desk. Each held a casket, lid open, half-filled with coins, gems, and artifacts. The Falconlord tugged loose a drawer, tipped its contents on to the table, and sifted through them with feverish fingers.

"It must be here somewhere," murmured Baron Skeer, clawing through bound scrolls and checking the seals of each.

The doors to his study were wide open, the booted sound of guards' feet echoing through the corridor beyond.

"What the devil's going on?"

The question came from the doorway, Skeer glancing up to find his guest, craning his head around the corner.

"I'm leaving," said Skeer briskly. "Ah, there you are!"

His eyes lit up as he snatched a scroll with a red wax seal: the Lionshead, King Leopold.

"Leaving? Are you insane, Skeer?"

"You'd leave, too, if you knew what was best."

The old Falcon checked the seal, making sure it remained unopened.

"What's the scroll?" said the visitor, striding into the room, looking back as another group of soldiers raced by in the corridor. They may have worn the brown, feather-trimmed cloaks of the Hawkguard, but each man there was now a soldier of the Lion. Windfell had been Leopold's foothold in the Barebones for fifteen years, in which time the soldiers had seen little by way of combat, growing careless and out of condition. Suddenly, conflict was approaching, and the Hawkguard's fear was palpable.

Skeer stashed the scroll in the belt of his robes.

"A decree made by the old king."

"That states what?" asked the Falcon's guest, trailing his hands over one of the open caskets that the servants held.

"That my position here as baron is lawful. Leopold asked me to rule here for the good of the Seven Realms."

His guest laughed, a rasping cackle that rattled in his chest.

"For the good of the Seven Realms? For the good of *you*, Skeer, and no one else!"

The guest slammed the casket lid shut, causing the

Falconlord to jump. The baron scooped up a further handful of trinkets and barged past his visitor, dumping them into another box.

"Why the concern over your position, old friend? Why the activity within the halls and corridors of Windfell? Why so fearful for your life all of a sudden, Skeer? Explain what's happening!"

Skeer stepped closer to his fellow Werelord, who was a good foot taller than the old bird. The baron stared up into the squinting off-center eyes of the crooked count.

"My cousins, Kesslar," said the Falcon. "The Hawklords return!"

"What do you *mean* they're returning?" shouted Kesslar as he marched after Skeer, the baron's servants getting under his feet as he tried to catch up. He shoved one out of the way, the young man crashing into the corridor wall and spilling half the contents of the casket on the floor.

"Pick those up!" squawked Skeer as his servant snatched up the jewels.

"How can the Hawklords return?" repeated Kesslar. "They're all dead, aren't they?"

"Not dead," corrected the Falcon. "Banished. Forbidden ever to return."

"Yet you say that's happening? How can you know?"

Skeer's eyes were frantic as he peered through one of the tall arches that looked out over the mountains beyond. He strode

to the stone sill, ducking his head from side to side, searching the sky fearfully. Beside the towering keep of Windfell,
the Steppen Falls crashed down through the Barebones, working their way to the Longridings far below. A line of bridges
spanned the falls, carrying a road from the city down to the
grasslands.

"Did you not *hear* it?"

"Hear what, Skeer? The waterfall? Of course I do. You
sound like a madman!"

"No! The Screaming Peak! It's calling them home. They're
returning to Windfell." He turned toward a set of double doors
guarded by soldiers.

"I thought only the Lord of Windfell could enter the crypt
of your ancestors?"

Skeer looked back at Kesslar briefly, as the Hawkguard
opened the great doors.

"Griffyn?" asked Kesslar. "That old buzzard's behind this?
I left him behind in Scoria—I'd be amazed if he got out of that
hellhole alive!"

"Well, he's out," grumbled Skeer. The soldiers followed
out of the doors and down a flight of steps into the huge circular courtyard within the keep. Curving granite walls rose
high around them, stone ledges lining them on every level, the
ancient seats of the Council of Hawklords. A carriage waited,
horses kicking their hooves impatiently, alongside a platoon of
Skeer's personal guard.

Kesslar was thinking fast as he stumbled down the steps behind the Falconlord.

"If Griffyn escaped Scoria . . ." he muttered. *Who else escaped the island of the Lizardlords? Surely few of them could have survived? If they find me here . . .*

Skeer spun, raising his voice.

"He *is* returning, and he brings the banished Hawklords with him!" he cried. "I don't give a flying spit about the where or why that helped him get here, but these are my *enemies*. They won't forget the part I played in this city's downfall. I was there when they chopped Griffyn's wings off, for Brenn's sake! If he's returning, do you think he'll be in forgiving mood?"

Kesslar watched the baron storm across the courtyard toward his waiting soldiers. He counted thirty of them, and they struck the Goatlord as an uninspiring bunch. Their armor and uniforms were pitted and shabby. A couple of the men glanced up at the skies nervously.

*This is what happens when you're posted to a ghost town in the peaks of the Barebones.*

"Why not stand and fight?" shouted Kesslar. "There may only be Griffyn returning."

"True," replied Skeer. "Then again, what if they all return?"

"Wave your precious scroll at them!"

"I'm not a fool, Kesslar: that scroll will provide me with protection throughout Lyssia, but in the eyes of the brethren whom I turned against? That's a risk I'm not prepared to take!"

"Where will you go?"

"You ask too many questions, old friend!" yelled Skeer as his men loaded his chests and personal belongings into the carriage. "If you hurry, there's a seat here for you! Make haste!"

Kesslar turned on his heel and ran, passing more soldiers who were hurriedly evacuating the keep. Following the curving corridors and sweeping staircases, the Goatlord crashed into the room he'd been occupying, dashing straight to the side of his bed. He reached under, gnarled hands catching hold of the five-foot trunk that was stowed beneath. With a heave it slid out. Kesslar took a key from his pocket and unlocked it.

The true fortune of Scoria lay inside: gems and jewels that had been captured from every continent. Rubies the size of fists; ingots of enchanted Sturmish steel; diamonds as big as apples; coins, crowns, and coronets; regal rings and magisters' rods. Kesslar allowed himself a momentary smile. That fool Ignus and his inbred brothers thought they'd get the better of him. Kesslar had already been plotting his heist, long before the Wolf boy and his allies decided to spoil the Lizards' party in the Furnace. If anything, their escape and the ensuing chaos helped Kesslar make his getaway.

He locked the trunk shut once more, heaved it across his back, and set off through the door. Kesslar shook his head as he ran, cursing his luck. With Haggard lost to him and his bridges with Scoria utterly burned, Windfell had been his last hope of a place to recuperate and re-form his plans. He and Skeer had always looked out for each other. Long ago the old Falcon had even sold Griffyn to him, along with his daughter, Shah. Their business relationship was about the longest standing friendship the Goat had ever known, Skeer being possibly the only therian he could ever truly trust.

His stay in Windfell should have been a quiet, relaxed affair. Let the rest of Lyssia crash and burn; he and Skeer would remain in the Barebones, looking down on the chaos below, ready to return once the victor was decided. Or, failing that, remain hidden away while all their foes slayed one another—it made little difference to Kesslar. Instead, the old wretch Griffyn had somehow sprouted a new pair of wings and flown back to Lyssia, even making it as far as the tomb on Tor Raptor. Kesslar couldn't hear the *Screaming*, as Skeer had described it, but he didn't doubt his friend for one moment. Something was coming.

The corridors were near deserted by the time Kesslar bounded down toward the double doors that led into the courtyard. He was too busy grunting, the box on his back heavy with treasure, to pay attention to what lay ahead. At the last moment he looked up, stumbling to a halt as his knees buckled beneath him.

In the brief time it had taken him to grab his trunk, the yard had been transformed into a scene of battle. The Hawkguard were trapped within the circular court, screaming and shouting as they defended themselves from aerial attack.

Their spears jabbed skyward, swords slashing at the air as they desperately sought shelter from their enemy. Many lay dead on the ground, and the unmistakable figure of Skeer could be seen with his back to the carriage while the chaos exploded around him, the horses bucking to break loose. He looked up, face stricken by terror.

A dozen therians rode the wind around the courtyard, great raptor wings keeping them aloft as they rained death down on the soldiers. Some wore breastplates, others were bare-chested; some carried axes and swords, others fired bows or threw javelins. While they favored different armor and weapons, they were inextricably linked as kinfolk; each was unmistakably a Hawklord, legendary warriors thought to be lost from Lyssia.

Their wings, with feathers of different shades of brown, red, and gray, rose majestically from their backs. Their muscular arms were still human in appearance, while their legs were those of birds of prey, wide splayed feet that ended in deadly talons. Most fearsome of all were their heads, hooked yellow beaks screeching with fury, dealing death in the blinking of a big black eye. They swooped through the Hawkguard, tearing them to shreds, ripping them apart, tossing their warm corpses into the air.

Skeer saw Kesslar and made a break toward his old friend. He darted through the screaming guards, deceptively agile, as dismembered bodies fell across the courtyard. The Hawklords were enjoying this moment, meting out long-awaited justice upon those who had pillaged Windfell. Even Kesslar, a man used to violence, blanched at the Werehawks' grisly work.

Skeer was close now, leaping up the steps toward the Goatlord. "Kesslar!" he wailed as he neared him, hands reaching out in desperation as a shadow passed overhead.

With a bone-shattering *crunch*, an Eaglelord landed on top of Skeer, knuckled yellow feet crushing the baron's body beneath him. He held a broadsword, but that wasn't the weapon he'd used on the turncoat Falcon. Dark talons clenched together, the hooked blades digging into the skin of Skeer's back, catching on his ribs and spine as they ground flesh and bone together on the stone steps. The Falcon cried out in horror, screaming Kesslar's name from his traitorous lips. The Eagle turned his head to stare at Kesslar, blinking briefly, before tearing Skeer apart with his feet.

Kesslar raced back inside, dropped the trunk, and slammed the doors shut, throwing the locking bars into place with a *clang*. His heart felt like it might explode, his hands shaking as he caught hold of the trunk handle again, dragging it away from the doors and the battle in the courtyard. He heaved the box over to the windows from where Skeer had, only moments earlier, stared out over the mountains. With few alternatives, Kesslar craned his neck out and looked down the keep's curved granite wall. There was a twenty-foot drop from the window to rough rock below. Windfell perched upon a sheer cliff face, protecting it from attack, the bridge road over the falls being the only way to reach it on foot. The cliffs were sharp and jagged, impassable to humankind, and to therians for that matter. *Most* therians.

He let the beast take over quickly, every moment's delay making his death more likely as the Hawklords hammered on the double doors. His chest expanded with three great cracks, ribs bursting to take on the Weregoat's mightier physique. He tore the robes from his back as wiry gray hair raced over his body. His legs transformed swiftly, huge, muscular thighs supported by powerful black hooves. His eyes shifted farther around his skull, long black pupils bisecting globs of molten gold. The horns emerged from his brow, thick as tree trunks, coiling around upon themselves—the devil incarnate.

Snatching up the trunk in one grotesque hand, the Weregoat clambered out of the window and jumped. Kesslar's hooves hit the rocks and somehow managed to take hold, his free hand grasping the wall for further support. To anyone other than the Goatlord such a feat would have proved deadly. Unperturbed, Kesslar shuffled and jumped his way around the keep's base, making his way around, past the outer walls that surrounded the city, toward the road ahead. Above, he heard the cries of Skeer's soldiers as they were chased through the palace, butchered where they were found.

Finally he approached the cliff road, a yawning chasm his only obstacle to freedom. The gap was fifteen feet, from a standing jump, but once more, Kesslar's faith in his therian ability and his own survival instinct provided all the impetus he needed. Shifting the trunk to his other arm, he crouched low and leaped, propelling himself forward as if his legs were spring-loaded. The Goat sailed through the air, landing safely on the road with some feet to spare.

Kesslar grinned triumphantly, glancing back at Windfell just the once.

"Good-bye, old friend," he said, before turning and sprinting toward the first bridge on his powerful therian legs.

The first bridge was the tallest and longest of all those that spanned the Steppen Falls, the white stone road riding the elegant arches that held it over the mighty torrent of water. Misty clouds from the waterfall shrouded the center of the bridge from view, the promise of freedom awaiting him beyond the veil. Kesslar kept his pace up, jogging away from the city, black hooves striking the white granite underfoot as he ran into the spray. He was unsure of where he was headed, but an opportunity would arise soon enough. Something would surprise him, sooner or later.

As it happened, he was surprised far sooner than he could have imagined. His hooves skittered to a halt on the wet road as the beating of wings caused the mists to part. A large shape loomed into view overhead, the spray swirling through the backdraft. With dread, Kesslar saw the Hawklord drop something from above, the dark mass landing on the bridge, barring his path. The figure rose to its full height, stepping forward, slowly materializing through the mist before Kesslar's bulging eyes.

"It cannot be!" the Goatlord gasped, staggering backward in disbelief.

Drew Ferran growled. The last of the Gray Wolves paced forward, Moonbrand raised and vengeance in his heart.

"Kesslar!" Drew shouted over the roar of the Steppen Falls.

# 2

# THE STEPPEN FALLS

**THE GOATLORD LOOKED** back the way he'd come, the cries of battle echoing from Windfell. He tugged a long, black knife free from his belt, holding it up defensively.

"Stop running, Kesslar," growled Drew. "Surrender now and I'll spare your life."

"You believe my life is *yours* to spare?"

"Drop the knife," said the Werewolf, his teeth bared as he stepped closer to the Ram.

"You think you can intimidate me, child?" shouted the Goat, but there was a tremble to his voice. "Your father was the same! Bullied his way across Lyssia, and what good did it ultimately do him? His own friends turned against him!"

Kesslar laughed, backing nervously through the mists, losing all sense of direction. Drew kept his eyes locked on the Goat, ready to leap upon him at a moment's notice.

"They'll turn on you, too, Wolf! All those you hold dear! History repeats itself, boy: you're your father's son!"

"Drop the dagger," said Drew. "You've nowhere to run."

Kesslar's hooves backed up to the edge, sending chalky pebbles scuttling off the bridge.

"Your weapon, Kesslar."

The noise of the waterfall was all around them, a constant, tumbling cymbal clash. Kesslar looked behind at the deadly drop, and then squinted at the dagger in his hand. The Wolf towered before him.

"I've had a good life, haven't I?" Kesslar chuckled, his laughter false and grim. "Spent so long putting people in cages, maybe it's time I tried the view from the inside out? Perhaps the change will do me good?"

"The knife."

The Goatlord tossed it across the bridge, metal clanging against stone as it skittered to a halt. Kesslar put his long box down in front of him and dropped to one knee, his head sagging forward. Drew, trying to remain calm, felt dizzy with triumph, having forced the Weregoat to surrender without even drawing blood. *There's always another way*, he reasoned silently to himself.

"You've done the right thing, Kesslar. I'm no monster. I'm taking you back to Windfell, let the Hawklords judge you. See what they—"

The sentence was cut short as the large wooden trunk was propelled forward by the Goat, shoved along the floor in front of him. Drew had no option but to jump into the air to avoid being hit. By the time he was returning to earth, Kesslar had already leaped, springing forward from his crouched position, his powerful horned head catching the Wolf square in the chest.

The Werewolf sailed through the mist, landing on his back with a crunch. Stars flashed as the world spun. His vision blurred as he tried to right himself. The hammering of hooves on the road approached rapidly. Drew raised Moonbrand up, his hold on the sword flimsy. A powerful kick from the Goatlord's hoof almost broke Drew's arm, the precious sword flying from his grasp.

With a wheeze he rolled over, the fingers of his hand scrabbling over the white stone as he searched in vain. Another kick to his guts sent him rolling, over and over, before he shuddered to a halt by the bridge's edge. Grunting, he pulled himself on to all fours, wincing as his bruised ribs grated, nerves firing with pain. He caught the sound of hooves through the mist once more. He raised his left arm up, the stump deflecting the blow at the last second and slamming Kesslar onto the ground.

Drew dived for the Goatlord, but his movement was

clumsy, the youth still stunned from the injuries he'd been dealt. Kesslar snatched at the Wolf's throat, throttling Drew as the lycanthrope's jaws snapped toward his face. The Wolf's claws came up next, his right hand tearing at Kesslar's chest, arms, and wrists, trying to shake the Goat loose. The golden eyes bulged, the Weregoat snorting with exertion as he put all his strength into the chokehold.

Drew tried to bring his legs around, tried to grapple with the lower half of the Goatlord, but Kesslar's powerful legs kicked him clear. Drew felt his stamina faltering, his limbs growing weak as the fight began to slip away. He focused his energies into his throat, straining against the Goat's grip, concentrating solely on not letting the beast snap his neck. *A little longer*, he prayed. *Just a little longer . . .*

Kesslar rolled him over, first straddling him and then standing. Drew's hand and stump fell away as the Goatloard choked the life from him.

"This is how you die, Wolf," grunted Kesslar. "At my hands. Alone."

"Not . . ." spluttered Drew, the Werewolf's mouth wide now, tongue lolling. The veins and muscles bulged around his shoulders and throat, a last stand against suffocation. Kesslar shook him, coaxing the final words from the dying lycanthrope.

"Speak, Wolf!"

"Not . . ." croaked Drew. "Alone . . ."

He lifted his weak hand, a clawed finger pointing through

the mist. Kesslar looked up and saw three figures appear through the mist. Their features were unreadable through the spray, but their outlines were instantly recognizable. The giant figure in the middle carried an enormous mallet in his hand, a hammer that would take the strength of two regular humans to lift it over their heads. The prowling woman stalked forward, her spear raised, ready for attack. Last of all came the heavy-set warrior carrying the spiked mace, swinging his deadly club menacingly.

"No!" shouted Kesslar, as the Werewolf threw his arm out.

The clawed hand tore at Kesslar's hamstring, the mighty leg buckling instantly, loosening the Goatlord's grip. Drew collapsed as the Goat staggered back, bringing his hand to his throat as the Wolf vanished, his therian energies exhausted. He lay on the ground as the Goatlord screamed, clutching his bloodied leg. Kesslar tried to back away, but it was no good. His enemies surrounded him in the mist, shadows that would have their revenge.

With a furious roar the Weretiger dashed forward, light-ning fast, her claws tearing across Kesslar's chest. Then he was flying in the other direction as Taboo caught him with another claw, this time across his throat. Then she was gone, returned to the mists.

"Turn on me, would you?" choked Kesslar, trying to staunch the wound at his neck. "They chanted your name in

Scoria, Taboo! I turned you into a goddess! This is how you repay me?"

The snorting sound from behind was the only warning the Were-rhino gave him. Krieg's huge horn punched into Kesslar's back, launching him into the air. Drew watched as the battered Weregoat sailed over him. He landed beside the trunk, his clawed hands fumbling over the wood as he struggled to rise, his back broken, leg snapped, and throat torn. The Goat still managed to pick up his precious box, holding his treasure close to his chest as the last therian gladiator advanced.

"Whatever he's paying you," spat Kesslar, his mouth frothing with bloody bubbles. "I'll triple it! I have here the treasure of Scoria. I'll share it with you. What do you say?"

The Behemoth brought his huge mallet back, his body shifting, doubling in size as his shadow filled the bridge. His broad head, tusks, and trunk rose through the air as he put all his weight behind the final blow. Drew looked away at the last, the Weremammoth's hammer flying, the stone block crashing through Kesslar's box, shattering the timber as if it wasn't there. The mallet shattered the Goatlord's ribcage as Kesslar's body took flight, disappearing off the bridge into the white spray, leaving a trail of blood, gems, and jewels raining through the air in its wake.

The Behemoth let the mallet fall to his side.

"Take it with you."

Krieg was at Drew's side, the horn slowly receding, the broad neck thinning once more as he cradled the young Wolflord in his arms.

"My throat . . ." whispered Drew, his voice hoarse.

"You'll live, Wolf," said the Rhino, as the Behemoth joined him.

"Thank you," Drew croaked.

"Thank your Hawklord friends," said Krieg as he helped the Wolflord to his feet.

Taboo slinked toward them, Moonbrand in her hand. For a moment, she examined the blade, checking its balance, giving it a few swipes through the air. Drew was momentarily transported back to Scoria and the wild, arrogant felinthrope he'd first met. That Taboo would have taken the sword for herself. She flipped the blade around, holding the round white metal handle out toward Drew.

"The king dropped his sword," she said, smiling, as the Steppen Falls thundered around them.

# 3

# THE RATLORD'S SKULL

**THE TORCHLIGHT SENT** shadows racing down the spiral staircase ahead of them, flickering phantoms that danced out of sight. Each curving step down the narrow stairs took them deeper into the belly of the citadel of Vermire, closer to the tomb of the Ratlords. Vanmorten led the way, the Lord Chancellor's long black robes dragging over the wet stone steps, threatening to trip up the magister following. Hector stayed close behind the Ratlord, grateful for the illumination, fearful he might stumble and fall at any moment.

"Mind your step, Lord Magister. I wouldn't want you breaking your neck."

*We can't have that happening, dear brother. Not when we're so near to our prize.*

447

Hector's Boarguard, increased in number, had accompanied him on the two-day ride north. There were now eight, Ringlin and Ibal complemented by the six Ugri warriors who had been the bodyguard to Slotha. Hector had been unaware of the Tuskun tradition that dictated that a defeated lord's or lady's vassals would immediately swear allegiance to the victor. He now had six of the mightiest warriors from the frozen wastes at his disposal. The thought was comforting to Hector, especially considering their destination.

Vanmorten and a platoon of the Lionguard had traveled also, escorting the Lord Magister up Grimm's Lane. Word must have been sent ahead that Hector was on his way, for the Vermirian army awaited them in number at the top of Grimm's Lane. Armored pikemen, mounted bowmen, filthy foot soldiers, and black-cowled scouts; the escort grew as they neared the city of the Rat King, all wanting to catch sight of the magister who had once been Vankaskan's apprentice. Hector kept the Boarguard close at all times. He knew that Vanmorten despised him, the very act of escorting the young Boar to Vermire repulsing the Rat. His business was unfinished with the Lord Chancellor, just as it was with his dead brother.

Two other members of the Rat King, Vorhaas and Vex, remained upstairs in the Citadel, watching over the Boarguard, while the eldest sibling led Hector into the tomb. War Marshal Vorjavik was away campaigning, leading the Lyssian army through the Dalelands alongside Onyx's Bastian force. His twin brother, Inquisitor Vorhaas, had remained behind in Vermire, looking after the Rat King's homeland. He'd shown surprise at the decision to allow the magister into their family crypt, but had held his tongue after a glare from Vanmorten. The youngest brother, Vex, had looked on from a distance, apparently studying the Boarlord's every move. Hector no longer spooked very easily, but Vex set his nerves on edge.

*You'll have to watch that one, brother,* Vincent had hissed.

Arriving at the base of the staircase, Vanmorten strode across to an unlit torch that hung from a bracket. Lighting it, he walked onto a rusted iron gate, feet slapping through the puddles. The stench of damp and stagnant water was overwhelming, while the constant sound of dripping echoed around the catacomb. Vanmorten reached a scarred, skeletal hand into his robes and withdrew a key, unlocking the metal door. It swung open with an ominous creak. Hector followed him through.

Stone coffins lined every wall of the room, some recessed within the crudely carved ore-stained rock. The scurrying of rats replaced the dripping noise, as Vanmorten's distant, diminutive cousins fled from the torchlight. A black marble box, less than two feet square, stood on a pedestal in the center of the low-ceilinged chamber, yet to be moved into the walls like those of the Rat King's ancestors.

"Here he is," muttered Vanmorten unenthusiastically. Hector had known from his years in Vankaskan's service that the brothers disliked one another.

"This is it?" asked Hector, surprised to be faced with a small box and not a coffin.

"What part of 'only his skull remaining' did you not understand, boy?" snarled Vanmorten.

"If you could leave me alone," said Hector, smiling politely.

"That's not going to happen, little pig. You may have fooled Opal and the prince, but I won't be tricked so easily. You've had your fun. Say your piece to his box and let's be on our way. I won't dance to your tune a moment longer."

"With respect, Lord Chancellor, my business with your brother is a sacred and magisterial matter. The Guild of Magisters' secrets go back to the Great Feast. To have you present while I bless his remains would be blasphemous."

Vanmorten sneered under his hood. Hector got a whiff of the decayed, burned flesh within the cowl as the Ratlord grated his teeth in annoyance.

"You can find your own way back up, piglet," said the Wererat, tossing him the key. "Lock up when you're done. And leave *everything* as you find it. I shall know if you've disturbed anything. Understand?"

Hector nodded, smiling. Vanmorten stormed from the chamber, disappearing up the spiral staircase. Hector followed to check he was gone before closing the door as quietly as its rusted hinges would allow. He locked it, making sure it was firmly shut. Then he turned, walking back to the black box. Hector removed the lid and placed it gently on the floor before reaching into the box and lifting the grotesque bleached-white skull of Vankaskan.

*Oh, dear brother,* gasped the Vincent-vile. *He's beautiful!*

"Now, my old master," he whispered, marveling at the partially transformed skull. "To work."

The chanting was fast and breathless, ancient words of magick known to only the few. The black candle burned brightly in Hector's right hand, oily black smoke billowing from the flame and gathering under the ceiling above. He tipped the candle over his open left hand, the molten wax pooling in his blackened palm, pouring between his fingers, searing the flesh and racing down his arm. All the while the chanting continued as the Boarlord sat, cross-legged.

The box had been removed from its plinth, the skull of the dead Ratlord now gracing the stone pedestal alone. A circle of brimstone was carefully laid out around it on the ground. Hector's words rattled from his mouth rapid-fire, unintelligible to anyone other than a magister. He stopped chanting suddenly, clenched his fist and slammed it down on to the stone floor once, twice, three times. The skull shuddered on the plinth.

"Rise, creature, and answer your master's bidding!"

Hector felt the cold rush into the room. The candle flame sputtered, fighting the breeze, clinging to the wick and refusing to die. While the candle remained lit, the rest of the crypt darkened as the shadows crept in all around, the blackness all-consuming. The coffins and walls were swallowed by the darkness, and the gate that led to the stairs vanished. Even the torch at the foot of the stairwell spluttered out, leaving the candlelight as the only illumination in the chiling chamber.

A low chuckle bloomed slowly in the center of the circle of brimstone, the yellow powder shifting as if caught by a breeze. The laughter rose, rasping like a blade on a file, causing the skin on Hector's arms to bristle.

*Well, this is a surprise*, hissed the spirit of Vankaskan, tied to the dead Ratlord's skull in the form of a vile.

Hector listened for Vincent, but heard nothing, his brother silent in the presence of a spirit as powerful and steeped in magick as Vankaskan.

"I've surprised myself, my lord," said Hector. "I wasn't sure your spirit would still be here. I thought you might have moved on."

*Alas no*, sighed Vankaskan. *My time in the mortal world isn't over by a long chalk. One cannot be surrounded and immersed in magick one's whole life and not be affected by it in death. Once one crosses over, the bridge remains, and as easy as it is for one to pass along it . . . things . . . can always come the other way. But then, you'll know that already, won't you, Hector?*

The young magister shivered at the mention of commun-

ing; the dead Ratlord was clearly already aware of Hector's dab-
bling in the dark arts.

"I'm in control, my lord," blustered Hector. "I know what
I'm doing."

*Do you? You've raised my spirit, awoken me from my slumber,
bottled my soul in the form of a vile. You know what you're doing? Can
you imagine how angry you've just made me, calling me to you like
some kind of plaything?*

Hector leaned back from the edge of the brimstone circle,
as he felt the cold breath of Vankaskan's vile wash over him.
He saw its shape now, a smoky black cloud of malevolence that
paced the yellow line like a caged beast.

*You think this sulfurous dust can stop me, Hector? You think I
won't find a way out of this little prison you've constructed for me? Why
did you summon me, Hector? Did you hope to get answers from me? An
apology perhaps for the path I set you upon?*

Vankaskan's words came thick and fast, loaded with hatred
for the young Boarlord. Hector recoiled, turning his face as if
the vile's spittle might spatter his cheek.

*I will find you, Hector,* hissed Vankaskan. *I'll come looking for
you, once I'm free of this crypt. You've woken me now, Boarlord! I shall
not sleep! I shall not return to the darkness!*

Hector turned toward the skull on the pedestal. Slowly,
very deliberately, he reached out with his wax-covered, blackened hand and placed it within the circle. The Vankaskan-vile
gasped as Hector drew his hand back, clearing away the yel-

low powder. He lifted his hand, the brimstone mixing with the cooling wax that was setting over his fist and forearm.

"I'm right here," said Hector.

*Are you* mad? gasped the Vankaskan-vile. *Is this suicide?*

"No," answered the young magister, rising to his feet and stepping into the broken circle. He felt the dead magister's vile now enveloping him, its claws moving around his throat, trying to prize open his mouth and see his insides. Hector ignored the spirit, picking up the skull in his right hand. He opened his left hand and clicked his fingers, the wax cracking and tumbling to the flagged floor.

"I'm here for everything, Vankaskan."

The Vincent-vile was onto the Ratlord's vile in an instant, tearing it off his brother.

*What is this? What's going on?*

"You don't understand, Vankaskan. There are more powerful creatures of magick than you out there. I met one; it shared its secrets with me."

The Ratlord's vile screamed as the Vincent-vile tore into it, biting and clawing at the shadowy form.

*Release your hound, Hector!*

"Every ounce of knowledge your rotten skull has held on to, every scrap and cantrip of magick lore, I'm going to take from you, Vankaskan."

Hector ran his scarred hand over his throat where the

wound from his encounter on the White Isle still remained. Vankaskan's spirit continued to wail as the Vincent-vile devoured it, bite after bite, smoky black morsels of pure magick torn from the air. Hector's heart and head pulsed as the vile feasted on the dead Rat's secrets. He stared at the skull in his hands, Vankaskan's power rushing through his body, filling every corner of his dark and dangerous soul.

"You took your time, Lord Magister," said Vanmorten as Hector arrived at the top of the staircase.

Behind the Ratlord, Vorhaas and Vex huddled, deep in conversation, looking every inch like a pair of villains plotting treason. Ringlin and Ibal rose from where they sat with their Ugri companions. The soldiers of the Rats had formed a circle around the eight Browncloaks, watching the Boarguard all the while.

"Well, you will bury your dead beneath the pits of hell, Lord Chancellor," replied Hector, a note of derision in his voice.

Vanmorten covered the distance between them in a swift stride, his long robes swirling around him, dark as night. The Boarguard moved for their weapons, but the Vermirians' swords and halberds were already poised to strike.

"How dare you come here, thinking you can speak to *me* in such a way! What makes you think I won't—"

Vanmorten's speech was cut short as Hector raised his ungloved left hand to his face, placing his forefinger to his lips. "Hush."

The hand was unrecognizable, the flesh withered and clinging to the bones, seemingly drained of all fluid. Fingers, palm, and forearm were all black, as if burned by a raging fire, giving the limb a skeletal appearance. The necrotic flesh remained taut as the knuckles clicked against one another.

"Your hand . . ." said Vanmorten, shocked by the appearance of Hector's mummified limb. The Ratlord lifted his own disfigured fingers to his throat, running them over the scarred flesh of his neck.

Hector opened his palm and examined it, as if noticing the changed appearance for the first time. He turned it one way and then the other, as though it belonged to another person, alien to the rest of his body. The skin of his face was the opposite, drained of blood, white as a skull. A sickly sheen of sweat glistened across his features as he smiled at the stunned Ratlord.

*Blackhand*, whispered the Vincent-vile.

"My hand?" repeated Hector. "Oh, my hand is strong, Lord Chancellor. I have your brother to thank for that."

# 4

## CROSSROADS

**A CROWD HAD** gathered in Windfell's great hall, returning Hawklords from the length and breadth of Lyssia and beyond.
Each stared at the rough stone wall behind the carved wooden
throne, their faces etched with sorrow. Drew stood among them,
watching with grim wonder. A pair of threadbare, tattered wings
hung staked to the brickwork, metal spikes having held them in
place for many miserable years. The skeletal frames now resembled
a moth-eaten spiderweb of thin white bones, the odd remaining
feather still clinging to the rotten remains.

"Take them down," said a choked Count Carsten.

One of the still-transformed Hawklords moved quickly,
flying toward Baron Griffyn's severed wings. Reverently, he
lifted the torn bones and feathers from the spikes, gently fold-

ing them close to his chest as he returned to the ground.

Thirty falconthropes filled the hall, each one ready for battle. More were sure to follow. Drew had expected them all to look similar to one another, but he couldn't have been more wrong. The Hawklords came in all shapes and sizes, as different as Krieg, Taboo, and the Behemoth were from each other: tall and rangy, short and wiry, heavyset, slight, young, old, fit, and out of shape. The tombwraiths had soared across the continent, seeking out the Hawklords wherever they hid, carrying Tor Raptor's screams to the four corners of Lyssia. Each had heard the call and answered.

As Griffyn's wings were taken away, the assembled Werelords looked to their most senior noblemen, Count Carsten and Baron Baum, the Eagles. Neither therian was as tall as Krieg or the Mammoth, but they were as imposing in their way, their muscular chests rippling beneath banded mail breastplates. The black-haired Carsten's broadsword remained sheathed in its scabbard, while the bald and bearded Baum leaned on his spear, the weapon fashioned from a deep red wood, filed and burned to a terrible point. Drew wondered if the spear was naturally that color or whether it remained stained from the recent battle.

"Take the throne!" called one of the Hawklords from the rear of the hall. A chorus of cheers broke out as the Werelords raised weapon and voice in support.

"The brothers!"

"Our new Lords of Windfell!"

Carsten raised his hands to quieten the crowd while his brother smiled and shook his head.

"Our enemies might have taken Griffyn from us before we could be reunited, but the baron's bloodline lives on," said Carsten.

"This throne is not ours to take," added Baum, his voice deep and rich. He lifted his spear and pointed it over his shoulder symbolically.

"Lady Shah is in the custody of King Faisal in Azra. *She* is the rightful Lady of Windfell and it's our duty to return her to her father's throne."

Nods and murmured agreements rumbled around the room, each Hawklord accepting the Eagles' words without question.

"How soon do we fly to her aid?" asked Red Rufus, his scrawny neck bobbing as he spoke. The scar that had been visible from the top of his head right down to his throat as a Werehawk was all the more livid in human form as it gouged through the left side of his face. He cut quite a different figure now from the fellow who'd wanted to kill Drew in the Tomb of the Hawklords.

Red Rufus continued. "How long has the Jackal held her prisoner? Wergar should have killed him when we had the chance. The only good Omiri's a dead one."

"It's not as simple as that, Red Rufus, as well you know,"

said Carsten, turning and holding his hand toward Drew.

The Wolflord looked surprised when Carsten beckoned him, painfully aware he was a stranger among these people—they didn't know him from the next man. The doubts had returned. What did Drew really know? What could he say that might convince them to aid him? Baum nodded, encouraging Drew to approach. Krieg's firm hand pushed him forward, through the crowd, the Hawklords parting as he walked toward the dais. He climbed the steps, standing between the two Eagles and turning to face the assembled room.

Humans had joined therians in the chamber, those hardy souls who still lived in the Barebones having returned after the sight of the Hawklords coming home to roost. Drew looked over to his companions. Krieg nodded encouragingly while the Behemoth looked on impassively. Taboo bared her teeth, somewhere between a snarl and a smile.

"Faisal isn't the enemy," Drew said at last turning to the assembled throng. "Azra's surrounded by the Jackal's foes: Doglords to the north and Hayfa to the south. Between them they'll overrun Azra."

"I fail to see why we should care about the demise of Faisal," said Red Rufus. It was clear to Drew that the old falconthrope still distrusted him.

"Aye," agreed another. "Leave the Hounds and Hyenas to tear one another apart. They're savages."

460

"The Azrans *aren't* savages. They're a proud people, not unlike yourselves."

Red Rufus scoffed, but Drew continued.

"Baron Griffyn's last wish was that his people should fly to Faisal's aid. That's why Shah remains there, already lending her wits and wisdom to the Jackal's cause. I understand the ill feeling you have for one another—the war you fought on Wergar's behalf has left wounds that have festered over the years. But a new enemy's at the gate. The world is changed."

"It's not so different," said Red Rufus. "I see we're still expected to follow a Wolf."

Drew winced. The old Hawklord's attitude was belligerent but well-founded. *Away from their homes for fifteen years and my first request is that they join me in battle? I'd feel the same.*

"This is *everyone's* fight. The threat won't go away. You can't stay out of a battle that rages around you—the Catlords will come knocking. We *need* you. I was told the Hawklords were the bravest warriors to fight by the Wolf's side, and loyal to the last."

"Loyal to old Wergar, young cub," said a voice from the rear of the group.

Another voice chimed in. "You expect us to swear fealty on account of the love we had for the dead Wolf?"

"We should fetch Shah!" cried a third Hawk. "Get her out of the desert. Leave the Omiri to butcher themselves."

Carsten and Baum watched and listened in silence, leaving the debating entirely to Drew.

*It's my task to convince these men that they should join me,* thought Drew. "It's not as simple as leaving them to fight it out," he said aloud. "The Catlords are behind the civil war in Omir. Canan's Doglords aided the Bastians' attack on Highcliff, and now Prince Lucas returns the favor. The young Lion sits on the throne, his counsel coming from the Rat King and the Werepanthers Onyx and Opal. So long as Lucas and his cronies rule, nobody is safe. They mean to take *everything*, to crush the uprising of the free people of the Seven Realms. The fighting in Westland and the Barebones, the battles in Omir—it's all one and the same. This is a war for Lyssia, and one that Bast is winning."

Drew felt his chest rising as he spoke, his words honest and true. His blood was up and his self-belief was solid. Although Red Rufus was the voice of doubt among the Hawklords, many of the old therian's brothers seemed unconcerned by him. They nodded as Drew spoke, jaws set, eyes glinting with steely resolve as they saw the fight that lay ahead. If Drew had doubted the cause previously, that reservation had been vanquished.

"Believe me, the Jackal's our ally. The Cats are the constant throughout. The Dogs, the Hyenas, the Crows, the Rats are just adding their muscle and might to these enemies of the free people of Lyssia. Lucas might reign in Highcliff, but he's a puppet, a mouthpiece. It's his friends from across the sea who seek control over the Seven Realms. Onyx and Opal are the power behind the throne. If we help defend Azra, break the back of this assault from Canan and Hayfa, then we have Faisal's army behind us. Each battle we win, we shall gain fresh allies. It starts with Azra. First we drive them out of Omir, then the Barebones and Westland. We chase them back across the Lyssian Straits, all the way back to Bast."

His voice had deepened now, his words coming out loud and heavy, bouncing off the walls of Windfell's great hall. Every man and therian watched intently, caught up in the Wolflord's passion.

"There are three other therians in this chamber who have joined me in the fight. None is Lyssian—each hails from a land far away. They fought me in the Scorian arena, and now they fight by my side: free therians, united against a common enemy. I trust each with my life."

He looked at his three friends from the Furnace. Each of them bowed back, as the assembled Hawklords stared reverently at them.

"These Werelords have traveled to a foreign land where they can expect little more than suspicious looks of fear and distrust. Their homelands have already been seized by the Catlords. They've seen firsthand what Onyx is capable of. I would return with them to Bast, once the fight here is won, lend my life to their cause in return for their sacrifice. They've put their faith in me, and Brenn be my witness, I won't let them down."

Drew glanced at the skin of his curled fist, the flesh now gray as the Wolf fought to emerge. His eyes had yellowed over, and he could see the Hawklords nodding as one. Falconthropes clapped one another on the shoulder, punched their chests, and raised their weapons.

"Join me," growled Drew. "Let's take the fight to the Beast of Bast."

The great hall of Windfell, silent for so many years, thundered with the sound of swords beating against shields and falconthropes cheering.

The Hawklords had returned.

Two hours had passed since Drew's passionate speech in the great hall, and that time hadn't been wasted. Windfell's circular courtyard was a hive of activity as the Werehawks prepared for battle. Drew, Taboo, Krieg, and the Behemoth had equipped themselves, replacing their battered gear and torn clothing with kit from the Hawklords' armory. Drew had found a studded black-leather breastplate, fashioned in the style of the Sturmish smiths, with buckles and clasps that allowed the armor to change shape as a therianthrope shifted. While there were steel breastplates and chain shirts that might provide stiffer defense against blade or bow, the leather felt right for Drew, more lightweight and less cumbersome. Besides which, the wide-eyed youth in Drew found himself grinning: it looked utterly fearsome. He even found a woodland cloak that wasn't a million miles from the tattered old Greencloak he'd been gifted by Bergan and, snatching it up, he was ready to depart.

The Hawklords looked resplendent, armed and armored, gathered and ready to take flight. News had spread quickly. The population of Windfell continued to swell with humans returning to the city. While the majority who'd left might never return, some had made new lives in nearby hamlets and settlements on the Barebones' slopes. With the sudden activity in the city above, they'd rushed home as if they'd heard Tor Raptor's screams themselves. Many now hurried around the halls of the mountain keep, helping their former lords make preparation for war.

In all, thirty-three Hawklords had returned, and thirty of them would fly to Omir. It wasn't the hundred Drew and the late Baron Griffyn had hoped for, but thirty falconthropes flying into battle was still a tremendous coup for the Wolf and his allies. Three would remain in the mountain city to prepare the people for what lay ahead, ensuring the last reminders of Skeer's reign were tossed from the parapets and Windfell was returned to its former glory.

The first "wing" of Hawklords had already taken flight, ten of them taking to the skies in the dim light of dusk. The second wing was now leaping skyward from the courtyard as they pursued their brethren into the clouds. Drew was the last of the therians from the Furnace to depart, Krieg, Taboo, and the Behemoth having been taken off in the first two wings. Two Hawklords had been needed to carry the Weremammoth, each holding an arm as they lifted the giant aloft.

Drew stood apart from the remaining Hawklords, lost in his own thoughts while they made the final adjustments to their armor ahead of the journey. He unsheathed Moonbrand and stared at the dark leather that spiraled about the handle, the wrappings centuries old yet unchanged by time. The white stone pommel was polished smooth, its likeness to the moon it was named after unmissable. In the warm light of day, the blade was steel gray, unremarkable.

"What tales you could tell," he whispered, imagining his ancestors' battles. An unending stream of questions ran through his head. *Will this sword help reunite me with my friends? With Hector, Whitley, and Gretchen? How many lives have been taken by this blade? How many wars won? Can one good soul really make a difference? Just a shepherd boy from the Cold Coast?*

"If ever a fight was just . . ." he murmured.

The flapping of the Hawklords indicated that the final wing was taking flight. He slid Moonbrand back into its scabbard before returning to the three remaining falconthropes. As he approached, two of them suddenly took to the heavens.

*And then there was one*, thought Drew, striding up to the Hawklord who would fly him into the heart of Omir.

"Hang loose like a bag o' bones, you hear me?" said Red Rufus, running his thumbs around the collar of his golden breastplate. "Limp as a dead man. That's what I need you to be."

The old therian was shifting as he spoke, rusty-colored feathers sprouting from his face as the yellow beak emerged. He straightened his bent frame as great red wings emerged through flaps of leather that ran down his armor's back. As old as Red Rufus was, he was in remarkable shape when in therian form, his legs transforming into those of a powerful, deadly raptor. The skin of his calves hardened, reminding Drew of the reptilian limbs of Ignus and Drake, while his feet split into four immense, long toes, ending in curling black talons. The big predator's eyes blinked as Rufus towered over the spellbound Wolflord.

"I'm carrying a precious cargo. I'd like to get you to the Jackal in one piece. Understand, boy?"

Drew nodded as Red Rufus shook his wings, ruffling the feathers. A shortbow hung from one hip and a quiver swung from the other.

"Ready, Wolf?"

Drew was about to answer when the clattering of a horse's hooves beyond the walls distracted him. It was swiftly followed by shouts from the men who remained in the keep. Drew made for the commotion as he saw a crowd gathering outside the gate.

"Where are you going? We need to be away—the last wing has already departed!" warned Red Rufus.

"A moment!" cried Drew, rushing off before the cantankerous old Hawklord could object further.

Directly outside the keep, the townsfolk had gathered around a horse, its rider slumped in the saddle. As Drew approached the man tumbled into the arms of the surrounding men and women. Some cried out when they noticed his cloak was dark with blood, broken arrow shafts protruding from his back.

Although he wore battered military clothes beneath the cloak, Drew reckoned he was much younger than himself. The youngster's face was ashen—a sheen of sweat glistening as his eyes fluttered. Drew counted four broken arrows in all, peppering his back and pinning his gray cloak to his torso. Recognizing the uniform instantly, Drew snatched his own waterskin from his hip. He bit the stopper off and held it to the boy's mouth. The boy drank greedily, spluttering on the liquid.

"Steady," said Drew.

"I'm a healer, my lord. I can tend to those wounds," said an old woman at Drew's shoulder, looking on with grave concern, but the Wolflord ignored her for the moment, pressing the injured Graycloak for answers.

"You're from Stormdale? A little young to be one of Manfred's men, aren't you?"

"His son," said the boy, a bout of coughing racking his chest.

"What news?" asked one of the men nearby.

"I have family in Stormdale," said another.

Drew raised his hand, calling for silence.

"Highwater's fallen. Stormdale's next. Villagers and farmers, women and children: surrounded," spluttered the boy, his voice fading. "No mercy. Crows and Rats. Kill us all . . ."

The crowd at Drew's back parted as Rufus stepped forward, flexing his wings and casting shadows over the townsfolk.

"Come, Wolf. You delay us. We need to go. We need to leave now."

Drew looked at the young Stag, the boy's eyes closed, his head lolling heavy to one side. Drew lifted him carefully, cradling him, feeling the fever-heat rolling off him. He turned to the old woman.

"Lead the way," he said, holding the boy close.

Rufus grabbed Drew by the shoulder, holding him fast. "You're not listening, Wolf!"

Drew tugged himself free from Rufus's grip, glaring at him. "We're not going to Omir."

"Have you lost your mind, pup?"

"Not at all, old bird," said Drew, his patience worn thin by the grumbling Hawklord. "You and I fly to Stormdale."

# Epilogue
## Man and Boy

**NO SOONER HAD** the lightning flashed than the thunder followed, tearing the sky apart above Moga. Ten ships blockaded the harbor, the Catlords' navy having chosen the Sturmish port as their base in the far north. Flags from Bast, Highcliff, and the Cluster Isles flapped in the fierce wind, the rain threatening to tear them from the masts. The fleet had arrived straight after the *Maelstrom*'s departure, on the hunt for the remainder of the Wolf's Council. While others had followed the pirate ship, the remaining force had taken Moga for their own.

Three men crept along the harbor road, hugging the walls and rushing between buildings. Passage was slow on account of the size of one of them, the man twice as big as his two companions. To be found on the streets after the ninth bell had tolled was punishable by death: fully two dozen Sturmish pirates swung from the gallows that had been set up in the crowded marketplace, two or three hanging from each of the scaffolds. Arriving at the ruined warehouse on the northern-most end of the docks, the two smaller men took up lookout positions in the shadows that shrouded the splintered building, while the enormous one squeezed through the broken door-way. The storm crashed overhead as the rain hammered down, the inside of the building exposed to the elements through the ramshackle roof. The big man shook the water from his heavy black cloak, the jewelry that adorned his hands and wrists jan-gling as he advanced into the heart of the warehouse. Another man emerged from the shadows, a weaselly looking fellow with a tatty black beard and a cutlass in his hand.

"My lord," he said, nodding humbly in the presence of the newcomer. The noble dismissed him with the wave of a fat, gem-laden hand.

"No time for pleasantries, Quigg. Where are they?"

The bearded pirate turned, leading the huge man deeper into the building. The floorboards groaned under the fat one's weight, threatening to splinter and carry them both into the harbor water below. The spluttering coughs of a young boy drew them through the shadows. The child sat on a barrel, a filthy old coat wrapped around him for warmth. He looked up as the two approached.

"Baron Bosa," said the boy, jumping down from the barrel to bow dramatically before the fat man. Bosa rolled his eyes at the lad's show of etiquette, considering the dire circumstances.

"You know me, child?"

"I've heard plenty about you, your lordship, from my ship-mates and my captain."

"And where's your ship now?"

"Dunno, sir; she sailed off without us. They done him in, sir. Least they tried to."

"How is it you didn't drown, boy? The Sturmish Sea could kill any man, yet you live?"

The boy shrugged.

"And you claim to have saved your captain's life?"

The boy supplied no answer, simply staring at Bosa with big brown eyes. The Whale of Moga turned to Quigg.

"Where is he?"

The black-bearded pirate pointed beyond the boy toward the dark recesses of the warehouse. The fat Whalelord strode past them, searching the shadows for his brother therian-thrope. He found the man lying within a grounded rowboat, a tarpaulin laid across him as a makeshift blanket. His face was white, eyes red-rimmed as he stared up at Bosa. The Whale reached down and pulled the tarpaulin to one side, revealing the injured man's torso; the usually pristine white shirt was stained dark.

"I see you have visitors in Moga," whispered the wounded sea captain, trying to smile through bloodied teeth. "How long have they been lodging with you?"

"My dear, sweet Vega." The Whale sighed, his voice thick with concern. "What have they done to you?"

# ACKNOWLEDGMENTS

I need to say a few words of thanks to the elite team of guys and gals at Puffin HQ who have not only supported me while I wrote the Wereworld series, but also got the books into readers' hands. Clever birds, these Puffins.

Much gratitude to Francesca Dow, MD extraordinaire, and to publishing director Sarah Hughes—I should probably restrict thanks to 140 characters as she's fluent in Twitspeak! #cheekynorthernblighter

Huge thanks to Jayde Lynch, Julia Teece, and Vanessa Godden who've had to endure my company—and obsession with Full Englishes—while we've toured schools and festivals the length and breadth of Britain.

Cheers to Samantha Mackintosh, Julia Bruce, and Mary-Jane Wilkins in editing, for polishing my dirty lumps of coal into something that sparkled.

Thanks to Zosia Knopp and her amazing rights team, including Jessica Hargreaves, Camilla Borthwick, Joanna Lawrie, Susanne Evans, and Jessica Adams. Thank-yous to Winsey

Samuels in production, Brigid Nelson and the children's division sales team, and Carl Rolfe and the Penguin sales reps, and *merci* to Rebecca Cooney in international sales.

And they say you should never judge a book by its cover. While there's a great deal of truth to that adage, I have to say that a spiffy cover really does bring a book to life. Thanks to fab designer Patrick Knowles and ace artist Andrew Farley for helping to make Wereworld turn folks' heads. A special word of thanks has to go to Jacqui McDonough, Puffin's art director and the first person I ever reached out to many, many years ago when I was trying to get into publishing as an illustrator. When I say "reached out," a more accurate description would be "pestered for two years." Whodathunk we'd finally get to work together after all that time, missus?

Last two thanks go to my left and right hands: my editor, Shannon Park, for believing in Wereworld from the get-go, and my wife, Emma, for spotting my shoddy grammar and enlightening me in the process. Cheers, m'dears!

Thank you all.

Read an excerpt from the fourth book,
*Wereworld: Nest of Serpents*

# I

# TAKE NO CHANCES

**"DID YOU HIT HIM, MASTER?"**

The Lionguard scout lowered his bow, ignoring his apprentice. He stared out across the Longridings, squinting through the twilight at the evading Greencloak. Gradually, the rider began to slouch in his saddle as his mount slowed, weaving up a rocky incline. The bowman grinned as he saw the distant figure keel to one side, sliding from his steed and hitting the frozen earth in a crumpled heap.

"Have you ever known me to miss?" the scout finally replied, stowing his bow alongside the quiver on his saddle before clambering back on to his own horse.

His companion, a youth yet to see eighteen summers,

grinned with delight. For one so young, he'd seen more than his fair share of bloodshed, having served his apprenticeship in the Lionguard scouts under his master's watchful eye. The boy wasn't shy about getting his blade wet: that would serve him well in the coming months as the Catlord armies mopped up the remnants of their enemies' ragtag force, scattered across the Seven Realms.

The scout had served in the army of Westland for three-score years, his bow having accounted for enemies of Wolf and Lion alike as they had fought for the throne. As a mortal man, he could never truly understand the noble therianthropes—their might, their majesty, and the old magicks—and it wasn't his place to question. His lieges may have changed over time, but the role had remained the same: a life spent in servitude to the shape-shifting Werelords who ruled Lyssia.

"Let's see what we've bagged," said the scout as he spurred his horse on, his young protégé riding close behind as they raced across the barren slopes towards the fallen Greencloak.

Traveling apart from their comrades allowed the scout and his apprentice to move swiftly and stealthily across the Longridings, deep into hostile territory. Powerful as the Catlord army was in the south, the grasslands were still untamed, harboring the enemies of Prince Lucas throughout. Many of the Horselords had fled to Calico, hiding behind the coastal city's enormous seawalls, while others remained in the wilds. The Werestallions weren't the only danger to the Lion's forces in the Longridings: the traveling people known as the Romari had sworn fealty to the Werelord known as Drew Ferran, last of the Werewolves and the sole reason why the Seven Realms fought this terrible, bloody civil war. The Romari were unpredictable and unconventional: they waged war through subterfuge and terrorism, striking the Catlord forces on their fringes, at their weakest points, before disappearing back into the grasslands. The scout and his charge had expected to run across the Romari: stumbling upon a Greencloak had been a surprise.

"What's a soldier of the Woodland Realm doing out in the Longridings, master?" called the youth from behind, his Redcloak clapping in the stiff winter breeze.

"A straggler or deserter, perhaps," the man cried back. "Maybe he was left behind after the taking of Cape Gala."

"He could be a spy from Brackenholme!"

It was well known that the men of the Woodland Realm were aligned with the Wolf, which made this fool fair game in the eyes of the scout. They had encountered one another by chance, the two Lionguard soldiers spying the lone rider as each had crested hillocks in the grasslands; they were dangerously close and within hailing distance. While the Greencloak had spurred his horse away, the scout had leapt down with practiced ease, his bow quick to hand, and sent an arrow sailing on its way. He had taken only one shot; he rarely took more.

"Whoever he was, and wherever he was heading, his message won't arrive." The man began to slow his mount as they neared the fallen woodlander, bringing their horses up the rock-strewn slope to where their enemy lay. "His war's over."

Twenty feet up the slope, the Greencloak lay motionless, face down on the frozen earth, his horse nearby, its head bowed solemnly. A quarterstaff lay beside the body, hinting at the soldier's profession: *a scout, perhaps?* The old tracker kept his eyes fixed on the fallen foe, although he could sense the movements of his companion in the saddle beside him, keen to investigate. He heard the dry *shlick* of the young Redcloak's hunting knife sliding out of its leather sheath. The apprentice jumped down and began walking forward, shifting the dagger in his grasp as he approached the still woodlander. The thick green cloak covered the body like a death shroud, the hood obscuring the back of the man's head, only the scuffed brown leather of his boots visible, poking out from the hem of the long emerald cloth. A sharp whistle made the youth stop and turn. His master's bow was drawn and aimed at the body on the floor. With a sharp *twang* the arrow whistled into the body, joining the earlier one, buried deep in the Greencloak's back. The apprentice's eyes widened momentarily before he nodded.

"Best take no chances," said the scout as the young Redcloak covered the remaining distance to the body.

The apprentice kicked one of the fallen rider's legs, and the booted foot wobbled lifelessly. He looked back at his master and smiled. It was a brief moment of contentment, followed swiftly by a sensation of pure horror as the leg he'd just kicked lashed

out, sweeping his own from under him and sending him crashing to the ground.

The scout's horse reared up, suddenly alarmed as the felled
Greencloak jumped into action. The old Lionguard let go of his
weapon, the saddle quiver spilling its contents as bow and arrows clattered to the ground. The rider snatched at his reins
in panic as the youth and the woodlander wrestled on the
ground. The apprentice lashed out with his dagger, and his enemy raised a forearm to deflect the blade. In the split second before the weapon struck home, the Redcloak caught sight of his
opponent's face. It wasn't a man at all, but a girl, her big brown
eyes wide and fearful as she fought for her life. The hunting
knife bit into her forearm, tearing flesh and scoring bone. The
girl let loose a roar of pain.

The scout heard it, clear as a bell. The cry was deep, ani-
malistic, primal. He'd heard it before, on the battlefield long
ago, back in the time of the last Werewar. He'd switched sides,
taking the Red at the first opportunity, and swearing fealty to
King Leopold as the Lion seized Westland from Wergar the
Wolf. The scout had been there when they'd brought Duke
Bergan, the lord of Brackenholme, to his knees at the gates of
Highcliff. That roar and this one were unmistakable. They were
the roars of a Bearlord and they chilled him to his core.

Whitley had struggled to imagine if there could be any greater
agony than that which accompanied an arrow in the back. She

5

hadn't had to wait for long, with a second arrow joining the first as the Lionguard scouts approached her motionless form. Gritting her teeth, she thanked Brenn that the thick cloth of her cloak had hidden the telltale trembling of her shaking body. By chance, the arrows had missed the vital organ of her heart, her leather armor having slowed the momentum of the shafts as they'd lanced through her torso. The injuries wouldn't prove fatal to a therian such as Whitley, but regardless, the pain was immeasurable. She could feel the blood pooling inside her breastplate, against the flesh of her belly, hot against her cold skin. The boot to her leg had told her it was time to act, her survival instinct kicking in as she brought the man to the ground in a tangle of limbs.

These two were dangerous, no doubt; scouts, just like her, searching for her friends. The Romari settlement wasn't a great distance away, full of women, children, and old folk: if the Redcloaks were to search the wider area they'd be bound to come across her comrades. Whitley wasn't only battling for her life: she was fighting for the future of her friends. While the older Lionguard struggled to control his horse, the younger man came at her fast with his knife, the blade jabbing straight for Whitley's neck. With only a moment to react, she'd brought her arm up defensively. She could see the knife wasn't silver—potentially deadly to a therianthrope like her—but it would still cause enormous damage if it struck her throat. The knife hit her arm, the steel ripping through muscle, blade squealing, scraping against bone like fingernails upon slate. The roar that escaped her throat was monstrous, a cocktail of pain and fury that heralded the arrival of the beast.

She snatched the Redcloak's hand in hers, the blood pumping from her torn forearm as they wrestled for control of the knife. Her knuckles popped and cracked as her hand contorted, shifting in size as her palm began to smother the Lionguard's. Whitley gritted her teeth, which were sharpening all the while, her gums slick with blood as the sweat beaded on her brow. The young soldier brought his other hand around, snatching at her transforming limb, trying to prise it loose as claws tore free from her flesh. His fingers splintered, crushed by her shifting hand as she ground them against the grip of his knife. He struck her across the face with his free hand, stunning her momentarily, loosening her grip enough to yank his maimed hand clear.

The hunting knife fell to the ground, and the Redcloak dived for it, snatching it up in his good hand and lunging at Whitley once more. The girl was already moving, though, reaching for her staff where it lay nearby, grabbing it by a steel-shod end and swinging it back at the young Lionguard. As he dived at her, the quarterstaff arced through the air, striking him cleanly across the temple and sending him spinning away. The Redcloak went down hard, his head hitting the nearby rocks with an awful, wet cracking sound, his body instantly still.

Panting hard, Whitley struggled to her knees. *Where was the other one?* She couldn't allow him to escape: if he rejoined his companions he'd return with more men, more Redcloaks. All would be lost. Her eyes scoured the surrounding slopes frantically. She caught sight of a billowing crimson cloak as the Lionguard tried to put distance between himself and the injured Bearlady. Wincing, she scrambled down the incline to where the rider had dropped his weapons, every painful movement reminding her that arrows were still buried in her back. She picked up the bow, her hands already shifting back to human form, her fingers fumbling for a missile. A good bow, well made, almost as good as the ones the Woodland Watch carried back in Brackenholme. It would suffice until she finally returned to her home in the Dyrewood. Raising the weapon she nocked an arrow, picking out the rider as he raced desperately, and ultimately vainly, to safety.

The bowstring sang, and the whispered words escaped Whitley's lips before the arrow struck its target.

"Take no chances."

# The Hanging Garden

# The Hanging Garden

*An Inspector Rebus Novel*

---

## IAN RANKIN

St. Martin's Press ❧ New York

The lyrics at the beginning of each book are from "The Hanging Garden"
by The Cure, reproduced by kind permission of Robert Smith and Fiction
Songs. Extract from "Burnt Norton" from *The Four Quartets* by T. S. Eliot
reproduced by kind permission of the Estate of T. S. Eliot and Faber and
Faber Ltd.

ISBN 0-312-19278-9

First published in Great Britain by Orion, an imprint of Orion Books Ltd.

First U.S. Edition: October 1998

10  9  8  7  6  5  4  3  2  1

For Miranda

'If all time is eternally present
All time is unredeemable.'

T.S. Eliot, 'Burnt Norton'


'I went to Scotland and found nothing there
that looks like Scotland'

Arthur Freed, Producer *Brigadoon*

# The Hanging Garden

# Book One

'In a Hanging Garden/Change the past'

They were arguing in the living-room.

'Look, if your bloody job's so precious ...'

'What do you want from me?'

'You know bloody well!'

'I'm working my arse off for the three of us!'

'Don't give me that crap.'

And then they saw her. She was holding her teddy bear, Pa Broon, by one well-chewed ear. She was peering round the doorway, thumb in her mouth. They turned to her.

'What is it, sweetie?'

'I had a bad dream.'

'Come here.' The mother crouched down, opening her arms. But the girl ran to her father, wrapped herself around his legs.

'Come on, pet, I'll take you back to bed.'

He tucked her in, started to read her a story.

'Daddy,' she said, 'what if I fall asleep and don't wake up? Like Snow White or Sleeping Beauty?'

'Nobody sleeps forever, Sammy. All it takes to wake them up is a kiss. There's nothing the witches and evil queens can do about that.'

He kissed her forehead.

'Dead people don't wake up,' she said, hugging Pa Broon. 'Not even when you kiss them.'

# 1

John Rebus kissed his daughter.

'Sure you don't want a lift?'

Samantha shook her head. 'I need to walk off that pizza.'

Rebus put his hands in his pockets, felt folded banknotes beneath his handkerchief. He thought of offering her some money – wasn't that what fathers did? – but she'd only laugh. She was twenty-four and independent; didn't need the gesture and certainly wouldn't take the money. She'd even tried to pay for the pizza, arguing that she'd eaten half while he'd chewed on a single slice. The remains were in a box under her arm.

'Bye, Dad.' She pecked him on the cheek.

'Next week?'

'I'll phone you. Maybe the three of us ...?' By which she meant Ned Farlowe, her boyfriend. She was walking backwards as she spoke. One final wave, and she turned away from him, head moving as she checked the evening traffic, crossing the road without looking back. But on the opposite pavement she half-turned, saw him watching her, waved her hand in acknowledgment. A young man almost collided with her. He was staring at the pavement, the thin black cord from a pair of earphones dribbling down his neck. Turn round and look at her, Rebus commanded. Isn't she incredible? But the youth kept shuffling along the pavement, oblivious to her world.

And then she'd turned a corner and was gone. Rebus could only imagine her now: making sure the pizza box was secure beneath her left arm; walking with eyes fixed firmly ahead of her; rubbing a thumb behind her right ear, which she'd recently had pierced for the third time. He knew that her nose would twitch when she thought of something funny. He knew that if she wanted to concentrate, she might tuck the corner of one jacket-lapel into her mouth. He knew that she wore a bracelet of braided leather, three silver rings, a cheap

watch with black plastic strap and indigo face. He knew that the brown of her hair was its natural colour. He knew she was headed for a Guy Fawkes party, but didn't intend staying long.

He didn't know nearly enough about her, which was why he'd wanted them to meet for dinner. It had been a tortuous process: dates rejigged, last-minute cancellations. Sometimes it was her fault, more often his. Even tonight he should have been elsewhere. He ran his hands down the front of his jacket, feeling the bulge in his inside breast pocket, his own little time-bomb. Checking his watch, he saw it was nearly nine o'clock. He could drive or he could walk – he wasn't going far.

He decided to drive.

Edinburgh on firework night, leaves blown into thick lines down the pavement. One morning soon he would find himself scraping frost from his car windscreen, feeling the cold like jabs to his kidneys. The south side of the city seemed to get the first frost earlier than the north. Rebus, of course, lived and worked on the south side. After a stint in Craigmillar, he was back at St Leonard's. He could make for there now – he was still on shift after all – but he had other plans. He passed three pubs on his way to his car. Chat at the bar, cigarettes and laughter, a fug of heat and alcohol: he knew these things better than he knew his own daughter. Two out of the three bars boasted 'doormen'. They didn't seem to be called bouncers these days. They were doormen or front-of-house managers, big guys with short hair and shorter fuses. One of them wore a kilt. His face was all scar tissue and scowl, the scalp shaved to abrasion. Rebus thought his name was Wattie or Wallie. He belonged to Telford. Maybe they all did. Graffiti on the wall further along: Won't Anyone Help? Three words spreading across the city.

Rebus parked around the corner from Flint Street and started walking. The street was in darkness at ground level, except for a cafe and amusement arcade. There was one lamppost, its bulb dead. The council had been asked by police not to replace it in a hurry – the surveillance needed all the help it could get. A few lights were shining in the tenement flats. There were three cars parked kerbside, but only one of them with people in it. Rebus opened the back door and got in.

A man sat in the driver's seat, a woman next to him. They looked cold and bored. The woman was Detective Constable Siobhan

Clarke, who had worked with Rebus at St Leonard's until a recent posting to the Scottish Crime Squad. The man, a Detective Sergeant called Claverhouse, was a Crime Squad regular. They were part of a team keeping twenty-four-hour tabs on Tommy Telford and all his deeds. Their slumped shoulders and pale faces bespoke not only tedium but the sure knowledge that surveillance was futile.

It was futile because Telford owned the street. Nobody parked here without him knowing who and why. The other two cars parked just now were Range Rovers belonging to Telford's gang. Anything but a Range Rover stuck out. The Crime Squad had a specially adapted van which they usually used for surveillance, but that wouldn't work in Flint Street. Any van parked here for longer than five minutes received close and personal attention from a couple of Telford's men. They were trained to be courteous and menacing at the same time.

'Undercover bloody surveillance,' Claverhouse growled. 'Only we're not undercover and there's nothing to survey.' He tore at a Snickers wrapper with his teeth and offered the first bite to Siobhan Clarke, who shook her head.

'Shame about those flats,' she said, peering up through the windscreen. 'They'd be perfect.'

'Except Telford owns them all,' Claverhouse said through a mouthful of chocolate.

'Are they all occupied?' Rebus asked. He'd been in the car a minute and already his toes were cold.

'Some of them are empty,' Clarke said. 'Telford uses them for storage.'

'But every bugger in and out of the main door gets spotted,' Claverhouse added. 'We've had meter readers and plumbers try to wangle their way in.'

'Who was acting the plumber?' Rebus asked.

'Ormiston. Why?'

Rebus shrugged. 'Just need someone to fix a tap in my bathroom.'

Claverhouse smiled. He was tall and skinny, with huge dark bags under his eyes and thinning fair hair. Slow-moving and slow-talking, people often underestimated him. Those who did sometimes discovered that his nickname of 'Bloody' Claverhouse was merited.

Clarke checked her watch. 'Ninety minutes till the changeover.'

'You could do with the heating on,' Rebus offered. Claverhouse turned in his seat.

'That's what I keep telling her, but she won't have it.'

'Why not?' He caught Clarke's eyes in the rearview. She was smiling.

'Because,' Claverhouse said, 'it means running the engine, and running the engine when we're not going anywhere is wasteful. Global warming or something.'

'It's true,' Clarke said.

Rebus winked at her reflection. It looked like she'd been accepted by Claverhouse, which meant acceptance by the whole team at Fettes. Rebus, the perennial outsider, envied her the ability to conform.

'Bloody useless anyway,' Claverhouse continued. 'The bugger knows we're here. The van was blown after twenty minutes, the plumber routine didn't even get Ormiston over the threshhold, and now here we are, the only sods on the whole street. We couldn't blend in less if we were doing panto.'

'Visible presence as a deterrent,' Rebus said.

'Aye, right, a few more nights of this and I'm sure Tommy'll be back on the straight and narrow.' Claverhouse shifted in his seat, trying to get comfortable. 'Any word of Candice?'

Sammy had asked her father the same thing. Rebus shook his head.

'You still think Taravicz snatched her? No chance she did a runner?'

Rebus snorted.

'Just because you want it to be them doesn't mean it was. My advice: leave it to us. Forget about her. You've got that Adolf thing to keep you busy.'

'Don't remind me.'

'Did you ever track down Colquhoun?'

'Sudden holiday. His office got a doctor's line.'

'I think we did for him.'

Rebus realised one of his hands was caressing his breast pocket. 'So is Telford in the cafe or what?'

'Went in about an hour ago,' Clarke said. 'There's a room at the back, he uses that. He seems to like the arcade, too. Those games where you sit on a motorbike and do the circuit.'

'We need someone on the inside,' Claverhouse said. 'Either that or wire the place.'

'We couldn't even get a plumber in there,' Rebus said. 'You think someone with a fistful of radio mikes is going to fare any better?'

'Couldn't do any worse.' Claverhouse switched on the radio, seeking music.

'Please,' Clarke pleaded, 'no country and western.'

Rebus stared out at the cafe. It was well-lit with a net curtain covering the bottom half of its window. On the top half was written 'Big Bites For Small Change'. There was a menu taped to the window, and a sandwich board on the pavement outside, which gave the cafe's hours as 6.30 a.m. – 8.30 p.m. The place should have been closed for an hour.

'How are his licences?'

'He has lawyers,' Clarke said.

'First thing we tried,' Claverhouse added. 'He's applied for a late-night extension. I can't see the neighbours complaining.'

'Well,' Rebus said, 'much as I'd love to sit around here chatting ...'

'End of liaison?' Clarke asked. She was keeping her humour, but Rebus could see she was tired. Disrupted sleep pattern, body chill, plus the boredom of a surveillance you know is going nowhere. It was never easy partnering Claverhouse: no great fund of stories, just constant reminding that they had to do everything 'the right way', meaning by the book.

'Do us a favour,' Claverhouse said.

'What?'

'There's a chippy across from the Odeon.'

'What do you want?'

'Just a poke of chips.'

'Siobhan?'

'Irn-Bru.'

'Oh, and John?' Claverhouse added as Rebus stepped out of the car. 'Ask them for a hot-water bottle while you're at it.'

A car turned into the street, speeding up then screeching to a halt outside the cafe. The back door nearest the kerb opened, but nobody got out. The car accelerated away, door still hanging open, but there was something on the pavement now, something crawling, trying to push itself upright.

'Get after them!' Rebus shouted. Claverhouse had already turned the ignition, slammed the gear-shift into first. Clarke was on the radio as the car pulled away. As Rebus crossed the street, the man

7

got to his feet. He stood with one hand against the cafe window, the other held to his head. As Rebus approached, the man seemed to sense his presence, staggered away from the cafe into the road.

'Christ!' he yelled. 'Help me!' He fell to his knees again, both hands scrabbling at his scalp. His face was a mask of blood. Rebus crouched in front of him.

'We'll get you an ambulance,' he said. A crowd had gathered at the window of the cafe. The door had been pulled open, and two young men were watching, like they were onlookers at a piece of street theatre. Rebus recognised them: Kenny Houston and Pretty-Boy. 'Don't just stand there!' he yelled. Houston looked to Pretty-Boy, but Pretty-Boy wasn't moving. Rebus took out his mobile, called in the emergency, his eyes fixing on Pretty-Boy: black wavy hair, eyeliner. Black leather jacket, black polo-neck, black jeans. Stones: 'Paint it Black'. But the face chalk-white, like it had been powdered. Rebus walked up to the door. Behind him, the man was beginning to wail, a roar of pain echoing into the night sky.

'We don't know him,' Pretty-Boy said.

'I didn't ask if you knew him, I asked for help.'

Pretty-Boy didn't blink. 'The magic word.'

Rebus got right up into his face. Pretty-Boy smiled and nodded towards Houston, who went to fetch towels.

Most of the customers had returned to their tables. One was studying the bloody palmprint on the window. Rebus saw another group of people, watching from the doorway of a room to the back of the cafe. At their centre stood Tommy Telford: tall, shoulders straight, legs apart. He looked almost soldierly.

'I thought you took care of your lads, Tommy!' Rebus called to him. Telford looked straight through him, then turned back into the room. The door closed. More screams from outside. Rebus grabbed the dishtowels from Houston and ran. The bleeder was on his feet again, weaving like a boxer in defeat.

'Take your hands down for a sec.' The man lifted both hands from his matted hair, and Rebus saw a section of scalp rise with them, like it was attached to the skull by a hinge. A thin jet of blood hit Rebus in the face. He turned away and felt it against his ear, his neck. Blindly he stuck the towel on to the man's head.

'Hold this.' Rebus grabbing the hands, forcing them on to the towel. Headlights: the unmarked police car. Claverhouse had his window down.

8

'Lost them in Causewayside. Stolen car, I'll bet. They'll be hoofing it.'

'We need to get this one to Emergency.' Rebus pulled open the back door. Clarke had found a box of paper hankies and was pulling out a wad.

'I think he's beyond Kleenex,' Rebus said as she handed them over.

'They're for you,' she said.

# 2

It was a three-minute drive to the Royal Infirmary. Accident &
Emergency was gearing up for firework casualties. Rebus went to
the toilets, stripped, and rinsed himself off as best he could. His
shirt was damp and cold to the touch. A line of blood had dried
down the front of his chest. He turned to look in the mirror, saw
more blood on his back. He had wet a clump of blue paper towels.
There was a change of clothes in his car, but his car was back near
Flint Street. The door of the toilets opened and Claverhouse came
in.

'Best I could do,' he said, holding out a black t-shirt. There was a
garish print on the front, a zombie with demon's eyes, wielding a
scythe. 'Belongs to one of the junior doctors, made me promise to
get it back to him.'

Rebus dried himself off with another wad of towels. He asked
Claverhouse how he looked.

'There's still some on your brow.' Claverhouse wiped the bits
Rebus had missed.

'How is he?' Rebus asked.

'They reckon he'll be okay, if he doesn't get an infection on the
brain.'

'What do you think?'

'Message to Tommy from Big Ger.'

'Is he one of Tommy's men?'

'He's not saying.'

'So what's his story?'

'Fell down a flight of steps, cracked his head at the bottom.'

'And the drop-off?'

'Says he can't remember.' Claverhouse paused. 'Eh, John ...?'

'What?'

'One of the nurses wanted me to ask you something.'

His tone told Rebus all he needed to know. 'AIDS test?'

'They just wondered.'

Rebus thought about it. Blood in his eyes, his ears, running down his neck. He looked himself over: no scratches or cuts. 'Let's wait and see,' he said.

'Maybe we should pull the surveillance,' Claverhouse said, 'leave them to get on with it.'

'And have a fleet of ambulances standing by to pick up the bodies?'

Claverhouse snorted. 'Is this sort of thing Big Ger's style?'

'Very much so,' Rebus said, reaching for his jacket.

'But not that nightclub stabbing?'

'No.'

Claverhouse started laughing, but there was no humour to the sound. He rubbed his eyes. 'Never got those chips, did we? Christ, I could use a drink.'

Rebus reached into his jacket for the quarter-bottle of Bell's.

Claverhouse didn't seem surprised as he broke the seal. He took a gulp, chased it down with another, and handed the bottle back. 'Just what the doctor ordered.'

Rebus started screwing the top back on.

'Not having one?'

'I'm on the wagon.' Rebus rubbed a thumb over the label.

'Since when?'

'The summer.'

'So why carry a bottle around?'

Rebus looked at it. 'Because that's not what it is.'

Claverhouse looked puzzled. 'Then what is it?'

'A bomb.' Rebus tucked the bottle back into his pocket. 'A little suicide bomb.'

They walked back to A&E. Siobhan Clarke was waiting for them outside a closed door.

'They've had to sedate him,' she said. 'He was up on his feet again, reeling all over the place.' She pointed to marks on the floor – airbrushed blood, smudged by footprints.

'Do we have a name?'

'He's not offered one. Nothing in his pockets to identify him. Over two hundred in cash, so we can rule out a mugging. What do you reckon for a weapon? Hammer?'

11

Rebus shrugged. 'A hammer would dent the skull. That flap looked too neat. I think they went for him with a cleaver.'

'Or a machete,' Claverhouse added. 'Something like that.'

Clarke stared at him. 'I smell whisky.'

Claverhouse put a finger to his lips.

'Anything else?' Rebus asked. It was Clarke's turn to shrug.

'Just one observation.'

'What's that?'

'I like the t-shirt.'

Claverhouse put money in the machine, got out three coffees. He'd called his office, told them the surveillance was suspended. Orders now were to stay at the hospital, see if the victim would say anything. The very least they wanted was an ID. Claverhouse handed a coffee to Rebus.

'White, no sugar.'

Rebus took the coffee with one hand. In the other he held a polythene laundry-bag, inside which was his shirt. He'd have a go at cleaning it. It was a good shirt.

'You know, John,' Claverhouse said, 'there's no point you hanging around.'

Rebus knew. His flat was a short walk away across The Meadows. His large, empty flat. There were students through the wall. They played music a lot, stuff he didn't recognise.

'You know Telford's gang,' Rebus said. 'Didn't you recognise the face?'

Claverhouse shrugged. 'I thought he looked a bit like Danny Simpson.'

'But you're not sure?'

'If it's Danny, a name's about all we can hope to get out of him. Telford picks his boys with care.'

Clarke came towards them along the corridor. She took the coffee from Claverhouse.

'It's Danny Simpson,' she confirmed. 'I just got another look, now the blood's been cleaned off.' She took a swallow of coffee, frowned. 'Where's the sugar?'

'You're sweet enough already,' Claverhouse told her.

'Why did they pick on Simpson?' Rebus asked.

'Wrong place, wrong time?' Claverhouse suggested.

12

'Plus he's pretty low down the pecking order,' Clarke added, 'making it a gentle hint.'

Rebus looked at her. Short dark hair, shrewd face with a gleam to the eyes. He knew she worked well with suspects, kept them calm, listened carefully. Good on the street, too: fast on her feet as well as in her head.

'Like I say, John,' Claverhouse said, finishing his coffee, 'any time you want to head off ...'

Rebus looked up and down the empty corridor. 'Am I in the way or something?'

'It's not that. But your job's *liaison* – period. I know the way you work: you get attached to cases, maybe even over-attached. Look at Candice. I'm just saying ...'

'You're saying, don't butt in?' Colour rose to Rebus's cheeks: *Look at Candice*.

'I'm saying it's our case, not yours. That's all.'

Rebus's eyes narrowed. 'I don't get it.'

Clarke stepped in. 'John, I think all he means is –'

'Whoah! It's okay, Siobhan. Let the man speak for himself.'

Claverhouse sighed, screwed up his empty cup and looked around for a bin. 'John, investigating Telford means keeping half an eye on Big Ger Cafferty and his crew.'

'And?'

Claverhouse stared at him. 'Okay, you want it spelling out? You went to Barlinnie yesterday – news travels in our business. You met Cafferty. The two of you had a chinwag.'

'He asked me to go,' Rebus lied.

Claverhouse held up his hands. 'Fact is, as you've just said, he asked you and you went.' Claverhouse shrugged.

'Are you saying I'm in his pocket?' Rebus's voice had risen.

'Boys, boys,' Clarke said.

The doors at the end of the corridor had swung open. A young man in dark business suit, briefcase swinging, was coming towards the drinks machine. He was humming some tune. He stopped humming as he reached them, put down his case and searched his pockets for change. He smiled when he looked at them.

'Good evening.'

Early-thirties, black hair slicked back from his forehead. One kiss-curl looped down between his eyebrows.

'Anyone got change of a pound?'

They looked in their pockets, couldn't find enough coins.

'Never mind.' Though the machine was flashing EXACT MONEY ONLY he stuck in the pound coin and selected tea, black, no sugar. He stooped down to retrieve the cup, but didn't seem in a hurry to leave.

'You're police officers,' he said. His voice was a drawl, slightly nasal: Scottish upper-class. He smiled. 'I don't think I know any of you professionally, but one can always tell.'

'And you're a lawyer,' Rebus guessed. The man bowed his head in acknowledgement. 'Here to represent the interests of a certain Mr Thomas Telford.'

'I'm Daniel Simpson's legal advisor.'

'Which adds up to the same thing.'

'I believe Daniel's just been admitted.' The man blew on his tea, sipped it.

'Who told you he was here?'

'Again, I don't believe that's any of your business, Detective ...?'

'DI Rebus.'

The man transferred his cup to his left hand so he could hold out his right. 'Charles Groal.' He glanced at Rebus's t-shirt. 'Is that what you call "plain clothes", Inspector?'

Claverhouse and Clarke introduced themselves in turn. Groal made great show of handing out business cards.

'I take it,' he said, 'you're loitering here in the hope of interviewing my client?'

'That's right,' Claverhouse said.

'Might I ask why, DS Claverhouse? Or should I address that question to your superior?'

'He's not my –' Claverhouse caught Rebus's look.

Groal raised an eyebrow. 'Not your superior? And yet he manifestly is, being an Inspector to your Sergeant.' He looked towards the ceiling, tapped a finger against his cup. 'You're not strictly colleagues,' he said at last, bringing his gaze back down to focus on Claverhouse.

'DS Claverhouse and myself are attached to the Scottish Crime Squad,' Clarke said.

'And Inspector Rebus isn't,' Groal observed. 'Fascinating.'

'I'm at St Leonard's.'

'Then this is quite rightly part of your division. But as for the Crime Squad ...'

'We just want to know what happened,' Rebus went on.

'A fall of some kind, wasn't it? How is he, by the way?'

'Nice of you to show concern,' Claverhouse muttered.

'He's unconscious,' Clarke said.

'And likely to be in an operating theatre fairly soon. Or will they want to X-ray him first? I'm not very up on the procedures.'

'You could always ask a nurse,' Claverhouse said.

'DS Claverhouse, I detect a certain hostility.'

'Just his normal tone,' Rebus said. 'Look, you're here to make sure Danny Simpson keeps his trap shut. We're here to listen to whatever bunch of shite the two of you eventually concoct for our delectation. I think that's a pretty fair summary, don't you?'

Groal cocked his head slightly to one side. 'I've heard about you, Inspector. Occasionally stories can become exaggerated but not, I'm pleased to say, in your case.'

'He's a living legend,' Clarke offered. Rebus snorted and headed back into A&E.

There was a woolly-suit in there, seated on a chair, his cap on his lap and a paperback book resting on the cap. Rebus had seen him half an hour before. The constable was sitting outside a room with its door closed tight. Quiet voices came from the other side. The woolly-suit was called Redpath and he worked out of St Leonard's. He'd been in the force a bit under a year. Graduate recruit. They called him 'The Professor'. He was tall and spotty and had a shy look about him. He closed the book as Rebus approached, but kept a finger in his page.

'Science fiction,' he explained. 'Always thought I'd grow out of it.'

'There are a lot of things we don't grow out of, son. What's it about?'

'The usual: threats to the stability of the time continuum, parallel universes.' Redpath looked up. 'What do you think of parallel universes, sir?'

Rebus nodded towards the door. 'Who's in there?'

'Hit and run.'

'Bad?' The Professor shrugged. 'Where did it happen?'

'Top of Minto Street.'

'Did you get the car?'

Redpath shook his head. 'Waiting to see if she can tell us anything. What about you, sir?'

15

'Similar story, son. Parallel universe, you could call it.'

Siobhan Clarke appeared, nursing a fresh cup of coffee. She nodded a greeting towards Redpath, who stood up: a courtesy which gained him a sly smile.

'Telford doesn't want Danny talking,' she said to Rebus.

'Obviously.'

'And meantime he'll want to even the score.'

'Definitely.'

She caught Rebus's eyes. 'I thought he was a bit out of order back there.' Meaning Claverhouse, but not wanting to name names in front of a uniform.

Rebus nodded. 'Thanks.' Meaning: you did right not to say as much at the time. Claverhouse and Clarke were partners now. It wouldn't do for her to upset him.

A door slid open and a doctor appeared. She was young, and looked exhausted. Behind her in the room, Rebus could see a bed, a figure on the bed, staff milling around the various machines. Then the door slid closed.

'We're going to do a brain scan,' the doctor was telling Redpath. 'Have you contacted her family?'

'I don't have a name.'

'Her effects are inside.' The doctor slid open the door again and walked in. There was clothing folded on a chair, a bag beneath it. As the doctor pulled out the bag, Rebus saw something. A flat white cardboard box.

A white cardboard pizza box. Clothes: black denims, black bra, red satin shirt. A black duffel-coat.

'John?'

And black shoes with two-inch heels, square-toed, new-looking except for the scuff marks, like they'd been dragged along the road.

He was in the room now. They had a mask over her face, feeding her oxygen. Her forehead was cut and bruised, the hair pushed away from it. Her fingers were blistered, the palms scraped raw. The bed she lay on wasn't really a bed but a wide steel trolley.

'Excuse me, sir, you shouldn't be in here.'

'What's wrong?'

'It's this gentleman —'

'John? John, what is it?'

Her earrings had been removed. Three tiny pin-pricks, one of them redder than its neighbours. The face above the sheet: puffy

16

blackened eyes, a broken nose, abrasions on both cheeks. Split lip, a graze on the chin, eyelids which didn't even flutter. He saw a hit and run victim. And beneath it all, he saw his daughter.

And he screamed.

Clarke and Redpath had to drag him out, helped by Claverhouse who'd heard the noise.

'Leave the door open! I'll kill you if you close that door!'

They tried to sit him down. Redpath rescued his book from the chair. Rebus tore it from him and threw it down the hall.

'How could you read a fucking book?' he spat. 'That's Sammy in there! And you're out here reading a book!'

Clarke's cup of coffee had been kicked over, the floor slippy, Redpath going down as Rebus pushed at him.

'Can you jam that door open?' Claverhouse was asking the doctor. 'And what about a sedative?'

Rebus was clawing his hands through his hair, bawling dry-eyed, his voice hoarse and uncomprehending. Staring down at himself, he saw the ludicrous t-shirt and knew that's what he'd take away from this night: the image of an Iron Maiden t-shirt and its grinning bright-eyed demon. He hauled off his jacket and started tearing at the shirt.

She was behind that door, he thought, and I was out here chatting as casual as you like. She'd been in there all the time he'd been here. Two things clicked: a hit and run; the car speeding away from Flint Street.

He grabbed at Redpath. 'Top of Minto Street. You're sure?'

'What?'

'Sammy ... top of Minto Street?'

Redpath nodded. Clarke knew straight away what Rebus was thinking.

'I don't think so, John. They were headed the opposite way.'

'Could have doubled back.'

Claverhouse had caught some of the exchange. 'I just got off the phone. The guys who did Danny Simpson, we picked up the car. White Escort abandoned in Argyle Place.'

Rebus looked at Redpath. 'White Escort?'

Redpath was shaking his head. 'Witnesses say dark-coloured.'

Rebus turned to the wall, stood there with his palms pressed to it. Staring at the paintwork, it was like he could see *inside* the paint.

Claverhouse put a hand on his shoulder. 'John, I'm sure she's going to be fine. The doctor's gone to fetch you a couple of tablets, but meantime what about one of these?'

Claverhouse with Rebus's jacket folded in the crook of his arm, the quarter-bottle in his hand.

The little suicide bomb.

He took the bottle from Claverhouse. Unscrewed its top, his eyes on the open doorway. Lifted the bottle to his lips.

Drank.

# Book Two

'In the Hanging Garden/No one sleeps'

*A seaside holiday: caravan park, long walks and sandcastles. He sat in a deck-chair, trying to read. Cold wind blowing, despite the sun. Rhona rubbed suntan lotion on Sammy, said you couldn't be too careful. Told him to keep an eye open, she was going back to the caravan for her book. Sammy was burying her father's feet in the sand.*

*He was trying to read, but thinking about work. Every day of the holiday, he sneaked off to a phone-box and called the station. They kept telling him to go and enjoy himself, forget about everything. He was halfway through a spy thriller. The plot had already lost him.*

*Rhona was doing her best. She'd wanted somewhere foreign, a bit of glamour and heat to go with the sunshine. Finances, however, were on his side. So here they were on the Fife coast, where he'd first met her. Was he hoping for something? Some memory rekindled? He'd come here with his own parents, played with Mickey, met other kids, then lost them again at the end of the fortnight.*

*He tried the spy novel again, but case-work got in the way. And then a shadow fell over him.*

*'Where is she?'*

*'What?' He looked down. His feet were buried in sand, but Sammy wasn't there. How long had she been gone? He stood up, scanned the seashore. A few tentative bathers, going in no further than their knees.*

*'Christ, John, where is she?'*

*He turned round, looked at the sand dunes in the distance.*

*'The dunes ...?'*

*They warned her. There were hollows in the dunes where the sand was eroding. Small dens had been created – a magnet for kids. Only they were prone to collapse. Earlier in the season, a ten-year-old boy had been dug out by frantic parents. He hadn't quite choked on the sand ...*

*They were running now. The dunes, the grass, no sign of her.*

*'Sammy!'*

'Maybe she went into the water.'

'You were supposed to be keeping an eye on her!'

'I'm sorry. I ...'

'Sammy!'

A small shape in one of the dens. Hopping on its hands and knees. Rhona reached in, pulled her out, hugged her.

'Sweetie, we told you not to!'

'I was a rabbit.'

Rebus looked at the fragile roof: sand meshed with the roots of plants and grasses. Punched it with a fist. The roof collapsed. Rhona was looking at him.

End of holiday.

# 3

John Rebus kissed his daughter.

'See you later,' he said, watching her as she left the coffee shop. Espresso and a slice of caramel shortbread – that's all she'd had time for – but they'd fixed another date for dinner. Nothing fancy, just a pizza.

It was October 30th. By mid-November, if Nature were feeling bloody, it would be winter. Rebus had been taught at school that there were four distinct seasons, had painted pictures of them in bright and sombre colours, but his native country seemed not to know this. Winters were long, outstaying their welcome. The warm weather came suddenly, people stripping to t-shirts as the first buds appeared, so that spring and summer seemed entwined into a single season. And no sooner had the leaves started turning brown than the first frost came again.

Sammy waved at him through the cafe window then was gone. She seemed to have grown up all right. He'd always been on the lookout for evidence of instability, hints of childhood traumas or a genetic predisposition towards self-destruction. Maybe he should phone Rhona some day and thank her, thank her for bringing Samantha up on her own. It couldn't have been easy: that was what people always said. He knew it would be nice if he could feel some responsibility for the success, but he wasn't *that* hypocritical. The truth was, while she'd been growing up, he'd been elsewhere. It was the same with his marriage: even when in the same room as his wife, even out at the pictures or around the table at a dinner party … the best part of him had been elsewhere, fixed on some case or other, some question that needed answering before he could rest.

Rebus lifted his coat from the back of his chair. Nothing left for it but to go back to the office. Sammy was headed back to her own office; she worked with ex-convicts. She had refused his offer of a

lift. Now that it was out in the open, she'd wanted to talk about her man, Ned Farlowe. Rebus had tried to look interested, but found that his mind was half on Joseph Lintz – in other words, same problem as always. When he'd been given the Lintz case, he'd been told he was well-suited to it: his Army background for one thing; and his seeming affinity for historical cases – by which Farmer Watson, Rebus's chief superintendent, had meant Bible John – for another.

'With respect, sir,' Rebus had said, 'that sounds like a load of balls. Two reasons for me getting lumbered with this: one, no other bugger will touch it with a barge-pole; two, it'll keep me out of the way for a while.'

'Your remit,' the Farmer had said, unwilling to let Rebus rile him, 'is to sift through what there is, see if any of it amounts to evidence. You can interview Mr Lintz if it'll help. Do whatever you think necessary, and if you find enough to warrant a charge ...'

'I won't. You know I won't.' Rebus sighed. 'Sir, we've been through this before. It's the whole reason the War Crimes section was shut down. That case a few years back – lot of hoo-haa about bugger all.' He was shaking his head. 'Who wants it all dragged up, apart from the papers?'

'I'm taking you off the Mr Taystee case. Let Bill Pryde handle that.'

So it was settled: Lintz belonged to Rebus.

It had started with a news story, with documents handed over to a Sunday broadsheet. The documents had come from the Holocaust Investigation Bureau based in Tel Aviv. They had passed on to the newspaper the name of Joseph Lintz, who had, they said, been living quietly in Scotland under an alias since the end of the war, and who was, in fact, Josef Linzstek, a native of Alsace. In June 1944, Lieutenant Linzstek had led the 3rd Company of an SS regiment, part of the 2nd Panzer Division, into the town of Villefranche d'Albarede in the Corrèze region of France. 3rd Company had rounded up everyone in the town – men, women, children. The sick were carried from their beds, the elderly pulled from their armchairs, babies hoisted from their cots.

A teenage girl – an evacuee from Lorraine – had seen what the Germans were capable of. She climbed into the attic of her house and hid there, watching from a small window in the roof-tiles. Everyone was marched into the village square. The teenager saw

24

her schoolfriends find their families. She hadn't been in school that day: a throat infection. She wondered if anyone would tell the Germans ...

There was a commotion as the mayor and other dignitaries remonstrated with the officer in charge. While machine guns were aimed at the crowd, these men – among them the priest, lawyer, and doctor – were set upon with rifle butts. Then ropes were produced, and strung over half a dozen of the trees which lined the square. The men were hauled to their feet, their heads pushed through the nooses. An order was given, a hand raised then dropped, and soldiers pulled on each rope, until six men were hanging from the trees, bodies writhing, legs kicking uselessly, the movements slowing by degrees.

As the teenager remembered it, it took an age for them to die. Stunned silence in the square, as if the whole village knew now, knew that this was no mere check of identity papers. More orders were barked. The men, separated from the women and children, were marched off to Prudhomme's barn, everyone else shepherded into the church. The square grew empty, except for a dozen or so soldiers, rifles slung over their shoulders. They chatted, kicked up dust and stones, shared jokes and cigarettes. One of them went into the bar and switched the radio on. Jazz music filled the air, competing with the rustle of leaves as a breeze twisted the corpses in the trees.

'It was strange,' the girl later said. 'I stopped seeing them as dead bodies. It was as if they'd become something else, parts of the trees themselves.'

Then the explosion, smoke and dust billowing from the church. A moment's silence, as though a vacuum had been created in the world, then screams, followed immediately by machine-gun fire. And when it finally stopped, she could still hear it. Because it wasn't just inside the church: it was in the distance, too.

Prudhomme's barn.

When she was finally found – by people from surrounding villages – she was naked except for a shawl she had found in a trunk. The shawl had belonged to her grandmother, dead the previous year. But she was not alone in escaping the massacre. When the soldiers had opened fire in Prudhomme's barn, they'd aimed low. The first row of men to fall had been wounded in the lower body, and the bodies which fell on them shielded them from further fire.

25

When straw was strewn over the mound and set alight, they'd waited as long as they could before starting to claw their way out from beneath, expecting at any moment to be shot. Four of them made it, two with their hair and clothes on fire, one dying later from his wounds.

Three men, one teenage girl: the only survivors.

The death toll was never finalised. No one knew how many visitors had been in Villefranche that day, how many refugees could be added to the count. A list was compiled of over seven hundred names, people who had most likely been killed.

Rebus sat at his desk and rubbed his eyes with his knuckles. The teenage girl was still alive, a pensioner now. The male survivors were all dead. But they'd been alive for the Bordeaux trial in 1953. He had summaries of their evidence. The summaries were in French. A lot of the material sitting on his desk was French, and Rebus didn't speak French. That was why he'd gone to the Modern Languages department at the university and found someone who could. Her name was Kirstin Mede, and she lectured in French, but also had a working knowledge of German, which was handy: the documents which weren't in French were in German. He had a one-page English summary of the trial proceedings, passed on from the Nazi hunters. The trial had opened in February 1953 and lasted just under a month. Of seventy-five men identified as having been part of the German force at Villefranche, only fifteen were present – six Germans and nine French Alsatians. Not one of them was an officer. One German received the death sentence, the others jail terms of between four and twelve years, but they were all released as soon as the trial finished. Alsace hadn't been enjoying the trial, and in a bid to unite the nation, the government had passed an amnesty. The Germans, meantime, were said to have already served their sentences.

The survivors of Villefranche had been horrified.

Even more extraordinary to Rebus's mind, the British had apprehended a couple of German officers involved in the massacre, but had refused to hand them over to the French authorities, returning them to Germany instead, where they lived long and prosperous lives. If Linzstek had been captured then, there would have been none of the present commotion.

Politics: it was all down to politics. Rebus looked up and Kirstin Mede was standing there. She was tall, deftly constructed, and

immaculately dressed. She wore make-up the way women usually did only in fashion adverts. Today she was wearing a check two-piece, the skirt just touching her knees, and long gold-coloured earrings. She had already opened her briefcase and was pulling out a sheaf of papers.

'Latest translations,' she said.

'Thanks.'

Rebus looked down at a note he'd made to himself: 'Corrèze trip necessary??' Well, the Farmer had said he could have whatever he wanted. He looked up at Kirstin Mede and wondered if the budget would stretch to a tour guide. She was sitting opposite him, putting on half-moon reading glasses.

'Can I get you a coffee?' he asked.

'I'm a bit pushed today. I just wanted you to see these.' She laid two sheets of paper on his desk so that they faced him. One sheet was the photocopy of a typed report, in German. The second sheet was her translation. Rebus looked at the German.

'– *Der Beginn der Vergeltungsmassnahmen hat ein merkbares Aufatmen hervorgerufen und die Stimmung sehr günstig beeinflusst.*'

'The beginning of reprisals,' he read, 'has brought about a marked improvement in morale, with the men now noticeably more relaxed.'

'It's supposed to be from Linzstek to his commander,' she explained.

'But no signature?'

'Just the typed name, underlined.'

'So it doesn't help us identify Linzstek.'

'No, but remember what we were talking about? It gives a reason for the assault.'

'A touch of R&R for the lads?'

Her look froze him. 'Sorry,' he said, raising his hands. 'Far too glib. And you're right, it's almost like the Lieutenant is trying to justify the whole thing in print.'

'For posterity?'

'Maybe. After all, they'd just started being the losing side.' He looked at the other papers. 'Anything else?'

'Some further reports, nothing too exciting. And some of the eyewitness testimony.' She looked at him with pale grey eyes. 'It gets to you after a while, doesn't it?'

Rebus looked at her and nodded.

The female survivor of the massacre lived in Juillac, and had been

questioned recently by local police about the man in charge of the German troops. Her story hadn't changed from the one she'd told at the trial: she'd seen his face only for a few seconds, and looking down from the attic of a three-storey house. She'd been shown a recent photo of Joseph Lintz, and had shrugged.

'Maybe,' she'd said. 'Yes, maybe.'

Which would, Rebus knew, be turfed out by the Procurator-Fiscal, who knew damned well what any defence lawyer with half a brain would do with it.

'How's the case coming?' Kirstin Mede asked. Maybe she'd seen some look cross his face.

'Slowly. The problem is all this stuff.' He waved towards the strewn desk. 'On the one hand I've got all this, and on the other I've got a wee old man from the New Town. The two don't seem to go together.'

'Have you met him?'

'Once or twice.'

'What's he like?'

What was Joseph Lintz like? He was cultured, a linguist. He'd even been a Professor at the university, back in the early 70s. Only for a year or two. His own explanation: 'I was filling a vacuum until they could find someone of greater standing'. He'd been Professor of German. He'd lived in Scotland since 1945 or 46 – he was vague about exact dates, blaming his memory. His early life was vague, too. He said papers had been destroyed. The Allies had had to create a duplicate set for him. There was only Lintz's word that these new papers were anything but an official record of lies he'd told and which had been believed. Lintz's story – birth in Alsace; parents and relatives all dead; forced enlistment in the SS. Rebus liked the touch about joining the SS. It was the sort of admission that would make officials decide: he's been honest about his involvement with that, so he's probably being honest about the other details. There was no actual record of a Joseph Lintz serving with any SS regiment, but then the SS had destroyed a lot of their own records once they'd seen the way the war was headed. Lintz's war record was vague, too. He mentioned shell-shock to explain the gaps in his memory. But he was vehement that he had never been called Linzstek and had never served in the Corrèze region of France.

'I was in the east,' he would say. 'That's where the Allies found me, in the east.'

The problem was that there was no convincing explanation as to how Lintz had found himself in the United Kingdom. He said he'd asked if he could go there and start a new life. He didn't want to return to Alsace, wanted to be as far away from the Germans as possible. He wanted water between him and them. Again, there was no documentation to back this up, and meantime the Holocaust investigators had come up with their own 'evidence', which pointed to Lintz's involvement in the 'Rat Line'.

'Have you ever heard of something called the Rat Line?' Rebus had asked at their first meeting.

'Of course,' Joseph Lintz had said. 'But I never had anything to do with it.'

Lintz: in the drawing-room of his Heriot Row home. An elegant four-storey Georgian edifice. A huge house for a man who'd never married. Rebus had said as much. Lintz had merely shrugged, as was his privilege. Where had the money come from?

'I've worked hard, Inspector.'

Maybe so, but Lintz had purchased the house in the late-1950s on a lecturer's salary. A colleague from the time had told Rebus everyone in the department suspected Lintz of having a private income. Lintz denied this.

'Houses were cheaper back then, Inspector. The fashion was for country properties and bungalows.'

Joseph Lintz: barely five foot tall, bespectacled. Parchment hands with liver spots. One wrist sported a pre-war Ingersoll watch. Glass-fronted bookcases lining his drawing-room. Charcoal-coloured suits. An elegant way about him, almost feminine: the way he lifted a cup to his lips; the way he flicked specks from his trousers.

'I don't blame the Jews,' he'd said. 'They'd implicate everyone if they could. They want the whole world feeling guilty. Maybe they're right.'

'In what way, sir?'

'Don't we all have little secrets, things we're ashamed of?' Lintz had smiled. 'You're playing their game, and you don't even know it.'

Rebus had pressed on. 'The two names are very similar, aren't they? Lintz, Linzstek.'

'Naturally, or they'd have absolutely no grounds for their accusations. Think, Inspector: wouldn't I have changed my name more radically? Do you credit me with a modicum of intelligence?'

'More than a modicum.' Framed diplomas on the walls, honorary

degrees, photos taken with university chancellors, politicians. When the Farmer had learned a little more about Joseph Lintz, he'd cautioned Rebus to 'ca' canny'. Lintz was a patron of the arts – opera, museums, galleries – and a great giver to charities. He was a man with *friends*. But also a solitary man, someone who was happiest when tending graves in Warriston Cemetery. Dark bags under his eyes, pushing down upon the angular cheeks. Did he sleep well?

'Like a lamb, Inspector.' Another smile. 'Of the sacrificial kind. You know, I don't blame you, you're only doing your job.'

'You seem to have no end of forgiveness, Mr Lintz.'

A careful shrug. 'Do you know Blake's words, Inspector? "And through all eternity/ I forgive you, you forgive me." I'm not so sure I can forgive the media.' This last word voiced with a distaste which manifested itself as a twist of facial muscles.

'Is that why you've set your lawyer on them?'

'"Set" makes me sound like a hunter, Inspector. This is a *newspaper*, with a team of expensive lawyers at its beck and call. Can an individual hope to win against such odds?'

'Then why bother trying?'

Lintz thumped both arms of his chair with clenched fists. 'For the principle, man!' Such outbursts were rare and short-lived, but Rebus had experienced enough of them to know that Lintz had a temper ...

'Hello?' Kirstin Mede said, angling her head to catch his gaze. 'What?'

She smiled. 'You were miles away.'

'Just across town,' he replied.

She pointed to the papers. 'I'll leave these here, okay? If you've any questions ...'

'Great, thanks.' Rebus got to his feet.

'It's okay, I know my way out.'

But Rebus was insistent. 'Sorry, I'm a bit ...' He waved his hands around his head.

'As I said, it gets to you after a while.'

As they walked back through the CID office, Rebus could feel eyes following them. Bill Pryde came up, preening, wanting to be introduced. He had curly fair hair and thick blond eyelashes, his nose large and freckled, mouth small and topped with a ginger moustache – a fashion accessory he could well afford to lose.

'A pleasure,' he said, taking Kirstin Mede's hand. Then, to Rebus: 'Makes me wish we'd swopped.'

Pryde was working on the Mr Taystee case: an ice-cream man found dead in his van. Engine left running in a lock-up, looking initially like suicide.

Rebus steered Kirstin Mede past Pryde, kept them moving. He wanted to ask her out. He knew she wasn't married, but thought there might be a boyfriend in the frame. Rebus was thinking: what would she like to eat – French or Italian? She spoke both those languages. Maybe stick to something neutral: Indian or Chinese. Maybe she was vegetarian. Maybe she didn't like restaurants. A drink then? But Rebus didn't drink these days.

'... So what do you think?'

Rebus started. Kirstin Mede had asked him something.

'Sorry?'

She laughed, realising he hadn't been listening. He began to apologise, but she shook it off. 'I know,' she said, 'you're a bit ...' And she waved her hands around her head. He smiled. They'd stopped walking. They were facing one another. Her briefcase was tucked under one arm. It was the moment to ask her for a date, any kind of date – let *her* choose.

'What's that?' she said suddenly. It was a shriek, Rebus had heard it, too. It had come from behind the door nearest them, the door to the women's toilets. They heard it again. This time it was followed by some words they understood.

'Help me, somebody!'

Rebus pushed open the door and ran in. A WPC was pushing at a cubicle door, trying to force it with her shoulder. From behind the door, Rebus could hear choking noises.

'What is it?' he said.

'Picked her up twenty minutes ago, she said she needed the loo.' The policewoman's cheeks wore a flush of anger and embarrassment.

Rebus grabbed the top of the door and hauled himself up, peering over and down on to a figure seated on the pan. The woman there was young, heavily made-up. She sat with her back against the cistern, so that she was staring up at him, but glassily. And her hands were busy. They were busy pulling a streamer of toilet-paper from the roll, stuffing it into her mouth.

'She's gagging,' Rebus said, sliding back down. 'Stand back'. He shouldered the door, tried again. Stood back and hit the lock with

31

the heel of his shoe. The door flew open, catching the seated woman on the knees. He pushed his way in. Her face was turning purple.

'Grab her hands,' he told the WPC. Then he started pulling the stream of white paper from her mouth, feeling like nothing so much as a cheap stage-show magician. There seemed to be half a roll in there, and as Rebus caught the WPC's eye, both of them let out a near-involuntary laugh. The woman had stopped struggling. Her hair was mousy-brown, lank and greasy. She wore a black skiing jacket and a tight black skirt. Her bare legs were mottled pink, bruising at one knee where the door had connected. Her bright red lipstick was coming off on Rebus's fingers. She had been crying, was crying still. Rebus, feeling guilty about the sudden laughter, crouched down so that he could look into her makeup-streaked eyes. She blinked, then held his gaze, coughing as the last of the paper was extracted.

'She's foreign,' the policewoman was explaining. 'Doesn't seem to speak English.'

'So how come she told you she needed the toilet?'

'There are ways, aren't there?'

'Where did you find her?'

'Down the Pleasance, brazen as you like.'

'That's a new patch on me.'

'Me, too.'

'Nobody with her?'

'Not that I saw.'

Rebus took the woman's hands. He was still crouching in front of her, aware of her knees brushing his chest.

'Are you all right?' She just blinked. He made his face show polite concern. 'Okay now?'

She nodded slightly. 'Okay,' she said, her voice husky. Rebus felt her fingers. They were cold. He was thinking: junkie? A lot of the working girls were. But he'd never come across one who couldn't speak English. Then he turned her hands, saw her wrists. Recent zigzag scar tissue. She didn't resist as he pushed up one sleeve of her jacket. The arm was a mass of similar inflictions.

'She's a cutter.'

The woman was talking now, babbling incoherently. Kirstin Mede, who had been standing back from proceedings, stepped forward. Rebus looked to her.

'It's not anything I understand ... not quite. Eastern European.'

32

'Try her with something.'

So Mede asked a question in French, repeating it in three or four other languages. The woman seemed to understand what they were trying to do.

'There's probably someone at the uni who could help,' Mede said.

Rebus started to stand up. The woman grabbed him by the knees, pulled him to her so that he nearly lost his balance. Her grip was tight, her face resting against his legs. She was still crying and babbling.

'I think she likes you, sir,' the policewoman said. They wrested her hands free, and Rebus stepped back, but she was after him at once, throwing herself forwards, like she was begging, her voice rising. There was an audience now, half a dozen officers in the doorway. Every time Rebus moved, she came after him on all fours. Rebus looked to where his exit was blocked by bodies. The cheap magician had become straight man in a comedy routine. The WPC grabbed her, pulled her back on to her feet, one arm twisted behind her back.

'Come on,' she said through gritted teeth. 'Back to the cell. Show's over, folks.'

There was scattered applause as the prisoner was marched away. She looked back once, seeking Rebus, her eyes pleading. For what, he did not know. He turned towards Kirstin Mede instead.

'Fancy a curry some time?'

She looked at him like he was mad.


'Two things: one, she's a Bosnian Muslim. Two, she wants to see you again.'

Rebus stared at the man from the Slavic Studies department, who'd come here at Kirstin Mede's request. They were talking in the corridor at St Leonard's.

'Bosnian?'

Dr Colquhoun nodded. He was short and almost spherical, with long black hair which was swept back either side of a bald dome. His puffy face was pockmarked, his brown suit worn and stained. He wore suede Hush Puppies – same colour as the suit. *This*, Rebus couldn't help feeling, was how dons were supposed to look. Colquhoun was a mass of nervous twitches, and had yet to make eye contact with Rebus.

'I'm not an expert on Bosnia,' he went on, 'but she says she's from Sarajevo.'

'Does she say how she ended up in Edinburgh?'

'I didn't ask.'

'Would you mind asking her now?' Rebus gestured back along the corridor. The two men walked together, Colquhoun's eyes on the floor.

'Sarajevo was hit hard in the war,' he said. 'She's twenty-two, by the way, she told me that.'

She'd looked older. Maybe she was; maybe she was lying. But as the door to the Interview Room opened and Rebus saw her again, he was struck by how unformed her face was, and he revised her age downwards. She stood up abruptly as he came in, looked like she might rush forward to him, but he held up a hand in warning, and pointed to the chair. She sat down again, hands cradling the mug of sweetened black tea. She never took her eyes off him.

'She's a big fan,' the WPC said. The policewoman – same one as the toilet incident – was called Ellen Sharpe. She was sitting on the room's other chair. There wasn't much space in the Interview Room: a table and two chairs just about filled it. On the table were twin video recorders and a twin cassette-machine. The video camera pointed down from one wall. Rebus gestured for Sharpe to give her seat to Colquhoun.

'Did she give you a name?' he asked the academic.

'She told me Candice,' Colquhoun said.

'You don't believe her?'

'It's not exactly ethnic, Inspector.' Candice said something. 'She's calling you her protector.'

'And what am I protecting her from?'

The dialogue between Colquhoun and Candice was gruff, guttural.

'She says firstly you protected her from herself. And now she says you have to continue.'

'Continue protecting her?'

'She says you own her now.'

Rebus looked at the academic, whose eyes were on Candice's arms. She had removed her skiing jacket. Underneath she wore a ribbed, short-sleeved shirt through which her small breasts were visible. She had folded her bare arms, but the scratches and slashes were all too apparent.

'Ask her if those are self-inflicted.'

Colquhoun struggled with the translation. 'I'm more used to literature and film than ... um ...'

'What does she say?'

'She says she did them herself.'

Rebus looked at her for confirmation, and she nodded slowly, looking slightly ashamed.

'Who put her on the street?'

'You mean ...?'

'Who's running her? Who's her manager?'

Another short dialogue.

'She says she doesn't understand.'

'Does she deny working as a prostitute?'

'She says she doesn't understand.'

Rebus turned to WPC Sharpe. 'Well?'

'A couple of cars stopped. She leaned in the window to talk with the drivers. They drove off again. Didn't like the look of the goods, I suppose.'

'If she can't speak English, how did she manage to "talk" to the drivers?'

'There are ways.'

Rebus looked at Candice. He began to speak to her, very softly. 'Straight fuck, fifteen, twenty for a blow job. Unprotected is an extra fiver.' He paused. 'How much is anal, Candice?'

Colour flooded her cheeks. Rebus smiled.

'Maybe not university tuition, Dr Colquhoun, but someone's taught her a few words of English. Just enough to get her working. Ask her again how she got here.'

Colquhoun mopped his face first. Candice spoke with her head lowered.

'She says she left Sarajevo as a refugee. Went to Amsterdam, then came to Britain. The first thing she remembers is a place with lots of bridges.'

'Bridges?'

'She stayed there for some time.' Colquhoun seemed shaken by the story. He handed her a handkerchief so she could wipe her eyes. She rewarded him with a smile. Then she looked at Rebus.

'Burger chips, yes?'

'Are you hungry?' Rebus rubbed his stomach. She nodded and

smiled. He turned to Sharpe. 'See what the canteen can come up with, will you?'

The WPC gave him a hard stare, not wanting to leave. 'Would you like anything, Dr Colquhoun?'

He shook his head. Rebus asked for another coffee. As Sharpe left, Rebus crouched down by the table and looked at Candice. 'Ask her how she got to Edinburgh.'

Colquhoun asked, then listened to what sounded like a long tale. He scratched some notes on a folded sheet of paper.

'The city with the bridges, she says she didn't see much of it. She was kept inside. Sometimes she was driven to some rendezvous ... You'll have to forgive me, Inspector. I may be a linguist, but I'm no expert on colloquialisms.'

'You're doing fine, sir.'

'Well, she was used as a prostitute, that much I can infer. And one day they put her in the back of a car, and she thought she was going to another hotel or office.'

'Office?'

'From her descriptions, I'd say some of her ... work ... was done in offices. Also private apartments and houses. But mostly hotel rooms.'

'Where was she kept?'

'In a house. She had a bedroom, they kept it locked.' Colquhoun pinched the bridge of his nose. 'They put her in the car one day, and next thing she knew she was in Edinburgh.'

'How long was the trip?'

'She's not sure. She slept part of the way.'

'Tell her everything's going to be all right.' Rebus paused. 'And ask her who she works for now.'

The fear returned to Candice's face. She stammered, shaking her head. Her voice sounded more guttural than ever. Colquhoun looked like he was having trouble with the translation.

'She can't tell you,' he said.

'Tell her she's safe.' Colquhoun did so. 'Tell her again,' Rebus said. He made sure she was looking at him while Colquhoun spoke. His face was set, a face she could trust. She reached a hand out to him. He took it, squeezed.

'Ask her again who she works for.'

'She can't tell you, Inspector. They'd kill her. She's heard stories.'

Rebus decided to try the name he'd been thinking of, the man who ran half the city's working girls.

'Cafferty,' he said, watching for a reaction. There was none. 'Big Ger. Big Ger Cafferty.' Her face remained blank. Rebus squeezed her hand again. There was another name ... one he'd been hearing recently.

'Telford,' he said. 'Tommy Telford.'

Candice pulled her hand away and broke into hysterics, just as WPC Sharpe pushed open the door.

Rebus walked Dr Colquhoun out of the station, recalling that just such a walk had got him into this in the first place.

'Thanks again, sir. If I need you, I hope you won't mind if I call?'

'If you must, you must,' Colquhoun said grudgingly.

'Not too many Slavic specialists around,' Rebus said. He had Colquhoun's business card in his hand, a home phone number written on its back. 'Well,' Rebus put out his free hand, 'thanks again.' As they shook, Rebus thought of something.

'Were you at the university when Joseph Lintz was Professor of German?'

The question surprised Colquhoun. 'Yes,' he said at last.

'Did you know him?'

'Our departments weren't that close. I met him at a few social functions, the occasional lecture.'

'What did you think of him?'

Colquhoun blinked. He still wasn't looking at Rebus. 'They're saying he was a Nazi.'

'Yes, but back then ...?'

'As I say, we weren't close. Are you investigating him?'

'Just curious, sir. Thanks for your time.'

Back in the station, Rebus found Ellen Sharpe outside the Interview Room door.

'So what do we do with her?' she asked.

'Keep her here.'

'You mean charge her?'

Rebus shook his head. 'Let's call it protective custody.'

'Does *she* know that?'

'Who's she going to complain to? There's only one bugger in the whole city can make out what she's saying, and I've just packed him off home.'

'What if her man comes to get her?'

'Think he will?'

She thought about it. 'Probably not.'

'No, because as far as he's concerned, all he has to do is wait, and we'll release her eventually. Meantime, she doesn't speak English, so what can she give us? And she's here illegally no doubt, so if she talks, all *we'd* probably do is kick her out of the country. Telford's clever ... I hadn't realised it, but he is. Using illegal aliens as prossies. It's sweet.'

'How long do we keep her?'

Rebus shrugged.

'And what do I tell my boss?'

'Direct all enquiries to DI Rebus,' he said, going to open the door.

'I thought it was exemplary, sir.'

He stopped. 'What?'

'Your knowledge of the charge-scale for prostitutes.'

'Just doing my job,' he said, smiling.

'One last question, sir ... ?'

'Yes, Sharpe?'

'Why? What's the big deal?'

Rebus considered this, twitched his nose. 'Good question,' he said finally, opening the door and going in.

And he knew. He knew straight away. She looked like Sammy. Wipe away the make-up and the tears, get some sensible clothes on her, and she was the spitting image.

And she was scared.

And maybe he could help her.

'What can I call you, Candice? What's your real name?'

She took hold of his hand, put her face to it. He pointed to himself.

'John,' he said.

'Don.'

'John.'

'Shaun.'

'John.' He was smiling; so was she. 'John.'

'John.'

He nodded. 'That's it. And you?' He pointed at her now. 'Who are you?'

She paused. 'Candice,' she said, as a little light died behind her eyes.

# 4

Rebus didn't know Tommy Telford by sight, but he knew where to find him.

Flint Street was a passageway between Clerk Street and Buccleuch Street, near the university. The shops had mostly closed down, but the games arcade always did good business, and from Flint Street Telford leased gaming machines to pubs and clubs across the city. Flint Street was the centre of his eastern empire.

The franchise had until recently belonged to a man called Davie Donaldson, but he'd suddenly retired on 'health grounds'. Maybe he'd been right at that: if Tommy Telford wanted something from you and you weren't forthcoming, predictions of your future health could suddenly change. Donaldson was now in hiding somewhere: hiding not from Telford but from Big Ger Cafferty, for whom he had been holding the franchise 'in trust' while Cafferty bided his time in Barlinnie jail. There were some who said Cafferty ran Edinburgh as effectively from inside as he ever had done outside, but the reality was that gangsters, like Nature, abhorred a vacuum, and now Tommy Telford was in town.

Telford was a product of Ferguslie Park in Paisley. At eleven he'd joined the local gang; at twelve a couple of woolly-suits had visited him to ask about a spate of tyre slashings. They'd found him surrounded by other gang members, nearly all of them older than him, but he was at the centre, no doubt about it.

His gang had grown with him, taking over a sizeable chunk of Paisley, selling drugs and running prostitutes, doing a bit of extortion. These days he had shares in casinos and video shops, restaurants and a haulage firm, plus a property portfolio which made him landlord to several hundred people. He'd tried to make his mark in Glasgow, but had found it sealed down tight, so had gone exploring elsewhere. There were stories he'd become friendly with

some big villain in Newcastle. Nobody could remember anything like it since the days when London's Krays had rented their muscle from 'Big Arthur' in Glasgow.

He'd arrived in Edinburgh a year ago, moving softly at first, buying a casino and hotel. Then suddenly he was inescapably *there*, like the shadow from a raincloud. With the chasing out of Davie Donaldson he'd given Cafferty a calculated punch to the gut. Cafferty could either fight or give up. Everyone was waiting for it to get messy ...

The games arcade called itself Fascination Street. The machines were all flashing insistence, in stark contrast to the dead facial stares of the players. Then there were shoot-'em-ups with huge video screens and digital imprecations.

'Think you're tough enough, punk?' one of them challenged as Rebus walked past. They had names like Harbinger and NecroCop, this latter reminding Rebus of how old he felt. He looked at the faces around him, saw a few he recognised, kids who'd been pulled into St Leonard's. They'd be on the fringes of Telford's gang, awaiting the call-up, hanging around like foster children, hoping The Family would take them. Most of them came from families who weren't families, latchkey kids grown old before their time.

One of the staff came in from the cafe.

'Who ordered the bacon sarnie?'

Rebus smiled as the faces turned to him. Bacon meant pig meant him. A moment's examination was all he warranted. There were more pressing demands on their attention. At the far end of the arcade were the really big machines: half-size motorbikes you sat astride as you negotiated the circuit on the screen in front of you. A small appreciative coterie stood around one bike, on which sat a young man dressed in a leather jacket. Not a market-stall jacket, something altogether more special. Quality goods. Shiny sharp-toed boots. Tight black denims. White polo neck. Surrounded by fawning courtiers. Steely Dan: 'Kid Charlemagne'. Rebus found a space for himself in the midst of the glaring onlookers.

'No takers for that bacon sarnie?' he asked.

'Who are you?' the man on the machine demanded.

'DI Rebus.'

'Cafferty's man.' Said with conviction.

'What?'

'I hear you and him go back.'

'I put him inside.'

'Not every cop gets visiting rights though.' Rebus realised that though Telford's gaze was fixed on the screen, he was watching Rebus in its reflection. Watching him, talking to him, yet still managing to control the bike through hairpin bends.

'So is there some problem, Inspector?'

'Yes, there's a problem. We picked up one of your girls.'

'My what?'

'She calls herself Candice. That's about as much as we know. But foreign lassies are a new one on me. And you're fairly new around here, too.'

'I'm not getting your drift, Inspector. I supply goods and services to the entertainment sector. Are you accusing me of being a pimp?'

Rebus stuck out a foot and pushed the bike sideways. On the screen, it spun and hit a crash barrier. A moment later, the screen changed. Back to the start of the race.

'See, Inspector,' Telford said, still not turning round. 'That's the beauty of games. You can always start again after an accident. Not so easy in real life.'

'What if I cut the power? Game over.'

Slowly, Telford swivelled from the hips. Now he was looking at Rebus. Close up, he looked so young. Most of the gangsters Rebus had known, they'd had a worn look, undernourished but overfed. Telford had the look of some new strain of bacteria, not yet tested or understood.

'So what is it, Rebus? Some message from Cafferty?'

'Candice,' Rebus said quietly, the slight tremor in his voice betraying his anger. With a couple of drinks in him, he'd have had Telford on the floor by now. 'From tonight, she's off the game, understood?'

'I don't know any Candice.'

'Understood?'

'Hang on, let's see if I've got this. You want me to agree with you that a woman I've never met should stop touting her hole?'

Smiles from the spectators. Telford turned back to his game. 'Where's this woman from anyway?' he asked, almost casually.

'We're not sure,' Rebus lied. He didn't want Telford knowing any more than was necessary.

'Must have been a great little chat the two of you had.'

'She's scared shitless.'

'Me, too, Rebus. I'm scared you're going to bore me to death. This Candice, did she give you a taste of the goods? I'm betting it's not every scrubber would get you this het up.'

Laughter, Rebus its brunt.

'She's off the game, Telford. Don't think about touching her.'

'Not with a bargepole, pal. Myself, I'm a clean-living sort of individual. I say my prayers last thing at night.'

'And kiss your cuddly bear?'

Telford looked at him again. 'Don't believe all the stories, Inspector. Here, grab a bacon sarnie on your way out, I think there's one going spare.' Rebus stood his ground a few moments longer, then turned away. 'And tell the mugs out front I said hello.'

Rebus walked back through the arcade and out into the night, heading for Nicolson Street. He was wondering what he was going to do with Candice. Simple answer: let her go, and hope she had the sense to keep moving. As he made to pass a parked car, its window slid down.

'Fucking well get in,' a voice ordered from the passenger seat. Rebus stopped, looked at the man who'd spoken, recognised the face.

'Ormiston,' he said, opening the back door of the Orion. 'Now I know what he meant.'

'Who?'

'Tommy Telford. I'm to tell you he said hello.'

The driver stared at Ormiston. 'Rumbled again.' He didn't sound surprised. Rebus recognised the voice.

'Hello, Claverhouse.'

DS Claverhouse, DC Ormiston: Scottish Crime Squad, Fettes's finest. On surveillance. Claverhouse: as thin as 'twa ply o' reek', as Rebus's father would have said. Ormiston: freckle-faced and with Mick McManus's hair – slick, pudding-bowl cut, unfeasibly black.

'You were blown before I walked in there, if that's any consolation.'

'What the fuck were you doing?'

'Paying my respects. What about you?'

'Wasting our time,' Ormiston muttered.

The Crime Squad were out for Telford: good news for Rebus.

'I've got someone,' he said. 'She works for Telford. She's frightened. You could help her.'

'The frightened ones don't talk.'

'This one might.'

Claverhouse stared at him. 'And all we'd have to do is ...?'

'Get her out of here, set her up somewhere.'

'Witness relocation?'

'If it comes to that.'

'What does she know?'

'I'm not sure. Her English isn't great.'

Claverhouse knew when he was being sold something. 'Tell us,' he said.

Rebus told them. They tried not to look interested.

'We'll talk to her,' Claverhouse said.

Rebus nodded. 'So how long has this been going on?'

'Ever since Telford and Cafferty squared off.'

'And whose side are we on?'

'We're the UN, same as always,' Claverhouse said. He spoke slowly, measuring each word and phrase. A careful man, DS Claverhouse. 'Meantime, you go charging in like some bloody mercenary.'

'I've never been a great one for tactics. Besides, I wanted to see the bastard close up.'

'And?'

'He looks like a kid.'

'And he's as clean as a whistle,' Claverhouse said. 'He's got a dozen lieutenants who'd take the fall for him.'

At the word 'lieutenants', Rebus's mind flashed to Joseph Lintz. Some men gave orders, some carried them out: which group was the more culpable?

'Tell me something,' he said, 'the teddy bear story ... is it true?'

Claverhouse nodded. 'In the passenger seat of his Range Rover. A fucking huge yellow thing, sort they raffle in the pub Sunday lunchtime.'

'So what's the story?'

Ormiston turned in his seat. 'Ever hear of Teddy Willocks? Glasgow hardman. Carpentry nails and a claw-hammer.'

Rebus nodded. 'You welched on someone, Willocks came to see you with the carpentry bag.'

'But then,' Claverhouse took over, 'Teddy got on the wrong side of some Geordie bastard. Telford was young, making a name for himself, and he very badly wanted an in with this Geordie, so he took care of Teddy.'

'And that's why he carries a teddy around with him,' Ormiston said. 'A reminder to everyone.'

Rebus was thinking. Geordie meant someone from Newcastle. Newcastle, with its bridges over the Tyne ...

'Newcastle,' he said softly, leaning forward in his seat.

'What about it?'

'Maybe Candice was there. Her city of bridges. She might link Telford to this Geordie gangster.'

Ormiston and Claverhouse looked at one another.

'She'll need a safe place to stay,' Rebus told them. 'Money, somewhere to go afterwards.'

'A first-class flight home if she helps us nail Telford.'

'I'm not sure she'll want to go home.'

'That's for later,' Claverhouse said. 'First thing is to talk to her.'

'You'll need a translator.'

Claverhouse looked at him. 'And of course you know just the man ... ?'

She was asleep in her cell, curled under the blanket, only her hair visible. The Mothers of Invention: 'Lonely Little Girl'. The cell was in the women's block. Painted pink and blue, a slab to sleep on, graffiti scratched into the walls.

'Candice,' Rebus said quietly, squeezing her shoulder. She started awake, as if he'd administered an electric shock. 'It's okay, it's me, John.'

She looked round blindly, focused on him slowly. 'John,' she said. Then she smiled.

Claverhouse was off making phone calls, squaring things. Ormiston stood in the doorway, appraising Candice. Not that Ormiston was known to be choosy. Rebus had tried Colquhoun at home, but there'd been no answer. So now Rebus was gesturing, letting her know they wanted to take her somewhere.

'A hotel,' he said.

She didn't like that word. She looked from him to Ormiston and back again.

'It's okay,' Rebus said. 'It's just a place for you to sleep, that's all, somewhere safe. No Telford, nothing like that.'

She seemed to soften, came off the bed and stood in front of him. Her eyes seemed to say, I'll trust you, and if you let me down I won't be surprised.

45

Claverhouse came back. 'All fixed,' he said, his examination falling on Candice. 'She doesn't speak any English?'

'Not as practised in polite society.'

'In that case,' Ormiston said, 'she should be fine with us.'

Three men and a young woman in a dark blue Ford Orion, heading south out of the city. It was late now, past midnight, black taxis cruising. Students were spilling from pubs.

'They get younger every year.' Claverhouse was never short of a cliche.

'And more of them end up joining the force,' Rebus commented.

Claverhouse smiled. 'I meant prossies, not students. We pulled one in last week, said she was fifteen. Turned out she was twelve, on the run. All grown up about it.'

Rebus tried to remember Sammy at twelve. He saw her scared, in the clutches of a madman with a grievance against Rebus. She'd had lots of nightmares afterwards, till her mother had taken her to London. Rhona had phoned Rebus a few years later. She just wanted to let him know he'd robbed Sammy of her childhood.

'I phoned ahead,' Claverhouse said. 'Don't worry, we've used this place before. It's perfect.'

'She'll need some clothes,' Rebus said.

'Siobhan can fetch her some in the morning.'

'How is Siobhan?'

'Seems fine. Hasn't half cut into the jokes and the language though.'

'Ach, she can take a joke,' Ormiston said. 'Likes a drink, too.'

This last was news to Rebus. He wondered how much Siobhan Clarke would change in order to blend with her new surroundings.

'It's just off the bypass,' Claverhouse said, meaning their destination. 'Not far now.'

The city ended suddenly. Green belt, plus the Pentland Hills. The bypass was quiet, Ormiston doing the ton between exits. They came off at Colinton and signalled into the hotel. It was a motorist's stop, one of a nationwide chain: same prices, same rooms. The cars which crowded the parking area were salesmen's specials, cigarette packets littering the passenger seats. The reps would be sleeping, or lying in a daze with the TV remote to hand.

Candice seemed reluctant to get out of the car, until she saw that Rebus was coming, too.

'You light up her life,' Ormiston offered.

46

At reception, they signed her in as one half of a couple – Mrs Angus Campbell. The two Crime Squad cops had the routine off pat. Rebus watched the hotel clerk, but a wink from Claverhouse told him the man was okay.

'Make it the first floor, Malcolm,' Ormiston said. 'Don't want anyone peeking in the windows.'

Room number 20. 'Will someone be with her?' Rebus asked as they climbed the stairs.

'Right there in the room,' Claverhouse said. 'The landing's too obvious, and we'd freeze our bums off in the car. Did you give me Colquhoun's number?'

'Ormiston has it.'

Ormiston was unlocking the door. 'Who's on first watch?'

Claverhouse shrugged. Candice was looking towards Rebus, seeming to sense what was being discussed. She snatched at his arm, jabbering in her native tongue, looking first to Claverhouse and then to Ormiston, all the time waving Rebus's arm.

'It's okay, Candice, really. They'll take care of you.'

She kept shaking her head, holding him with one hand and pointing at him with the other, prodding his chest to make her meaning clear.

'What do you say, John?' Claverhouse asked. 'A happy witness is a willing witness.'

'What time's Siobhan expected?'

'I'll hurry her up.'

Rebus looked at Candice again, sighed, nodded. 'Okay.' He pointed to himself, then to the room. 'Just for a little while, okay?'

Candice seemed satisfied with this, and went inside. Ormiston handed Rebus the key.

'I don't want you young things waking the neighbours now ...'

Rebus closed the door on his face.

The room was exactly as expected. Rebus filled the kettle and switched it on, dumped a tea-bag into a cup. Candice pointed to the bathroom, made turning motions with her hands.

'A bath?' He gestured with his arm. 'Go ahead.'

The curtain over the window was closed. He parted it and looked out. A grassy slope, occasional lights from the bypass. He made sure the curtains were closed tight, then tried adjusting the heating. The room was stifling. There didn't seem to be a thermostat, so he went back to the window and opened it a fraction. Cold night air, and the

47

swish of nearby traffic. He opened the pack of custard creams, two small biscuits. Suddenly he felt ravenous. He'd seen a snack machine in the lobby. Plenty of change in his pockets. He made the tea, added milk, sat down on the sofa. For want of any other distractions, he turned the TV on. The tea was fine. The tea was absolutely fine, no complaints there. He picked up the phone and called Jack Morton.

'Did I wake you?'

'Not really. How's it going?'

'I wanted a drink today.'

'So what's new?'

Rebus could hear his friend making himself comfortable. Jack had helped Rebus get off the booze. Jack had said he could phone any time he liked.

'I had to talk to this scumbag, Tommy Telford.'

'I know the name.'

Rebus lit a cigarette. 'I think a drink would have helped.'

'Before or after?'

'Both.' Rebus smiled. 'Guess where I am now?'

Jack couldn't, so Rebus told him the story.

'What's your angle?' Jack asked.

'I don't know.' Rebus thought about it. 'She seems to need me. It's been a long time since anyone's felt like that.' As he said the words, he feared they didn't tell the whole story. He remembered another argument with Rhona, her screaming that he'd exploited every relationship he'd ever had.

'Do you still want that drink?' Jack was asking.

'I'm a long way from one.' Rebus stubbed out his cigarette. 'Sweet dreams, Jack.'

He was on his second cup of tea when she came back in, wearing the same clothes, her hair wet and hanging in rat's-tails.

'Better?' he asked, making the thumbs-up sign. She nodded, smiling. 'Do you want some tea?' He pointed to the kettle. She nodded again, so he made her a cup. Then he suggested a trip to the snack machine. Their haul included crisps, nuts, chocolate, and a couple of cans of Coke. Another cup of tea finished off the tiny cartons of milk. Rebus lay along the sofa, shoes off, watching soundless television. Candice lay on the bed, fully-clothed, sliding the occasional crisp from its packet, flicking channels. She seemed to have forgotten he was there. He took this as a compliment.

He must have fallen asleep. The touch of her fingers on his knee brought him awake. She was standing in front of him, wearing the t-shirt and nothing else. She stared at him, fingers still resting on his knee. He smiled, shook his head, led her back to bed. Made her lie down. She lay on her back, arms stretched. He shook his head again and pulled the duvet over her.

'That's not you any more,' he told her. 'Goodnight, Candice.'

Rebus retreated to the sofa, lay down again, and wished she would stop saying his name.

The Doors: 'Wishful Sinful' ...

A tapping at the door brought him awake. Still dark outside. He'd forgotten to close the window, and the room was cold. The TV was still playing, but Candice was asleep, duvet kicked off, chocolate wrappers strewn around her bare legs and thighs. Rebus covered her up, then tiptoed to the door, peered through the spyhole, and opened up.

'For this relief, much thanks,' he whispered to Siobhan Clarke.

She was carrying a bulging polythene bag. 'Thank God for the twenty-four-hour shop.' They went inside. Clarke looked at the sleeping woman, then went over to the sofa and started unpacking the bag.

'For you,' she whispered, 'a couple of sandwiches.'

'God bless the child.'

'For sleeping beauty, some of my clothes. They'll do till the shops open.'

Rebus was already biting into the first sandwich. Cheese salad on white bread had never tasted finer.

'How am I getting home?' he asked.

'I called you a cab.' She checked her watch. 'It'll be here in two minutes.'

'What would I do without you?'

'It's a toss-up: either freeze to death or starve.' She closed the window. 'Now go on, get out of here.'

He looked at Candice one last time, almost wanting to wake her to let her know he wasn't leaving for good. But she was sleeping so soundly, and Siobhan could take care of everything.

So he tucked the second sandwich into his pocket, tossed the room-key on to the sofa, and left.

Four-thirty. The taxi was idling outside. Rebus felt hungover. He went through a mental list of all the places he could get a drink at

this time of night. He didn't know how many days it had been since he'd had a drink. He wasn't counting.

He gave his address to the cabbie, and settled back, thinking again of Candice, so soundly asleep, and protected for now. And of Sammy, too old now to need anything from her father. She'd be asleep too, snuggling into Ned Farlowe. Sleep was innocence. Even the city looked innocent in sleep. He looked at the city sometimes and saw a beauty his cynicism couldn't touch. Someone in a bar – recently? years back? – had challenged him to define romance. How could he do that? He'd seen too much of love's obverse: people killed for passion and from lack of it. So that now when he saw beauty, he could do little but respond to it with the realisation that it would fade or be brutalised. He saw lovers in Princes Street Gardens and imagined them further down the road, at the crossroads where betrayal and conflict met. He saw valentines in the shops and imagined puncture wounds, real hearts bleeding.

Not that he'd voiced any of this to his public bar inquisitor.

'Define romance,' had been the challenge. And Rebus's response? He'd picked up a fresh pint of beer and kissed the glass.

He slept till nine, showered and made some coffee. Then he phoned the hotel, and Siobhan assured him all was well.

'She was a bit startled when she woke up and saw me instead of you. Kept saying your name. I told her she'd see you again.'

'So what's the plan?'

'Shopping – one quick swoop on The Gyle. After that, Fettes. Dr Colquhoun's coming in at noon for an hour. We'll see what we get.'

Rebus was at his window, looking down on a damp Arden Street. 'Take care of her, Siobhan.'

'No problem.'

Rebus knew there'd be no problem, not with Siobhan. This was her first real action with the Crime Squad, she'd be doing her damnedest to make it a success. He was in the kitchen when the phone rang.

'Is that Inspector Rebus?'

'Who's speaking?' A voice he didn't recognise.

'Inspector, my name is David Levy. We've never met. I apologise for calling you at home. I was given this number by Matthew Vanderhyde.'

Old man Vanderhyde: Rebus hadn't seen him in a while.

'Yes?'

'I must say, I was astonished when it transpired he knew you.' The voice was tinged with a dry humour. 'But by now nothing about Matthew should surprise me. I went to him because he knows Edinburgh.'

'Yes?'

Laughter on the line. 'I'm sorry, Inspector. I can't blame you for being suspicious when I've made such a mess of the introductions. I am a historian by profession. I've been contacted by Solomon Mayerlink to see if I might offer assistance.'

Mayerlink ... Rebus knew the name. Placed it: Mayerlink ran the Holocaust Investigation Bureau.

'And exactly what "assistance" does Mr Mayerlink think I need?'

'Perhaps we could discuss it in person, Inspector. I'm staying in a hotel on Charlotte Square.'

'The Roxburghe?'

'Could we meet there? This morning, ideally.'

Rebus looked at his watch. 'An hour?' he suggested.

'Perfect. Goodbye, Inspector.'

Rebus called into the office, told them where he'd be.

# 5

They sat in the Roxburghe's lounge, Levy pouring coffee. An elderly couple in the far corner, beside the window, pored over sections of newspaper. David Levy was elderly, too. He wore black-rimmed glasses and had a small silver beard. His hair was a silver halo around a scalp the colour of tanned leather. His eyes seemed constantly moist, as if he'd just chewed on an onion. He sported a dun-coloured safari suit with blue shirt and tie beneath. His walking-stick rested against his chair. Now retired, he'd worked in Oxford, New York State, Tel Aviv itself, and several other locations around the globe.

'I never came into contact with Joseph Lintz, however. No reason why I should, our interests being different.'

'So why does Mr Mayerlink think you can help me?'

Levy put the coffee pot back on its tray. 'Milk? Sugar?' Rebus shook his head to both, then repeated his question.

'Well, Inspector,' Levy said, tipping two spoonfuls of sugar into his own cup, 'it's more a matter of moral support.'

'Moral support?'

'You see, many people before you have been in the same position in which you now find yourself. I'm talking about objective people, professionals with no axe to grind, and no real stake in the investigation.'

Rebus bristled. 'If you're suggesting I'm not doing my job ...'

A pained look crossed Levy's face. 'Please, Inspector, I'm not making a very good job of this, am I? What I mean is that there will be times when you will doubt the validity of what you are doing. You'll doubt its worth.' His eyes gleamed. 'Perhaps you've already had doubts?'

Rebus said nothing. He had a drawerful of doubts, especially now

that he had a real, living, breathing case – Candice. Candice, who might lead to Tommy Telford.

'You could say I'm here as your conscience, Inspector.' Levy winced again. 'No, I didn't put that right, either. You already have a conscience, that's not under debate.' He sighed. 'The question you've no doubt been pondering is the same one I've asked myself on occasions: can time wash away responsibility? For me, the answer would have to be no. The thing is this, Inspector.' Levy leaned forward. 'You are not investigating the crimes of an old man, but those of a young man who now happens to be old. Focus your mind on that. There have been investigations before, half-hearted affairs. Governments wait for these men to die rather than have to try them. But each investigation is an act of remembrance, and remembrance is never wasted. Remembrance is the only way we learn.'

'Like we've learned with Bosnia?'

'You're right, Inspector, as a race we've always been slow to take in lessons. Sometimes they have to be hammered home.'

'And you think I'm your carpenter? Were there Jews in Villefranche?' Rebus couldn't remember reading of any.

'Does it matter?'

'I'm just wondering, why the interest?'

'To be honest, Inspector, there is a slight ulterior motive.' Levy sipped coffee, considering his words. 'The Rat Line. We'd like to show that it existed, that it operated to save Nazis from possible tormentors.' He paused. 'That it worked with the tacit approval – the *more* than tacit approval – of several western governments and even the Vatican. It's a question of general complicity.'

'What you want is for everyone to feel guilty?'

'We want recognition, Inspector. We want the truth. Isn't that what you want? Matthew Vanderhyde would have me believe it is your guiding principle.'

'He doesn't know me very well.'

'I wouldn't be so sure of that. Meantime, there are people out there who want the truth to stay hidden.'

'The truth being ...?'

'That known war criminals were brought back to Britain – and elsewhere – and offered new lives, new identities.'

'In exchange for what?'

'The Cold War was starting, Inspector. You know the old saying: My enemy's enemy is my friend. These murderers were protected

by the secret services. Military Intelligence offered them jobs. There are people who would rather this did not become general knowledge.'

'So?'

'So a trial, an open trial, would expose them.'

'You're warning me about spooks?'

Levy put his hands together, almost in an attitude of prayer. 'Look, I'm not sure this has been a completely satisfactory meeting, and for that I apologise. I'll be staying here for a few days, maybe longer if necessary. Could we try this again?'

'I don't know.'

'Well, think about it, won't you?' Levy extended his right hand. Rebus took it. 'I'll be right here, Inspector. Thank you for seeing me.'

'Take care, Mr Levy.'

'*Shalom*, Inspector.'

At his desk, Rebus could still feel Levy's handshake. Surrounded by the Villefranche files, he felt like the curator of some museum visited only by specialists and cranks. Evil had been done in Villefranche, but had Joseph Lintz been responsible? And even if he had, had he perhaps atoned during the past half-century? Rebus phoned the Procurator-Fiscal's office to let them know how little progress he was making. They thanked him for calling. Then he went to see the Farmer.

'Come in, John, what can I do for you?'

'Sir, did you know the Crime Squad had set up a surveillance on our patch?'

'You mean Flint Street?'

'So you know about it?'

'They keep me informed.'

'Who's acting as liaison?'

The Farmer frowned. 'As I say, John, they keep me informed.'

'So there's no liaison at street level?' The Farmer stayed silent. 'By rights there should be, sir.'

'What are you getting at, John?'

'I want the job.'

The Farmer stared at his desk. 'You're busy on Villefranche.'

'I want the job, sir.'

'John, liaison means diplomacy. It's never been your strongest suit.'

So Rebus explained about Candice, and how he was already tied into the case. 'And since I'm already in, sir,' he concluded, 'I might as well act as liaison.'

'What about Villefranche?'

'That remains a priority, sir.'

The Farmer looked into his eyes. Rebus didn't blink. 'All right then,' he said at last.

'You'll let Fettes know?'

'I'll let them know.'

'Thank you, sir.' Rebus turned to leave.

'John ...?' The Farmer was standing behind his desk. 'You know what I'm going to say.'

'You're going to tell me not to tread on too many toes, not to go off on my own little crusade, to keep in regular contact with you, and not betray your trust in me. Does that just about do it, sir?'

The Farmer shook his head, smiling. 'Bugger off,' he said.

Rebus buggered off.


When he walked into the room, Candice rose so quickly from her chair that it fell to the floor. She came forward and gave him a hug, while Rebus looked at the faces around them – Ormiston, Claverhouse, Dr Colquhoun, and a WPC.

They were in an Interview Room at Fettes, Lothian and Borders Police HQ. Colquhoun was wearing the same suit as the previous day and the same nervous look. Ormiston was picking up Candice's chair. He'd been standing against one wall. Claverhouse was seated at the table beside Colquhoun, a pad of paper in front of him, pen poised above it.

'She says she's happy to see you,' Colquhoun translated.

'I'd never have guessed.' Candice was wearing new clothes: denims too long for her and turned up four inches at the ankle; a black woollen v-neck jumper. Her skiing jacket was hanging over the back of her chair.

'Get her to sit down again, will you?' Claverhouse said. 'We're pushed for time.'

There was no chair for Rebus, so he stood next to Ormiston and the WPC. Candice went back to the story she'd been telling, but glanced regularly towards him. He noticed that beside Claverhouse's

pad of paper sat a brown folder and an A4-sized envelope. On top of the envelope sat a black and white surveillance shot of Tommy Telford.

'This man,' Claverhouse asked, tapping the photo, 'she knows him?'

Colquhoun asked, then listened to her answer. 'She ...' He cleared his throat. 'She hasn't had any direct dealings with him.' Her two-minute commentary reduced to this. Claverhouse dipped into the envelope, spread more photos before her. Candice tapped one of them.

'Pretty-Boy,' Claverhouse said. He picked up the photo of Telford again. 'But she's had dealings with this man, too?'

'She's ...' Colquhoun mopped his face. 'She's saying something about Japanese people ... Oriental businessmen.'

Rebus shared a look with Ormiston, who shrugged.

'Where was this?' Claverhouse asked.

'In a car ... more than one car. You know, a sort of convoy.'

'She was in one of the cars?'

'Yes.'

'Where did they go?'

'They headed out of town, stopping once or twice.'

'Juniper Green,' Candice said, quite clearly.

'Juniper Green,' Colquhoun repeated.

'They stopped there?'

'No, they stopped before that.'

'To do what?'

Colquhoun spoke with Candice again. 'She doesn't know. She thinks one of the drivers went into a shop for some cigarettes. The others all seemed to be looking at a building, as if they were interested in it, but not saying anything.'

'What building?'

'She doesn't know.'

Claverhouse looked exasperated. She wasn't giving him much of anything, and Rebus knew that if there was nothing she could trade, Crime Squad would dump her straight back on the street. Colquhoun was all wrong for this job, completely out of his depth.

'Where did they go after Juniper Green?'

'Just drove around the countryside. For two or three hours, she thinks. They would stop sometimes and get out, but just to look at

the scenery. Lots of hills and ...' Colquhoun checked something. 'Hills and flags.'

'Flags? Flying from buildings?'

'No, stuck into the ground.'

Claverhouse gave Ormiston a look of hopelessness.

'Golf courses,' Rebus said. 'Try describing a golf course to her, Dr Colquhoun.'

Colquhoun did so, and she nodded agreement, beaming at Rebus. Claverhouse was looking at him, too.

'Just a guess,' Rebus said with a shrug. 'Japanese businessmen, it's what they like about Scotland.'

Claverhouse turned back to Candice. 'Ask her if she ... accommodated any of these men.'

Colquhoun cleared his throat again, colour flooding his cheeks as he spoke. Candice looked down at the table, moved her head in the affirmative, started to speak.

'She says that's why she was there. She was fooled at first. She thought maybe they just wanted a pretty woman to look at. They had a nice lunch ... the beautiful drive ... But then they came back into town, dropped the Japanese off at a hotel, and she was taken up to one of the hotel rooms. Three of them ... she, as you put it yourself, DS Claverhouse, she "accommodated" three of them.'

'Does she remember the name of the hotel?'

She didn't.

'Where did they have lunch?'

'A restaurant next to flags and ...' Colquhoun corrected himself. 'Next to a golf course.'

'How long ago was this?'

'Two or three weeks.'

'And how many of them were there?'

Colquhoun checked. 'The three Japanese, and maybe four other men.'

'Ask her how long she's been in Edinburgh,' Rebus asked.

Colquhoun did so. 'She thinks maybe a month.'

'A month working the street ... funny we haven't picked her up.'

'She was put there as a punishment.'

'For what?' Claverhouse asked. Rebus had the answer.

'For making herself ugly.' He turned to Candice. 'Ask her why she cuts herself.'

Candice looked at him and shrugged.

'What's your point?' Ormiston asked.

'She thinks the scars will deter punters. Which means she doesn't like the life she's been leading.'

'And helping us is her only sure ticket out?'

'Something like that.'

So Colquhoun asked her again, then said: 'They don't like that she does it. That's why she does it.'

'Tell her if she helps us, she won't ever have to do anything like that again.'

Colquhoun translated, glancing at his watch.

'Does the name Newcastle mean anything to her?' Claverhouse asked.

Colquhoun tried the name. 'I've explained to her that it's a town in England, built on a river.'

'Don't forget the bridges,' Rebus said.

Colquhoun added a few words, but Candice only shrugged. She looked upset that she was failing them. Rebus gave her another smile.

'What about the man she worked for?' Claverhouse asked. 'The one before she came to Edinburgh.'

She seemed to have plenty to say about this, and kept touching her face with her fingers while she talked. Colquhoun nodded, made her stop from time to time so he could translate.

'A big man ... fat. He was the boss. Something about his skin ... a birthmark maybe, certainly something distinctive. And glasses, like sunglasses but not quite.'

Rebus saw Claverhouse and Ormiston exchange another look. It was all too vague to be much use. Colquhoun checked his watch again. 'And cars, a lot of cars. This man crashed them.'

'Maybe he got a scar on his face,' Ormiston offered.

'Glasses and a scar aren't going to get us very far,' Claverhouse added.

'Gentlemen,' Colquhoun said, while Candice looked towards Rebus, 'I'm afraid I'm going to have to leave.'

'Any chance of coming back in later, sir?' Claverhouse asked.

'You mean today?'

'I thought maybe this evening ...?'

'Look, I do have other commitments.'

'We appreciate that, sir. Meantime, DC Ormiston will run you back into town.'

'My pleasure,' Ormiston said, all charm. They needed Colquhoun, after all. They had to keep him sweet.

'One thing,' Colquhoun said. 'There's a refugee family in Fife. From Sarajevo. They'd probably take her in. I could ask.'

'Thank you, sir,' Claverhouse said. 'Maybe later on, eh?'

Colquhoun seemed disappointed as Ormiston led him away.

Rebus walked over to Claverhouse, who was shuffling his photos together.

'Bit of an oddball,' Claverhouse commented.

'Not used to the real world.'

'Not much help either.'

Rebus looked towards Candice. 'Mind if I take her out?'

'What?'

'Just for an hour.' Claverhouse stared at him. 'She's been cooped up here, and only her hotel room to look forward to. I'll drop her back there in an hour, hour and a half.'

'Bring her back in one piece, preferably with a smile on her face.'

Rebus motioned for Candice to join him.

'Japanese and golf courses,' Claverhouse mused. 'What do you think?'

'Telford's a businessman, we know that. Businessmen do deals with other businessmen.'

'He runs bouncers and slot machines: what's the Japanese connection?'

Rebus shrugged. 'I leave the hard questions to the likes of you.' He opened the door.

'And, John?' Claverhouse warned, nodding towards Candice. 'She's Crime Squad property, okay? And remember, *you* came to *us*.'

'No bother, Claverhouse. And by the way, I'm your B Division liaison.'

'Since when?'

'With immediate effect. If you don't believe me, ask your boss. This might be your case, but Telford works out of *my* territory.'

He took Candice by the arm and marched her from the room.

He stopped the car on the corner of Flint Street.

'It's okay, Candice,' he said, seeing her agitation. 'We're staying in the car. Everything's all right.' Her eyes were darting around, looking for faces she didn't want to see. Rebus started the car again

and drove off. 'Look,' he told her, 'we're leaving.' Knowing she couldn't understand. 'I'm guessing this is where you started from that day.' He looked at her. 'The day you went to Juniper Green. The Japanese would be staying in a central hotel, somewhere pricey. You picked them up, then headed east. Along Dalry Road maybe?' He was speaking for his own benefit. 'Christ, I don't know. Look, Candice, anything you see, anything that looks familiar, just let me know, okay?'

'Okay.'

Had she understood? No, she was smiling. All she'd heard was that final word. All she knew was that they were heading away from Flint Street. He took her down on to Princes Street first.

'Was it a hotel here, Candice? The Japanese? Was it here?' She gazed from the window with a blank look.

He headed up Lothian Road. 'Usher Hall,' he said. 'Sheraton ... Any of it ring a bell?' Nothing did. Out along the Western Approach Road, Slateford Road, and on to Lanark Road. Most of the lights were against them, giving her plenty of time to study the buildings. Each newsagent's they passed, Rebus pointed it out, just in case the convoy had paused there to buy cigarettes. Soon they were out of town and entering Juniper Green.

'Juniper Green!' she said, pointing at the signpost, delighted to have something to show him. Rebus attempted a smile. There were plenty of golf courses around the city. He couldn't hope to take her to every one of them, not in a week never mind an hour. He stopped for a few moments by the side of a field. Candice got out, so he followed, lit a cigarette. There were two stone gateposts next to the road, but no sign of a gate between them, or any sort of path behind them. Once there might have been a track, and a house at the end of it. Atop one of the pillars sat the badly worn representation of a bull. Candice pointed towards the ground behind the other pillar, where another lump of carved stone lay, half-covered by weeds and grass.

'Looks like a serpent,' Rebus said. 'Maybe a dragon.' He looked at her. 'It'll all mean something to somebody.' She looked back at him blankly. He saw Sammy's features, reminded himself that he wanted to help her. He was in danger of letting that slip, of focusing on how she might help them get to Telford.

Back in the car, he branched off towards Livingston, intending to head for Ratho and from there back into town. Then he noticed that Candice had turned to look out of the back window.

'What is it?'

She came out with a stream of words, her tone uncertain. Rebus turned the car anyway, and drove slowly back the way they'd just come. He stopped at the side of the road, opposite a low dry-stone wall, beyond which lay the undulations of a golf course.

'Recognise it?' She mumbled more words. Rebus pointed. 'Here? Yes?'

She turned to him, said something which sounded apologetic.

'It's okay,' he told her. 'Let's take a closer look anyway.' He drove to where a vast iron double-gate stood open. A sign to one side read POYNTINGHAME GOLF AND COUNTRY CLUB. Beneath it: 'Bar Lunches and A La Carte, Visitors Welcome'. As Rebus drove through the gates, Candice started nodding again, and when an oversized Georgian house came into view she almost bounced in her seat, slapping her hands against her thighs.

'I think I get the picture,' Rebus said.

He parked outside the main entrance, squeezing between a Volvo estate and a low-slung Toyota. Out on the course, three men were finishing their round. As the final putt went in, hands went to wallets and money changed hands.

Two things Rebus knew about golf: one, to some people it was a religion; two, a lot of players liked a bet. They'd bet on final tally, each hole, even every shot if they could.

And didn't the Japanese have a passion for gambling?

He took Candice's arm as he escorted her into the main building. Piano music from the bar. Panatella smoke and oak-panelling. Huge portraits of self-important unknowns. A few old wooden putters, framed behind glass. A poster advertised a Halloween dinner-dance for that evening. Rebus walked up to reception, explained who he was and what he wanted. The receptionist made a phone call, then led them to the Chief Executive's office.

Hugh Malahide, bald and thin, mid-forties, already had a slight stammer, which intensified when Rebus asked his first question. By throwing it back at the questioner, he seemed to be playing for time.

'Have we had any Japanese visitors recently? Well, we do get a few golfers.'

'These men came to lunch. Maybe a fortnight, three weeks back. There were three of them, plus three or four Scottish men. Probably driving Range Rovers. The table may have been reserved in the name of Telford.'

'Telford?'

'Thomas Telford.'

'Ah, yes ...' Malahide wasn't enjoying this at all.

'You know Mr Telford?'

'In a manner of speaking.'

Rebus leaned forward in his chair. 'Go on.'

'Well, he's ... look, the reason I seem so reticent is because we don't want this made common knowledge.'

'I understand, sir.'

'Mr Telford is acting as go-between.'

'Go-between?'

'In the negotiations.'

Rebus saw what Malahide was getting at. 'The Japanese want to buy Poyntinghame?'

'You understand, Inspector, I'm just the manager here. I mean, I run the day-to-day business.'

'But you're the Chief Executive.'

'With no personal share in the club. The actual owners were set against selling at first. But an offer has been made, and I believe it's a very good one. And the potential buyers ... well, they're persistent.'

'Have there been any threats, Mr Malahide?'

He looked horrified. 'What sort of threats?'

'Forget it.'

'The negotiations haven't been *hostile*, if that's what you mean.'

'So these Japanese, the ones who had lunch here ... ?'

'They were representing the consortium.'

'The consortium being ... ?'

'I don't know. The Japanese are always very secretive. Some big company or corporation, I'd guess.'

'Any idea why they want Poyntinghame?'

'I've wondered that myself.'

'And?'

'Everyone knows the Japanese love golf. It might be a prestige thing. Or it could be that they're opening a plant of some kind in Livingston.'

'And Poyntinghame would become the factory social club?'

Malahide shivered at the thought. Rebus got to his feet.

'You've been very helpful, sir. Anything else you can tell me?'

'Look, this has been off the record, Inspector.'

'I've no problem with that. I don't suppose you've got any names?'

'Names?'

'Of the diners that day.'

Malahide shook his head. 'I'm sorry, not even credit card details. Mr Telford paid cash as usual.'

'Did he leave a big tip?'

'Inspector,' smiling, 'some secrets are sacrosanct.'

'Let's keep this conversation that way, too, sir, all right?'

Malahide looked at Candice. 'She's a prostitute, isn't she? I thought as much the day they were here.' There was revulsion in his voice. 'Tarty little thing, aren't you?'

Candice stared at him, looked to Rebus for help, said a few words neither man understood.

'What's she saying?' Malahide asked.

'She says she once had a punter who looked just like you. He dressed in plus-fours and made her whack him with a mashie-niblick.'

Malahide showed them out.

# 6

Rebus telephoned Claverhouse from Candice's room.

'Could be something or nothing,' Claverhouse said, but Rebus could tell he was interested, which was good: the longer he stayed interested, the longer he'd want to hang on to Candice. Ormiston was on his way to the hotel to resume babysitting duties.

'What I want to know is, how the hell did Telford land something like this?'

'Good question,' Claverhouse said.

'It's way out of his previous sphere, isn't it?'

'As far as we know.'

'A chauffeur service for Jap companies ...'

'Maybe he's after the contract to supply their gaming machines.'

Rebus shook his head. 'I still don't get it.'

'Not your problem, John, remember that.'

'I suppose so.' There was a knock at the door. 'Sounds like Ormiston.'

'I doubt it. He's just left.'

Rebus stared at the door. 'Claverhouse, wait on the line.'

He left the receiver on the bedside table. The knock was repeated. Rebus motioned for Candice, who'd been flicking through a magazine on the sofa, to move into the bathroom. Then he crept up to the door and put his eye to the spy-hole. A woman: the day-shift receptionist. He unlocked the door.

'Yes?'

'Letter for your wife.'

He stared at the small white envelope which she was trying to hand him.

'Letter,' she repeated.

There was no name or address on the envelope, no stamp. Rebus

took it and held it to the light. A single sheet of paper inside, and something flat and square, like a photograph.

'A man handed it in at reception.'

'How long ago?'

'Two, three minutes.'

'What did he look like?'

She shrugged. 'Tallish, short brown hair. He was wearing a suit, took the letter out of a briefcase.'

'How do you know who it's for?'

'He said it was for the foreign woman. He described her to a T.'

Rebus was staring at the envelope. 'Okay, thanks,' he mumbled. He closed the door, went back to the telephone.

'What is it?' Claverhouse asked.

'Someone's just dropped off a letter for Candice.' Rebus tore open the envelope, holding the receiver between shoulder and chin. There was a Polaroid photo and a single sheet, handwritten in small capitals. Foreign words.

'What does it say?' Claverhouse asked.

'I don't know.' Rebus tried a couple of words aloud. Candice had emerged from the bathroom. She snatched the paper from him and read it quickly, then fled back into the bathroom.

'It means something to Candice,' Rebus said. 'There's a photo, too.' He looked at it. 'She's on her knees gamming some fat bloke.'

'Description?'

'The camera's not exactly interested in his face. Claverhouse, we've got to get her away from here.'

'Hang on till Ormiston arrives. They might be trying to panic you. If they want to snatch her, one cop in a car isn't going to cause much of a problem. Two cops just might.'

'How did they know?'

'We'll think about that later.'

Rebus was staring at the bathroom door, remembering the locked cubicle at St Leonard's. 'I've got to go.'

'Be careful.'

Rebus put down the receiver.

'Candice?' He tried the door. It was locked. 'Candice?' He stood back and kicked. The door wasn't as strong as the one in St Leonard's; he nearly took it off its hinges. She was seated on the toilet, a plastic safety razor in her hand, slashing it across her arms. There was blood on her t-shirt, blood spraying the white tiled floor.

She started screaming at him, the words collapsing into monosyllables. Rebus grabbed the razor, nicked his thumb in the process. He pulled her off the toilet, flushed the razor, and started wrapping towels around her arms. The note was lying in the bath. He waved it in her face.

'They're trying to scare you, that's all.' Not even half-believing it himself. If Telford could find her this quickly, if he had the means of writing to her in her own language, then he was much stronger, much cleverer than Rebus had suspected.

'It's going to be okay,' he went on. 'I promise. It's all okay. We'll look after you. We'll get you out of here, take you somewhere he can't get to you. I promise, Candice. Look, this is me talking.'

But she was bawling, tears dripping from her cheeks, head shaking from side to side. For a time, she'd actually believed in knights on white chargers. Now, she was realising how stupid she'd been ...

The coast seemed to be clear.

Rebus took her in his car, Ormiston tucked in behind. No other way to play it. It was a trade-off: a speedy exit versus hanging around for a cavalry escort. And the way Candice was bleeding, they couldn't afford to wait. The drive to the hospital was nerve-tingling, then there was the wait while her wounds were checked and some of them sewn up. Rebus and Ormiston waited in A&E, drinking coffee from beakers, asking one another questions they couldn't answer.

'How did he know?'

'Who did he get to write the note?'

'Why give us a warning? Why not just grab her?'

'What does the note say?'

It struck Rebus that they were near the university. He took Dr Colquhoun's card from his pocket and phoned his office. Colquhoun was in. Rebus read the message out to him, spelling some of the words.

'They sound like addresses,' Colquhoun said. 'Untranslatable.'

'Addresses? Are any towns named?'

'I don't think so.'

'Sir, we'll be taking her to Fettes if she's well enough ... any chance you could meet us there? It's important.'

'Everything with you chaps is important.'

'Yes, sir, but this is *important*. Candice's life may be in danger.'

66

Colquhoun took time answering. 'I suppose in that case ...'

'I'll send a car for you.'

After an hour, she was well enough to leave. 'The cuts weren't too deep,' the doctor said. 'Not life-threatening.'

'They weren't meant to be.' Rebus turned to Ormiston. 'She thinks she's going back to Telford, that's why she did it. She *knows* she's going back to him.'

Candice looked as though all the blood had been drained from her. Her face seemed more skeletal than before, and her eyes darker. Rebus tried to recall what her smile looked like. He doubted he'd be seeing one for a while. She kept her arms folded protectively in front of her, and wouldn't meet his eyes. Rebus had seen suspects act that way in custody: people for whom the world had become a trap.

At Fettes, Claverhouse and Colquhoun were already waiting. Rebus handed over the note and photo.

'As I said, Inspector,' Colquhoun stated, 'addresses.'

'Ask her what they mean,' Claverhouse demanded. They were in the same room as before. Candice knew her place, and was already seated, her arms still folded, showing cream-coloured bandages and pink plasters. Colquhoun asked, but it was as though he'd ceased to exist. Candice stared at the wall in front of her, unblinking, her only motion a slight rocking to and fro.

'Ask her again,' Claverhouse said. But Rebus interrupted before Colquhoun could start.

'Ask her if people she knows live there, people who are important to her.'

As Colquhoun formed the question, the rocking grew slightly in intensity. There were fresh tears in her eyes.

'Her mother and father? Brothers and sisters?'

Colquhoun translated. Candice tried to stop her mouth trembling.

'Maybe she left a kid behind ...'

As Colquhoun asked, Candice flew from her chair, shouting and screaming. Ormiston tried to grab her, but she kicked out at him. When she'd calmed, she subsided in a corner of the room, arms over her head.

'She's not going to tell us anything,' Colquhoun translated. 'She was stupid to believe us. She just wants to go now. There's nothing she can help us with.'

Rebus and Claverhouse shared a look.

'We can't hold her, John, not if she wants to leave. It's been

dodgy enough keeping her away from a lawyer. Once she starts asking to go ...' He shrugged.

'Come on, man,' Rebus hissed, 'she's shit-scared, and with good reason. And now you've got all you're going to get out of her, you're just going to hand her back to Telford?'

'Look, it's not a question of –'

'He'll kill her, you know he will.'

'If he was going to kill her, she'd be dead.' Claverhouse paused. 'He's cleverer than that. He knows damned well all he had to do was give her a fright. He *knows* her. It sticks in my craw, too, but what can we do?'

'Just keep her a few days, see if we can't ...'

'Can't what? You want to hand her over to Immigration?'

'It's an idea. Get her the hell away from here.'

Claverhouse pondered this, then turned to Colquhoun. 'Ask her if she wants to go back to Sarajevo.'

Colquhoun asked. She slurred some answer, choking back tears.

'She says if she goes back, they'll kill everyone.'

Silence in the room. They were all looking at her. Four men, men with jobs, family ties, men with lives of their own. In the scheme of things, they seldom realised how well off they were. And now they realised something else: how helpless they were.

'Tell her,' Claverhouse said quietly, 'she's free to walk out of here at any time, if that's what she really wants. If she stays, we'll do our damnedest to help her ...'

So Colquhoun spoke to her, and she listened, and when he'd finished she pushed herself back on to her feet and looked at them. Then she wiped her nose on her bandages, pushed the hair out of her eyes, and walked to the door.

'Don't go, Candice,' Rebus said.

She half-turned towards him. 'Okay,' she said.

Then she opened the door and was gone.

Rebus grabbed Claverhouse's arm. 'We've got to pull Telford in, warn him not to touch her.'

'You think he needs telling?'

'You think he'd listen?' Ormiston added.

'I can't believe this. He scared her half to death, and as a result we let her walk? I really can't get my head round this.'

'She could always have gone to Fife,' Colquhoun said. With Candice out of the room, he seemed to have perked up a bit.

'Bit late now,' Ormiston said.

'He beat us this time, that's all,' Claverhouse said, his eyes on Rebus. 'But we'll take him down, don't worry.' He managed a thin, humourless smile. 'Don't think we're giving up, John. It's not our style. Early days yet, pal. Early days ...'

She was waiting for him out in the car park, standing by the passenger-door of his battered Saab 900.

'Okay?' she said.

'Okay,' he agreed, smiling with relief as he unlocked the car. He could think of only one place to take her. As he drove through The Meadows, she nodded, recognising the tree-lined playing fields.

'You've been here before?'

She said a few words, nodded again as Rebus turned into Arden Street. He parked the car and turned to her.

'You've been *here*?'

She pointed upwards, fingers curled into the shape of binoculars.

'With Telford?'

'Telford,' she said. She made a show of writing something down, and Rebus took out his notebook and pen, handed them over. She drew a teddy bear.

'You came in Telford's car?' Rebus interpreted. 'And he watched one of the flats up there?' He pointed to his own flat.

'Yes, yes.'

'When was this?' She didn't understand the question. 'I need a phrasebook,' he muttered. Then he opened his door, got out and looked around. The cars around him were all empty. No Range Rovers. He signalled for Candice to get out and follow him.

She seemed to like his living-room, went straight to the record collection but couldn't find anything she recognised. Rebus went into the kitchen to make coffee and to think. He couldn't keep her here, not if Telford knew about the place. Telford ... why had he been watching Rebus's flat? The answer was obvious: he knew the detective was linked to Cafferty, and therefore a potential threat. He thought Rebus was in Cafferty's pocket. Know your enemy: it was another rule Telford had learned.

Rebus phoned a contact from the *Scotland on Sunday* business section.

'Japanese companies,' Rebus said. 'Rumours pertaining to.'

'Can you narrow that down?'

'New sites around Edinburgh, maybe Livingston.'

Rebus could hear the reporter shuffling papers on his desk. 'There's a whisper going round about a microprocessor plant.'

'In Livingston?'

'That's one possibility.'

'Anything else?'

'Nope. Why the interest?'

'Cheers, Tony.' Rebus put down the receiver, looked across at Candice. He couldn't think where else to take her. Hotels weren't safe. One place came to mind, but it would be risky ... Well, not so very risky. He made the call.

'Sammy?' he said. 'Any chance you could do me a favour ... ?'

Sammy lived in a 'colonies' flat in Shandon. Parking was almost impossible on the narrow street outside. Rebus got as close as he could.

Sammy was waiting for them in the narrow hallway, and led them into the cramped living-room. There was a guitar on a wicker chair and Candice lifted it, setting herself on the chair and strumming a chord.

'Sammy,' Rebus said, 'this is Candice.'

'Hello there,' Sammy said. 'Happy Halloween.' Candice was putting chords together now. 'Hey, that's Oasis.'

Candice looked up, smiled. 'Oasis,' she echoed.

'I've got the CD somewhere ...' Sammy examined a tower of CDs next to the hi-fi. 'Here it is. Shall I put it on?'

'Yes, yes.'

Sammy switched the hi-fi on, told Candice she was going to make some coffee, and beckoned for Rebus to follow her into the kitchen.

'So who is she?' The kitchen was tiny. Rebus stayed in the doorway.

'She's a prostitute. Against her will. I don't want her pimp getting her.'

'Where's she from again?'

'Sarajevo.'

'And she doesn't have much English?'

'How's your Serbo-Croat?'

'Rusty.'

Rebus looked around. 'Where's your boyfriend?'

'Out working.'

'On the book?' Rebus didn't like Ned Farlowe. Partly it was that name: 'Neds' were what the *Sunday Post* called hooligans. They robbed old ladies of their pension books and walking-frames. Those were the Neds of this world. And Farlowe meant Chris Farlowe: 'Out of Time', a number one that should have belonged to the Stones. Farlowe was researching a history of organised crime in Scotland.

'Sod's law,' Sammy said. 'He needs money to buy the time to write the thing.'

'So what's he doing?'

'Just some freelance stuff. How long am I babysitting?'

'A couple of days at most. Just till I find somewhere else.'

'What will he do if he finds her?'

'I'm not that keen to find out.'

Sammy finished rinsing the mugs. 'She looks like me, doesn't she?'

'Yes, she does.'

'I've got some time off coming. Maybe I'll phone in, see if I can stay here with her. What's her real name?'

'She hasn't told me.'

'Has she any clothes?'

'At a hotel. I'll get a patrol car to bring them.'

'She's really in danger?'

'She might be.'

Sammy looked at him. 'But I'm not?'

'No,' her father said. 'Because it'll be our secret.'

'And what do I tell Ned?'

'Keep it short, just say you're doing your dad a favour.'

'You think a journalist's going to be content with that?'

'If he loves you.'

The kettle boiled, clicked off. Sammy poured water into three mugs. Through in the living-room, Candice's interest had shifted to a pile of American comic books.

Rebus drank his coffee, then left them to their music and their comics. Instead of going home, he made for Young Street and the Ox, ordering a mug of instant. Fifty pee. Pretty good deal, when you thought about it. Fifty pence for ... what, half a pint? A pound a pint? Cheap at twice the price. Well, one-point-seven times the price, which would take it to the price of a beer ... give or take.

Not that Rebus was counting.

The back room was quiet, just somebody scribbling away at the table nearest the fire. He was a regular, a journalist of some kind. Rebus thought of Ned Farlowe, who would want to know about Candice, but if anyone could keep him at bay, Sammy could. Rebus took out his mobile, phoned Colquhoun's office.

'Sorry to bother you again,' he said.

'What is it now?' The lecturer sounded thoroughly exasperated.

'Those refugees you mentioned. Any chance you could have a word with them?'

'Well, I ...' Colquhoun cleared his throat. 'Yes, I suppose I could talk to them. Does that mean ...?'

'Candice is safe.'

'I don't have their number here.' Colquhoun sounded fuddled again. 'Can it wait till I go home?'

'Phone me when you've talked to them. And thanks.'

Rebus rang off, finished his coffee, and called Siobhan Clarke at home.

'I need a favour,' he said, feeling like a broken record.

'How much trouble will it get me in?'

'Almost none.'

'Can I have that in writing?'

'Think I'm stupid?' Rebus smiled. 'I want to see the files on Telford.'

'Why not just ask Claverhouse?'

'I'd rather ask you.'

'It's a lot of stuff. Do you want photocopies?'

'Whatever.'

'I'll see what I can do.' Voices were raised in the front bar. 'You're not in the Ox, are you?'

'As it happens, yes.'

'Drinking?'

'A mug of coffee.'

She laughed in disbelief and told him to take care. Rebus ended the call and stared at his mug. People like Siobhan Clarke, they could drive a man to drink.

# 7

It was 7 a.m. when the buzzer sounded, telling him there was someone at his tenement's main door. He staggered along the hall to the intercom, and asked who the bloody hell it was.

'The croissant man,' a rough English voice replied.

'The what?'

'Come on, dick-brain, wakey-wakey. Memory's not so hot these days, eh?'

A name tilted into Rebus's head. 'Abernethy?'

'Now open up, it's perishing down here.'

Rebus pushed the buzzer to let Abernethy in, then jogged back to the bedroom to put on some clothes. His mind felt numb. Abernethy was a DI in Special Branch, London. The last time he'd been in Edinburgh had been to chase terrorists. Rebus wondered what the hell he was doing here now.

When the doorbell sounded, Rebus tucked in his shirt and walked back down the hall. True to his word, Abernethy was carrying a bag of croissants. He hadn't changed much: same faded denims and black leather bomber, same cropped brown hair spiked with gel. His face was heavy, pockmarked, and his eyes an unnerving, psychopath's blue.

'How've you been, mate?' Abernethy slapped Rebus's shoulder and marched past him into the kitchen. 'Get the kettle on then.' Like they did this every day of the week. Like they didn't live four hundred miles apart.

'Abernethy, what the hell are you doing here?'

'Feeding you, of course, same thing the English have always done for the Jocks. Got any butter?'

'Try the butter-dish.'

'Plates?'

Rebus pointed to a cupboard.

'Bet you drink instant: am I right?'

'Abernethy ...'

'Let's get this ready first, then talk, okay?'

'The kettle boils quicker if you switch it on at the plug.'

'Right.'

'And I think there's some jam.'

'Any honey?'

'Do I look like a bee?'

Abernethy smirked. 'Old Georgie Flight sends his love, by the way. Word is, he'll be retiring soon.'

George Flight: another ghost from Rebus's past. Abernethy had unscrewed the top from the coffee jar and was sniffing the granules.

'How fresh is this?' He wrinkled his nose. 'No class, John.'

'Unlike you, you mean? When did you get here?'

'Hit town half an hour ago.'

'From London?'

'Stopped a couple of hours in a lay-by, got my head down. That A1 is murder though. North of Newcastle, it's like coming into a third-world country.'

'Did you drive four hundred miles just to insult me?'

They took everything through to the table in the living-room, Rebus shoving aside books and notepads, stuff about the Second World War.

'So,' he said, as they sat down, 'I'm assuming this isn't a social call?'

'Actually it is, in a way. I could have just telephoned, but I suddenly thought: wonder how the old devil's getting on? Next thing I knew, I was in the car and heading for the North Circular.'

'I'm touched.'

'I've always tried to keep track of what you're up to.'

'Why?'

'Because last time we met ... well, you're different, aren't you?'

'Am I?'

'I mean, you're not a team player. You're a loner, bit like me. Loners can be useful.'

'Useful?'

'For undercover, jobs that are a bit out of the ordinary.'

'You think I'm Special Branch material?'

'Ever fancied moving to London? It's where the action is.'

'I get action enough up here.'

Abernethy looked out of the window. 'You couldn't wake this place with a fifty-megaton warhead.'

'Look, Abernethy, not that I'm not enjoying your company or anything, but why *are* you here?'

Abernethy brushed crumbs from his hands. 'So much for the social niceties.' He took a gulp of coffee, squirmed at its awfulness. 'War Crimes,' he said. Rebus stopped chewing. 'There's a new list of names. You know that, because you've got one of them living on your doorstep.'

'So?'

'So I'm heading up the London HQ. We've established a temporary War Crimes Unit. My job's to collate gen on the various investigations, create a central register.'

'You want to know what I know?'

'That's about it.'

'And you drove through the night to find out? There's got to be more to it.'

Abernethy laughed. 'Why's that?'

'There just has. A collator's job is for someone good at office work. That's not you, you're only happy in the field.'

'What about you? I'd never have taken you for a historian.' Abernethy tapped one of the books on the table.

'It's a penance.'

'What makes you think it's any different with me? So, what's the score with Herr Lintz?'

'There's no score. So far all the darts have missed the board. How many cases are there?'

'Twenty-seven originally, but eight of those are deceased.'

'Any progress?'

Abernethy shook his head. 'We got one to court, trial collapsed first day. Can't prosecute if they're ga-ga.'

'Well, for your information, here's where the Lintz case stands. I can't prove he was and is Josef Linzstek. I can't disprove his story of his participation in the war, or how he came to Britain.' Rebus shrugged.

'Same tale I've been hearing up and down the country.'

'What did you expect?' Rebus was picking at a croissant.

'Shame about this coffee,' Abernethy said. 'Any decent caffs in the neighbourhood?'

So they went to a cafe, where Abernethy ordered a double

75

espresso, Rebus a decaf. There was a story on the front of the *Record* about a fatal stabbing outside a nightclub. The man reading the paper folded it up when he'd finished his breakfast and took it away with him.

'Any chance you'll be talking to Lintz today?' Abernethy asked suddenly.

'Why?'

'Thought I might tag along. It's not often you get to meet someone who might have killed seven hundred Frenchies.'

'Morbid attraction?'

'We're all a bit that way inclined, aren't we?'

'I've nothing new to ask him,' Rebus said, 'and he's already been muttering to his lawyer about harassment.'

'He's well-connected?'

Rebus stared across the table. 'You've done your reading.'

'Abernethy the Conscientious Cop.'

'Well, you're right. He has friends in high places, only a lot of them have been hiding behind the curtains since this all started.'

'Sounds like you think he's innocent.'

'Until proven guilty.'

Abernethy smiled, lifted his cup. 'There's a Jewish historian been going around. Has he contacted you?'

'What's his name?'

Another smile. 'How many Jewish historians have you been in touch with? His name's David Levy.'

'You say he's been going around?'

'A week here, a week there, asking how the cases are going.'

'He's in Edinburgh just now.'

Abernethy blew on his coffee. 'So you've spoken with him?'

'Yes, as it happens.'

'And?'

'And what?'

'Did he try his "Rat Line" story?'

'Again, why the interest?'

'He's tried it with everyone else.'

'What if he has?'

'Jesus, do you always answer a question with a question? Look, as collator, this guy Levy's name has popped up on my computer screen more than once. That's why I'm interested.'

'Abernethy the Conscientious Cop.'

76

'That's right. So shall we go see Lintz?'

'Well, seeing you've come all this way ...'

On the way back to the flat, Rebus stopped at a newsagent's and bought the *Record*. The stabbing had taken place outside Megan's Nightclub, a new establishment in Portobello. The fatality had been a 'doorman', William Tennant, aged 25. The story had made the front page because a Premier League footballer had been on the periphery of the incident. A friend who'd been with him had received minor cuts. The attacker had fled on a motorbike. The footballer had offered no comment to reporters. Rebus knew him. He lived in Linlithgow and a year or so back had been caught speeding in Edinburgh, with – in his own words – a 'wee bitty Charlie', meaning cocaine, on his person.

'Anything interesting?' Abernethy asked.

'Someone killed a bouncer. Quiet little backwater, eh?'

'A story like that, in London it wouldn't rate a column inch.'

'How long are you staying here?'

'I'll be off today, want to drop in on Carlisle. They're supposed to have another old Nazi. After that, it's Blackpool and Wolverhampton before home.'

'A sucker for punishment.'

Rebus drove them the tourist route: down The Mound and across Princes Street. He double parked in Heriot Row, but Joseph Lintz wasn't home.

'Never mind,' he said. 'I know where he'll probably be.' He took them down Inverleith Row and turned right into Warriston Gardens, stopping at the cemetery gates.

'What is he, a gravedigger?' Abernethy got out of the car and zipped his jacket.

'He plants flowers.'

'Flowers? What for?'

'I'm not sure.'

A cemetery should have been about death, but Warriston didn't feel that way to Rebus. Much of it resembled a rambling park into which some statuary had been dropped. The newer section, with stone driveway, soon gave way to an earthen path between fading inscriptions. There were obelisks and Celtic crosses, lots of trees and birds, and the electric movements of squirrels. A tunnel beneath a walkway took you to the oldest part of the cemetery, but between tunnel and driveway sat the heart of the place, with its roll-call of

Edinburgh's past. Names like Ovenstone, Cleugh, and Flockhart, and professions such as actuary, silk merchant, ironmonger. There were people who'd died in India, and some who'd died in infancy. A sign at the gate informed visitors that the place had been the subject of a compulsory purchase by the City of Edinburgh, because previous private owners had let it fall into neglect. But that same neglect was at least part of its charm. People walked their dogs here, or came to practise photography, or just mused among the tombstones. Gays came looking for company, others for solitude.

After dark, of course, the place had another reputation entirely. A Leith prostitute – a woman Rebus had known and liked – had been found murdered here earlier in the year. Rebus wondered if Joseph Lintz knew about that ...

'Mr Lintz?'

He was trimming the grass around a headstone, doing so with a half-sized pair of garden shears. There was a sheen of sweat on his face as he forced himself upright.

'Ah, Inspector Rebus. You have brought a colleague?'

'This is DI Abernethy.'

Abernethy was examining the headstone, which belonged to a teacher called Cosmo Merriman.

'They let you do this?' he asked, his eyes finally finding Lintz's.

'No one has tried to stop me.'

'Inspector Rebus tells me you plant flowers, too.'

'People assume I am a relative.'

'But you're not, are you?'

'Only in so far as we are the family of man, Inspector Abernethy.'

'You're a Christian then?'

'Yes, I am.'

'Born and bred?'

Lintz took out a handkerchief and wiped his nose. 'You're wondering if a Christian could commit an atrocity like Villefranche. It's perhaps not in my interest to say this, but I think it entirely possible. I've been explaining this to Inspector Rebus.'

Rebus nodded. 'We've had a couple of talks.'

'Religious belief is no defence, you see. Look at Bosnia, plenty of Catholics involved in the fighting, plenty of good Muslims, too. "Good" in that they are believers. And what they believe is that their faith gives them the right to kill.'

Bosnia: Rebus saw a sharp image of Candice escaping the terror, only to end up more terrified still, and more trapped than ever.

Lintz was stuffing the large white handkerchief into the pocket of his baggy brown cord trousers. In the outfit – green rubber overshoes, green woollen jersey, tweed jacket – he did look like a gardener. Little wonder he attracted so little attention in the cemetery. He blended in. Rebus wondered how artful it was, how deeply he'd learned the skill of invisibility.

'You look impatient, Inspector Abernethy. You're not a man for theories, am I right?'

'I wouldn't know about that, sir.'

'In that case, you must not know very much. Now Inspector Rebus, he listens to what I have to say. More than that, he looks *interested*. Whether he is or not, I can't judge, but his performance – if performance it be – is exemplary.' Lintz always spoke like this, like he'd been rehearsing each line. 'Last time he visited my home, we discussed human duality. Would you have any opinion on *that*, Inspector Abernethy?'

The look on Abernethy's face was cold. 'No, sir.'

Lintz shrugged: case against the Londoner proven. 'Atrocities, Inspector, occur by an effort of the collective will.' Spelling it out; sounding like the lecturer he had once been. 'Because sometimes all it takes to turn us into devils is the fear of being an outsider.'

Abernethy sniffed, hands in pockets. 'Sounds like you're justifying war crimes, sir. Sounds to me like you might even have been there yourself.'

'Do I need to be a spaceman to imagine Mars?' He turned to Rebus, gave him the fraction of a smile.

'Well, maybe I'm just a bit too simple, sir,' Abernethy said. 'I'm also a bit parky. Let's walk back to the car and carry on our discussion there, all right?'

While Lintz packed his few small tools into a canvas bag, Rebus looked around, saw movement in the distance, between headstones. The crouched figure of a man. Split-second glimpse of a face he recognised.

'What is it?' Abernethy asked.

Rebus shook his head. 'Nothing.'

The three men walked in silence back to the Saab. Rebus opened the back door for Lintz. To his surprise, Abernethy got into the back, too. Rebus took the driver's seat, felt warmth returning slowly

to his toes. Abernethy had his arm along the back of the seat, his body twisted towards Lintz.

'Now, Herr Lintz, my role in all this is quite straightforward. I'm collating all the information on this latest outbreak of alleged old Nazis. You understand that with allegations such as these, very serious allegations, we have a duty to investigate?'

'Spurious allegations rather than "serious" ones.'

'In which case you've nothing to worry about.'

'Except my reputation.'

'When you're exonerated, we'll take care of that.'

Rebus was listening closely. None of this sounded like Abernethy. The hostile graveside tone had been replaced by something much more ambiguous.

'And meantime?' Lintz seemed to be picking up whatever the Londoner was saying between the lines. Rebus felt deliberately excluded from the conversation, which was why Abernethy had got into the back seat in the first place. He'd placed a physical barrier between himself and the officer investigating Joseph Lintz. There was something going on.

'Meantime,' Abernethy said, 'cooperate as fully as you can with my colleague. The sooner he's able to reach his conclusions, the sooner this will all be over.'

'The problem with conclusions is that they should be conclusive, and I have so little proof. This was wartime, Inspector Abernethy, a lot of records destroyed ...'

'Without proof either way, there's no case to answer.'

Lintz was nodding. 'I see,' he said.

Abernethy hadn't voiced anything Rebus himself didn't feel; the problem was, he'd voiced it to the suspect.

'It would help if your memory improved,' Rebus felt obliged to add.

'Well, Mr Lintz,' Abernethy was saying, 'thanks for your time.' His hand was on the elderly man's shoulder: protective, comforting. 'Can we drop you somewhere?'

'I'll stay here a little longer,' Lintz said, opening the door and easing himself out. Abernethy handed the bag of tools to him.

'Take care now,' he said.

Lintz nodded, gave a small bow to Rebus, and shuffled back towards the gate. Abernethy climbed into the passenger seat.

'Rum little bugger, isn't he?'

'You as good as told him he was off the hook.'

'Bollocks,' Abernethy said. 'I told him where he stands, let him know the score. That's all.' He saw the look on Rebus's face. 'Come on, do you really want to see him in court? An old professor who keeps cemeteries tidy?'

'It doesn't make it any easier if you sound like you're on his side.'

'Even supposing he *did* order that massacre – you think a trial and a couple of years in clink till he snuffs it is the answer? Better to just give them all a bloody good scare, stuff the trial, and save the taxpayer millions.'

'That's not our job,' Rebus said, starting the engine.

He took Abernethy back to Arden Street. They shook hands, Abernethy trying to sound like he wanted to stay a little longer.

'One of these days,' he said. And then he was gone. As his Sierra drew away, another car pulled into the space he'd just vacated. Siobhan Clarke got out, bringing with her a supermarket carrier-bag.

'For you,' she said. 'And I think I'm owed a coffee.'

She wasn't as fussy as Abernethy, accepted the mug of instant with thanks and ate a spare croissant. There was a message on the answering machine, Dr Colquhoun telling him the refugee family could take Candice tomorrow. Rebus jotted down the details, then turned his attention to the contents of Siobhan's carrier-bag. Maybe two hundred sheets of paper, photocopies.

'Don't get them out of order,' she warned. 'I didn't have time to staple them.'

'Fast work.'

'I went back into the office last night. Thought I'd get it done while no one was about. I can summarise, if you like.'

'Just tell me who the main players are.'

She came to the table and pulled a chair over beside him, found a sequence of surveillance shots. Put names to the faces.

'Brian Summers,' she said, 'better known as "Pretty-Boy". He runs most of the working girls.' Pale, angular face, thick black lashes, a pouting mouth. Candice's pimp.

'He's not very pretty.'

Clarke found another picture. 'Kenny Houston.'

'From Pretty-Boy to Plug-Ugly.'

'I'm sure his mother loves him.' Prominent teeth, jaundiced skin.

'What does he do?'

'He runs the doormen. Kenny, Pretty-Boy and Tommy Telford grew up on the same street. They're at the heart of The Family.' She sifted through more photos. 'Malky Jordan ... he keeps the drugs flowing. Sean Haddow ... bit of a brainbox, runs the finances. Ally Cornwell ... he's muscle. Deek McGrain ... There's no religious divide in The Family, Prods and Papes working together.'

'A model society.'

'No women though. Telford's philosophy: relationships get in the way.'

Rebus picked up a sheaf of paper. 'So what have we got?'

'Everything but the evidence.'

'And surveillance is supposed to provide that?'

She smiled over the top of her mug. 'You don't agree?'

'It's not my problem.'

'And yet you're interested.' She paused. 'Candice?'

'I don't like what happened to her.'

'Well, just remember: you didn't get this stuff from me.'

'Thanks, Siobhan.' He paused. 'Everything going all right?'

'Fine. I like Crime Squad.'

'Bit livelier than St Leonard's.'

'I miss Brian.' Meaning her one-time partner, now out of the force.

'You ever see him?'

'No, do you?'

Rebus shook his head, got up to show her out.

He spent about an hour sifting through the paperwork, learning more about The Family and its convoluted workings. Nothing about Newcastle. Nothing about Japan. The core of The Family – eight or nine of them – had been at school together. Three of them were still based in Paisley, taking care of the established business. The rest were now in Edinburgh, and busy prying the city away from Big Ger Cafferty.

He went through lists of nightclubs and bars in which Telford had an interest. There were incident reports attached: arrests in the vicinity. Drunken brawls, swings taken at bouncers, cars and property damaged. Something caught Rebus's eye: mention of a hot-dog van, parked outside a couple of the clubs. The owner questioned: possible witness. But he'd never seen anything worth the recall. Name: Gavin Tay.

Mr Taystee.

Recent dodgy suicide. Rebus gave Bill Pryde a bell, asked how that investigation was going.

'Dead end street, pal,' Pryde said, not sounding too concerned. Pryde: too long the same rank, and not going anywhere. Beginning the long descent into retirement.

'Did you know he ran a hot-dog stall on the side?'

'Might explain where he got the cash from.'

Gavin Tay was an ex-con. He'd been in the ice-cream business a little over a year. Successful, too: new Merc parked outside his house. His financial records hadn't hinted at money to spare. His widow couldn't account for the Merc. And now: evidence of a job on the side, selling food and drink to punters stumbling out of nightclubs.

Tommy Telford's nightclubs.

Gavin Tay: previous convictions for assault and reset. A persistent offender who'd finally gone straight ... The room began to feel stuffy, Rebus's head clotted and aching. He decided to get out.

Walked through The Meadows and down George IV Bridge, took the Playfair Steps down to Princes Street. A group was sitting on the stone steps of the Scottish Academy: unshaven, dyed hair, torn clothes. The city's dispossessed, trying their best not to be ignored. Rebus knew he had things in common with them. In the course of his life, he'd failed to fit several niches: husband, father, lover. He hadn't fit in with the Army's ideas of what he should be, and wasn't exactly 'one of the lads' in the police. When one of the group held out a hand, Rebus offered a fiver, before crossing Princes Street and heading for the Oxford Bar.

He settled into a corner with a mug of coffee, got out his mobile, and called Sammy's flat. She was home, all was well with Candice. Rebus told her he had a place for Candice, she could move out tomorrow.

'That's fine,' Sammy said. 'Hold on a second.' There was a rustling sound as the receiver was passed along.

'Hello, John, how are you?'

Rebus smiled. 'Hello, Candice. That's very good.'

'Thank you. Sammy is ... uh ... I am teaching how to ...' She broke into laughter, handed the receiver back.

'I'm teaching her English,' Sammy said.

'I can tell.'

'We started with some Oasis lyrics, just went from there.'

'I'll try to come round later. What did Ned say?'

'He was so shattered when he came home, I think he barely noticed.'

'Is he there? I'd like to talk to him.'

'He's out working.'

'What did you say he was doing again?'

'I didn't.'

'Right. Thanks again, Sammy. See you later.'

He took a swig of coffee, washed it around his mouth. Abernethy: he couldn't just let it go. He swallowed the coffee and called the Roxburghe, asked for David Levy's room.

'Levy speaking.'

'It's John Rebus.'

'Inspector, how good to hear from you. Is there something I can do?'

'I'd like to talk to you.'

'Are you in your office?'

Rebus looked around. 'In a manner of speaking. It's a two-minute walk from your hotel. Turn right out of the door, cross George Street, and walk down to Young Street. Far end, the Oxford Bar. I'm in the back room.'

When Levy arrived, Rebus bought him a half of eighty-bob. Levy eased himself into a chair, hanging his walking-stick on the back of it. 'So what can I do for you?'

'I'm not the only policeman you've spoken to.'

'No, you're not.'

'Someone from Special Branch in London came to see me today.'

'And he told you I'd been travelling around?'

'Yes.'

'Did he warn you against speaking to me?'

'Not in so many words.'

Levy took off his glasses, began polishing them. 'I told you, there are people who'd rather this was all relegated to history. This man, he came all the way from London just to tell you about me?'

'He wanted to see Joseph Lintz.'

'Ah.' Levy was thoughtful. 'Your interpretation, Inspector?'

'I was hoping for yours.'

'My utterly subjective interpretation?' Rebus nodded. 'He wants to be sure of Lintz. This man works for Special Branch, and as

everyone knows Special Branch is the public arm of the secret services.'

'He wanted to be confident I wasn't going to get anything out of Lintz?'

Levy nodded, staring at the smoke from Rebus's cigarette. This case was like that: one minute you could see it, the next you couldn't. Like smoke.

'I have a little book with me,' Levy said, reaching into his pocket. 'I'd like you to read it. It's in English, translated from the Hebrew. It's about the Rat Line.'

Rebus took the book. 'Does it prove anything?'

'That depends on your terms.'

'Concrete proof.'

'Concrete proof exists, Inspector.'

'In this book?'

Levy shook his head. 'Under lock and key in Whitehall, kept from scrutiny by the Hundred Year Rule.'

'So there's no way to prove anything.'

'There's one way ...'

'What?'

'If someone talks. If we can get just *one* of them to talk ...'

'That's what this is all about: wearing down their resistance? Looking for the weakest link?'

Levy smiled again. 'We have learned patience, Inspector.' He finished his drink. 'I'm so grateful you called. This has been a much more satisfactory meeting.'

'Will you send your bosses a progress report?'

Levy chose to ignore this. 'We'll talk again, when you've read the book.' He stood up. 'The Special Branch officer ... I've forgotten his name?'

'I didn't give it.'

Levy waited a moment, then said, 'Ah, that explains it then. Is he still in Edinburgh?' He watched Rebus shake his head. 'Then he's probably on his way to Carlisle, yes?'

Rebus sipped coffee, offered no comment.

'My thanks again, Inspector,' Levy said, undeterred.

'Thanks for dropping by.'

Levy took a final look around. 'Your office,' he said, shaking his head.

# 8

The Rat Line was an 'underground railway', delivering Nazis – sometimes with the help of the Vatican – from their Soviet persecutors. The end of the Second World War meant the start of the Cold War. Intelligence was necessary, as were intelligent, ruthless individuals who could provide a certain level of expertise. It was said that Klaus Barbie, the 'Butcher of Lyons', had been offered a job with British Intelligence. It was rumoured that high-profile Nazis had been spirited away to America. It wasn't until 1987 that the United Nations released its full list of fugitive Nazi and Japanese war criminals, forty thousand of them.

Why so late in releasing the list? Rebus thought he could understand. Modern politics had decreed that Germany and Japan were part of the global brotherhood of capitalism. In whose interests would it be to reopen old wounds? And besides, how many atrocities had the Allies themselves hidden? Who fought a war with clean hands? Rebus, who'd grown to adulthood in the Army, could comprehend this. He'd done things ... He'd served time in Northern Ireland, seen trust disfigured, hatred replace fear.

Part of him could well believe in the existence of a Rat Line.

The book Levy had given him went into the mechanics of how such an operation might have worked. Rebus wondered: was it really possible to disappear completely, to change identity? And again, the recurring question: did any of it matter? There did exist sources of identification, and there *had* been court cases – Eichmann, Barbie, Demjanjuk – with others ongoing. He read about war criminals who, rather than being tried or extradited, were allowed to return home, running businesses, growing rich, dying of old age. But he also read of criminals who served their sentences and became 'good people', people who *had* changed. These men said war itself was the real culprit. Rebus recalled one of his first conversations with Joseph

Lintz, in the drawing-room of Lintz's home. The old man's voice was hoarse, a scarf around his throat.

'At my age, Inspector, a simple throat infection can feel like death.'

There didn't seem to be many photographs around. Lintz had explained that a lot had gone missing during the war.

'Along with other mementoes. I do have these photos though.'

He'd shown Rebus half a dozen framed shots, dating back to the 1930s. As he'd explained who the subjects were, Rebus had suddenly thought: what if he's making it up? What if these are just a bunch of old photos he picked up somewhere and had framed? And the names, the identities he now gave to the faces – had he invented them? He'd seen in that instant, for the first time, how easy it might be to construct another life.

And then, later in their conversation that day, Lintz, sipping honeyed tea, had started discussing Villefranche.

'I've been thinking a lot about it, Inspector, as you might imagine. This Lieutenant Linzstek, he was in charge on the day?'

'Yes.'

'But presumably under orders from above. A lieutenant is not so very far up the pecking order.'

'Perhaps.'

'You see, if a soldier is under orders ... then they must carry out those orders, no?'

'Even if the order is insane?'

'Nevertheless, I'd say the person was at the very least *coerced* into committing the crime, and a crime that very many of us would have carried out under similar circumstances. Can't you see the hypocrisy of trying someone, when you'd probably have done the same thing yourself? One soldier standing out from the crowd ... saying no to the massacre: would you have made that stand yourself?'

'I hope so.' Rebus thinking back to Ulster and the 'Mean Machine' ...

Levy's book didn't prove anything. All Rebus knew was that Josef Linzstek's name was on a list as having used the Rat Line, posing as a Pole. But where had the list originated? In Israel. Again, it was highly speculative. It wasn't *proof*.

And if Rebus's instincts told him Lintz and Linzstek were one and the same, they were still failing to tell him whether it mattered.

*

He dropped the book back to the Roxburghe, asked the receptionist to see that Mr Levy got it.

'I think he's in his room, if you'd like to ...'

Rebus shook his head. He hadn't left any message with the book, knowing Levy might interpret this as a message in itself. He went home for his car, drove down to Haymarket and along to Shandon. As usual, parking near Sammy's flat was a problem. Everyone was home from work and tucked in front of their televisions. He climbed the stone steps, wondering how treacherous they'd get when the frosts came, and rang the bell. Sammy herself led him into the living room, where Candice was watching a game show.

'Hello, John,' she said. 'Are you my wonderwall?'

'I'm nobody's wonderwall, Candice.' He turned to Sammy. 'Everything all right?'

'Just fine.'

At that moment, Ned Farlowe walked in from the kitchen. He was eating soup from a bowl, dunking a folded slice of brown bread into it.

'Mind if I have a word?' Rebus said.

Farlowe shook his head, then jerked it in the direction of the kitchen.

'Can I eat while we talk? I'm starving.' He sat down at the foldaway table, got another slice of bread from the packet and spread margarine on it. Sammy put her head round the doorway, saw the look on her father's face, and made a tactical retreat. The kitchen was about seven foot square and too full of pots and appliances. Swinging a cat, you could have done a lot of damage.

'I saw you today,' Rebus said, 'skulking in Warriston Cemetery. Coincidence?'

'What do you think?'

'I'm asking you.' Rebus leaned his back against the sink unit, folded his arms.

'I'm watching Lintz.'

'Why?'

'Because I'm being paid to.'

'By a newspaper?'

'Lintz's lawyer has interim interdicts flying around. Nobody can afford to be seen near him.'

'But they still want him watched?'

'If there's a court case coming, they want to know as much as possible, stands to reason.'

By court case, Farlowe didn't mean any trial of Lintz, but rather of the newspapers themselves, for libel.

'If he catches you …'

'He doesn't know me from Adam. Besides, there'd always be somebody to take my place. Now do I get to ask a question?'

'Let me say something first. You know I'm investigating Lintz?' Farlowe nodded. 'That means we're too close. If you find out anything, people might think it came from me.'

'I haven't told Sammy what I'm doing, *specifically* so there's no conflict of interests.'

'I'm just saying others might not believe it.'

'A few more days, I'll have enough money to fund the book for another month.' Farlowe had finished his soup. He carried the empty bowl over to the sink, stood next to Rebus.

'I don't want this to be a problem, but the bottom line is: what can you do about it?'

Rebus stared at him. His instinct was to stuff Farlowe's head into the sink, but how would that look with Sammy?

'Now,' Farlowe said, 'do I get to ask my question?'

'What is it?'

'Who's Candice?'

'A friend of mine.'

'So what's wrong with *your* flat?'

Rebus realised he was no longer dealing with his daughter's boyfriend. He was confronted with a journalist, someone with a nose for a story.

'Tell you what,' said Rebus, 'say I didn't see you in the cemetery. Say we didn't just have this little chat.'

'And I don't ask about Candice?' Rebus stayed quiet. Farlowe considered the deal. 'Say I get to ask you a few questions for my book.'

'What sort of questions?'

'About Cafferty.'

Rebus shook his head. 'I could talk about Tommy Telford though.'

'When?'

'When we've got him behind bars.'

Farlowe smiled. 'I could be on the pension by then.' He waited, saw Rebus was going to give him nothing.

'She's only here till tomorrow anyway,' Rebus said.

'Where's she off to?'

Rebus just winked. Left the kitchen, returned to the living-room. Talked to Sammy while Candice's game show reached its climax. Whenever she heard audience laughter, she joined in. Rebus made arrangements for the following day, then left. There was no sign of Farlowe. He'd either hidden himself in the bedroom or else gone back out. It took Rebus a few moments to remember where he'd parked his car. He drove home carefully; stopped for all the lights.

The parking spaces were all taken in Arden Street. He left the Saab on a yellow line. As he approached his tenement door, he heard a car door open and spun towards the sound.

It was Claverhouse. He was on his own. 'Mind if I come in?'

Rebus thought of a dozen reasons for saying yes. But he shrugged and made for the door. 'Any news of the stabbing at Megan's?' he asked.

'How did you know we'd be interested?'

'A bouncer gets stabbed, the attacker flees on a waiting motorbike. It was premeditated. And the majority of the bouncers work for Tommy Telford.'

They were climbing the stairs. Rebus's flat was on the second floor.

'Well, you're right,' Claverhouse said. 'Billy Tennant worked for Telford. He controlled the traffic in and out of Megan's.'

'Traffic as in dope?'

'The footballer's friend, the one who got wounded, he's a known dealer. Works out of Paisley.'

'Therefore connected to Telford, too.'

'We're speculating he was the target, Tennant just got in the way.'

'Leaving only one question: who was behind it?'

'Come on, John. It was Cafferty, obviously.'

'Not Cafferty's style,' Rebus said, unlocking his door.

'Maybe he's learned a thing or two from the Young Pretender.'

'Make yourself at home,' Rebus said, walking down the hall. The breakfast things were still on the dining table. Siobhan's bag of goodies was down the side of a chair.

'A guest.' Claverhouse had noticed the two mugs, two plates. He looked around. 'She's not here now though?'

'She wasn't here for breakfast either.'

'Because she's at your daughter's.'

Rebus froze.

'I went to settle up with the hotel. They said a police car had come and taken all her things away. So then I asked around, and the driver gave me Samantha's address as the drop-off.' Claverhouse sat down on the sofa, crossed one leg over the other. 'So what's the game, John, and how come you've seen fit to leave me on the bench?' He sounded calm now, but Rebus could tell there'd been a storm.

'Do you want a drink?'

'I want an answer.'

'When she walked out ... she waited beside my car. I couldn't think where to take her, so I brought her here. But she recognised the street. Telford had been watching my flat.'

Claverhouse looked interested. 'Why?'

'Maybe because I know Cafferty. I couldn't let Candice stay here, so I took her to Sammy's.'

'Is she still there?' Rebus nodded. 'So what happens now?'

'There's a place she can go, the refugee family.'

'For how long?'

'What do you mean?'

Claverhouse sighed. 'John, she's ... the only life she's known here is prostitution.'

Rebus went over to the hi-fi for something to do, looked through his tapes. He needed to do *some*thing.

'What's she going to do for money? Are you going to provide? What does that make you?'

Rebus dropped a CD, turned on his heels. 'Nothing like that,' he spat.

Claverhouse had his hands up, palms showing. 'Come on, John, you know yourself there's –'

'I don't know anything.'

'John ...'

'Look, get out, will you?' It wasn't just that it had been a long day, more that it felt like the day would never end. He could feel the evening stretch to infinity, no rest available to him. In his head, bodies were swaying gently from trees while smoke engulfed a

church. Telford was on his arcade motorbike, cannoning off spectators. Abernethy was touching an old man's shoulder. Soldiers were rifle-butting civilians. And John Rebus ... John Rebus was in every frame, trying hard to remain an onlooker.

He put Van Morrison on the hi-fi: *Hardnose the Highway*. He'd played this music on East Neuk beaches and tenement stakeouts. It always seemed to heal him, or at least patch the wounds. When he turned back into the room, Claverhouse was gone. He looked out of his window. Two kids lived in the second-floor flat across from his. He'd watched them often from this window, and they never once saw him, for the simple reason that they never so much as glanced outside. Their world was complete and all-absorbing, anything outside their window an irrelevance. They were in bed now, their mother closing the shutters. Quiet city. Abernethy was right about that. There were large chunks of Edinburgh where you could live your whole life and never encounter a spot of bother. Yet the murder rate in Scotland was double that of its southern neighbour, and half those murders took place in the two main cities.

Not that the statistics mattered. A death was a death. Something unique had disappeared from the world. One murder or several hundred ... they all meant something to the survivors. Rebus thought of Villefranche's sole existing survivor. He hadn't met her, probably never would. Another reason it was hard to get passionate about a historical case. In a contemporary one, you had many of the facts to hand, and could talk to witnesses. You could gather forensic evidence, question people's stories. You could measure guilt and grief. You became part of the whole story. This was what interested Rebus. The people interested him; their stories fascinated him. When part of their lives, he could forget his own.

He noticed the answering-machine was flashing: one message.

'Oh, hello there. I'm ... um, I don't know how to put this ...' Placed the voice: Kirstin Mede. She sighed. 'Look, I can't do this any more. So please don't ... I'm sorry, I just can't. There are other people who can help you. I'm sure one of them ...'

End of message. Rebus stared down at the machine. He didn't blame her. *I can't do this any more*. That makes two of us, Rebus thought. The only thing was, *he* had to keep going. He sat down at his table and pulled the Villefranche paperwork towards him: lists of names and occupations, ages and dates of birth. Picat, Mesplede, Rousseau, Deschamps. Wine merchant, china painter, cartwright,

housemaid. What did any of it mean to a middle-aged Scot? He pushed it aside and lifted Siobhan's paperwork on to the table.

Off with Van the Man; on with side one of *Wish You Were Here*. Scratched to hell. He remembered it had come in a black polythene wrapper. When opened, there'd been this smell, which afterwards he'd learned was supposed to be burning flesh ...

'I need a drink,' he said to himself, sitting forward in his chair. 'I want a drink. A few beers, maybe with whiskies attached.' Something to smooth the edges ...

He looked at his watch; not even near to closing time. Not that it mattered much in Edinburgh, the land that closing time forgot. Could he make it to the Ox before they shut up shop? Yes, too easily. It was nicer to have a challenge. Wait an hour or so and then repeat the debate.

Or call Jack Morton.

Or go out, right now.

The telephone rang. He picked it up.

'Hello?'

'John?' Making it sound like 'Sean'.

'Hello, Candice. What's up?'

'Up?'

'Is there a problem?'

'Problem, no. I just wanting ... I say to you, see you tomorrow.'

He smiled. 'Yes, see you tomorrow. You speak very good English.'

'I was chained to a razor blade.'

'What?'

'Line from song.'

'Oh, right. But you're not chained to it now?'

She didn't seem to understand. 'I'm ... uh ...'

'It's okay, Candice. See you tomorrow.'

'Yes, see you.'

Rebus put down the receiver. Chained to a razor blade ... Suddenly he didn't want a drink any more.

# 9

He picked Candice up the next afternoon. She had two carrier bags, her worldly belongings. She gave Sammy as much of a hug as her bandaged arms would allow.

'See you again, Candice,' Sammy said.

'Yes, see you. Thanks ...' Lost for an ending to the sentence, Candice opened her arms wide, bags swinging.

They stopped off at McDonald's (her choice) for something to eat. Zappa and the Mothers: 'Cruising for Burgers'. The day was bright and crisp, just right for crossing the Forth Bridge. Rebus took it slowly, so Candice could take in the view. He was heading towards Fife's East Neuk, a cluster of fishing villages popular with artists and holidaymakers. Out of season, Lower Largo seemed practically deserted. Though Rebus had an address, he stopped to ask directions. Finally, he parked in front of a small terraced house. Candice stared at the red door until he gestured for her to follow him. He hadn't been able to make her understand what they were doing here. Hoped Mr and Mrs Petrec would make a better job of it.

The door was opened by a woman in her early-forties. She had long black hair, and peered at him over half-moon glasses. Then her attention shifted to Candice, and she said something in a language both women understood. Candice replied, looking a little shy, not sure what was going on.

'Come in, please,' Mrs Petrec said. 'My husband is in the kitchen.'

They sat around the kitchen table. Mr Petrec was heavily built, with a thick brown moustache and wavy brown and silver hair. A pot of tea was produced, and Mrs Petrec drew her chair beside Candice's and began talking again.

'She's explaining to the girl,' Mr Petrec said.

Rebus nodded, sipped the strong tea, listened to a conversation he

could not understand. Candice, cautious at first, grew more animated as she told her story, and Mrs Petrec was a skilled listener, sympathising, showing shared horror and exasperation.

'She was taken to Amsterdam, told there would be a job there for her,' Mr Petrec explained. 'I know this has happened to other young women.'

'I think she left a child behind.'

'A son, yes. She's telling my wife about him.'

'What about you?' Rebus asked. 'How did you end up here?'

'I was an architect in Sarajevo. No easy decision, leaving your whole life behind.' He paused. 'We went to Belgrade first. A refugee bus brought us to Scotland.' He shrugged. 'That was nearly five years ago. Now I am a house painter.' A smile. 'Distance no object.'

Rebus looked at Candice, who had started crying, Mrs Petrec comforting her.

'We will look after her,' Mrs Petrec said, staring at her husband.

Later, at the door, Rebus tried to give them some money, but they wouldn't take it.

'Is it all right if I come and see her sometime?'

'But of course.'

He stood in front of Candice.

'Her real name is Dunya,' Mrs Petrec said quietly.

'Dunya.' Rebus tried out the word. She smiled, her eyes softer than Rebus remembered them, as if some transformation were beginning. She bent forward.

'Kiss the girl,' she said.

A peck on both cheeks. Her eyes filling with tears again. Rebus nodded, to let her know he understood everything.

At his car, he waved once, and she blew him another kiss. Then he drove around the corner and stopped, gripping the steering-wheel hard. He wondered if she'd cope. If she'd learn to forget. He thought again of his ex-wife's words. What would she think of him now? Had he exploited Dunya? No, but he wondered if that was only because she hadn't been able to give him anything on Telford. He felt he had somehow failed to do the right thing. So far, the only choice she'd had to make was when she'd waited for him by his car rather than going back to Telford. Before then and after, all the decisions had been taken for her. In a sense, she was still as trapped as ever, because the locks and chains were in her mind; they were

what she expected from life. It would take time for her to change, to begin trusting the world again. The Petrecs would help her.

Heading south down the coast, thinking about families, he decided to visit his brother.

Mickey lived on an estate in Kirkcaldy, his red BMW parked in the driveway. He was just home from work and suitably surprised to see Rebus.

'Chrissie and the kids are at her mum's,' he said. 'I was going to grab a curry for dinner. How about a beer?'

'Maybe just a coffee,' Rebus said. He sat in the lounge until Mickey returned, toting a couple of old shoe-boxes.

'Look what I dug out of the attic last weekend. Thought you might like a look. Milk and sugar?'

'A spot of milk.'

While Mickey went to the kitchen to fetch the coffee, Rebus examined the boxes. They were filled with packets of photographs. The packets had dates on them, some with questionmarks. Rebus opened one at random. Holiday snaps. A fancy dress parade. A picnic. Rebus didn't have any pictures of his parents, and the photos startled him. His mother had thicker legs than he remembered, but a tidy body, too. His father used the same grin in every shot, a grin Rebus shared with Mickey. Digging further into the box, he found one of himself with Rhona and Sammy. They were on a beach somewhere, the wind playing havoc. Peter Gabriel: 'Family Snapshot'. Rebus couldn't place it at all. Mickey came back through with a mug of coffee and a bottle of beer.

'There are some,' he said, 'I don't know who the people are. Relatives maybe? Grandma and Granddad?'

'I'm not sure I'd be much help.'

Mickey handed over a menu. 'Here,' he said, 'best Indian in town. Pick what you want.'

So Rebus chose, and Mickey phoned the order in. Twenty minutes till delivery. Rebus was on to another packet. These photos were older still, the 1940s. His father in uniform. The soldiers wore hats like McDonald's counter staff. They also wore long khaki shorts. 'Malaya' written on the backs of some, 'India' on the others.

'Remember, the old man got himself wounded in Malaya?' Mickey said.

'No, he didn't.'

'He showed us the wound. It was in his knee.'

Rebus was shaking his head. 'Uncle Jimmy told me it was a cut Dad got playing football. He kept picking the scab off, ended with a scar.'

'He told us it was a war wound.'

'He was fibbing.'

Mickey had started on the other box. 'Here, look at these ...' Handing over an inch-thick collection of postcards and photographs, secured with an elastic band. Rebus pulled the band off, turned the cards over, saw his own writing. The photos were of him, too: posed snaps, badly taken.

'Where did you get these?'

'You always used to send me a card or a photo, don't you remember?'

They were all from Rebus's own Army days. 'I'd forgotten,' he said.

'Once a fortnight, usually. A letter to Dad, a card for me.'

Rebus sat back in his chair and started to go through them. Judging by the postmarks, they were in chronological sequence. Training, then service in Germany and Ulster, more exercises in Cyprus, Malta, Finland, and the desert of Saudi Arabia. The tone of each postcard was breezy, so that Rebus failed to recognise his own voice. The cards from Belfast consisted of almost nothing but jokes, yet Rebus remembered that as one of the most nightmarish periods of his life.

'I used to love getting them,' Mickey said, smiling. 'I'll tell you, you almost had me joining up.'

Rebus was still thinking of Belfast: the closed barracks, the whole compound a fortress. After a shift out on the streets, there was no way to let off steam. Booze, gambling and fights – all taking place within the same four walls. All culminating in the Mean Machine ... And here were these postcards, here was the image of Rebus's past life that Mickey had lived with these past twenty-odd years.

And it was all a lie.

Or was it? Where did the reality lie, other than in Rebus's own head? The postcards were fake documents, but they were also the only ones in existence. There was nothing to contradict them, nothing except Rebus's word. It was the same with the Rat Line, the same with Joseph Lintz's story. Rebus looked at his brother and knew he could break the spell right now. All he had to do was tell him the truth.

'What's the matter?' Mickey asked.

'Nothing.'

'Ready for that beer yet? The food'll be here any second.'

Rebus stared at the cooling mug of coffee. 'More than ready,' he said, putting the rubber band back around his past. 'But I'll stick to this.' He lifted the mug, toasted his brother.

# 10

Next morning, Rebus went to St Leonard's, telephoned the NCIS centre at Prestwick and asked if they had anything connecting British criminals to European prostitution. His reasoning: *someone* had brought Candice – she was still Candice to him – from Amsterdam to Britain, and he didn't think it was Telford. Whoever it was, Rebus would get to them somehow. He wanted to show Candice her chains could be broken.

He got NCIS to fax him what information they had. Most of it concerned the 'Tippelzone', a licensed car park where drivers went for sex. It was worked by foreign prostitutes mainly, most of them lacking work permits, many smuggled in from Eastern Europe. The main gangs seemed to be from former Yugoslavia. NCIS had no names for any of these kidnappers-cum-pimps. There was nothing about prostitutes making the trip from Amsterdam to Britain.

Rebus went into the car park to smoke his second cigarette of the day. There were a couple of other smokers out there, a small brotherhood of social pariahs. Back in the office, the Farmer wanted to know if there was any progress on Lintz.

'Maybe if I brought him in and slapped him around a bit,' Rebus suggested.

'Be serious, will you?' the Farmer growled, stalking back to his office.

Rebus sat down at his desk and pulled forward a file.

'Your problem, Inspector,' Lintz had said to him once, 'is that you're afraid of being taken seriously. You want to give people what you think they expect. I mention the Ishtar gate, and you talk of some Hollywood movie. At first I thought this was meant to rouse me to some indiscretion, but now it seems more a game you are playing against *yourself*.'

Rebus: seated in his usual chair in Lintz's drawing-room. The

view from the window was of Queen Street Gardens. They were kept locked: you had to pay for a key.

'Do educated people frighten you?'

Rebus looked at the old man. 'No.'

'Are you sure? Don't you perhaps wish you were more like them?' Lintz grinned, showing small, discoloured teeth. 'Intellectuals like to see themselves as history's victims, prejudiced against, arrested for their beliefs, even tortured and murdered. But Karadzic thinks himself an intellectual. The Nazi hierarchy had its thinkers and philosophers. And even in Babylon ...' Lintz got up, poured himself more tea. Rebus declined a refill.

'Even in Babylon, Inspector,' Lintz continued, getting comfortable again, 'with its opulence and its artistry, with its enlightened king ... do you know what they did? Nebuchadnezzar held the Jews captive for seventy years. This spendid, awe-inspiring civilisation ... Do you begin to see the madness, Inspector, the flaws that run so deep in us?'

'Maybe I need glasses.'

Lintz threw his cup across the room. 'You need to listen and to learn! You need to understand!'

The cup and saucer lay on the carpet, still intact. Tea was soaking into the elaborate design, where it would become all but invisible ...

He parked on Buccleuch Place. The Slavic Studies department was housed in one of the tenements. He tried the secretary's office first, asked if Dr Colquhoun was around.

'I haven't seen him today.'

When Rebus explained what he wanted, the secretary tried a couple of numbers but didn't find anyone. Then she suggested he take a look in their library, which was one floor up and kept locked. She handed him a key.

The room was about sixteen feet by twelve, and smelled stuffy. The shutters across the windows were closed, giving the place no natural light. A No Smoking sign sat on one of four desks. On another sat an ashtray with three butts in it. One entire wall was shelved, filled with books, pamphlets, magazines. There were boxes of press cuttings, and maps on the walls showing Yugoslavia's changing demarcation lines. Rebus lifted down the most recent box of cuttings.

Like a lot of people he knew, Rebus didn't know much about the

war in ex-Yugoslavia. He'd seen some of the news reports, been shocked by the pictures, then had got on with his life. But if the cuttings were to be believed, the whole region was being run by war criminals. The Implementation Force seemed to have done its damnedest to avoid confrontation. There had been a few arrests recently, but nothing substantial: out of a meagre seventy-four suspects charged, only *seven* had been apprehended.

He found nothing about slave traders, so thanked the secretary and gave her back her key, then crawled through the city traffic. When the call came on his mobile, he nearly went off the road.

Candice had disappeared.

Mrs Petrec was distraught. They'd had dinner last night, breakfast this morning, and Dunya had seemed fine.

'There was a lot she said she couldn't tell us,' Mr Petrec said, standing behind his seated wife, hands stroking her shoulders. 'She said she wanted to forget.'

And then she'd gone out for a walk down to the harbour, and hadn't returned. Lost maybe, though the village was small. Mr Petrec had been working; his wife had gone out, asking people if they'd seen her.

'And Mrs Muir's son,' she said, 'he told me she'd been taken away in a car.'

'Where was this?' Rebus asked.

'Just a couple of streets away,' Mr Petrec said.

'Show me.'

Outside his home on Seaford Road, Eddie Muir, aged eleven, told Rebus what he'd seen. A car stopping beside a woman. A bit of chat, though he couldn't hear it. The door opening, the woman getting in.

'Which door, Eddie?'

'One of the back ones. Had to be, there were two of them in the car already.'

'Men?'

Eddie nodded.

'And the woman got in by herself? I mean, they didn't grab her or anything?'

Eddie shook his head. He was straddling his bike, keen to be going. One foot kept testing a pedal.

'Can you describe the car?'

'Big, a bit flash. Not from round here.'

'And the men?'

'Didn't really get a good look. Driver was wearing a Pars shirt.'

Meaning a football shirt, Dunfermline Athletic. Which would mean he was from Fife. Rebus frowned. A pick-up? Could that be it? Candice back to her old ways so soon? Not likely, not in a place like this, on a street like this. It was no chance encounter. Mrs Petrec was right: she'd been snatched. Which meant someone had known where to find her. Had Rebus been followed yesterday? If he had, they'd been invisible. Some device on his car? It seemed unlikely, but he checked wheel-arches and the underbody: nothing. Mrs Petrec had calmed a little, her husband having administered medicinal vodka. Rebus could use a shot himself, but turned down the offer.

'Did she make any phone calls?' he asked. Petrec shook his head. 'What about strangers hanging around the street?'

'I would have noticed. After Sarajevo, it's hard to feel safe, Inspector.' He opened his arms. 'And here's the proof – nowhere's safe.'

'Did you tell anyone about Dunya?'

'Who would we tell?'

Who knew? That was the question. Rebus did. And Claverhouse and Ormiston knew about the place, because Colquhoun had mentioned it.

Colquhoun knew. The nervy old Slavic Studies specialist knew … On the way back to Edinburgh, Rebus tried phoning him at office and home: no reply. He'd told the Petrecs to let him know if Candice came back, but he didn't think she'd be coming back. He remembered the look she'd given him early on when he'd asked her to trust him. *I won't be surprised if you let me down.* Like she'd known back then that he'd fail. And she'd given him a second chance, waiting for him beside his car. And he'd let her down. He got back on his mobile and called Jack Morton.

'Jack,' he said, 'for Christ's sake, talk me out of having a drink.'

He tried Colquhoun's home address and the Slavic Studies office: both locked up tight. Then he drove to Flint Street and looked for Tommy Telford in the arcade. But Telford wasn't there. He was in the cafe's back office, surrounded as usual by his men.

'I want to talk to you,' Rebus said.

'So talk.'

'Without the audience.' Rebus pointed to Pretty-Boy. 'That one can stay.'

Telford took his time, but finally nodded, and the room began to empty. Pretty-Boy stood against a wall, hands behind his back. Telford had his feet up on his desk, leaning back in his chair. They were relaxed, confident. Rebus knew what *he* looked like: a caged bear.

'I want to know where she is.'

'Who?'

'Candice.'

Telford smiled. 'Still on about her, Inspector? How should I know where she is?'

'Because a couple of your boys grabbed her.' But as he spoke, Rebus realised he was making a mistake. Telford's gang was a *family*: they'd grown up together in Paisley. Not many Dunfermline supporters that distant from Fife. He stared at Pretty-Boy, who ran Telford's prostitutes. Candice had arrived in Edinburgh from a city of bridges, maybe Newcastle. Telford had Newcastle connections. And the Newcastle United strip – vertical black and white lines – was damned close to Dunfermline's. Probably only a kid in Fife could make the mistake.

A Newcastle strip. A Newcastle car.

Telford was talking, but Rebus wasn't listening. He walked straight out of the office and back to the Saab. Drove to Fettes – the Crime Squad offices – and started looking. He found a contact number for a DS Miriam Kenworthy. Tried the number but she wasn't there.

'Fuck it,' he told himself, getting back into his car.

The A1 was hardly the country's fastest road – Abernethy was right about that. Still, without the daytime traffic Rebus made decent time on his way south. It was late evening when he arrived in Newcastle, pubs emptying, queues forming outside clubs, a few United shirts on display, looking like prison bars. He didn't know the city. Drove around it in circles, passing the same signs and landmarks, heading further out, just cruising.

Looking for Candice. Or for girls who might know her.

After a couple of hours, he gave up, headed back into the centre. He'd had the idea of sleeping in his car, but when he found a hotel with an empty room, the thought of en-suite facilities suddenly seemed too good to miss.

He made sure there was no mini-bar.

A long soak with his eyes closed, mind and body still racing from the drive. He sat in a chair by his window and listened to the night: taxis and yells, delivery lorries. He couldn't sleep. He lay on the bed, watching soundless TV, remembering Candice in the hotel room, asleep under sweet wrappers. Deacon Blue: 'Chocolate Girl.'

He woke up to breakfast TV. Checked out of the hotel and had breakfast in a cafe, then called Miriam Kenworthy's office, relieved to find she was an early starter.

'Come right round,' she said, sounding bemused. 'You're only a couple of minutes away.'

She was younger than her telephone voice, face softer than her attitude. It was a milkmaid's face, rounded, the cheeks pink and plump. She studied him, swivelling slightly in her chair as he told her the story.

'Tarawicz,' she said when he'd finished. 'Jake Tarawicz. Real name Joachim, probably.' Kenworthy smiled. 'Some of us around here call him Mr Pink Eyes. He's had dealings – meetings anyway – with this guy Telford.' She opened the brown folder in front of her. 'Mr Pink Eyes has a lot of European connections. You know Chechnia?'

'In Russia?'

'It's Russia's Sicily, if you know what I mean.'

'Is that where Tarawicz comes from?'

'It's one theory. The other is that he's Serbian. Might explain why he set up the convoy.'

'What convoy?'

'Running aid lorries to former Yugoslavia. A real humanitarian, our Mr Pink.'

'But also a way of smuggling people out?'

Kenworthy looked at him. 'You've been doing your homework.'

'Call it an educated guess.'

'Well, it gets him noticed. He got a papal blessing six months ago. Married to an Englishwoman – not for love. She was one of his girls.'

'But it gives him residency here.'

She nodded. 'He hasn't been around that long, five or six years ...'

Like Telford, Rebus thought.

'But he's built himself a rep, muscled in where there used to be Asians, Turks ... Story is, he started with a nice line in stolen icons. A ton of stuff has been lifted out of the Soviet bloc. And when that operation started drying, he moved into prossies. Cheap girls, and he could keep them docile with a bit of crack. The crack comes up from London – the Yardies control that particular scene. Mr Pink spreads their goods around the north-east. He also deals heroin for the Turks and sells some girls to Triad brothels.' She looked at Rebus, saw she had his attention. 'No racial barriers when it comes to business.'

'So I see.'

'Probably also sells drugs to your friend Telford, who distributes them through his nightclubs.'

'"Probably"?'

'We've no hard proof. There was even a story going around that Pink wasn't selling to Telford, he was *buying*.'

Rebus blinked. 'Telford's not that big.'

She shrugged.

'Where would he get the stuff?'

'It was a story, that's all.'

But it had Rebus thinking, because it might help explain the relationship between Tarawicz and Telford ...

'What does Tarawicz get out of it?' he asked, making his thoughts flesh.

'You mean apart from money? Well, Telford trains a good bouncer. Jock bouncers get respect down here. Then, of course, Telford has shares in a couple of casinos.'

'A way for Tarawicz to launder his cash?' Rebus thought about this. 'Is there anything Tarawicz *doesn't* have a finger in?'

'Plenty. He likes businesses which are fluid. And he's still a relative newcomer.'

Eagles: 'New Kid in Town'.

'We think he's been dealing arms: a lot of stuff crossing into Western Europe. The Chechens seem to have weaponry to spare.' She sniffed, gathered her thoughts.

'Sounds like he's one step ahead of Tommy Telford.' Which would explain why Telford was so keen to do business with him. He was on a learning curve, learning how to fit into the bigger picture. Yardies and Asians, Turks and Chechens, and all the others. Rebus

saw them as spokes on a huge wheel which was trundling mercilessly across the world, breaking bones as it went.

'Why "Mr Pink Eyes"?' he asked.

She'd been awaiting the question, slid a colour photo towards him.

It was the close-up of a face, the skin pink and blistered, white lesions running through it. The face was puffy, bloated, and in its midst sat eyes hidden by blue-tinted glasses. There were no eyebrows. The hair above the jutting forehead was thin and yellow. The man looked like some monstrous shaved pig.

'What happened to him?' he asked.

'We don't know. That's the way he looked when he arrived.'

Rebus remembered the description Candice had given: sunglasses, looks like a car-crash victim. Dead ringer.

'I want to talk to him,' Rebus said.

But first, Kenworthy gave him a guided tour. They took her car, and she showed him where the street girls worked. It was mid-morning, no action to speak of. He gave her a description of Candice, and she promised she'd put the word out. They spoke with the few women they met. They all seemed to know Kenworthy, weren't hostile towards her.

'They're the same as you or me,' she told him, driving away. 'Working to feed their kids.'

'Or their habit.'

'That too, of course.'

'In Amsterdam, they've got a union.'

'Doesn't help the poor sods who're shipped there.' Kenworthy signalled at a junction. 'You're sure he has her?'

'I don't think Telford does. Someone knew addresses back in Sarajevo, addresses that were important to her. Someone shipped her out of there.'

'Sounds like Mr Pink all right.'

'And he's the only one who can send her back.'

She looked at him. 'Why would he do a thing like that?'

Just as Rebus was thinking their surroundings couldn't get any grimmer – all industrial decay, gutted buildings and pot-holes – Kenworthy signalled to turn in at the gates of a scrapyard.

'You're kidding?' he said.

Three Alsatians, tethered by thirty-foot chains, barked and bounded towards the car. Kenworthy ignored them, kept driving. It was like being in a ravine. Either side of them stood precarious canyon walls of car wrecks.

'Hear that?'

Rebus heard it: the sound of a collision. The car entered a wide clearing, and he saw a yellow crane, dangling a huge grab from its arm, pluck up the car it had dropped and lift it high, before dropping it again on to the carcass of another. A few men were standing at a safe distance, smoking cigarettes and looking bored. The grab dropped on to the roof of the top car, denting it badly. Glass shimmered on the oily ground, diamonds against black velvet.

Jake Tarawicz – Mr Pink Eyes – was in the crane, laughing and roaring as he picked up the car again, worrying it the way a cat might play with a mouse without noticing it was dead. If he'd seen the new additions to his audience, it didn't show. Kenworthy hadn't got out of her car immediately. First, she'd fixed on a face from her repertoire. When finally she was ready, she nodded to Rebus and they opened their doors simultaneously.

As Rebus stood upright, he saw that the grab had dropped the car and was swinging towards them. Kenworthy folded her arms and stood her ground. Rebus was reminded of those arcade games where you had to pick up a prize. He could see Tarawicz in the cab, manipulating the controls like a kid with a toy. He remembered Tommy Telford on his arcade bike, and saw at once something the two men had in common: neither had ever really grown up.

The motorised hum stopped suddenly, and Tarawicz dropped from the cab. He was wearing a cream suit and emerald shirt, open at the neck. He'd borrowed a pair of green wellies from somewhere, so as to keep his trousers clean. As he walked towards the two detectives, his men stepped into line behind him.

'Miriam,' he said, 'always a pleasure.' He paused. 'Or so the rumour goes.' A couple of his men grinned. Rebus recognised one face: 'The Crab', that's what he'd been called in central Scotland. His grip could crush bones. Rebus hadn't seen him in a long time, and had never seen him so smartly groomed and dressed.

'All right, Crab?' Rebus said.

This seemed to disconcert Tarawicz, who half-turned towards his minion. The Crab stayed quiet, but colour had risen to his neck.

Up close, it was hard not to stare at Mr Pink Eyes's face. His eyes

demanded that you meet them, but you really wanted to study the flesh in which they sat.

He was looking at Rebus now.

'Have we met?'

'No.'

'This is Detective Inspector Rebus,' Kenworthy explained. 'He's come all the way from Scotland to see you.'

'I'm flattered.' Tarawicz's grin showed small sharp teeth with gaps between them.

'I think you know why I'm here,' Rebus said.

Tarawicz made a show of astonishment. 'Do I?'

'Telford needed your help. He needed a home address for Candice, a note to her in Serbo-Croat ...'

'Is this some sort of riddle?'

'And now you've taken her back.'

'Have I?'

Rebus took a half-step forward. Tarawicz's men fanned out either side of their boss. There was a sheen on Tarawicz's face which could have been sweat or some medical cream.

'She wanted out,' Rebus told him. 'I promised I'd help her. I never break a promise.'

'She wanted out? She told you that?' Tarawicz's voice was teasing.

One of the men behind cleared his throat. Rebus had been wondering about this man, so much smaller and more reticent than the others, better dressed and with sad drooping eyes and sallow skin. Now he knew: lawyer. And the cough was his way of warning Tarawicz that he was saying too much.

'I'm going to take Tommy Telford down,' Rebus said quietly. 'That's my promise to you. Once he's in custody, who knows what he'll say?'

'I'm sure Mr Telford can look after himself, Inspector. Which is more than can be said for Candice.' The lawyer coughed again.

'I want her kept off the streets,' Rebus said.

Tarawicz stared at him, tiny black pupils like spots of absolute darkness.

'Can Thomas Telford go about his daily business unfettered?' he said at last. Behind him, the lawyer almost choked.

'You know I can't promise that,' Rebus said. 'It's not me he has to worry about.'

'Take a message to your friend,' Tarawicz said. 'And afterwards, stop being his friend.'

Rebus realised then: Tarawicz was talking about *Cafferty*. Telford had told him that Rebus was Cafferty's man.

'I think I can do that,' Rebus said quietly.

'Then do it.' Tarawicz turned away.

'And Candice?'

'I'll see what I can do.' He stopped, slid his hands into his jacket pockets. 'Hey, Miriam,' he said, his back still to them, 'I like you better in that red two-piece.'

Laughing, he walked away.

'Get in the car,' Kenworthy said through gritted teeth. Rebus got into the car. She looked nervous, dropped her keys, bent to retrieve them.

'What's wrong?'

'Nothing's wrong,' she snapped.

'The red two-piece?'

She glared at him. 'I don't have a red two-piece.' She did a three point-turn, hitting brakes and accelerator with a little more force than necessary.

'I don't get it.'

'Last week,' she said, 'I bought some red underwear ... bra and pants.' She revved the engine. 'Part of his little game.'

'So how does he know?'

'That's what I'm wondering.' She shot past the dogs and out of the gate. Rebus thought of Tommy Telford, and how he'd been watching Rebus's flat.

'Surveillance isn't always one-way,' he said, knowing now who'd taught Telford the skill. A little later he asked about the scrapyard.

'He owns it. He's got a compacter, but before the cars get squashed he likes to play with them. And if you cross him, he welds your seatbelt shut.' She looked at him. 'You become part of his game.'

Never get personally involved: it was *the* golden rule. And practically every case he worked, Rebus broke it. He sometimes felt that the reason he became so involved in his cases was that he had no life of his own. He could only live *through* other people.

Why had he become so involved with Candice? Was it down to her physical resemblance to Sammy? Or was it that she had seemed

109

to need *him*? The way she'd clung to his leg that first day ... Had he wanted – just for a little while – to be someone's knight in shining armour, the real thing, not some mockery?

John Rebus: complete bloody sham.

He phoned Claverhouse from his car, filled him in. Claverhouse told him not to worry.

'Thanks for that,' Rebus said. 'I feel a whole lot better now. Listen, who's Telford's supplier?'

'For what? Dope?'

'Yes.'

'That's the real joker in the pack. I mean, he does business with Newcastle, but we can't be certain who's dealing and who's buying.'

'What if Telford's selling?'

'Then he's got a line from the continent.'

'What do Drugs Squad say?'

'They say not. If he's landing the stuff from a boat, it means transporting it from the coast. Much more likely he's buying from Newcastle. Tarawicz has the contacts in Europe.'

'Makes you wonder why he needs Tommy Telford at all ...'

'John, do yourself a favour, switch off for five minutes.'

'Colquhoun seems to be keeping his head down ...'

'Did you hear me?'

'I'll talk to you soon.'

'Are you heading back?'

'In a manner of speaking.' Rebus cut the call and drove.

# 11

'Strawman,' said Morris Gerald Cafferty, as he was escorted into the room by two prison guards.

Earlier in the year, Rebus had promised Cafferty he would put a Glasgow gangster, Uncle Joe Toal, behind bars. It hadn't worked, despite Rebus's best efforts. Toal, pleading old age and illness, was still a free man, like a war criminal excused for senility. Ever since then, Cafferty had felt Rebus owed him.

Cafferty sat down, rolled his neck a few times, loosening it.

'So?' he asked.

Rebus nodded for the guards to leave, waited in silence until they'd gone. Then he slipped a quarter-bottle of Bell's from his pocket.

'Keep it,' Cafferty told him. 'From the look of you, I'd say your need was greater than mine.'

Rebus put the bottle back in his pocket. 'I've brought a message from Newcastle.'

Cafferty folded his arms. 'Jake Tarawicz?'

Rebus nodded. 'He wants you to lay off Tommy Telford.'

'What does he mean?'

'Come on, Cafferty. That bouncer who got stabbed, the dealer wounded ... There's war breaking out.'

Cafferty stared at the detective. 'Not my doing.'

Rebus snorted, but looking into Cafferty's eyes, he found himself almost believing.

'So who was it?' he asked quietly.

'How do I know?'

'Nevertheless, war is breaking out.'

'That's as may be. What's in it for Tarawicz?'

'He does business with Tommy.'

'And to protect that, he needs to have *me* warned off by a cop?' Cafferty was shaking his head. 'You really buy that?'

'I don't know,' Rebus said.

'One way to finish this.' Cafferty paused. 'Take Telford out of the game.' He saw the look on Rebus's face. 'I don't mean top him, I mean put him away. That should be *your* job, Strawman.'

'I only came to deliver a message.'

'And what's in it for you? Something in Newcastle?'

'Maybe.'

'Are you Tarawicz's man now?'

'You know me better than that.'

'Do I?' Cafferty sat back in his chair, stretched out his legs. 'I wonder about that sometimes. I mean, it doesn't keep me awake at night, but I wonder all the same.'

Rebus leaned on the table. 'You must have a bit salted away. Why can't you just be content with that?'

Cafferty laughed. The air felt charged; there might have been only the two of them left in the world. 'You want me to retire?'

'A good boxer knows when to stop.'

'Then neither of us would be much cop in the ring, would we? Got any plans to retire, Strawman?'

Despite himself, Rebus smiled.

'Thought not. Do I have to say something for you to take back to Tarawicz?'

Rebus shook his head. 'That wasn't the deal.'

'Well, if he does come asking, tell him to get some life insurance, the kind with death benefits.'

Rebus looked at Cafferty. Prison might have softened him, but only physically.

'I'd be a happy man if someone took Telford out of the game,' Cafferty went on. 'Know what I mean, Strawman? It'd be worth a lot to me.'

Rebus stood up. 'No deal,' he said. 'Personally, I'd be happy if you wiped one another out. I'd be jumping for joy at ring-side.'

'Know what happens at ring-side?' Cafferty rubbed at his temples. 'You tend to get spattered with blood.'

'As long as it's someone else's.'

112

The laughter came from deep within Cafferty's chest. 'You're not a spectator, Strawman. It's not in your nature.'

'And you're some kind of psychologist?'

'Maybe not,' said Cafferty. 'But I know what gets people excited.'

# Book Three

'Cover my face as the animals cry.'

*Running through the hospital, stopping nurses to ask directions. Sweat dripping off him, tie hanging loose around his neck. Taking right turns, left turns, looking for signs. Whose fault? He kept asking himself that. A message which failed to reach him. Because he was on a surveillance. Because he wasn't in radio contact. Because the station didn't know how important the message was.*

*Now running, a stitch in his side. He'd run all the way from the car. Up two flights of stairs, down corridors. The place was quiet. Middle of the night.*

*'Maternity!' he called to a man pushing a trolley. The man pointed to a set of doors. He pushed through them. Three nurses in a glass cubicle. One of them came out.*

*'Can I help?'*

*'I'm John Rebus. My wife ...'*

*She gave him a hard look. 'Third bed along.' Pointing ... Third bed along, curtains closed around it. He pulled the curtains open. Rhona lay on her side, face still flushed, hair sticking to her brow. And beside her, nuzzling into her, a tiny perfection with wisps of brown hair and black, unfocused eyes.*

*He touched the nose, ran a finger round the curves of an ear. The face twitched. He bent past it to kiss his wife.*

*'Rhona ... I'm really sorry. They didn't get the message to me until ten minutes ago. How did it ... ? I mean ... he's beautiful.'*

*'He's a she,' his wife said, turning away from him.*

# 12

Rebus was sitting in his boss's office. It was nine-fifteen and he had slept for probably forty-five minutes the previous night. There'd been the hospital vigil and Sammy's operation: something about a blood clot. She was still unconscious, still 'critical'. He'd called Rhona in London. She'd told him she'd catch the first train she could. He'd given her his mobile number, so she could let him know when she arrived. She'd started to ask ... her voice had cracked. She'd put down the receiver. He'd tried to find some feeling for her. Richard and Linda Thompson: 'Withered and Died'.

He'd called Mickey, who said he'd drop by the hospital some time today. And that was it for the family. There were other people he could call, people like Patience, who had been his lover for a time, and Sammy's landlady until far more recently. But he didn't. He knew in the morning he'd call the office where Sammy worked. He wrote it in his notebook so he wouldn't forget. And then he'd called Sammy's flat and given Ned Farlowe the news.

Farlowe had asked a question nobody else had: 'How about you? Are you all right?'

Rebus had looked around the hospital corridor. 'Not exactly.'

'I'll be right there.'

So they'd spent a couple of hours in one another's company, not really saying very much at first. Farlowe smoked, and Rebus helped him empty the pack. He couldn't reciprocate with whisky – there was nothing in the bottle – but he'd bought the young man several cups of coffee, since Farlowe had spent nearly all his money on the taxi from Shandon ...

'Wakey-wakey, John.'

Rebus's boss was shaking him gently. Rebus blinked, straightened in his chair.

'Sorry, sir.'

Chief Superintendent Watson went around the desk and sat down. 'Hellish sorry to hear about Sammy. I don't really know what to say, except that she's in my prayers.'

'Thank you, sir.'

'Do you want some coffee?' The Farmer's coffee had a reputation throughout the station, but Rebus accepted a mug gladly. 'How is she anyway?'

'Still unconscious.'

'No sign of the car?'

'Not the last I heard.'

'Who's handling it?'

'Bill Pryde started the ball rolling last night. I don't know who's taken it from him.'

'I'll find out.' The Farmer made an internal call, Rebus watching him over the rim of his mug. The Farmer was a big man, imposing behind a desk. His cheeks were a mass of tiny red veins and his thin hair lay across the dome of his head like the lines of a well-furrowed field. There were photos on his desk: grandchildren. The photos had been taken in a garden. There was a swing in the background. One of the children was holding a teddy bear. Rebus felt his throat start to ache, tried to choke it back.

The Farmer put down the receiver. 'Bill's still on it,' he said. 'Felt if he worked straight through we might get a quicker result.'

'That's good of him.'

'Look, we'll let you know the minute we get something, but meantime you'll probably want to go home ...'

'No, sir.'

'Or to the hospital.'

Rebus nodded slowly. Yes, the hospital. But not right this minute. He had to talk to Bill Pryde first.

'And meantime, I'll reassign your cases.' The Farmer started writing. 'There's this War Crimes thing, and your liaison on Telford. Are you working on anything else?'

'Sir, I'd prefer it if you ... I mean, I want to keep working.'

The Farmer looked at him, then leaned back in his chair, pen balanced between his fingers.

'Why?'

Rebus shrugged. 'I want to keep busy.' Yes, there was that. And

119

he didn't want anyone else taking his work. It was *his*. He owned it; it owned him.

'Look, John, you're going to want some time off, right?'

'I can handle things, sir.' His gaze met the Farmer's. 'Please.'

Across the hall in the CID room he nodded as everyone came up to say how sorry they were. One person stayed at their desk – Bill Pryde knew Rebus was coming to see him.

'Morning, Bill.'

Pryde nodded. They'd met in the wee small hours at the Infirmary. Ned Farlowe had been napping in a chair, so they'd stepped into the corridor to talk. Pryde looked tireder now. He had loosened the top button of his dark green shirt. His brown suit looked lived-in.

'Thanks for sticking with it,' Rebus said, drawing over a chair. Thinking: *I'd rather have had someone else, someone sharper ...*

'No problem.'

'Any news?'

'A couple of good eyewitnesses. They were waiting to cross at the lights.'

'What's their story?'

Pryde considered his reply. He knew he was dealing with a father as well as a cop. 'She was crossing the road. Looked like she was heading down Minto Street, maybe making for the bus stop.'

Rebus shook his head. 'She was walking, Bill. Going to a friend's in Gilmour Road.'

She'd said as much over the pizza, apologising that she couldn't stay longer. Just one more coffee at the end of the meal ... one more coffee and she wouldn't have been there at that moment. Or if she'd accepted his offer of a lift ... When you thought about life, you thought of it as chunks of time, but really all it was was a series of connected moments, any one of which could change you completely.

'The car was heading south out of town,' Pryde went on. 'Looks like he ran a red light. Motorist sitting behind him seemed to think so.'

'Reckon he was drunk?'

Pryde nodded. 'Way he was driving. I mean, could be he just lost control, but in that case why didn't he stop?'

'Description?'

Pryde shook his head. 'We've got a dark car, a bit sporty. Nobody caught the licence plate.'

'It's a busy enough street, must've been other cars around.'

'A couple of people have called in.' Pryde flicked through his notes. 'Nothing helpful, but I'm going to interview them, see if I can jog a memory or two.'

'Could the car have been nicked? Maybe that's why he was in a hurry.'

'I can check.'

'I'll help you.'

Pryde considered this. 'You sure?'

'Try and stop me, Bill.'

'No skid marks,' Pryde said, 'no sign that he tried braking, either before or after.'

They were standing at the junction of Minto Street and Newington Road. The cross-streets were Salisbury Place and Salisbury Road. Cars, vans and buses queued at the traffic lights as pedestrians crossed the road.

It could have been any one of you, Rebus thought. Any one of them could have taken Sammy's place ...

'She was about here,' Pryde went on, pointing to a spot where, just past the lights, a bus lane started. The carriageway was wide, a four-lane road. She hadn't crossed at the lights. She'd been lazy, carrying on down Minto Street a few strides, then crossing in a diagonal. When she'd been a child, they'd taught her about crossing the road. Green Cross Code, all of that. Drummed it into her. Rebus looked around. At the top of Minto Street were some private houses and Bed & Breakfasts. On one corner stood a bank, on another a branch of Remnant Kings, with a takeaway next door.

'The takeaway would have been open,' Rebus said, pointing. On the third corner stood a Spar. 'That place, too. Where did you say she was?'

'The bus lane.' She'd crossed three lanes, been only a yard or two from safety. 'Witnesses say she was nearly at the kerb when he hit her. I think he was drunk, lost it for a second.' Pryde nodded towards the bank. There were two phone boxes in front of it. 'Witness called from there.' The wall behind the phone boxes had a poster glued to it. Grinning maniac behind a steering-wheel, and some writing: 'So many pedestrians, so little time'. A computer game ...

'It would have been so easy to avoid her,' Rebus said quietly.

'Sure you're okay? There's a cafe up the road.'

'I'm fine, Bill.' He looked around, took a deep breath. 'Looks like offices behind the Spar, doubtful anyone would have been there. But there are flats above Remnant Kings and the bank.'

'Want to talk to them?'

'And the Spar and the kebab shop. You take the B&Bs and the houses, meet back here in half an hour.'

Rebus talked to everyone he could find. In the Spar, there was a new shift on, but he got home phone numbers from the manager and called up the workers from the previous night. They hadn't seen or heard anything. First they'd known had been the flashing lights of the ambulance. The kebab shop was closed, but when Rebus banged on the door a woman came through from the back, wiping her hands on a tea-towel. He pressed his warrant card to the glass door, and she let him in. The shop had been busy last night. She didn't see the accident – she called it that, 'the accident'. And that's what it was: the word really hadn't sunk in until she said it. Elvis Costello: 'Accidents Will Happen'. Was the next line really 'It's only hit and run'?

'No,' the woman said, 'the first thing that caught my attention was the crowd. I mean, only three or four people, but I could see they were standing around something. And then the ambulance came. Will she be all right?'

The look in her eyes was one Rebus had encountered before. It almost wanted the victim dead, because then there was a story to be told.

'She's in hospital,' he said, unable to look at the woman any longer.

'Yes, but the paper said she's in a coma.'

'What paper?'

She brought him the first edition of the day's *Evening News*. There was a paragraph on one of the inside pages – 'Hit and Run Coma Victim'.

It wasn't a coma. She was unconscious, that was all. But Rebus was thankful for the story. Maybe someone would read it and come forward. Maybe guilt would begin to press down on the driver. Maybe there'd been a passenger ... It was hard to keep secrets, usually you told *some*one.

He tried Remnant Kings, but of course they had been closed last night, so he climbed to the flats above. There was no one home at

the first flat. He wrote a brief message on the back of a business card and pushed it through the letterbox, then jotted down the surname on the door. If they didn't call him, he'd call them. A young man answered the second door. He was just out of his teens and pushed a thick lock of black hair away from his eyes. He wore Buddy Holly glasses and had acne scars around his mouth. Rebus introduced himself. The hand went to the hair again, a backward glance into the flat.

'Do you live here?' Rebus asked.

'Mm, yeah. Like, I'm not the owner. We rent it.'

There were no names on the door. 'Anyone else in at the moment?'

'Nope.'

'Are you all students?'

The young man nodded. Rebus asked his name.

'Rob. Robert Renton. What's this about?'

'There was an accident last night, Rob. A hit and run.' So many times he'd been in this situation, passing on the bland news of another changed life. It was a whole hour since he'd telephoned the hospital. In the end, they'd taken his mobile number, said it might be easier if they phoned him whenever there was news. They meant easier for them, not him.

'Oh, yes,' Renton was saying, 'I saw it.'

Rebus blinked. 'You saw it?'

Renton was nodding, hair bobbing in front of his eyes. 'From the window. I was up changing a CD, and –'

'Is it okay if I come in for a minute? I want to see what kind of view you had.'

Renton puffed out his cheeks, exhaled. 'Well, I suppose ...'

And Rebus was in.

The living-room was fairly tidy. Renton went ahead of him, crossed to where a hi-fi rack sat between two windows. 'I was putting on a new CD, and I looked out of the window. You can see the bus stop, and I wondered if I might catch Jane coming off a bus.' He paused. 'Jane's Eric's girlfriend.'

The words washed over Rebus. He was looking down on the street, where Sammy had been walking. 'Tell me what you saw.'

'This girl was crossing the road. She was nice-looking ... I thought so anyway. Then this car came through the lights, swerved and sent her flying.'

Rebus closed his eyes for a second.

'She must have gone ten feet in the air, hit that hedge, bounced back on to the pavement. She didn't move after that.'

Rebus opened his eyes. He was at the window, Renton standing just behind his left shoulder. Down on the street, people were crossing the road, walking over the spot where Sammy had been hit, the spot where she'd landed. Flicking ash on to the pavement where she'd lain.

'I don't suppose you saw the driver?'

'Not from this angle.'

'Any passengers?'

'Couldn't tell.'

He wears glasses, Rebus thought. How reliable is he?

'When you saw it happen, you didn't go down?'

'I'm not a medical student or anything.' He nodded towards an easel in the corner, and Rebus noticed a shelf of paints and brushes. 'Someone ran to the phone box, so I knew help was coming.'

Rebus nodded. 'Anyone else see it?'

'They were in the kitchen.' Renton paused. 'I know what you're thinking.' Rebus doubted it. 'You're thinking I wear specs, so maybe I didn't see it right. But he definitely swerved. You know ... deliberately. I mean, like he was aiming for her.' He nodded to himself.

'*Aiming* for her?'

Renton made a movement with his hand, imitating a car gliding off one course and on to another. 'He steered straight for her.'

'The car didn't lose control?'

'That would have been jerkier, wouldn't it?'

'What colour was the car?'

'Dark green.'

'And the make?'

Renton shrugged. 'I'm hopeless with cars. Tell you what though ...'

'What?'

Renton took off his glasses, started polishing them. 'Why don't I try sketching it for you?'

He moved the easel over to the window and got to work. Rebus went into the hall and called the hospital. The person he got through to didn't sound too surprised.

'No change, I'm afraid. She's got a couple of visitors with her.'

Mickey and Rhona. Rebus terminated the call, made another to Pryde's mobile.

'I'm in one of the flats over Remnant Kings. I've got an eyewitness.'

'Yes?'

'He saw the whole thing. And he's an art student.'

'Yes?'

'Come on, Bill. Do you want me to draw it for you?'

There was silence for a moment, then Pryde said 'Ah'.

# 13

Rebus held the mobile to his ear as he walked through the hospital.

'Joe Herdman's put together a list,' Bill Pryde was saying. 'Rover 600 series, the newer Ford Mondeos, Toyota Celica, plus a couple of Nissans. Rank outsider is the BMW 5-series.'

'It narrows things down a bit, I suppose.'

'Joe says the Rover, Mondeo and Celica are favourites. He's given me a few more details – chrome around the number-plates, stuff like that. I'm going to call our artist friend, see if anything clicks.'

A nurse was glaring at Rebus as he walked towards her.

'Let me know what he says. Talk to you later, Bill.' Rebus slipped the phone back into his pocket.

'You're not supposed to use those things in here,' the nurse snapped.

'Look, I'm in a bit of a hurry ...'

'They can interfere with the machines.'

Rebus pulled up, colour leaving his face. 'I forgot,' he said. He put a shaking hand to his forehead.

'Are you all right?'

'Fine, fine. Look, I won't do it again, okay?' He started to move off. 'You can rely on that.'

Rebus took a photocopy of Renton's drawing from his pocket. Joe Herdman was a desk sergeant who knew everything about cars. He'd been useful before, turning a vague description into something more concrete. Rebus looked at the drawing as he walked. All the details were there: buildings in the background, the hedge, the onlookers. And Sammy, caught at the point of impact. She'd half-turned, was stretching out her hands as if she could push the car to a stop. But Renton had drawn fine lines issuing from the back of the car, representing the air being pushed, representing speed. Where there

should have been a face, he had left a blank oval. The back half of the car was very clearly defined, the front a blur of disappearing perspective. Renton said he'd left out anything he couldn't be sure of. He promised he hadn't let his imagination fill in the blanks.

It was the face, or the lack of it … it disturbed Rebus more than anything else in the picture. He drew himself into the scene, wondered what he'd have done. Would he have concentrated on the car, caught its licence plate? Or would his attention have been focused on Sammy? Which would have prevailed: cop instincts or fatherhood? Someone at the station had said, 'Don't worry, we'll get him.' Not, 'Don't worry, she'll be all right.' Which brought it all down to two things: him – meaning the driver – and retribution, rather than her – the victim – and recovery.

'I'd just have been another witness,' Rebus said quietly. Then he folded the drawing and put it away.

Sammy had a room to herself, all tubes and machinery, the way he'd seen it in films and on TV. Only here the room was dingier, paint flaking from the walls and around the window-frames. The chairs had metal legs and rubber feet and moulded plastic seats. A woman rose as he came in. They embraced. He kissed the side of her forehead.

*Aiming for her. Didn't anyone say that?*

'Hello, Rhona.'

'Hello, John.'

She looked tired, of course, but her hair was stylishly cut and dyed the colour of a dull golden harvest. Her clothes were smart and she wore jewellery. He studied her eyes. Their colour was wrong. Coloured contacts. Not even her eyes were going to betray her past.

'Christ, Rhona, I'm sorry.'

He was whispering, not wanting to disturb Sammy. Which was ludicrous, because right now all he wanted in the world was for her to wake up.

'How is she?' he asked.

'Much the same.'

Mickey stood up. There were three chairs arranged in a sort of semi-circle. Mickey and Rhona had been sitting with an empty chair between them. As Rhona broke from Rebus's embrace, his brother took her place.

'This is so fucking awful,' Mickey said, his voice low. He looked the same as ever: a party animal who'd stopped getting the invites.

Niceties dispensed with, Rebus went to Sammy's bedside. Her face was still bruised, and now he could place the probable cause of each abrasion: hedge, wall, pavement. One leg was broken, both arms heavily bandaged. A teddy bear, missing one ear, lay by her head. Rebus smiled.

'You brought Pa Broon.'

'Yes.'

'Do they know yet if there's any ... ?' His eyes were on Sammy as he spoke.

'What?' Rhona wanted him to spell it out. No hiding place.

'Brain damage,' he said.

'Nobody's told us anything,' she said, sounding snubbed.

*Aiming for her. Didn't anyone say that?* No, none of the other onlookers had even hinted as much, but then they hadn't had Renton's grandstand view.

'Has nobody been in?'

'Not since I got here.'

'And I was here before Rhona,' Mickey added. 'Haven't seen a soul.'

It was enough. Rebus strode from the room. A doctor and two nurses were standing chatting at the end of the corridor. One of the nurses was leaning against a wall.

'What's going on?' Rebus exploded. 'Nobody's been near my daughter all morning!'

The doctor was young, male. Blond hair cut short with a parting.

'We're doing everything we can.'

'What does that mean?'

'I can appreciate that you're —'

'Fuck you, pal. Why hasn't the big man been to look at her? Why's she just lying there like a —' Rebus choked back the words.

'Your daughter was seen by two specialists this morning,' the doctor said quietly. 'We're waiting for some test results to determine whether to operate again. There's some brain swelling. The tests take a little time to process, there's nothing we can do about it.'

Rebus felt cheated: still angry, but nothing to feel angry *about*, not here. He nodded, turned away.

Back in the room, he explained the situation to Rhona. A suitcase and large holdall were sitting behind one of the machines.

'Listen,' he told her, 'it'd make sense if you stayed at the flat. It's only ten minutes away, and I could let you have the car.'

She was shaking her head. 'We're booked into the Sheraton.'

'The flat's nearer, and I tend not to charge ...' *We?* Rebus looked at Mickey, whose eyes were on the bed. Then the door opened and a man came in. Short, thickly built, breathing hard. He was rubbing his hands to let everyone know he'd been to the toilet. Loose folds of flesh furrowed his brow and bulged from his shirt collar. His hair was thick and black, like an oil-slick. He stopped when he saw Rebus.

'John,' Rhona said, 'this is a friend of mine, Jackie.'

'Jackie Platt,' the man said, reaching out a plump hand.

'When Jackie heard, he insisted on driving me up.'

Platt shrugged, his head almost disappearing into his shoulders. 'Couldn't have her training it up on her ownio.'

'Hell of a drive,' Mickey said, his tone hinting at repetition.

'Could have done without the roadworks,' Jackie Platt agreed. Rebus's eyes caught Rhona's; she looked away quickly, dodging reproach.

To Rebus, this bulk didn't belong. It was as if a character had wandered on to the wrong set. Platt hadn't been in the script.

'She looks so peaceful, don't she?' the Londoner was saying, making for the bed. He touched her arm, Sammy's bandaged arm, grazing it with the back of his hand. Rebus's fingernails dug into his palms.

Then Platt yawned. 'You know, Rhona, it might not be good manners, but I think I'm about to crash. See you back at the hotel?' She nodded, relieved. Platt picked up the suitcase. As he passed her, his hand went into his trouser pocket, came out with a fold of banknotes.

'Get a cab back, all right?'

'All right, Jackie. See you later.'

'Cheers, pet.' And he squeezed her hand. 'Take care, Mickey. All the best, John.' A huge, face-creasing wink, then he was gone. They waited in silence for a few seconds. Rhona held up her free hand, the one without the wad of notes.

'Not a word, okay?'

'Furthest thing from my mind,' Rebus said, sitting down. '"Think I'm about to crash". Tactful or what?'

'Come on, Johnny,' Mickey said. Johnny: only Mickey could do that, using the name so that the years fell from both of them. Rebus

looked at his brother and smiled. Mickey was a therapist by profession; he knew the things to say.

'Why the cases?' Rebus asked Rhona.

'What?'

'You're going to a hotel, why not leave them in his car?'

'I thought about staying here. They said I could if I wanted to. Only then I saw her ... and I changed my mind.' Tears started down her face, smudging already-smudged mascara. Mickey had a handkerchief ready.

'John, what if she ... ? Oh, Jesus Christ, why did this have to happen?' She was wailing now. Rebus went over to her chair, crouched in front of it, his hands resting on hers. 'She's all we've got, John. She's all we ever had.'

'She's still here, Rhona. She's right here.'

'But why her? Why Samantha?'

'I'll ask him when I find him, Rhona.' He kissed her hair, his eyes on Mickey. 'And believe me, I'm going to find him.'

Later, when Ned Farlowe visited, Rebus took him outside. There was drizzle falling, but the air felt good.

'One of the eye-witnesses,' Rebus said, 'thinks it was deliberate.'

'I don't understand.'

'He thinks the driver meant to hit Sammy.'

'I still don't get it.'

'Look, there are two scenarios. One, he was intent on hitting a pedestrian, and anyone would have done. Two, Sammy was his target. He'd been following her, saw his chance when she crossed the road, only the lights were against him so he had to jump them. Then she was so close to the kerb he had to switch lanes.'

'But why?'

Rebus stared at him. 'This is Sammy's dad and her lover, right? For the purposes of what follows, I want you to stop being a reporter.'

Farlowe stared back, nodded slowly.

'I've had a few run-ins with Tommy Telford,' Rebus said. He was seeing teddy bears: Pa Broon, and the one Telford kept in his car. 'This might have been a message for me.' Telford or Tarawicz: flip a coin. 'Or for you, if you've been asking questions about Telford.'

'You think my book ...'

'I'm keeping an open mind. I've been working the Lintz case ... and so have you.'

'Someone warning us off Lintz?'

Rebus thought of Abernethy, shrugged. 'Then there's Sammy's job, working with ex-cons. Maybe one of them had a grudge.'

'Jesus.'

'She hadn't mentioned anyone following her? Nobody odd in the area?' Same question he'd put to the Petrecs, only different victim ...

Farlowe shook his head. 'Look,' he said, 'until five minutes ago I thought this was an accident. Now you're saying it was attempted murder. Are you *sure*?'

'I'm trusting a witness.' But he knew what Bill Pryde thought: a drunk driver, a crazy man. And a grandstand spectator who wore glasses and had read it wrong. He took out the drawing again.

'What's that?'

Rebus handed it over. 'This is what someone saw last night.'

'What kind of car is it?'

'Rover 600, Ford Mondeo, something like that. Dark green. Ring any bells?'

Ned Farlowe shook his head, then looked at Rebus. 'Let me help. I can ask around.'

'One kid in a coma's enough.'


The rest of the office had packed up and gone home. Now there were only Rebus and Sammy's boss, a woman called Mae Crumley. The light from half a dozen desk-lamps illuminated the haphazard office, which was on the top floor of an old four-storey building off Palmerston Place. Rebus knew Palmerston Place: there was a church there where the AA held meetings. He'd been to a couple. He could still taste whisky at the back of his throat. Not that he'd had any so far today, not in daylight hours. But then he hadn't phoned Jack Morton either.

The address might have been posher than Rebus was expecting, but the accommodation was cramped. The office was in the eaves of the building, so that you couldn't stand up in half the available space, which hadn't stopped desks being sited in the most awkward corners.

'Which is hers?' Rebus asked. Mae Crumley pointed to the desk next to her own. There was a computer there somewhere, but only

131

its screen was showing. Loose sheets of paper, books and pamphlets and reports, the whole lot spilled on to the chair and from there down on to the floor.

'She works too hard,' Crumley said. 'We all do.'

Rebus sipped the coffee she'd made him. Cafe Hag.

'When Sammy came here,' she went on, 'the first thing she said was that her father was CID. She never tried to hide it.'

'And you'd no qualms about taking her on?'

'None at all.' Crumley folded her arms. They were big arms; she was a big woman. Her hair was a fiery red, long and frizzy and tied back with a black ribbon. She wore an oatmeal linen shirt with a denim jacket over the top of it. Her eyebrows had been plucked into thin arches over pale grey eyes. Her desk was relatively tidy, but only, as she'd explained to Rebus, because she tended to stay later than anyone else.

'What about her clients?' Rebus asked. 'Could any of them have held a grudge?'

'Against her or against you?'

'Against me *through* her.'

Crumley considered this. 'To the extent that they'd run her over just to make a point? I very much doubt it.'

'I'd be interested to see her client list.'

She shook her head. 'Look ... you shouldn't be doing this. It's too personal, you know that. I mean, who am I talking to here: Sammy's father, or a copper?'

'You think I've a score to settle?'

'Well haven't you?'

Rebus put down the coffee mug. 'Maybe.'

'And that's why you shouldn't be doing this.' She sighed. 'Number one on my wish list: Sammy back on her feet and back here. But what about if meantime I do a bit of poking around? I stand a better chance of getting them to talk than you do.'

Rebus nodded. 'I'd appreciate that.' He got to his feet. 'Thanks for the coffee.'

Outside, he checked the list the Juice Church had given him. He kept it in his pocket, didn't refer to it often. There was a meeting at Palmerston Place in about an hour and a half. No good. He knew he'd spend the time beforehand in a pub. Jack Morton had introduced him to Al-Anon, but Rebus hadn't really taken to it, though the stories had affected him.

'See,' one man had told the group, 'I had problems at work, problems with my wife, my kids. I had money problems and health problems and everything else. Practically the only problem I didn't have was with the drink. And that's because I was a drunk.'

Rebus lit himself a cigarette and drove home.

He sat in his chair and thought about Rhona. They'd shared so much over so many years ... and then it had all stopped. He'd chosen his job over his marriage, and that could not be forgiven. Last time he'd seen her had been in London, wearing her new life like armour. Nobody had warned him about Jackie Platt. His phone rang, and he snatched it from the floor.

'Rebus.'

'It's Bill.' Pryde sounded halfway to excited, which was as far as he ever ventured.

'What have you got?'

'Dark green Rover 600 – I think the owner called it "Sherwood Green" – stolen yesterday evening about an hour before the collision.'

'Where from?'

'Metered parking on George Street.'

'What do you reckon?'

'My advice is, keep an open mind. Having said that, at least now we've got a licence plate. Owner reported it at six-forty last night. It hasn't turned up anywhere, so I've upped the alert status.'

'Give me the reg.' Pryde read out the letters and numbers. Rebus thanked him and put down the phone. He was thinking of Danny Simpson, dumped outside Fascination Street around the time Sammy was being hit. Coincidence? Or a double message, Telford and Rebus. Which put Big Ger Cafferty in the frame. He called the hospital, was told there was no change. Farlowe was in visiting. The nurse said he had his laptop with him.

Rebus recalled Sammy growing up – a series of isolated images. He hadn't been there for her. He saw her in a series of fast jerky impressions, as if the film had been spliced. He tried not to think about the hell she had gone through at the hands of Gordon Reeve ...

He saw good people doing bad things and bad people doing good, and he tried dividing the two into groups. He saw Candice and Tommy Telford and Mr Pink Eyes. And encompassing it all, he saw Edinburgh. He saw the mass of the people just getting on with their

lives, and he saluted them. They *knew* things and felt things, things he'd never feel. He used to think he knew things. As a kid, he'd known *everything*. Now he knew differently. The only thing you could be sure of was the inside of your head, and even that could deceive you. I don't even know myself, he thought. So how could he ever hope to know Sammy? And with each year, he understood less.

He thought of the Oxford Bar. Even on the wagon, he'd stayed a regular, drinking cola and mugs of coffee. A pub like the Ox was about so much more than just the hooch. It was therapy and refuge, entertainment and art. He checked his watch, thinking he could head down there now. Just a couple of whiskies and a beer, something to make him feel good about himself until the morning.

The phone rang again. He picked it up.

'Evening, John.'

Rebus smiled, leaned back in his chair. 'Jack, you must be a bloody mind reader ...'

# 14

Mid-morning, Rebus walked through the cemetery. He'd been to the hospital to check on Sammy – no change. Now, he felt he had time to kill ...

'A bit cooler today, Inspector.' Joseph Lintz rose from his knees and pushed his glasses back up to the bridge of his nose. There were damp patches on his trousers from where he'd been kneeling. He dropped his trowel on to a white polythene bag. Beside the bag stood pots of small green plants.

'Won't the frost get them?' Rebus asked. Lintz shrugged.

'It gets all of us, but we're allowed to bloom for a while.'

Rebus turned away. Today, he wasn't in the mood for games. Warriston Cemetery was vast. In the past, it had been a history lesson to Rebus – headstones telling the story of nineteenth-century Edinburgh – but now he found it a jarring reminder of mortality. They were the only living souls in the place. Lintz had pulled out a handkerchief.

'More questions?' he asked.

'Not exactly.'

'What then?'

'Truth is, Mr Lintz, I've got other things on my mind.'

The old man looked at him. 'Maybe all this archaeology is beginning to bore you, Inspector?'

'I still don't get it, planting things before the first frost?'

'Well, I can't plant very much afterwards, can I? And at my age ... any day now I could be lying in the ground. I like to think there might be a few flowers surviving above me.' He'd lived in Scotand the best part of half a century, but there was still something lurking beneath the local accent, peculiarities of phrasing and tone that would be with Joseph Lintz until he died, reminders of his far less recent history.

'So,' he said now, 'no questions today?' Rebus shook his head. 'You're right, Inspector, you do seem preoccupied. Is it something I can help with?'

'In what way?'

'I don't really know. But you've come here, questions or no. I take it there's a reason?'

A dog was bounding through the long grass, crunching on the fallen leaves, nose brushing the ground. It was a yellow labrador, short-haired and overweight. Lintz turned towards it and almost growled. Dogs were the enemy.

'I was just wondering,' Rebus was saying, 'what you're capable of.' Lintz looked puzzled. The dog began to paw at the ground. Lintz reached down, picked up a stone, and hurled it. It didn't reach the dog. The labrador's owner was rounding the corner. He was young, crop-haired and skinny.

'That thing should be kept on its lead!' Lintz roared.

'*Jawohl!*' the owner snapped back, clicking his heels. He was laughing as he passed them.

'I am a famous man now,' Lintz reflected, back to his old self after the outburst. 'Thanks to the newspapers.' He looked up at the sky, blinked. 'People send me hate by the Royal Mail. A car was parked outside my home the other night ... they put a brick through the windscreen. It wasn't my car, but they didn't know that. Now my neighbours keep clear of that spot, just in case.'

He spoke like the old man he was, a little tired, a little defeated.

'This is the worst year of my life.' He stared down at the border he'd been tending. The earth, newly turned, looked dark and rich, like crumbs of chocolate cake. A few worms and wood lice had been disturbed and were still looking for their old homes. 'And it's going to get worse, isn't it?'

Rebus shrugged. His feet were cold, the damp seeping in through his shoes. He was standing on the rough roadway, Lintz six inches above him on the grass. And still Lintz didn't reach his height. A little old man: that's what he was. And Rebus could study him, talk with him, go to his home and see what few photographs remained – according to Lintz – from the old days.

'What did you mean back there?' he said. 'What was it you said? Something about what I was capable of?'

Rebus stared at him. 'It's okay, the dog just showed me.'

'Showed you what?'

'What you're like with the enemy.'

Lintz smiled. 'I don't like dogs, it's true. Don't read too much into it, Inspector. That's the journalists' job.'

'Your life would be easier without dogs, wouldn't it?'

Lintz shrugged. 'Of course.'

'And easier without me, too?'

Lintz frowned. 'If it weren't you, it would be someone else, a boor like your Inspector Abernethy.'

'What do you think he was telling you?'

Lintz blinked. 'I'm not sure. Someone else came to see me. A man called Levy. I refused to talk to him – one privilege still open to me.'

Rebus shuffled his feet, trying to get some warmth into them. 'I have a daughter, did I ever tell you that?'

Lintz looked baffled. 'You might have mentioned it.'

'You know I have a daughter?'

'Yes ... I mean, I think I knew before today.'

'Well, Mr Lintz, the night before last, someone tried to kill her, or at least do her some serious damage. She's in hospital, still unconscious. And *that* bothers me.'

'I'm so sorry. How did it ... ? I mean, how do you ... ?'

'I think maybe someone was trying to send me a message.'

Lintz's eyes widened. 'And you believe *me* capable of such a thing? My God, I thought we had come to understand one another, at least a little.'

Rebus was wondering. He was wondering how easy it would be to put on an act, when you'd spent half a century practising. He was wondering how easy it would be to steel yourself to killing an innocent ... or at least ordering their death. All it took was an order. A few words to someone else who would carry out your bidding. Maybe Lintz had it in him. Maybe it wouldn't be any more difficult than it had been for Josef Linzstek.

'Something you should know,' Rebus said. 'Threats don't scare me off. Quite the opposite.'

'It's good that you are so strong.' Rebus looked for meaning behind the words. 'I'm on my way home. Can I offer you some tea?'

Rebus drove, and then sat in the drawing-room while Lintz busied himself in the kitchen. Started flicking through a pile of books on a desk.

'Ancient History, Inspector,' Lintz said, bringing in the tray – he always refused offers of help. 'Another hobby of mine. I'm

fascinated by that intersection at which history and fiction meet.' The books were all about Babylonia. 'Babylon is an historical fact, you see, but what about the Tower of Babel?'

'A song by Elton John?' Rebus offered.

'Always making jokes.' Lintz looked up. 'What is it you're afraid of?'

Rebus took one of the cups. 'I've heard of the Gardens of Babylon,' he admitted, putting the book down. 'What other hobbies do you have?'

'Astrology, hauntings, the unknown.'

'Have you ever been haunted?'

Lintz seemed amused. 'No.'

'Would you like to be?'

'By seven hundred French villagers? No, Inspector, I wouldn't like that at all. It was astrology that first brought me to the Chaldeans. They came from Babylonia. Have you ever heard of Babylonian numbers ...?'

Lintz had a way of turning conversations in directions *he* wanted them to take. Rebus wasn't going to be deflected this time. He waited till Lintz had the cup to his lips.

'Did you try to kill my daughter?'

Lintz paused, then sipped, swallowed.

'No, Inspector,' he said quietly.

Which left Telford, Tarawicz and Cafferty. Rebus thought of Telford, surrounded by his Family but wanting to play with the big boys. How different was a gang war from any other kind? You had soldiers, and orders given to them. They had to prove themselves, or lose face, show themselves cowards. Shoot a civilian, run down a pedestrian. Rebus realised that he didn't want the driver as such – he wanted the person who'd *driven* them to do it. Lintz's defence of Linzstek was that the young lieutenant had been under orders, that war itself was the real culprit, as though humans had no say in the matter ...

'Inspector,' the old man was saying, 'do *you* think I'm Linzstek?'

Rebus nodded. 'I know you are.'

A wry smile. 'Then arrest me.'

'Here comes the blue-nose,' Father Conor Leary said. 'Out to steal Ireland's God-given Guinness.' He paused, eyes narrowing. 'Or are you still on that abstention kick?'

'I'm trying,' Rebus said.

'Well, I won't tempt you then.' Leary smiled. 'But you know me, John. I'm not one to judge, but a wee drop never harmed a soul.'

'Problem is, you put lots of wee drops together and you get a bloody big fall.'

Father Leary laughed. 'But aren't we all the fallen? Come away in.'

Father Leary was priest of Our Lady of Perpetual Help. Years back, someone had defaced the board outside to turn 'Help' into 'Hell'. The board had been corrected many times, but Rebus always thought of the place as 'Perpetual Hell': it was what the followers of Knox and Calvin would have believed. Father Leary took him through to the kitchen.

'Here, man, sit yourself down. I haven't seen you in so long, I thought you'd renounced me.' He went to the fridge and lifted out a can of Guinness.

'Are you operating a pharmacy on the side?' Rebus asked. Father Leary looked at him. Rebus nodded towards the fridge. 'The shelves of medicine.'

Father Leary rolled his eyes. 'At my age, you go to the doctor with angina and they dose you for every conceivable ailment. They think it makes old folk feel better.' He brought a glass to the table, placed it next to his can. Rebus felt a hand fall on his shoulder.

'I'm hellish sorry about Sammy.'

'How did you hear?'

'Her name was in one of the rags this morning.' Father Leary sat down. 'Hit and run, they said.'

'Hit and run,' Rebus echoed.

Father Leary shook his head wearily, one hand rubbing slowly over his chest. He was probably in his late-sixties, though he'd never said. Well-built, with a thatch of silver hair. Tufts of grey sprouted from his ears, nose and dog-collar. His hand seemed to smother the can of Guinness. But when he poured, he poured gently, almost with reverence.

'It's a terrible thing,' he said quietly. 'Coma, is it?'

'Not until the doctors say so.' Rebus cleared his throat. 'It's only been a day and a half.'

'You know what we believers say,' Father Leary went on. 'When something like this happens, it's a test for all of us. It's a way of making us stronger.' The head on his Guinness was perfect. He took

a swallow, licked his lips thoughtfully. 'That's what we *say*; it may not be what we think.' He looked into his drink.

'It didn't make me strong. I went back to the whisky.'

'I can understand that.'

'Until a friend reminded me it was the lazy way out, the cowardly way.'

'And who's to say he's not right?'

'"Faint-Heart and the Sermon",' Rebus said with a smile.

'What's that?'

'A song. But maybe it's us, too.'

'Get away, we're just two old boys having a natter. So how are you holding up, John?'

'I don't know.' He paused. 'I don't think it was an accident. And the man I think is behind it ... Sammy isn't the first woman he's tried to destroy.' Rebus looked into the priest's eyes. 'I want to kill him.'

'But so far you haven't?'

'I haven't even talked to him.'

'Because you're worried what you might do?'

'Or not do.' Rebus's mobile sounded. He gave a look of apology and switched it on.

'John, it's Bill.'

'Yes, Bill?'

'Green Rover 600.'

'Yes?'

'We've got it.'


The car had been parked illegally on the street outside Piershill Cemetery. There was a parking ticket on its windscreen, dated the previous afternoon. If anyone had checked, they'd have found the driver's-side door unlocked. Maybe someone had: the car was empty, no coins, no map-books or cassettes. The fascia had been removed from the radio/cassette. There were no keys in the ignition. A car transporter had arrived, and the Rover was being winched aboard.

'I called in a favour at Howdenhall,' Bill Pryde was saying, 'they've promised to fingerprint it today.'

Rebus was studying the front passenger side. No dents, nothing to suggest this car had been used as a battering-ram against his daughter.

'I think maybe we need your permission, John.'

'What for?'

'Someone should go to the Infirmary and print Sammy.'

Rebus stared at the front of the car, then got out the drawing. Yes, she'd put out a hand. Her prints might be there, invisible to him.

'Sure,' he said. 'No problem. You think this is it?'

'I'll tell you once we print it.'

'You steal a car,' Rebus said, 'then you hit someone with it, and leave it a couple of miles away.' He looked around. 'Ever been on this street before?' Pryde shook his head. 'Me neither.'

'Someone local?'

'I'm wondering why they stole it in the first place.'

'Stick false plates on and sell it,' Pryde suggested. 'Spot of joy-riding maybe.'

'Joy-riders don't leave cars looking like this.'

'No, but they'd had a fright. They'd just knocked someone down.'

'And they drove all the way over here before deciding to dump it?'

'Maybe it was stolen for a job, turn over a petrol station. Then they hit Sammy and decide to jump ship. Maybe the job was this side of town.'

'Or Sammy *was* the job.'

Pryde put a hand on his shoulder. 'Let's see what the boffins turn up, eh?'

Rebus looked at him. 'You don't go for it?'

'Look, it's a feeling you've got, and that's fair enough, but right now all you've got is that student's word for it. There were other witnesses, John, and I asked them all again, and they told me the same thing: it looked like the driver lost control, that's all.'

There was an edge of irritation to Pryde's voice. Rebus knew why: long hours.

'Will Howdenhall let you know tonight?'

'They promised. And I'll phone you straight away, okay?'

'On my mobile,' Rebus said. 'I'm going to be on the move.' He looked around. 'There was something about Piershill Cemetery recently, wasn't there?'

'Kids,' Pryde said, nodding. 'They pushed over a load of gravestones.'

Rebus remembered now. 'Just the Jewish headstones, wasn't it?'
'I think so.'
And there, sprayed on the wall near the gates, the same piece of graffiti: Won't Anyone Help?

It was late evening, and Rebus was driving. Not the M90 into Fife: tonight, he was on the M8, heading west, heading for Glasgow. He'd spent half an hour at the hospital, followed by an hour and a half with Rhona and Jackie Platt, their guest for dinner at the Sheraton. He'd worn a fresh suit and shirt. He hadn't smoked. He'd drunk a bottle of Highland Spring.

They were planning yet more tests on Sammy. The neurologist had taken them into his office and talked them through the procedures. There would probably be another operation at the end of it. Rebus could barely remember what the man had said. Rhona had asked for the occasional explanation, but these seemed no more lucid than what had gone before.

Dinner had been a subdued affair. Jackie Platt, it turned out, sold second-hand cars.

'See, John, where I really score is the obituaries. Check the local paper, hare round there and see if they've left a car behind. Quick cash offer.'

'Sammy doesn't drive, sorry,' Rebus had said, causing Rhona to drop her cutlery on to her plate.

At the end of the meal, she'd seen him out to his car, gripped one of his arms hard.

'Get the bastard, John. I want to look him in the face. Just get the bastard who did this to us.' Her eyes were blazing.

He nodded. Stones: 'Just Wanna See His Face'. Rebus wanted it, too.

The M8, which could be a nightmare at rush-hour, was a quiet drive in the evenings. Rebus knew he was making good time, and that he would soon see the outline of the Easterhouse estate against the sky. When his phone sounded, he didn't hear it at first: blame Wishbone Ash. As *Argus* finished, he picked up.

'Rebus.'

'John, it's Bill.'

'What've you got?'

'Forensics were good as gold. There are prints all over the car,

interior and exterior. Several sets.' He paused, and Rebus thought the connection had gone. 'One good palm and finger set on the front of the bonnet ...'

'Sammy's?'

'For definite.'

'So we've got our car.'

'The owner's given us a set so we can eliminate him. When we've done that ...'

'We're still not home and dry, Bill. The car sat unlocked outside that cemetery, we don't know someone didn't clean it out.'

'Owner says the radio/cassette fascia was there when he left it. Also half a dozen tapes, a packet of Paracetamol, receipts for petrol and a road map. So someone cleaned it out, whether it's the bastard we want or just some scavenger.'

'At least we know it's the car.'

'I'll check again with Howdenhall tomorrow, collect any other prints and start trying to match them. Plus I'll ask around Piershill, see if anyone saw someone dumping it.'

'Meantime get some sleep, eh?'

'Try and stop me. What about you?'

'Me?' Two cups of espresso after dinner. And with the knowledge of what lay ahead. 'I'll get my head down soon enough, Bill. Talk to you tomorrow.'

On the outskirts of Glasgow, headed for Barlinnie Prison.

He'd phoned ahead, made sure they were expecting him. It was way outside any visiting hours, but Rebus had made up a story about a murder inquiry. 'Follow-up questions,' was what he'd said.

'At this time of night?'

'Lothian and Borders Police, pal. Motto: Justice Never Sleeps.'

Morris Gerald Cafferty probably didn't sleep much either. Rebus imagined him lying awake at night, hands under his head, staring into the darkness.

Scheming.

Running things through his mind: how to keep his empire from falling, how best to combat threats like Tommy Telford. Rebus knew that Cafferty employed a lawyer – a middle-aged pinstripe from the New Town – to carry messages back to his gang in Edinburgh. He thought of Charles Groal, Telford's lawyer. Groal was young and sharp, like his paymaster.

'Strawman.'

He was waiting in the Interview Room, arms folded, chair set well away from the table. And of course his opening gambit was his nickname for Rebus.

'A lovely surprise, two visits in a week. Don't tell me you've another message from the Pole?'

Rebus sat down opposite Cafferty. 'Tarawicz isn't Polish.' He glanced towards the guard who stood by the door, lowered his voice. 'Another of Telford's boys got a doing.'

'How clumsy.'

'He was all but scalped. Are you looking for war?'

Cafferty drew his chair in to the table, leaned across towards Rebus. 'I've never backed down from a fight.'

'My daughter got hurt. Funny that, so soon after we'd had our little chat.'

'Hurt how?'

'Hit and run.'

Cafferty was thoughtful. 'I don't pick on civilians.'

Yes, Rebus thought, but she wasn't a civilian, because *he* had lured her on to the battlefield.

'Convince me,' Rebus said.

'Why should I bother?'

'The conversation we had ... What you asked me to do.'

'Telford?' A whisper. Cafferty sat back for a moment to consider. When he leaned forward again, his eyes bored into Rebus's. 'There's something you've forgotten. I lost a son, remember. Think I could do that to another father? I'd do a lot of things, Rebus, but not that, never that.'

Rebus held the stare. 'All right,' he said.

'You want me to find who did it?'

Rebus nodded slowly.

'That's your price?'

Rhona's words: *I want to look him in the face.* Rebus shook his head. 'I want them *delivered* to me. I want you to do that, whatever it takes.'

Cafferty placed his hands on his knees, seemed to take his time positioning them just so. 'You know it's probably Telford?'

'Yes. If it's not you.'

'You'll be going after him then?'

'Any way I can.'

Cafferty smiled. 'But your ways aren't my ways.'

'You might get to him first. I want him *alive*.'

'And meantime, you're my man?'

Rebus stared at him. 'I'm your man,' he said.

# 15

Rebus got a phone call early the next morning from Leith CID, telling him Joseph Lintz was dead. The bad news was, it looked like murder: the body found hanging from a tree in Warriston Cemetery.

By the time Rebus appeared at the scene, they were cordoning it off, the doctor having concluded that most suicides wouldn't have bothered administering a violent blow to their own head before commencing with operations.

The corpse of Joseph Lintz was being zipped into a body bag. Rebus got a look at the face. He'd seen elderly corpses before, and mostly they'd looked wonderfully at peace, their faces shiny and child-like. But Joseph Lintz looked like he'd suffered. He didn't look to be at rest at all.

'You'll have come to thank us, no doubt,' a man said, walking towards Rebus. His shoulders were hunched inside a navy raincoat and he walked with head bowed, hands in pockets. His hair was thick and silver and wiry, his skin an almost jaundiced yellow – the remains of an autumn holiday tan.

'Hiya, Bobby,' Rebus said.

Bobby Hogan was Leith CID.

'To get back to my initial observation, John ...'

'What am I supposed to be thanking you for?'

Hogan nodded towards the body bag. 'Taking Mr Lintz off your hands. 'Don't tell me you were *enjoying* digging into all that?'

'Not exactly.'

'Any idea who might have wanted him dead?'

Rebus puffed out his cheeks. 'Where do you want me to start?'

'I mean, I'm right to rule out the usual, aren't I?' Hogan held up three fingers. 'It wasn't suicide, muggers aren't quite this creative, and it surely wasn't an accident.'

'Someone was making a point, no doubt about it.'

'But what sort of point?'

Scene of Crime officers were busying themselves, filling the *locus* with noise and movement. Rebus gestured for Hogan to walk with him. They were deep in the cemetery, the part Lintz had loved so much. As they walked, the place grew wilder, more overgrown.

'I was here with him yesterday morning,' Rebus said. 'I don't know if he had a routine exactly, but he came here most days.'

'We found a bag of gardening tools.'

'He planted flowers.'

'So if someone knew he'd be coming, they could have been waiting?'

Rebus nodded. 'An assassination.'

Hogan was thoughtful. 'Why hang him?'

'It's what happened at Villefranche. The town elders were strung up in the square.'

'Jesus.' Hogan stopped walking. 'I know you've got other stuff on the go, but can you help out on this, John?'

'Any way I can.'

'A list of possibles would do for a start.'

'How about an old woman living in France, and a Jewish historian who walks with a stick?'

'Is that all you've got?'

'Well, there's always me. Yesterday I as good as accused him of trying to kill my daughter.' Hogan stared at him. 'I don't think he did it.' Rebus paused, thinking of Sammy: he'd called the hospital first thing. She was still unconscious; they still weren't using the word 'coma'. 'One more thing,' he said. 'Special Branch, a guy called Abernethy. He was here talking to Lintz.'

'What's the connection?'

'Abernethy's co-ordinating the various war crimes investigations. He's street-tough, not your typical desk-jockey.'

'A strange choice for the job?' Rebus nodded. 'Which hardly makes him a suspect.'

'I'm doing my best, Bobby. We could check Lintz's house, see if we can turn up any of the hate mail he claimed he'd been getting.'

'"Claimed"?'

Rebus shrugged. 'You were never sure where you were with Lintz. Do you have any idea what happened?'

'From what you've told me, I'd guess he came down here as usual

to do his gardening stint – he's certainly dressed for it. Someone was waiting. They smacked him over the head, stuck his neck in a noose, and hauled him up into the tree. The rope was tied around a headstone.'

'Did the hanging kill him?'

'Doctor says yes. Haemorrhages in the eyes. What do you call them?'

'Tardieu spots.'

'That's it. The blow to the head was just to knock him out. Something else – bruising and cuts on the face. Looks like someone kicked him when he was down.'

'Knock him cold, thump him in the face, then string him up.'

'Big-time grudge.'

Rebus looked around. 'Someone with a flair for theatre.'

'And not afraid to take risks. This place might never get exactly crowded, but it's a public space and that tree's in open view. Anyone could have walked past.'

'What time are we talking about?'

'Eight, eight-thirty. I'm guessing Mr Lintz would have wanted to do his digging in daylight.'

'Could have been earlier,' Rebus suggested. 'A pre-arranged meeting.'

'Then why the tools?'

'Because by the time it got light, the meeting would be over.'

Hogan looked doubtful.

'And if it *was* a meeting,' Rebus said, 'there might be some record of it at Lintz's home.'

Hogan looked at him, nodded. 'My car or yours?'

'Better get his keys first.'

They started back up the slope.

'Searching through a dead man's pockets,' Hogan said to himself. 'Why is that never mentioned during recruitment?'

'I was here yesterday,' Rebus said. 'He invited me back for tea.'

'No family?'

'None.'

Hogan looked around the hallway. 'Big place. What happens to the money when it's sold?'

Rebus looked at him. 'We could split it two ways.'

'Or we could just move ourselves in. Basement and ground for me, you can have first and second.'

Hogan smiled, tried one of the doors off the hall. It opened on to an office. 'This could be my bedroom,' he said, going in.

'When I came here before, he always took me upstairs.'

'On you go. We'll take a floor each, then swop.'

Rebus headed up the staircase, running his hand over the varnished banister: not a speck of dust. Cleaning ladies could be invaluable informants.

'If you find a chequebook,' he called down to Hogan, 'look for regular payments to a Mrs Mop.'

Four doors led off the first-floor landing. Two were bedrooms, one a bathroom. The last door led into the huge drawing-room, where Rebus had asked his questions and listened to the stories and philosophy that Lintz had used in place of answers.

'Do you think guilt has a genetic component, Inspector?' he'd asked one time. 'Or are we taught it?'

'Does it matter, so long as it's there?' Rebus had said, and Lintz had nodded and smiled, as if the pupil had given some satisfactory answer.

The room was big, not too much furniture. Huge sash windows – recently cleaned – looked down on to the street. There were framed prints and paintings on the walls. They could have been priceless originals or junk-store stuff – Rebus was no expert. He liked one painting. It showed a ragged white-haired man seated on a rock, surrounded by a barren plain. He had a book open on his lap, but was staring skywards in horror or awe as a shining light appeared there, picking him out. It had a Biblical look, but Rebus couldn't quite place it. He knew the look on the man's face though. He'd seen it before when some suspect's carefully crafted alibi had suddenly come tumbling down.

Over the marble fireplace was a large gilt-framed mirror. Rebus studied himself in it. Behind him he could see the room. He knew he didn't fit here.

One bedroom was for guests, the other was Lintz's. A faint smell of embrocation, half a dozen medicine bottles on the bedside table. Books, too, a pile of them. The bed had been made, a dressing-gown draped across it. Lintz was a creature of habit; he'd been in no special hurry this morning.

The next floor up, Rebus found two further bedrooms and a

toilet. There was a slight smell of damp in one room, and the ceiling was discoloured. Rebus didn't suppose Lintz got many visitors; no impetus to redecorate. Out on the landing again, he saw that one of the stair-rails was missing. It had been propped against the wall, awaiting repair. A house this size, things would always be going wrong.

He went back downstairs. Hogan was in the basement. The kitchen had a door on to a back garden – stone patio, lawn covered in rotting leaves, an ivy-covered wall giving privacy.

'Look what I found,' Hogan said, coming back from the utility room. He was holding a length of rope, frayed at one end where it had been cut.

'You think it'll match with the noose? That would mean the killer got it from here.'

'Meaning Lintz knew them.'

'Anything in the office?'

'It's going to take a bit of time. There's an address book, lots of entries, but most of them seem to go back a while.'

'How can you tell?'

'Old STD codes.'

'Computer?'

'Not even a typewriter. He used carbons. Lots of letters to his solicitor.'

'Trying to shut the media up?'

'You get a couple of mentions, too. Anything upstairs?'

'Go take a look. I'll check the office.'

Rebus climbed upstairs and stood in the office doorway, looking around. Then he sat down at the desk and imagined the room was his. What did he do here? He conducted his daily business. There were two filing-cabinets, but to get to them he'd have to stand up from the desk. And he was an old man. Say the cabinets were for dead correspondence. More recent stuff would be closer to hand.

He tried the drawers. Found the address book Hogan had mentioned. A few letters. A small snuff-box, its contents turned solid. Lintz hadn't even allowed himself that small vice. In a bottom drawer were some files. Rebus lifted out the one marked 'General/ Household'. It comprised bills and guarantees. A large brown envelope was marked BT. Rebus opened it and took out the phone bills. They went back to the beginning of the year. The most recent bill was at the front. Rebus was disappointed to find that it wasn't

150

itemised. Then he noticed that all the other statements *were*. Lintz had been meticulous, placing names beside calls made, double-checking British Telecom's totals at the foot of each page. The whole year was like that ... right up until recently. Frowning, Rebus realised that the penultimate statement was missing. Had Lintz mislaid it? Rebus couldn't see him mislaying anything. A missing bill would have hinted at chaos in his ordered world. No, it had to be somewhere.

But Rebus was damned if he could find it.

Lintz's correspondence was all business, either to lawyers or else to do with local charities and committees. He'd been resigning from his committees. Rebus wondered if pressure had been applied. Edinburgh could be cruel and cold that way.

'Well?' Hogan said, sticking his head round the door.

'I'm just wondering ...'

'What?'

'Whether to add on a conservatory and knock through from the kitchen.'

'We'd lose some garden space,' Hogan said. He came in, rested against the desk. 'Anything?'

'A missing phone bill, and a sudden change from being itemised.'

'Worth a call,' Hogan admitted. 'I found a chequebook in his bedroom. Stubs show payments of £60 a month to E. Forgan.'

'Where in the bedroom?'

'Marking his place in a book.' Hogan reached into the desk's top drawer, lifted out the address book.

Rebus got up. 'Pretty rich street this. Wonder how many of them do their own dusting.'

Hogan shut the book. 'No listing for an E. Forgan. Think the neighbours will know?'

'Edinburgh neighbours know *everything*. It's just that they most often keep it to themselves.'

# 16

Joseph Lintz's neighbours: an artist and her husband on one side; a retired advocate and his wife on the other. The artist used a cleaning lady called Ella Forgan. Mrs Forgan lived in East Claremont Street. The artist gave them a telephone number.

Conclusions drawn from the two interviews: shock and horror that Lintz was dead; praise for the quiet, considerate neighbour. A Christmas card every year, and an invitation to drinks one Sunday afternoon each July. Hard to tell when he'd been at home and when he'd been out. He went off on holiday without telling anyone except Mrs Forgan. Visitors to his home had been few – or few had been noticed, which wasn't quite the same thing.

'Men? Women?' Rebus had asked. 'Or a mixture?'

'A mixture, I'd say,' the artist had replied, measuring her words. 'Really, we knew very little about him, to say we've been neighbours these past twenty-odd years ...'

Ah, and that was Edinburgh for you, too, at least in this price bracket. Wealth was a very private thing in the city. It wasn't brash and colourful. It stayed behind its thick stone walls and was at peace.

Rebus and Hogan held a doorstep conference.

'I'll call the cleaning lady, see if I can meet her, preferably here.' Hogan looked back at Lintz's front door.

'I'd love to know where he got the money to buy this place,' Rebus said.

'That could take some excavating.'

Rebus nodded. 'Solicitor would be the place to start. What about the address book? Worth tracking down some of these elusive friends?'

'I suppose so.' Hogan looked dispirited at the prospect.

'I'll follow up on the phone bills,' Rebus said. 'If that'll help.'

Hogan was nodding. 'And remember to get me copies of your files. Are you busy otherwise?'

'Bobby, if time was money, I'd be in hock to every lender in town.'

Mae Crumley reached Rebus on his mobile.

'I thought you'd forgotten me,' he told Sammy's boss.

'Just being methodical, Inspector. I'm sure you'd want no less.' Rebus stopped at traffic lights. 'I've been in to see Sammy. Is there any news?'

'Nothing much. So you've talked to her clients?'

'Yes, and they all seemed genuinely upset and surprised. Sorry to disappoint you.'

'What makes you think I'm disappointed?'

'Sammy has a good rapport with all her clients. None of them would have wanted her hurt.'

'What about the ones who didn't want to be her clients?'

Crumley hesitated. 'There was one man ... When he was told Sammy had a police inspector for a father, he'd have nothing to do with her.'

'What's his name?'

'It couldn't have been him though.'

'Why not?'

'Because he killed himself. His name was Gavin Tay. He used to drive an ice-cream van ...'

Rebus thanked her for her call, and put down the phone. If someone had tried to kill Sammy on purpose, the question was: why? Rebus had been investigating Lintz; Ned Farlowe had been following him. Rebus had twice confronted Telford; Ned was writing a book about organised crime. Then there was Candice ... Could she have *told* Sammy something, something which might have threatened Telford, or even Mr Pink Eyes? Rebus just didn't know. He knew the most likely culprit – the most vicious – was Tommy Telford. He remembered their first meeting, and the young gangster's words to him: *That's the beauty of games. You can always start again after an accident. Not so easy in real life.* At the time it had sounded like bravado, a performance for the troops. But now it sounded like a plain threat.

And now there was Mr Taystee, connecting Sammy to Telford.

Mr Taystee had worked Telford's clubs; Mr Taystee had rejected Sammy. Rebus knew he'd have to talk to the widow.

There was just the one problem. Mr Pink Eyes had intimated that if Telford wasn't left alone, Candice would suffer. He kept seeing images of Candice: torn from home and homeland; used and abused; abusing herself in the hope of respite; clinging to a stranger's legs ... He recalled Levy's words: *Can time wash away responsibility?* Justice was a fine and noble thing, but revenge ... revenge was an *emotion*, and so much stronger than an abstract like justice. He wondered if Sammy would want revenge. Probably not. She'd want him to help Candice, which meant yielding to Telford. Rebus didn't think he could do that.

And now there was Lintz's murder, unconnected but resonant.

'I've never felt comfortable with the past, Inspector,' Lintz had said once. Funny, Rebus felt the same way about the present.

Joanne Tay lived in Colinton: a newish three-bedroomed semi with the Merc still parked in the drive.

'It's too big for me,' she explained to Rebus. 'I'll have to sell it.'

He wasn't sure if she meant the house or the car. Having declined her offer of tea, he sat in the busy living-room, ornaments on every flat surface. Joanne Tay was still in mourning: black skirt and blouse, dark grooves beneath her eyes. He'd interviewed her back at the start of the inquiry.

'I still don't know why he did it,' she said now, reluctant to see her husband's death as anything other than suicide.

But the pathology and forensic tests had cast this into doubt.

'Have you ever heard,' Rebus asked, 'of a man called Tommy Telford?'

'He runs a nightclub, doesn't he? Gavin took me there once.'

'So Gavin knew him?'

'Seemed to.'

Yes: because no way was Mr Taystee setting up his hot-dog pitch outside Telford's premises without Telford's okay. And Telford's okay almost certainly meant payment of some kind. A percentage maybe ... or a favour.

'The week before Gavin died,' Rebus went on, 'you said he'd been busy?'

'Working all hours.'

'Days as well as nights?' She nodded. 'The weather was lousy that week.'

'I know. I told him: you'll never get them buying ice-cream, a day like this. Pelting down outside. But still he went out.'

Rebus shifted in his chair. 'Did he ever mention SWEEP, Mrs Tay?'

'He had some woman would visit him ... red hair.'

'Mae Crumley?'

She nodded, eyes staring at the coal-effect fire. She asked him again if he wanted some tea. Rebus shook his head and made to leave. Did pretty well: knocked over just the two ornaments on his way to the door.

The hospital was quiet. When he pushed open the door to Sammy's room, he saw that another bed had been added, a middle-aged woman sleeping in it. Her hands lay on the bedcovers, a white identity tag around one wrist. She was hooked up to a machine, and her head was bandaged.

Two women were sitting by Sammy's bed. Rhona, and Patience Aitken. Rebus hadn't seen Patience in a while. The women were sitting close together. Their whispered conversation stopped as he came in. He lifted a chair and placed it beside Patience's. She leaned over and squeezed his hand.

'Hello, John.'

He smiled at her, spoke to Rhona. 'How is she?'

'The specialist says those last tests were very positive.'

'What does that mean?'

'It means there's brain activity. She's not in deep coma.'

'Is that his version?'

'He thinks she'll come out of it, John.' Her eyes were bloodshot. He noticed a handkerchief gripped in one hand.

'That's good,' he said. 'Which doctor was it?'

'Dr Stafford. He's just back from holiday.'

'I can't keep track of them all.' Rebus rubbed his forehead.

'Look,' Patience said, checking her watch, 'I really should be going. I'm sure the two of you ...'

'Stay as long as you like,' Rebus told her.

'I'm already late for an appointment, actually.' She got to her feet. 'Nice to meet you, Rhona.'

'Thanks, Patience.' The two women shook hands a little awkwardly, then Rhona got up and they hugged, and the awkwardness vanished. 'Thanks for coming.'

Patience turned to Rebus. She looked radiant, he decided. Light really seemed to emanate from her skin. She was wearing her usual perfume, and had had her hair restyled.

'Thanks for looking in,' he said.

'She's going to be fine, John.' She took his hands in hers, leaned towards him. A peck on the cheek, a kiss between friends. Rebus saw Rhona watching them.

'John,' she said, 'see Patience out, will you?'

'No, that's all —'

'Of course, yes,' Rebus said.

They left the room together. Walked the first few steps in silence. Patience spoke first.

'She's great, isn't she?'

'Rhona?'

'Yes.'

Rebus was thoughtful. 'She's terrific. Have you met her paramour?'

'He's gone back to London. I've ... I asked Rhona if she wanted to come stay with me. Hotels can be ...'

Rebus smiled tiredly. 'Good idea. Then all you'd have to do is invite my brother over and you'd have the whole set.'

Her face cracked into an embarrassed grin. 'I suppose it must look a bit like I'm collecting you all.'

'The perfect hand of Unhappy Families.'

She turned to him. They were at the main doors of the hospital. She touched his shoulder. 'John, I'm really sorry about Sammy. Anything I can do, you've only got to ask.'

'Thanks, Patience.'

'But asking for things has never been your strong point, has it? You just sit in silence and hope they come to you.' She sighed. 'I can't believe I'm saying this, but I miss you. I think that's why I took in Sammy. If I couldn't be close to you, at least I could be close to someone who was. Does that make any sense? Is this where you say something about not deserving me?'

'You've seen the script.' He pulled back a little from her, just so he could look at her face. 'I miss you, too.'

All the nights slumped at the bar, or in his chair at home, the long midnight drives so he could keep his restlessness alive. He'd have the TV and the hi-fi on at the same time, and the flat would still feel empty. Books he tried reading, finding he was ten pages in and

156

couldn't remember anything. Gazing from his window at the darkened flats across the street, imagining lives at rest.

All because he didn't have *her*.

They embraced in silence for a while. 'You're going to be late,' he said.

'God, John, what are we going to do?'

'See one another?'

'That sounds like a start.'

'Tonight? Mario's at eight?' She nodded and they kissed again. He squeezed her hand. Her head was turned to look at him as she pushed open the doors.

Emerson, Lake and Palmer: 'Still ... You Turn Me On.'

Rebus felt a little giddy as he walked back to Sammy's room. Only it wasn't any more, wasn't 'Sammy's room'. Now there was another patient there. They'd said there was always that possibility — shortage of space, cutbacks. The woman was still asleep or unconscious, breathing noisily. Rebus ignored her and sat where Patience had been sitting.

'I've got a message for you,' Rhona said. 'From Dr Morrison.'

'Who's he when he's at home?'

'I've no idea. All he said was, could he have his t-shirt back?'

The ghoul with the scythe ... Rebus picked up Pa Broon, turned the bear in his hands. They sat in silence for a while, until Rhona shifted in her chair. 'Patience is really nice.'

'Did the two of you have a good chat?' She nodded. 'And you told her what a perfect husband I'd been?'

'You must be crazy, walking out on her.'

'Sanity's never exactly been my strong point.'

'But you used to know a good thing when you saw it.'

'Trouble is, that's never what I see when I look in the mirror.'

'What do you see?'

He looked at her. 'Sometimes I don't see anything at all.'

Later, they took a coffee-break, went to the machine.

'I lost her, you know,' Rhona said.

'What?'

'Sammy, I lost her. She came back here. She came back to you.'

'We hardly see one another, Rhona.'

'But she's *here*. Don't you get it? It's you she wants, not me.' She turned away from him, fumbled for her handkerchief. He stood

157

close behind her, then couldn't think of anything to say. He was all out of words; every line of sympathy rang hollow to him, just another cliche. He touched the back of her neck, rubbed it. She lowered her head a little, didn't resist. Massage: there'd been a lot of massage early on in their relationship. By the end, he hadn't even given her time for a handshake.

'I don't know why she came back, Rhona,' he said at last. 'But I don't think she was running away, and I don't think it had much to do with seeing me.'

A couple of nurses ran past, urgency in their movements.

'I'd better get back,' Rhona said, rubbing a hand over her face, pulling it into something resembling composure.

Rebus went with her to the room, then said he had to be going. He bent down to kiss Sammy, feeling the breath from her nostrils against his cheek.

'Wake up, Sammy,' he cajoled. 'You can't stay in bed all your life. Time to get up.'

When there was no movement, no response, he turned and left the room.

# 17

David Levy was no longer in Edinburgh. At least, he wasn't at the Roxburghe Hotel. Rebus could think of only one way of contacting him. Seated at his desk, he called the Holocaust Investigation Bureau in Tel Aviv and asked to speak with Solomon Mayerlink. Mayerlink wasn't available, but Rebus identified himself and said he needed to contact him as a matter of urgency. He got a home telephone number.

'Is there news on Linzstek, Inspector?' Mayerlink's voice was a harsh rasp.

'Of a kind, yes. He's dead.'

Silence on the line, then a slow release of breath. 'That's a pity.'

'It is?'

'People die, a little bit of history dies with them. We would have preferred to see him in court, Inspector. Dead, he's worthless.' Mayerlink paused. 'I take it this ends your inquiry?'

'It changes the nature of the investigation. He was murdered.'

Static on the line; an eight-beat pause. 'How did it happen?'

'He was hung from a tree.'

There was a longer silence on the line. 'I see,' Mayerlink said at last. There was a slight echo on his voice. 'You think the allegations led to his murder?'

'What would you say?'

'I'm not a detective.'

But Rebus knew Mayerlink was lying: detection was *exactly* the role he'd chosen in life. A detective of history.

'I need to talk to David Levy,' Rebus said. 'Do you have his address and phone number?'

'He came to see you?'

'You know he did.'

'It's not that simple with David. He doesn't work for the Bureau.

159

He's self-motivated. I ask him for help occasionally. Sometimes he helps, sometimes he doesn't.'

'But you do have some way of contacting him?'

It took Mayerlink a full minute to come up with the details. An address in Sussex, plus telephone number.

'Is David your number one suspect, Inspector?'

'Why do you ask?'

'I could tell you you're barking up the wrong tree.'

'The same tree Joseph Lintz swung from?'

'Can you really see David Levy as a murderer, Inspector?'

Safari suit, walking stick. 'It takes all sorts,' Rebus said, putting down the phone.

He tried Levy's number. It rang and rang. He gave it a couple of minutes, drank a coffee, tried again. Still no answer. He called British Telecom instead, explained what he needed, was finally put through to the right person.

'My name's Justine Graham, Inspector. How can I help?'

Rebus gave her Lintz's details. 'He used to get itemised bills, then he switched.'

He heard her fingers hammer a keyboard. 'That's right,' she told him. 'The customer asked for itemised billing to be discontinued.'

'Did he say why?'

'No record of that. You don't need to give an excuse, you know.'

'When was this?'

'A couple of months back. The customer had requested monthly billing several years previously.'

Monthly billing: because he was meticulous, kept his accounts by the month. A couple of months back – September – the Lintz/Linzstek story had blown up in the media. And, suddenly, he hadn't wanted his phone calls to be a matter of record.

'Do you have records of his calls, even the *un*itemised ones?'

'Yes, we should have that information.'

'I'd like to see a list. Everything from the first unitemised call through to this morning.'

'Is that when he died – this morning?'

'Yes.'

She was thoughtful. 'Well, I'll need to check.'

'Please do. But remember, Ms Graham, this is a murder inquiry.'

'Yes, of course.'

'And your information could be absolutely crucial.'

'I'm quite aware of –'

'So if I could have that by the end of today ...?'

She hesitated. 'I'm not sure I can promise that.'

'And one last thing. The bill for September is missing. I'd like a copy of it. Let me give you the fax number here, speed things up.'

Rebus congratulated himself with another cup of coffee and a cigarette in the car park. She might or might not deliver later in the day, but he was confident she'd be trying her best. Wasn't that all you could ask of anybody?

Another call: Special Branch in London. He asked for Abernethy.

'I'll just put you through.'

Someone picked up: a grunt in place of an acknowledgement.

'Abernethy?' Rebus asked. He heard liquid being swallowed. The voice became clearer.

'He's not here. Can I help?'

'I really need to speak to him.'

'I could have him paged, if it's urgent.'

'My name's DI Rebus, Lothian and Borders Police.'

'Oh, right. Have you lost him or something?'

Rebus's expression turned quizzical. His voice carried a false note of humour. 'You know what Abernethy's like.'

A snort. 'Don't I just.'

'So any help appreciated.'

'Yeah, right. Look, give me your number. I'll get him to call you.'

*Have you lost him or something?* 'You've no idea where he is then?'

'It's your city, chum. Take your best shot.'

*He's up here*, Rebus thought. *He's right here.*

'I bet the office is quiet without him.'

Laughter on the line, then the sounds of a cigarette being lit. A long exhalation. 'It's like being on holiday. Keep him as long as you like.'

'So how long have you been without him?'

A pause. As the silence lengthened, Rebus could feel the change of atmosphere.

'What did you say your name was?'

'DI Rebus. I was only asking when he left London.'

'This morning, soon as he heard. So what have I won: the hatchback or the hostess trolley?'

Rebus's turn to laugh. 'Sorry, I'm just nosy.'

'I'll be sure to tell him that.' A single click, then the sound of an open line.

Later that afternoon, Rebus chased up British Telecom, then tried Levy's house again. This time he got through to a woman.

'Hello, Mrs Levy? My name's John Rebus. I was wondering if I could have a word with your husband?'

'You mean my father.'

'I'm sorry. Is your father there?'

'No, he's not.'

'Any idea when ... ?'

'Absolutely none.' She sounded peeved. 'I'm just his cook and cleaner. Like I don't have a life of my own.' She caught herself. 'Sorry, Mr ... ?'

'Rebus.'

'It's just that he never says how long he's going to be away.'

'He's away just now?'

'Has been for the best part of a fortnight. He rings two or three times a week, asks if there've been any calls or letters. If I'm lucky, he *might* remember to ask how *I'm* doing.'

'And how are you doing?'

A smile in her voice. 'I know, I know. I sound like I'm his mother or something.'

'Well, you know, fathers ...' Rebus stared into the middle distance ... 'if you don't tell them anything's wrong, they're happy to assume the best and hold their peace.'

'You speak from experience?'

'Too much experience.'

She was thoughtful. 'Is it something important?'

'Very.'

'Well, give me your name and number, and next time he calls I'll have him phone you.'

'Thanks.' Rebus reeled off two numbers: home and mobile.

'Got that,' she said. 'Any other message?'

'No, just have him call me.' Rebus thought for a moment. 'Has he had any other calls?'

'You mean, people trying to reach him? Why do you ask?'

'I just ... no real reason.' He didn't want to say he was a policeman; didn't want her spooked. 'No reason,' he repeated.

As he came off the phone, someone handed him another coffee. 'That receiver must be red hot.'

He touched it with the tips of his fingers. It was pretty warm. Then it rang and he picked it up again.

'DI Rebus,' he said.

'John, it's Siobhan.'

'Hiya, how's tricks?'

'John, you remember that guy?' Her tone was warning him of something.

'What guy?' The humour was gone from his voice.

'Danny Simpson.' He of the flappy skull; Telford's lackey.

'What about him?'

'I've just found out he's HIV positive. His GP let the hospital know.'

Blood in Rebus's eyes, his ears, dribbling down his neck ...

'Poor guy,' he said quietly.

'He should have said something at the time.'

'When?'

'When we got him to the hospital.'

'Well, he had other things on his mind, and some of them were in danger of falling off.'

'Christ, John, be serious for a minute!' Her voice was loud enough to have people glance up from their desks. 'You need to get a blood test.'

'Fine, no problem. How is he, by the way?'

'Back home but poorly. And sticking to his story.'

'Do I detect the influence of Telford's lawyer?'

'Charles Groal? That one's so slimy, he's practically primordial.'

'Saves you the cost of a valentine.'

'Look, just phone the hospital. Talk to a Dr Jones. She'll fix an appointment. They can do a test right away. Not that it'll be the last word – there's a three-month incubation.'

'Thanks, Siobhan.'

Rebus put down the receiver, drummed his fingers against it. Wouldn't *that* be a nice irony? Rebus out to get Telford, does the Good Samaritan bit for one of his men, gets AIDS and dies. Rebus stared at the ceiling.

*Nice one, Big Man.*

The phone rang again. Rebus snatched it up.

'Switchboard,' he said.

'Is that you, John?' Patience Aitken.

'The one and only.'

'Just wanted to check we're still on for tonight.'

'To be honest, Patience, I'm not sure I'll be at my most sparkling.'

'You want to cancel?'

'Absolutely not. But I have something to take care of. At the hospital.'

'Yes, of course.'

'No, I don't think you understand. It's not Sammy this time, it's me.'

'What's wrong?'

So he told her.

She went with him. Same hospital Sammy was in, different department. Last thing he wanted was to bump into Rhona, have to explain everything to her. Possibly HIV-infected: chances were, she'd red-card him from the bedside.

The waiting room was white, clean. Lots of information on the walls. Leaflets on every table, as if paperwork was the real virus.

'I must say, it's very pleasant for a leper colony.'

Patience didn't say anything. They were alone in the room. Someone on reception had dealt with him first, then a nurse had come out and taken some details. Now another door opened.

'Mr Rebus?'

A tall thin woman in a white coat, standing in the doorway: Dr Jones, he presumed. Patience took his arm as they walked towards her. Halfway across the floor, Rebus turned on his heels and bolted.

Patience caught up with him outside, asked what was wrong.

'I don't want to know,' he told her.

'But, John ...'

'Come on, Patience. All I got was a bit of blood splashed on me.'

She didn't look convinced. 'You need to take the test.'

He looked back towards the building. 'Fine.' Started walking away. 'But some other time, eh?'

It was one in the morning when he drove back into Arden Street. No dinner date with Patience: instead, they'd visited the hospital, sat with Rhona. He'd made a silent pact with the Big Man: bring her

back and I'll keep off the booze. He'd driven Patience home. Her last words to him: 'Take that test. Get it over and done with.'

As he locked his car, a figure appeared from nowhere.

'Mr Rebus, long time no see.'

Rebus recognised the face. Pointy chin, misshapen teeth, the breathing a series of small gasps. The Weasel: one of Cafferty's men. He was dressed like a down-and-out, perfect camouflage for his role in life. He was Cafferty's eyes and ears on the street.

'We need to talk, Mr Rebus.' His hands were deep in the pockets of a tweed coat meant for someone eight inches taller. He glanced towards the tenement door.

'Not in my flat,' Rebus stated. Some things were sacrosanct.

'Cold out here.'

Rebus just shook his head, and the Weasel sniffed hard.

'You think it was a hit?' he said.

'Yes,' Rebus answered.

'She was meant to die?'

'I don't know.'

'A pro wouldn't fuck up.'

'Then it was a warning.'

'We could do with seeing your notes.'

'Can't do that.'

The Weasel shrugged. 'Thought you wanted Mr Cafferty's help?'

'I can't give you the notes. What about if I summarise?'

'It'd be a start.'

'Rover 600, stolen from George Street that afternoon. Abandoned on a street by Piershill Cemetery. Radio and some tapes lifted – not necessarily by the same person.'

'Scavengers.'

'Could be.'

The Weasel was thoughtful. 'A warning ... That would mean a professional driver.'

'Yes,' Rebus said.

'And not one of ours ... Doesn't leave too many candidates. Rover 600 ... what colour?'

'Sherwood Green.'

'Parked on George Street?'

Rebus nodded.

'Thanks for that.' The Weasel made to turn away, then paused. 'Nice doing business with you again, Mr Rebus.'

Rebus was about to say something, then remembered he needed the Weasel more than the Weasel needed him. He wondered how much crap he'd take from Cafferty ... how long he'd have to take it. All his life? Had he made a contract with the devil?

For Sammy, he'd have done much, much worse ...

In his flat, he stuck on the CD of *Rock 'n' Roll Circus*, skipping to the actual Stones tracks. His answering machine was flashing. Three messages. The first: Hogan.

'Hello, John. Just thought I'd check, see if there's been any word from BT.'

Not by the time Rebus had left the office. Message two: Abernethy.

'Me again, bad penny and all that. Heard you've been trying to catch me. I'll call you tomorrow. Cheers.'

Rebus stared at the machine, willing Abernethy to say more, to give some hint of a location. But the machine was on to the final message. Bill Pryde.

'John, tried you at the office, left a message. But I thought you'd want to know, we've had final word on those prints. If you want to try me at home, I'm on ...'

Rebus took down the number. Two in the morning, but Bill would understand.

After a minute or so, a woman picked up. She sounded groggy.

'Sorry,' Rebus said. 'Is Bill there?'

'I'll get him.'

He heard background dialogue, then the receiver being hoisted.

'So what's this about prints?' he asked.

'Christ, John, when I said you could call, I didn't mean the middle of the night!'

'It's important.'

'Yes, I know. How's she doing anyway?'

'Still out cold.'

Pryde yawned. 'Well, most of the prints inside the car belong to the owner and his wife. But we found one other set. Problem is, looks like they belong to a kid.'

'What makes you so sure?'

'The size.'

'Plenty of adults around with small hands.'

'I suppose so ...'

'You sound sceptical.'

'More likely to be one of two scenarios. One, Sammy was hit by a joyrider. I know what you think, but it does happen. Two, the prints belong to whoever rifled the car after it was left at the cemetery.'

'The kid who took the cassette player and tapes?'

'Exactly.'

'No other prints? Not even partials?'

'The car was clean, John.'

'Exterior?'

'Same three sets on the doors, plus Sammy's on the bonnet.' Pryde yawned again. 'So what about your grudge theory?'

'Still holds. A pro would be wearing gloves.'

'That's what I was thinking. Not too many pros out there though.'

'No.' Rebus was thinking of the Weasel: *I'm dealing with slime to catch a slug*. Nothing he hadn't done before, only this time there were personal reasons.

And he didn't think there'd be a trial.

# 18

Breakfast was on Hogan: bacon rolls in a brown paper bag. They ate them in the CID room at St Leonard's. A Murder Room had been established in Leith, and that's where Hogan should have been.

Only he wanted Rebus's files, and he knew better than to trust Rebus to deliver them.

'Thought I'd save you the hassle,' was what he said.

'You're a gentleman,' Rebus answered, examining the interior of his roll. 'Tell me, are pigs an endangered species?'

'I lifted half a slice from you.' Hogan pulled a string of fat from his mouth, tossed it into a bin. 'Thought I was doing you a favour: cholesterol and all that.'

Rebus put the roll to one side, took a swig from the can of Irn–Bru – Hogan's idea of a morning beverage – and swallowed. What was sugar consumption compared to HIV? 'What did you get from the cleaning lady?'

'Grief. Soon as she heard her employer was dead, the taps were on.' Hogan brushed flour from his fingers: mealtime over. 'She never met any of his friends, never had occasion to answer his telephone, hadn't noticed any change in him recently, and doesn't think he was a mass murderer. Quote: "If he'd killed that many people, I'd have known".'

'What is she, psychic or something?'

Hogan shrugged. 'About all I got from her was a glowing character reference and the fact that as she was paid in advance, she owes his estate a partial refund.'

'There's your motive.'

Hogan smiled. 'Speaking of motives ...'

'You've got something?'

'Lintz's lawyer has come up with a letter from the deceased's

bank.' He handed Rebus a photocopy. 'Seems our man made a cash withdrawal of five grand ten days ago.'

'*Cash?*'

'We found ten quid on his person, and about another thirty bar in the house. No five grand. I'm beginning to think blackmail.'

Rebus nodded. 'What about his address book?'

'Slow work. A lot of old numbers, people who've moved on or died. Plus a few charities, museums ... an art gallery or two.' Hogan paused. 'What about you?'

Rebus opened his drawer, pulled out the fax sheets. 'Waiting for me this morning. The calls Lintz wanted kept secret.'

Hogan looked down the list. 'Calls plural, or one in particular?'

'I've just started going through them. Best guess: there'll be callers he spoke to regularly. Those numbers will show up on the other statements. We're looking for anomalies, one–offs.'

'Makes sense.' Hogan looked at his watch. 'Anything else I should know?'

'Two things. Remember I told you about the Special Branch interest?'

'Abernethy?'

Rebus nodded. 'I tried calling him yesterday.'

'And?'

'According to his office, he was on his way up here. He'd already heard the news.'

'So I've got Abernethy sniffing around, and you don't trust him? Terrific. What's the other thing?'

'David Levy. I spoke with his daughter. She doesn't know where he is. He could be anywhere.'

'With a grudge against Lintz?'

'It's possible.'

'What's his phone number?'

Rebus patted the topmost file on his desk. 'Ready for you to take away.'

Hogan studied the foot-high pile, looking glum.

'I whittled it down to what's absolutely necessary,' Rebus told him.

'There's a month's reading there.'

Rebus shrugged. 'My case is your case, Bobby.'

With Hogan gone, Rebus went back to the British Telecom list. It

was as detailed as he could have wished for. Lots of calls to Lintz's solicitor, a few to one of the city's taxi firms. Rebus tried a couple of numbers, found himself connected to charity offices: Lintz would have been phoning to tender his resignation. There were a few calls that stood out from the crowd: the Roxburghe Hotel – duration four minutes; Edinburgh University – twenty-six minutes. The Roxburghe had to mean Levy. Rebus knew Levy had talked to Lintz – Lintz himself had admitted it. Talking to him – being confronted by him – was one thing; calling him at his hotel quite another.

The number for Edinburgh University connected Rebus to the main switchboard. He asked to be put through to Lintz's old department. The secretary was very helpful. She'd been in the job over twenty years, was due to retire. Yes, she remembered Professor Lintz, but he hadn't contacted the department recently.

'Every call that comes through here, I know about it.'

'He might have got straight through to a tutor though?' Rebus suggested.

'No one's mentioned speaking to him. There's nobody here from the Professor's day.'

'He doesn't keep in touch with the department?'

'I haven't spoken to him in years, Inspector. Too many years for me to remember ...'

So who had he been talking to for over twenty minutes? Rebus thanked the secretary and put down the phone. He went through the other numbers: a couple of restaurants, a wine shop, and the local radio station. Rebus told the receptionist what he was after, and she said she'd do her best. Then he went back to the restaurants, asked them to check if Lintz had been making a reservation.

Within half an hour, the calls started coming in. First restaurant: a booking for dinner, just the one cover. The radio station: they'd asked Lintz to appear on a programme. He'd said he'd consider it, then had called back to decline. Second restaurant: a lunch reservation, two covers.

'Two?'

'Mr Lintz and one other.'

'Any idea who the "other" might have been?'

'Another gentleman, quite elderly, I think ... I'm sorry, I don't really remember.'

'Did he walk with a stick?'

'I wish I could help, but it's a madhouse here at lunchtime.'

'You remember Lintz though?'

'Mr Lintz is a regular ... was a regular.'

'Did he usually eat alone, or with company?'

'Mostly alone. He didn't seem to mind. He'd bring a book with him.'

'Do you happen to recall any of his other guests?'

'I remember a young woman ... his daughter maybe? Or granddaughter?'

'So when you say "young" ...?'

'Younger than him.' A pause. 'Maybe much younger.'

'When was this?'

'I really don't remember.' The voice impatient now.

'I appreciate your help, sir. Just one more minute of your time ... This woman, did he bring her more than once?'

'I'm sorry, Inspector. The kitchen needs me.'

'Well, if you think of anything else ...'

'Of course. Goodbye.'

Rebus put the phone down, made some notes. Just one number left. He waited for an answer.

'Yeah?' The voice grudging.

'Who's this?'

'This is Malky. Who the fuck are you?'

A voice in the background: 'Tommy says that new machine's fucked.' Rebus put the phone down. His hand was shaking. *That new machine* ... Tommy Telford on his arcade motorbike. He remembered The Family mugshots: Malky Jordan. Tiny nose and eyes in a balloon of a face. *Joseph Lintz talking to one of Telford's men? Phoning Telford's office??* Rebus found the number of Hogan's mobile.

'Bobby,' he said. 'If you're driving, better slow down right now ...'

Hogan's notion: five in cash was just Telford's style. Blackmail? But where was the connection? Something else ...?

Hogan's play: he'd talk to Telford.

Rebus's notion: five was a bit steep for a hit-man. All the same, he wondered about Lintz ... paying five thou' to Telford to set up the 'accident'. Motive: give Rebus a fright, scare him off? It put Lintz back in the frame, potentially.

Rebus had fixed up another meeting, one he didn't want anyone

171

knowing about. Haymarket Station was nice and anonymous. The bench on platform one. Ned Farlowe was already waiting. He looked tired: worry over Sammy. They talked about her for a couple of minutes. Then Rebus got down to business.

'You know Lintz has been murdered?'

'I didn't think this was a social call.'

'We're looking at a blackmail angle.'

Farlowe looked interested. 'And he didn't pay up?'

Oh, he paid up all right, Rebus thought. He paid up, and someone still took him out of the game.

'Look, Ned, this is *all* off the record. By rights I should take you in for questioning.'

'Because I followed him for a few days?'

'Yes.'

'And that makes me a suspect?'

'It makes you a possible witness.'

Farlowe thought about it. 'One evening. Lintz left his house, walked down the road, made a call from a phone-box, then went straight back home.'

Not wanting to use his home phone ... afraid it was bugged? Afraid of the number being traced? Telephone bugging: a favourite ploy of Special Branch.

'And something else,' Farlowe was saying. 'He met this woman on his doorstep. Like she was waiting for him. They had a few words. I think she was crying when she left.'

'What did she look like?'

'Tall, short dark hair, well-dressed. She had a briefcase with her.'

'Wearing?'

Farlowe shrugged. 'Skirt and jacket ... matching. Black and white check. You know ... elegant.'

He was describing Kirstin Mede. Her phone message to Rebus: *I can't do this any more ...*

'There's something I want to ask you,' Farlowe was saying. 'That girl Candice.'

'What about her?'

'You asked me if anything unusual had happened just before Sammy got hit.'

'Yes?'

'Well, *she* happened, didn't she?' Farlowe's eyes narrowed. 'Does she have anything to do with it?'

172

Rebus looked at Farlowe, who started nodding.

'Thanks for the confirmation. Who was she?'

'One of Telford's girls.'

Farlowe leaped to his feet, paced the platform. Rebus waited for him to sit down again. When he did, there could be no doubting the fury in his eyes.

'You hid one of Telford's girls with your own *daughter*?'

'I didn't have much choice. Telford knows where I live. I ...'

'You were using us!' He paused. 'Telford did this, didn't he?'

'I don't know,' Rebus said. Farlowe leaped to his feet again. 'Look, Ned, I don't want you —'

'Quite frankly, *Inspector*, I don't think you're in any position to give advice.' He started walking, and though Rebus called after him, he never once looked back.

As Rebus walked into the Crime Squad office, a paper plane glided past and crashed into the wall. Ormiston had his feet up on the desk. Country and western music was playing softly in the background, its source a tape player on the window ledge behind Claverhouse's desk. Siobhan Clarke had pulled a chair over beside him. They were poring over some report.

'Not exactly the "A-Team" in here, is it?' Rebus retrieved the plane, straightened its crumpled nose, and sent it back to Ormiston, who asked what he was doing there.

'Liaising,' Rebus told him. 'My boss wants a progress report.'

Ormiston glanced towards Claverhouse, who was tipping himself back in his chair, hands behind his head.

'Want to take a guess at the headway we've made?'

Rebus sat down opposite Claverhouse, nodded a greeting to Siobhan.

'How's Sammy?' she asked.

'Just the same,' Rebus answered. Claverhouse looked abashed, and Rebus suddenly realised that he could use Sammy as a lever, play on people's sympathy. Why not? Hadn't he used her in the past? Wasn't Ned Farlowe on the nail there?

'We've pulled the surveillance,' Claverhouse said.

'Why?'

Ormiston snorted, but it was Claverhouse who answered.

'High maintenance, low returns.'

'Orders from above?'

'It isn't as if we were close to getting a result.'

'So we just let him get on with getting on?'

Claverhouse shrugged. Rebus wondered if news would get back to Newcastle. Jake Tarawicz would be happy. He'd think Rebus was fulfilling his part of the bargain. Candice would be safe. Maybe.

'Any news on that nightclub killing?'

'Nothing to link it to your chum Cafferty.'

'He's *not* my chum.'

'Whatever you say. Stick the kettle on, Ormie.' Ormiston glanced towards Clarke, then rose grudgingly from his chair. Rebus had thought the tension in the office was all to do with Telford. Not a bit of it. Claverhouse and Clarke close together, *involved*. Ormiston off on his own, a kid making paper planes, seeking attention. An old Status Quo song: 'Paper Plane'. But the status quo here had been disturbed: Clarke had usurped Ormiston. The office junior was absolved from making the tea.

Rebus could see why Ormiston was pissed off.

'I hear Herr Lintz was a bit of a swinger,' Claverhouse said.

'Now there's a joke I haven't heard before.' Rebus's pager sounded. The display gave him a number to call.

He used Claverhouse's phone. It sounded like he was connected to a pay-phone. Street sounds, heavy traffic close by.

'Mr Rebus?' Placed the voice at once: the Weasel.

'What is it?'

'A couple of questions. The tape player from the car, any idea of the make?'

'Sony.'

'The front bit detachable?'

'That's right.'

'So all they got was the front bit?'

'Yes.' Claverhouse and Clarke, back at their report, pretending they weren't listening.

'What about the tapes? You said some tapes got stolen?'

'Opera – *The Marriage of Figaro* and Verdi's *Macbeth*.' Rebus squeezed his eyes shut, thinking. 'And another tape with film music on it, famous themes. Plus Roy Orbison's *Greatest Hits*.' This last the wife's. Rebus knew what the Weasel was thinking: whoever took the stuff, they'd try flogging it round the pubs or at a car boot sale. Car boot sales were clearing houses for knock-off. But getting whoever had lifted the stuff from the unlocked car wasn't going to

174

nail the driver ... Unless the kid – the one who'd lifted the stuff, whose prints were on the car – had *seen* something: been hanging around on the street, watched the car screeching to a stop, a man getting out and hoofing it ...

An eye witness, someone who could describe the driver.

'The only prints we got were small, maybe a kid's.'

'That's interesting.'

'Anything else I can do,' Rebus said, 'just let me know.'

The Weasel hung up.

'Sony's a good make,' Claverhouse said, fishing.

'Some stuff lifted from a car,' Rebus told him. 'It might have turned up.'

Ormiston had made the tea. Rebus went to fetch himself a chair, saw someone walk past the open doorway. He dropped the chair and ran into the corridor, grabbed at an arm.

Abernethy spun quickly, saw who it was and relaxed.

'Nice one, son,' he said. 'You almost had knuckles for teeth.' He was working on a piece of chewing gum.

'What are you doing here?'

'Visiting.' Abernethy looked back at the open door, walked towards it. 'What about you?'

'Working.'

Abernethy read the sign on the door. 'Crime Squad,' he said, sounding amused, taking in the office and the people in it. Hands in pockets, he sauntered in, Rebus following.

'Abernethy, Special Branch,' the Londoner said by way of introduction. 'That music's a good idea: play it at interrogations, sap the suspect's will to live.' He was smiling, surveying the premises like he was thinking of moving in. The mug meant for Rebus was on the corner of the desk. Abernethy picked it up and slurped, made a face, started chewing again. The three Crime Squad officers were like a frozen tableau. Suddenly they looked like a unit: it had taken Abernethy to do that.

Had taken him all of ten seconds.

'What you working on?' No one answered. 'Must've got the sign on the door wrong,' Abernethy said. 'Should be Mime Squad.'

'Is there something we can do for you?' Claverhouse asked, his voice level, hostility in his eyes.

'I don't know. It was John pulled me in here.'

'And I'm pulling you out again,' Rebus said, taking his arm.

Abernethy shrugged free, bunched his fists. 'A word in the corridor ... please.'

Abernethy smiled. 'Manners maketh the man, John.'

'What does that maketh you?'

Abernethy turned his head slowly, looked at Siobhan Clarke who'd just spoken.

'I'm just a regular guy with a heart of gold and twelve big inches of ability.' He grinned at her.

'To go with your twelve big points of IQ,' she said, going back to the report. Ormiston and Claverhouse weren't trying too hard to conceal their laughter as Abernethy stormed out of the room. Rebus hung back long enough to watch Ormiston pat Clarke on the back, then headed off after the Special Branch man.

'What a bitch,' Abernethy said. He was making for the exit.

'She's a friend of mine.'

'And they say you can choose your friends ...' Abernethy shook his head.

'What brings you back?'

'You have to ask?'

'Lintz is dead. Case closed as far as you're concerned.'

They emerged from the building.

'So?'

'So,' Rebus persisted, 'why come all the way back here? What is there that couldn't be done with a phone or fax?'

Abernethy stopped, turned to face him. 'Loose ends.'

'What loose ends?'

'There aren't any.' Abernethy gave a cheerless smile and took a key from his pocket. As they approached his car, he used the remote to unlock it and disable the alarm.

'What's going on, Abernethy?'

'Nothing to worry your pretty little head about.' He opened the driver's-side door.

'Are you glad he's dead?'

'What?'

'Lintz. How do you feel about him being murdered?'

'I've no feelings either way. He's dead, which means I can cross him off my list.'

'That last time you came up here, you were warning him.'

'Not true.'

176

'Was his phone bugged?' Abernethy just snorted. 'Did you know he might be killed?'

Abernethy turned on Rebus. 'What's it to you? I'll tell you: nothing. Leith CID are on the murder, and you're out of it. End of story.'

'Is it the Rat Line? Too embarrassing if it all came to light?'

'Christ, what *is* it with you? Just give it a rest.' Abernethy got into the car, closed the door. Rebus didn't move. The engine turned and caught, Abernethy's window slid down. Rebus was ready.

'They sent you four hundred miles just to check there were no loose ends.'

'So?'

'So there's rather a large loose end, isn't there?' Rebus paused. 'Unless you know who Lintz's killer was.'

'I leave that sort of thing to you guys.'

'Heading down to Leith?'

'I have to talk to Hogan.' Abernethy stared at Rebus. 'You're a hard bastard, aren't you? Maybe even a bit selfish.'

'How's that?'

'If I'd a daughter in hospital, police work would be the last thing on my mind.'

As Rebus lunged towards the open window, Abernethy gunned the car. Footsteps behind: Siobhan Clarke.

'Good riddance,' she said, watching the car speed off. A finger appeared from Abernethy's window. She gave a two-fingered reply. 'I didn't want to say anything in the office ...' she began.

'I took the test yesterday,' Rebus lied.

'It'll be negative.'

'Are you positive?'

She smiled a little longer than the joke merited. 'Ormiston chucked your tea away, said he was going to disinfect the mug.'

'Abernethy has that effect on people.' He looked at her. 'Remember, Ormiston and Claverhouse go back years.'

'I know. I think Claverhouse has a crush on me. It'll pass, but until it does ...'

'Tread carefully.' They started walking back towards the main entrance. 'And don't let him tempt you into the broom cupboard.'

# 19

Rebus went back to St Leonard's, saw that the office was coping quite well without him, and headed over to the hospital with Dr Morrison's Iron Maiden t-shirt in a plastic bag. A third bed had been moved into Sammy's room. An elderly woman lay in it. Though awake, she stared fixedly at the ceiling. Rhona was at Sammy's bedside, reading a book.

Rebus stroked his daughter's hair. 'How is she?'

'No change.'

'Any more tests planned?'

'Not that I know of.'

'That's it then? She just stays like this?'

He lifted a chair over, sat down. It had turned into a sort of ritual now, this bedside vigil. It felt almost ... the word he wanted to use was 'comfortable'. He squeezed Rhona's hand, sat there for twenty minutes, saying almost nothing, then went to find Kirstin Mede.

She was in her office at the French Department, marking scripts. She sat at a big desk in front of the window, but moved from this to a coffee-table with half a dozen chairs arranged around it.

'Sit down,' she said. Rebus sat down.

'I got your message,' he told her.

'Hardly matters now, does it? The man's dead.'

'I know you spoke with him, Kirstin.'

She glanced towards him. 'I'm sorry?'

'You waited for him outside his house. Did the two of you have a nice chat?'

Colour had risen to her cheeks. She crossed her legs, tugged the hem of her skirt towards her knee. 'Yes,' she said at last, 'I went to his house.'

'Why?'

'Because I wanted to see him close up.' Her eyes were on his now, challenging him. 'I thought maybe I could tell from his face ... the look in his eyes. Maybe something in his tone of voice.'

'And could you?'

She shook her head. 'Not a damned thing. No window to the soul.'

'What did you say to him?'

'I told him who I was.'

'Any reaction?'

'Yes.' She folded her arms. 'His words: "My dear lady, will you kindly piss off".'

'And did you?'

'Yes. Because I knew then. Not whether he was Linzstek or not, but something else.'

'What?'

'That he was at the end of his tether.' She was nodding. 'Absolutely at breaking point.' She looked at Rebus again. 'And capable of anything.'

The problem with the Flint Street surveillance was that it had been so open. A hidden operation – deep cover – that's what was needed. Rebus had decided to scout out the territory.

The tenement flats across the road from Telford's cafe and arcade were served by a single main door. It was locked, so Rebus chose a buzzer at random – marked HETHERINGTON. Waited, pushed again. An elderly voice came on the intercom.

'Who is it, please?'

'Mrs Hetherington? Detective Inspector Rebus, I'm your Community CID officer. Can I talk to you about home security? There've been a few break-ins around here, especially with elderly victims.'

'Gracious, you'd better come up.'

'Which floor?'

'The first.' The door buzzed, and Rebus pushed it open.

Mrs Hetherington was waiting for him in her doorway. She was tiny and frail-looking, but her eyes were lively and her movements assured. The flat was small, well-maintained. The sitting-room was heated by a two-bar electric fire. Rebus wandered over to the window, found himself looking down on to the arcade. Perfect location for a surveillance. He pretended to check her windows.

179

'These seem fine,' he said. 'Are they always locked?'

'I open them a bit in the summer,' Mrs Hetherington said, 'and when they need washing. But I always lock them again afterwards.'

'One thing I should warn you about, and that's bogus officials. People coming to your door, telling you they're so-and-so. Always ask to see some ID, and don't open up until you're satisfied.'

'How can I see it without opening the door?'

'Ask them to push it through the letterbox.'

'I didn't see *your* identification, did I?'

Rebus smiled. 'No, you didn't.' He took it out and showed her. 'Sometimes the fake stuff can look pretty convincing. If you're unsure, keep the door locked and call the police.' He looked around. 'You have a phone?'

'In the bedroom.'

'Any windows in there?'

'Yes.'

'Can I take a look?'

The bedroom window also looked out on to Flint Street. Rebus noticed travel brochures on the dressing-table, a small suitcase standing near the door.

'Off on holiday, eh?' With the flat empty, maybe he could move the surveillance in.

'Just a long weekend,' she said.

'Somewhere nice?'

'Holland. Wrong time of year for the bulb-fields, but I've always wanted to go. It's a nuisance flying from Inverness, but so much cheaper. Since my husband died ... well, I've done a bit of travelling.'

'Any chance of taking me with you?' Rebus smiled. 'This window's fine, too. I'll just check your door, see if it could do with more locks.' They went into the narrow hall.

'You know,' she said, 'we've always been very lucky here, no break-ins or anything like that.'

Hardly surprising with Tommy Telford as proprietor.

'And with the panic button, of course ...'

Rebus looked at the wall next to the front door. A large red button. He'd assumed it was for the stairhead lights or something.

'Anyone who calls, anyone at all, I'm supposed to press it.'

Rebus opened the door. 'And do you?'

Two very large men were standing right outside.

'Oh, yes,' Mrs Hetherington said. 'I always do.'

For thugs, they were very polite. Rebus showed them his warrant card and explained the nature of his visit. He asked them who they were, and they told him they were 'representatives of the building's owner'. He knew the faces though: Kenny Houston, Ally Cornwell. Houston – the ugly one – ran Telford's doormen; Cornwell, with his wrestler's bulk, was general muscle. The little charade was carried out with humour and good nature on both sides. They accompanied him downstairs. Across the street, Tommy Telford was standing in the cafe doorway, wagging his finger. A pedestrian crossed Rebus's line of vision. Too late, Rebus saw who it was. Had his mouth open to shout something, then saw Telford hang his head, hands going to his face. Screeching.

Rebus ran across the road, pulled the pedestrian round: Ned Farlowe. A bottle dropped from Farlowe's hand. Telford's men were closing in. Rebus held tight to Farlowe.

'I'm placing this man under arrest,' he said. 'He's *mine*, understood?'

A dozen faces glaring at him. And Tommy Telford down on his knees.

'Get your boss to the hospital,' Rebus said. 'I'm taking this one to St Leonard's ...'

Ned Farlowe sat on the ledge in one of the cells. The walls were blue, smeared brown near the toilet-pan. Farlowe was looking pleased with himself.

'Acid?' Rebus said, pacing the cell. '*Acid*? All this research must have gone to your head.'

'It's what he deserved.'

Rebus glared at him. 'You don't know what you've done.'

'I know *exactly* what I've done.'

'He'll kill you.'

Farlowe shrugged. 'Am I under arrest?'

'You'd better believe it, son. I want you kept out of harm's way. If I hadn't been there ...' But he didn't want to think about that. He looked at Farlowe. Looked at Sammy's lover, who'd just staged a full-frontal assault on Telford, the kind of assault Rebus knew wouldn't work.

Now Rebus would have to redouble his efforts. Because

otherwise, Ned Farlowe was a dead man ... and when Sammy came round, he didn't want news like that to be waiting for her.

He drove back towards Flint Street, parked at a distance from it, and headed there on foot. Telford had the place sewn up, no doubt about it. Letting his flats to old folk might have been a charitable act but he'd made damned sure it served its purpose. Rebus wondered if, given the same circumstances, Cafferty would have been clever enough to think of panic-buttons. He suspected not. Cafferty wasn't thick, but most of what he did he did by instinct. Rebus wondered if Tommy Telford had ever made a rash move in his life.

He was staking out Flint Street because he needed an *in*, needed to find the weak link in the chain around Telford. After ten minutes of windchill, he thought of a better idea. On his mobile, he called one of the city's taxi firms. Identified himself and asked if Henry Wilson was on shift. He was. Rebus told the switchboard to put a call out to Henry. It was as simple as that.

Ten minutes later, Wilson turned up. He drank in the Ox occasionally, which was his problem really. Drunk in charge of a taxi-cab. Luckily Rebus had been around to smooth things over, as a result of which Wilson owed him a lifetime of favours. He was tall, heavily built, with short black hair and a long black beard. Ruddy-faced, and he always wore check shirts. Rebus thought of him as 'The Lumberjack'.

'Need a lift?' Wilson said, as Rebus got into the front passenger-seat.

'First thing I need is a blast of the heater.' Wilson obliged. 'Second thing I need is to use your taxi as cover.'

'You mean, sit here?'

'That's what I mean.'

'With the meter running?'

'You've got an engine problem, Henry. Your cab's out of the game for the rest of the afternoon.'

'I'm saving up for Christmas,' Wilson complained. Rebus stared him out. The big man sighed and lifted a newspaper from the side of his seat. 'Help me pick a few winners then,' he said, turning to the racing pages.

They sat for over an hour at the end of Flint Street, and Rebus stayed in the front of the cab. His reasoning: a cab parked with a passenger in the back looked suspicious. A cab parked with two guys

in the front, and you'd just think they were on their break, or at shift's end – two cabbies sharing stories and a flask of tea.

Rebus took one sip from the plastic cup and winced. Half a bag of sugar in the flask.

'I've always had a sweet tooth,' Wilson explained. He had a packet of crisps open on his lap: pickled onion flavour.

Finally, Rebus saw two Range Rovers being driven into Flint Street. Sean Haddow – Telford's money man – was driving the lead car. He got out and went into the arcade. On the passenger seat, Rebus could see a huge yellow teddy bear. Haddow was coming out again, bringing Telford with him. Telford: back from the hospital already, hands bandaged, gauze patches on his face like he'd had a particularly ropey shave. But not about to let a little thing like an acid attack get in the way of business. Haddow held the back door open, and Telford got in.

'This is us, Henry,' Rebus said. 'You're going to be following those two Range Rovers. Stay back as far as you like. Those things are so high off the ground, we'll be able to see them over anything smaller than a double-decker.'

Both Range Rovers headed out of Flint Street. The second car carried three of Telford's 'soldiers'. Rebus recognised Pretty-Boy. The other two were younger recruits, well-dressed with groomed hair. One hundred percent business.

The convoy headed for the city centre, stopped outside a hotel. Telford had a word with his men, but entered the building alone. The cars stayed where they were.

'Are you going in?' Wilson asked.

'I think I'd be noticed,' Rebus said. The drivers of both Range Rovers had got out and were enjoying a smoke, but keeping a keen eye on people entering and leaving the hotel. A couple of prospects looked into the cab, but Wilson shook his head.

'I could be making a mint here,' he muttered. Rebus offered him a Polo. Wilson accepted with a snort.

'Brilliant,' Rebus said. Wilson looked back towards the hotel. A parking warden was talking to Haddow and Pretty-Boy. She had her notebook out. They were tapping their watches, attempting charm. Double yellow lines kerbside: no parking any time.

Haddow and Pretty-Boy held up their hands in surrender, had a quick confab, then it was back into the Range Rovers. Pretty-Boy made circling motions with one hand, letting his passengers know

they were going to circle the block. The warden stood her ground till they'd moved off. Haddow was on his mobile: doubtless letting his boss know the score.

Interesting: they hadn't tried to strongarm the warden, or bribe her, nothing like that. Law-abiding citizens. Telford's rules, no doubt. Again, Rebus couldn't see any of Cafferty's men giving in so quickly.

'You going in then?' Wilson asked.

'Not much point, Henry. Telford will already be in a bedroom or somebody's suite. If he's doing business, it'll be behind closed doors.'

'So that was Tommy Telford?'

'You've heard of him?'

'I'm a taxi driver, we hear things. He's after Big Ger's cab business.' Wilson paused. 'Not that Big Ger *has* a cab business, you understand.'

'Any idea how Telford plans to wrest it away from Cafferty?'

'Scare off the drivers, or get them to switch sides.'

'What about your company, Henry?'

'Honest, legal and decent, Mr Rebus.'

'No approach by Telford?'

'Not yet.'

'Here they come again.' They watched as the two Range Rovers turned back into the street. There was no sign of the warden. A couple of minutes later, Telford emerged from the hotel, bringing with him a Japanese man with spiky hair and a shiny aquamarine suit. He carried a briefcase but didn't look like a businessman. Maybe it was the sunglasses, worn in late-afternoon twilight; maybe it was the cigarette slouching from the corner of the downturned mouth. Both men got into the back of the lead car. The Japanese leaned forward and ruffled the teddy bear's ears, making some joke. Telford didn't look amused.

'Do we follow them?' Wilson asked. He saw the look on Rebus's face, turned the key in the ignition.

They were heading west out of town. Rebus already had an inkling of their ultimate destination, but he wanted to know what route they'd take. Turned out it was much the same route he'd taken with Candice. She hadn't recognised anything until Juniper Green, but it wasn't as if there were many landmarks. On Slateford Road the back car signalled that it was pulling over.

'What do I do?' Wilson asked.

'Keep going. Make the first left you can, and turn the cab round. We'll wait for them to go past us.'

Haddow had gone into a newspaper shop. Same story as with Candice. Strange, during what was a business trip, that Telford would allow a stop. And what about the building which, according to Candice, he'd seemed so interested in? There it was: an anonymous brick edifice. A warehouse maybe? Rebus could think of reasons why a warehouse might be of interest to Tommy Telford. Haddow stayed in the shop three minutes – Rebus timed him. No one else came out, so it wasn't as if he'd had to queue. Back into the car, and the little convoy set off again. They were heading for Juniper Green, and after that Poyntinghame Country Club. Little point in tagging along: the further they got out of town, the more conspicuous the cab would be. Rebus told Henry to turn around.

He got the cabbie to drop him off at the Oxford Bar. Wilson slid down his window as he was about to move off.

'Are we square now?' he called.

'Till next time, Henry.' Rebus pushed open the door and walked into the pub.

Perched on a stool, daytime TV and Margaret the barmaid for company, Rebus ordered a mug of coffee and a corned beef and beetroot roll. For his main course Margaret suggested a bridie.

'Excellent choice,' Rebus agreed. He was thinking about the Japanese businessman. Who hadn't really looked like a businessman at all. He'd been all sharp edges, chiselled face. Fortified, Rebus walked from the Ox back to the hotel, and kept watch on it from an overpriced bar across the street. He passed the time making calls on his mobile. By the time the battery died, he'd spoken with Hogan, Bill Pryde, Siobhan Clarke, Rhona and Patience, and had been about to call Torphichen cop-shop, see if anyone there could identify the building on Slateford Road. Two hours crawled by. He broke his 'personal best' for slow drinking: two Cokes. The bar wasn't exactly crowded; no one seemed to mind. The music was on a tape-loop. 'Psycho Killer' was coming round for the third time when the Range Rovers stopped outside the hotel. Telford and the Jap shook hands, made slight bows. Telford and his men drove off.

Rebus left the bar, crossed the road, and entered the hotel. The lift doors were closing on Mr Aquamarine. Rebus walked up to reception, showed his ID.

'The guest who just came in, I need his name.'

The receptionist had to check. 'Mr Matsumoto.'

'First name?'

'Takeshi.'

'When did he arrive?'

She checked the register again. 'Yesterday.'

'How long's he staying?'

'Three more days. Look, I should call my supervisor ...'

Rebus shook his head. 'That's all I needed to know, thanks. Mind if I sit in the lounge for a while?'

She shook her head, so Rebus wandered into the residents' lounge. He settled on a sofa – perfect view of the reception area through the glass double-doors – and picked up a newspaper. Matsumoto was in town on Poyntinghame business, but Rebus had a whiff of something altogether less savoury. Hugh Malahide's story had been that a corporation wanted to buy the club, but Matsumoto didn't look like he worked in any above-board business. When he finally emerged into reception, he'd changed into a white suit, black open-necked shirt, and Burberry trenchcoat, topped off with a woollen tartan scarf. He had a cigarette in his mouth, but didn't light it until he was outside the hotel. With the collar of his coat turned up, he started walking. Rebus followed him for the best part of a mile, and kept checking that no one was following *him*. It was possible, after all, that Telford would want to keep tabs on Matsumoto. But if there was surveillance, it was exceptional. Matsumoto wasn't playing the tourist, wasn't dawdling. He kept his head down, protecting his face from the wind, and seemed to have some destination in mind.

When he disappeared into a building, Rebus paused, studying the glass door behind which stood a flight of red-carpeted stairs. He knew where he was, didn't need the sign above the door to tell him. He was outside the Morvena Casino. The place used to be owned by a local villain called Topper Hamilton and managed by a man called Mandelson. But Hamilton was in retirement, and Mandelson had scarpered. The new owner was still an unknown quantity – or had been till now. Rebus guessed he wouldn't be far wrong if he placed Tommy Telford and his Japanese friends in the frame. He looked around, checking the parked cars: no Range Rovers.

'What the hell,' he said to himself, pushing open the door and starting to climb the stairs.

In the upstairs foyer he was eyeballed by security: two of them looking uncomfortable in their black suits and bowties, white shirts. One skinny – he'd be all about speed and manoeuvres; one a real heavyweight – slow muscle to back up the fast moves. Rebus seemed to pass whatever test they'd just given him. He bought a twenty's worth of chips and walked into the gaming room.

At one time, it would have been the drawing-room of a Georgian house. There were two huge bay windows, and ornate cornicing connected the twenty-foot-high cream walls to the pastel-pink ceiling. Now it was home to gaming tables: blackjack, dice, roulette. Hostesses moved between the tables, taking orders for drinks. There was very little noise: the gamblers took their work seriously. Rebus wouldn't have called the place busy, but what clientele there was comprised a veritable United Nations. Matsumoto's coat had disappeared into the cloakroom, and he was seated at the roulette table. Rebus sat down beside two men at the blackjack table, nodded a greeting. The dealer – young, but obviously sure of himself – smiled. Rebus won with his first hand. Lost with his second and third. Won again with his fourth. There was a voice just behind his right ear.

'Something to drink, sir?'

The hostess had bent forward to speak to him, showing plenty of cleavage.

'Coke,' he told her. 'Ice and lemon.' He pretended to watch her move away. Really, he was scoping the room. He'd sat in on the game quickly: walking around the room would have attracted everyone's interest, and he couldn't be sure if there'd be anyone here who'd know him.

He needn't have worried. The only person he recognised was Matsumoto, rubbing his hands as the croupier pushed chips towards him. Rebus stuck on eighteen. The dealer got twenty. Rebus had never been a great gambler. He'd tried the football pools, sometimes the horses, and now occasionally the lottery. But fruit machines didn't interest him; the poker sessions organised in the office didn't interest him. He had other ways of losing money.

Matsumoto lost and gave what sounded like a curse, a little bit louder than the room liked. The skinny security ape put his head around the door, but Matsumoto ignored him, and when Mr Skinny saw who was making the noise, he retreated fast. Matsumoto laughed: he might not have much English, but he knew he had

power in this place. He told everyone something in a stream of Japanese, nodding, trying for eye contact. Then a hostess brought him a big tumbler of whisky and ice. He handed her a couple of chips as a tip. The croupier was telling everyone to place their bets. Matsumoto quietened down and went back to work.

Rebus's drink was a while coming, Coke the unlikely beverage of the high roller. He'd won a couple of hands, felt a bit better. Stood up to accept the drink. The table knew to leave him out of the next deal.

'Where are you from?' he asked the hostess. 'I can't place your accent.'

'I am from Ukraine.'

'You speak good English.'

'Thank you.' She turned away. Conversation was not house policy, it kept the punters away from their games. Ukraine: Rebus wondered if she was another of Tarawicz's imports. Like Candice ... A few things seemed clear to him. Matsumoto was comfortable here, therefore known. And the staff were wary of him, therefore he had clout, had Telford behind him. Telford wanted him kept sweet. It wasn't much return for all Rebus's work, but it was something.

Then someone walked in. Someone Rebus knew. Dr Colquhoun. He saw Rebus immediately and fear jumped into his face. Colquhoun: with his sick line to the university; his enforced holiday; no forwarding address. Colquhoun: who'd known Rebus was taking Candice to the Petrecs.

Rebus watched him back towards the doors. Watched him turn and run.

Options: go after him, or stay with Matsumoto? Which was the more important to him now, Candice or Telford? Rebus stayed. But now Colquhoun was back in town, he'd track him down.

For definite.

After an hour and a quarter's play, he was considering cashing a cheque for more chips. Twenty quid down in a little over an hour, and Candice fighting for some space in his crowded head. He took a break, moved to a row of fruit machines, but the lights and buttons defeated him. He wasted three nudges and ran out of time on some accumulator. Another two quid gone – this time in a couple of minutes. Little wonder clubs and pubs wanted slot machines. Tommy Telford was in the right business. His hostess came to see him again, asked if he wanted another drink.

'I'm fine,' he said. 'Not much action tonight.'

'It's early,' she told him. 'Wait till after midnight ...'

No way was he sticking around that long. But Matsumoto surprised him, threw up his hands and came out with another rush of Japanese, nodding and grinning, gathering up his chips. He cashed them and left the casino. Rebus waited all of thirty seconds, then followed. He said a breezy goodnight to the security men, felt their eyes on him all the way back down the stairs.

Matsumoto was buttoning his coat, wrapping the scarf tight around his neck. He was headed back in the direction of the hotel. Rebus, suddenly bone-tired, stopped in his tracks. He was thinking of Sammy and Lintz and the Weasel, thinking of all the time he seemed to be wasting.

'Fuck this for a game of soldiers.'

Turned on his heels and went to collect his car. Ten Years After: 'Goin' Home'.

It was a twenty-minute walk to Flint Street, a lot of it uphill and with the wind doing nobody any favours. The city was quiet: people huddled at bus stops; students munching on baked potatoes, chips with curry sauce. A few souls marching home with the concentrated tread of the sozzled. Rebus stopped, frowned, looked around. This was where he'd left the Saab. He was positive ... no, not 'positive' – the word had taken on malign overtones. He was *sure*, yes, sure he'd left the Saab right here. Where now a black Ford Sierra was parked, and behind that a Mini. But no sign of Rebus's car.

'Aw, Christ,' he exploded. There were no signs of glass by the roadside, which meant they hadn't taken a brick to one of his windows. Oh, there'd be jokes in the office about this though, whether he got the car back or not. A taxi came along and he flagged it down, then remembered he'd no cash, so waved it off again.

His flat in Arden Street wasn't that far off, but had he been a camel, he'd have been keeping well clear of any straw.

# 20

He was asleep in his chair by the living-room window, duvet pulled up to his neck, when the buzzer sounded. He couldn't remember setting the alarm. Consciousness brought the dawning realisation that it was his door. He staggered to his feet, found his trousers and put them on.

'All right, all right,' he called, heading for the hall. 'Keep your hair on.'

He opened the door and saw Bill Pryde.

'Jesus, Bill, is this some sort of twisted revenge?' Rebus looked at his watch: two-fifteen.

'Afraid not, John,' Pryde said. His face and voice told Rebus something bad had happened.

Something very bad indeed.

'I've been off the booze for weeks.'

'Sure about that?'

'Definite.' Rebus's eyes burned into those of DCI Gill Templer. They were in her office at St Leonard's. Pryde was there, too. His jacket was off and his sleeves rolled up. Gill Templer looked bleary from interrupted sleep. Rebus was pacing what floor there was, unable to stay seated.

'I've had nothing to drink all day but coffee and Coke.'

'Really?'

Rebus ran his hands through his hair. He felt groggy, and his head was throbbing. But he couldn't ask for Paracetamol and water: they'd assume hangover.

'Come on, Gill,' he said, 'I'm being shafted here.'

'Who authorised your surveillance?'

'Nobody. I did it in my own time.'

'How do you work that out?'

'The Chief Super said I could take a bit of time off.'

'He meant so you could visit your daughter.' She paused. 'Is that what this was all about?'

'Maybe.'

'This Mr ...' she checked her notes '... Matsumoto, he was connected to Thomas Telford. And your theory is that Telford was behind the attack on your daughter?'

Rebus thumped the wall with his fists. 'It's a set-up, oldest trick in the book. I've yet to see one perfected. There's got to be something at the scene ... something out of kilter.' He turned to his colleagues. 'You've got to let me go there, take a look around.'

Templer looked to Bill Pryde. Pryde folded his arms, shrugged assent. But it was Templer's play, she was the senior officer here. She tapped her pen against her teeth, then dropped it on to the desk.

'Will you submit to a blood test?'

Rebus swallowed. 'Why not?' he said at last.

'Come on then,' she said, getting to her feet.

The story was: Matsumoto had been on his way back to his hotel. Crossing the road, he'd been hit by a car travelling at speed. The driver hadn't stopped, not right away. But the car had travelled only another couple of hundred yards before mounting the pavement with its front wheels. It had been abandoned there, driver's door open.

A Saab 900, its identity known to half the Lothian and Borders force.

The interior reeked of whisky, the screw-top from a bottle lying on the passenger seat. No sign of the bottle, no sign of the driver. Just the car, and two hundred yards further back, the body of the Japanese businessman, growing cold by the roadside.

Nobody had seen anything. Nobody had heard anything. Rebus could believe it: never one of the city centre's busier routes, at this hour the place was dead.

'When I followed him from his hotel, he didn't come this way,' Rebus told Templer. She stood with shoulders hunched, hands deep in her coat pockets, keeping out the cold.

'So?' she asked.

'Long way round for a short-cut.'

'Maybe he wanted to see the sights,' Pryde suggested.

'What time's this supposed to have happened?' Rebus asked.

Templer hesitated. 'There's a margin of error.'

'Look, Gill, I know this is awkward. You shouldn't have brought me here, you shouldn't answer my questions. I'm the number one suspect, after all.' Rebus knew how much she had to lose. Over two hundred male Chief Inspectors in Scotland; only *five* women. Bad odds, and a lot of people waiting for her to fail. He held up his hands. 'Look, if I was blind drunk and I hit somebody, think I'd leave the car at the scene?'

'You might not know you'd hit anyone. You hear a thunk, lose control and mount the kerb, and some survival instinct tells you it's time to get out and walk.'

'Only I hadn't been drinking. I left the car near Flint Street, and that's where they took it from. Any signs it was broken into?'

She didn't say anything.

'I'll guess not,' Rebus went on. 'Because professionals don't leave marks. But to get it started, they must have wired it or got into the steering column. That's what you should be looking for.'

The car had been towed. First thing in the morning, forensics would be all over it.

Rebus laughed, shaking his head. 'It's nice though, isn't it? First they make Sammy look like a hit and run, and now they try to pin me for the same thing.'

'Who's "they"?'

'Telford and his men.'

'I thought you said they were doing business with Matsumoto?'

'They're all gangsters, Gill. Gangsters fall out.'

'What about Cafferty?'

Rebus frowned. 'What about him?'

'He's got an old grudge against you. This way, he stitches you up *and* annoys Telford.'

'So you do think I'm being stitched up?'

'I'm giving you the benefit of the doubt.' She paused. 'Not everyone will. What was Matsumoto's business with Telford?'

'Something to do with a country club – on the surface at least. Some Japanese were buying it, and Telford was clearing the way.' He shivered: should have worn a coat over his jacket. He rubbed his arm where the blood sample had been taken to test his alcohol level. 'Of course, a check of the deceased's hotel room might throw up something.'

192

'We've already been there,' Pryde said. 'Nothing out of the ordinary.'

'Which deadbeat did you send?'

'I went myself,' Gill Templer said, voice as icy as the wind. Rebus bowed his head in apology. She had a point though: Matsumoto and Telford had been doing business. There had been nothing about their farewell to one another to suggest a break-up, and Matsumoto had seemed happy and confident at the casino. What had Telford to gain by bumping him off?

Apart from maybe getting Rebus off his back.

Templer had mentioned Cafferty: was Big Ger capable of such a move? What did *he* stand to gain? Apart from settling a long-held grudge against Rebus, giving Telford a headache, and maybe gaining Poyntinghame and the Japanese deal for himself.

Balance the two – Telford against Cafferty. Cafferty's side tipped, went clunk as it hit the ground.

'Let's get back to the station,' Templer said. 'I'm reaching the early stages of frostbite.'

'Can I go home then?'

'We're not done with you yet, John,' she said, getting into the car. 'Not by a long chalk.'

But eventually they had to let him go. He wasn't being charged, not yet. There was work still to be done. He knew they could make a case against him if they wanted to, knew it only too well. *He'd* followed Matsumoto out of the club. *He* was the one with the grudge against Telford. *He* was the one who'd see poetic justice in sending Telford a message by driving over one of his associates.

He, John Rebus, was firmly in the frame. It was tightly constructed and quite elegant in its way. The scales suddenly tipped back towards Telford again, so much subtler than Cafferty.

Telford.

Rebus visited Farlowe in his cell. The reporter wasn't asleep.

'How long do I have to stay here?' he asked.

'As long as possible.'

'How's Telford?'

'Minor burns. Don't expect him to press charges. He'll want you on the outside.'

'Then you'll have to let me go.'

'Don't bet on it, Ned. *We* can press charges. We don't need Telford.'

Farlowe looked at him. 'You're going to prosecute me?'

'I saw the whole thing. Unwarranted attack on an innocent man.'

Farlowe snorted, then smiled. 'Ironic, isn't it? Charging me for my own good.' He paused. 'I won't be able to see Sammy, will I?'

Rebus shook his head.

'I didn't think of that. Fact is, I didn't *think*.' He looked up from his ledge. 'I just did. And right up until the moment I did it, it felt ... brilliant.'

'And afterwards?'

Farlowe shrugged. 'What does afterwards matter? It's only the rest of my life.'

Rebus didn't go home, knew he wouldn't sleep. And he'd no car, so he couldn't go driving. Instead, he visited the hospital, sat down by Sammy's bedside. He took her hand, rested it against his face.

When a nurse came in and asked if he wanted anything, he asked if she'd any Paracetamol.

'In a hospital?' she said, smiling. 'I'll see what I can do.'

# 21

Rebus was due for further questioning at St Leonard's at ten o'clock, so when his pager sounded at eight-fifteen, he assumed it was a reminder. But the phone number it wanted him to call was the mortuary down in the Cowgate. He called from the hospital payphone, and was put through to Dr Curt.

'Looks like I've drawn the short straw,' Curt told him.

'You're about to start work on Matsumoto?'

'For my sins. Look, I've heard the stories ... don't suppose there's any truth in them?'

'I didn't kill him.'

'Glad to hear it, John.' Curt seemed to be struggling to say something. 'There are questions of ethics, of course, so I can't suggest that you come down here ...'

'There's something you think I should see?'

'That I can't say.' Curt cleared his throat. 'But if you happened to be here ... and the place is always very quiet this time of the morning ...'

'I'm on my way.'

The Infirmary to the mortuary: a ten-minute walk. Curt himself was waiting to lead Rebus to the body.

The room was all white tile, bright light and stainless steel. Two of the dissecting-tables lay empty. Matsumoto's naked body lay on the third. Rebus walked around it, stunned by what he saw.

Tattoos.

And not just the kilted piper on a sailor's arm. These were works of art, and they were massive. A scaly green dragon, breathing pink and red fire, covered one shoulder and crept down the arm towards the wrist. Its back legs reached around the body's neck, while its front ones rested on the chest. There were other smaller dragons, and a landscape – Mount Fuji reflected in water. There were

Japanese symbols and the visored face of a kendo champion. Curt put on rubber gloves, and had Rebus do the same. Then the two men rolled the body over, displaying a further gallery across Matsumoto's back. A masked actor, something out of a Noh play, and a warrior in full armour. Some delicate flowers. The effect was mesmerising.

'Stunning, aren't they?' Curt said.

'Phenomenal.'

'I've visited Japan a few times, given papers at conferences.'

'So you recognise some of these?'

'A few of the references, yes. Thing is, tattoos – especially on this scale – usually mean you're a gang member.'

'Like the Triads?'

'The Japanese are called Yakuza. Look here.' Curt held up the left hand. The pinkie had been severed at the first joint, the skin healed in a rough crust.

'That's what happens when they screw up, isn't it?' Rebus said, the word 'Yakuza' bouncing around in his head. 'Someone cuts off a finger every time.'

'I think so, yes,' Curt said. 'Just thought you might like to know.'

Rebus nodded, eyes glued to the corpse. 'Anything else?'

'Well, I haven't started on him yet, really. All looks fairly standard: evidence of impact with a moving vehicle. Crushed ribcage, fractures to the arms and legs.' Rebus noticed that a bone was protruding from one calf, obscenely white against the skin. 'There'll be a lot of internal damage. Shock probably killed him.' Curt was thoughtful. 'I must let Professor Gates know. Doubt he'll have seen anything like it.'

'Can I use your phone?' Rebus asked.

He knew one person who might know about the Yakuza – she'd seemed knowledgeable about every other country's criminal gangs. So he spoke to Miriam Kenworthy in Newcastle.

'Tattoos and missing fingers?' she said.

'Bingo.'

'That's Yakuza.'

'Actually, it's only the top bit missing from one little finger. That's done to them when they step out of line, isn't it?'

'Not quite. They do it to *themselves* as a way of saying they're

196

sorry. I'm not sure I know much more than that.' There was the sound of papers being shifted. 'I'm just looking for my notes.'

'What notes?'

'When I was connecting all these gangs, different cultures, I did some research. Might be something on the Yakuza ... Look, can I call you back?'

'How long?'

'Five minutes.'

Rebus gave her Curt's number, then sat and waited. Curt's room wasn't so much an office as a walk-in cupboard. Files were stacked high on his desk, and a dictaphone lay on top of them, along with a fresh pack of tapes. The room reeked of cigarettes and bad ventilation. On the walls: schedules of meetings, postcards, a couple of framed prints. The place was a bolt-hole, a necessity; Curt spent most of his time elsewhere.

Rebus took out Colquhoun's business card, tried home and office. As far as his secretary was concerned, Dr Colquhoun was still off sick.

Maybe, but he was well enough to visit a casino. One of Telford's casinos. No coincidence surely ...

Kenworthy was good as gold.

'Yakuza,' she said, sounding like she was lifting from her script. 'Ninety thousand members split into something like two and a half thousand groupings. Utterly ruthless, but also highly intelligent and sophisticated. Very hierarchical structure, almost impenetrable to outsiders. Like a secret society. They even have a sort of middle management level, called the Sokaiya.'

Rebus was writing it all down. 'How do you spell that?'

She told him. 'Back in Japan they run *pachinko* parlours – that's a sort of gaming thing – and have fingers in most other illegal pies.'

'Unless they've lopped them off. What about outside Japan?'

'Only thing I've got down here is that they ship expensive designer stuff back home to sell on the black market, also stolen art, ship it back to wealthy buyers ...'

'Wait a minute, you told me Jake Tarawicz started out smuggling icons out of Russia.'

'You're saying Pink Eyes might connect to the Yakuza?'

'Tommy Telford's been chauffeuring them around. There's a warehouse everyone seems interested in, plus a country club.'

'What's in the warehouse?'

197

'I don't know yet.'

'Maybe you should find out.'

'It's on my list. Something else, these *pachinko* parlours ... would those be like amusement arcades?'

'Pretty much.'

'Another connection with Telford: he puts gaming machines into half the pubs and clubs on the east coast.'

'You think the Yakuza saw someone they could do a deal with?'

'I don't know.' He tried stifling a yawn.

'Too early in the morning for big questions?'

He smiled. 'Something like that. Thanks for your help, Miriam.'

'No problem. Keep me posted.'

'Sure. Anything new on Tarawicz?'

'Nothing I've heard. No sign of Candice either, sorry.'

'Thanks again.'

''Bye.'

Curt was standing in the doorway. He'd stripped off gown and gloves, and his hands smelled of soap.

'Not much I can do till my assistants get in.' He looked at his watch. 'Fancy a spot of breakfast?'

'You have to appreciate how this looks, John. The media could be all over us. I can think of a few journalists who'd give their drinking-arm to nail you.'

Chief Superintendent Watson was in his element. Seated behind his desk, hands folded, he had the serenity of a large stone Buddha. The occasional crises with which John Rebus presented him had hardened the Farmer to life's lesser knocks and taught him calm acceptance.

'You're going to suspend me,' Rebus stated with conviction – he'd been here before. He finished the coffee his boss had given him, but kept his hands locked around the mug. 'Then you're going to open an investigation.'

'Not straight away,' Watson surprised him by saying. 'What I want first of all is your statement – and I mean a full and frank explanation – of your recent movements, your interest in Mr Matsumoto and Thomas Telford. Bring in anything you want about your daughter's accident, any suspicions you've had, and above all the *validity* of those suspicions. Telford already has a lawyer asking awkward questions about our Japanese friend's untimely end. The

lawyer ...' Watson looked to Gill Templer, seated by the door, mouth a thin unimpressed line.

'Charles Groal,' she said flatly.

'Groal, yes. He's been asking at the casino. He got a description of a man who came in just after Matsumoto, and left immediately after him. He seems to think it's you.'

'Are you telling him otherwise?' Rebus asked.

'We're telling him nothing, not until our own inquiries have established ... et cetera. But I can't hold him off forever, John.'

'Have you asked anyone what Matsumoto was doing here?'

'He works for a firm of management consultants. He was here at a client's behest, finalising the takeover of a country club.'

'With Tommy Telford in tow.'

'John, let's not lose sight of ...'

'Matsumoto was a member of the Yakuza, sir. The closest I've come to one of those before has been on a TV screen. Now suddenly they're in Edinburgh.' Rebus paused. 'Don't you find that just a *wee* bit curious? I mean, doesn't it worry you at all? I don't know, maybe I'm getting my priorities all wrong, but it seems to me we're splashing about in puddles while a tidal wave's coming in!'

The pressure of his hands around the mug had been increasing by degrees. Now the thing broke, a piece falling to the floor as Rebus winced. He picked one ceramic shard out of his palm. Drops of blood hit the carpet. Gill Templer had come forward, was reaching for his hand.

'Here, let me.'

He spun away from her. 'No!' Way too loud. Fumbling in his pocket for a handkerchief.

'I've got some paper ones in my bag.'

'It's all right.' Blood dripping on to his shoes. Watson was saying something about the mug having a crack; Templer was staring at him. He wrapped white cotton around the wound.

'I'll go wash it,' he said. 'With your permission, sir?'

'On you go, John. Sure you're all right?'

'I'll be fine.'

It wasn't a bad cut. Cold water helped. He dried off with paper towels, which he flushed down the toilet, waiting to see they'd gone. A first aid box next: half a dozen plasters, cover the nick good and proper. He bunched his fist, saw no sign of leakage. Had to be content with that.

Back at his desk, he started on his memoirs – as ordered by Watson. Gill Templer came past, decided he needed a few soft words.

'None of us thinks you did it, John. But something like this ... questions being asked by the Japanese consul ... it has to be done by the book.'

'It all comes down to politics in the end, eh?' He was thinking of Joseph Lintz.

At lunchtime he dropped in on Ned Farlowe, asked him if he needed anything. Farlowe wanted sandwiches, books, newspapers, company. He looked drawn, weary of imprisonment. Maybe soon he'd think to ask for a lawyer. A lawyer – any lawyer – would get him out.

Rebus handed his report to Watson's secretary and headed out of the station. He'd gone fifty yards when a car pulled up alongside. Range Rover. Pretty-Boy telling him to get in. Rebus looked into the back of the car.

Telford. Ointment on his blistered face. Looking like a scaled-down Jake Tarawicz ...

Rebus hesitated. The cop shop was a short sprint away.

'Get in,' Pretty-Boy repeated. Sucker for a free offer, Rebus got in.

Pretty-Boy turned the car. The giant yellow teddy had been strapped into the passenger seat.

'I don't suppose,' Rebus said, 'it's worth my while asking you to leave Ned Farlowe be?'

Telford's mind was on other things. 'He wants war, he's going to get war.'

'Who?'

'Your boss.'

'I don't work for Cafferty.'

'Don't give me that.'

'I'm the one who put him inside.'

'And you've been snuggling up ever since.'

'I didn't kill Matsumoto.'

Telford looked at him for the first time, and Rebus could see he was itching for violence.

'You know I didn't,' Rebus went on.

'What do you mean?'

'Because you did it, and you want me to –'

Telford's hands were around Rebus's neck. Rebus shrugged them off, tried pinning Telford down. Impossible with the car in motion, cramped in the back seat. Pretty-Boy stopped the car and got out, opened Rebus's door and dragged him on to the pavement. Telford followed, face beetroot-red, eyes bulging.

'You're not going to pin this on me!' he roared. Drivers slowed to watch. Pedestrians crossed the road to safety.

'Who else?' Rebus's voice was shaky.

'Cafferty!' Telford screeched. 'It's you and Cafferty, trying to shut me down!'

'I'm telling you, I didn't do it.'

'Boss,' Pretty-Boy was saying, 'let's screw the head, eh?' He was looking around, nervous of the attention they were attracting. Telford saw his point, let his shoulders relax a little.

'Get in the car,' he said to Rebus. Rebus just stared at him. 'It's okay. Just get in. I want to show you a couple of things.'

Rebus, world's craziest cop, got back in.

There was silence for a couple of minutes, Telford rearranging the dressings on his fingers, which had come loose during the fight.

'I don't think Cafferty wants war,' Rebus said.

'What makes you so sure?'

*Because I've done a deal with him – it's me who's going to shut you down.* They were heading west. Rebus tried not to think about possible destinations.

'You were in the Army, weren't you?' Telford asked.

Rebus nodded.

'Paratroops, then the SAS.'

'I didn't get past training.' Rebus thinking: he's well-informed.

'So you decided to become a cop instead.' Telford was completely calm again. He'd brushed down his suit and checked the knot in his tie. 'Thing is, working for structures like those – Army, cops – you need to obey orders. I hear you're not very good at it. You wouldn't last long with me.' He looked out of the window. 'What's Cafferty planning?'

'No idea.'

'Why were you watching Matsumoto?'

'Because he tied into you.'

'Crime Squad pulled their surveillance.' Rebus said nothing. 'But you kept yours going.' Telford turned towards him. 'Why?'

'Because you tried to kill my daughter.'

Telford stared at him, unblinking. 'Is that what this is about?'

'It's why Ned Farlowe tried to blind you He's her boyfriend.'

Telford choked out a disbelieving laugh, started to shake his head. 'I'd nothing to do with your daughter. Where's the reason?'

'To get at me. Because she helped me with Candice.'

Telford was thoughtful. 'Okay,' he said, nodding, 'I can see your thinking, and I don't suppose my word's going to count for much, but for what it's worth, I know absolutely nothing about your daughter.' He paused. Rebus could hear sirens nearby. 'Is that what took you to Cafferty?'

Rebus said nothing, which seemed, to Telford's mind, to confirm his suspicions. He smiled again.

'Pull over,' Telford said. Pretty-Boy stopped the car. The road ahead was blocked anyway, police diverting traffic down side-streets. Rebus realised he'd been smelling smoke for some time. The tenements had hidden it from view, but now he could see the fire. It was in the lot where Cafferty kept his taxis. The shed used as an office had been reduced to ash. The garage behind, where the cabs were worked on and cleaned up, was about to lose its corrugated roof. A row of vehicles was burning nicely.

'We could have sold tickets,' Pretty-Boy said. Telford turned from the spectacle to Rebus.

'Fire Brigade's going to be stretched. Two of Cafferty's offices are spontaneously combusting ...' he checked his watch ... 'right about now, as is that beautiful house of his. Don't worry, we waited till his wife was out shopping. Final ultimatums have been delivered to his men – they can shuffle out of town or off this mortal coil.' He shrugged. 'Makes no odds to me. Go tell Cafferty: he's finished in Edinburgh.'

Rebus licked his lips. 'You've just said I'm wrong about you, that you had nothing to do with my daughter. What if *you're* wrong about Cafferty?'

'Wake up, will you? The stabbing at Megan's, then Danny Simpson ... Cafferty's not exactly subtle.'

'Did Danny say it was Cafferty's men?'

'He knows, same as I do.' Telford tapped Pretty-Boy's shoulder. 'Back to base.' To Rebus: 'Another little message for you to take to Barlinnie. Here's what I told Cafferty's men – any of them left in this city after midnight are fair game ... and I don't take prisoners.'

202

He sniffed, seemed pleased with himself, settled back in the seat. 'You won't mind if I drop you at Flint Street? Only I've a business meeting in fifteen minutes.'

'With Matsumoto's bosses?'

'If they want Poyntinghame, they'll keep dealing with me.' He looked at Rebus. 'You should deal with me, too. Think about this: who'd want you pissed off with me? It comes back to Cafferty: hitting your daughter, setting up Matsumoto ... It *all* comes back to Cafferty. Think it over, then maybe we should talk again.'

After a couple of minutes, Rebus broke the silence.

'You know a man called Joseph Lintz?'

'Bobby Hogan mentioned him.'

'He phoned your office in Flint Street.'

Telford shrugged. 'I'll tell you what I told Hogan. Maybe it was a wrong number. Whatever it was, *I* didn't speak to any old Nazi.'

'You're not the only one uses that office though.' Rebus saw Pretty-Boy watching him in the rearview mirror. 'What about you?'

'Never heard of the cat.'

A car was parked in Flint Street – a huge white limousine with blackened windows. There was a TV aerial on the boot, and the hubcaps were painted pink.

'Christ,' Telford said in amusement, 'look at his latest toy.' He seemed to have forgotten all about Rebus. He was out of the car and loping towards the man who was emerging from the back of the limo. White suit, panama hat, big cigar, and a bright red paisley shirt. None of which stopped you staring at the scarred face and blue-tinted glasses. Telford was commenting on the attire, the car, the audacity, and Mr Pink Eyes was loving it. He put a hand around Telford's shoulder, steering him towards the amusement arcade. But then he stopped, clicked his fingers, turned back to the limo and reached out a hand.

And now a woman was emerging. Short black dress and black tights, fur jacket keeping out the chills. Tarawicz rubbed a hand over her backside; Telford kissed her on the neck. She smiled, eyes slightly glazed. Then Tarawicz and Telford turned towards the Range Rover. They were both staring at Rebus.

'Trip's over, Inspector,' Pretty-Boy said, telling Rebus it was time to get out. He did so, his eyes on Candice. But she wasn't looking at him. She was snuggling into Mr Pink Eyes, head on his chest. He was still rubbing her backside, the dress rising and falling. He was

watching Rebus, eyes alight, face pulled into a latex grin. Rebus walked over to them, and now Candice saw him, and looked frightened.

'Inspector,' Tarawicz said, 'good to see you again. Come to whisk the damsel away to safety?'

Rebus ignored him. 'Come on, Candice.' His hand, not quite steady, held out towards her.

She looked at him and shook her head. 'Why would I want that?' she said, and was rewarded with another kiss from Tarawicz.

'You were abducted. You can press charges.'

Tarawicz was laughing, leading her into the cafe.

'Candice.' Rebus reached for her arm, but she pulled away and followed her master inside.

Two of Telford's men were blocking the door. Pretty-Boy was behind Rebus.

'No cheap heroics?' he asked, making to pass the policeman.

Back at St Leonard's, Rebus took Farlowe his food and newspapers, then hitched a lift in a patrol car to Torphichen. The man he wanted was DI 'Shug' Davidson, and Davidson was in the CID office, looking frazzled.

'Somebody torched a taxi rank,' he told Rebus.

'Any idea who?'

Davidson's eyes narrowed. 'The rank was owned by Jock Scallow. Is there something you're trying to tell me?'

'Who really owned the outfit, Shug?'

'You know damned well.'

'And who's muscling in on Cafferty's patch?'

'I've heard rumours.'

Rebus rested against Davidson's desk. 'Tommy Telford's going into combat, unless we can stop him.'

'"We"?'

'I want you to take me somewhere,' Rebus said.

Shug Davidson was happily married to an understanding wife, and had kids who didn't see as much of him as they deserved. A year back, he'd won forty grand on the Lottery. Everyone in his station got a drink. The rest of the money had been salted away.

Rebus had worked with him before. He wasn't a bad cop, maybe lacking a little in imagination. They had to work their way around

the scene of the fire. A further mile and a half on, Rebus told him to stop.

'What is it?' Davidson asked.

'That's what I want you to tell me.' Rebus was looking towards the brick building, the same one which so interested Tommy Telford.

'It's Maclean's,' Davidson said.

'And what's Maclean's when it's at home?'

Davidson smiled. 'You really don't know?' He opened his car door. 'Come on, I'll show you.'

They had to have their identities checked at the main entrance. Rebus noticed a lot of security, albeit subtle: cameras trained down from the corners of the building, catching every angle of approach. A phone call was made, and a man in a white coat came down to sign them in. They pinned visitor's badges to their jackets, and the tour began.

'I've been here before,' Davidson confided. 'If you ask me, it's the best kept secret in the city.'

They climbed steps, walked down passageways. Everywhere there was security: guards checked their badges; doors had to be unlocked; cameras charted their progress. Which puzzled Rebus, for it was such an unassuming building, really. And nothing spectacular was happening.

'What is it, Fort Knox?' he asked. But then their guide handed them white coats to put on, before pushing open the door to a laboratory, and Rebus started to understand.

People were working with chemicals, examining test-tubes, writing notes. There were all sorts of weird and wonderful machines, but in essence it was a school chemistry-lab on a slightly grander scale.

'Welcome,' Davidson said, 'to the world's biggest drugs factory.'

Which wasn't quite correct, for Maclean's was only the world's largest *legal* producer of heroin and cocaine, something the guide explained.

'We're licensed by the government. Back in 1961 there was an international agreement: every country in the world was allowed just one producer, and we're it for Britain.'

'So what do you make?' Rebus was staring at the rows of locked fridges.

'All sorts of things: methadone for heroin addicts, pethedine for

women in labour. Diamorphine to ease terminal illnesses and cocaine for use in medical procedures. The company started out supplying laudanum to the Victorians.'

'And these days?'

'We produce about seventy tonnes of opiates a year,' the guide said. 'And around two million pounds' worth of pure cocaine.'

Rebus rubbed his forehead. 'I begin to see the need for security.'

The guide smiled. 'The MoD has asked us for advice – that's how good our security is.'

'No break-ins?'

'A couple of attempts, nothing we couldn't deal with.'

No, Rebus thought, but then you've never had to deal with Tommy Telford and the Yakuza ... not yet.

Rebus walked around the lab, smiled and nodded at a woman who just seemed to be standing there, not doing anything.

'Who's she?' he asked the guide.

'Our nurse. She's on stand-by.'

'What for?'

The guide nodded towards where a man was operating one of the machines. 'Etorphine,' he said. 'Forty thousand pounds a kilo, and extremely potent. The nurse has the antidote, just in case.'

'So what's it used for, this etorphine?'

'Knocking out rhinos,' the guide said, like the answer should have been obvious.

The cocaine was produced from coca leaves flown in from Peru. The opium came from plantations in Tasmania and Australia. The pure heroin and cocaine were kept in a strongroom. Each lab had its share of locked safes. The storage warehouse boasted infrared detectors and movement sensors. Five minutes in the place told Rebus *exactly* why Tommy Telford was interested in Maclean's. And he'd brought the Yakuza in on the plan either because he needed their help – which was unlikely – or to brag about the exploit.

Back at the car, Davidson asked the obvious question.

'What's this all about, John?'

Rebus pinched the bridge of his nose. 'I think Telford's planning to hit this place.'

Davidson snorted. 'He'd never get in. Like you said yourself, it's Fort bloody Knox.'

'It's a prestige thing, Shug. If he can empty the place, it'll make

his name. He'll have beaten Cafferty hands down.' It was the same with the fire-bombings: they weren't just a message to Cafferty, but a sort of 'red carpet' for Mr Pink Eyes – welcome to Edinburgh, and look what I can do.

'I'm telling you,' Davidson said, 'there's no way in. Christ, that's cheap!' Davidson's attention had been diverted by signs on the window of the corner shop. Rebus looked, too. Cut-price cigarettes. Cheap sandwiches and hot rolls. Plus five pence off any morning paper.

'Competition around here must be crippling,' Davidson said. 'Fancy a roll?'

Rebus was watching workers leaving the gates of Maclean's. Afternoon break maybe. Saw them cross the road, dodging traffic. Counting small change from their pockets as they pushed open the door to the shop.

'Yes,' Rebus said quietly, 'why not?'

The small shop was packed out. Davidson got in the queue, while Rebus looked at the rack of papers and magazines. The workers were sharing jokes and gossip. Two staff worked behind the counter – young males, mixing banter with less-than-efficient service.

'What do you fancy, John? Bacon?'

'Fine,' Rebus said. Remembered he hadn't had lunch. 'Make it two.'

Two bacon rolls came in at one pound exactly. They sat in the car to eat.

'You know, Shug, the usual ploy with a shop like that is to take a beating on one or two necessities to get the punters in.' Davidson nodded, attacked his roll. 'But that place looked like Bargain City.' Rebus had stopped eating. 'Do us both a favour: find out the shop's history, who owns it, who those two are behind the counter.'

Davidson's chewing slowed. 'You think ... ?'

'Just check it out, all right?'

# 22

Back at St Leonard's, his telephone was ringing. He sat down and prised the lid from a beaker of coffee. On the drive back he'd been thinking about Candice. Two swigs of coffee and he lifted the receiver.

'DI Rebus,' he said.

'What the fuck is that little shite up to?' The voice of Big Ger Cafferty.

'Where are you?'

'Where do you think I am?'

'Sounds like a mobile.'

'Amazing the things that find their way into Barlinnie. Now tell me, what is happening over there?'

'You've heard then.'

'He torched my house! My *house*! Am I supposed to let him get away with that?'

'Look, I think I may have found a way to get to him.'

Cafferty calmed a little. 'Tell me?'

'Not yet, I want to –'

'And all my taxis,' Cafferty exploded again. 'The little bastard!'

'Look, the point is: what's he expecting you to do? He's waiting for instant retaliation.'

'And he's going to get it.'

'He'll be ready. Wouldn't it be better to catch him off-guard?'

'That little bastard hasn't been off-guard since he was lifted from the cradle.'

'Shall I tell you why he did it?'

Cafferty's anger ebbed again. 'Why?'

'Because he says you killed Matsumoto.'

'Who?'

'A business acquaintance. Whoever did it made it look like I was behind the wheel.'

'It wasn't me.'

'Try telling Telford that. He thinks you ordered me to do it.'

'We know differently.'

'That's right. *We* know someone was setting me up, trying to get me out of the way.'

'What was his name again, the dead one?'

'Matsumoto.'

'Is that Japanese?'

Rebus wished he could see Cafferty's eyes. Even then, it was hard to tell when the man was playing games.

'He was Japanese,' Rebus stated.

'What the hell did he have to do with Telford?'

'Sounds to me like your intelligence has gone to pot.'

There was silence on the line. 'About your daughter ...'

Rebus froze. 'What about her?'

'A secondhand shop in Porty.' Meaning Portobello. 'The owner bought some stuff from a seller. Including opera tapes and Roy Orbison. Stuck in his mind. They don't naturally go together.'

Rebus's hand tightened on the receiver. 'Which shop? What did the seller look like?'

Cold laughter. 'We're working on it, Strawman, just leave everything to us. Now, about this Japanese fellow ...?'

'I said *I'd* put Telford out of the game. That was the agreement.'

'I've yet to see any action.'

'I'm working on it!'

'I want to hear about him anyway.'

Rebus paused.

'How is Samantha anyway?' Cafferty asked. 'That's her name, isn't it?'

'She's ...'

'Because it looks like I'll be fulfilling *my* side of our bargain any day. While you, on the other hand ...'

'Matsumoto was Yakuza: heard of them?'

A moment's silence. 'I've heard of them.'

'Telford's helping them buy a country club.'

'What in God's name do they want with that?'

'I'm not sure.'

Cafferty was silent again. Rebus almost thought his mobile had

died. Then: 'He's got big ideas, hasn't he?' Like there was just a touch of respect there, battling the sense of territorial breach.

'We've both seen people overreach themselves.' An idea formed in Rebus's mind, a sudden notion of where everything was headed.

'Looks like Telford's got plenty of stretch left in him though,' Cafferty was saying. 'And me, I'm not even halfway through *my* stretch.'

'Know something, Cafferty? Every time you start to sound beaten, that's when I know you're just coming to the boil.'

'You know I'm going to have to retaliate, whether I want to or not. A little ritual we have to go through, like shaking hands.'

'How many men have you got?'

'More than enough.'

'Listen, one last thing ...' Rebus couldn't believe he was telling his arch-enemy this. 'Jake Tarawicz arrived here today. I think the fireworks were meant to impress him.'

'Telford torched my house just so he'd have something to show that ugly Russian bastard?'

Like a kid showing off to his elders, Rebus was thinking. Overreaching himself ...

'That's it, Strawman!' Cafferty was back to being furious. 'All bets are off. Those two want to get dirty with Morris Gerald Cafferty, I'll give them both anthrax. I'll infect the pair of them. They'll think they've caught full-blown fucking AIDS by the time I'm finished!'

Which was about as much as Rebus could take. He put down the phone, drank his cold coffee, checked his messages. Patience wondered if he could make it to supper. Rhona said they'd carried out another scan. Bobby Hogan wanted a word.

He called the hospital first. Rhona said something about a new scan to assess the amount of damage done to the brain.

'Then why the hell didn't they give her *that* scan straight away?'

'I don't know.'

'Did you ask?'

'Why don't *you* come down here? Why don't *you* ask? Seems like when I'm not here, you're happy enough spending time with Samantha, even sleeping in the chair. What is it – do I scare you off?'

'Look, Rhona, I'm sorry. It's been a rough day.'

'For you and everyone else.'

'I know. I'm a selfish bastard.'

The rest of their conversation was predictable. It was a relief to say goodbye. He tried Patience, got her answering machine, and told it he'd be happy to accept the invitation. Then he called Bobby Hogan.

'Hiya, Bobby, what've you got?'

'Not much. I had a word with Telford.'

'I know, he told me.'

'You've been speaking to him?'

'Says he never knew Lintz. Did you talk to The Family?'

'The ones who frequent the office. Same story.'

'Did you mention the five thou'?'

'Think I'm stupid? Listen, I thought you might be able to help me.'

'Fire away.'

'Lintz's address book, I found a couple of addresses for a Dr Colquhoun. Thought at first it must be his GP.'

'He's a Slavic Studies lecturer.'

'Only Lintz seems to have been keeping track of him. Three changes of address, going back twenty years. First two addresses have phone numbers with them, but not the most recent. I checked, and Colquhoun's only been at this latest address three years.'

'So?'

'So Lintz didn't have his home phone number. So if he wanted to speak to him ...'

Rebus twigged. 'He'd phone the university.' The call on Lintz's bill: twenty-odd minutes. Rebus was remembering what Colquhoun had said about Lintz.

*I met him at a few social functions ... our departments weren't that close ... As I say, we weren't close ...*

'They weren't in the same department,' Rebus said. 'Colquhoun told me they'd barely met ...'

'So how come Lintz has been keeping up with Colquhoun's various moves around the city?'

'Beats me, Bobby. Have you asked him?'

'No, but I intend to.'

'He's lying low. I've been trying to talk to him for a week.' Last seen at the Morvena: did Colquhoun link Telford to Lintz?

'Well, he's back now.'

'What?'

'I've an appointment with him at his office.'

'Count me in,' Rebus said, getting to his feet.

As Rebus parked in Buccleuch Place – he was in an unmarked Astra, courtesy of St Leonard's – he saw the car in the neighbouring bay make to leave. He waved, but Kirstin Mede didn't see him, and by the time he'd found the horn, she'd pulled away. He wondered how well she knew Colquhoun. After all, she'd been the one to suggest him as a translator ...

Hogan, standing by the railings, had seen Rebus's attempts at communication.

'Someone you know?'

'Kirstin Mede.'

Hogan placed the name. 'The one who did those translations?'

Rebus looked up at the Slavic Studies building. 'Have you tracked down David Levy?'

'Daughter still hasn't heard from him.'

'How long has that been?'

'Long enough to seem suspicious in itself, only she doesn't seem too bothered.'

'How do you want to play this?' Rebus asked.

'Depends what he's like.'

'You ask your questions. Me, I just want to be there.'

Hogan looked at him, then shrugged and pushed open the door. They started to climb the worn stone steps. 'Hope they haven't put him in the penthouse.'

Colquhoun's name was on a piece of card stuck to a door on the second floor. They pushed it open, and were confronted with a short hallway and another five or six doors. Colquhoun's office was first on the right, and he was already standing in the doorway.

'Thought I heard you. Sound carries in this place. Come in, come in.' He wasn't expecting Hogan to have company. His words dried up when he saw Rebus. He walked back into his office, motioned for both officers to sit, then fussed about moving their chairs around so they'd be facing his desk.

'Terrible muddle,' he said, kicking over a pile of books.

'Know the feeling, sir,' Hogan said.

Colquhoun peered in Rebus's direction. 'My secretary says you used the library.'

'Filling in some of the gaps, sir.' Rebus kept his voice level.

'Yes, Candice ...' Colquhoun was thoughtful. 'Is she ... ? I mean, did she ... ?'

'But today, sir,' Hogan interrupted, 'we want to talk to you about Joseph Lintz.'

Colquhoun sat down heavily in his wooden chair, which creaked under the weight. Then he sprang to his feet again. 'Tea, coffee? You must excuse the mess. Not normally this disorganised ...'

'Not for us, sir,' Hogan said. 'If you'd just take a seat?'

'Of course, of course.' Again, Colquhoun collapsed on to his chair.

'Joseph Lintz, sir,' Hogan prompted.

'Terrible tragedy ... terrible. They think it's murder, you know.'

'Yes, sir, we do know.'

'Of course you do. Apologies.'

The desk in front of Colquhoun was venerable and spotted with woodworm. The shelves were bowed under the weight of textbooks. There were old framed prints on the walls, and a blackboard with the single word CHARACTER on it. University paperwork was piled on the window ledge, all but blacking out the bottom two panes. The smell in the room was that of intellect gone awry.

'It's just that Mr Lintz had your name in his address book, sir,' Hogan continued. 'And we're talking to all his friends.'

'Friends?' Colquhoun looked up. 'I wouldn't call us "friends" exactly. We were colleagues, but I don't think I met him socially more than three or four times in twenty-odd years.'

'Funny, he seems to have taken an interest in you, sir.' Hogan flipped open his notebook. 'Starting with your address in Warrender Park Terrace.'

'I haven't lived there since the seventies.'

'He also has your telephone number there. After that, it's Currie.'

'I thought I was ready for the rural life ...'

'In Currie?' Hogan sounded sceptical.

Colquhoun tipped his head. 'I eventually realised my mistake.'

'And moved to Duddingston.'

'Not at first. I rented a few properties while I was looking for a place to buy.'

'Mr Lintz has your telephone number in Currie, but not for the Duddingston address.'

'Interesting. I went ex-directory when I moved.'

'Any reason for that, sir?'

Colquhoun swayed in his chair. 'Well, I'm sure it sounds awful ...'

'Try us.'

'I didn't want students bothering me.'

'Did they do that?'

'Oh, yes, phoning to ask questions, advice. Worried about exams or wanting deadlines extended.'

'Do you remember giving Mr Lintz your address, sir?'

'No, I don't.'

'You're sure of that?'

'Yes, but it wouldn't have been hard for him to find out. I mean, he could just have asked one of the secretaries.'

Colquhoun was beginning to look more agitated than ever. The little chair could barely contain him.

'Sir,' Hogan said, 'is there anything you want to tell us about Mr Lintz, anything at all?'

Colquhoun just shook his head, staring at the surface of his desk.

Rebus decided to use their joker. 'Mr Lintz made a phone call to this office. He was talking for over twenty minutes.'

'That's ... simply not true.' Colquhoun mopped his face with a handkerchief. 'Look, gentlemen, I'd like to help, but the fact is, I barely knew Joseph Lintz.'

'And he didn't phone you?'

'No.'

'And you've no idea why he'd keep note of your Edinburgh addresses for the past three decades?'

'No.'

Hogan sighed theatrically. 'Then we're wasting your time and ours.' He got to his feet. 'Thank you, Dr Colquhoun.'

The look of relief on the old academic's face told both detectives all they needed to know.

They said nothing as they walked back downstairs – like Colquhoun had said, sound could travel. Hogan's car was nearest. They rested against it as they talked.

'He was worried,' Rebus said.

'Hiding something. Think we should go back up?'

Rebus shook his head. 'Let him sweat for a day or so, then hit him.'

'He didn't like the fact you were there.'

'I noticed.'

'That restaurant ... Lintz dining with an elderly gent.'

'We could tell him we've got a description from the restaurant staff.'

'Without going into specifics?'

Rebus nodded. 'See if it flushes him out.'

'What about the other person Lintz took to lunch, the young woman?'

'No idea.'

'Posh restaurant, old man, young woman ...'

'A call girl?'

Hogan smiled. 'Do they still call them that?'

Rebus was thoughtful. 'It might explain the phone call to Telford. Only I doubt Telford's daft enough to discuss business like that from his office. Besides, his escort agency runs from another address.'

'Fact is, he called Telford's office.'

'And nobody's owned up to talking to him.'

'Escort agency stuff, could be very innocent. He doesn't want to eat alone, hires some company. Afterwards, a peck on the cheek and separate taxis.' Hogan exhaled. 'This one's running in circles.'

'I know the feeling, Bobby.'

They looked up at the second-floor windows. Saw Colquhoun staring down, handkerchief to his face.

'Let's leave him to it,' Hogan said, unlocking his car.

'I've been meaning to ask: how did you get on with Abernethy?'

'He didn't give me too much trouble.' Hogan avoided Rebus's eyes.

'So he's gone?'

Hogan had disappeared into the driver's seat. 'He's gone. See you, John.'

Leaving Rebus on the pavement, a frown on his face. He waited till Hogan's car had turned the corner, then went back into the stairwell and climbed the steps again.

Colquhoun's office door was open, the old man fidgeting behind his desk. Rebus sat down opposite him, said nothing.

'I've been ill,' Colquhoun said.

'You've been hiding.' Colquhoun started shaking his head. 'You told them where to find Candice.' Head still shaking. 'Then you got worried, so they hid you away, maybe in a room at the casino.' Rebus paused. 'How am I doing?'

'I've no comment to make,' Colquhoun snapped.

'What if I just keep talking then?'

'I want you to leave now. If you don't go, I'll have to call my lawyer.'

'Name of Charles Groal?' Rebus smiled. 'They might have spent the last few days tutoring you, but they can't change what you've done.' Rebus stood up. '*You* sent Candice back to them. *You* did that.' He leaned down over the desk. 'You knew all along who she was, didn't you? That's why you were so nervous. How come you knew who she was, Dr Colquhoun? How come you're so chummy with a turd like Tommy Telford?'

Colquhoun picked up the receiver, his hands shaking so badly he kept missing the digits.

'Don't bother,' Rebus said. 'I'm going. But we'll talk again. And you *will* talk. You'll talk because you're a coward, Dr Colquhoun. And cowards always talk eventually ...'

# 23

The Crime Squad office at Fettes: home of country and western; Claverhouse terminating a phone call. No sign of Ormiston and Clarke.

'They're out on a call,' Claverhouse said.

'Any progress on that stabbing?'

'What do you think?'

'I think there's something you should know.' Rebus seated himself behind Siobhan Clarke's desk, admiring its tidy surface. He opened a drawer: it was tidy, too. Compartments, he thought to himself. Clarke was very good at dividing her life into separate compartments. 'Jake Tarawicz is in town. He's got this outrageous white limo, hard to miss.' Rebus paused. 'And he's brought Candice with him.'

'What's he doing here?'

'I think he's here for the show.'

'What show?'

'Cafferty and Telford, fifteen rounds of bare-knuckle and no referee.' Rebus leaned forward, arms on the desk. 'And I've got an idea where it's headed.'

Rebus went home, called Patience and told her he might be late.

'How late?' she asked.

'How late can I be without us falling out?'

She thought about it. 'Half-nine.'

'I'll be there.'

He checked his answering machine: David Levy, saying he could be reached at home.

'Where the hell have you been?' Rebus asked, when Levy's daughter had put her father on.

'I had business elsewhere.'

'You know your daughter's been worried. You might have phoned her.'

'Does this counselling service come free?'

'My fee cancels out when you answer a few questions. You know Lintz is dead?'

'I've heard.'

'Where were you when you *heard*?'

'I've told you, I had business ... Inspector, am I a suspect?'

'Practically the only one we've got.'

Levy gave a harsh laugh. 'This is preposterous. I'm not a ...' He couldn't say the word. Rebus guessed his daughter was within hearing distance. 'Hold on a moment, please.' The receiver was muffled: Levy ordering his daughter out of the room. He came back on, voice lower than before.

'Inspector, for the record, I feel I must let you know how *angry* I felt when I heard the news. Justice may have been done or not done – I can't argue those points just now – but what is absolutely certain is that history has been cheated here!'

'Of the trial?'

'Of course! And the Rat Line, too. With each suspect who dies, we're that much less likely to prove its existence. Lintz isn't the first, you know. One man, the brakes failed on his car. Another fell from an upstairs window. There've been two apparent suicides, six more cases of what look like natural causes.'

'Am I going to get the full conspiracy theory?'

'This isn't a joke, Inspector.'

'Did you hear me laughing? What about you, Mr Levy? When did you leave Edinburgh?'

'Before Lintz died.'

'Did you see him?' Rebus knowing he had, but seeking a lie.

Levy paused. '*Confronted* would be a more apposite term.'

'Just the once?'

'Three times. He wasn't keen to talk about himself, but I stated my case nonetheless.'

'And the phone call?'

Levy paused. 'What phone call?'

'When he called you at the Roxburghe.'

'I wish I'd recorded it for posterity. Rage, Inspector. Foul-mouthed rage. I'm positive he was mad.'

'Mad?'

'You didn't hear him. He's very good at seeming perfectly normal
– he must be, or he wouldn't have gone undetected for so long. But
the man is ... was ... mad. Truly mad.'

Rebus was remembering the crooked little man in the cemetery,
and how he'd suddenly let fly at a passing dog. Poise, to rage, to
poise again.

'The story he told ...' Levy sighed.

'Was this in the restaurant?'

'What restaurant?'

'Sorry, I thought the two of you went out to lunch.'

'I can assure you we didn't.'

'So what story is this then?'

'These men, Inspector, they come to justify their actions by
blanking them out, or by transference. Transference is the more
common.'

'They tell themselves someone else did it?'

'Yes.'

'And that was Lintz's story?'

'Less believable than most. He said it was all a case of mistaken
identity.'

'And who did he think you were mistaking him for?'

'A colleague at the university ... a Dr Colquhoun.'


Rebus called Hogan, gave him the story.

'I told Levy you'd want to speak to him.'

'I'll phone him right now.'

'What do you think?'

'Colquhoun a war criminal?' Hogan snorted.

'Me, too,' Rebus said. 'I asked Levy why he didn't think any of
this worth telling us.'

'And?'

'He said as he gave it no credence, it was worthless.'

'All the same, we'd better talk to Colquhoun again. Tonight.'

'I've other plans for tonight, Bobby.'

'Fair enough, John. Look, I really appreciate all your help.'

'You're going to talk to him alone?'

'I'll have someone with me.'

Rebus hated being left out. If he cancelled that late supper ...

'Let me know how you get on.' Rebus put the telephone down.
On the hi-fi: Eddie Harris, upbeat and melodic. He went and soaked

in a bath, facecloth across his eyes. Everyone, it seemed to him, lived their lives out of little boxes, opening different ones for different occasions. Nobody ever gave their whole self away. Cops were like that, each box a safety mechanism. Most people you met in the course of your life, you never even learned their names. Everybody was boxed off from everybody else. It was called society.

He was wondering about Joseph Lintz, always questioning, turning every conversation into a philosophy lesson. Stuck in his own little box, identity blocked off elsewhere, his past a necessary mystery ... Joseph Lintz, furious when cornered, possibly clinically mad, driven there by ... what? Memories? Or the lack of them? Driven there by other people?

The Eddie Harris CD was on its last track by the time he emerged from the bathroom. He put on the clothes he'd be wearing to Patience's. Only he had a couple of stops to make first: check on Sammy at the hospital, and then a meeting at Torphichen.

'The gang's all here,' he said, walking into the CID room.

Shug Davidson, Claverhouse, Ormiston, and Siobhan Clarke, all seated around the one big desk, drinking coffee from identical Rangers mugs. Rebus pulled a chair over.

'Have you filled them in, Shug?'

Davidson nodded.

'What about the shop?'

'I was just getting to that.' Davidson picked up a pen, played with it. 'The last owner went out of business, not enough passing trade. The shop was shut the best part of a year, then suddenly reopened — under new management and with prices that stopped the locals looking elsewhere.'

'And got the workers at Maclean's interested, too,' Rebus added. 'So how long's it been going?'

'Five weeks, selling cut-price everything.'

'No profit motive, you see.' Rebus looked around the table. This was mostly for the benefit of Ormiston and Clarke; he'd given Claverhouse the story already.

'And the owners?' Clarke asked.

'Well, the shop's *run* by a couple of lads called Declan Delaney and Ken Wilkinson. Guess where they come from?'

'Paisley,' Claverhouse said, keen to hurry things on.

'So they're part of Telford's gang?' Ormiston asked.

'Not in so many words, but they're connected to him, no doubt about that.' Davidson blew his nose loudly. 'Of course, Dec and Ken are running the shop, but they don't own it.'

'Telford does,' Rebus stated.

'Okay,' Claverhouse said. 'So we've got Telford owning a loss-making business, in the hope of gathering intelligence.'

'I think it goes further than that,' Rebus said. 'I mean, listening in on gossip is one thing, but I don't suppose any of the workers are standing around talking about the various security systems and how to beat them. Dec and Ken are garrulous, perfect for the job Telford's given them. But it's going to look suspicious if they start asking too many questions.'

'So what's Telford looking for?' Ormiston asked. Siobhan Clarke turned to him.

'A mole,' she said.

'Makes sense,' Davidson went on. 'That place *is* well-protected, but not impregnable. We all know any break-in's going to be a lot easier with someone on the inside.'

'So what do we do?' Clarke asked.

'We fight Telford's sting with our own,' Rebus explained. 'He wants a man on the inside, *we* give him one.'

'I'm seeing the head of Maclean's later on tonight,' Davidson said.

'I'll come with you,' Claverhouse said, keen not to be left out.

'So we put someone of our own inside the factory.' Clarke was working it out for herself. 'And they shoot their mouth off in the shop, making them an attractive proposition. And we sit and pray that Telford approaches *them* rather than anyone else?'

'The less luck we have to rely on the better,' Claverhouse said. 'Got to do this right.'

'Which is why we work it like this.' Rebus said. 'There's a bookie called Marty Jones. He owes me one big favour. Say our man's just been into Telford's shop. As he's coming out, a car pulls up. Marty and a couple of his men. Marty wants some bets paid off. Big argy-bargy, and a punch in the guts as warning.'

Clarke could see it. 'He stumbles back into the shop, sits down to catch his breath. Dec and Ken ask him what's going on.'

'And he gives them the whole sorry story: gambling debts, broken marriage, whatever.'

'To make him more attractive still,' Davidson said, 'we make him a security guard.'

221

Ormiston looked at him. 'You think Maclean's will go for it?'

'We'll persuade them,' Claverhouse said quietly.

'More importantly,' Clarke asked, 'will *Telford* go for it?'

'Depends how desperate he is,' Rebus answered.

'A man on the inside ...' Ormiston's eyes were alight. 'Working for Telford – it's what we've always wanted.'

Claverhouse nodded. 'Just one thing.' He looked at Rebus and Davidson. 'Who's it going to be? Telford knows us.'

'We get someone from outside,' Rebus said. 'Someone I've worked with before. Telford won't have heard of him. He's a good man.'

'Is he willing?'

There was silence around the table.

'Depends who's asking,' a voice called from the doorway. A stocky man with thick, well-groomed hair and narrow eyes. Rebus got up, shook Jack Morton's hand, made the introductions.

'I'll need a history,' Morton said, all business. 'John's explained the deal, and I like it. But I'll need a flat, something scruffy and local.'

'First thing tomorrow,' Claverhouse said. 'Look, we need to talk to our bosses about this, make sure it's cleared.' He looked at Morton. 'What did you tell your own boss, Jack?'

'I've got a few days off, didn't think it was worth mentioning.'

Claverhouse nodded. 'I'll talk to him as soon as we get the go-ahead.'

'We need that go-ahead *tonight*,' Rebus said. 'Telford's men may already have lined someone up. If we hang around, we might lose it.'

'Agreed,' Claverhouse said, checking his watch. 'I'll make a few phone calls, interrupt a few post-prandial whiskies.'

'I'll back you up if need be,' Davidson said.

Rebus looked at Jack Morton – his friend – and mouthed the word 'thanks'. Morton shrugged it off. Then Rebus got to his feet.

'I'm going to have to leave you to it,' he told the assembly. 'You've got my pager number and mobile if you need me.'

He was halfway down the hall when Siobhan Clarke caught him.

'I just wanted to say thanks.'

Rebus blinked. 'What for?'

'Ever since you got Claverhouse excited, the tape machine's stayed off.'

# 24

Supper was fine. He talked to Patience about Sammy, Rhona, his obsession with sixties music, his ignorance of fashion. She talked about work, an experimental cookery class she'd been taking, a trip to Orkney she was thinking of. They ate fresh pasta with a homemade mussel and prawn sauce, and shared a bottle of Highland Spring. Rebus tried his damnedest to forget about the sting operation, Tarawicz, Candice, Lintz … She could see at least half his mind was elsewhere; tried not to feel betrayed. She asked him if he was going home.

'Is that an invitation?'

'I'm not sure … I suppose so.'

'Let's pretend it wasn't, then I won't feel like complete scum when I turn it down.'

'That sounds reasonable. Things on your mind?'

'I'm surprised you can't see them leaking out of my ears.'

'Do you want to talk about any of it? I mean, you may not have noticed, but we've talked about practically everything tonight except *us*.'

'I don't think talking would help.'

'But bottling it up does?' She threw out an arm. 'Behold the Scottish male, at his happiest when in denial.'

'What am I denying?'

'For a start, you're denying *me* access to your life.'

'Sorry.'

'Christ, John, get the word put on a t-shirt.'

'Thanks, maybe I will.' He got up from the sofa.

'Oh, hell, I'm sorry.' She smiled. 'Look, you've got me at it now.'

'Yes, it's catching, all right.'

She stood up, touched his arm. 'You're worried about taking the test?'

'Right now, believe it or not, that's the least of my worries.'

'It should be. Everything's going to be fine.'

'Hunky dory.'

'Hunky dory,' she repeated, smiling again. She pecked him on the cheek. 'You know, I've never quite understood what that meant.'

'*Hunky Dory?*'

She nodded.

'It's a David Bowie album.' He kissed her brow.

He would never know what instinct made him decide on the detour, but he was glad he'd made it. For there, parked outside the Morvena casino, stood the white stretch limo. The driver leaned against it, smoking a cigarette, looking bored. From time to time he took out a mobile phone and had a short conversation. Rebus stared at the Morvena, thinking: Tommy Telford has a slice of the place; the hostesses come from Eastern Europe, provided by Mr Pink Eyes. Rebus wondered how closely entwined the two empires – Telford's and Tarawicz's – really were. And add a third strand: the Yakuza. Something refused to add up.

*What was Tarawicz getting out of it?*

Miriam Kenworthy had suggested muscle: Scottish hardmen trained in Telford's organisation then shipped south. But it wasn't *enough* of a trade. There had to be more. Was Mr Pink Eyes due a share of the Maclean's pay-out? Was Telford tempting him with some Yakuza action? What about the theory that Telford was Tarawicz's supplier?

At quarter to midnight, another phone call had the driver springing into action. He flicked his cigarette on to the road, started opening doors. Tarawicz and his entourage breezed out of the casino looking like they owned the world. Candice was wearing a black full-length coat over a shimmering pink dress which didn't quite reach her knees. She was carrying a bottle of champagne. Rebus counted three of Tarawicz's men, remembering them from the scrapyard. Two no-shows: the lawyer, and the Crab. Telford was there, too, with a couple of minders, one of them Pretty-Boy. Pretty-Boy was making sure his jacket hung right, trying to decide whether it would look better buttoned. But his eyes raked the darkened street. Rebus had parked away from the street-lights, confident he was invisible. They were piling into the limo. Rebus watched it move off, waited

until it had signalled and turned a corner before switching on his own headlamps and starting the engine.

They drove to the same hotel Matsumoto had stayed at. Telford's Range Rover was parked outside. Pedestrians – late-night couples hurrying home from the pub – turned to stare at the limo. Saw the entourage spill out, probably mistook them for pop stars or film people. Rebus as casting director: Candice's startlet being mauled by sleazy producer Tarawicz. Telford a sleek young operator on his way up, looking to learn from the producer before toppling him. The others were bit players, except maybe Pretty-Boy, who was hanging on to his boss's coattails, maybe readying himself for his own big break …

If Tarawicz had a suite, there might be room for them all. If not, they'd be in the bar. Rebus parked, followed them inside.

The lights hurt his eyes. The reception area was all mirrors and pine, brass and pot-plants. He tried to look like he'd been left behind by the party. They were settling down in the bar, through a double set of swing-doors with glass panels. Rebus hung back. Sitting target in the empty reception; bigger target in the bar. Retreat to the car? Someone was standing up, shrugging off a long black coat. Candice. Smiling now, saying something to Tarawicz, who was nodding. Took her hand and planted a kiss in the palm. Went further: a slow lick across the palm and up her wrist. Everyone laughing, whistling. Candice looking numb. Tarawicz got to the inside of her elbow and took a bite. She squealed, pulled back, rubbed her arm. Tarawicz had his tongue out, playing to the gallery. Give Tommy Telford credit: he wasn't grinning along with everyone else.

Candice stood there, a stooge to her owner's little act. Then he waved her off with a flick of his hand. Permission granted, she started for the doors. Rebus moved back into a recess where the public telephones sat. She turned right out of the doors, disappeared into the ladies'. At the table, they were busy ordering more champagne – and an orange juice for Pretty-Boy.

Rebus looked around, took a deep breath. Walked into the ladies' toilets like it was the most natural thing in the world.

She was splashing her face with water. A little brown bottle sat next to the sink. Three yellow tablets lying ready. Rebus swept them on to the floor.

'Hey!' She turned, saw him, put a hand to her mouth. She tried backing away, but there was nowhere to go.

'Is this what you want, Dunya?' Using her real name as a weapon: friendly fire.

She frowned, shook her head: incomprehension on her face. He grabbed her shoulders, squeezed.

'Sammy,' he hissed. 'Sammy's in hospital. Very ill.' He pointed towards the hotel bar. '*They* tried to kill her.'

The gist got through. Candice shook her head. Tears were smudging her mascara.

'Did you tell Sammy anything?'

She frowned again.

'Anything about Telford or Tarawicz? Did you talk to Sammy about them?'

A slow, determined shake of the head. 'Sammy ... hospital?'

He nodded. Turned his hands into a steering-wheel, made engine noises, then slammed a fist into his open palm. Candice turned away, grabbed the sink. She was crying, shoulders jerking. She scrabbled for more tablets. Rebus tore them from her hand.

'You want to blank it all out? Forget it.' He threw them on to the floor, crushed them under his heel. She crouched down, licked a finger and dabbed at the powder. Rebus hauled her to her feet. Her knees wouldn't lock; he had to keep holding her upright. She wouldn't look him in the eyes.

'It's funny, we first met in a toilet, remember? You were scared. You hated your life so much you'd slashed your arms.' He touched her scarred wrists. 'That's how much you hated your life. And now you're straight back in it.'

Her face was against his jacket, tears dropping on to his shirt.

'Remember the Japanese?' he cooed. 'Remember Juniper Green, the golf club?'

She drew back, wiped her nose on her bare wrist. 'Juniper Green,' she said.

'That's right. And a big factory ... the car stopped, and everyone looked at the factory.'

She was nodding.

'Did anyone talk about it? Did they say *anything*?'

She was shaking her head. 'John ...' Her hands on his lapels. She sniffed, swiped at her nose again. She slid down his jacket, his shirt. She was on her knees, looking up at him, blinking tears, while her

damp fingers scored white powder from the tiles. Rebus crouched down in front of her.

'Come with me,' he said. 'I'll help you.' He pointed towards the door, towards the world outside, but she was busy in her own world now, fingers going to her mouth. Someone pushed open the door. Rebus looked up.

A woman: young, drunk, hair falling into her eyes. She stopped and studied the two people on the floor, then smiled and headed for a cubicle.

'Save some for me,' she said, sliding the lock.

'Go, John.' There was powder at the corners of Candice's mouth. A tiny piece of tablet had lodged between her front two teeth. 'Please, go now.'

'I don't want you getting hurt.' He sought her hands, squeezed them.

'I do not hurt any more.'

She got to her feet and turned from him. Checked her face in the mirror, wiped away the powder and dabbed at her mascara. Blew her nose and took a deep breath.

Walked out of the toilets.

Rebus waited a moment, time enough for her to reach the table. Then he opened the door and made his exit. Walked back to his car on legs that seemed to belong to someone else.

Drove home, not quite crying.

But not quite not.

# 25

Four in the morning, the blessed telephone pulled him out of a nightmare.

Prison-camp prostitutes with teeth filed to points were kneeling in front of him. Jake Tarawicz, in full SS regalia, held him from behind, telling him resistance was useless. Through the barred window, Rebus could see black berets – the *maquis*, busy freeing the camp but leaving his billet till last. Alarm bells ringing, everything telling him that salvation was at hand ...

... alarm becoming his telephone ... he staggered from his chair, picked it up.

'Yes.'

'John?' The Chief Super's voice: Aberdonian, instantly recognisable.

'Yes, sir?'

'We've got a spot of bother. Get down here.'

'What kind of bother?'

'I'll tell you when you get here. Now *shift*.'

Night shift, to be precise. The city asleep. St Leonard's was lit up, the tenements around it dark. No sign of the Farmer's 'spot of bother'. The Chief Super's office: the Farmer in conference with Gill Templer.

'Sit down, John. Coffee?'

'No, thanks, sir.'

While Templer and the Chief Super were deciding who should speak, Rebus helped them out.

'Tommy Telford's businesses have been hit.'

Templer blinked. 'Telepathy?'

'Cafferty's offices and taxis got firebombed. So did his house.' Rebus shrugged. 'We knew there'd be payback.'

'Did we?'

What could he say? *I did, because Cafferty told me*. He didn't think they'd like that. 'I just put two and two together.'

The Farmer poured himself a mug of coffee. 'So now we've got open war.'

'What got hit?'

'The arcade on Flint Street,' Templer said. 'Not too much damage: the place has a sprinkler system.' She smiled: an amusement arcade with a sprinkler system ... not that Telford was careful or anything.

'Plus a couple of nightclubs,' the Farmer added. 'And a casino.'

'Which one?'

The Chief Super looked to Templer, who answered: 'The Morvena'.

'Any injuries?'

'The manager and a couple of friends: concussion and bruising.'

'Which they got ...?'

'Falling over each other as they ran down the stairs.'

Rebus nodded. 'Funny how some people have trouble with stairs.' He sat back. 'So what does all this have to do with me? Don't tell me: having disposed of Telford's Japanese partner, I decided to take up fire-raising?'

'John ...' The Farmer got up, rested his backside against the desk. 'The three of us, we know you had nothing to do with that. Tell me, we found an untouched half-bottle of malt under your driver's seat ...'

Rebus nodded. 'It's mine.' Another of his little suicide bombs.

'So why would you be drinking a supermarket blend?'

'Is that what the screw-top was? The cheap bastards.'

'No alcohol in your blood either. Meantime, as you say, Cafferty's in the frame for this. And Cafferty and you ...'

'You want me to talk to him?'

Gill Templer leaned forward in her chair. 'We don't want war.'

'Takes two to make a ceasefire.'

'I'll talk to Telford,' she said.

'He's a sharp little bugger, watch out for him.'

She nodded. 'Will you talk to Cafferty?'

Rebus didn't want a war. It would take Telford's mind off the Maclean's heist. He'd need all the troops he could get; the shop might even have to close. No, Rebus didn't want a war.

'I'll talk to him,' he said.

Breakfast-time at Barlinnie.

Rebus jangling after the drive, knowing a whisky would smooth out his nerve-endings. Cafferty waiting for him, same room as before.

'Top of the morning, Strawman.' Arms folded, looking pleased with himself.

'You've had a busy night.'

'On the contrary, I slept as well as I ever have done in this place. What about you?'

'I was up at four o'clock, checking damage reports. I could have done without driving all the way here. Maybe if you gave me the number of your mobile ...?'

Cafferty grinned. 'I hear the nightclubs were gutted.'

'I think your boys are making themselves look good.' Cafferty's grin tightened. 'Telford's premises seem to have state of the art fire prevention. Smoke sensors, sprinklers, fire-doors. The damage was minimal.'

'This is just the start,' Cafferty said. 'I'll have that little arse-wipe.'

'I thought that was supposed to be *my* job?'

'I've seen precious little from you, Strawman.'

'I've got something in the pipeline. If it comes off, you'll like it.'

Cafferty's eyes narrowed. 'Give me details. Make me believe you.'

But Rebus was shaking his head. 'Sometimes, you just have to have faith.' He paused. 'Deal?'

'I must have missed something.'

Rebus spelled it out. 'Back off. Leave Telford to me.'

'We've been through this. He hits me and I do nothing, I look like something you'd step around on the pavement.'

'We're talking to him, warning him off.'

'And meantime I'm supposed to trust you to get the job done?'

'We shook hands on it.'

Cafferty snorted. 'I've shaken hands with a lot of bastards.'

'And now you've met an exception to the rule.'

'You're an exception to a lot of rules, Strawman.' Cafferty looked thoughtful. 'The casino, the clubs, the arcade ... they weren't badly hit?'

'My guess is the sprinklers will have done as much damage as anything.'

Cafferty's jaw hardened. 'Makes me look even more of a mug.'

Rebus sat in silence, waiting for him to finish whatever chess-game was being played inside his head.

'Okay,' the gangster said at last, 'I'll call off the troops. Maybe it's time to do some recruiting anyway.' He looked up at Rebus. 'Time for some fresh blood.'

Which reminded Rebus of another job he'd been putting off.

Danny Simpson lived at home with his mother in a terraced house in Wester Hailes.

This bleak housing-scheme, designed by sadists who'd never had to live anywhere near it, had a heart which had shrivelled but refused to stop pumping. Rebus had a lot of respect for the place. Tommy Smith had grown up here, practising with socks stuffed into the mouth of his sax, so as not to disturb the neighbours through the thin walls of the high-rise. Tommy Smith was one of the best sax players Rebus had ever heard.

In a sense, Wester Hailes existed outside the real world: it wasn't on a route from anywhere to anywhere. Rebus had never had cause to drive *through* it – he only went there if he had business there. The city bypass flew past it, offering many drivers their only encounter with Wester Hailes. They saw: high-rise blocks, terraces, tracts of unused playing field. They didn't see: people. Not so much concrete jungle as concrete vacuum.

Rebus knocked on Danny Simpson's door. He didn't know what he was going to say to the young man. He just wanted to see him again. He wanted to see him without the blood and the pain. Wanted to see him whole and of a piece.

Wanted to see him.

But Danny Simpson wasn't in, and neither was his mother. A neighbour, lacking her top set of dentures, came out and explained the situation.

The situation took Rebus to the Infirmary, where, in a small, gloomy ward not easily found, Danny Simpson lay in bed, head bandaged, sweating like he'd just played a full ninety minutes. He wasn't conscious. His mother sat beside him, stroking his wrist. A nurse explained to Rebus that a hospice would be the best place for Danny, supposing they could find him a bed.

'What happened?'

'We think infection must have set in. When you lose your resistance ... the world's a lethal place.' She shrugged, looked like she'd been through it all once too often. Danny's mother had seen them talking. Maybe she thought Rebus was a doctor. She got up and came towards him, then just stood there, waiting for him to speak.

'I came to see Danny,' he said.

'Yes?'

'The night he ... the night of his accident, I was the one who brought him here. I just wondered how he was doing.'

'See for yourself.' Her voice was breaking.

Rebus thought: a five-minute walk from here, he'd be in Sammy's room. He'd thought her situation unique, because it was unique to *him*. Now he saw that within a short radius of Sammy's bed, other parents were crying, and squeezing their children's hands, and asking why.

'I'm really sorry,' he said. 'I wish ...'

'Me, too,' the woman said. 'You know, he's never been a bad laddie. Cheeky, but never bad. His problem was, he was always itching for something new, something to stop him getting bored. We all know where that can lead.'

Rebus nodded, suddenly not wanting to be here, not wanting to hear Danny Simpson's life story. He had enough ghosts to contend with as it was. He squeezed the woman's arm.

'Look,' he said, 'I'm sorry, but I have to go.'

She nodded distractedly, wandered off in the direction of her son's bed. Rebus wanted to curse Danny Simpson for the mere *possibility* that he'd passed on the virus. He realised now that if they'd met on the doorstep, that's the way their conversation would have gone, and maybe Rebus would have gone further.

He wanted to curse him ... but he couldn't. It would be every bit as efficacious as cursing the Big Man. A waste of time and breath. So instead he went to Sammy's room, to find that she was back on her own. No other patients, no nursing staff, no Rhona. He kissed her forehead. It tasted salty. Sweat: she needed wiping down. There was a smell he hadn't noticed before. Talcum powder. He sat down, took her warm hands in his.

'How are you doing, Sammy? I keep meaning to bring in some Oasis, see if that would bring you round. Your mum sits here listening to classical. I wonder if you can hear it. I don't even know

if you like that sort of stuff. Lots of things we've never got round to talking about.'

He saw something. Stood up to be sure. Movement behind her eyelids.

'Sammy? Sammy?'

He hadn't seen her do that before. Pushed the button beside her bed. Waited for a nurse to come. Pushed it again.

'Come on, come on.'

Eyelids fluttering … then stopping.

'Sammy!'

Door opening, nurse coming in.

'What is it?'

Rebus: 'I thought I saw … she was moving.'

'Moving?'

'Just her eyes, like she was trying to open them.'

'I'll fetch a doctor.'

'Come on, Sammy, try again. Wakey-wakey, sweetheart.' Patting her wrists, then her cheeks.

The doctor arrived. He was the same one Rebus had shouted at that first day. Lifted her eyelids, shone a thin torch into them, pulling it away, checking her pupils.

'If you saw it, I'm sure it was there.'

'Yes, but does it mean anything?'

'Hard to say.'

'Try anyway.' Eyes boring into the doctor's.

'She's asleep. She has dreams. Sometimes when you dream you experience REM: Rapid Eye Movement.'

'So it could be …' Rebus sought the word '… involuntary?'

'As I say, it's hard to tell. Latest scans show definite improvement.' He paused. '*Minor* improvement, but certainly there.'

Rebus nodding, trembling. The doctor saw it, asked if he needed anything. Rebus shaking his head. The doctor checking his watch, other places to be. The nurse shuffling her feet. Rebus thanked them both and headed out.

HOGAN: You agree to this interview being taped, Dr Colquhoun?

COLQUHOUN: I've no objections.

HOGAN: It's in your interests as well as ours.

COLQUHOUN: I've nothing to hide, Inspector Hogan. (*Coughs.*)

HOGAN: Fine, sir. Maybe we'll just start then?

COLQUHOUN: Might I ask a question? Just for the record, you want to ask me about Joseph Lintz – nothing else?

HOGAN: What else might there be, sir?

COLQUHOUN: I just wanted to check.

HOGAN: You wish to have a solicitor present?

COLQUHOUN: No.

HOGAN: Right you are, sir. Well, if I can begin ... it's really just a question of your relationship with Professor Joseph Lintz.

COLQUHOUN: Yes.

HOGAN: Only, when we spoke before, you said you didn't know Professor Lintz.

COLQUHOUN: I think I said I didn't know him very well.

HOGAN: Okay, sir. If that's what you said ...

COLQUHOUN: It is, to the best of my recollection.

HOGAN: Only, we've had some new information ...

COLQUHOUN: Yes?

HOGAN: That you knew Professor Lintz a little better than that.

COLQUHOUN: And this is according to ...?

HOGAN: New information in our possession. The informant tells us that Joseph Lintz accused you of being a war criminal. Anything to say to that, sir?

COLQUHOUN: Only that it's a lie. An outrageous lie.

HOGAN: He didn't think you were a war criminal?

COLQUHOUN: Oh, he thought it all right! He told me to my face on more than one occasion.

HOGAN: When?

COLQUHOUN: Years back. He got it into his head ... the man was mad, Inspector. I could see that. Driven by demons.

HOGAN: What did he say exactly?

COLQUHOUN: Hard to remember. This was a long time ago, the early 1970s, I suppose.

HOGAN: It would help us if you could ...

COLQUHOUN: He came out with it in the middle of a party. I believe it was some function to welcome a visiting professor. Anyway, Joseph insisted on taking me to one side. He looked feverish. Then he came out with it: I was some sort of Nazi, and I'd come to this country by some circuitous route. He kept on about it.

HOGAN: What did you do?

COLQUHOUN: Told him he was drunk, babbling.

HOGAN: And?

234

COLQUHOUN: And he was. Had to be taken home in a taxi. I said no more about it. In academic circles, one becomes used to a certain amount of ... eccentric behaviour. We're obsessive people, it can't be helped.

HOGAN: But Lintz persisted?

COLQUHOUN: Not really, no. But every few years ... there'd ... he'd say something, allege some atrocity ...

HOGAN: Did he approach you outside the university?

COLQUHOUN: For a time, he telephoned my home.

HOGAN: You moved?

COLQUHOUN: Yes.

HOGAN: To an unlisted phone number?

COLQUHOUN: Eventually.

HOGAN: To stop him calling you?

COLQUHOUN: I suppose that was part of it.

HOGAN: Did you speak to anyone about Lintz?

COLQUHOUN: You mean the authorities? No, no one. He was a nuisance, nothing more.

HOGAN: And then what happened?

COLQUHOUN: Then these stories started appearing in the papers, saying Joseph might be a Nazi, a war criminal. And suddenly he was on my back again.

HOGAN: He phoned you at your office?

COLQUHOUN: Yes.

HOGAN: You lied to us about that?

COLQUHOUN: I'm sorry. I panicked.

HOGAN: What was there to panic about?

COLQUHOUN: Just ... I don't know.

HOGAN: So you met him? To straighten things out?

COLQUHOUN: We had lunch together. He seemed ... lucid. Only what he was saying, it was the stuff of madness. He had a whole history mapped out, only it wasn't mine. I kept saying to him, 'Joseph, when the war ended I wasn't out of my teens.' Besides, I was born and raised here. It's all on record.

HOGAN: What did he say to that?

COLQUHOUN: He said records could be faked.

HOGAN: Faked records ... one way Josef Linzstek could have gone undetected.

COLQUHOUN: I know.

HOGAN: You think Joseph Lintz was Josef Linzstek?

COLQUHOUN: I don't know. Maybe the stories got to him ... he started to believe ... I don't know.

HOGAN: Yes, but these accusations, they began before the media circus – decades before.

COLQUHOUN: That's true.

HOGAN: So he was hounding you. Did he say he would go to the media with his version of events?

COLQUHOUN: He may have ... I can't remember.

HOGAN: Mmm.

COLQUHOUN: You're looking for a motive, aren't you? You're looking for reasons why I'd want him dead.

HOGAN: Did you kill him, Dr Colquhoun?

COLQUHOUN: Emphatically not.

HOGAN: Any idea who did?

COLQUHOUN: No.

HOGAN: Why didn't you tell us? Why tell lies?

COLQUHOUN: Because I knew this would happen. These suspicions. Stupidly, I thought I could circumvent them.

HOGAN: Circumvent?

COLQUHOUN: Yes.

HOGAN: A young woman was seen dining with Lintz, same restaurant he took you to. Any idea who she might be?

COLQUHOUN: None.

HOGAN: You knew Professor Lintz a long time ... what did you think were his sexual proclivities?

COLQUHOUN: Never thought about it.

HOGAN: No?

COLQUHOUN: No.

HOGAN: What about yourself, sir?

COLQUHOUN: I don't see what that ... well, for the record, Inspector, I'm monogamous and heterosexual.

HOGAN: Thank you, sir. I appreciate your frankness.

Rebus switched off the tape.

'I'll bet you did.'

'What do you think?' Bobby Hogan asked.

'I think you mistimed the did-you-do-it. Otherwise, not bad.' Rebus tapped the tape machine. 'Is there much more?'

'Not a lot.'

Rebus switched it back on.

HOGAN: When you met in the restaurant, it was the same routine as before?

COLQUHOUN: Oh, yes. Names, dates ... countries I was taken through on my way into Britain from the continent.

HOGAN: He told you how this was achieved?

COLQUHOUN: He called it the Rat Line. Said it was operated by the Vatican, if you can believe that. And all the western governments were in cahoots to get the top Nazis – the scientists and intellectuals – away from the Russians. I mean, really ... it's Ian Fleming meets John Le Carre, isn't it?

HOGAN: But he was very detailed?

COLQUHOUN: Yes, but it can be that way with obsessives.

HOGAN: There have been books written alleging the same thing Professor Lintz was talking about.

COLQUHOUN: Have there?

HOGAN: Nazis smuggled overseas ... war criminals rescued from the gallows.

COLQUHOUN: Well, yes, but those are just stories. You don't seriously think ...?

HOGAN: I'm just collecting information, Dr Colquhoun. In my job, we don't throw anything away.

COLQUHOUN: Yes, I can see that. The problem is, sorting out the wheat from the chaff.

HOGAN: You mean the truths from the lies? Yes, that's one problem.

COLQUHOUN: I mean, the stories you hear about Bosnia and Croatia ... slaughterhouses, mass torture, the guilty being spirited away .... It's hard to know what's *true*.

HOGAN: Just before we finish ... any idea what happened to the money?

COLQUHOUN: What money?

HOGAN: The withdrawal Lintz made from his bank. Five thousand pounds in cash.

COLQUHOUN: This is the first I've heard of it. Another motive?

HOGAN: Thank you for your time, Dr Colquhoun. It might be necessary for us to talk again. I'm sorry, but you shouldn't have lied to us, it makes our job that much more difficult.

COLQUHOUN: I'm sorry, Inspector Hogan. I quite understand, but I hope you can comprehend why I did it.

HOGAN: My mum always told me never to lie, sir. Thanks again for your time.

Rebus looked at Hogan. 'Your mum?'

Hogan shrugged. 'Maybe it was my granny.'

Rebus drained his coffee. 'So we know one of Lintz's mealtime companions.'

'And we know he was hounding Colquhoun.'

'Is he a suspect?'

'I'm not exactly snowed under with them.'

'Fair point, but all the same ...'

'You think he's on the level?'

'I don't know, Bobby. He sounded like he had it rehearsed. And he was relieved at the end.'

'You don't think I got it all? I could bring him in again.'

Rebus was thinking: *stories you hear ... the guilty being spirited away*. Not stories you *read*, but ones you *hear* ... Who might he have heard them from? Candice? Jake Tarawicz?

Hogan rubbed the bridge of his nose. 'I need a drink.'

Rebus dropped his beaker into a waste-bin. 'Message received and understood. By the way, any word from Abernethy?'

'He's a bloody nuisance,' Hogan said, turning away.

# 26

'He's in place,' Claverhouse said, when Rebus phoned him to ask about Jack Morton. 'Got him a little one-bedroom shit-hole in Polwarth. Measured him up for his uniform, and he's now officially a member of on-site security.'

'Is anyone else in on it?'

'Just the big boss. His name's Livingstone. We had a long session with him last night.'

'Won't the other security men find it a bit odd, a stranger arriving in their midst?'

'It's down to Jack to put them at ease. He was pretty confident.'

'What's his cover?'

'Secret drinker, open gambler, busted marriage.'

'He doesn't drink.'

'Yes, he told me. Doesn't matter, so long as everyone *thinks* he does.'

'Is he in character?'

'Getting there. He's going to be working double shifts. That way he makes more trips to the shop, some in the evening when the place is quieter. More chance to get to know Ken and Dec. We've no contact with him during the day. Debriefing takes place once he's reached home. Telephone only, can't risk too many meetings.'

'You think they'll watch him?'

'If they're being thorough. And *if* they fall for the plan.'

'Did you talk to Marty Jones?'

'That's set for tomorrow. He'll bring a couple of heavies, but they'll go easy on Jack.'

'Isn't tomorrow a bit soon?'

'Can we afford to wait? They might already have someone in mind.'

'We're asking a lot of him.'

'He was *your* idea.'

'I know.'

'You don't think he's up to it?'

'It's not that ... but he's stepping into a war.'

'Then get the ceasefire sorted out.'

'It is.'

'That's not what I hear ...'

Rebus heard it too, as soon as he got off the phone. He knocked on the Chief Super's door. The Farmer was in conference with Gill Templer.

'Did you talk to him?' the Farmer asked.

'He agreed to a ceasefire,' Rebus said. He was looking at Templer. 'What about you?'

She took a deep breath. 'I spoke to Mr Telford – his solicitor was present throughout. I kept telling him what we wanted, and the lawyer kept telling me I was blackening his client's name.'

'And Telford?'

'Just sat there, arms folded, smiling at the wall.' Colour was creeping up her face. 'I don't think he looked at me once.'

'But you gave him the message?'

'Yes.'

'You said Cafferty would comply?'

She nodded.

'Then what the hell's happening?'

'We can't let it get out of control,' the Farmer said.

'Looks to me like it already is.'

The latest score-line: two of Cafferty's men, their faces mashed to something resembling fruit-pulp.

'Lucky they're not dead,' the Farmer went on.

'You know what's happening?' Rebus said. 'It's Tarawicz, *he's* the problem. Tommy's playing up to him.'

'It's times like this you yearn for independence,' the Farmer agreed. 'Then we could just extradite the bugger.'

'Why don't we?' Rebus suggested. 'Tell him his presence here is no longer acceptable.'

'And if he stays?'

'We shadow him, make sure everyone knows we're doing it. We make *nuisances* of ourselves.'

'You think that would work?' Gill Templer sounded sceptical.

'Probably not,' Rebus agreed, slumping into a chair.

'We've no real leverage,' the Farmer said, glancing at his watch. 'Which isn't going to please the Chief Constable. He wants me in his office in half an hour.' He got on the phone, ordered a car, rose to his feet.

'Look, see if you can thrash something out between you.'

Rebus and Templer exchanged a look.

'I'll be back in an hour or two.' The Farmer looked around, as if he were suddenly lost. 'Lock the door when you leave.' With that and a wave of his hand, he left. There was silence in the room.

'Has to keep his office locked,' Rebus said, 'to stop people stealing the secret of his terrible coffee.'

'Actually, it's been getting better recently.'

'Maybe your taste buds are being corroded. So, Chief Inspector ...' Rebus turned his chair to face hers. 'What about thrashing it out then, eh?'

She smiled. 'He thinks he's losing it.'

'Is he in for a bollocking?'

'Probably.'

'So it's down to us to come to the rescue?'

'I don't really see us as the Dynamic Duo, do you?'

'No.'

'Then there's always that part of you that says, let them tear each other apart. So long as no civilians get caught in the crossfire.'

Rebus thought of Sammy, of Candice. 'Thing is,' he said, 'they always do.'

She looked at him. 'How are you doing?'

'Same as ever.'

'As bad as that?'

'It's my calling.'

'You're done with Lintz though?'

Rebus shook his head. 'There's half a chance he ties in to Telford.'

'You still think Telford was behind the hit-and-run?'

'Telford or Cafferty.'

'Cafferty?'

'Setting up Telford, the way someone tried to set *me* up for Matsumoto.'

'You know you're not out of the woods?'

He looked at her. 'An internal inquiry? The men with rubber

soles?' She nodded. 'Bring them on.' He sat forward in his chair, rubbed his temples. 'No reason they should be left out of the party.'

'What party?'

'The one inside my head. The party that never stops.' Rebus leaned across the desk to answer the phone. 'No, he's not here. Can I take a message? This is DI Rebus.' A pause; he was looking at Gill Templer. 'Yes, I'm working that case.' He found pen and paper, started writing. 'Mmm, I see. Yes, sounds like. I'll let him know when he gets back.' Eyes *boring into* hers. Then the punchline: 'How many did you say were dead?'

Just the one. Another fled the scene, holding his arm, all but severed from the shoulder. He turned up at a local hospital later, needing surgery and a huge transfusion of blood.

In broad daylight. Not in Edinburgh, but Paisley. Telford's hometown, the town he still ruled. Four men, dressed in council work jackets, like a road team. But in place of picks and shovels, they'd toted machetes and a large-calibre revolver. They'd chased two men into a housing scheme. Kids playing on tricycles; kicking a ball up the street. Women hanging out of their windows. And grown men itching to hurt one another. A machete swung overhead, coming down hard. The wounded man kept running. His friend tried hurdling a fence, wasn't agile enough. Three inches higher and he'd have made it. As it was, his toe caught, and he fell. He was pushing himself back up when the barrel of the gun touched the back of his head. Two shots, a fine drizzle of blood and brain. The children not playing any more, the women screaming for them to run. But something had been satisfied by those two shots. The chase was over. The four men turned and jogged back down the street, towards a waiting van.

A public execution, in Tommy Telford's heartland.

The two victims: known money-lenders. The one in hospital was called 'Wee' Stevie Murray, age twenty-two. The one in the mortuary was Donny Draper – known since childhood as 'Curtains'. They'd be making jokes about that. Curtains was two weeks shy of his twenty-fifth birthday. Rebus hoped he'd made the most of his short time on the planet.

Paisley police knew about Telford's move to Edinburgh, knew there were some problems there. A courtesy call had been placed to Chief Superintendent Watson.

The caller said: the men were two of Telford's brightest and best.

The caller said: descriptions of the attackers were vague.

The caller said: the children weren't talking. They were being shielded by their parents, fearful of reprisals. Well, they might not be talking to the *police*, but Rebus doubted they'd be so reticent when Tommy Telford came calling, armed with his own questions and determined to have answers.

This was bad. This was *escalation*. Fire-bombings and beatings: these could be remedied. But murder ... murder put the grudge-match on to a much higher plane.

'Is it worth talking to them again?' Gill Templer asked. They were in the canteen, sandwiches untouched in front of them.

'What do you think?'

He knew what she thought. She was talking because she thought talking was better than doing nothing. He could have told her to save her breath.

'They used a machete,' he said.

'Same thing they took to Danny Simpson's scalp.' Rebus nodded. 'I've got to ask ...' she said.

'What?'

'About Lintz ... what you said?'

He drained the last inch of his cold coffee. 'Fancy another?'

'John ...'

He looked at her. 'Lintz had some phone calls he was trying to hide. One of them was to Tommy Telford's office in Flint Street. We don't know how it ties in, but we think it *does* tie in.'

'What could Lintz and Telford have had in common?'

'Maybe Lintz went to him for help. Maybe he rented prossies off him. Like I say, we don't *know*. Which is why we're keeping it under the table.'

'You want Telford very badly, don't you?'

Rebus stared at her, thought about it. 'Not as much as I did. He's not enough any more.'

'You want Cafferty, too?'

'And Tarawicz ... and the Yakuza ... and anybody else who's along for the ride.'

She nodded. 'This is the party you were talking about?'

He tapped his head. 'They're all in here, Gill. I've tried kicking them out, but they won't leave.'

'Maybe if you stopped playing their kind of music?'

He smiled tiredly. 'Now there's an idea. What do you reckon: ELP? The Enid? How about a Yes triple album?'

'Your department, not mine, thank God.'

'You don't know what you're missing.'

'Yes, I do: I was there first time round.'

Old Scottish proverb: he who has had knuckles rapped will want to rap someone else's. Which is why Rebus found himself back in Watson's office. The Farmer's cheeks were still red from his meeting with the Chief Constable. When Rebus made to sit, Watson told him to get back on his feet.

'You'll sit when you're told and not before.'

'Thank you, sir.'

'What the bloody hell's going on, John?'

'Pardon, sir?'

The Farmer looked at the note Rebus had left on his desk. 'What's this?'

'One dead, one seriously wounded in Paisley, sir. Telford's men. Cafferty's hitting him where it hurts. Probably reckons that Telford's territory's spun a bit thin. Leaves him open to breaches.'

'Paisley.' The Farmer stuffed the note in his drawer. 'Not our problem.'

'It will be, sir. When Telford hits back, it'll be right here.'

'Never mind that, Inspector. Let's talk about Maclean's Pharmaceuticals.'

Rebus blinked, relaxed his shoulders. 'I was going to tell you, sir.'

'But instead I had to hear it from the Chief Constable?'

'Not really my baby, sir. Crime Squad are pushing the pram.'

'But who put the baby *in* the pram?'

'I was going to tell you, sir.'

'Know how it makes me look? I walk into Fettes and I don't know something one of my junior officers knows? I look like a mug.'

'With respect, sir, I'm sure that's not the case.'

'I look like a *mug*!' The Farmer slammed the desk with both palms. 'And it's not as though this was the first time. I've always tried to do my best for you, you know that.'

'Yes, sir.'

'Always been fair.'

'Absolutely, sir.'

'And you pay me back like this?'

'It won't happen again, sir.'

The Farmer stared at him; Rebus held it, returned it.

'I bloody well hope not.' The Farmer leaned back in his chair. He'd calmed down a little. Bollocking as therapy. 'Nothing else you want to tell me, is there, while I've got you here?'

'No, sir. Except ... well ...'

'Go on.' The Farmer sat forward again.

'It's the man in the flat above me, sir,' Rebus said. 'I think he might be Lord Lucan.'

# 27

Leonard Cohen: 'There is a War'.

They were waiting for Telford's retaliatory strike. The Chief Constable's idea: 'visible presence as deterrent'. It came as no surprise to Rebus: probably even less so to Telford, who had Charles Groal ready, claiming harassment the minute the patrol cars turned up in Flint Street. How was his client supposed to carry on with his legitimate and substantial business interests, as well as his many community developments, under the pressure of unwarranted and intrusive police surveillance? 'Community developments' meaning the pensioners and their rent-free flats: Telford wouldn't hesitate to use them as pawns. The media would love it.

The patrol cars would be pulled, it was just a matter of time. And afterwards: firework night all over again. That's what everyone was expecting.

Rebus went to the hospital, sat with Rhona. The room, so familiar to him now, was an oasis where calm and order reigned, where each hour of the day brought its comforting rituals.

'They've washed her hair,' he said.

'She's had another scan,' Rhona explained. 'They had to get the gunk off afterwards.' Rebus nodded. 'They said you'd noticed eye movement?'

'I thought I did.'

Rhona touched his arm. 'Jackie says he might manage to come up again at the weekend. Call this fair warning.'

'Received and understood.'

'You look tired.'

He smiled. 'One of these days someone's going to tell me how terrific I'm looking.'

'But not today,' Rhona said.

'Must be all the booze, clubbing and women.'

Thinking: Coke, the Morvena Casino, and Candice.

Thinking: why do I feel like piggy in the middle? Are Cafferty and Telford *both* playing games with me?

Thinking: I hope Jack Morton's okay.

The phone was ringing when he got back to Arden Street. He picked up just as the answering machine was cutting in.

'Hold on till I stop this thing.' Found the right button and hit it.

'Technology, eh, Strawman?'

Cafferty.

'What do you want?'

'I've heard about Paisley.'

'You mean you've been talking to yourself?'

'I had nothing to do with it.'

Rebus laughed out loud.

'I'm telling you.'

Rebus fell into his chair. 'And I'm supposed to believe you?' Games, he was thinking.

'Whether you believe me or not, I wanted you to know.'

'Thanks, I'm sure I'll sleep better for that.'

'I'm being set up, Strawman.'

'Telford doesn't *need* to set you up.' Rebus sighed, stretched his neck to left and right. 'Look, have you considered another possibility?'

'What?'

'Your men have lost it. They're going behind your back.'

'I'd know.'

'You'd know what your own lieutenants tell you. What if they're lying? I'm not saying it's the whole gang, could be just two or three gone rogue.'

'I'd know.' The emotion had drained from Cafferty's voice. He was thinking it over.

'Fine, okay, you'd know: who'd be the first to tell you? Cafferty, you're on the other side of the country. You're in *prison*. How hard would it be to keep stuff from you?'

'These are men I'd trust with my life.' Cafferty paused. 'They'd tell me.'

'*If* they knew. *If* they hadn't been warned not to tell you. See what I'm saying?'

'Two or three gone rogue ...' Cafferty echoed.

'You must have candidates?'

'Jeffries would know.'

'Jeffries? Is that the Weasel's name?'

'Don't let him hear you call him that.'

'Give me his number. I'll talk to him.'

'No, but I'll get him to call you.'

'And if he's part of the breakaway?'

'We don't know there is one.'

'But you admit it makes sense?'

'I admit Tommy Telford's trying to put me in a box.'

Rebus stared from his window. 'You mean literally?'

'I've heard word of a contract.'

'But you've got protection?'

Cafferty chuckled. 'Strawman, you almost sound concerned.'

'You're imagining things.'

'Look, there are only two ways out of this. One, *you* deal with Telford. Two, *I* deal with him. Are we agreed on that? I mean, I'm not the one who went poaching players and territory and putting out frighteners.'

'Maybe he's just more ambitious than you. Maybe he reminds you of the way you used to be.'

'Are you saying I've gone soft?'

'I'm saying it's adapt or die.'

'Have *you* adapted, Strawman?'

'Maybe a little.'

'Aye, a fucking speck, if that.'

'We're not talking about me though.'

'You're as involved as anyone. Remember that, Strawman. And sweet dreams.'

Rebus put down the phone. He felt exhausted, and depressed. The kids across the way were in bed, shutters closed. He looked around the room. Jack Morton had helped him paint it, back when Rebus was thinking of selling. Jack had helped him off the sauce, too ...

He knew he wouldn't be able to sleep. Got back into the car and headed for Young Street. The Oxford Bar was quiet. A couple of philosophers in the corner, and through in the back-room three musicians who'd packed up their fiddles. He drank a couple of cups of black coffee, then drove to Oxford Terrace. Parked the car outside Patience's flat, turned off the ignition and sat there for a while, jazz

on the radio. He hit a good streak: Astrid Gilberto, Stan Getz, Art Pepper, Duke Ellington. Told himself he'd wait till a bad record came on, then go knock on Patience's door.

But by then it was too late. He didn't want to turn up unannounced. It would be ... it wouldn't look right. He didn't mind that it smacked of desperation, but he didn't want her to think he was pushing. He started the engine again and moved off, drove around the New Town and down to Granton. Sat by the edge of the Forth, window down, listening to water and the nighttime traffic of HGVs.

Even with eyes closed, he couldn't shut out the world. In fact, in those moments before sleep came, his images were at their most vivid. He wondered what Sammy dreamed about, or even if she dreamed at all. Rhona said that Sammy had come north to be with him. He couldn't think what he'd done to deserve her.

Back into town for an espresso at Gordon's Trattoria, then the hospital: easy to find a parking space this time of night. A taxi was idling outside the entrance. He made his way to Sammy's room, was surprised to see someone there. His first thought: Rhona. The only illumination in the room was that given through the closed curtains. A woman, kneeling by the bed, head resting on the covers. He walked forwards. She heard him, turned, face glistening with tears.

Candice.

Her eyes widened. She stumbled to her feet.

'I wanting see her,' she said quietly.

Rebus nodded. In shadows, she looked even more like Sammy: same build, similar hair and shape to her face. She wore a long red coat, fished in the pocket for a paper hankie.

'I like her,' she said. He nodded again.

'Does Tarawicz know where you are?' he asked.

She shook her head.

'The taxi outside?' he guessed.

She nodded. 'They went casino. I said sore head.' She spoke falteringly, checking each word was right before using it.

'Will he find out you've gone?'

She thought about it, shook her head.

'You sleep in the same room?' Rebus asked.

She shook her head again, smiled. 'Jake not liking women.'

This was news to Rebus. Miriam Kenworthy had said something about him marrying an Englishwoman ... but put that down to immigration. He remembered the way Tarawicz had pawed Candice,

realised now it had been for *Telford's* benefit. He'd been showing Telford that he could control his women. While Telford ... well, Telford had let her get arrested, then be taken in by the Crime Squad. A small sign of rivalry between the two partners. Something to be exploited?

'Is she ... will she ...?'

Rebus shrugged. 'We hope so, Candice.'

She looked down at the floor. 'My name is Dunya.'

'Dunya,' he echoed.

'Sarajevo was ...' She looked up at him. 'You know, like *really*. I was escaping ... lucky. They all said to me: "You lucky, you lucky".' She stabbed at her chest with a finger. 'Lucky. Survivor.' She broke down again, and this time he held her.

The Stones: 'Soul Survivor'. Only sometimes it was the body alone that survived, the soul eaten into, chewed up by experience.

'Dunya,' he said, repeating her name, reinforcing her true identity, trying to get through to the one part of her she'd kept hidden since Sarajevo. 'Dunya, sshhh. It's going to be all right. Sshhh.' And stroking her hair, her face, his other hand on her back, feeling her tremble. Blinking back his own tears, and watching Sammy's body. The atmosphere in the room crackled like electricity: he wondered if any part of it was reaching Sammy's brain.

'Dunya, Dunya, Dunya ...'

She pulled away, turned her back on him. He wouldn't let her go. Walked up to her and rested his hands on her shoulders.

'Dunya,' he said, 'how did Tarawicz find you?' She seemed not to understand. 'In Lower Largo, his men found you.'

'Brian,' she said quietly.

Rebus frowned. 'Brian Summers?' Pretty-Boy ...

'He tell Jake.'

'He told Tarawicz where you were?' But why not just take her back to Edinburgh? Rebus thought he knew: she was too dangerous; she'd been too close to the police. Best get her out of the way. Not a killing: that would have implicated all of them. But Tarawicz could control her. Mr Pink Eyes bailing out his friend one more time ...

'He brought you here so he could gloat over Telford.' Rebus was thoughtful. He looked at Candice. What could he do with her? Where would be safe? She seemed to sense his thoughts, squeezed his hand.

'You know I have a …' She made a cradling motion with her hands.

'A boy,' Rebus said. She nodded. 'And Tarawicz knows where he is?'

She shook her head. 'The lorries … they took him.'

'Tarawicz's refugee lorries?' She nodded again. 'And you don't know where he is?'

'Jake knows. He says his man …' she made scuttling motions with her hands '… will kill my boy if …'

Scuttling motions: the Crab. Something struck Rebus. 'Why isn't the Crab up here with Tarawicz?' She was looking at him. 'Tarawicz here,' he said, 'Crab in Newcastle. Why?'

She shrugged, looked thoughtful. 'He don't come.' She was remembering some snippet of conversation. 'Danger.'

'Dangerous?' Rebus frowned. 'Who for?'

She shrugged again. Rebus took her hands.

'You can't trust him, Dunya. You have to leave him.'

She smiled up at him, eyes glinting. 'I tried.'

They looked at one another, held one another for a while. Afterwards, he walked her back out to her taxi.

# 28

In the morning he called the hospital, found out how Sammy was doing, then asked to be transferred.

'How's Danny Simpson getting on?'

'I'm sorry, are you family?'

Which told him everything. He identified himself, asked when it had happened.

'In the night,' the nurse said.

Body at its lowest ebb: the dying hours. Rebus called the mother, identified himself again.

'Sorry to hear the news,' he said. 'Is the funeral ...?'

'Just family, if you don't mind. No flowers. We're asking for donations to be sent to an ... to a charity. Danny was well thought of, you know.'

'I'm sure.'

Rebus took down details of the charity – an AIDS hospice; the mother couldn't bring herself to say the word. Terminated the call. Got an envelope out and put in ten pounds, plus a note: 'In memory of Danny Simpson'. He wondered about going for that test ... His phone rang and he picked it up.

'Hello?'

Lots of static and engine noise: car-phone, on the move at speed.

'This takes persecution to new levels.' *Telford.*

'What do you mean?' Rebus trying to compose himself.

'Danny Simpson's been dead six hours, and already you're on the phone to his mum.'

'How do you know?'

'I was *there*. Paying my respects.'

'Same reason I phoned then. Know what, Telford? I think *you're* taking persecution complexes to new levels.'

'Yes, and Cafferty's not out to shut me down.'

252

'He says he didn't have anything to do with Paisley.'

'I bet you believed in the Tooth Fairy when you were a kid.'

'I still do.'

'You'll need more than a good fairy if you side with Cafferty.'

'Is that a threat? Don't tell me: Tarawicz is in the car with you?' Silence. Bingo, Rebus thought. 'You think Tarawicz will respect you because you bad-mouth cops? He's got no respect for you whatsoever – look how he's waving Candice in your face.'

Mixing levity with fury: 'Hey, Rebus, you and Candice in that hotel – what was she like? Jake tells me she's vindaloo.' Background laughter: Mr Pink Eyes, who, according to Candice, had never touched her. For 'laughter' read 'bravado'. Telford and Tarawicz, playing games between themselves, playing games with the world.

Rebus found the tone of voice he wanted. 'I tried to help her. If she's too stupid to know that, she deserves the likes of you and Tarawicz.' Telling them he had no further interest in her. 'Anyway, Tarawicz didn't have any trouble taking her off *your* hands.' Rebus jabbing away, looking for gaps in the armour of the Telford/ Tarawicz relationship.

'What if Cafferty wasn't behind Paisley?' he asked into the silence.

'It was his men.'

'Gone rogue.'

'He can't control them, that's his look-out. He's a *joke*, Rebus. He's finished.'

Rebus didn't say anything; listened instead to a muted conversation. Then Telford again: 'Mr Tarawicz wants a word.' The phone was handed over.

'Rebus? I thought we were civilised men?'

'In what way?'

'When we met in Newcastle ... I thought we came to an understanding?'

The unspoken agreement: leave Telford alone, have nothing more to do with Cafferty, and Candice and her son would be safe. What was Tarawicz getting at?

'I've kept my side.'

A forced chuckle. 'You know what Paisley represents?

'What?'

'The beginning of the end of Morris Gerald Cafferty.'

'And I bet you'd send flowers to the grave.'

Dead flowers at that.

Rebus went into St Leonard's, got settled in front of his computer screen, and took a look at the Crab.

The Crab: William Andrew Colton. Plenty of form. Rebus decided he'd like to read the files. Phoned in and requested them, backed up the request in writing. Buzzed from downstairs: a man to see him, no name supplied. Description: the Weasel.

Rebus went downstairs.

The Weasel was outside, smoking a cigarette. He was wearing a green waxed jacket, torn at both pockets. A lumberjack hat with its flaps down protected his ears from the wind.

'Let's walk,' Rebus said. The Weasel got into step with him. They wandered through an estate of new flats: satellite dishes and windows picked from Lego boxes. Behind the flats sat Salisbury Crags.

'Don't worry,' Rebus said, 'I'm not in the mood for rock-climbing.'

'I'm in the mood for indoors.' The Weasel tucked his chin into the upturned collar of his coat.

'What's the news on my daughter?'

'We're close, I told you.'

'How close?'

The Weasel measured his response. 'We've got the tapes from the car, the guy who sold them. He says he got them from another party.'

'And he is ...?'

A sly smile: the Weasel knew he had control over Rebus. He'd play it out as long as possible.

'You're going to be meeting him fairly shortly.'

'Even so ... say the tapes got taken from the car after it was abandoned?'

The Weasel was shaking his head. 'That's not how it was.'

'Then how was it?' He wanted to pull his tormentor down on to the ground and start hammering his skull on the pavement.

'Give us a day or two, we'll have everything you need.' The wind gusted some grit towards them. They turned their faces. Rebus saw a heavy-set man loitering sixty yards behind.

'Don't worry,' the Weasel said, 'he's with me.'

'Getting jittery?'

'After Paisley, Telford's out for blood.'

'What do you know about Paisley?'

The Weasel's eyes became slits. 'Nothing.'

'No? Cafferty's beginning to suspect some of his own men might have gone rogue.' Rebus watched the Weasel shake his head.

'I don't know the first thing about it.'

'Who's your boss's main man?'

'Ask Mr Cafferty.' The Weasel was looking around, as if bored by the conversation. He made a signal to the back-marker, who passed it along. Seconds later, a newish Jaguar – arterial-red paint-job – cruised to a stop beside them. Rebus saw: a driver itching for a less sedentary occupation; cream leather interior; the back-marker jogging forwards, opening the door for the Weasel.

'It's you,' Rebus said. The Weasel: Cafferty's eyes and ears on the street; the man with the look and dress-code of a down-and-out. The Weasel was running the show. All the lieutenants in the various outposts ... all the tailor-made suits ... the collective which, according to police intelligence, ran Cafferty's kingdom in their master's absence ... they were a smokescreen. The hunched man pulling off his lumberjack hat, the man with bad teeth and a blunt razor, *he* was in charge.

Rebus actually laughed. The bodyguard got into the car's passenger seat, having made sure his boss was comfortable in the back. Rebus tapped on the window. The Weasel lowered it.

'Tell me,' Rebus asked, 'have you got the bottle to wrest it away from him?'

'Mr Cafferty trusts me. He knows I'll do right by him.'

'What about Telford?'

The Weasel stared at him. 'Telford's not my concern.'

'Then who is?'

But the window was rising again, and the Weasel – Cafferty had called him Jeffries – had turned his face away, dismissing Rebus from his mind.

He stood there, watching the car drive off. Was Cafferty making a big mistake, putting the Weasel in charge? Was it just that his best men had scarpered or gone over to the other side?

Or was the Weasel every bit as sly, clever and vicious as his namesake?

\*

Back at the station, Rebus sought out Bill Pryde. Pryde was shrugging his shoulders even before Rebus had reached his desk.

'Sorry, John, no news.'

'Nothing at all? What about the stolen tapes?' Pryde shook his head. 'That's funny, I've just been talking to someone who claims to know who sold them on, and who *he* got them from.'

Pryde sat back in his chair. 'I wondered why you hadn't been chasing me up. What've you done, hired a private eye?' Blood was rising to his face. 'I've been working my arse off on this, John, you know I have. Now you don't trust me to do the job?'

'It's not like that, Bill.' Rebus suddenly found himself on the defensive.

'Who've you got working for you, John?'

'Just people on the street.'

'Well-connected people by the sound of it.' He paused. 'Are we talking villains?'

'My daughter's in a coma, Bill.'

'I'm well aware of that. Now answer my question!'

People around them were staring. Rebus lowered his voice. 'Just a few of my grasses.'

'Then give me their names.'

'Come on, Bill ...'

Pryde's hands gripped the table. 'These past days, I've been thinking you'd lost interest. Thinking maybe you didn't *want* an answer.' He was thoughtful. 'You wouldn't go to Telford ... Cafferty?' His eyes widened. 'Is that it, John?'

Rebus turned his head away.

'Christ, John ... what's the deal here? He hands over the driver, what do *you* hand *him*?'

'It's not like that.'

'I can't believe you'd trust Cafferty. You put him away, for Christ's sake!'

'It's not a question of trust.'

But Pryde was shaking his head. 'There's a line we don't cross.'

'Get a grip, Bill. There's no line.' Rebus spread his arms. 'If there is, show me it.'

Pryde tapped his forehead. 'It's up here.'

'Then it's a fiction.'

'You really believe that?'

Rebus sought an answer, slumped against the desk, ran his hands over

his head. He remembered something Lintz had once said: *when we stop believing in God, we don't suddenly believe in 'nothing' ... we believe anything.*

'John?' someone called. 'Phone call.'

Rebus stared at Pryde. 'Later,' he said. He walked across to another desk, took the call.

'Rebus here.'

'It's Bobby.' Bobby Hogan.

'What can I do for you, Bobby?'

'For a start, you can help get that Special Branch arsehole off my back.'

'Abernethy?'

'He won't leave me alone.'

'Keeps phoning you?'

'Christ, John, aren't you listening? He's *here*.'

'When did he get in?'

'He never went away.'

'Whoah, hold on.'

'And he's driving me round the twist. He says he knows you from way back, so how about having a word?'

'Are you at Leith?'

'Where else?'

'I'll be there in twenty minutes.'

'I got so pissed off, I went to my boss – and that's something I seldom have to resort to.' Bobby Hogan was drinking coffee like it was something best taken intravenously. The top button of his shirt was undone, tie hanging loose.

'Only,' he went on, '*his* boss had a word with my *boss's* boss, and I ended up with a warning: co-operate or else.'

'Meaning?'

'I wasn't to tell anyone he was still around.'

'Thanks, pal. So what's he actually doing?'

'What *isn't* he doing? He wants to be in on any interviews. He wants copies of tapes and transcripts. He wants to see all the paperwork, wants to know what I'm planning to do next, what I had for breakfast ...'

'I don't suppose he's managing to be helpful in any shape or form?'

Hogan's look gave Rebus his answer.

'I don't mind him taking an interest, but this verges on the obstructive. He's slowing the case to a dead stop.'

'Maybe that's his plan.'

Hogan looked up from his cup. 'I don't get it.'

'Neither do I. Look, if he's being obstructive, let's put on a show, see how he reacts.'

'What sort of show?'

'What time will he be in?'

Hogan checked his watch. 'Half an hour or so. That's when my work stops for the day, while I fill him in.'

'Half an hour's enough. Mind if I use your phone?'

# 29

When Abernethy arrived, he didn't manage not to look surprised. The space put aside for the investigation – Hogan's space – now contained three bodies, and they were working at the devil's own pace.

Hogan was on the telephone to a librarian. He was asking for a run-down of books and articles about 'the Rat Line'. Rebus was sorting through paperwork, putting it in order, cross-referencing, laying aside anything he didn't think useful. And Siobhan Clarke was there, too. She appeared to be on the phone to some Jewish organisation, and was asking them about lists of war criminals. Rebus nodded towards Abernethy, but kept on working.

'What's going on?' Abernethy asked, taking off his raincoat.

'Helping out. Bobby's got so many leads to work on ...' He nodded towards Siobhan. 'And Crime Squad are interested, too.'

'Since when?'

Rebus waved a piece of paper. 'This might be bigger than we think.'

Abernethy looked around. He wanted to speak to Hogan, but Hogan was still on the phone. Rebus was the only one with time to talk.

Which was just the way Rebus had planned it.

He'd only had five minutes in which to brief Siobhan, but she was a born actress, even holding a conversation with the dialling tone. Hogan's fantasy librarian, meantime, was asking him all the right questions. And Abernethy was looking glazed.

'What do you mean?'

'In fact,' Rebus said, putting down a file, 'you might be able to help.'

'How?'

'You're Special Branch, and Special Branch has access to the secret services.' Rebus paused. 'Right?'

Abernethy licked his lips and shrugged.

'See,' Rebus went on, 'we're beginning to wonder something. There could be a dozen reasons why someone would want to kill Joseph Lintz, but the one we've been practically ignoring' (ignoring at Abernethy's suggestion, according to Hogan) 'is the one that just might provide the answer. I'm talking about the Rat Line. What if Lintz's murder had something to do with that?'

'How could it?'

It was Rebus's turn to shrug. 'That's why we need your help. We need any and all information we can get on the Rat Line.'

'But it never existed.'

'Funny, a lot of books seem to say it did.'

'They're wrong.'

'Then there are all these survivors ... except they haven't survived. Suicides, car crashes, a fall from a window. Lintz is just one of a long line of dead men.'

Siobhan Clarke and Bobby Hogan had finished their calls and were listening.

'You're climbing the wrong tree,' Abernethy said.

'Well, you know, if you're in a forest, climbing any tree will give you a better view.'

'There is no Rat Line.'

'You're an expert?'

'I've been collating ...'

'Yes, yes, all the investigations. And how far have you got? Is any one of them going to make it to trial?'

'It's too early to tell.'

'And soon it may be too late. These men aren't getting any younger. I've seen the same thing all around Europe: delay the trial until the defendants are so old they snuff it or go doolally. Result's the same: no trial.'

'Look, this has nothing to do with ...'

'Why are you here, Abernethy? Why did you come up that time to speak to Lintz?'

'Look, Rebus, it's not ...'

'If you can't tell us, talk to your boss. Get *him* to do it. Otherwise, the way we're digging, we're bound to throw up an old bone sooner or later.'

Abernethy stood back a pace. 'I think I get it,' he said. And he began to smile. 'You're trying to stiff me.' He was looking at Hogan. 'That's what this is.'

'Not at all,' Rebus answered. 'What I'm saying is: we'll redouble our efforts. We'll sniff into every little corner. The Rat Line, the Vatican, turning Nazis into cold war spies for the allies ... it could all count as evidence. The other men on your list, the other suspects ... we'll need to talk to all of them, see if they knew Joseph Lintz. Maybe they met him on the trip over.'

Abernethy was shaking his head. 'I'm not going to let you do that.'

'You're going to obstruct the investigation?'

'That's not what I said.'

'No, but it's what you'll *do*.' Rebus paused. 'If you think we're climbing the wrong tree – and, incidentally, that should be *barking up* – go ahead and prove it. Give us everything you've got on Lintz's past.'

Abernethy's eyes were fierce.

'Or we go on digging and sniffing.' Rebus opened another file, lifted out the first sheet. Hogan picked up his telephone, made another call. Siobhan Clarke looked at a list of numbers and chose one.

'Hello, is that the City Synagogue?' Hogan was saying. 'Yes, it's Detective Inspector Hogan here, Leith CID. Do you by any chance have information on a Joseph Lintz?'

Abernethy grabbed his coat, turned on his heels and left. They waited thirty seconds, then Hogan put the receiver down.

'He looked nettled.'

'That's one Christmas wish I can chalk off,' Siobhan Clarke said.

'Thanks for your time, Siobhan,' Rebus said.

'Happy to oblige. But why did it have to be me?'

'Because he knows you're Crime Squad. I wanted him to think interest was escalating. And because the two of you didn't exactly hit it off last time you met. Antagonism always helps.'

'And what did we accomplish?' Bobby Hogan asked, beginning to gather together the files, half of which belonged to other cases.

'We rattled his cage,' Rebus said. 'He's not up here for the good of his health – or yours, come to that. He's here because Special Branch in London want to know all about the investigation. And to me, that means they're scared of something.'

'The Rat Line?'

'That would be my guess. Abernethy's been keeping an eye on all the new cases nationwide. Someone in London is getting a bit sweaty.'

'They're worried this Rat Line will connect to whoever killed Lintz?'

'I'm not sure it goes that far,' Rebus said.

'Meaning?'

He looked at Clarke. 'Meaning I'm not sure it goes that far.'

'Well,' Hogan said, 'looks like he's off my back for a little while at least, for which I'm grateful.' He got to his feet. 'Get anyone a coffee?'

Clarke checked her watch. 'Go on then.'

Rebus waited till Hogan was gone, then thanked Siobhan again. 'I wasn't sure you'd be able to spare the time.'

'We're giving Jack Morton a wide berth,' she explained. 'Nothing to do but bite our fingernails and wait. What about you, what are you up to?'

'Keeping my nose clean.'

She smiled. 'I'll bet.'

Hogan came back with three coffees. 'Powdered milk, sorry.'

Clarke wrinkled her nose. 'Actually, I've got to be getting back.' She stood up and put on her coat.

'That's one I owe you,' Hogan said, shaking her hand.

'I won't let you forget.' She turned to Rebus. 'See you later.'

'Cheers, Siobhan.'

Hogan put her cup beside his own. 'So we got Abernethy off my back, but did we get anything else?'

'Wait and see, Bobby. I didn't exactly have much time to devise a strategy.'

The phone rang, just as Hogan took a mouthful of scalding coffee. Rebus picked up.

'Hello?'

'Is that you, John?' Country and western twanging in the background: Claverhouse.

'You've just missed her,' Rebus told him.

'It's not Clarke I wanted, it's you.'

'Oh?'

'Something I thought you might be interested in. It's just filtered down from NCIS.' Rebus heard Claverhouse pick up a sheet of

paper. 'Sakiji Shoda ... I think I've pronounced that right. Flew into Heathrow from Kansai Airport yesterday. South-East Regional Crime Squad were apprised.'

'Terrific.'

'He didn't hang around, caught a connection to Inverness. Stayed the night in a local hotel, and now I hear he's in Edinburgh.'

Rebus looked out of the window. 'Not exactly golfing weather.'

'I don't think he's up here for the golf. According to the original report, Mr Shoda is a high-ranking member of the ... can't make it out on the fax. Socky-something.'

'Sokaiya?' Rebus sat up.

'That looks about right.'

'Where is he now?'

'I tried a couple of hotels. He's staying at the Caly. What's the Sokaiya?'

'It's the upper echelons of the Yakuza.'

'How does it read to you?'

'I was going to suggest he's Matsumoto's replacement, but it sounds to me like he's a few grades higher.'

'Matsumoto's boss?'

'Which means he's probably here to find out what happened to his boy.' Rebus tapped a pen against his teeth. Hogan was listening, but not getting any of it. 'Why Inverness? Why not direct to Edinburgh?'

'I've been wondering that.' Claverhouse sneezed. 'How pissed off will he be?'

'Somewhere between "mildly" and "very". More importantly, how are Telford and Mr Pink Eyes going to react?'

'You think Telford will drop Maclean's?'

'On the contrary, I think he'll want to show Mr Shoda that he can do *some* things right.' Rebus thought back to something Claverhouse had said. 'South-East Crime Squad?'

'Yes.'

'Rather than Scotland Yard?'

'Maybe the two are the same?'

'Maybe. Do you have a contact number?'

Claverhouse gave it to him.

'You'll speak to Jack Morton tonight?' Rebus asked.

'Yes.'

'Better tell him about this.'

'Talk to you again.'

Rebus put down the receiver, picked it up again, got an outside line and made the call. Explained his reason for calling and asked if there was anyone who could help him.

He was told to hold.

'Is this to do with Telford?' Hogan asked. Rebus nodded.

'Hey, Bobby, did you ever talk to Telford again?'

'I tried a couple of times. He just kept saying: "It must've been a wrong number".'

'And this was echoed by his staff?'

Hogan nodded, smiled. 'Tell you a funny thing. I walked into Telford's office, and someone was at his desk, back to me. I apologised, said I'd come back when he'd finished with the lady. Well, the "lady" turns, face like fury ...'

'Pretty-Boy?'

Hogan nodded. 'And pretty fucking angry the last I saw him.' Hogan laughed.

'Putting you through,' the switchboard told Rebus.

'How can I help you?' The voice sounded Welsh.

'My name's DI Rebus, Scottish Crime Squad.' Rebus winked at Hogan: the lie would give him more clout.

'Yes, Inspector?'

'And you are ...?'

'DI Morgan.'

'We had this message this morning ...'

'Yes?'

'Concerning Sakiji Shoda.'

'That would be my boss has sent you that.'

'What I'm wondering is, what's your interest?'

'Well, Inspector, I'm more of an expert on *vory v zakone*.'

'That clears things up then.'

Morgan chuckled. '"Thieves within the code". Meaning *mafiya*.'

'Russian mafia?'

'That's it.'

'You'll have to help me here. What's that got to do with ...?'

'Why do you want to know?'

Rebus took a sip of coffee. 'We've had a spot of bother with the Yakuza up here. One victim so far. My guess is that Shoda is the victim's boss.'

'And he's up there for a sort of unofficial committal?'

'We don't have the committal stage in Scotland, DI Morgan.'

'Well, pardon me for breathing.'

'Thing is, we've also got a Russian gangster up here. I say he's Russian, word is he's Chechen.'

'Is it Jake Tarawicz?'

'You've heard of him?'

'That's my job, sonny boy.'

'Well, anyway, with the Yakuza and the Chechens in town ...'

'You've got a nightmare scenario. Understood. Well, look ... What about if you give me your number there, and I'll call back in five minutes? Need to put some facts together first.'

Rebus gave him the number, then waited ten minutes for the call back.

'You were checking me out,' he told the Welshman.

'Got to be careful. Bit naughty of you to say you were Crime Squad.'

'Let's just say I'm the next best thing. So is there anything you can tell me?'

Morgan took a deep breath. 'We've been chasing a lot of dirty money around the world.'

Rebus couldn't find a clean sheet of paper to write on. Hogan gave him a pad.

'See,' Morgan was saying, 'the old Soviet Asia is now the biggest supplier of raw opium in the world. And wherever there's drugs, there's money needs laundering.'

'And this money makes its way to Britain?'

'On its way elsewhere. Companies in London, private banks in Guernsey ... the money gets filtered down, getting cleaner all the time. Everyone wants to do business with the Russians.'

'Why?'

'Because they make everyone money. Russia's one giant bazaar. You want weapons, counterfeit goods, money, fake passports, even plastic surgery? You want any of that, it's in Russia. The place has open borders, airports nobody knows exist ... it's ideal.'

'If you happen to be an international mobster.'

'Exactly. And the *mafiya* have made links with their Sicilian cousins, with the Camorra, the Calabrians ... I could go on forever. British villains go shopping there. They all love the Russians.'

'And now they're here?'

'Oh, they're here all right. Running protection and prossies, dealing drugs ...'

Prostitutes, drugs: Mr Pink Eyes's territory; Telford's territory.

'Any evidence of a hook-up with the Yakuza?'

'Not that I know of.'

'But if they moved into Britain ...?'

'They'd be trying to control drugs and prostitution. They'd be laundering money.'

Ways to launder money: through legitimate businesses such as country clubs and the like; by swopping dirty money for casino chips at an establishment like the Morvena.

Rebus already knew that the Yakuza liked to smuggle artworks back into Japan. Rebus already knew Mr Pink had made his early money smuggling icons out of Russia. Put the two together.

Then add Tommy Telford to the equation.

Did they need the haul from Maclean's? It didn't sound to Rebus like they did. So why was Tommy Telford doing it? Two possible reasons: one, to show off; two, *because they'd told him to*. Some rite of passage ... If he wanted to play with the big boys, he had to prove himself. He had to wipe out Cafferty, and pull off what would be the biggest heist in Scottish history.

Something hit Rebus between the eyes.

Telford wasn't meant to succeed. Telford was meant to fail.

Telford was being set up by Tarawicz and the Yakuza.

Because he had something they wanted: a steady supply of drugs; a kingdom waiting to be plucked from his grasp. Miriam Kenworthy had said as much: rumour was, the drugs were going south from Scotland. Which meant Telford had a supply ... something *nobody* knew about.

With Cafferty out of the way, there'd be no competition. The Yakuza would have their British base – solid, respectable, reliable. The electronics factory would act as perfect cover, maybe even as a laundering operation itself. Every way Rebus looked at it, Telford was unnecessary to the equation, like a zero that could be safely cancelled out.

Which was where Rebus wanted Telford ... only not at the price being asked.

'Thanks for your help,' he said. He noticed that Hogan had stopped listening and was staring into space. Rebus put the phone down.

'Sorry to have bored you.'

Hogan blinked. 'No, nothing like that. It's just that I thought of something.'

'What?'

'Pretty-Boy. I mistook him for a woman.'

'You're probably not the first.'

'Exactly.'

'I'm not sure I follow you?'

'In the restaurant ... Lintz and a young woman.' Hogan shrugged. 'It's a long shot.'

Rebus saw it. 'Talking business?'

Hogan nodded. 'Pretty-Boy runs Telford's stable.'

'And takes a personal interest in the higher-price models. It's worth a try, Bobby.'

'What do you think – bring him in?'

'Definitely. Beef up the restaurant angle. Say there's a positive ID. See what he says to that.'

'Same gag we pulled with Colquhoun? Pretty-Boy's bound to deny it.'

'Doesn't mean it ain't so.' Rebus patted Hogan on the shoulder. 'What about your call?'

'My call?' Rebus looked at his scrawled notes. Gangsters preparing to carve up Scotland. 'It wasn't the worst news I've ever had.'

'And is that saying much?'

'Afraid not, Bobby,' Rebus said, putting on his jacket. 'Afraid not.'

# 30

By the end of play, Rebus still hadn't received the files on the Crab, but he had fielded a frank and foul-mouthed call from Abernethy, accusing him of everything from obstruction – which was pretty rich, considering – to racism, which Rebus thought nicely ironic.

They'd given him back his car. Someone had run their finger through the dirt crusted on the boot, creating two messages: TERMINAL CASE, and WASHED BY STEVIE WONDER. The Saab, affronted, started first time and seemed to have shrugged off some of its repertoire of clanks and thunks. On the drive home, Rebus kept the windows open so he wouldn't smell the whisky that had soaked into the upholstery.

The evening had turned out fine, the sky clear, temperature dropping sharply. The low red sun, curse of the city's drivers, had disappeared behind the rooftops. Rebus left his coat unbuttoned as he walked down to the chip shop. He bought a fish supper, two buttered rolls, and a couple of cans of Irn-Bru, then returned to the flat. Nothing on the TV, so he put on a record. Van Morrison: *Astral Weeks*. The record had more scratches than a dog with eczema.

The opening track contained the refrain 'To be born again'. Rebus thought of Father Leary, shored up by a fridge full of medicine. Then he thought of Sammy, crowned with electrodes, machines rising either side of her, like she was being offered to them in sacrifice. Leary often talked of faith, but it was hard to have faith in a human race that never learned, that seemed ready to accept torture, murder, destruction. He opened his newspaper: Kosovo, Zaire, Rwanda. Punishment beatings in Northern Ireland. A young girl found murdered in England, another girl's disappearance termed 'a cause for concern'. The predators were out there, no

doubt about it. Strip the veneer, and the world had moved only a couple of steps from the cave.

*To be born again* ... But sometimes only after a baptism of fire.

Belfast, 1970. A sniper's bullet blew open the skull of a British squaddie. The victim was nineteen, came from Glasgow. Back in the barracks, there'd been little mourning, just an overspill of anger. The assassin would never be caught. He'd slipped back into the shadows of a tower-block, and from there deep into the Catholic housing estate.

Leaving one more newspaper story, one early statistic in the 'Troubles'.

And anger.

The ring-leader went by the nickname of 'Mean Machine'. He was a lance-corporal, came from somewhere in Ayrshire. Cropped blond hair, looked like he'd played rugby, liked to work out, even if it was just press-ups and sit-ups in the barracks. He started the campaign for retribution. It was to be covert – meaning behind the backs of the 'brass'. It was to be a release-valve for the frustration, the pressure that was building in the cramped confines of the barracks. The world outside was enemy terrain, everyone a potential foe. Knowing there was no way to punish the sniper, Mean Machine had decided to hold the entire community to blame: collective responsibility, for which there would be collective justice.

The plan: a raid on a known IRA bar, a place where sympathisers drank and colluded. The pretext: a man with a handgun, chased into the bar, necessitating a search. Maximum harassment, ending with the beating of the local IRA fundraiser.

And Rebus went along with it ... because it *was* collective. You were either part of the team, or you were dead meat. And Rebus wasn't in the market for pariah status.

But all the same, he knew the line between 'good guys' and 'bad guys' had become blurred. And during the incursion, it disappeared altogether.

Mean Machine went in hardest, teeth bared, eyes ablaze. He swung with his rifle, cracking skulls. Tables flew, pint glasses shattered. Initially the other soldiers seemed shocked by the sudden violence. They looked to each other for guidance. Then one of them lashed out, and the others fell in beside him. A mirror dissolved into glittering stars, stout and lager washed over the wooden floor. Men were shouting, begging, crawling on hands and knees across the

glass minefield. Mean Machine had the IRA man pinned to a wall, kneeing him in the groin. He twisted his body, threw him to the floor, then started pummelling him with the rifle-butt. More soldiers were pouring into the drinking-club: armoured cars arriving outside. A chair crashed into the row of optics. The smell of whisky was almost overpowering.

Rebus tried to shut it out, his own teeth bared not in anger but anguish. Then he aimed his rifle at the ceiling and let loose a single shot, and everything froze ... A final kick to the bloodied figure on the floor and Mean Machine turned and walked out of the club. The others hesitated again, then followed. He'd proved something to the other men: for all his lowly rank, he'd become their leader.

They enjoyed themselves that night in the barracks, chiding Rebus for letting his trigger-finger slip. They cracked open cans of beer and told stories, stories which were already being exaggerated, turning the event into a myth, giving it a grandeur it had lacked.

Turning it into a lie.

A few weeks later, the same IRA man was found shot dead in a stolen car south of the city, on a farm road with a view of hills and grazing land. Protestant paramilitaries took the blame, but Mean Machine, though he admitted nothing, would wink and grin when the incident was mentioned. Bravado or confession – Rebus was never sure. All he knew was that he wanted out, away from Mean Machine's newly minted code of ethics. So he did the one thing he could – applied to join the SAS. Nobody would think him a coward or a turncoat for applying to join the elite.

*To be born again.*

Side one had finished; Rebus turned the record over, switched off the lights and went to sit in his chair. He felt a chill run through him. Because he *knew* how events like Villefranche could come to be. Because he *knew* how the world's continuing horrors could come to be perpetrated at the cusp of the twentieth century. He knew that mankind's instinct was raw, that every act of bravery and kindness was countered by so many acts of savagery.

And he suspected that if his daughter had been that sniper's victim, he'd have run into the bar with his trigger-finger already working.

Telford's gang ran in a pack, too, trusted their leader. But now *he* wanted to run with an even bigger gang ...

The phone rang and he picked up.

'John Rebus,' he said.

'John, it's Jack.' Jack Morton. Rebus put down his can.

'Hello, Jack. Where are you?'

'In the poky one-bedroomed flat our friends at Fettes so graciously provided.'

'It has to fit the image.'

'Aye, I suppose so. Got a phone though. Coin job, but you can't have everything.' He paused. 'You okay, John? You sound ... not all there.'

'That just about sums me up, Jack. What's it like being a security guard?'

'A dawdle, pal. Should have taken it up years ago.'

'Wait till your pension's safe.'

'Aye, right.'

'And it went okay with Marty Jones?'

'Oscars all round. They were just heavy enough. I stumbled back into the shop, said I had to sit down. The Gruesome Twosome were very solicitous, then started asking me all these questions ... Not very subtle.'

'You don't think they twigged?'

'Like you, I was a bit dubious about setting it up so fast, but I think they fell for it. Whether their boss goes along is a different story.'

'Well, he's under a lot of pressure.'

'With the war going on?'

'I don't think that's the whole story, Jack. I think he's under pressure from his partners.'

'The Russian and the Japs?'

'I think they're setting him up for a fall, and Maclean's is the precipice.'

'Evidence?'

'Gut feeling.'

Jack was thoughtful. 'So where do I stand?'

'Just ca' canny, Jack.'

'I never thought of that.'

Rebus laughed. 'When do you think they'll make contact?'

'They followed me home – that's how desperate they are. They're sitting outside right now.'

'They must think you're a good thing.'

Rebus could see the way it was going. Dec and Ken getting

271

panicky, needing a quick result – feeling vulnerable so far away from Flint Street, not knowing if they'd be Cafferty's next victims. Telford, pressure applied by Tarawicz, and now with the Yakuza boss in town ... needing a result, something to show he was top dog.

'What about you, John? It's been a while.'

'Yes.'

'How are you holding up?'

'I'm on soft drinks only, if that's what you mean.' And a car doused in whisky ... he could taste it in his lungs.

'Hang on,' Jack said. 'Someone's at the door. I'll call you back.'

'Be careful.'

The phone went dead.

Rebus gave it an hour. When Jack hadn't called, he got on the blower to Claverhouse.

'It's okay,' Claverhouse told him from his mobile. 'Tweedledee and Tweedledum came calling, took him off somewhere.'

'You're watching the flat?'

'Decorator's van parked down the street.'

'So you've no idea where they've taken him?'

'I'd guess he's at Flint Street.'

'With no back-up?'

'That's how we all wanted it.'

'Christ, I don't know ...'

'Thanks for the vote of confidence.'

'It's not you in the firing line. And I'm the one who volunteered him.'

'He knows the score, John.'

'So now you wait for him either to come home or end up on a slab?'

'Christ, John, Calvin was Charlie Chester compared to you.' Claverhouse had lost all patience. Rebus tried to think of a comeback, slammed the phone down instead.

Suddenly he couldn't be doing with Van the Man; put on Bowie instead, *Aladdin Sane*: nicely discordant, Mike Garson's piano in key with his thoughts.

Empty juice cans and a dead pack of cigarettes stared up at him. He didn't know Jack's address. The only person who'd give it to him was Claverhouse, and he didn't want to pick up their conversation. He took Bowie off halfway through side one,

substituted *Quadrophenia*. Liner notes: 'Schizophrenic? I'm bleeding Quadrophenic'. Which was just about right.

Quarter past midnight, the phone rang. It was Jack Morton.

'Back home safe and sound?' Rebus asked.

'Right as nails.'

'Have you spoken to Claverhouse?'

'He can wait his turn. I said I'd phone you back.'

'So what did you get?'

'The third degree, basically. Some guy with dyed black hair, frizzy ... tight jeans.'

'Pretty-Boy.'

'Wears mascara.'

'Looks like. So what was the gist?'

'Second hurdle passed. Nobody's mentioned what the job is yet. Tonight was a sort of preface. Wanted to know all about me, told me my money worries could be over. If I could help them with a "little problem" – Pretty-Boy's words.'

'You asked what the problem was?'

'He wasn't saying. If you ask me, he goes to Telford, talks it through. Then there's another meeting, and that's where they tell me the plan.'

'And you'll be miked up?'

'Yes.'

'And if they strip you?'

'Claverhouse has access to some miniaturised stuff, cuff-links and the like.'

'And your character would obviously wear cuff-links.'

'True enough. Maybe fit a transmitter into a bookie's pencil.'

'Now you're thinking.'

'I'm thinking I'm wiped out.'

'What was the mood like?'

'Fraught.'

'Any sign of Tarawicz or Shoda?'

'Nope, just Pretty-Boy and the Gruesome Twosome.'

'Claverhouse calls them Tweedledum and Tweedledee.'

'He's obviously classically educated.' Morton paused. 'You've spoken to him?'

'When you didn't call back.'

'I'm touched. Do you think he's up to it?'

'Claverhouse?' Rebus thought about it. 'I'd feel better if *I* was in charge. But that probably puts me in a minority.'

'I didn't say that.'

'You're a pal, Jack.'

'They're running a check on me. But that's all in place. With luck, I'll pass.'

'What did they say to your sudden arrival at Maclean's?'

'I've been transferred from another plant. If they go looking, I'm in the personnel files.' Morton paused again. 'One thing I want to know ...'

'What?'

'Pretty-Boy handed me a hundred quid on account: what do I do with it?'

'That's between you and your conscience, Jack. See you soon.'

'Night, John.'

For the first time in a while, Rebus actually made it as far as his bed. His sleep was deep and dreamless.

# 31

Doctors in white coats were doing things to Sammy when Rebus arrived at the hospital next morning: taking her pulse, shining lights in her eyes. They were setting up another scanner, a nurse trying to untangle the thin coloured leads. Rhona looked like she'd lost some sleep. She jumped up and ran towards him.

'She woke up!'

It took him a second to take it in. Rhona was holding his arms, shaking him.

'She woke *up*, John!'

He pushed his way to the bedside.

'When?'

'Last night.'

'Why didn't you phone me?'

'I tried three, four times. You were engaged. I tried Patience, but there was no answer there.'

'What happened?' To him, Sammy looked the same as ever.

'She just opened her eyes ... No, first off, it was like she was moving her eyeballs. You know, with her eyelids closed. Then she opened her eyes.'

Rebus could see that the medical personnel were finding their work hampered. Half of him wanted to lash out – *We're her fucking parents!* The other half wanted them to do all they could to bring her round again. He took Rhona by the shoulder and guided her out into the hallway.

'Did she ... Did she look at you? Did she say anything?'

'She was just staring at the ceiling, where the strip-light is. Then I thought she was going to blink, but she closed her eyes again and they stayed shut.' Rhona burst into tears. 'It was like ... I lost her all over again.'

275

Rebus took her in his arms. She hugged him back.

'She did it once,' he whispered into her ear, 'she'll do it again.'

'That's what one of the doctors said. He said they're "very hopeful". Oh, John, I wanted to tell you! I wanted to tell *everyone*!'

And he'd been busy with work: Claverhouse, Jack Morton. And he'd got Sammy into all this in the first place. Sammy and Candice – pebbles dropped into a pool. And now the ripples had grown so that he'd all but forgotten about the centre, the starting point. Just like when he was married, work consuming him, becoming an end in itself. And Rhona's words: *You've exploited every relationship you ever had.*

*To be born again ...*

'I'm sorry, Rhona,' he said.

'Can you let Ned know?' She started crying again.

'Come on,' he said, 'let's get some breakfast. Have you been here all night?'

'I couldn't leave.'

'I know.' He kissed her cheek.

'The person in the car ...'

'What?'

She looked at him. 'I don't care any more. I don't care who they were or whether they get caught. All I want is for her to wake up.'

Rebus nodded, told her he understood. Told her breakfast was on him. He kept the talk going, his mind not really on it. Instead, her words bounced around in his head: *I don't care who they were or whether they get caught ...*

Whichever stress he put on it, he couldn't make it sound like surrender.


At St Leonard's, he broke the news to Ned Farlowe. Farlowe wanted to go to the hospital, but Rebus shook his head. Farlowe was crying as Rebus left his cell. Back at his desk, the files on the Crab were waiting.

The Crab: real name, William Andrew Colton. He had form going back to his teens, celebrated his fortieth birthday on Guy Fawkes Day. Rebus hadn't had many dealings with him during his time in Edinburgh. Looked like the Crab had lived in the city for a couple of years in the early-80s, and again in the early-90s. 1982: Rebus gave evidence against him in a conspiracy trial. Charges dropped. 1983: he was in trouble again – a fight in a pub left one

man in a coma and his girlfriend needing sixty stitches to her face. Sixty stitches: you could knit a pair of mittens with less.

The Crab had held various jobs: bouncer, bodyguard, general labourer. The Inland Revenue had a go at him in 1986. By '88, he was on the West Coast, which was presumably where Tommy Telford had found him. Knowing good muscle when he saw it, he'd put the Crab on the doors of his club in Paisley. More blood-spilling; more accusations. Nothing came of them. The Crab had lived a charmed life, the sort of life that niggled at cops the world over: witnesses too scared to testify; withdrawing or refusing to give evidence. The Crab didn't often make it to trial. He'd served three adult sentences – a total of twenty-seven months – in a career that was now entering its fourth decade. Rebus went through the paperwork again, picked up the phone and called CID in Paisley. The man he wanted to speak to had been transferred to Motherwell. Rebus made the call, eventually got through to Detective Sergeant Ronnie Hannigan, and explained his interest.

'It's just that reading between the lines, you suspected the Crab of a lot more than ever got put down on paper.'

'You're right.' Hannigan cleared his throat. 'Never got close to proving anything though. You say he's south of the border now?'

'Telford placed him with a gangster in Newcastle.'

'Have criminal tendencies, will travel. Well, let's hope they keep him. He was a one-man reign of terror, and that's no exaggeration. Probably why Telford palmed him off on someone else: the Crab was getting out of control. My theory is, Telford tried him out as a hit-man. Crab wasn't suitable, so Telford needed to jettison him.'

'What was the hit?'

'Down in Ayr. Must've been ... four years ago? Lot of drugs swilling around, most of them inside a dance-club ... can't remember its name. I don't know what happened: maybe a deal went sour, maybe someone was skimming. Whatever, there was a hit outside the club. Guy got his face half torn off with a carving knife.'

'You put the Crab in the frame?'

'He had an alibi, of course, and the eye-witnesses all seemed to have suffered temporary blindness. Could be a plot for the *X-Files* in that.'

A knife attack outside a nightclub ... Rebus tapped his desk with a pen. 'Any idea how the attacker got away?'

'On a motorbike. The Crab likes bikes. Crash helmet makes a good disguise.'

'We had an almost identical attack recently. Guy on a motorbike went for a drug dealer outside one of Tommy Telford's nightclubs. Killed a bouncer instead.'

And Cafferty denied any involvement ...

'Well, like you say, the Crab's in Newcastle.'

Yes, and staying put ... *scared* to come north. Warned off by Tarawicz. Because Edinburgh was too dangerous ... people might *remember* him.

'Do you know how far away Newcastle is?'

'A couple of hours?'

'No distance at all by bike. Anything else I should know?'

'Well, Telford tried the Crab in the van, but he wasn't much good.'

'What van?'

'The ice-cream van.'

Rebus nearly dropped the phone. 'Explain,' he said.

'Easy: Telford's boys were selling dope from an ice-cream van. The "five-pound special", they called it. You handed over a fiver and got back a cone or wafer with a wee plastic bag tucked inside ...'

Rebus thanked Hannigan and terminated the call. Five-pound specials: Mr Taystee with his clients who ate ice-cream in all weathers. His daytime pitches: near schools. His nighttime pitches: outside Telford's clubs. Five-pound specials on the menu, Telford taking his cut ... The new Merc: Mr Taystee's big mistake. Telford's moneymen wouldn't have taken long to work out their boy was skimming. Telford would have decided to turn Mr Taystee into a lesson ...

It was coming together. He spun his pen, caught it, and made another call, this time to Newcastle.

'Nice to hear from you,' Miriam Kenworthy said. 'Any sign of your lady friend?'

'She's turned up here.'

'Great.'

'In tow with Mr Pink Eyes.'

'Not so great. I wondered where he'd gone.'

'And he's not here to see the sights.'

'I'll bet he isn't.'

'Which is really why I'm calling.'

'Mmm?'

'I'm just wondering if he's ever been linked to machete attacks.'

'Machetes? Let me think ...' She was so quiet for so long, he thought the connection had failed. 'You know, that *does* ring a bell. Let me put it up on the screen.' Clackety-clack of her keyboard. Rebus was biting his bottom lip, almost drawing blood.

'God, yes,' she said. 'A year or so back, a battle on an estate. Rival gangs, that was the story, but everyone knew what was behind it: namely, drugs and pitch incursions.'

'And where there's drugs, there's Tarawicz?'

'There was a rumour his men were involved.'

'And they used machetes?'

'One of them did. His name's Patrick Kenneth Moynihan, known to all and sundry as "PK".'

'Can you give me a description?'

'I can fax you his picture. But meantime: tall, heavy build, curly black hair and a black beard.'

He wasn't part of the Tarawicz retinue. Two of Mr Pink's best muscle-men had been left behind in Newcastle. For safety's sake. Rebus put PK down as one of the Paisley attackers – Cafferty again in the clear.

'Thanks, Miriam. Listen, about that rumour ...'

'Remind me.'

'Telford supplying Tarawicz rather than the other way round: anything to back it up?'

'We tracked Pink Eyes and his men. A couple of jaunts to the continent, only they came back clean.'

'Leading you up the garden path?'

'Which made us start reassessing.'

'Where would Telford be getting the stuff?'

'We didn't reassess that far.'

'Well, thanks again ...'

'Hey, don't leave me hanging: what's the story?'

'Morning Glory. Cheers, Miriam.'

Rebus went and got a coffee, put sugar in it without realising, had finished half the cup before he noticed. Tarawicz was attacking Telford. Telford was blaming Cafferty. The resulting war would destroy Cafferty and weaken Telford. Then Telford would pull off the Maclean's break-in but be grassed up ...

And Tarawicz would fill the vacuum. That had been the plan all

along. Bluesbreakers: 'Double-Crossing Time'. Christ, it was beautiful: set the two rivals against one another and wait for the carnage to end ...

The prize: something Rebus didn't yet know. There had to be something big. Tarawicz, the theory went, was sourcing his drugs not from London but from Scotland. From Tommy Telford.

What did Telford know? What was it that made *his* supply so valuable? Did it have something to do with Maclean's? Rebus got another coffee, washed down three Paracetamol with it. His head felt ready to explode. Back at his desk, he tried Claverhouse, couldn't get him. Paged him instead, and got an immediate call back.

'I'm in the van,' Claverhouse said.

'I've something to tell you.'

'What?'

Rebus wanted to know what was happening. Wanted in on the action. 'It's got to be face to face. Where are you parked?'

Claverhouse sounded suspicious. 'Down from the shop.'

'White decorator's van?'

'This definitely isn't a good idea ...'

'You want to hear what I've got?'

'Sell me the idea.'

'It clears everything up,' Rebus lied.

Claverhouse waited for more, but Rebus wasn't obliging. Theatrical sigh: life was hard on Claverhouse.

'I'll be there in half an hour,' Rebus said. He put down the phone, looked around the office. 'Anyone got a set of overalls?'

'Nice disguise,' Claverhouse said, as Rebus squeezed into the front seat.

Ormiston was in the driver's seat, plastic piece-box open in front of him. A flask of tea had been opened, steaming up the windscreen. The back of the van was full of paint-tins, brushes and other paraphernalia. A ladder was strapped to the roof, and another was leaning against the wall of the tenement beside which the van had been parked. Claverhouse and Ormiston were in white overalls, daubed with swatches of old paint. The best Rebus could come up with was a blue boilersuit, tight at the waist and chest. He pulled the first few studs open as he settled in.

'Anything happening?'

'Jack's been in twice this morning.' Claverhouse looked towards

the shop. 'Once for ciggies and a paper, once for a can of juice and a filled roll.'

'He doesn't smoke.'

'He does for this operation: perfect excuse to nip to the shop.'

'He hasn't given you any signal?'

'You expecting him to put the flags out?' Ormiston exhaled fish-paste.

'Just asking.' Rebus checked his watch. 'Either of you want a break?'

'We're fine,' Claverhouse said.

'What's Siobhan up to?'

'Paperwork,' Ormiston said with a smile. 'Ever come across a woman house painter?'

'Done much house painting yourself, Ormie?'

This brought a smile from Claverhouse. 'So, John,' he said, 'what is it you've got for us?'

Rebus filled them in quickly, noting Claverhouse's mounting interest.

'So Tarawicz is planning to double-cross Telford?' Ormiston said at the end.

Rebus shrugged. 'That's my guess.'

'Then why the hell are we bothering to set up a sting? Just let them get on with it.'

'That wouldn't give us Tarawicz,' Claverhouse said, his eyes slitted in concentration. 'If he sets up Telford for a fall, *he's* home and dry. Telford gets put away, and all we've done is replace one villain with another.'

'And an altogether nastier species at that,' Rebus said.

'What? And Telford's Robin Hood?'

'No, but at least with him, we know what we're dealing with.'

'And the old dears in his flats love him,' Claverhouse said.

Rebus thought of Mrs Hetherington, readying herself for her trip to Holland. The only drawback: she had to fly from Inverness ... Sakiji Shoda had flown from London to Inverness ...

Rebus started laughing.

'What's so funny?'

He shook his head, still laughing, wiping his eyes. It wasn't funny, not really.

'We could let Telford know what we know,' Claverhouse said,

studying Rebus. 'Set him against Tarawicz, let them eat each other alive.'

Rebus nodded, took a deep breath. 'That's certainly one option.'

'Give me another.'

'Later,' Rebus said. He opened the door.

'Where are you off to?' Claverhouse asked.

'Got to fly.'

# 32

But in fact he was driving. A long drive, too. North through Perth and from there into the Highlands, taking a route which could be cut off during the worst of the winter. It wasn't a bad road, but traffic was heavy. He'd get past one slow-moving lorry only to catch up with another. He knew he should be thankful for small mercies: in the summer, caravans could end up fronting mile-long tailbacks.

He did pass a couple of caravans outside Pitlochry. They were from the Netherlands. Mrs Hetherington had said it was out of season for a trip to Holland. Most people her age would go in the spring, ready to fill their senses with the bulb-fields. But not Mrs Hetherington. Telford's offer: go when I say. Telford probably provided spending money, too. Told her to have a good time, not worry about a thing ...

As he neared Inverness, Rebus hit dual carriageway again. He'd been on the road well over two hours. Sammy might be coming round again; Rhona had his mobile number. Inverness Airport was signposted from the road into town. Rebus parked and got out, stretched his legs and arched his back, feeling the vertebrae pop. He went into the terminal and asked for security. He got a small balding man with glasses and a limp. Rebus introduced himself. The man offered coffee, but Rebus was jumpy enough after the drive. Hungry though: no lunch. He gave the man his story, and eventually they tracked down a representative of Her Majesty's Customs. During his tour of the facilities, Rebus got the impression of a low-key operation. The Customs official was in her early-thirties, rosy-cheeked and with black curly hair. There was a purple birthmark, the size of a small coin, in the middle of her forehead, looking for all the world like a third eye.

She took Rebus into the Customs area and found a room they could use for their conversation.

'They've just started direct international flights,' she said, in answer to his question. 'It's shocking really.'

'Why?'

'Because at the same time, they've cut back on manpower.'

'You mean in Customs?'

She nodded.

'You're worried about drugs?'

'Of course.' She paused. 'And everything else.'

'Are there flights to Amsterdam?'

'There will be.'

'But as of now ... ?'

She shrugged. 'You can fly to London, make the connection there.'

Rebus was thoughtful. 'There was a guy a few days ago, flew from Japan to Heathrow, then got a flight to Inverness.'

'Did he stop off in London?'

Rebus shook his head. 'Caught the first connection.'

'That counts as an international connection.'

'Meaning?'

'His luggage would be put on the plane in Japan, and he wouldn't see it again until Inverness.'

'So you'd be the first Customs point?'

She nodded.

'And if his flight came in at some horrible hour ...?'

She shrugged again. 'We do what we can, Inspector.'

Yes, Rebus could imagine: a lone, bleary-eyed Customs official, wits not at their sharpest ...

'So the bags change planes at Heathrow, but no one checks them there?'

'That's about it.'

'And if you were flying from Holland to Inverness via London?'

'Same deal.'

Rebus knew now, knew the brilliance of Tommy Telford's thinking. *He* was supplying drugs for Tarawicz, and Christ knew how many others. His little old ladies and men were bringing them in past early-morning or late-night Customs posts. How difficult would it be to slip something into a piece of luggage? Then Telford's men would be on hand to take everyone back to

Edinburgh, carry their luggage upstairs ... and surreptitiously remove each package.

Old age pensioners as unwitting drugs couriers. It was stunning.

And Shoda hadn't flown into Inverness so he could check out the local tourist amenities. He'd flown in so he could see how easy it was, what a brilliant route Telford had found, quick and efficient with a minimum of risk. Rebus had to laugh again. The Highlands had its own drugs problem these days: bored teenagers and cash-rich oil-workers. Rebus had smashed one north-east ring back in early summer, only to have Tommy Telford come along ...

Cafferty would never have thought of it. Cafferty would never have been so daring. But Cafferty would have kept it quiet. He wouldn't have sought to expand, wouldn't have brought partners into the scheme.

Telford was still a kid in some respects. The passenger-seat teddy bear was proof of that.

Rebus thanked the Customs official and went in search of food. Parked in the middle of town and grabbed a burger, sat at a window table and thought it all through. There were still aspects that didn't make sense, but he could cope with that.

He made two calls: one to the hospital; one to Bobby Hogan. Sammy hadn't woken up again. Hogan was interviewing Pretty-Boy at seven o'clock. Rebus said he'd be there.

The weather was kind on the trip south, the traffic manageable. The Saab seemed to enjoy long drives, or maybe it was just that at seventy miles an hour the engine noise disguised all the rattles and bumps.

He drove straight to Leith cop-shop, looked at his watch and found he was quarter of an hour late. Which didn't matter, since they were just starting the interview. Pretty-Boy was there with Charles Groal, all-purpose solicitor. Hogan was sitting with another CID officer, DC James Preston. A tape-recorder had been set up. Hogan looked nervous, realising how speculative this whole venture was, especially with a lawyer present. Rebus gave him a reassuring wink and apologised for having been detained. The burger had given him indigestion, and the coffee he'd had with it had done nothing for his frayed nerves. He had to shake his head clear of Inverness and all its implications and concentrate on Pretty-Boy and Joseph Lintz.

Pretty-Boy looked calm. He was wearing a charcoal suit with a

yellow t-shirt, black suede winkle-picker boots. He smelt of expensive aftershave. In front of him on the desk: a pair of tortoiseshell Ray-Bans and his car keys. Rebus knew he'd own a Range Rover – it was mandatory for Telford employees – but the key-ring boasted the Porsche marque, and on the street outside Rebus had parked behind a cobalt blue 944. Pretty-Boy showing a touch of individuality ...

Groal had his briefcase open on the floor beside him. On the desk in front of him: an A4 pad of ruled paper, and a fat black Mont Blanc pen.

Lawyer and client oozed money easily made and just as easily spent. Pretty-Boy used his money to buy class, but Rebus knew his background: working-class Paisley, a granite-hard introduction to life.

Hogan identified those present for the benefit of the tape-recorder, then looked at his own notes.

'Mr Summers ...' Pretty-Boy's real name: Brian Summers. 'Do you know why you're here?'

Pretty-Boy made an O of his glossy lips and stared ceilingwards.

'Mr Summers,' Charles Groal began, 'has informed me that he is willing to co-operate, Inspector Hogan, but that he'd like some indication of the accusations against him and their validity.'

Hogan stared at Groal, didn't blink. 'Who said he's accused of anything?'

'Inspector, Mr Summers works for Thomas Telford, and your police force's harassment of that individual is on record ...'

'Nothing to do with me, Mr Groal, or this station.' Hogan paused. 'Nothing at all to do with my present inquiries.'

Groal blinked half a dozen times in quick succession. He looked at Pretty-Boy, who was now studying the tips of his boots.

'You want me to say something?' Pretty-Boy asked the lawyer.

'I'm just ... I'm not sure if ...'

Pretty-Boy cut him off with a wave of his hand, then looked at Hogan.

'Ask away.'

Hogan made show of studying his notes again. 'Do you know why you're here, Mr Summers?'

'General vilification as part of your witch-hunt against my employer.' He smiled at the three CID men. 'Bet you didn't think

I'd know a word like "vilification".' His gaze rested on Rebus, then he turned to Groal.

'DI Rebus isn't based at this station.'

Groal took the hint. 'That's true, Inspector. Might I ask by what authority you've been allowed to sit in on this interview?'

'That will become clear,' Hogan said, '*if* you'll allow us to begin?'

Groal cleared his throat, but said nothing. Hogan let the silence lie for a few moments, then began.

'Mr Summers, do you know a man called Joseph Lintz?'

'No.'

The silence stretched out. Summers recrossed his feet. He looked up at Hogan, and blinked, the blink deteriorating into a momentary twitch of one eye. He sniffed, rubbed at his nose – trying to make out that the twitch meant nothing.

'You've never met him?'

'No.'

'The name means nothing to you?'

'You've asked me about him before. I'll tell you same as I told you then: I never knew the cat.' Summers sat up a bit straighter in his chair.

'You've never spoken to him by telephone?'

Summers looked at Groal.

'Hasn't my client made himself clear, Inspector?'

'I'd like an answer.'

'I don't know him,' Summers said, forcing himself to relax again, 'I've never spoken to him.' He gave Hogan his stare again, and this time held it. There was nothing behind the eyes but naked self-interest. Rebus wondered how anyone could ever think him 'pretty', when his whole outlook on life was so fundamentally ugly.

'He didn't phone you at your ... business premises?'

'I don't have any business premises.'

'The office you share with your employer.'

Pretty-Boy smiled. He liked those phrases: 'business premises'; 'your employer'. They all knew the truth, yet played this little game ... and he liked playing games.

'I've already said, I never spoke to him.'

'Funny, the phone company says differently.'

'Maybe they made a mistake.'

'I doubt that, Mr Summers.'

'Look, we've been through this before.' Summers sat forward in

287

his chair. 'Maybe it was a wrong number. Maybe he spoke to one of my associates, and they *told* him he had a wrong number.' He opened his arms. 'This is going nowhere.'

'I agree with my client, Inspector,' Charles Groal said, scribbling something down. 'I mean, is this leading anywhere?'

'It's leading, Mr Groal, to an identification of Mr Summers.'

'Where and by whom?'

'In a restaurant with Mr Lintz. The same Mr Lintz he claims never to have met, never to have spoken to.'

Rebus saw hesitation cross Pretty-Boy's face. *Hesitation*, rather than surprise. He made no immediate denial.

'An identification made by a member of staff at the restaurant,' Hogan continued. 'Corroborated by another diner.'

Groal looked to his client, who wasn't saying anything, but the way he was staring at the table, Rebus wondered a smoking hole didn't start appearing in it.

'Well,' Groal went on, 'this is fairly irregular, Inspector.'

Hogan wasn't interested in the lawyer. It was Pretty-Boy and him now.

'What about it, Mr Summers? Care to revise your version of events? What were you talking about with Mr Lintz? Was he looking for female company? I believe that's your particular area of expertise.'

'Inspector, I must insist ...'

'Insist away, Mr Groal. It won't change the facts. I'm just wondering what Mr Summers will say in court when he's asked about the phone call, the meeting ... when the witnesses identify him. I'm sure he's got a fund of stories, but he'll have to find a bloody good one.'

Summers slapped the desk with both palms, half-rose to his feet. There wasn't an ounce of fat on him. Veins stood out on the backs of his hands.

'I told you, I've never met him, never talked to him. Period, end of story, finito. And if you've got witnesses, they're lying. Maybe *you've* told them to lie. And that's all I've got to say.' He sat back down, put his hands in his pockets.

'I've heard,' Rebus said, as though attempting to liven up a flagging conversation between friends, 'that you run the more upmarket girls, the three-figure jobs rather than the gam-and-bam merchants.'

Summers snorted and shook his head.

'Inspector,' Groal said, 'I can't allow these accusations to continue.'

'Was that what Lintz wanted? Did he have expensive tastes?'

Summers continued shaking his head. He seemed about to say something, but caught himself, laughed instead.

'I would like to remind you,' Groal went on, unheeded by anyone, 'that my client has co-operated fully throughout this outrageous ...'

Rebus caught Pretty-Boy's eyes, held their stare. There was so much he wasn't telling ... so much he very nearly *wanted* to tell. Rebus thought of the length of rope in Lintz's house.

'He liked to tie them up, didn't he?' Rebus asked quietly.

Groal stood up, yanking Summers to his feet.

'Brian?' Rebus asked.

'Thank you, gentlemen,' Groal said. He was stuffing his notepad into his case, closing its brass locks. 'If you should find yourselves with any questions worth my client's time, we'll be pleased to assist. But otherwise, I'd advise you to ...'

'Brian?'

DC Preston had turned off the tape recorder and gone to open the door. Summers picked up his car keys, slipped his sunglasses on.

'Gentlemen,' he said, 'it's been educational.'

'S&M,' Rebus persisted, getting in Pretty-Boy's face. 'Did he tie them up?'

Pretty-Boy snorted, shook his head again. He paused as his lawyer led him past Rebus.

'It was for *him*,' he said in an undertone.

It was for him.

Rebus drove to the hospital. Sat with Sammy for twenty minutes. Twenty minutes of meditation and head-clearing. Twenty reviving minutes, at the end of which he squeezed his daughter's hand.

'Thanks for that,' he said.

Back at the flat, he thought of ignoring the answering-machine until after he'd had a bath. His shoulders and back were aching from the drive to Inverness. But something made him press the button. Jack Morton's voice: 'I'm on for a meeting with TT. Let's meet after. Half-ten at the Ox. I'll aim for that, but can't promise. Wish me luck.'

\*

He walked in at eleven.

There was folk music in the back room. The front would have been quiet if it weren't for two loud-mouths who looked like they'd been at it since their office closed for the night. They still wore work-suits, newspapers rolled in their pockets. They were drinking G&T.

Rebus asked Jack Morton what he wanted.

'A pint of orange and lemonade.'

'So how did it go?' Rebus ordered the drink. In forty minutes, he'd managed to put away two Cokes, and was now on coffee.

'They seem keen.'

'So who was at the meeting?'

'My sponsors from the shop, plus Telford and a couple of his men.'

'The transmitter worked okay?'

'Sound as a pound.'

'Did they search you?'

Morton shook his head. 'They were sloppy, seemed really sweaty about something. Want to hear the plan?' Rebus nodded. 'Middle of the night, truck arrives at the factory, and I let it through the gates. My story is, I had a phone call from the boss okaying the delivery. So I wasn't suspicious.'

'Only your boss never made the call?'

'That's right. So I was duped by a voice. And that's all I need to tell the police.'

'We'd sweat the truth out of you.'

'Like I say, John, the whole plan's half-baked. I'll give them this though – they did check my background. Seemed satisfied.'

'Who's going to be in the truck?'

'Ten men, armed to the teeth. I'm to get a rough plan of the place to Telford tomorrow, let him know how many people will be around, what the alarm system's like ...'

'What's in it for you?'

'Five grand. He's judged that right: five gets my debts repaid and puts a wedge in my pocket.'

Five grand: the amount Joseph Lintz had taken out of his bank ...

'Your story's holding?'

'They've staked out my flat.'

'And they didn't follow you here?'

Morton shook his head, and Rebus filled him in on what he'd

learned and what he suspected. While Morton was taking it in, Rebus threw a question at him.

'How does Claverhouse want to play it?'

'The tape evidence is good: Telford talking, me making sure I called him "Mr Telford" and "Tommy" a few times. It's obviously him on the recording. But ... Claverhouse wants Telford's crew caught red-handed.'

'"Got to do it right".'

'That seems to be his catch-phrase.'

'Is there a date?'

'Saturday, all being well.'

'What's the betting we get a tip-off on Friday?'

'If your theory's right.'

'If I'm right,' he agreed.

# 33

The tip-off didn't come until Saturday lunchtime, but when it did, Rebus knew his hunch had been right.

Claverhouse was the first to congratulate him, which surprised Rebus, because Claverhouse had a lot on his plate and had acted very casually when the call had come. Pinned to the walls of the Crime Squad office were detailed maps of the drugs plant, along with staff rosters. Coloured stickers showed where personnel would be stationed. During the night, it was security only, unless some big order was demanding overtime. Tonight, the usual security staff would be augmented by Lothian & Borders Police. Twenty people inside the plant, with marksmen stationed on roofs and at certain key windows. A dozen cars and vans as back-up. It was the biggest operation of Claverhouse's career; a lot was expected of him. He kept saying 'it has to be done right'. He said he would leave 'nothing to chance'. Those two phrases had become his mantra.

Rebus had listened to a recording of the snitch call: 'Be at Maclean's factory in Slateford tonight. Two in the morning, it's going to be turned over. Ten men, tooled up, driving a lorry. If you're canny, you can catch all of them.'

Scots accent, but sounding long distance. Rebus smiled, looked at the turning spools, and said 'Hello again, Crab' out loud.

No mention of Telford, which was interesting. Telford's men were loyal: they'd go down without saying a word. And Tarawicz wasn't grassing up Telford. He couldn't know the police already had taped evidence of Telford's involvement. Which meant he was planning on letting Telford go ... No, think it through. With the plan dead in the water and ten of his best men in custody, Tarawicz didn't *need* Telford under lock and key. He wanted him out in the open and worried, Yakuza breathing down his neck, all his frailties exposed. He could be picked off at any time, or made to hand over

*everything*. No blood-letting required; it would be a simple business proposition.

'It has to be ...'

'Done right,' Rebus said. 'Claverhouse, we *know*, okay?'

Claverhouse lost it. 'You're only here because I tolerate you! So let's get that straight for a start. I snap my fingers and you're out of the game, understood?'

Rebus just stared at him. A line of sweat was running down Claverhouse's left temple. Ormiston was looking up from his desk. Siobhan Clarke, briefing another officer beside a wall-chart, stopped talking.

'I promise I'll be a good boy,' Rebus said quietly, 'if you'll promise to stop with the broken record routine.'

Claverhouse's jaw was working, but eventually he produced a near-smile of apology.

'Let's get on with it then.'

Not that there was much for them to do. Jack Morton was working a double shift, wouldn't start till three o'clock. They'd be watching the place from then on, just in case Telford changed the game-plan. This meant personnel were going to miss the big match: Hibs against Hearts at Easter Road. Rebus had his money on a 3–2 home win.

Ormiston's summing-up: 'Easiest quid you'll ever lose.'

Rebus retired to one of the computers and got back to work. Siobhan Clarke had already come round snooping.

'Writing it up for one of the tabloids?'

'No such luck.'

He tried to keep it simple, and when he was happy with the finished product he printed off two copies. Then he went out to buy a couple of nice, bright folders ...

He dropped off one of the folders, then returned home, too restless to be much use at Fettes. Three men were waiting in his tenement stairwell. Two more came in behind him, blocking the only escape route. Rebus recognised Jake Tarawicz and one of his muscle-men from the scrapyard. The others were new to him.

'Up the stairs,' Tarawicz ordered. Rebus was a prisoner under escort as they climbed the steps.

'Unlock the door.'

'If I'd known you were coming, I'd have got in some beers,'

Rebus said, searching his pockets for keys. He was wondering which was safer: let them in, or keep them out? Tarawicz made the decision for him, nodded some signal. Rebus's arms were grabbed, hands went into his jacket and trousers, found his keys. He kept his face blank, eyes on Tarawicz.

'Big mistake,' he said.

'In,' Tarawicz ordered. They pushed Rebus into the hallway, walked him to the living room.

'Sit.'

Hands pushed Rebus on to the sofa.

'At least let me make a pot of tea,' he said. Inside he was trembling, knowing everything he couldn't afford to give away.

'Nice place,' Mr Pink Eyes was saying. 'Lacks the feminine touch though.' He turned to Rebus. 'Where is she?' Two of the men had peeled off to search the place.

'Who?'

'I mean, who else would she turn to? Not your daughter ... not now she's in a coma.'

Rebus stared at him. 'What do you know about that?' The two men returned, shook their heads.

'I hear things.' Tarawicz pulled out a dining-chair and sat down. There were two men behind the sofa, two in front.

'Make yourselves at home, lads. Where's the Crab, Jake?' Reasoning: a question he might be expected to ask.

'Down south. What's it to you?'

Rebus shrugged.

'Shame about your daughter. Going to make a recovery, is she?' Rebus didn't answer. Tarawicz smiled. 'National Health Service ... I wouldn't trust it myself.' He paused. 'Where is she, Rebus?'

'Using my finely honed detective's skills, I'll assume you mean Candice.' Meaning she'd done a runner. Trusting to herself for once. Rebus was proud of her.

Tarawicz snapped his fingers. Arms grabbed Rebus from behind, pinning back his shoulders. One man stepped forward and punched him solidly on the jaw. Stepped back again. Second man forward: gut punches. A hand tugged his hair, forcing his eyes up to the ceiling. He didn't see the flat-handed chop aiming for his throat. When it came, he thought he was going to cough out his voice-box. They let him go, and he pitched forward, hands going to his throat,

retching for breath. A couple of teeth felt loose, and the skin inside his cheek had burst. He got out a handkerchief, spat blood.

'Unfortunately,' Tarawicz was saying, 'I have no sense of humour. So I hope you'll understand I'm not joking when I say that I'll kill you if I have to.'

Rebus shook his head free of all the secrets he knew, all the power he held over Tarawicz. He told himself: *you don't know anything.*

He told himself: *you're not going to die.*

'Even ... if ... I did know ...' Fighting for breath. 'I wouldn't tell you. If the two of us were standing in a minefield, I wouldn't let you know. Want me ... to tell you why?'

'Sticks and stones, Rebus.'

'It's not because of *who* you are, it's *what* you are. You trade in human beings.' Rebus dabbed at his mouth. 'You're no better than the Nazis.'

Tarawicz put a hand to his chest. 'I'm struck to the quick.'

'Chance would be a fine thing.' Rebus coughed again. 'Tell me, why do you want her back?' Rebus knowing the answer: because he was about to head south, leaving Telford in Shit Street. Because to return to Newcastle without her was a small but palpable defeat. Tarawicz wanted it *all*. He wanted every last crumb on the plate.

'My business,' Tarawicz said. Another signal, and the hands grabbed him again, Rebus resisting this time. Packing-tape was being wound around his mouth.

'Everybody tells me how *genteel* Edinburgh is,' Tarawicz was saying. 'Can't have the neighbours complaining about the screams. Put him on a chair.'

Rebus was lifted up. He struggled. A kidney punch buckled his knees. They forced him down on to a dining-chair. Tarawicz was removing his jacket, undoing gold cufflinks so he could roll up the sleeves of his pink and blue striped shirt. His arms were hairless, thick, and the same mottled colour as his face.

'A skin complaint,' he explained, removing his blue-tinted glasses. 'Some distant cousin of leprosy, they tell me.' He loosened his top button. 'I'm not as pretty as Tommy Telford, but I think you'll find me his master in every other respect.' A smile to his troops, a smile Rebus wasn't supposed to understand. 'We can start anywhere you want, Rebus. And *you* get to choose when we stop. Just nod your head, tell me where she is, and I walk out of your life forever.'

He got in close to Rebus, the sheen on his face like a protective

seal. His pale blue eyes had tiny black pupils. Rebus thought: consumer as well as pusher. Tarawicz waited for a nod which didn't come, then retreated. Found an anglepoise lamp next to Rebus's chair. Planted both feet on its base and yanked on the mains cable, ripping it free.

'Bring him over here,' he ordered. Two men pulled both Rebus and chair over towards where Tarawicz was checking that the cable was plugged into the wall and that the socket was switched on. Another man closed the curtains: no free show for the kids across the way. Tarawicz was dangling the cable, letting Rebus see the loose wires – the very *live* wires. Two-hundred-and-forty volts just waiting to make his acquaintance.

'Believe me,' Tarawicz said, 'this is nothing. The Serbs had torture down to a fine art. Much of the time, they weren't even looking for a confession. I've helped a few of the more intelligent ones, the ones who knew when it was time to run. There was money to be made in the early days, power for the taking. Now the politicians are moving in, bringing trial-judges with them.' He looked at Rebus. 'The intelligent ones always know when it's time to quit. One last chance, Rebus. Remember, a nod of the head ...' The wires were inches from his cheek. Tarawicz changed his mind, moved them towards his nostrils, then his eyeballs.

'A nod of the head ...'

Rebus was twisting, arms holding him down – his legs, arms, shoulders. Hands holding his head, chest. Wait! The shock would pass straight through Tarawicz's men! Rebus saw it for a bluff. His eyes met Tarawicz's, and they both knew. Tarawicz pulled back.

'Tape him to the chair.' Two-inch-wide runs of tape, fixing him in place.

'This time for real, Rebus.' To his men: 'Hold him till I get close. Pull away when I say.'

Rebus thinking: there'd be a split-second after they let go ... A moment in which to break free. The tape wasn't the strongest he'd seen, but there was plenty of it. Maybe too much. He flexed his chest against it, felt no sign that it would break.

'Here we go,' Tarawicz said. 'First the face ... then the genitals. You *will* tell me, we both know it. How much bravado you want to show is up to you, but don't think it means anything.'

Rebus said something behind the gag.

'No point talking,' Tarawicz said. 'The only thing I want from you is a nod, understood?'

Rebus nodded.

'Was that a nod?'

Forcing a smile, Rebus shook his head.

Tarawicz didn't look impressed. His mind was on business. That was all Rebus was to him. He aimed the wire at Rebus's cheek.

'Let go!'

The pressure on Rebus fell away. He pushed against his bonds, couldn't budge them. Electricity flashed through his nervous system, and he went rigid. His heart felt like it had doubled in size, his eyeballs bulged, tongue pushing against the gag. Tarawicz lifted the cable away.

'Hold him.'

Arms fell on Rebus again, finding less resistance than before.

'Doesn't even leave a mark,' Tarawicz said. 'And the real beauty is, you end up paying for it from your own electric bill.'

His men laughed. They were beginning to enjoy themselves.

Tarawicz crouched down, face to face. His eyes sought Rebus's.

'For your information, that was a five-second jolt. Things only start to get interesting at the half-minute mark. How's your heart? For your sake, I hope it's in good condition.'

Rebus felt like he'd just mainlined adrenaline. Five seconds: it had seemed much longer. He was changing strategies, trying to think up some new lies Mr Pink might believe, anything to get him out of the flat ...

'Undo his trousers,' Tarawicz was saying. 'Let's see what a jolt down there will do.'

Behind the gag, Rebus started screaming. His tormentor was looking around the room again.

'Definitely lacks the feminine touch.'

Hands were loosening his trouser-belt. They stopped when a buzzer sounded. There was someone at the main door.

'Just wait,' Tarawicz said quietly. 'They'll go away.'

The buzzer sounded again. Rebus wrestled with his bonds. Silence. Then the buzzer again, more insistent now. One of the men went for the window.

'Don't!' Tarawicz snapped.

Buzzer again. Rebus hoped it would go on forever. Couldn't think who it might be: Rhona? Patience? A sudden thought ... what if

they persisted, and Tarawicz decided to allow them inside? Rhona or Patience ...

Time stretched. No more buzzing. They'd gone away. Tarawicz was beginning to relax, focusing his mind on his work once more.

Then there was a knock at the flat door. The person had got into the tenement. Now they were on the landing outside. Knocking again. Lifting the flap of the letterbox.

'Rebus!'

A male voice. Tarawicz looked to his men, nodded another signal. Curtains were opened; Rebus's bonds cut; the tape ripped from his face. Tarawicz rolled down his sleeves, put his jacket back on. Left the flex lying on the floor. One last word to Rebus: 'We'll speak again.' Then he marched his men to the door, opened it.

'Excuse us.'

Rebus was left sitting on the chair. He couldn't move, felt too shaky to stand up.

'Hang on a minute, chief!'

Rebus placed the voice: Abernethy. It didn't sound as if Tarawicz was heeding the Special Branch man.

'What's the score?' Now Abernethy was in the living-room, looking around.

'Business meeting,' Rebus croaked.

Abernethy came forward. 'Funny old business where you have to unzip your flies.'

Rebus looked down, started to make repairs.

'Who was that?' Abernethy persisted.

'A Chechen from Newcastle.'

'Likes to travel mob-handed, does he?' Abernethy walked around the room, found the bare flex and tut-tutted, unplugged it at the socket. 'Fun and games,' he said.

'Don't worry,' Rebus told him, 'it's under control.'

Abernethy laughed.

'What do you want anyway?'

'Brought someone to see you.' He nodded towards the doorway. A distinguished-looking man was standing there, dressed in three-quarter-length black woollen coat and white silk scarf. He was completely bald, with a huge dome of a head and cheeks reddened from cold. He had a sniffle, and was wiping his nose with a handkerchief.

'Thought we might pop out somewhere,' the man said, locution

impeccable, his eyes everywhere but on Rebus. 'Get a spot to eat, if you're hungry.'

'I'm not,' Rebus said.

'Something to drink then.'

'There's whisky in the kitchen.'

The man looked reluctant.

'Look, pal,' Rebus told him, 'I'm staying right here. You can join me or you can bugger off.'

'I see,' the man said. He put the handkerchief away and stepped forward, stretched out a hand. 'Name's Harris, by the way.'

Rebus took the hand, expecting sparks to leap from his fingertips.

'Mr Harris, let's sit at the dining-table.' Rebus got to his feet. He was shaky, but his knees held till he'd crossed the floor. Abernethy appeared from the kitchen with the bottle and three glasses. Left again, and returned with a milk-jug of water.

Ever the host, Rebus poured, sizing up the trembling in his right arm. He felt disoriented. Adrenaline and electricity coursing through him.

'*Slainte*,' he said, lifting the glass. But he paused with it at his nostrils. Pact with the Big Man: no drinking, and Sammy back. His throat hurt when he swallowed, but he put the glass down untouched. Harris was pouring too much water into his own glass. Even Abernethy looked disapproving.

'So, Mr Harris,' Rebus said, rubbing his throat, 'just who the hell are you?'

Harris affected a smile. He was playing with his glass.

'I'm a member of the intelligence community, Inspector. I know what that probably conjures up in your mind, but I'm afraid the reality is far more prosaic. Intelligence-gathering means just that: lots of paperwork and filing.'

'And you're here because of Joseph Lintz?'

'I'm here because DI Abernethy says you're determined to link the murder of Joseph Lintz with the various accusations which have been made against him.'

'And?'

'And that, of course, is your prerogative. But there are matters not necessarily germane which might prove ... embarrassing, if brought into the open.'

'Such as that Lintz really was Linzstek, and was brought to this country by the Rat Line, probably with help from the Vatican?'

'As to whether Lintz and Linzstek were the same man ... I can't tell you. A lot of the documentation was destroyed just after the war.'

'But "Joseph Lintz" was brought to this country by the Allies?'

'Yes.'

'And why did we do that?'

'Lintz was useful to this country, Inspector.'

Rebus poured a fresh whisky for Abernethy. Harris hadn't touched his. 'How useful?'

'He was a reputable academic. As such he was invited to attend conferences and give guest lectures all round the world. During this time, he did some work for us. Translation, intelligence-gathering, recruitment ...'

'He recruited people in other countries?' Rebus stared at Harris. 'He was a *spy*?'

'He did some dangerous and ... influential work for this country.'

'And got his reward: the house in Heriot Row?'

'He earned every penny in the early days.'

Harris's tone told Rebus something. 'What happened?'

'He became ... unreliable.' Harris lifted the glass to his nose, sniffed it, but put it down again untouched.

'Drink it before it evaporates,' Abernethy chided. Harris looked at him, and the Londoner mumbled an apology.

'Define "unreliable",' Rebus said, pushing aside his own glass.

'He began to ... fantasise.'

'He thought a colleague at the university had been in the Rat Line?'

Harris was nodding. 'He became obsessed with the Rat Line, began to imagine that everyone around him had been involved in it, that we were *all* culpable. Paranoia, Inspector. It affected his work and eventually we had to let him go. This was years back. He hasn't worked for us since.'

'So why the interest? What does it matter if any of this comes out?'

Harris sighed. 'You're right, of course. The problem is not the Rat Line *per se*, or the notion of Vatican involvement or any of the other conspiracy theories.'

'Then what is ...?' Rebus broke off, realised the truth. 'The problem is the personnel,' he stated. 'The other people brought in

by the Rat Line.' He nodded to himself. 'Who are we talking about? Who might be implicated?'

'Senior figures,' Harris admitted. He'd stopped playing with the glass. His hands were flat on the table. He was telling Rebus: this is *serious*.

'Past or present?'

'Past ... plus people whose children have gone on to achieve positions of power.'

'MPs? Government ministers? Judges?'

Harris was shaking his head. 'I can't tell you, Inspector. I haven't been trusted with that knowledge myself.'

'But you could hazard a guess.'

'I don't deal in guesswork.' He looked at Rebus. There was steel behind the eyes. 'I deal in known quantities. It's a good maxim – one you should try.'

'But whoever killed Lintz did so *because* of his past.'

'Are you sure?'

'It doesn't make sense otherwise.'

'DI Abernethy tells me there's a link with some criminal elements in Edinburgh, perhaps a question of prostitution. It all sounds sordid enough to be believable.'

'And if it's believable, that's good enough for you?'

Harris stood up. 'Thank you for listening.' He blew his nose again, looked to Abernethy. 'Time to go, I believe. DI Hogan is waiting for us.'

'Harris,' Rebus said, 'you said yourself, Lintz had gone loopy, become a liability. Who's to say *you* didn't have him killed?'

Harris shrugged. 'If we'd arranged it, his demise would not have been quite so obvious.'

'Car crash, suicide, falling from a window ...?'

'Goodbye, Inspector.'

As Harris walked to the door, Abernethy stood up and locked eyes with Rebus. He didn't say anything, but the message was there.

*This is deeper water than either of us wants to be in. So do yourself a favour, swim for shore.*

Rebus nodded, reached out a hand. The two men shook.

# 34

Two in the morning.

Frost on the car windscreens. They couldn't clear them: had to blend in with the other cars on the street. Back-up – four units – parked in a builder's yard just round the corner. Bulbs had been removed from street-lights, leaving the area in almost total darkness. Maclean's was like a Christmas tree: security lights, every window blazing, same as every other night.

No heating in the unmarked cars: heat would melt the frost; exhaust fumes a dead giveaway.

'This all seems very familiar,' Siobhan Clarke said. The surveillance on Flint Street seemed a lifetime ago to Rebus. Clarke was in the driving seat, Rebus in the back. Two to each car. That way, they had space to duck should anyone come snooping. Not that they expected anyone to do that: the whole heist was half-baked. Telford desperate *and* with his mind on other things. Sakiji Shoda was still in town – a quiet word with the hotel manager had revealed a Monday morning check-out. Rebus was betting Tarawicz and his men had already gone.

'You look pretty snug,' Rebus said, referring to her padded ski-jacket. She brought a hand out of her pocket, showed him what it was holding. It looked like a slim lighter. Rebus lifted it from her palm. It was warm.

'What the hell is it?'

Clarke smiled. 'I got it from one of those catalogues. It's a handwarmer.'

'How does it work?'

'Fuel rods. Each one lasts up to twelve hours.'

'So you've got one warm hand?'

She brought her other hand out, showed him an identical rod. 'I bought two,' she said.

'You might have said.' Rebus closed his fingers around the handwarmer, stuck it deep into his pocket.

'That's not fair.'

'Call it a privilege of rank.'

'Lights,' she warned. They dived for cover, surfaced again when the car had sped past: false alarm.

Rebus checked his watch. Jack Morton had been told to expect the truck some time between one-thirty and two-fifteen. Rebus and Clarke had been in the car since just after midnight. The snipers on the roof, poor bastards, had been in position since one o'clock. Rebus hoped they had a good supply of fuel rods. He still felt jittery from the afternoon's events. He didn't like that he owed Abernethy such a huge favour; indeed, maybe owed him his life. He knew he could cancel it out by agreeing – along with Hogan – to soft-pedal on the Lintz inquiry. He didn't like the idea, but all the same ... And the day's silver lining: Candice had made the break from Tarawicz.

Clarke's police radio was silent. They had maintained silence since before midnight. Claverhouse's words: 'The first person to speak will be me, understood? Anyone uses a radio before me, they're in farmyard shit. And I won't utter a sound until the truck's entered the compound. Is that clear?' Nods all around. 'They could be listening in, so this is *important*. We've got to do this *right*.' Averting his eyes from Rebus as he said it. 'I'd wish us all luck, but the less luck's involved the better I'll like it. A few hours from now, if we stick to the plan, we should have broken up Tommy Telford's gang.' He paused. 'Just let that sink in. We'll be heroes.' He swallowed, realising the immensity of the prize.

Rebus couldn't get so excited. The whole enterprise had shown him a simple truth: no vacuum. Where you had society, you had criminals. No belly without an underbelly.

Rebus knew his own criteria came cheaply: his flat, books, music and clapped-out car. And he realised that he had reduced his life to a mere shell in recognition that he had completely failed at the important things: love, relationships, family life. He'd been accused of being in thrall to his career, but that had never been the case. His work sustained him only because it was an easy option. He dealt every day with strangers, with people who didn't mean anything to him in the wider scheme. He could enter their lives, and leave again just as easily. He got to live other people's lives, or at least portions

of them, experiencing things at one remove, which wasn't nearly as challenging as the real thing.

Sammy had brought home to him these essential truths: that he was not only a failed father but a failed human being; that police work kept him sane, yet was a substitute for the life he could have had, the kind of life everyone else seemed to lead. And if he became obsessed with his case-work, well, that was no different from being obsessed with train numbers or cigarette cards or rock albums. Obsession came easy – especially to men – because it was a cheap way of achieving *control*, albeit control over something practically worthless. What did it matter if you could reel off the track listing to every '60s Stones album? It didn't matter a damn. What did it matter if Tommy Telford got put away? Tarawicz would take his place, and if he didn't, there was always Big Ger Cafferty. And if not Cafferty, then someone else. The disease was endemic, no cure in sight.

'What are you thinking about?' Clarke asked, switching her rod from left hand to right.

'My next cigarette.' Patience's words: *happiest when in denial* ...

They heard the truck before they saw it: changing gears noisily. Slid down into their seats, then up again as it made to pull into Maclean's. A wheeze of air-brakes as it jolted to a stop at the gates. A guard came out to talk to the driver. He carried a clip-board.

'Jack really suits a uniform,' Rebus said.

'Clothes maketh the man.'

'You reckon your boss has got it right?' He meant Claverhouse's plan: when the truck was in the compound, they'd use a megaphone and show the marksmen to whoever was in the driver's cab, tell them to come out. The rest of the men could stay locked in the back of the vehicle. They'd have them toss out any arms and then come out one at a time.

It was either that or wait until they were *all* out of the truck. Merit of this second plan: they'd know what they were dealing with. Merit of the first: most of the gang would be nicely stowed in the truck, and could be dealt with as and when.

Claverhouse had plumped for plan one.

Marked and unmarked cars were to move in as soon as the truck had come to a stop – engine off – in the compound. They would block the exit, then watch from safety while Claverhouse, at a first-floor window with his megaphone, and the marksmen (roof; ground-

floor windows) did their stuff. 'Negotiation with force' was how Claverhouse had described it.

'Jack's opening the gates,' Rebus said, peering through the side window.

Engine roar, and the truck jerked forward.

'Driver seems a bit nervous,' Clarke commented.

'Or isn't used to HGVs.'

'Okay, they're in.'

Rebus stared at the radio, willing it to burst into life. Clarke had turned the ignition one click away from starting. Jack Morton was watching the truck move into the compound. He turned his head towards the line of cars parked across the way.

'Any second ...'

The truck's brake-lights came on, then went off again. Air-brakes sounded.

The radio fizzed a single word: '*Now!*'

Clarke turned the engine, revved hard. Five other cars did the same. Exhaust smoke billowed suddenly into the night air. The noise was like the start of a stock-car race. Rebus wound his window down, the better to hear Claverhouse's megaphone diplomacy. Clarke's car leaped forward, first to the gates. Both she and Rebus jumped out, keeping their heads down, the car a shield between themselves and the truck.

'Engine's still running,' Rebus hissed.

'What?'

'The truck. Its engine's still running!'

Claverhouse's voice, warbling – partly nerves, partly megaphone quality: 'Armed police. Open the cab doors slowly and come out one at a time, hands held high. I repeat: armed police. Discard weapons before coming out. I repeat: discard weapons.'

'Do it!' Rebus hissed. Then: 'Tell them to switch off the bloody engine!'

Claverhouse: 'The gate is blocked, there's no escape, and we don't want anyone getting hurt.'

'Tell them to throw out the keys.' Cursing, Rebus dived back into the car, grabbed the handset. 'Claverhouse, tell them to ditch the bloody keys!'

Windscreen frosted over; he couldn't see a thing. Heard Clarke's yell: '*Get out!*'

Saw: dim white lights. The truck was reversing. At speed. A roar from its engine, veering crazily but heading for the gates.

Heading straight for him.

An explosion: bricks flying from the factory's front wall.

Rebus dropped the handset, got his arm stuck in the seatbelt. Clarke was screaming as he leaped clear.

A second later, truck and car connected in a rending of metal and smashing of glass. Domino effect: Clarke's car hit the one behind, throwing officers off balance. The road was like a skating rink, the truck pushing one car, two cars, then three cars back on to the highway.

Claverhouse was on the megaphone, choking on dust: 'No shooting! Officers too close! Officers too close!'

Yes, all they needed now was to be pinned down by sniper fire. Men and women were slipping, losing their footing, clambering from their cars. Some of them armed, but dazed. The truck's back doors, buckled by the initial collision, flew open, seven or eight men hit the ground running. Two of them had handguns, and loosed off three or four shots apiece.

Shouts, screams, the megaphone. The glass wall of the gatehouse exploded as a bullet hit it. Rebus couldn't see Jack Morton ... couldn't see Siobhan. He was lying on his front on a section of grass verge, hands over his head: classic defence/defeat posture and bloody useless with it. The whole area was picked out by floodlights, and one of the gunmen – Declan from the shop – was now aiming at those. Other members of the gang had headed out into the street and were running for it. They carried shotguns, pickaxe handles. Rebus recognised a few more faces: Ally Cornwell, Deek McGrain. The streetlights were dead, of course, giving them all the cover they could want. Rebus hoped the backup cars from the builder's yard were coming.

Yes: turning the corner now, all lights blazing, sirens howling. Tenement curtains were twitching, palms rubbing at windows. And right in front of Rebus, about an inch from his nose, a thickly rimed blade of grass. He could make out each sliver of frost, and the complex patterns which had formed. But he realised it was melting fast as his breath hit it. And his front was growing cold. And the marksmen were running from the building, lit up like a firing-range.

And Siobhan Clarke was safe: he could see her lying beneath a car. Good girl.

And one policewoman, also lying low, had been wounded in the knee. She kept touching it with her hand, then pulling the hand away to stare at the blood.

And there was still no sign of Jack Morton.

The gunmen were returning fire, scattering shots, smashing windscreens. Uniforms were ordered out of the front back-up car. Four of the gang got in.

Second car: uniforms out, three of the gang got in. No windscreens, but they were rolling. Yelling and whooping, waving their weapons. The two remaining gunmen were cool. They were taking a good look round, assessing the situation. Did they want to be here when the marksmen arrived? Maybe they did. Maybe they fancied their chances in that arena, too. Their luck had held *this* far, after all. Claverhouse: *the less luck's involved, the better I'll like it.*

Rebus got on to his knees, then his feet, staying at a crouch. He felt moderately safe. After all, *his* luck had held today, too.

'You okay, Siobhan?' Voice low, eyes on the gunmen. The two getaway cars added up to seven men. Two still left. Where was number ten?

'Fine,' Clarke said. 'What about you?'

'I'm okay.' Rebus left her, worked his way round to the front of the truck. The driver was unconscious behind his wheel, head bleeding where it had connected after the collision. There was some kind of grenade launcher on the seat beside him. It had left a bloody great hole in the wall of Maclean's. Rebus checked the driver for firearms, found none. Then checked the pulse: steady. Recognised the face: one of the arcade regulars; looked about nineteen, twenty. Rebus took out his handcuffs, hooked the driver to the steering-wheel, threw the grenade launcher on to the road.

Then headed for the gatehouse. Jack Morton, in uniform but missing his cap, prone on the floor, covered by a glass shroud. The bullet had pierced his right breast-pocket. Pulse was weak.

'Christ, Jack ...'

There was a telephone in the booth. Rebus punched 999 and asked for ambulances.

'Police officers down at the Maclean's factory on Slateford Road!' Staring down at his friend.

'Whereabouts on Slateford Road?'

'Believe me, they won't be able to miss it.'

Five marksmen, dressed in black, aimed rifles at Rebus from

outside. Saw him on the phone, saw him shake his head, moved on. Saw their targets out on the road, getting into a patrol car. Yelled the order to stop, warning that they would fire.

Response: muzzle-flash. Rebus ducked again. Fire was returned, the noise deafening but momentary.

Shouts from the road: 'Got them!'

A plaintive wail: one of the gunmen wounded. Rebus looked. The other was lying quite still on the road. Marksmen yelling to the wounded man: 'Drop the weapon, turn on to your front, hands behind your back.'

Response: 'I'm shot!'

Rebus to himself: 'Bastard's only wounded. Finish him off.'

Jack Morton unconscious. Rebus knew better than to move him. He could staunch the bleeding, that was all. Removed his jacket, folded it and pressed it to his friend's chest. Must've hurt, but Jack was out of it. Rebus dug the fuel rod out of his own pocket, the tiny canister still warm. Pressed it into Jack's right hand, curled the fingers around it.

'Stick around, pal. Just keep sticking around.'

Siobhan Clarke at the doorway, tears welling in her eyes.

Rebus pushed past her, slid his way across the road to where the Armed Response Team were cuffing the wounded man. Nobody much bothering with his dead partner. A little group of onlookers, keeping their distance. Rebus walked right up to the corpse, prised the handgun from its fingers, walked back around the front of the car. Heard someone call out: 'He's got a gun!'

Rebus bending down until the barrel of the gun touched the back of the wounded man's neck. Declan from the shop: breath coming in short gasps, hair matted with sweat, burrowing his face into the tarmac.

'John ...'

Claverhouse. No megaphone needed. Standing right behind him. 'You really want to be like them?'

Like them ... Like Mean Machine. Like Telford and Cafferty and Tarawicz. He'd crossed the line before, made several trips forth and back. His foot was on Declan's neck, the gun barrel so hot it was singeing nape-skin.

'Please, no ... oh, Christ, please ... don't ... don't ...'

'Shut up,' Rebus hissed. He felt Claverhouse's hand close over his, flick on the safety.

'My responsibility, John. My fuck-up, don't make it yours, too.'

'Jack ...'

'I know.'

Rebus's vision blurred. 'They're getting away.'

Claverhouse shook his head. 'Road blocks. Back-up are already on it.'

'And Telford?'

Claverhouse checked his watch. 'Ormie will be picking him up right about now.'

Rebus grabbed Claverhouse's lapels. 'Nail him!'

Sirens nearing. Rebus shouted for the drivers to move their cars, make room for the ambulance. Then he ran back to the gatehouse. Siobhan Clarke was kneeling beside Jack, stroking his forehead. Her face was streaked with tears. She looked up at Rebus and shook her head.

'He's gone,' she said.

'No.' But he knew the truth. Which didn't stop him saying the word over and over again.

# 35

They divided the gang between two different locations – Torphichen and Fettes – and took Telford and a few of his 'lieutenants' to St Leonard's. Result: a logistical nightmare. Claverhouse was washing Pro-Plus down with double-strength coffee, part of him wanting to do things right, the other part knowing he was answerable for the blood-bath at Maclean's. One officer dead, six wounded or otherwise injured – one of them seriously. One gunman dead, one wounded – not seriously enough to some people's minds.

The getaway cars had been apprehended and arrests made – shots exchanged but no bloodshed. None of the gang was saying anything, not a single damned word.

Rebus was sitting in an empty Interview Room at St Leonard's, arms on the table, head resting on arms. He'd been sitting there for a while, just thinking about loss, about how suddenly it could strike. A life, a friendship, just snatched away.

Irretrievable.

He hadn't cried, and didn't think he would. Instead, he felt numb, as if his soul had been spiked with novocaine. The world seemed to have slowed, like the mechanism was running down. He wondered if the sun would have the energy to rise again.

*And I got him into it.*

He had wallowed before in feelings of guilt and inadequacy, but nothing to measure up to this. This was overwhelming. Jack Morton, a copper with a quiet patch in Falkirk ... murdered in Edinburgh because a friend had asked a favour. Jack Morton, who'd brought himself back to life by swearing off cigarettes and booze, getting into shape, eating right, taking *care* of himself ... Lying in the mortuary, deep-body temperature dropping.

*And I put him there.*

310

He jumped up suddenly, threw the chair at the wall. Gill Templer walked into the room.

'All right, John?'

He wiped his mouth with the back of his hand.

'Fine.'

'My office is empty if you want to get your head down.'

'No, I'll be fine. Just ...' He looked around. 'Is this place needed?'

She nodded.

'Right. Okay.' He picked up the chair. 'Who is it?'

'Brian Summers,' she said.

Pretty-Boy. Rebus straightened his back.

'I can make him talk.'

Templer looked sceptical.

'Honest, Gill.' Hands trembling. 'He doesn't know what I've got on him.'

She folded her arms. 'And what's that?'

'I just need ...' He checked his watch. 'An hour or so; two hours tops. Bobby Hogan needs to be here. And I want Colquhoun brought in pronto.'

'Who's he?'

Rebus found the business card and handed it over. 'Pronto,' he repeated. He worked at his tie, making himself presentable. Smoothed back his hair. Said nothing.

'John, I'm not sure you're in any state to ...'

He pointed at her, turned it into a wagging finger. 'Don't presume, Gill. If I say I can break him, I mean it.'

'No one else has said a single word.'

'Summers will be different.' He stared at her. 'Believe me.'

Looking back at him, she believed. 'I'll hold him back till Hogan gets here.'

'Thanks, Gill.'

'And, John?'

'Yes?'

'I'm really sorry about Jack Morton. I didn't know him, but I've heard what everyone's saying.'

Rebus nodded.

'They're saying he'd be the last one to blame you.'

Rebus smiled. 'Right at the back of the queue.'

'There's only one person in the queue, John,' she said quietly. 'And you're it.'

311

*

Rebus phoned the night-desk at the Caledonian Hotel, learned that Sakiji Shoda had checked out unexpectedly, less than two hours after Rebus had dropped off the green folder which had cost him fifty-five pence at a stationer's on Raeburn Place. Actually, the folders had come in three-packs at one sixty-five. He had the other two in his car, only one of them empty.

Bobby Hogan was on his way. He lived in Portobello. He said to give him half an hour. Bill Pryde came over to Rebus's desk and said how sorry he was about Jack Morton, how he knew the two of them had been old friends.

'Just don't get too close to me, Bill,' Rebus told him. 'The people closest to me tend to lose their health.'

He got a message from reception: someone there to see him. He headed downstairs, found Patience Aitken.

'Patience?'

She had all her clothes on, but not necessarily in the right order, like she'd dressed in a power-cut.

'I heard on the radio,' she said. 'I couldn't sleep, so I had the radio on, and they said about this police raid and how people were dead ... And you weren't in your flat, so I ...'

He hugged her. 'I'm okay,' he whispered. 'I should have called you.'

'It's my fault, I ...' She looked at him. 'You were there, I can see it on your face.' He nodded. 'What happened?'

'I lost a friend.'

'Oh, Christ, John.' She hugged him again. She was still warm from the bedclothes. He could smell shampoo on her hair, perfume on her neck. *The people closest to me* ... He pulled away gently, planted a kiss on her cheek.

'Go get some sleep,' he told her.

'Come for breakfast.'

'I just want to go home and crash.'

'You could sleep at my place. It's Sunday. We could stay in bed.'

'I don't know what time I'll finish here.'

She found his eyes. 'Don't feed on it, John. Don't keep it all inside.'

'Okay, Doc.' He pecked her cheek again. 'Now vamoose.'

He managed a smile and a wink: both felt treacherous. He stood at the door and watched her leave. A lot of times while he'd been married, he'd thought of just walking. There were times when all

the responsibilities and the shite at work and the pressure and the *need* would make him dream of escape.

He was tempted again now. Push open the door and head off to somewhere that wasn't here, to do something that wasn't this. But that, too, would be treachery. He had scores to settle, and a reason to settle them. He knew Telford was somewhere in the building, probably consulting with Charles Groal, saying nothing to anyone else. He wondered how the team were playing it. When would they let Telford know about the tape? When would they tell him the security guard had been a plant? When would they tell him that same man was now dead?

He hoped they were being clever. He hoped they were rattling Telford's cage.

He couldn't help wondering – and not for the first time – if it was all worth it. Some cops treated it like a game, others like a crusade, and for most of the rest it was neither, just a way of earning their daily bread. He asked himself why he'd invited Jack Morton in. Answers: because he'd wanted a *friend* involved, someone who'd keep *him* in the game; because he'd thought Jack was bored, and would enjoy the challenge; because tactics had demanded an outsider. There were plenty of reasons. Claverhouse had asked if Morton had any family, anyone who should be informed. Rebus had told him: divorced, four kids.

Did Rebus blame Claverhouse? Easy to be wise after the event, but then Claverhouse's reputation had been built on being wise *before* the event. And he'd failed ... monumentally.

Icy roads: they'd needed the gates closed. The blockade had been too easy to move with the horsepower available to a truck.

Marksmen in the building: fine in the enclosed space of the yard, but they'd failed to keep the truck there, and the marksmen had been ineffectual once the truck had reversed out.

More armed officers *behind* the truck: producing little but a crossfire hazard.

Claverhouse should have got them to turn off the ignition, or – better still – waited for it to be turned off before making his presence known.

Jack Morton should have kept his head down.

And Rebus should have warned him.

Only, a shout would have turned the gunmen's attention towards him. Cowardice: was that what was at the bottom of his feelings?

Simple human cowardice. Like in the bar in Belfast, when he hadn't said anything, fearing Mean Machine's wrath, fearing a rifle-butt turned on *him*. Maybe that was why – no, *of course* that was why – Lintz had got beneath Rebus's skin. Because when it came down to it, if Rebus had been in Villefranche ... drunk on failure, the dream of conquest over ... if he'd been under orders, just a lackey with a gun ... if he'd been primed by racism and the loss of comrades ... who was to say what he'd have done?

'Christ, John, how long have you been out here?'

It was Bobby Hogan, touching his face, prising the folder from frozen fingers.

'You're like ice, man, let's get you inside.'

'I'm fine,' Rebus breathed. And it had to be true: how else to explain the sweat on his back and his brow? How else to explain that he only started shivering *after* Bobby led him indoors?

Hogan got two mugs of sweet tea into him. The station was still buzzing: shock, rumour, theories. Rebus filled Hogan in.

'They'll have to let Telford walk, if nobody talks.'

'What about the tape?'

'They'll want to spring that later ... if they're being canny.'

'Who's in with him?'

Rebus shrugged. 'Farmer Watson himself, last time I heard. He was doing a double-act with Bill Pryde, but I saw Bill later, so they've either taken a break or else done a swop.'

Hogan shook his head. 'What a fucking business.'

Rebus stared at his tea. 'I hate sugar.'

'You drank the first mug all right.'

'Did I?' He took a mouthful, squirmed.

'What the hell did you think you were doing out there?'

'Catching a breath.'

'Catching your death more like.' Hogan patted down an unruly clump of hair. 'I had a visit from a man called Harris.'

'What are you going to do?'

Hogan shrugged. 'Let it go, I suppose.'

Rebus stared at him. 'You might not have to.'

# 36

Colquhoun didn't look happy to be there.

'Thanks for coming in,' Rebus told him.

'I didn't have much choice.' He had a solicitor sitting beside him, a middle-aged man: one of Telford's? Rebus couldn't have cared less.

'You might have to get used to not having choices, Dr Colquhoun. Know who else is in here tonight? Tommy Telford; Brian Summers.'

'Who?'

Rebus shook his head. 'You're getting your script wrong. It's okay for you to know who they are: we talked about them in front of Candice.'

Colquhoun's face flushed.

'You remember Candice, don't you? Her real name's Dunya: did I ever tell you that? She's got a son somewhere, only they took him away. Maybe she'll find him one day, maybe not.'

'I don't see what this —'

'Telford and Summers are going to be spending a while behind bars.' Rebus sat back. 'If I want to, I could have a damned good go at putting you in there with them. How would you like that, Dr Colquhoun? Conspiracy to pervert, et cetera.'

Rebus could feel himself relaxing into his work; doing it for Jack.

The solicitor was about to say something, but Colquhoun got in first. 'It was a mistake.'

'A mistake?' Rebus hooted. 'One way of putting it, I suppose.' He sat forward, resting his elbows on the table. 'Time to talk, Dr Colquhoun. You know what they say about confession ...'

Brian 'Pretty-Boy' Summers looked immaculate.

He had a lawyer with him, too, a senior partner who looked like

an undertaker and wasn't taking kindly to being kept waiting. As they settled at the table in the Interview Room, and Hogan slotted tapes into cassette machine and video recorder, the lawyer started the protest he'd spent the past hour or two preparing in his head.

'On behalf of my client, Inspector, I feel duty bound to say that this is some of the most appalling behaviour I've –'

'You think you've seen appalling behaviour?' Rebus answered. 'In the words of the song, you ain't seen nothing yet.'

'Look, it's clear to me that you –'

Rebus ignored him, slapped the folder down on to the table, slid it towards Pretty-Boy.

'Take a look.'

Pretty-Boy was wearing a charcoal suit and purple shirt, open at the neck. No sunglasses or car-keys. He'd been brought in from his flat in the New Town. Comment from one of the men who'd gone to fetch him: 'Biggest hi-fi I've seen in my life. Bugger was wide awake, listening to Patsy Cline.'

Rebus started whistling 'Crazy': that got Pretty-Boy's attention and a wry smile, but he kept his arms folded.

'I would if I were you,' Rebus said.

'Ready,' Hogan said, meaning he had the tapes running. They went through the formalities: date and time, location, individuals present. Rebus looked towards the lawyer and smiled. He looked pretty expensive. Telford would have ordered the best, same as always.

'Know any Elton John, Brian?' Rebus asked. 'He's got this song: "Someone Saved My Life Tonight". You'll be singing it to me once you've looked inside.' He tapped the folder. 'Go on, you know it makes sense. I'm not playing some trick, and you don't have to say anything. But you really should do yourself a favour ...'

'I've got nothing to say.'

Rebus shrugged. 'Just open the folder, take a look.'

Pretty-Boy looked to his lawyer, who seemed uncertain.

'Your client won't be incriminating himself,' Rebus explained. 'If you want to read what's in there first, that's fine. It might not mean much to you, but go ahead.'

The lawyer opened the folder, found a dozen sheets of paper.

'Sorry in advance for any mistakes,' Rebus said. 'I typed it in a bit of a rush.'

Pretty-Boy didn't so much as glance towards the material. He kept his eyes on Rebus, while the lawyer sifted through the papers.

'These allegations,' the lawyer finally said, 'you must realise they're worthless?'

'If that's your opinion, fair enough. I'm not asking Mr Summers to admit or deny anything. Like I said, he can do a deaf and dumb routine for all I care, so long as he uses his *eyes*.'

A smile from Pretty-Boy, then a glance towards his lawyer, who shrugged his shoulders, saying there was nothing here to fear. A glance back at Rebus, and Pretty-Boy unfolded his arms, picked up the first sheet, and started reading.

'Just so we have a record for the tape,' Rebus said, 'Mr Summers is now reading a draft report prepared by myself earlier today.' Rebus paused. 'Actually, I mean yesterday, Saturday. He's reading my interpretation of recent events in and around Edinburgh, events concerning his employer, Thomas Telford, a Japanese business consortium – which is really, in my opinion, a Yakuza front – and a gentleman from Newcastle by the name of Jake Tarawicz.'

He paused. The lawyer said: 'Agreed, thus far.' Rebus nodded and continued.

'My version of events is as follows. Jake Tarawicz became an associate of Thomas Telford only because he wanted something Telford had: namely, a slick operation to bring drugs into Britain without raising suspicion. Either that or it was only later on, once their relationship had become established, that Tarawicz decided he could move in on Telford's turf. To facilitate this, he manufactured a war between Telford and Morris Gerald Cafferty. This was easily accomplished. Telford had moved in aggressively on Cafferty's territory, probably with Tarawicz egging him on. All Tarawicz had to do was make sure things escalated. To this end, he had one of his men attack a drug dealer outside one of Telford's night-clubs, Telford immediately placing the blame on Cafferty. He also had some of his men attack a Telford stronghold in Paisley. Meanwhile, there were attacks on Cafferty's territory and associates, retaliation by Telford for perceived wrongs.'

Rebus cleared his throat, took a sip of tea – a fresh cup, no sugar.

'Does this sound familiar, Mr Summers?' Pretty-Boy said nothing. He was busy reading. 'My guess is that the Japanese were never meant to become involved. In other words, they had no knowledge of what was happening. Telford was showing them

around, easing the way for them as they tried to buy a country club. Rest and recreation for their members, plus a good way of laundering money – less suspect than a casino or similar operation, especially when an electronics factory is about to open, so that the Yakuza slip into the country as just a few more Japanese businessmen.

'I think when Tarawicz saw this, he began to worry. He didn't want to get rid of Tommy Telford just to leave the way open for other competitors to muscle in. So he decided they'd have to become part of his plan. He had Matsumoto followed. He had him killed, and in a nice twist made *me* the chief suspect. Why? Two reasons. First, Tommy Telford had me pegged as Cafferty's man, so by fingering me, Tarawicz was fingering Cafferty. Second, he wanted me out of the game, because I'd gone to Newcastle, and had met one of his men, a guy called William 'The Crab' Cotton. I knew the Crab of old, and it so happened Tarawicz had used him for the hit on the drug dealer. He didn't want me putting two and two together.'

Rebus paused again. 'How's it sounding, Brian?'

Pretty-Boy had finished reading. His arms were folded again, eyes on Rebus.

'We've yet to see any evidence, Inspector,' the lawyer said.

Rebus shrugged. 'I don't need evidence. See, the same file you've got there, I delivered a copy to a Mr Sakiji Shoda at the Caledonian Hotel.' Rebus watched Pretty-Boy's eyelids flutter. 'Now, the way I see it, Mr Shoda is going to be a bit pissed off. I mean, he's already pissed off, that's why he was here. He'd seen Telford screw up, and wanted to see if he could do anything *right*. I don't suppose the raid on Maclean's will have given him any renewed sense of confidence. But he was also here to find out why one of his men had been killed, and who was responsible. This report tells him Tarawicz was behind it, and if he chooses to believe that, he'll go after Tarawicz. In fact, he checked out of his hotel yesterday evening – seems he was in a bit of a rush. I'm wondering if he was on his way home via Newcastle. Doesn't matter. What matters is that he'll *still* be pissed off at Telford for letting it happen. And meantime Jake Tarawicz is going to be wondering who shopped him to Shoda. The Yakuza are not nice people, Brian. You lot are nursery school by comparison.' Rebus sat back in his chair.

'One last point,' he said. 'Tarawicz's base is Newcastle. I'm

betting he had eyes and ears here in Edinburgh. In fact, I know he did. I've just been having a chat with Dr Colquhoun. You remember him, Brian? You'd heard about him from Lintz. Then when Tarawicz offered East Europeans as working girls, you reckoned maybe Tommy should have a few foreign phrases to hand. Colquhoun did the teaching. You told him stories about Tarawicz, about Bosnia. Catch was, he's the only person round these parts who knew the subject, so when we picked up Candice, we ended up using him, too. Colquhoun sussed straight off what was happening. He wasn't sure if he had anything to fear: he'd never met her, and her answers were reassuringly vague – or he kept them that way. All the same, he came to you. Your solution: ship Candice to Fife, then snatch her, and take Colquhoun out of the game till the heat died.'

Rebus smiled. 'He told *you* about Fife. Yet it was *Tarawicz* who got Candice. I think Tommy will find that a bit odd, don't you? So, here we sit. And I can tell you that the minute you walk out of here, you're going to be a marked man. Could be the Yakuza, could be Cafferty, could be your own boss or Tarawicz himself. You haven't got any friends, and nowhere's safe any more.' Rebus paused. 'Unless *we* help you. I've talked to Chief Superintendent Watson, and he's agreeing to witness protection, new identity, whatever you want. There may be a short sentence to serve – just so it looks right – but it'll be a soft option, room of your own, no other prisoners allowed near. And afterwards, you'll be home and dry. That's a big commitment on our part, and we'll need a big commitment from *you*. We'll want everything.' Rebus counted off on his fingers. 'The drug shipments, the war with Cafferty, the Newcastle connection, the Yakuza, the prostitutes.' He paused again, drained his tea. 'Tall order, I know. Your boss had a meteoric rise, Brian, and he nearly made it. But that's all over. Best thing you can do now is talk. It's either that or spend the rest of your days waiting for the bullet or the machete to strike ...'

The lawyer started to protest. Rebus held up a hand.

'We'll need all of it, Brian. Including Lintz.'

'Lintz,' Pretty-Boy said dismissively. 'Lintz is nothing.'

'So where's the harm?'

The look in Pretty-Boy's eyes was a mix of anger, fear and disorientation. Rebus stood up.

'I need something else to drink. What about you gentlemen?'

'Coffee,' the lawyer said, 'black, no sugar.'

Pretty-Boy hesitated, then said, 'Get me a Coke.' And at that point – for the very first time – Rebus knew a deal might be done. He stopped the interview, Hogan switched off the tapes, and both men left the room. Hogan patted him on the back.

Farmer Watson was coming along the corridor towards them. Rebus moved to meet him, leading them away from the door.

'I think we might be in with a shout, sir,' Rebus said. 'He'll try to twist the deal, give us less than we want, but I think there's a chance.'

Watson beamed a smile, as Rebus leaned against the wall, eyes closed. 'I feel about a hundred years old.'

'Experience tells,' Hogan said.

Rebus growled at him, then they went to fetch the drinks.

'Mr Summers,' the lawyer said, as Rebus handed him his cup, 'would like to tell you the story of his relationship with Joseph Lintz. But first we'll need some assurances.'

'What about everything else I mentioned?'

'These can be negotiated.'

Rebus stared at Pretty-Boy. 'You don't trust me?'

Pretty-Boy picked up his can, said 'No', and drank.

'Fine.' Rebus walked over to the far wall. 'In that case, you're free to go.' He checked his watch. 'Soon as you've finished your drinks, I want you out of here. Interview Rooms are at a premium tonight. DI Hogan, mark up the tapes, will you?'

Hogan ejected both cassettes. Rebus sat down beside him and they started discussing work, as though Pretty-Boy had been dismissed from their minds. Hogan examined a sheet of paper, checking who was due to be interviewed next.

From the corner of his eye, Rebus saw Pretty-Boy leaning in towards his lawyer, whispering something. He turned on them.

'Can you do that outside, please? We need to vacate this room.'

Pretty-Boy *knew* Rebus was bluffing ... knew the policeman needed him. But he realised, too, that Rebus was *not* bluffing about giving the file to Shoda, and he was far too intelligent not to be scared. He didn't move from the chair, and held his lawyer's arm so he had to stay and listen. Eventually the lawyer cleared his throat.

'Inspector, Mr Summers is willing to answer your questions.'

'*All* my questions?'

The lawyer nodded. 'But I must insist on hearing more of the "deal" you're proposing.'

Rebus looked at Hogan. 'Go get the Chief Super.'

Rebus left the room, stood in the hallway while Hogan was away. Cadged a cigarette off a passing uniform. He'd just got it lit when Farmer Watson came barrelling towards him, Hogan behind as though attached to Watson by an invisible leash.

'No smoking, John, you know that.'

'Yes, sir,' Rebus said, crimping the tip. 'I was just holding it for Inspector Hogan.'

Watson nodded towards the door. 'What do they want?'

'We've been talking possible immunity from prosecution. At the very least, he'll want a soft sentence, and a safe one, plus new ID afterwards.'

Watson was thoughtful. 'We haven't had a cheep out of any of them. Not that it matters greatly. There's the gang we caught red-handed, plus Telford on the audio tape ...'

'Summers is a real insider, knows Telford's organisation.'

'So how come he's willing to spill?'

'Because he's scared, and his fear is overwhelming his loyalty. I'm not saying we'll get every last detail out of him, but we'll probably get enough to start pressing the other members. Once they know someone's yapping, they'll all want a trade.'

'What's his lawyer like?'

'Expensive.'

'No point shilly-shallying then.'

'I couldn't have put it better myself, sir.'

The Chief Super pinned back his shoulders. 'All right, let's do a deal.'


'When did you first meet Joseph Lintz?'

Pretty-Boy's arms were no longer folded. He was resting them on the desk, head in his hands. His hair flopped forward, making him look younger than ever.

'About six months ago. We'd spoken on the phone before that.'

'He was a punter?'

'Yes.'

'Meaning what exactly?'

Pretty-Boy looked at the turning spools. 'You want me to explain for all our listeners?'

'That's right.'

'Joseph Lintz was a client of the escort service for which I worked.'

'Come on, Brian, you were a bit more than a flunkey. You ran it, didn't you?'

'If you say so.'

'Anytime you want to walk, Brian ...'

Eyes burning. 'Okay, I *ran* it for my employer.'

'And Mr Lintz phoned wanting an escort?'

'He wanted one of our girls to go to his home.'

'And?'

'And that was it. He'd sit there opposite her and just stare for half an hour.'

'Both of them fully clothed?'

'Yes.'

'Nothing else?'

'Not at first.'

'Ah.' Rebus paused. 'You must have been curious.'

Pretty-Boy shrugged. 'Takes all sorts, doesn't it?'

'I suppose it does. So how did your business relationship progress?'

'Well, on a gig like that, there's always a chaperone.'

'Yourself?'

'Yes.'

'You didn't have better things to do?'

Another shrug. 'I was curious.'

'About what?'

'The address: Heriot Row.'

'Mr Lintz had ... class?'

'Coming out his ears. I mean, I've met plenty fat cats, corporate types looking for a shag in their hotel, but Lintz was a long way from that.'

'He just wanted to look at the girls.'

'That's right. And this huge house he had ...'

'You went in? You didn't just wait in the car?'

'Told him it was company policy.' A smile. 'Really, all I wanted was to snoop.'

'Did you talk to him?'

'Later, yes.'

'You became friends?'

'Not really ... maybe. He knew things, had a real brain on him.'

'You were impressed.'

Pretty-Boy nodded. Yes, Rebus could imagine. His previous role model had always been Tommy Telford, but Pretty-Boy had aspirations. He *wanted* class. He wanted people to acknowledge him for his mind. Rebus knew how seductive Lintz's storytelling could be. How much more seductive would Pretty-Boy have found it?

'Then what happened?'

Pretty-Boy shifted. 'His tastes changed.'

'Or his real tastes started to emerge?'

'That's what I wondered.'

'So what did he want?'

'He wanted the girls ... he had this length of rope ... he'd made it into a noose.' Pretty-Boy swallowed. His lawyer had stopped writing, was listening intently. 'He wanted the girls to slip it over their heads, then lie down like they were dead.'

'Dressed or naked?'

'Naked.'

'And?'

'And he'd ... he'd sit on his chair and get off. Some of the girls wouldn't go along. He wanted the works: bulging eyes, tongue sticking out, neck twisted ...' Pretty-Boy rubbed his hands through his hair.

'Did you ever talk about it?'

'With him? No, never.'

'So what did you talk about?'

'All sorts of things.' Pretty-Boy looked up at the ceiling, laughed. 'He told me once, he believed in God. Said the problem was, he wasn't sure God believed in him. That seemed clever at the time ... he always managed to get me thinking. And this was the same guy who tossed himself off over bodies with ropes round their necks.'

'All this personal attention you were giving him,' Rebus said, 'you were sizing him up, weren't you?'

Pretty-Boy looked into his lap, nodded.

'For the tape, please.'

'Tommy always wanted to know if a punter was worth squeezing.'

'And ... ?'

Pretty-Boy shrugged. 'We found out about the Nazi stuff, realised we couldn't hurt him any more than he was already being hurt. Turned into a bit of a joke. There we were, thinking of threatening

him with exposure as a perv, and at the same time the papers were saying he was a mass murderer.' He laughed again.

'So you dropped that idea?'

'Yes.'

'But he paid you five grand?' Rebus fishing.

Pretty-Boy licked his lips. 'He'd tried topping himself. He told me that. Tying the rope to the top of his banister and jumping off. Only it didn't work. Banister snapped and he fell half a flight.'

Rebus remembering: the broken stair-rail.

Rebus remembering: Lintz with a scarf around his neck, his voice hoarse. Telling Rebus he had a throat bug.

'He told you this?'

'He phoned the office, said we had to meet. That was unusual. In the past, he'd always used phone boxes and got me on my mobile. Safe old bugger, I'd always thought. Then he calls from home, right to the office.'

'Where did you meet?'

'In a restaurant. He bought me lunch.' The young woman ... 'Told me he'd tried killing himself and couldn't do it. He kept saying he'd proved himself a "moral coward", whatever that means.'

'So what did he want?'

Pretty-Boy stared up at Rebus. 'He needed someone to help him.'

'You?'

Pretty-Boy shrugged.

'And the price was right?'

'No haggling necessary. He wanted it done in Warriston Cemetery.'

'Did you ask him why?'

'I knew he liked the place. We met at his house, really early. I drove him down there. He seemed the same as ever, except he kept thanking me for my "resolve". I wasn't sure what he meant by that. To me, Resolve is something you take after a hard night.'

Rebus smiled, as was expected. 'Go on,' he said.

'Not much more to tell, is there? *He* put the noose over his head. *He* told me to pull on the rope. I had a last go at talking him out of it, but the bugger was determined. It's not murder, is it? Assisted suicide: a lot of places, it's legal.'

'How did the dunt get on his head?'

'He was heavier than I thought. First time I hauled him up, the rope slipped and he fell, thumped himself on the ground.'

Bobby Hogan cleared his throat. 'Brian, did he say anything ...
right at the end?'

'Famous last words and all that?' Pretty-Boy shook his head. 'All
he said was "thank you". Poor old sod. One thing: he wrote it all
down.'

'What?'

'About me helping him. A sort of insurance, in case anyone ever
linked us. Letter says he paid me, begged me to help.'

'Where is this?'

'In a safe. I can get it for you.'

Rebus nodded, stretched his back. 'Did you ever talk about
Villefranche?'

'A little bit, mostly about the way the papers and TV were
hounding him, how difficult it made it when he wanted ...
company.'

'But not the massacre itself?'

Pretty-Boy shook his head. 'Know something else? Even if he *had*
told me, I wouldn't tell you.'

Rebus tapped his pen against the desk. He knew the Lintz story
was as closed as it was ever going to be. Bobby Hogan knew it, too.
They had the secret at last, the story of how Lintz had died. They
knew he'd been helped by the Rat Line, but they'd never know
whether he'd been Josef Linzstek or not. The circumstantial
evidence was overwhelming, but so was the evidence that Lintz had
been hounded to death. He'd started putting the escorts into nooses
only *after* the accusations had been made.

Hogan caught Rebus's eye and shrugged, as if to say: what does it
matter? Rebus nodded back. Part of him wanted to take a break, but
now that Pretty-Boy was rolling it was important to keep up the
steam.

'Thanks for that, Mr Summers. We may come back to Mr Lintz
if we think of any more questions. But meantime, let's move on to
the relationship between Thomas Telford and Jake Tarawicz.'

Pretty-Boy shifted, as if trying to get comfortable. 'This could
take a while,' he said.

'Take as long as you like,' Rebus told him.

# 37

They got it all, in time.

Pretty-Boy had to rest, and so did they. Other teams came in, worked on different areas. The tapes were filling up, being listened to elsewhere, notes and transcripts made. Back-up questions were forwarded to the Interview Room. Telford wasn't talking. Rebus went and took a look at him, sat across from him. Telford didn't blink once. He sat ramrod-straight, hands on knees. And all the while, Pretty-Boy's confession was being used to squeeze other gang members – without letting slip who was singing.

The ranks broke, slowly at first and then in a cataract of accusation, self-defence and denial. And they got it all.

Telford and Tarawicz: European prostitutes heading north; muscle and dope heading south.

Mr Taystee: taking more than his fair share; dealt with accordingly.

The Japanese: using Telford as their introduction to Scotland, finding it a good base of operations.

Only now Rebus had scuppered that. In his folder to Shoda he'd warned the gangster to leave Poyntinghame alone, or he'd be 'implicated in ongoing criminal investigations'. The Yakuza weren't stupid. He doubted they'd be back ... for a while at least.

His last trip of the night: Rebus went down to the cells, unlocked one of the doors and told Ned Farlowe he was free. Told him he had nothing to fear ...

Unlike Mr Pink Eyes. The Yakuza had a score to settle. And it didn't stay unsettled long. He was found in his car-crusher, seatbelt welded shut. His men had started running.

Some of them were running still.

Rebus sat in his living-room, staring at the door Jack Morton had

stripped and varnished. He was thinking about the funeral, about how the Juice Church would be there in force. He wondered if they'd blame him. Jack's kids would be there, too. Rebus had never met them; didn't think he wanted to see them.

Wednesday morning, he was back in Inverness, meeting Mrs Hetherington off her flight. She'd been delayed in Holland, answering Customs questions. They'd laid a little trap, caught a man called De Gier – a known trafficker – planting the kilo package of heroin in Mrs Hetherington's luggage: a secret compartment in her suitcase, the suitcase itself a gift from her landlord. Several of Telford's other elderly tenants were enjoying short breaks in Belgium. They'd be questioned by local police.

Home again, Rebus telephoned David Levy.

'Lintz committed suicide,' he told him.

'That's your conclusion?'

'It's the truth. No conspiracy, no cover-up.'

A sigh. 'It's of little consequence, Inspector. What matters is that we've lost another one.'

'Villefranche doesn't mean a thing to you, does it? The Rat Line, that's all you care about.'

'There's nothing we can do about Villefranche.'

Rebus took a deep breath. 'A man called Harris came to see me. He works for British Intelligence. They're protecting some big names, high-level people. Rat Line survivors, maybe their children. Tell Mayerlink to keep digging.'

There was silence for a moment. 'Thank you, Inspector.'


Rebus was in a car. It was the Weasel's Jag. The Weasel was in the back with him. Their driver was missing a big chunk of his left ear. The shape made him resemble a pixie – but only from the side, and you wouldn't want to tell him to his face.

'You did well,' the Weasel was saying. 'Mr Cafferty's pleased.'

'How long have you been holding him?'

The Weasel smiled. 'Nothing gets past you, Rebus.'

'Rangers have offered me a trial in goal. How long have you had him?'

'A few days. Had to be sure we had the right one, didn't we?'

'And now you're sure?'

'Absolutely positive.'

Rebus looked out of the window at the passing parade of shops,

pedestrians, buses. The car was heading down towards Newhaven and Granton. 'You wouldn't be setting up some loser to take the blame?'

'He's genuine.'

'You could have spent the past few days making sure he was going to say the right things.'

The Weasel seemed amused. 'Such as?'

'Such as that he was in Telford's pay.'

'Rather than Mr Cafferty's, you mean?' Rebus glared at the Weasel, who laughed. 'I think you'll find him a pretty convincing candidate.'

The way he said it made Rebus shiver. 'He's still alive, isn't he?'

'Oh, yes. How long he remains so is entirely up to you.'

'You think I want him dead?'

'I know you do. You didn't go to Mr Cafferty because you wanted justice. You went out of *revenge*.'

Rebus stared at the Weasel. 'You don't sound like yourself.'

'You mean I don't sound like my persona – different thing entirely.'

'And do many people get behind the persona?' The Who: 'Can You See the Real Me?'

The Weasel smiled again. 'I thought you deserved it, after all the trouble you've gone to.'

'I didn't break Telford just to please your boss.'

'Nevertheless ...' The Weasel slid across his seat towards Rebus. 'How's Sammy, by the way?'

'She's fine.'

'Recuperating?'

'Yes.'

'That's good news. Mr Cafferty will be pleased. He's disappointed you haven't been to see him.'

Rebus took a newspaper from his pocket. It was folded at a story: FATAL STABBING AT JAIL.

'Your boss?' he said, handing the paper over.

The Weasel made show of reading it. '"Aged twenty-six, from Govan ... stabbed through the heart in his cell ... no witnesses, no weapon recovered despite a thorough search."' He tutted. 'Bit careless.'

'He'd taken up the contract on Cafferty?'

'Had he?' The Weasel looked amazed.

'Fuck off,' Rebus said, turning back to his window.

'By the way, Rebus, if you decide not to go to trial with the driver ...' The Weasel was holding something out. A homemade screw-driver, filed to a point, grip covered in packing-tape. Rebus looked at it in disgust.

'I washed the blood off,' the Weasel assured him. Then he laughed again. Rebus felt like he was being ferried straight to hell. In front of him he could see the grey expanse of the Firth of Forth, and Fife beyond it. They were coming into an area of docks, gas-plant and warehouses. It had been earmarked for a development spill-over from Leith. The whole city was changing. Traffic routes and priorities were altered overnight, cranes were kept busy on building-sites, and the council, who always complained about being broke, had all manner of schemes underway to further alter the shape and scope of his chosen home.

'Nearly there,' the Weasel said.

Rebus wondered if there'd be any turning back.

They stopped at the gates to a warehouse complex. The driver undid the padlock, pulled the chain free. The gates swung open. In they went. The Weasel ordered the driver to park around the back. There was a plain white van there, more rust than metal. Its back windows had been painted over, turning it into a suitable hearse should occasion demand.

They got out into a salt wind. The Weasel shuffled over towards a door and banged once. The door was pushed open from within. They stepped inside.

A huge open space, filled with only a few packing cases, a couple of pieces of machinery covered with oil-cloth. And two men: the one who'd let them in, and another at the far end. This man was standing in front of a wooden chair. There was a figure tied to the chair, half-hidden by the man. The Weasel led the procession. Rebus tried to control his breathing, which was growing painfully shallow. His heart was racing, nerves jangling. He pushed back the anger, wasn't sure he could hold it.

When they were eight feet from the chair, the Weasel nodded and the man stood away, revealing to Rebus the terrified figure of a kid.

A boy.

Nine or ten, no older.

One black eye, nose caked with blood, both cheeks bruised and a

graze on his chin. Burst lip beginning to heal, trousers torn at the knees, one shoe missing.

And a smell, as if he'd wet himself, maybe even worse.

'What the hell is this?' Rebus asked.

'This,' the Weasel said, 'is the little bastard who stole the car. This is the little bastard who lost his nerve at a red light and gunned through it, losing control of the pedals because he could barely reach them. This ...' The Weasel stepped forward, planted a hand on the kid's shoulder. 'This is the culprit.'

Rebus looked at the faces around him. 'Is this your idea of a joke?'

'No joke, Rebus.'

He looked at the boy. Dried tear-tracks. Eyes bloodshot from crying. Shoulders trembling. They'd tied his arms behind him. Tied his ankles to the chair-legs.

'Puh-please, mister ...' Dry, cracked voice. 'I ... help me, puh-please ...'

'Nicked the car,' the Weasel recited, 'then did the hit and run, got scared, and dumped the car near where he lives. Took the cassette and the tapes. He wanted the car for a race. That's what they do, race cars around the schemes. This little runt can start an engine in ten seconds flat.' He rubbed his hands together. 'So ... here we all are.'

'Help me ...'

Rebus recalling the city's graffiti: Won't Anyone Help? The Weasel nodding towards one of his men, the man producing a pickaxe-handle.

'Or the screwdriver,' the Weasel said. 'Or whatever you like, really. We are at your command.' And he gave a little bow.

Rebus could hardly speak. 'Cut the ropes.'

Silence in the warehouse.

'*Cut those fucking ropes!*'

A sniff from the Weasel. 'You heard the man, Tony.'

Ca-chink of a flick-knife opening. Ropes severed like cutting through butter. Rebus walked to within inches of the boy.

'What's your name?'

'J-Jordan.'

'Is that your first name or your second?'

The boy looked at him. 'First.'

'Okay, Jordan.' Rebus leaned down. The boy flinched, but did not

resist as Rebus picked him up. He weighed almost nothing. Rebus started walking with him.

'What now, Rebus?' the Weasel asked. But Rebus didn't answer. He carried the boy to the threshold, kicked open the door, stepped out into sunshine.

'I'm ... I'm really sorry.' The boy had a hand across his eyes, unused to the light. He was starting to cry.

'You know what you did?'

Jordan nodded. 'I've been ... ever since that night. I knew it was bad ...' Now the tears came.

'Did they say who I was?'

'Please don't kill me.'

'I'm not going to kill you, Jordan.'

The boy blinked, trying to clear tears from his eyes, the better to know whether he was being lied to.

'I think you've been through enough, pal,' Rebus said. Then added: 'I think we both have.'

So after everything, it had come to this. Bob Dylan: 'Simple Twist of Fate'. Segue to Leonard Cohen: 'Is This What You Wanted?'

Rebus didn't know the answer to that.

# 38

Clean and sober, he went to the hospital. An open ward this time, set hours for visitors. No more darkened vigils. No return visit by Candice, though nurses spoke of regular phone calls by someone foreign-sounding. No way of knowing where she was. Maybe out there searching for her son. It didn't matter, so long as she was safe. So long as she was in control.

When he reached the ward's far end, two women rose from their chairs so he could kiss them: Rhona and Patience. He had a carrier-bag with him, magazines and grapes. Sammy was sitting up, supported by three pillows, Pa Broon propped beside her. Her hair had been washed and brushed, and she was smiling at him.

'Women's magazines,' he said, shaking his head. 'They should be on the top-shelf.'

'I need a few fantasies to sustain me in here,' Sammy said. Rebus beamed at her, said hello, then bent down and kissed his daughter.

The sun was shining as they walked through The Meadows — a rare day off for both. They held hands and watched people sunbathing and playing football. He knew Rhona was excited, and thought he knew why. But he wasn't going to spoil things with speculation.

'If you had a daughter, what would you call her?' she asked.

He shrugged. 'Haven't really thought about it.'

'What about a son?'

'I quite like Sam.'

'Sam?'

'When I was a kid, I had a bear called Sam. My mum knitted it for me.'

'Sam ...' She tried the name out. 'It would work both ways, wouldn't it?'

He stopped, circled his arms around her waist. 'How do you mean?'

'Well, it could be Samuel or Samantha. You don't get many of those — names that work both ways.'

'I suppose not. Rhona, is there ...?'

She put a finger to his lips, then kissed him. They walked on. There didn't seem to be a cloud in the whole damned sky.

# Afterword

My fictional French village of Villefranche d'Albarede owes its existence to the real village of Oradour-sur-Glane, which was the subject of an attack by the 3rd Company of the SS 'Der Führer' regiment.

On the afternoon of Saturday 10 June 1944, 3rd Company – known as 'Das Reich' – entered the village and rounded up everyone. The women and children were herded into the church, while the men were split into groups and marched to various barns and other buildings around the village. Then the slaughter began.

Some 642 victims have been accounted for, but the estimate is that up to a thousand people may have perished that day. Only fifty-three corpses were ever identified. One boy from Lorraine, having first-hand knowledge of SS atrocities, managed to flee when the troops entered the village. Five men escaped the massacre in Laudy's barn. Wounded, they were able to crawl from the burning building and hide until the next day. One woman escaped from the church, climbing out of a window after playing dead beside the corpse of her child.

Soldiers went from house to house, finding villagers too sick or elderly to leave their beds. These people were shot and their houses set alight. Some of the bodies were hidden in mass graves, or dumped down wells and in bread ovens.

General Lammerding was the commanding officer. On 9 June he'd ordered the deaths of ninety-nine hostages in Tulle. He also gave the order for the Oradour massacre. Later on in the war, Lammerding was captured by the British, who refused his extradition to France. Instead, he was returned to Dusseldorf, where he ran a successful company until his death in 1971.

In the general euphoria of the Normandy landings, the tragedy at Oradour went almost unnoticed. Eventually, in January 1953, the

trial opened in Bordeaux of sixty-five men identified as having been involved in the massacre. Of these sixty-five, only twenty-one were present: seven Germans, and fourteen natives of French Alsace. None of the men was of officer rank.

Every individual found guilty at the Bordeaux trial left court a free man. A special Act of Amnesty had been passed, in the interests of national unity. (People in Alsace were disgruntled that their countrymen had been picked out for condemnation.) Meantime, the Germans were said to have already served their terms.

As a result, Oradour broke off all relations with the French state, a rupture which lasted seventeen years.

In May 1983, a man stood trial in East Berlin, charged with having been a lieutenant in 'Das Reich' during the Oradour massacre. He admitted everything, and was sentenced to life imprisonment.

In June 1996, it was reported that around 12,000 foreign volunteers to the Waffen SS are still receiving pensions from the Federal German government. One of these pensioners, a former Obersturmbannfuhrer, was a participant at Oradour ...

Oradour still stands as a shrine. The village has been left just the way it was on that day in June 1944.